EMPATH FOUND

THE COMPLETE TRILOGY

EMPATH FOUND

COLETTE RHODES

THE COMPLETE TRILOGY

FOR THE READERS WHO NEVER STOPPED BELIEVING
IN FAIRYTALES.

THEY JUST PREFER THEM SPICY THESE DAYS.

The Terrible Gift

"HERE YOU LEAVE TODAY AND ENTER THE WORLD OF YESTERDAY, TOMORROW, AND FANTASY."

- WALT DISNEY

FFION

CHAPTER 1

The icy wind blew in from the River Thames through the shattered window of the grimy club storage room I was standing in.

I gaped out the broken window in horror at what I had just done. I didn't regret stopping Kayden; the guy was a creep—his malicious intent had crashed against my skin like rancid waves of sewer water—but I wasn't 100% sure I hadn't killed him. *Crap*, murder was not what I had in mind for my Thursday night. Honestly, I'd just come out intending to get laid.

Kayden's creepy friends had herded me through the club here, into the downstairs storage room, and locked the door behind me. I remember him advancing on me. I remember being consumed by rage. Then, somehow, he went flying—*flying*—through the glass window above him. He must have gone another few feet over the barricade, since I heard the splash of him landing in the river.

Shoot, shoot, shoot! If he was alive, he was going to be furious. And confused, which would make two of us.

I could still *feel* his stupid friends standing outside the door, and I looked between that and the broken window, trying to determine which was the lesser of two evils.

Kayden had stayed in the same group home as me for a while, and he'd always struggled with taking no for an answer. And he wanted me, which sounds obnoxious, but I knew he wanted me because I felt it. Feeling other people's emotions was sort of my bag. And it was exhausting. I'd always assumed I'd been cursed as a baby or something. After blasting 150 pounds of man through a window without laying a finger on him, I was questioning if I was even human.

Perhaps I was a demon? Maybe a half demon? My dark brown eyes were distinctly ordinary and un-demonic, and I had no horns or fun tail to speak of.

I also had an absurdly high sex drive, which is why I had been at the club in the first place, looking for a quick fix for my raging libido. Drunk people's emotions were slightly less taxing on my hypersensitive emotional radar, and sometimes it was worth the headache to scratch that itch with a partner.

Maybe that made me a succubus? Whatever I was, I was confident it was evil.

The other theory is that I'm just plain crazy, and all of my quirks were a figment of my imagination. *I'd rather be a demon.* No one wanted to admit they were crazy.

I inched towards the broken window, glad that the noise of the club must have drowned out the sound of shattering glass. Should I look for Kayden? What if he retaliated? I wasn't sure if I could do my blasting trick again, if I even wanted to.

You need to make sure he's alive, Fi. My subconscious was so rude.

I really hoped I hadn't murdered someone. Even if he was a monster, I didn't want his death on my conscience.

Resigning myself to at least making sure I wasn't a murderer, I pushed a crate of beer over to the remains of the window and climbed out, scratching my arms and stomach on shards of glass and cursing the tiny crop top and skinny jeans I'd worn out tonight. My jacket was in the club's coat room, but there was no way I was risking going back in there. God knows what Kayden's mates would do if I emerged from that room and he didn't.

Clambering up onto the footpath, ignoring the stabbing sensation behind my eyes from the cocktail of emotions pouring out of the club behind me, I reached out with my spidey-senses and pinpointed Kayden's confused rage. Ah, he was definitely still alive then. I couldn't determine his exact location, but I doubted he'd have been able to climb out of the river that quickly.

Counting my blessings that I hadn't accidentally killed a person and hoping the freezing river water wouldn't finish the job for me, I slipped down a side street and hurried to the nearest tube station. I wasn't about to hang around and wait for Kayden to turn that anger on me—or worse, for him to call the authorities. After a lifetime in foster care, I had several issues with the man, plus an inconvenient inability to tell lies.

What a bust. I'd developed a new freaky skill, almost killed a dude, and had zero sex. Plus, I had to get up for my shitty, pre-dawn cleaning job in a couple of hours. Maybe I'd try my luck in a club in Shoreditch tomorrow. It looked like I'd be getting myself off tonight.

 BRYN

CHAPTER 2

I made my way through the winding forest path to Master Gwyneira's treehouse cabin, wondering what kind of assignment she'd give me today. Now I was in my third year at the Academy of Avalon; the dean had been entrusting me with more and more tracking missions to collect new students. Master Gwyneira had been gifted guardian magic by the gods that helped her discover any young fae in need of the Academy's guidance, and she utilized my gods-gifted tracking magic to lead us right to them.

"Bryn, come in." Mawrth, one of Master Gwyneira's mates, ushered me into the small reception room at the front of the treehouse. The cabin was more luxurious than most at the Academy, but it was fitting since Gwyneira was one of the most revered fae in Avalon. She also needed the space for her *three* mates. Only immensely powerful females had more than two.

I waited next to the couch for Gwyneira to arrive, the large tapestry of the gods that dominated one wall drawing my attention. I didn't know why Gwyneira still bothered displaying it; the gods had forsaken the fae. Many fae were now lucky to have any magic at all—they were practically human. I was exceptionally fortunate to have both a fire elemental affinity and the gift of tracking magic.

"Ah Bryn, I am glad you are here," Gwyneira said as she glided into the room and sat in the armchair as I took a seat on the couch. She was powerful,

400 years old, and there were few fae I respected more. "I have a sensitive assignment for you to undertake, and I would like you to go alone."

"Alone?"

I had never been on an assignment alone before. The situations we were going into were often dangerous, and at 20 years old, I was hardly qualified for solo extraction work.

I couldn't tell whether to be flattered or alarmed that Gwyneira was suggesting it at all.

"This is an unusual case. You will be collecting her from Albion and, so far as I can tell, she was raised there. While I do not believe she is being held against her will or poorly treated, it is highly unlikely that she knows she is fae. I think you will find that she believed herself to be a human, perhaps up until she used a large burst of magic a few hours ago, which is how she came to my attention."

I had been to the human realm before on tracking assignments for runaways, but I didn't think there had ever been a fae *raised* in Albion as a human. I wasn't entirely sure how it was possible.

How could someone not realize they weren't human? It sounded suspicious to me.

"With all due respect, Master Gwyneira, I'm not sure I'm the best qualified candidate for explaining the situation to her. Maybe Tesni should accompany me?" I suggested.

Tesni and I had worked together on multiple tracking assignments for the Academy. She had a way of keeping the newbies calm while we removed them from their situations and brought them to the Academy. She was also spectacular in bed, and I wouldn't mind the company.

Gwyneira looked at me with an odd glint in her eye that I'd never seen before. "I feel strongly that Tesni's presence would be detrimental to this assignment. In fact, I am confident that only you can convince the young woman to accompany you back to Avalon."

I wasn't at all confident she was right, but who was I to question a 400-year-old fae?

Gwyneira closed her eyes and cupped her hands in front of her, drawing forth the missing fae's magic signature so I could latch onto it and track it to the source. Usually, a magical signature appears as an orb of glowing color, influenced by the holder's magical ability. The orb that appeared in Gwyneira's hands was like nothing I'd ever seen before. It almost looked like *smoke*. It was a beautiful swirling globe of gray and silver, wispy yet powerful.

Gwyneira gave a quizzical look at the smokey orb in her palms as I ran my hands through it. My tracking magic left a glittery golden trail behind it, each particle latching on to the magic's signature. Something about this magic was calling to me, deep in my soul.

"May the gods be with you on your travels, Bryn Edan," Gwyneira said with a parting smile, and I allowed my tracking magic to lead me out the door to the edge of campus, commissioning a carriage and rider to take me to the portal.

The comforting feel of this fae's magic had set me on edge. It was time to find out who she was.

Gods, Albion reeked. London's stench was particularly potent—the reek of the pollution clung to the more human-friendly clothes I had to wear in this realm. I was counting down the minutes until I could collect the fae and get the hell out of here, back to the fresh, clean air and brimming magic of Avalon.

Once upon a time, humans knew about Avalon. Some had even visited, but none since the last human king, Arthur, had visited and died there centuries ago. It was a place of myth to humans now over the centuries of stories and retellings, and that's how we liked it. Humans had historically not reacted kindly to those they believed had magic.

At least now, at four am, the streets of London were still relatively quiet. I could probably drop the glamour if I wanted to, though I wasn't about to take any risks. I tracked the fae's magical signature through the city until I ended up across from a large, imposing building. The walls were made of glass, and with the painfully bright lights humans were so fond of on inside, I had an unobstructed view of her. Frustratingly, I was too far away to get a better read on her magic, but I could be patient.

I watched the girl as she worked, cleaning the floor of a large empty building. She looked utterly human—too short to be fae, with bronze skin, thick black curly hair bundled up in a mass on top of her head, and a plain face. I would dearly love a touch of Second Sight at times like these so I could see through glamours, because nothing about her looked fae at all.

No, it had to be a glamour, and a powerful one at that. I couldn't help but be curious how she'd ended up in Albion in the first place. I trusted Gwyneira knew what she was doing in sending me to collect her, but I had a sinking feeling that she hadn't grown up in Avalon for a reason, and that reason might come back to haunt her if she joined our world.

I don't know why that thought bothered me so much. She was nothing to me.

As she began collecting her things like she was going to leave, I made my way to the back entrance of the building, hoping to catch her away from prying eyes. Doing my best to look non-threatening, I hoped her curiosity would outweigh her nerves. Even if she knew nothing about what she was, I was confident she would sense that I was like her. If the large burst of magic she'd used a few hours ago had been the first time she'd used it, she might at least be open to getting some answers.

She opened the door, and her big, dark brown eyes immediately latched onto mine. I inhaled deeply as an intoxicating mix of vanilla and wildflowers reached my nose, and a hard pull in my chest almost yanked me towards the shell-shocked fae, who was standing in the doorway staring at me.

Fuck.

That was the *Pull of Cúpláil*, the pull that showed a compatible mate, and it was by far the strongest I had ever felt it. This seemingly human, somehow exiled fae female was a powerful match for me.

And I wanted nothing to do with her.

FFION

CHAPTER 3

Oh. My. God.

I didn't want to entirely lose my head over an attractive guy, but this boy—no, man—was inhumanly beautiful. Literally. There was no way he could be human. I should have probably been freaking out about that more, but maybe we were the same thing? Perhaps he could sense emotions and throw people around without touching them too.

I really hoped we weren't related, or the response my body was having to him would have been super awkward.

He was unusually tall, 6.5ft at least, and lean but strong, built like a swimmer. His hair was a thick mop of loose black curls that flopped across his forehead and were long enough to brush the collar of his shirt. He fixed his deep blue eyes on me, narrowed in irritation.

Something weird was happening to me that was separate from my usual, everyday weirdness. I felt like there was a magnet buried deep in my sternum and the opposing magnet was this beautiful man. I had a powerful urge to go up to him and climb him like a tree, which was an awful idea, but something about him ignited a fiery passion deep in my soul that I didn't know I had. I wanted to fuck him and fight him, then do it all over again.

Oh god, he smelled so good. Like the embers of a bonfire.

The only thing stopping me from moving forward—since my common sense had apparently gone out the window—is that I could *feel* how much he'd have hated it.

I usually experienced other people's emotions like they were a vast ocean of waves lapping against me. They'd brush up against my skin, touching me, but unless I sought them out or focused on them, the sensation was uncomfortable but fleeting.

Not so with the ridiculously fine specimen in front of me. I felt his emotions like they were embedded in my skin, burrowing into my bones.

I stood frozen, trying to process his emotions in this much more intimate form. A healthy dose of resentment sat like a heavy weight on my lungs, making each breath feel hard won. His anger coursed hot through my veins like bubbling lava. It both irritated me and sent a wave of crushing disappointment through my chest that I really didn't understand. I didn't even *know* this guy.

Why should I care if he didn't like me?

Despite his instant dislike, I also sensed the faintest morsel of his curiosity tingling behind my ears, and a fiery, almost desperate lust that had all of my most sensitive nerves lighting up.

I was reasonably confident the last two emotions were his, anyway. I'd never found it so difficult to differentiate someone's feelings from my own. After staring for an inappropriately long moment, I finally found my voice, breathy as it was.

"Who are you?"

"Bryn Edan." His tone was flat, and his eyes bored into mine with an intensity that made me squirm.

Right, a man of few words then. His expression gave away none of the maelstrom of conflicting emotions he was feeling.

"How can I help you, Bryn Edan? You look like you're waiting for something."

"I was waiting for you."

"Why would you be waiting for me? Do I know you?" I asked mildly, trying not to let the strong reaction I was having to him show.

I felt his irritation at my questions chafing at my skin, but what did he expect? He'd said all of seven words to me so far. I needed a little more to go on.

He looked around as if checking that we were alone in the alleyway, and I used the moment of distraction to search for any nefarious intent in his emotional state, finding nothing.

"It appears you got yourself in a spot of bother earlier tonight, fae."

My heart dropped. Shit, was he one of Kayden's friends here for revenge? Somehow, I didn't think so. Something in my gut told me this guy would never be friends with Kayden.

Hold on a minute. Fae?

"My name is Fi. *F-e-e*," I said cautiously. "Not Fae."

Bryn snorted, and his amusement tickled my skin. It was a weird, not entirely unpleasant sensation.

"I don't care what your name is. Fae is what you are. What we both are. I'm here to take you back to your people in Avalon."

Several questions were whirling around in my brain, but before I had the chance to ask any of them, a group of people emerged from around the corner, laughing loudly.

Crap, this really didn't seem like the right venue for this conversation. If nothing else, someone might hear us and call the asylum. I took a step forward so we wouldn't be overheard and ignored the sting of rejection when Bryn immediately tensed.

"Can you tell lies?" I asked in a low voice and felt another tickle of amusement. My in-built lie prevention mechanism had screwed me over on more than one occasion—the words would literally choke in my throat before I could get them out. I'd feel a lot better about continuing this conversation if I knew Bryn couldn't outright lie to me either.

"Obviously not," he drawled, and his sincerity pulsed through my veins. Odd. Well, at least I wasn't a total anomaly.

"Are you intending to hurt me?"

A flash of annoyance crossed his face. "*No.* I'm here to take you home."

Even if he couldn't lie, I didn't dare to believe him. I'd never had a home in my life.

"Fine. Let's go somewhere we can talk, and I'll assess whether or not you're insane," I said with far more confidence than I felt. I started heading down the footpath towards a quiet spot I liked to visit nearby, rightly assuming Bryn would follow.

Fae. *Fae.* Were fae the same as fairies? Fairies were tiny. With wings. And pointy ears. Like Tinkerbell! I was definitely human-sized, wingless, and there was nothing remotely distinctive about my ears.

Maybe he was insane after all.

I led Bryn across the street and through a cobblestone alley to the little courtyard garden outside an old Victorian church that I cut through every morning on my way to work. It was a little slice of brightly colored heaven in a busy gray city. Even when there were people inside the building, their emotions were in a concentrated state of calm that didn't aggravate me as much as other feelings did. Besides, I liked the flowers.

I had always felt a strong pull to be close to nature, but I hadn't built up the courage to move away from the city yet. This is where I was found as an abandoned toddler. The little girl inside of me couldn't bear the thought of leaving, in case someone ever came looking for me.

I dropped onto a bench in the courtyard and Bryn followed suit, sitting as far away from me on the bench as physically possible. The garden looked a little grim this time of year—it was nearly winter, and nothing was flowering. I pulled my threadbare wool coat tighter around me and looked expectantly at Bryn to talk.

I sighed when he continued to say nothing. "Look, I need more information. You've just shown up out of nowhere and started going on about fairies. How did you find me? Why were you looking for me?"

Bryn scoffed as though the idea was utterly ridiculous. "First, *'fae,'* not *'fairy.'* Second, not me. The dean of the Academy of Avalon, Master Gwyneira, possesses powerful guardian magic. She can sense when there is a young fae in need of help the Academy can provide. I have tracking magic.

She showed me your magic signature, and I followed it here on her orders."

I blinked at him. Guardian magic? Tracking magic? Magic signatures? I didn't even know where to begin.

"We assumed you came to her attention because you were in some kind of trouble and had to use a sizable amount of magic," Bryn continued, raising an expectant eyebrow, challenging me to respond.

"Right. Earlier tonight. Someone I knew from foster care. He's much bigger these days," I explained absently. I felt a hot flood of anger from Bryn, snapping me out of my musing, which was kind of odd considering he seemed to despise me. "Anyway, he tried to grab me, and all I remember thinking is that I really didn't want him to. Then somehow, he was flying backward through a closed window and over the railing into the river. I guess that was the, er, magic?"

It sounded even more ridiculous out loud. I really was losing my mind.

Bryn's anger was still bubbling through my veins. "You were in a closed room? No open windows or doors?"

"Right. That was the guy's intention."

"Then you have an air affinity, I assume. Only powerful fae can manipulate an element to that degree, and only one specialty element. Mine is fire, for example."

Bryn looked around, checking again that we were alone, before flipping his hand palm up between us on the bench. Tiny, bright orange flames flickered to life from his fingertips. I watched in amazement as the fire seemed to lick harmlessly at his fingers.

It was mesmerizing. I really hoped I wasn't hallucinating this whole thing.

"Not all fae can do that?" I murmured, sucking in a startled breath as the flames suddenly vanished like they'd been absorbed into his palm.

"Not anymore. All fae have an affinity with one of the four primary elements—earth, water, fire, and air. We can all manipulate an element that's right in front of us. For example, I can manipulate small amounts of water if I have a bowl of water in my hands, but I can't conjure the liquid into existence the way I can with my affinity, fire. If you were in a closed room without a breeze to manipulate, it would appear you conjured it. That would be enough to catch Gwyneira's attention, especially from Albion. Magic died out in this realm centuries ago."

Bryn's annoyance died down and his excitement rose significantly while he was explaining the mechanics of magic, and I wondered if he was a bit of a nerd like me? Learning gave me the kind of happy buzz that only orgasms could beat.

"And what about the other thing I can do?" I pressed. "You said you have tracking magic, and the dean has guardian magic, so maybe mine is unique to me."

His eyebrows snapped together, and I felt his doubt like a curdling in my gut, even while his curiosity tingled behind my ears.

"Only fae blessed by the gods are gifted magic beyond their elemental abilities. What is it you think you can do?" he asked condescendingly.

Behind the pretty face, this guy really was such an asshole. I shouldn't have been surprised—the devastatingly beautiful ones always were. I looked him dead in the eye so he could see the honesty in my expression.

"Right now, you are feeling doubtful that I have other magic, angry—which you've been feeling since the minute we met—and a mixture of lust and resentment."

I chickened out of eye contact on the last bit. Bryn blinked at me slowly, and I felt his doubt morphing into an icky discomfort.

"You can feel emotions? Anyone's emotions?"

"Since I was a kid. I've always been able to do it."

"Anything else? Can you influence people to your will?" His panic was shooting through me like sharp splints.

"No! I would never do that. Is that a thing? I don't even like being *near* people for long periods of time. Too many emotions give me migraines."

I hated *feeling* other people's emotions, I definitely didn't want to *influence* them. Unless I could influence people to stay away from me, that honestly didn't sound so bad.

"What am I?" I meant for it to sound confident, but my voice was little more than a dread-filled whisper.

"Trouble," Bryn muttered, running a hand through his hair. "And rare. Extinct, in fact. There are plenty of fae who would love to get their hands on someone who can scout emotions, and most of them don't have honorable intentions."

He was confirming every worst fear I'd ever had about myself. I'd always known that whatever I was, it was no good.

Bryn stood, looking resigned. "Come on, *scout*. We need to go to Gwyneira before you attract the wrong attention from Avalon."

The walk back to the tube station with Bryn trailing a few steps behind me was a blur. I hadn't made any promises about going to a magical fairy realm—I wasn't quite that impulsive—but I hadn't entirely dismissed him as crazy yet either. In the meantime, I felt more comfortable continuing this conversation in the privacy of the room I rented in a boarding house.

Theoretically, bringing a strange boy I just met home was a terrible idea, but I felt a strange, overwhelming urge to trust Bryn, and it wasn't just because he'd *told* me he wasn't going to hurt me. I *felt* physically safe in his company, as well incredibly turned on, but it probably wasn't the best time to bring that up.

"How do you live in Albion? The pollution here is suffocating. You probably can't even feel your magic," Bryn muttered, wrinkling his nose as he stomped down the steps to the station at my side.

"What do you mean by 'Albion'?" I replied, ignoring his snide commentary.

"This," he said vaguely, gesturing at our surroundings. "All of the human realm is called 'Albion'. The original portal was at Stonehenge. The giants who occupied the area at the time called it Albion and the name stuck."

I blinked. "Giants? At Stonehenge?"

If he was spinning a story, it was an elaborate one.

"Obviously. They built it," Bryn scoffed.

"There aren't any giants in Britain. Or on Earth. I think we'd notice."

"First, 'they' not 'we'. You are fae, not human. And there aren't any giants here now, Albion is solely inhabited by humans. The remaining giant population moved to Avalon to recover their numbers and live peacefully."

Holy crap. *Giants.*

"Next you'll tell me dragons are real," I joked. Bryn looked at me like I was the stupidest person he'd ever met.

After that, we fell into silence as we made our way through the still quiet station and on the fairly long ride to my stop. I *wanted* to ask more questions, but Bryn didn't look particularly amenable to conversation. He looked a little like he was about to be sick.

Maybe they didn't have high speed trains in fairyland?

He lost some of the greenish tinge in his cheeks after we disembarked and made the brief walk back to my place. The silence had been helpful since I needed a minute to think about what I would do. I sort of felt that now the genie was out of the bottle, I couldn't get it back in. My magic trick—*literal magic*, apparently—to protect myself from Kayden had already brought attention to myself. What if someone else from this magical place had noticed it too?

I could sense Bryn's sincerity when he warned me that there were people with less-than-honorable intentions who would be interested in my abilities.

Maybe going with him to meet this Gwyneira person wouldn't be the worst idea. Surely, I could just talk to her? There was little I hated more than feeling uninformed. Knowledge was power, after all.

I let us into my small room in Mrs. Davey's boarding house, grateful that my lodgings were on the ground floor, closest to the front door. It had a big window facing the street and a smaller window on the side of the house, both of which were hidden by the curtains I hadn't bothered to draw before I'd left for work after my power nap. There were three other residents, all upstairs in the converted Victorian house.

The room was sparsely furnished with a sink, mini-fridge, kettle, a single bed, and a dresser to store my clothes—all of which had seen better days. It wasn't like I had a great job, and London was hella expensive. Still, I'd happily take this tiny little place over some of the fancier foster homes they had placed me in over the years.

"This is where you live?"

"Ah, he speaks," I muttered, cutting him a glare. "Yes, this is where I live. It's a boarding house. The landlady lives upstairs."

He frowned at that. "Are you close to her? She may alert the human authorities when you leave."

"First — 'if,' not 'when.' I haven't agreed to anything. No, she and I aren't particularly close. I'm sure if I left her a note and some money for rent, she'd be okay with never seeing me again." The words came out unwittingly, and the rational part of my brain wondered why I was giving him so much information.

"Appears you've really endeared yourself to humans during your time here, scout," he scoffed.

I wanted to slap him and then pin him against the wall kiss him stupid. My hormones were really clashing with my better judgment right now.

"Foster care has a way of making people distrustful," I snapped. "And my name is—,"

A loud knock on the front door that made me jump interrupted my retort. Bryn narrowed his eyes at me.

"Expecting company, scout?"

"No, but plenty of people live here," I snapped, crossing the room to peek out through the curtains.

Shit.

Two police officers stood on the front steps, looking impatiently up at the house.

Could be anything. They could be here for anything. They weren't for sure here for me. Right? Right.

My phone buzzed in my bag where I'd left it during my shift, and I pulled it out uneasily.

Unknown Number:

My face blanched, the phone in my hand shaking. Was this seriously happening? The dude had locked me in a room to assault me, and *he'd* reported *me* to the police? What had he even told them? That piece of shit.

Bryn strode into my personal space like he had every right to be there, reading the message over my shoulder before leaning out to look through the curtains, rolling his eyes impatiently as the police knocked again. He, at least, was taking this development oddly well.

Shit, any moment now the knocking would wake someone upstairs. Mrs. Davey would probably kick me out just for having the cops darken her doorstep, worried about what the neighbors would think.

"Look, I don't really have any vested interest in convincing you to come to the Academy. The dean sent me here to get you, so here I am," Bryn grumbled irritably, and I wondered if the insane connection I felt to him was completely one-sided.

"You're really selling it," I deadpanned, carefully letting the curtain fall shut. The knocking on the front door grew louder and waves of the officers' impatience lapped at my skin.

"Ffion Smith? Are you there? We'd just like to talk to you."

Bryn's annoyance was an uncomfortable chafing sensation over my arms, and I couldn't help but glare at him. It's not like I wanted to be in this situation.

"Your job is awful, and you live in a tiny, damp room, spending your days avoiding people so you don't get headaches. At the Academy, you'll have comfortable accommodations, receive a stipend while you study, and learn more about your abilities," Bryn listed, huffing like I was being difficult.

That did sound like a vast improvement over my current setup...

The officers were bickering on the front step, and I could already hear the creak of floorboards upstairs as someone got out of bed. My heart was doing double time in my chest. I wouldn't be able to lie to the police if I talked to them. I'd spend the rest of my life in a straitjacket if I told them I blasted Kayden away with *magic*.

"Plus, I doubt you'll be able to avoid those emotion-induced migraines in prison," Bryn added smugly. "Grab a bag, we're leaving out the side window. Unless you want to hang around with the humans and see how this plays out?"

He was an insufferable asshole, but he was an insufferable asshole who was making some excellent points.

Open the door and chance it with the cops, or sneak out the window with a sexy fairy? Fuck it. Maybe I could lie low for a while and come back when Kayden inevitably got himself arrested for doing something shady. It didn't seem worth taking the risk with the authorities.

Why was I fighting for the right to stay in a tiny room and work the graveyard shift as a cleaner, anyway?

I took a deep breath. Time to take a chance with a fae. Maybe I'd figure out how to make that air magic happen on demand and never be vulnerable again.

FFION

CHAPTER 4

As quickly as I could, I left Mrs. Davey enough money to cover the next month's rent on my dresser and a note saying sorry—not a lie—before shoving my meager belongings into a backpack. Bryn muttered a stream of complaints the entire time since, apparently, synthetic materials would quickly deteriorate in Avalon. Still, I had worked hard for the few things I owned; I felt more comfortable having them with me.

His comment made me pay closer attention to his clothes, though. I'd initially assumed he was some kind of trendy London hipster, but maybe his clothes were standard fae apparel? His pants were dark navy, but made of a linen fabric and loose, stopping just above his ankles. It looked like he had a white tunic type shirt underneath and a thick gray woolen jumper over it, the tails of the shirt hanging below the jumper.

On his feet were soft leather boots that looked straight out of the Middle Ages, lacing up over his ankles and underneath the bottom of his trousers.

I held my breath as we climbed onto my bed and then out the side window, Bryn leading the way, then used the rubbish bins to boost ourselves over the fence into the side alleyway. My muscles were burning, and I'd never been more grateful to live on the ground floor. We moved through the backstreets of the suburban South London neighborhood where I lived in silence, with me looking nervously over my shoulder the entire time.

Between what Bryn had told me, the physical response I was having to his presence and the powerful way his emotions were affecting me, I didn't trust myself to speak. I was finding it difficult to separate my feelings from his, and it was messing with my head.

After walking for fifteen minutes, Bryn awkwardly flagged down a cab and directed the driver to take us to the southernmost limits of the city. I wasn't sure how this whole magical realm thing worked—if it was even real—but Bryn acted like he'd been here before, in an unsure tourist kind of way.

It was already a gray day, and the sun had barely risen when we pulled up outside an ominous-looking pile of ruins.

"You sure this is where you want to be dropped, mate?" the driver called to Bryn. "It's an old cement quarry, hasn't been used since the war."

Bryn's irritation chafed at my skin again, but I was getting used to it. Irritated seemed to be his permanent state of being. Before he could snap at the poor driver, I assured him this was where we wanted to get out as Bryn paid him. Luckily, he had some cash on hand since I'd cleared myself out with the rent money for Mrs. Davey.

"Come on, then," Bryn grumbled, offering absolutely no explanation as he ducked under a 'No Entry' sign and began picking his way across the broken cement flooring and around rusted bits of machinery.

"It is an abandoned quarry, but it has also been glamoured to repel curious humans. It's a good site for a portal, close enough to London to be convenient, but out of the way of passersby."

Shocked that he was bothering to tell me any of this—without me even asking—I kept my mouth shut, so I wouldn't jinx it. I was also focusing on not getting tetanus from all the old bits of rusted metal sticking out in every direction.

I'd been planning on going home after work and crashing in bed for a few hours, then possibly hitting up the library later, and a club tonight. My life had taken a *very* strange turn in the past few hours since I had met this infuriating man, I was hoping that 'death by rust' wasn't my legacy.

We climbed a creaking metal staircase before Bryn stepped out onto a ledge in front of a large vat. It looked out of place amongst the ruins—too shiny and new to belong here—and filled with what *could* have been water, but I doubted it. It had a strange silver sheen to it that definitely didn't look like anything of this world.

Holy crap. This whole fairy thing was looking more real by the second.

"Welcome to the portal. You need to be carrying a token on you to pass through it so the Assembly can monitor who enters and exits. It also stops humans from accidentally getting into Avalon." Bryn looked at me, and his suspicion felt like a layer of tar coating my insides. "Your glamour will disappear when you pass through the portal. As will mine."

"My what?"

"Your glamour," he repeated slowly, like I had a hearing problem. I rolled my eyes. *Such a pompous ass.* "The enchantment that is making you look like a human."

"Oh, I don't think I have one of those. This is just what I look like," I said, shrugging nonchalantly. This was the same face I'd had my entire life. Surely I'd know if it had changed.

I eyed the shimmering vat suspiciously. "I'm not jumping into that if it's a one-way trip. I want your word that I can return here if I want to."

I had a funny feeling that if Bryn gave his word, he would honor it. I'd always felt a weird sense of significance whenever I had given my word; maybe it was a fae thing?

I felt the striking sensation of Bryn's sincerity again when he reached out to shake my hand. I clasped it, fighting the urge to shiver at the feel of his skin on mine. *Don't embarrass yourself, Fi.*

"You have my word. You can return to Albion if you wish. The Academy has no interest in imprisoning you," Bryn said solemnly, yanking his hand back like he couldn't get away fast enough.

He reached into his pocket before handing me two silver coins that had a small circular hole in the middle and tiny engravings around the edges. "The tokens. One will disintegrate in transit, but the other is for you to keep so you can come back to Albion if you wish to, as agreed."

I closed my fingers tightly around them, trying to decide if they *felt* magical or not, whatever magic felt like.

"See you on the other side," Bryn announced.

And with that, he jumped.

Of course he just freaking left me there. Why was I surprised? I'd known Bryn for maybe an hour, and it was exactly the kind of thing I expected him to do. I inched closer to the vat, peering into it for a few seconds, deliberating what to do. The vibe I'd gotten from Bryn before he jumped hadn't been malicious, it was challenging. He was daring me to do this on my own.

Was I really going to rise to his baiting?

Probably.

Yes, definitely.

I crouched down and began lowering myself slowly into the vat, idly wondering if I'd lost my freaking mind in the process. The liquid came alive once I was submerged, gently coaxing me through a swirling mass of silver mist. It felt like icy water against my skin, but my clothes didn't feel wet, and I seemed to be breathing just fine. *Weird.* So very weird.

After what felt like a few seconds, I broke the surface of a pond filled with the same silvery substance as the vat had been. I shot Bryn a quick glare as I pulled myself up next to him on the bank. *Thanks for waiting for me, asshole.*

I would have known we weren't in the human world anymore without even opening my eyes. The air here was so different, so clean and full of... something. Magic? It was something intangible, but I felt it deep in my bones, right down to my soul. There was an intoxicating rush in my veins, like a warm welcome home from the realm itself.

I'd just vat-dived into a different world. What the hell.

The portal was much nicer on the fae side than the human side—no tetanus-y old concrete mixers or broken glass in sight. It was housed in a meadow that shimmered in brilliant shades of orange and gold, full of the most spectacular flowers I had ever seen. They were far more vibrant than any I'd ever seen in London, or even on day trips to the country—they almost... glittered? Was that even possible?

Bryn stood, and I went to follow, stumbling slightly when my limbs failed to cooperate with me. *My long limbs,* I thought, staring down at my body with a frown.

"You're taller," Bryn said gruffly, staring intently at my significantly longer legs.

My skirt had been two inches above the knee when we'd left London, but now it was practically a belt. I pulled off my jacket, which had become restrictively tight under my arms, and found that my hoodie was basically a crop top, leaving a generous strip of stomach on display. Holy hell, how tall was I? My breathing quickened as I looked at my long limbs in a panic. I'd somehow grown a foot in the past three minutes, I needed a moment to freak out about this.

Bryn cleared his throat uncomfortably as his lust shot through the roof. Not helping. I felt every flash of his desire as an aching pulse between my thighs and a heaviness in my breasts. If this was going to be a regular thing here, I'd be taking cold showers every ten minutes.

"You're about average height for a female fae. That was quite the glamour you had on you," Bryn reassured me while managing to sound snide at the same time. It was quite a talent. His suspicion laced through my system like tar, and I had to grit my teeth to stop myself from snapping at him. At least until after his tour guide duties were over and I had some semblance of where the hell I was.

"What else looks different?" I asked politely, examining my arms and legs and ignoring Bryn's suspicion. He reached forward and tugged a long lock of curly hair toward my face.

"Your hair is lighter. It has gold tones. Same as your eyes." I tilted my face up to him. What he was saying didn't even sound that ludicrous—his eyes were brighter too, his entire already attractive face less *mundane* than it had been a few minutes ago. "They're amber, with gold flecks. Your features are sharper too."

I felt my face warm a little at how close he was standing, staring at me intensely. Bryn may be a total dickhead, but he was fine as hell and my hormones were doing a merry dance at his proximity.

Bryn pushed my mass of curls back to one side and ran his finger lightly over the shell of my ear. I immediately shuddered, biting back a moan while Bryn dropped his hand like I had burned him. What the hell was that? My ears had never felt that sensitive before.

This was not helping with my excitable hormone situation.

"Your ears are pointed. You look like a fae. Congratulations."

Bryn spun on his heel and marched through the grass without a backward glance, stomping to the edge of the meadow where a horse and carriage—an honest to god *horse and carriage*—were waiting. The driver appeared to be napping on the ground, but jumped up like he'd been electrocuted when Bryn's furious footsteps got closer.

I felt the driver's nerves skittering along the back of my neck, but not the strange tugging feeling in my chest. Apparently, feeling the emotions on my body was a fae-specific thing, but the magnetic pull was just a Bryn-specific thing. I had no idea how to make heads or tails of these fresh developments in my life. Everything from how I felt, how I looked, to the very *air* I was breathing was foreign.

The lust Bryn was feeling continued to pulse impatiently in my body, but there was also a healthy dose of his embarrassment burning in my cheeks that wasn't there before. I suspected it had to do with the whole ear-touching thing. I desperately wanted to see his fae ears underneath his messy hair, but it felt too personal to ask.

Without his glamour, Bryn's hair wasn't black like it had been back in London, it was more like a dark, midnight blue—the kind of color girls back home would pay good money to achieve. The blue in his eyes was as bright as sapphires, and he was still half a foot taller than me, but we were definitely much closer in height than we were in London.

The thought didn't excite me. My limbs felt uncomfortably long and gawky, like I was inhabiting someone else's 6ft tall body, but I guessed I'd get used to them?

Bryn muttered a few words to the driver while indicating the carriage I assumed we were traveling in. I climbed in and attempted to get comfortable on the thinly padded bench with Bryn following not long after, sitting opposite me and staring resolutely out the window. His emotions were all anger now, but they felt forced, and I wondered if he was trying to mask his other feelings by using rage as a cover. It was a smart tactic.

"Get comfortable, scout. Sleep if you like. It's about an hour's journey from here to the Academy." Bryn didn't look at me at all, and I decided not to push it.

Sleep probably wasn't the worst way to handle an hour enclosed in a tiny space with a man who inspired more lust in me than I had ever experienced. Particularly since he, rather inconveniently, seemed to despise me and all, but I couldn't bring myself to do it. As soon as the carriage started moving, I couldn't take my eyes off the majestic scenery outside the window. Avalon was nothing like London.

We traveled along a dirt path that wound through miles of forest, occasionally broken up by a meadow or rolling fields. The foliage was far more *alive* than anything I'd ever seen back home. Each flower was perfectly formed and had an iridescent sheen to it. Occasionally it looked like they were moving all on their own, rather than blowing in the breeze, but maybe it was just a trick of the light? I didn't know what to think. There were also fruit trees *everywhere*. Particularly apples. They didn't grow in an orchard, the fruit trees just seemed to sprout up naturally in the middle of the forest.

When we arrived at the portal, everything was bathed in gold from the low sun. Now it seemed like the sky was darkening, which was weird since we'd left London in the wee hours of the morning. Was there a time difference in realm travel? I had so many burning questions, but Bryn didn't seem to be in the mood for chit-chat.

My toes pinched uncomfortably in my now too-small shoes. Bryn had kicked off his boots already, and I noticed the driver wasn't wearing any shoes either, so I pulled mine off as discreetly as I could and shoved them in my bag. Probably not the best first impression, but I think my feet had grown an extra couple of sizes when I came through the portal. The shoes were a write-off.

Bryn was still staring resolutely out of his window, and I wondered idly if he'd moved at all the entire trip. Either the route we were traveling was quite remote or Avalon was less populated than the human realm. The only emotions I could pick up on the ride were Bryn's sickly unease, with the occasional smattering of anger, and the driver's warm contentment that wrapped around me like a familiar blanket. The contrasting emotions clashed uncomfortably within me, and if this was what life here would always be like, I wasn't sure if I'd be able to handle it.

The carriage pulled to a stop, and I was stunned to see an enormous treehouse above me that extended up to three stories into the uppermost branches. I gaped at it in awe. Was this where the dean lived? I probably should have asked Bryn for more information about where we were going. Did all fae live in trees? I'd always been obsessed with tree climbing, as far back as I could remember. Maybe that was my fae side showing?

We slid out of the carriage, and I slung my backpack over my shoulders as Bryn started up the rough-hewn log staircase that wound around the tree trunk without a word to me. I guess his brief, helpful stint of explaining things to me was over. It had been nice while it lasted.

A stately looking woman who could only be the dean greeted us at the door. She looked to be in her 90s, with deep lines defining her face and silver hair pulled back into a long braid all the way down her back. Her floor-length dark green dress was the same linen-fabric that Bryn was wearing. However, she also wore a thick wool cape with a high collar, held together by a silver brooch that looked like the Celtic knots I'd seen guys tattoo on themselves back home.

She had an air of authority and confidence rolling off her in waves. Still, I sensed genuine compassion, like a comforting arm wrapped around my shoulders that immediately put me at ease.

"Welcome to the Academy of Avalon. I am Master Gwyneira, the dean.

You may call me Gwyneira."

"Hello," I said, feeling a little awkward with her formality. "I'm Ffion Smith."

"Ffion, a beautiful name. Mr. Edan, thank you for your assistance. Come sit, both of you. Let us have tea." Bryn looked like he'd rather be anywhere else, but it seemed he couldn't turn down a direct request from the dean.

We sat in a simple sitting room with two comfortable dark blue armchairs, a glossy wooden coffee table, and a small emerald green couch. Bryn and I sat on the couch, leaning as far away from each other as possible, while Gwyneira took the armchair opposite.

Almost everything in the room was wood as far as the eye could see. Wooden floors, wooden walls, wooden ceiling, wooden furniture. There were candles scattered throughout the room, housed in little glass orbs. *They should really consider getting electricity here.* All of those candles were a major fire hazard.

The focal point of Gwyneira's sitting room was a large tapestry that covered most of one wall. It looked ancient; the colors had mostly faded, but some threads looked like they were spun gold and glinted in the light. In the middle of the tapestry, it depicted six figures in a circle, holding hands. They were indistinguishable from each other, all wearing the same long white robes with hoods that covered their faces. In the middle of the circle was a glowing orb where most of the gold thread was concentrated.

Each corner of the tapestry depicted one element. The top left had waves that looked like they were coming from the corner of the tapestry and crashing on the circle of figures. The top right depicted fire, licking flames and curling smoke creeping towards the center of the image. The bottom left showed earth with long, twisting vines covered in blooming flowers. Finally, the bottom right of the tapestry showed air, a furious, twisting tornado spiraling towards the six serene-looking beings in the center.

It was fascinating—though not particularly beautiful—but whatever it was portraying resonated deeply in my soul.

A dignified-looking man entered the room with a tray of tea and fruit.

Both Gwyneira and the man were barefoot too, I guessed that was just the style here? I was feeling pretty self-conscious in my denim miniskirt, cropped hoodie and bare feet. With my sudden growth spurt, my outfit was bordering on indecent.

"Ffion, will you tell me about yourself?" Gwyneira asked as she poured tea, and the man quietly excused himself. I felt his affection for her. Must be her husband.

While Bryn and Gwyneira's emotions weren't raising any alarm bells, I didn't feel ready to spill all my secrets to total strangers, so I kept it vague. "I was raised in foster care. I don't know my parents. I had some strange abilities and a lot of medical issues that put families off adopting me, so I stayed in care until I aged out. I've been working as a cleaner for the past three years in London."

"How old are you now?"

"I recently turned 20."

I left out the part about being found wandering around outside the orphanage as a three-year-old, dressed in oversized rags and no shoes, with 'Ffion' written on my arm. A conversation for another day. I was curious, but I didn't want Gwyneira to think I was in any rush to track down the parents who had abandoned me.

"Can you tell me more about these strange abilities and the medical issues you mentioned?" Gwyneira pressed.

"I guess I'm good at reading people," I said vaguely, shifting uncomfortably on the couch. "I get migraines if there are a lot of people around."

"She's an empath." Gwyneira sucked in a breath at Bryn's blunt declaration. "She read my emotions. And by the sounds of it, she has an air affinity." It could have been a compliment, but Bryn's tone was unaffected.

"I thought you must be powerful to draw my attention all the way from Albion," Gwyneira said, smiling kindly. "Once upon a time, most fae had powerful elemental magic, but it is increasingly rare these days. It is also difficult to use magic in Albion, where there is none in the atmosphere to draw from. Though there is always magic inside you that can be called upon—it is an essential part of what makes us fae."

"So, I have magic inside me? But there's also more magic in this, er, realm? And not on Earth?" I asked, my curiosity burning hot. Bryn bristled with irritation, but I felt Gwyneira's satisfaction with my questions.

"All fae have magic in their blood, even those who do not have an elemental affinity. While the fae's magic weakens with each generation, the magic of Avalon is constant, and it helps us harness our abilities. Albion, or Earth as you called it, was once filled with magic too," Gwyneira explained before turning to Bryn, who immediately straightened under her attention.

"An empath, you say?" she asked before her gaze met mine. "I do not mean to alarm you, Ffion, but I think it would be best to keep that information between the three of us for now. There were many empaths, once upon a time. Their abilities were coveted, and they were often hunted."

An icy trickle of fear ran down my spine that belonged entirely to me. "Once you fully come into your gift, you can use it to defend yourself. Until then, it would be safer for you to have mentoring sessions with me privately to learn more about your gift."

Bryn's surge of surprise shot acutely through my gut. Apparently, being personally mentored by the dean wasn't the norm.

"Unfortunately, although you are the same age as our third-year students, you will be in the first-year classes." She looked at me sympathetically. "I will arrange tutors for you where possible to get you caught up. Meet me at the arena tomorrow at nine am. We will do a simple test to confirm that you have an affinity for air magic and complete your class schedule then."

"I'm not actually sure yet if I want to attend the Academy. It's kind of a lot just up and leaving my entire life, you know? Even if I'm not human, that's all I've ever known..."

Not that I really had anything to go back to. I was curious about this supposedly powerful air magic I had, but I wasn't sure I wanted to explore my empath ability. I hadn't forgotten Bryn's words about influencing people, and that idea was terrifying.

Gwyneira smiled, and her emotions mostly read as respect rather than the irritation I expected.

"I imagine we have given you much to think about. Perhaps you could commit to a two-week trial period? You can leave whenever you wish, you are not a prisoner here. I think it would be beneficial for you to get involved and get to know the Academy before you decide. What do you think?"

"I have your word that I can leave?" I was pretty confident that this was a significant fae custom. It had worked to get the second token from Bryn— it was sitting heavily in the pocket of my skirt.

"You have my word that you can leave. We will never detain you here." Gwyneira reached out her hand and we shook on it, sincerity striking at my chest as it had with Bryn.

"You must be exhausted from your journey. Bryn, would you kindly walk Ffion to the dorms? I have cleared cabin 47 for her use."

His irritation chafed my arms again as he reluctantly agreed, staring resolutely at the floor. We were almost out the door when Gwyneira spoke again.

"You two are a strong match, highly compatible I'm sure."

Bryn's panic spiked as he stormed off ahead of me into the forest.

CHAPTER 5

I had a much better view of the campus on foot than I'd had from the carriage. It looked nothing like the large, stately universities I'd often walked past in London. The Academy of Avalon appeared to have been built in the middle of a forest, with as little clearing of trees done as possible. Almost every enormous tree in sight had a treehouse or two built onto it, all interconnected by swinging rope bridges.

'Treehouse' was definitely underselling it. They were more like tiny houses built around the trunks, with branches passing through the walls and ceilings. *Please, fairy gods, let me be living in a treehouse.*

There were lanterns dotted along the bridges and on the stoop of each treehouse that made the whole forest canopy twinkle. At that moment, it was really hitting me that I was somewhere *magical*.

On the ground were a collection of small buildings and open-air structures I assumed were classrooms. They were made of an assortment of materials—some wood, some stone, others looked sort of like clay. I could see other paths leading deeper into the forest, and I was desperately curious to explore them.

Bryn marched ahead of me until we approached a cluster of treehouses with a beautiful wooden staircase winding around a tree trunk to the ground. As we neared it, Bryn snagged the arm of a pretty, dainty girl with dusty pink hair who was walking past with a basket of dirty plates and napkins. I clamped down on the urge to grab his hand and either stake my claim or take a swipe at him to punish him for touching her. What the hell was happening to me? Maybe it's the air here in Avalon? I'd never felt this kind of jealousy and possessiveness before. I didn't even *like* Bryn.

"Briallen, this is Ffion," he said, letting go of her arm now he had her attention and easing the wave of violent anger that had just surged through me. "She's a new student, just arrived from Albion a couple of hours ago. Assume she knows nothing about anything. Cabin 47. I'll let you take over from here. See you around, scout."

And with that charming introduction, he stormed off into the night without a look backward. He really was such an asshole.

Briallen laughed, a musical sound that reminded me of wind chimes. There was something very pixie-like about her. Now my irrational jealousy had passed, I thought we may end up getting along—Briallen's emotions were so warm and fuzzy, they were giving me a contact high. Her happiness was *potent*. It felt like summer sunshine on my skin, and soft, tingly vibrations that ran over my skin to the tips of my fingers and toes. I barely resisted the urge to rub against her like a cat.

"I should have known Bryn would fight the mating pull. Never mind him; he'll come around. Eventually. As he said, my name is Briallen, Briallen Edan."

She smiled brightly, and I couldn't help but return it even though I was confused as hell about what she'd said about Bryn. I almost asked her to explain—Gwyneira had said something similar—but I suddenly wasn't sure if I wanted to know. I had enough on my plate, what with moving worlds and all, adding in boy complications seemed like a recipe for disaster.

"Another Edan?" I asked. "My name is Ffion, but most people call me Fi. Nice to meet you, uh, sorry about all this. I hope I didn't disrupt your evening."

"Not to worry, my mate, Leigh, is on guard duty tonight; I just brought him dinner," she said in her lilting voice, hoisting the basket further up her arm. *Mate?* "And yes, another Edan. Bryn and I are cousins." *Poor girl.*

"So you were visiting Albion? Why would Bryn tell me to assume you know nothing?" she pondered.

"Not visiting," I told her. "I grew up there. Bryn showed up a few hours ago and told me I'm a fae and that I can do magic?" I hadn't meant for it to come out as a question, but it all still felt extremely surreal.

"You didn't know you were fae? How is that possible?" Briallen blinked slowly at me, and I felt her shock surging through my gut.

"I guess I thought I was a strange human," I laughed nervously. *How was this my life?*

"Right, then." Briallen laughed and clapped her hands together, rattling the basket on her arm. "Shall I show you to your room to wash up? I can go find you some food from the commons in the meantime. I've never traveled between realms, but I imagine it would make you work up an appetite."

"That would be amazing," I said as my stomach rumbled embarrassingly loudly. "Also, perhaps you could help me find some clothes? I don't want everyone to realize right away that I'm not from around here."

Briallen was wearing a pale blue linen wrap dress that was loose and hung to her knees. Over the top was a bulky brown woolen cardigan. Like everyone else I'd met in Avalon, she didn't have shoes. Her blush-colored hair was French braided across her crown and hung down over one shoulder.

Briallen smiled kindly. "Your room will be stocked with some basic clothes. Come, I'll show you."

Cabin 47 was a small but beautiful treehouse built above someone else's. Briallen let me in before disappearing to find me some food and let me explore.

Apparently, I had the cabin to myself, which was a pleasant surprise. There was a platform either side of the room in the rafters, accessible by ladders, that each had a double bed on them. On the main floor, there was a washbasin in the main room and a separate little closet with a toilet and a rainfall showerhead in it, accessible by a couple of stairs.

The room was comfortably furnished with an antique wardrobe, two cozy armchairs, a wooden desk and some shelves, and a small square table with two chairs. Next to the wardrobe was a heavy wooden chest, which I peeked in and found some spare linens and thick woolen blankets. A potbelly stove sat against one wall next to the armchairs, with an ancient-looking kettle resting on top. There were heavy rugs, gauzy curtains, and pastel-colored patchwork quilts on the beds. The whole place felt homey and perfect.

I'd certainly lived in worse places.

One of the cabin windows was larger than the others, easily big enough to climb out of, and I noticed a small wooden platform underneath the window to stand on. I clambered out to look around. The platform was only big enough for me to take a step in either direction but looking up at the strings and pegs mounted overhead of me; it was clear this area was for drying clothes. Maybe the washbasin was multipurpose?

Before Briallen could return, I had a quick, tepid shower since apparently treehouses didn't get boiling water. I wasn't complaining—at least there was indoor plumbing, and I'd never had a bathroom to myself before.

Wrapped in a cotton towel, I quickly crossed the room to the freestanding wardrobe, pulling the double doors open to see what I could find. It was pretty well-stocked considering I wasn't being charged anything to study here—yet, at least. Everything appeared to be wool, linen or cotton, and I felt sort of medieval peasant-chic even as I picked out a simple singlet and matching shorts in a khaki color that sort of looked like pajamas. I grabbed a cream-colored woolen cardigan to wear over the top before looking through the small baskets on the bottom shelf that housed new-looking undergarments.

I mean, new was good. I was grateful for that. Slightly alarmed at how thin and unsupportive everything was compared to what I was used to. The underwear seemed to sort of lace-up and tie at the sides, and I tugged it up clumsily, knotting it before pulling on the shorts and tightening the drawstring. The singlet was too large, but I wasn't about to tackle the bikini-like bra just to sleep, so I wrapped the cardigan tightly around me and used the attached belt to secure it in place.

With the size of my breasts, I was sure I'd be dreaming about underwire bras when I fell asleep tonight. The idea of living my life in a bikini top was almost more terrifying than the prospect of *feeling* everyone else's emotions as though they were my own.

Almost.

"Are you decent?" Briallen called, knocking on the cabin door. I quickly let her in, and she solidified her spot as my favorite fae by bringing an enormous bowl of salad, filled with nuts and vegetables, and a side of fruit.

"No meat?" I joked, accepting the bowl and taking it over to the small table.

She looked at me in horror. "Fae don't eat meat!"

Oh good. Already putting my foot in it, and I only just got here.

"Ah, I guess I'll need to rethink my diet," I laughed awkwardly, playing off my faux pas as I grabbed a fork and dug in. It wasn't bad as far as salads go. Maybe giving up meat wouldn't be that much of a hardship. Then again, grilled chicken would take this salad from 'good' to 'spectacular'...

Briallen perched on the armchair, and I didn't need my special emotion reading abilities, sorry—*empath "gift"*—to tell she was nervous about something.

"Spit it out Briallen, I promise I won't bite," I smiled, trying to put her at ease. I wanted to make sure Briallen felt comfortable around me so she'd hang out with me again. I was getting a light buzz from all the positive vibes she was putting out.

"Ah, did Gwyneira talk to you at all about the *Pull of Cúpláil,* or mating circles?"

I cocked an eyebrow at her. "She sort of mentioned something about Bryn and I being, er, compatible? I guess she was more focused on the basics. You know, 'what is a fae,' 'how magic works' that kind of thing."

All of these words felt so foreign on my tongue, like I was describing a fairytale instead of my actual life.

"Right," Briallen laughed nervously. "Usually, I wouldn't bring it up, but I don't want you to go into tomorrow unprepared, especially as you and Bryn are already feeling the pull. If you're compatible with a fae as strong as Bryn, there's a good chance you'll feel the pull with some other unmated male fae at the Academy. Those who aren't mated because they haven't encountered a female fae as strong as you before."

I stared at her a little too long as I tried to process what she was saying. I would feel a pull? To powerful unmated males?

"*Pull of Cúpláil* means the pull of mating. It's felt by two people whose magic is strong enough to support one another. It doesn't mean you have to claim that person as your mate; we always have free will. Chances are you will meet many people with whom you feel some kind of pull, but the stronger the feeling, the better the match for both your magic and your soul. A powerful pull indicates compatible magic and kindred souls," Briallen continued.

I blinked, her sincerity giving me that strange, gong-striking feeling in my chest. "So that weird tugging feeling in my chest I had around Bryn was the... mating pull?"

Briallen's eyes lit up, and she grinned. Her excitement made my skin almost vibrate all over my body. "Yes! I mean, I assumed that's why he was acting so strange, but you've just confirmed it."

I felt my cheeks heating. Maybe I shouldn't have said that?

"Ah, perhaps don't bring it up around him. Or anyone. You said we have a choice to, um, pursue things, right? I highly doubt Bryn and I will be pursuing anything."

"We'll see." She winked like she knew something I didn't. "You're right about the choice to pursue, though. To cement a mating bond, you have to actually claim each other. It's a private ceremony of sorts between the two in question, and then consummated."

She didn't look embarrassed in the least to be explaining this to me while I felt like burying my head in a pillow like a kid getting the birds and the bees talk.

"If you feel the mating pull and decide to get to know them better, they become your 'suitor.' Once you claim each other, they're your 'mate.' Fae mate for life," Briallen explained.

"Well, I'm confident I don't want to spend my life with Bryn. We'd drive each other insane," I replied instantly.

"You never know. You may need one of your mates to challenge you while the others balance him out."

"*One* of my mates? The *others*?" I choked out. I was definitely missing something here.

Briallen looked a little sheepish. "Sorry, humans usually only take one mate at a time, right? Fae females have a mating circle. I have one mate and enough magic for one more; that's standard in Avalon. You feel powerful, and you've already felt a mating pull to one of the strongest male fae in the Academy, so I assume you'll have three. Lucky girl."

There was that wink again. Lordy, this girl was too much.

"Why would I want three, er, *mates*?" I asked, stumbling slightly over the odd word. "I didn't even want one boyfriend in what's it called? Albion? I definitely don't need three at once."

"A human suitor wouldn't have been suited to you since he had no magic. You wouldn't feel any kind of pull to be with them. Fae can't sustain a relationship without the mating pull. Some try, or have casual flings—fae have more relaxed attitudes towards our bodies and sexuality than humans as I understand it. But long-term relationships do not survive without a strong mating pull to build from."

I mulled this over in my mind as Briallen told me about how she'd met her mate, Leigh, during their first week at the Academy before claiming each other six weeks later.

"Six weeks?" I spluttered. "Isn't that kind of quick considering the whole mating-for-life thing?"

Briallen laughed, and I let out a small sigh of relief that I hadn't offended her. It was stressful not knowing the parameters of acceptable behavior in this unfamiliar world I'd found myself in.

"Not for fae. When we feel a powerful pull, we're all in straight away. Your soul knows, your magic knows, so why wait? Besides, the closer you get to them, the more the mating pull encourages you to claim them. It's hard to hold off for more than a couple of months if you spend a lot of time together."

"Do you still feel the mating pull then? Since you've already got a mate? You said your magic could support two? Wouldn't Leigh be jealous?"

She smiled at my volley of questions. "I do still feel the mating pull from time-to-time, but much weaker than the pull I felt to Leigh. Knowing how strong that connection was, I couldn't settle for anything weaker. As for Leigh, he'll be there every step of the way when I find someone I want to pursue as a second mate. He'll get to know him, and hopefully they'll be fast friends. I wouldn't pursue anything that made Leigh unhappy, but if the new male was highly compatible with me, he and Leigh would probably have a lot in common. My fathers do. My mother met them three years apart, but you'd never know one had been around longer than the other."

"I have so many questions from what you just said, but I think I should probably sleep on it and give my brain some time to absorb all of this," I replied, blinking slowly at her. Did everyone here have multiple dads?

Did I have multiple dads?

Had I been abandoned by not one, not two, but *three* parents?

Briallen laughed. "Sorry Fi, I really didn't mean to overwhelm you. There are quite a few strong male fae in the senior year, and amongst the teaching assistants. If you don't feel a pull to at least one of them, I will clean your cabin for a week; that is how confident I am. Get some rest, we'll come to collect you tomorrow morning at eight, and we can go to breakfast together."

I showed Briallen out before clambering up the ladder to the bed. It was a cold evening, and I had no idea how to start a fire, so I curled up in bed instead, pulling the soft linen sheets and heavy patchwork quilt up around me. There was a fur coverlet strewn across the bottom of the bed, but I felt weird using it. God knows what kind of fur it was. I'd make do with the nice, safe quilt.

The bed itself was a mattress on the floor of the platform. It was encased in a large rectangular wooden frame, but there was no headboard. I burrowed into the impossibly soft mattress, pushing my fingers deep into the fabric. I think it was genuinely made of feathers? Whatever it was, I had never slept on something so comfortable in all my life.

There was a heavy, inky blue curtain that could be pulled along the edge of the platform for privacy, and above the bed was an enormous circular skylight that gave me a perfect view of the stars. Even without a roommate, I'd be pulling the curtain across. I loved the idea of cocooning myself in my own little world each night, just the endless night sky and me.

Laying in bed, staring up at the sky, I reflected on the insane few hours I'd just had. As much as I tried to distract myself, my thoughts kept drifting back to my conversation with Briallen.

"I sincerely hope she's wrong," I muttered.

I had an unfamiliar world to adjust to, air magic to learn, plus this super-rare-highly-coveted-empath-ability, which I had to hide. I had more than enough on my plate without adding a man or three into the mix.

FFION

CHAPTER 6

I woke up to the gentle, whimsical chiming of bells. Early morning sunlight streamed in through the skylight above my head as I stirred slowly, grateful for the warmth on my face and lack of blaring alarm. I felt more rested than I had ever remembered feeling.

Maybe it was the fresh air?

Something in Avalon seemed to agree with me, and I felt more curious than apprehensive about my first day of classes.

Pulling back the privacy curtain, I could spot the clock on the wall downstairs. *Perfect, half an hour until Briallen was due to arrive.* I headed into the bathroom to wash my face and tame my curls as best I could, pulling them into a low ponytail secured with a strip of linen, and hoped for the best given there was no mirror in the cabin or curl-friendly products. It definitely made getting ready in the morning a lot quicker.

Flicking through the array of dresses and tunics in the antique wardrobe, I noticed that despite the fabrics they used, fae fashion wasn't quite as old-fashioned as I first assumed. Still, it was definitely different from my human wardrobe. Almost everything was made of linen, though there were some heavy woolen items in there that would suffice for colder weather. It seemed as though the fae's nature-based lifestyle extended to their fabrics.

I chose a loose indigo-colored dress with a boat neck top and short, batwing sleeves. It fell to just under my knees, and there was a thin belt that I pulled tight at the waist. Just because everything was baggy doesn't mean I had to look like I was wearing a potato sack. I pulled a long cream woolen cardigan over the top. It wasn't nearly as cold as it had been in London, but the air was fresh and brisk.

I had a few minutes to spare before Briallen was due to arrive, so I pulled out my phone intending to kill some time. I wasn't entirely shocked to see that it seemed to have died on the way to Avalon. Digging around in my backpack, I found my clothes already looked like they were falling apart, just as Bryn had warned me they would. Was it the magic in the air? They looked like they'd been attacked by a swarm of moths overnight.

I gave a final, longing look at my favorite pair of jeans before conceding that I'd be limited to wearing linen dresses like all the other females here. I suppose I should be grateful. With my sudden growth spurt, my human clothes wouldn't fit me anymore.

Hearing a knock on the door, I opened it to find Briallen and a tall man who I assumed was Leigh. All I could really tell about him was he had light brown hair—he was standing behind Briallen with his entire face buried in her neck, nuzzling her from behind. She had mentioned last night that fae were pretty chill about sex. Maybe PDA was more of an accepted thing here?

"Good morning!" Briallen chirped, her happiness rolling off her and over my skin like a soothing wave. "I hope you slept well?"

"Very well, thank you. Is this Leigh?"

"Indeed," she giggled. "Leigh Edan, this is the new friend I was telling you about, Fi."

"Pleasure to meet ya, Fi," he tossed me a cheeky grin and a wink, then returned his attention to Briallen's neck. His accent differed from Briallen's; it had an almost Irish lilt to it. *How big was Avalon?* These were the kinds of questions I should have asked instead of learning the ins and outs of mating circles.

"Edan?" I asked, grabbing the canvas satchel next to the door that held a slate board, a couple of pencils and an empty glass bottle with a lid I assumed was for water. Leigh and Briallen carried similar bags, though theirs looked a lot heavier. Hopefully, I would get my textbooks in class. The slate board was throwing me for a loop.

"Are you wondering if we're related?" Briallen giggled as I locked the door and we began walking down the stairs to the grass below. "Don't worry, Fi. It's nothing like that! Mated males take the female's name. It would be incredibly confusing otherwise."

"Right, of course. That totally makes sense. So do you two have affinities as well? I meant to ask you last night, Briallen, but you distracted me." I gave her a pointed look, and she grinned in response.

"I have an earth affinity, and Leigh has an air affinity. I assume you had at least an affinity, since you felt a strong pull to Bryn," Briallen stated carefully.

"Air, I think. I have to go to the arena this morning to test it and find out for sure," I replied, excited that I had met someone who also had an air affinity. Maybe Leigh could give me some pointers.

"We're both fourth years, so we won't be in any of your classes. But if you have any questions at all, we'd be happy to help," Briallen said kindly, as if reading my mind.

"Briallen reckons you've got some kind of secret gifted ability that you're not telling anyone about. There's naught I love more than a challenge, Fi. What do you say? Can I wager you for it? A game of cards? Chess? If I win, you tell me your secret," Leigh offered with a cheeky smile, and I felt only genuine enthusiasm and burning curiosity coming from him. As if it was totally normal to extract secrets from someone you literally just met. Maybe it was a fae thing?

"Ah, no. I mean, I'll play a game of cards with you, but if I win, you don't get to ask about my magic again, and if you win... well, I still won't tell you about my magic. Regardless, we'll play a game of cards and get to know one another."

I gave him a slight smile to soften my words, but I absolutely was not telling this fae anything personal. Leigh only grinned in response, clearly interpreting my words as a challenge.

"Briallen mentioned you were on guard duty last night. What's that about?" I asked, not-so-subtly changing the subject.

"Eh, nothing exciting. All the male students are rostered on guard duty twice a week to protect the campus. Nothing ever happens, it's usually very anticlimactic," he said with a shrug.

"No need to sound so disappointed, Leigh. Are you hoping for a near-death experience? A maiming perhaps?" I teased, and Leigh laughed. *How come only the male students had to do guard duty?* Apparently, it wasn't just the clothes that were a little old-fashioned here.

"Briallen, my love, I bet you the choice of the next three date nights that young Fi here will be a strong match for our Marlen!" Leigh's excitement was rolling off him in waves, and I idly noticed that it was the second bet Leigh had made in just the past several minutes. Was it a Leigh thing or a fae thing? I was partial to a good wager myself.

"I'm not taking that bet," Briallen laughed. "There's no question they'll have a powerful pull."

"I'm really not looking for any, um, mates or suitors or whatever, Leigh."

"Mmm," Leigh responded noncommittally. "We're just going to make one quick stop before we head to the commons, then I promise we'll get breakfast. Come along Fi, we won't be long."

I noticed the subtle deflection and marveled at how different it was interacting with fae who couldn't lie after a lifetime of talking to humans who could.

Leigh ducked up the stairs to a treehouse while Briallen and I waited on the grass below, and she pointed out various buildings where classes took place. A few minutes later, Leigh reappeared with a beautiful, tall, red-headed man at his side, and I felt the same forceful yank in my chest I'd experienced just yesterday. His fresh, woodsy pine scent surrounded me, consuming my senses the moment he appeared.

"Fi—this is my best friend, Marlen Ferris. Marlen, meet Ffion Smith. She's new here; just arrived from Albion yesterday."

Leigh's giddy excitement was so intense that it broke through the haze of lust and wonder I was in, and I shook my head a little to clear it. *Focus, Fi!*

Marlen was so handsome though, it was hard not to stare at him. His hair was a vibrant, dark red, and he had a decent five o'clock shadow around his cut jawline. Like all fae, his eyes were so brilliant they almost glowed. Marlen's were a bright emerald, and I wanted to stare into them for hours. His pale skin was so smooth and flawless, I kind of wanted to bite it.

Did no one have blemishes here? There weren't any mirrors for me to check, but when I washed my face this morning, I noticed that my skin felt fantastic.

"Hello, Marlen, nice to meet you."

I tried to play it cool even though I felt anything but. His gaze was lasered in on me and filled with heat; it really wasn't helping.

"Lovely to meet you," he took my hand and brushed his lips gently over my knuckles. *Is this what swooning felt like?* I'm pretty sure I was swooning.

"Come," Marlen said, offering me his arm to take. *What a gentleman.* "Let's get some breakfast, and you can tell me everything there is to know about you."

Marlen and I walked arm-in-arm through the campus towards the commons where food was served. I berated myself internally the entire time as the mating pull did a happy jig in my chest, thrilled at the physical contact between us.

A couple of times, I felt a swell of emotion that would indicate a crowd nearby which I assumed was the commons. I had a sneaking suspicion that Leigh and Briallen were leading us along the scenic route, so Marlen and I had more time to talk.

"So, Fi, how long were you in Albion for?" Marlen asked curiously.

"Er, forever?" I answered, a little taken off guard by the question. "I grew up there."

Surprise rolled off him in waves. "So your family is in Albion?"

"I'm not entirely sure," I admitted. "I thought I was human until yesterday."

I had contemplated not telling anyone that, but it seemed better than everyone thinking I was just useless at magic and an idiot about all things fae.

"I... Wow. Honestly, I'm not even sure how to respond to that," Marlen said, bewildered. I appreciated that he wasn't pretending that my situation wasn't several shades of screwed up.

I laughed, but it was a little hollow. "I'm not sure what to think about all of this, my head is kind of a mess right now. What about you? What's your story?"

"Nothing as interesting as yours, I'm afraid. I'm the youngest of four. My parents are bakers in a tiny village a few hours away from here. I'm in my fourth year at the Academy..." he trailed off, seemingly thinking about what he could say next. Marlen was full to the brim with playful, positive emotions, but flashes of self-doubt would appear at random. I doubted anyone realized that this seemingly suave, confident man experienced such frequent bouts of insecurity.

I wasn't going to approach *that* topic though. I needed to keep the conversation light, lest I give him the wrong impression about where this was heading. This mating pull thing had to go.

"So, how do you know Leigh and Briallen?"

Marlen's eyes lit up. "Leigh and I met at a sporting competition when we were ten. The contests are a way for young fae from all over Avalon to meet each other. We roomed together at the competition and ended up writing to each other after we went home. I was thrilled when I found out he'd be attending the Academy too."

Marlen's excitement and love for his friend felt genuine, and it endeared me to him a little more. He was obviously a loyal person. *No! No encouraging the mating pull. Stop it.*

"I met Briallen the same time Leigh did," he continued. "They were pulled together during our first week and have been inseparable ever since. She's a wonderful friend. I relied on her a lot when I was missing my sister."

He gave me a slight smile, but I felt his wave of sadness.

"I only met Briallen last night when I arrived at the Academy," I offered. "She has been very kind to me."

"That's B," Marlen said, perking up.

"What's B?" Briallen asked, her and Leigh appearing out of nowhere. "Are you two hitting it off?"

I rolled my eyes affectionately at her lack of subtlety. "I believe I was promised breakfast, you two."

"Right you are, Fi," Leigh laughed. "A fae never goes back on their word. Let's away!" he said with a flourish, and took off with Briallen in tow.

"Come on, let's get you fed," Marlen smiled, guiding me by the arm after them.

FFION

CHAPTER 7

The commons were a large, circular building made of some kind of whitewashed clay with a thatched roof and wooden floor. It felt very rustic and homey. We had come in through the main double doors, but there were other exits all around the room that students were streaming in and out of. The room was filled with tables of various sizes, with benches and mismatched wooden chairs scattered haphazardly throughout.

One side of the room was dominated by an enormous food station. There was the most elaborate salad bar I'd ever seen with every kind of vegetable, and a variety of non-meat proteins. Next to that was a buffet table with assorted flatbreads and fruit. It all looked very... healthy.

I scanned the buffet table eagerly for coffee, but all I could see were assorted flavors of tea and freshly squeezed juices.

"Looking for something in particular?" Marlen asked. "I like the blackcurrant tea personally."

"I don't suppose you have coffee here?"

Briallen grimaced, "Gods no, why would you want that? Caffeine is terrible for your magic."

Marlen shot her a glare. "Which Fi wouldn't know, having only found out about magic yesterday."

It was sweet of him to jump to my defense when he didn't even know me.

He really was dangerously easy to like.

"Some fruit here doesn't grow in Albion. Why don't you sit down, and I'll bring you over a plate of stuff to try?" Marlen gave me an affable smile, and I couldn't help but return it. I wasn't going to get into all of that mating nonsense with him, but I could definitely see his appeal.

The boys left to get breakfast for the four of us, and I felt a sharp tug in my chest that drew my gaze towards Bryn. I found his beautiful ocean blue eyes already on me, looking so intently it felt like he was gazing into my soul. Then I noticed the petite little blonde on his lap sucking on his neck like a leech, and anger welled up in me like bubbling lava.

Was this how I would always feel around him? Bryn clearly didn't want me, and obviously I didn't want him. Was I forever going to respond like a raging bull whenever I saw him getting handsy with another woman? It would drive me crazy.

Not even all the emotions I was picking up from everyone else in the room could drown out my reaction.

After a few tense moments of eye contact, Bryn stood and towed the little blonde through a door behind him. My rage lessened once they weren't right in front of me, but I had a pretty good feeling I knew what they were off to do, and that thought made me feel a little ill. Turning to Briallen, I found her staring at the door Bryn had just disappeared through with a slight frown on her face.

Her emotions were a mix of disappointment and irritation, which seemed so uncharacteristic of sunny Briallen that I snapped out of my own funk.

"Hey, don't worry about that. We already knew Bryn wasn't interested in me, remember? I don't want any mates anyway," I murmured softly.

"I always knew he would struggle with a strong mating pull. Bryn values control, and a strong pull challenges that. But I never thought he would continue pursuing his barely there connection with Saffir."

Briallen's frown deepened, her eyes still narrowed on the now closed door.

"Continue things? As in they're already together?" The idea that he already had a girlfriend sent a sharp pain through my chest, right where I felt the mating pull. "He shouldn't end things with her on my behalf. He doesn't want me."

The words tasted like ash on my tongue, but I knew they were right. I didn't want to rip someone else's relationship apart, regardless of the magnetic feeling in my chest that insisted Bryn should be mine.

"The mating pull changes things, though," she said quietly, before shaking her head as if to clear it, leading me over to a free table and dropping into a seat.

"Sorry about before, for the caffeine thing," Briallen added sheepishly. "It's so surreal to me you didn't grow up here and don't know about this world. I didn't mean to be rude."

"I'm not mad," I quickly assured her, sensing her sincerity. "I'll probably say stupid things a lot, though, just so you're prepared. It would have never occurred to me that my diet would affect magic."

"I wonder if you'll have some kind of detox period," she mused. "Lots of things in Albion are bad for fae magic. Pollution, synthetic materials, food additives, the unnatural environment... You were eating meat too, right?"

"Er, yes," I mumbled, feeling oddly embarrassed about it.

"You won't find that at the Academy—all fae are vegetarians. A lot only eat raw food, and that's the easiest way to cater to so many students, so that's most of what you'll find in the commons. They load the food table up from sunrise to sunset. Just help yourself whenever."

She waved her hand in the direction of the buffet table, and I wept a little internally. A lifetime of salad? Maybe I wouldn't love Avalon after all.

The boys arrived at that moment, halting my pity party before it could properly kick off. Marlen told me about each item of food he'd chosen, and I dutifully tried all of it, although I forgot the names of everything almost straight away. It wasn't bad or anything, just not the greasy bacon and eggs that *I* considered a quality breakfast. Surely I would get used to the diet once I was eating it regularly. I appreciated Marlen explaining everything to me; my curious brain soaked up everything he was saying.

Briallen and Leigh sat opposite us, and I covertly admired how well suited they seemed to be. They were always laughing, flirting, and touching one another. The love they felt toward each other radiated off them and made me feel all gooey inside.

"You two have matching tattoos?" I blurted out, spotting the similar inky black lines on their inner left wrists. "That's kind of cute."

They both laughed, and Marlen gave me an indulgent smile like I was adorable.

"They're not tattoos," Marlen said, tipping his chin at the marks. "They're claiming marks. They appear after the ceremony. The mark itself is an ancient rune, determined by the female's magic."

Briallen held out her wrist so I could get a better look. "Mine is unfinished, see?" She grabbed Leigh's wrist and yanked it towards me, so I could compare. Sure enough, Briallen's lines looked about half done.

"Why?" I asked curiously.

"My mating circle isn't complete. When I claim my second mate, the rest of it will appear. It's how I can be certain I'll only have two mates. If I had three, only a third of the mark would have shown up when Leigh and I claimed each other. Leigh's mark is the finished rune."

It was fascinating, and I appreciated them for taking the time to explain it, even if I felt a little uncomfortable discussing anything mating-related with Marlen and his super-strong mating pull sitting right there. I'd save my questions about what the rune symbolized for later when Marlen wasn't around.

Besides, the commons was filling up and the emotional bombardment was getting to be too much. My head was pounding, and my muscles hurt from tensing up so tightly.

"Are you okay, Fi?" Marlen moved closer and rested his hand gently on my lower back. His presence was so soothing that I relaxed into him instinctually. I'd worry about the ramifications of that later. When my brain wasn't exploding.

"I have a bit of a thing about crowds," I muttered vaguely. "I might head out; I need to find the arena, anyway. Thank you for breakfast," I added, offering him a weak smile.

"I have this lesson free; I'll walk you there," Marlen said, already standing and gathering our satchels. I told my goodbyes to Leigh and Briallen and exhaled in relief as we left the commons and the sea of feelings behind.

Marlen guided me through a maze of small buildings, some made of clay and some stone until we came to a dirt path that followed the forest's treeline.

"You really don't need to walk me the entire way. Just point me in the right direction," I assured him self-consciously.

"Don't worry, Fi, I'll wait outside. I'd have hated an audience for my elemental testing." Marlen threw me another one of his disarming, cheeky grins. Spending time with him was effortless. It had 'danger' written all over it.

"Is that because it'll be embarrassing? I'm not sure what they're expecting—I used air magic once by accident. If it wasn't for the pointy ears, I'd be convinced I was still human and you were all screwing with me. I'm still kind of on the fence about it."

Marlen chuckled. "There's no doubt in my mind that you're fae, foxglove."

He absentmindedly rubbed the spot in his chest where I could feel the mating pull and a primal part of me delighted at knowing I had an effect on him. The rational part of my brain was clearly on the fritz.

"Foxglove?"

"You don't like it? Ffion means foxglove."

Oh no, that was way too cute.

"I don't *not* like it," I admitted, and he gave me a crooked grin.

"Foxglove it is," Marlen said, his handsome face lighting up. "Don't worry about your lack of experience with magic, no one will expect you to be proficient after living in Albion your whole life. It's pretty inhospitable to magic there now, except for glamours. Even the weakest fae can at least glamour their ears, hair, and eye color. It's a self-preservation thing."

My brain did a happy dance as I absorbed all the fae knowledge Marlen was giving me. The migraines and constant moving around had made it hard for me to enjoy school, and I'd ended up leaving early for the peace and solitude of my cleaning job. Being here was an opportunity to indulge in the learning I'd always wanted to indulge in, so long as I could keep the migraines at bay.

"Do you know why Albion is inhospitable to magic now?" I asked curiously.

What I really wanted to ask was how I had a glamour on me when I hadn't put it there myself, since that didn't fit the description Marlen had given of how glamours worked. Unless I'd been subconsciously disguising myself somehow? Surely I wouldn't have been able to do that as a toddler though...

I deliberated on whether I should bring it up, but decided it was a better question for Gwyneira instead. I'd only just met this guy.

Marlen gave me an apologetic look and I caught a flash of his insecurity again. "Sorry, Fi. I was never much good in theory classes. You'll have a History of Albion course at some point in your second year, I think." He shrugged and grinned at me. "I'd be happy to tutor you for combat class, though?" he asked hopefully, and I felt a brief surge of his lust between my thighs that was probably Marlen's. Probably.

"Are you sure you're not just looking for an excuse to get your hands on me?" I flirted back, then internally cursed because I wasn't supposed to be encouraging this. *Idiot!*

"Always," he replied, voice filled with sinful promise. Every part of me tingled in response, and I exhaled in relief as we arrived at a gigantic stone structure that looked like an arena. If we'd had to walk alone together any further, I was at risk of pinning him against a tree and begging him to have his way with me. Damn Kayden for interrupting my plans to get laid the previous night. My libido was at genuine risk of overruling my common sense.

The arena was a circular structure, made entirely of stone, with stairs scattered throughout to lead spectators up to the higher seats. It reminded me of the Roman ruins I'd visited once on a school trip, though this was in much better shape.

"I'll wait out here," Marlen assured me with another one of those guard-destroying smiles, leaning against the wall next to a large archway.

"You don't have to," I protested. "I don't even know how long it'll take."

I was a little taken aback by his kindness; we'd just met *this morning*. I had been The New Kid many times over in my life, and no one had ever given me so much of their attention.

I would have put it down to the mating pull, but Bryn couldn't have gotten away from me faster.

"The test doesn't take long. Don't stress, foxglove. I'll wait, I enjoy your company. Plus, you'll probably get lost trying to get back on your own."

I laughed, already heading through the archway and waving him goodbye. "Okay, I won't argue with you. Wish me luck."

"Ffion," Gwyneira greeted me warmly as I exited the gladiator-style corridor into the arena. She stood next to a serious, imposing-looking man, but his emotions weren't concerning. He felt studious, assessing, and a little impatient.

"This is Master Eurig. He is the head of the air mastery discipline here at the Academy and teaches fourth-year students. Master Eurig, this is Ffion Smith. She just arrived here from Albion last night. Ffion grew up there and has not experimented with the elements yet. We believe she has an air affinity."

That definitely piqued his curiosity, and elicited a healthy dose of doubt. I hadn't asked anyone about how often fae grew up in Albion, but based on everyone's reaction, it must be unusual.

Master Eurig gave me a curt nod. "If you have reason to believe you have an air affinity, let's start there."

He placed a heavy-looking leather ball down at my feet.

"I want you to use your air magic to move this weighted ball across the arena. There's a breeze today. Fae without an affinity could manipulate it to nudge the ball slightly. You should be able to generate a much stronger gust of wind if you have an affinity, and move the ball a significant distance."

His doubtfulness was seriously aggravating me, but I wasn't entirely sure I'd be able to prove him wrong since I'd only used magic once as far as I knew.

I stared at the ball at my feet for a few minutes and willed it to move with my mind, but that didn't feel right. *Ugh, obviously, Fi.* Air magic. I tried to imagine a gust of wind picking the ball up and gently depositing it on the other side of the arena, but it merely wobbled in place. I was quite impressed by that, but my audience clearly wasn't.

"Close your eyes," Gwyneira commanded softly from somewhere behind me. "Remember the way your magic felt the last time you used it. Let it come naturally. It's part of you, Ffion, an extension of your very soul."

I closed my eyes and tried to remember how my magic felt, but all I could feel was Kayden's twisted lust, his vicious rage, his triumph as that door locked behind me. Anger rose under my skin, coursing through my veins like a hurricane. *No, not anger.* This was magic. It was raw power, ready to come to my aid, to protect me.

I threw my hands out in front of me to expel the aching energy under my skin. I opened my eyes in time to see the heavy ball embed itself in the solid stone barricade on the other side of the arena with a deafening crack.

There was silence behind me, but Gwyneira and Master Eurig's shock was coming through loud and clear. I was pretty shocked myself. How was Kayden even alive? If I'd thrown him into the wall instead of through a window into the river, he'd be dead for sure. My stomach churned uncomfortably at how close I'd been to becoming a murderer.

"Right," Master Eurig cleared his throat awkwardly. "I believe we have confirmed you hold an air affinity. A strong one," he added. He was feeling a little sheepish, but his excitement was growing too. I didn't relish the thought of bringing more attention to myself.

Gwyneira patted my shoulder kindly, sensing my discomfort. "As your body adjusts and the human toxins leave your system, you will find it easier to feel your magic and release it in a controlled way."

She probably meant for that to be reassuring. All I could focus on was the fact that until my body adjusted, magic would explode out of me like releasing a high-pressure valve.

They got me to try manipulating water, fire, and earth while they discussed my class schedule between them and drew it up on paper. Once, I think I made a ripple in the basin of water I was experimenting with, but I may have just been breathing too close to it.

"Right, here is your class schedule, Ffion," Gwyneira said, handing me a handwritten schedule. "We have configured it so you can move up to second-year air mastery early if need be, but you will be in the first-year class for now. I have also written a letter introducing you and explaining your situation for you to show the masters," she added, handing me a long note that I fully intended to read once I was out of her sight.

"Please come by my cabin after your last class this afternoon for your first mentoring session." Gwyneira didn't elaborate, and Master Eurig's curiosity burned hot against my skin. "I am confident Bryn would show you the way if you cannot recall it," Gwyneira added kindly, and I snorted under my breath.

I was confident that if I asked Bryn for directions, he would bark at me to find Briallen and vanish into the ether. I hadn't even known him for 24 hours, but I felt strangely sure of my ability to read him, and it had nothing to do with me being an empath.

Gwyneira and Master Eurig dismissed me, and I hurried back through the tunnel. Marlen was still resting against the wall, lean, muscled arms crossed over his broad chest with one leg propped up at the knee, dark red hair shining in the sun. He looked *beautiful*, and my breath caught at the sharp tug in my chest, urging me to rush over and act on the intense attraction I felt to him.

I took a deep head-clearing breath and could have sworn I saw him do the same.

"So," Marlen said, cocking an eyebrow at me. "I heard the distinctive crack of stone, foxglove. Was that the Academy's strongest air fae giving you a demonstration, or were you massively underselling your talent on the way over here?"

"Neither," I said slowly, my cheeks heating. "I guess my magic is a little hard to wrangle while I'm all dosed up on human poisons or whatever. It sort of exploded out of me."

"It *was* you?" Marlen asked, his surprise spiking. "You'd still need a strong base of raw power to draw from to use that kind of force. Shit, foxglove, you might just give Arthus a run for his money. He was the strongest air affinity at the Academy since Master Eurig."

Marlen laughed, seemingly unperturbed by the fact that I'd cracked a solid stone wall with a ball. Fae were crazy.

"Come on, it's time for class," he said, reaching for my schedule. "Let's give you somewhere productive to direct all that magic."

FFION

CHAPTER 8

It was somewhat mortifying to show Marlen my class schedule filled with first-year courses, knowing he was a fourth year and I was almost the same age as him, but he hadn't judged me at all. He'd even promised to tutor me to help catch me up. He walked me to the entrance of the small stone building my first fire elemental class would be in, and his face lit up when we reached a group of younger students milling around the door.

"Aderyn! You're in this class? Perfect!"

He pulled the redheaded woman into a hug that had me crawling out of my skin with jealousy, despite sensing only annoyance from her. My irritation died as he moved back and I got a good look at the girl he'd called Aderyn—she was almost a carbon copy of Marlen. *Rein it in Fi. She's clearly his sister.* They looked like they could be twins, but then surely she'd be a fourth-year too?

"Foxglove, this is... Aderyn Ferris." Marlen's voice faltered slightly, and I felt a wave of sadness from him and a prickling of shame from her. There were definitely some complicated family dynamics at play. "She's a first-year. Hopefully you'll have a few classes together. I trust her to take excellent care of you. Aderyn, this is Ffion Smith." He didn't elaborate, but the mischievous glint in Aderyn's eye made me think he didn't need to.

"Hello," I said, giving Aderyn an awkward wave. I felt uncharacteristically shy, like I was meeting the in-laws even though Marlen was basically a total stranger at this point. "You can call me 'Fi' if you like, it's nice to meet you. You don't need to babysit me, I wouldn't want to get in your way."

"Nonsense, it would be my pleasure to get to know Marlen's new friend." Aderyn gave me a brilliant smile, and I felt nothing but genuine warmth and excitement from her. "Come! Let's go find a seat. Bye, Marlen!"

She pulled me away from Marlen before I had a chance to say goodbye, and we headed into the classroom. I was relieved she'd taken the decision out of my hands since I was feeling all kinds of conflicted about this connection with Marlen. I'd have probably done something weird like shake his hand or go for a fist bump or something equally awkward.

Aderyn was awesome. She had Marlen's playfulness but also a quieter, more reserved nature that kind of reminded me of me. But, if I had picked up slight tremors of insecurity from Marlen, they crashed over me in waves from Aderyn. It made me wonder what their family was like to make them feel this way.

She listened with rapt attention as I told her about growing up in Albion and arriving in Avalon the day before. I sensed less shock from Aderyn than I had from any of the others at my story. She seemed like the kind of person—or fae, rather—who just took everything in her stride.

Aderyn was also doing a lot better in this class than I was, despite the term only starting a few weeks ago. I had been worried about going into this class since, as far as I knew, I didn't have any fire magic. I'd never used it before if I did. As it turned out, everyone in this class was in the same boat. The students who had a fire affinity were in a separate 'mastery' class, as I would be for my air magic.

We spent the class learning to grow and shrink the flame of a small candle. Aderyn manipulated her fire a couple of times, but most students had little to no control, and I had even less than that. *Nothing* happened. Not a single thing. For a freaking magic school, the entire thing felt kind of anticlimactic.

"Do you have an affinity element?" I asked Aderyn as I focused on growing the tiny flame.

"Ah, no, I don't," Aderyn replied stiffly. I felt a mixture of embarrassment and disappointment rolling off her and immediately regretted asking the question. *Way to make a good impression, Fi.* "I'm assuming you do? Do you have a strong mating pull to Marlen? He has a water affinity and a gifted ability—healing magic."

That information threw me. I hadn't asked Marlen about his magic because I didn't want him asking about mine—I couldn't lie if he asked me point blank about gifted abilities. Though healing magic sounded much better than my supposedly gods-given gift.

"I haven't really used it much or anything, but apparently I have an air affinity," I mumbled, cursing myself for starting this entire conversation.

"You must think I'm kind of lame, not having an affinity, let alone a gift." She smiled sadly.

"Not at all!" I exclaimed, horrified at the suggestion. "I don't think that, Aderyn."

"Really?" I sensed her curiosity. "Maybe it's because you're from Albion. We have a caste system here, of sorts. Those with gifted abilities and elemental affinities are at the top, just affinities are the next step down, and regular, low-magic fae like me are at the bottom. We're the most common type throughout Avalon, but the least respected. Here at the Academy, I'm the only student without an affinity."

"That's awful," I told her, holding her eye so she could see my sincerity. "I don't think any less of you because of whatever magic you do or don't have." I was relieved to feel some of her confidence coming back.

"It wasn't always like this. Centuries ago, all fae had an affinity, and most had gifted abilities. They were granted at birth by the gods and only taken away if they were abused. And all fae had wings, like huge butterfly wings." She had a dreamy expression on her face.

"How many centuries ago? What happened?"

"My great-great-grandparents were the last generation, maybe a thousand years ago. Anyway, no one really knows what happened. The gods suddenly stopped blessing the babies with gifts, except for a select few. A century later, the affinities started to disappear too. There are theories why—perhaps the gods are punishing us for something. I think they're dying," she added the last part quietly.

Great-great-grandparents... *A thousand years ago?* I made a note to ask someone about lifespans. That seemed like critical information. Was I going to live for hundreds of years or something crazy like that? I wasn't sure I wanted to.

Both Bryn and Gwyneira had mentioned fae having different types and levels of magic, but no one had told me fae magic was dying. Then again, most of the people I had met were on the powerful end of the spectrum by the sounds of it, and I wondered if there was more to this situation than I was being led to believe.

I pondered the magic drought for the rest of the day and on my walk through the forest to Gwyneira's cabin for our mentoring session. I had a lot of questions for her.

Gwyneira welcomed me into her reception room where a tray of tea and fruit was already laid out for us. I had been a little apprehensive about coming here alone, however I hadn't sensed any worrisome emotions from Gwyneira, and she was probably the best person to talk to about my freaky magic.

"Good afternoon, Ffion. I hope you enjoyed your first full day at the Academy?"

"It has been very... interesting."

"Oh? Is there something on your mind?" Gwyneira asked, furrowing her brow. "You look concerned."

"I guess I'm a little confused why I have all this magic. I knew there were different levels of magic and that my empath abilities were unusual, but I found out about the gods today and how fae have less and less magic, and no wings. It's kind of messing with my head."

Gwyneira's sadness rolled off her as she glanced at the tapestry of the six figures on the wall. "Yes, unfortunately so. The gods have not told us their reasons for granting us less magic. We have to trust in their wisdom. My guess is that if things continue as they have been, within the next two generations, fae will be born with no magic at all."

That answer didn't really satisfy me. Why did a select few of us have so much more? If there were fae gods—and everyone seemed to be in consensus on that—surely this magic wasn't being distributed at random? Aderyn seemed like a wonderful person. Why wasn't she deemed worthy of having an affinity or a gift?

"I was also wondering about life spans. How long do fae live for?" I asked, mulling over the unfairness of it all.

I felt Gwyneira's surprise. "My apologies, Ffion. I should have thought to mention some of this to you or sourced some reference materials for you. This must all be so strange for you. Most fae live for roughly 500 years."

I gaped at her in horror. What was I supposed to *do* for 500 years? It sounded kind of awful.

"Shouldn't Avalon be massively overpopulated then?" I blurted out, trying to make sense of everything.

Gwyneira laughed lightly at my train of thought. "The gods accounted for that. Fae women only have a window of fertility every 50 years until age 350. Seven children usually, without multiple births."

Weird. So, so weird. I guess that explains why I'd never gotten my period. I thought I was just a late bloomer.

A really late bloomer.

"Is it rude to ask how old you are...?" I asked hesitantly, and Gwyneira's eyes shone with amusement.

"Usually, though, I do not mind indulging you. I recently celebrated my 400th birthday." She looked freaking great, all things considered. I suppose living that long wouldn't be so awful if I was still in good health.

"I understand that this is probably fascinating, but unfortunately we must move on to less pleasant subjects," Gwyneira said with a slight grimace. "I would like us to focus on your empath abilities and how best to keep you safe from those who may hunt you for them. Before empaths disappeared, they were hounded by those who wished to either steal their magic and use it themselves, or those who forced the empaths to work for them. It was particularly dangerous for those who could influence crowds. It is a powerful ability to bring a group of people to tears, make them angry enough to riot, feel such powerful lust it makes them delirious..." she trailed off as I stared at her in horror.

I didn't want to do any of that. Just the idea that I *could* was terrifying.

"I thought we might start by talking about what you can do already. I have found some ancient reference books for you to study. Still, it has been at least six centuries since the empaths went extinct, and even before then, the empaths were very secretive about their abilities, rightly so. Most of what you will read here are secondhand accounts," Gwyneira continued.

"Any knowledge is better than none. At least I have a starting point," I said uneasily, dreading what I would find. I steeled my spine and imagined putting my big girl pants on. The only thing worse than knowing would be not knowing.

"How do your abilities work? Have you noticed any changes since you entered Avalon?" Gwyneira asked, tilting her head to one side as she waited for my answer.

"I don't really know how they work; I can't control them, and they're different here in Avalon. With humans, the best comparison would be the sea—emotions sort of roll off people like waves and lap against me. I don't seek them out; I feel anyone within a ten-foot or so radius, but I have to concentrate on figuring out which emotion belongs to which person if I'm in a crowded room. I always tried to avoid that. Crowds give me a headache," I explained slowly. "With fae, I feel their emotions physically in my body like they're my own. It's a more intense sensation, but my head feels much clearer since I entered Avalon. Perhaps because there is less emotional noise. Though crowds are still not great. Breakfast in the commons was a little overwhelming."

"I think it is likely that the magic in Avalon's atmosphere is helping you process the emotions more easily. Do you feel emotions differently if they are centered around you?"

I thought about it, going through each interaction I'd had since I arrived here. "Yes, I suppose the emotions feel more potent if they're directed at me. It's not something I noticed all that much until I came here. I tried my best to be as invisible as possible in London—that's why I worked as a cleaner. But Bryn's irritation felt much stronger when it was directed at me rather than the carriage driver."

I felt my face heat. *Why did I say that?* I totally ratted him out to the dean.

Gwyneira chuckled. "Bryn has always had a rather serious disposition. You will be good for him."

She had the same mischievous glint in her eye that Briallen did when she was talking about mating, so I quickly deflected to safer territory. I didn't want to talk to Gwyneira about the weird mating pull I had towards Bryn. I didn't want to talk to *anybody* about it. Even if I didn't *want* the whole mating thing, his blatant rejection before he'd even gotten to know me was hurting my pride.

"Do you know if there's a way to block out the emotions?" I asked hopefully.

"I cannot be sure that it will work, but fae used to practice putting up mental shields to block empath magic. It may not be suitable since you will be trying to block out your own magic rather than someone else's, but it is something I thought we could try during these sessions," Gwyneira suggested.

Despite the clear warning in her eyes not to get my hopes up, a tiny ember of it flared in my chest anyway at the thought of getting everyone else's emotions off my skin and out of my head.

"What do you know about other empath abilities? Will mine grow stronger as I work on my air magic? Honestly, I don't want them to; the headaches already drive me crazy. Plus, people always felt uncomfortable around me when they realized I had a strange sense of intuition. I don't need any more reasons to scare people away," I rambled nervously.

A different older man to the one who brought in the tea yesterday came in and whispered something in Gwyneira's ear, affectionately kissing her temple before he left. Another one of her mates? This whole multiple mates thing was screwing with my head. Everyone seemed so chill about it, but having a whole harem of lovers definitely veered into kink-territory in my head. Did ancient Gwyneira and her two dudes get it on together?

Why had my thoughts taken me in this horrific direction?

"My apologies, Ffion. I will have to cut this session short. Duty calls." She chuckled, carefully handing me a stack of ancient books about empaths.

"You need not worry about your empath abilities growing by chance, or because of your elemental training. It is potent magic. Any growth requires powerful magic for balance. Once you claim your mates, you will see an increase in your empath abilities, provided you choose mates whose magic is as strong as yours. I will send word to your cabin to schedule another session as soon as I can. Be well, Ffion." And with that bombshell, she swept out of the room.

Well, if I was hesitant about the whole mating concept before, I was outright hostile to it now.

FFION

CHAPTER 9

Overwhelmed by my first day of classes, mentoring with Gwyneira and my first full day of not being human, I shuffled into the commons and dropped into a seat next to Briallen. She gave me a sympathetic smile before wordlessly disappearing to make a plate of food for me. I was already feeling attached to this girl; she was so kind. Then I remembered what Gwyneira had said about empaths being hunted for their abilities and questioned the wisdom of being friends with Briallen. I didn't intend to tell her about my abilities any time soon, and it seemed unfair to befriend her and potentially paint a target on her back without full disclosure.

As she returned with my food, she surreptitiously sat across from me as Marlen slid into the chair next to me. I cocked an eyebrow at Briallen. *Subtle.* Marlen offered me a charming smile, and the excitement rolling off him was enough to lift my spirits a little.

"Hey, foxglove. How was day one?"

"It was a lot. Like a lot to take in. A lot to remember. Just a lot."

I felt a spike of concern from Marlen that made my resolve melt a little. He had no reason to feel worried about me, or to be so kind to me at all. I was going to get myself into trouble with this boy, I could feel it in my waters.

Leigh joined us, and I found my spirits lifting as he relayed his escapades from the day. He told us how he'd spent his air mastery lesson sneakily swapping everyone's satchels around from the row in front of him by gusting them along the floor, baffling his classmates at the end of the lesson. Apparently, Leigh had a healthy dose of mischief in him, and a knack for discreetly casting air magic without drawing attention. I wondered if he'd be interested in tutoring me.

I stood and grabbed my glass to get more water. "Allow me, foxglove," Marlen said cheerily, grabbing my glass and magically filling it with water. I stared at the glass in awe. That was a handy trick.

"Top me up, would you?" Leigh asked, and I felt a wave of amusement from Marlen as he reached for Leigh's glass, filling it up.

Leigh took a sip and promptly spat it back out. "Without the salt," he scowled playfully, making us all chuckle. My laughter died in my throat as a strong wrench in my chest pulled my gaze up to meet Bryn's glare from a table across the room. The blonde from this morning talked a mile a minute in his ear, but Bryn's attention was fixed on me.

Uncomfortable with the intensity of his stare and feeling a little overwhelmed by the growing dinner crowd, I stood and said my goodnights to everyone. I was eager to get back to the solitude of my treehouse after being surrounded by people all day. Hopefully I'd have enough energy to crack into one of the books Gwyneira had loaned me.

"Let me walk you back. We took a pretty confusing route here this morning," Marlen said, giving Leigh and Briallen a pointed smile.

"That would be helpful," I admitted. I didn't actually have any idea how to get back to my cabin on my own. We grabbed our satchels and Marlen steered me out of the commons, his large hand resting lightly at the base of my spine. I felt Bryn's eyes burning holes into my back the whole way out of the room.

"I thought I could show you the library sometime, foxglove. I think you'd like it," Marlen said as we walked out into the cool evening air, shooting me a crooked grin. It was a little unsettling that he'd known just what I would like. I hadn't mentioned my love of books to him. "Well, I hope you'd like it. You just seem like you're quite independent and would enjoy the chance to research things on your own," Marlen rambled, filling in the silence when I didn't respond. Another wave of his insecurity crawled over my skin.

I rested my hand on his forearm to get his attention and caught his eye. "I would love that. Thank you. I was just surprised you suggested it to me, that's all." His insecurity faded and was replaced with relief.

"I was thinking about what I'd want if I were in your situation. A source of knowledge would be my priority—I wouldn't feel comfortable asking people so many questions all the time."

Marlen shrugged like it was no big deal that he'd spoken my exact game plan into existence. Was this what Briallen had meant by kindred souls?

We reached my cabin and Marlen paused at the entryway while I hovered awkwardly in the doorway.

"Want me to get the fire going for you before I leave? No funny business, I swear. It's easier to get it hot with a bit of elemental magic."

Sensing his honest intentions—and feeling a little chilly—I moved back to let him in. Marlen moved straight to the potbelly stove, and I watched closely as he stacked the kindling and lit the fire with a match. He held his hands out and closed his eyes, concentrating hard for a few minutes until the flames grew. Marlen tossed on two logs of wood, then stood to look at me.

I kept my face neutral while I panicked internally. Would he try to kiss me? *Please don't kiss me. I have a very tenuous hold on my hormones right now.*

Marlen gently picked my hand up from where it hung loosely at my side, raising it to his mouth and brushing a soft kiss across my knuckles, the same way he had this morning when we met. His eyes stayed intently on mine as if to check that I was okay with what he was doing, and I could feel the nerves that he so carefully kept from showing on his face.

"Goodnight, foxglove," he murmured.

"Goodnight, Marlen," I said, cursing my breathy voice.

I let him out, then leaned my back on the closed door, inhaling deeply to clear my head. It didn't help. Marlen's woodsy, pine scent clung to everything he'd touched, making me crave more. Suddenly, Avalon's rudimentary plumbing didn't seem so bad. A cold shower was exactly what I needed.

Instead of Briallen and Leigh, it was Marlen who greeted me at my door with an angelic smile the following morning to walk me to breakfast. He proceeded to walk me to my first class, then found me a couple of hours later during my lunch break in the commons.

Logically, I knew I should have been weirded out that we were spending so much time together so quickly. Still, the mating pull in my chest seemed to override logic. Being close to Marlen made the pull in my chest feel warm and comfortable, heating my body from the inside out. Whenever Bryn was around, it felt like there was a separate mating pull in my chest, burrowing uncomfortably into my bones and forcing me to acknowledge his presence against my will.

My elemental classes were as unsuccessful as the day before. I'd been excited about my air mastery class, only to sit on the sidelines because Master Aures was worried I was a hazard to my classmates until all the human toxins were out of my system. Remembering how that ball had embedded in a solid stone wall, I figured she was probably right. Regardless, I was a little bitter that I didn't get to take part in the one class I could actually do magic in.

By the time I reached the commons for dinner, I was in a foul mood. Marlen rested his hand lightly on my lower back, his thumb rubbing comforting circles over the fabric of my dress throughout dinner. His touch was so comforting, it felt like he was drawing the negativity right out of my body.

"A few of us are heading out to a clearing at the edge of campus tonight for a bonfire, since there aren't any classes tomorrow. We'll have ale and snacks and music. It'd be a great way to take your mind off all of *this*—" Marlen gestured absently at the room "—if only for a few hours. Want to come with?"

His tone was casual, but he looked so hopeful, like nothing was more important than my answer.

I could feel his nerves and it only endeared him to me more. Marlen's nervousness felt like something I had all to myself. He presented such a cocky facade to the rest of the world, but was a sensitive soul underneath all that bravado; it gave me a burning urge to protect him and his secret vulnerabilities. Which was crazy because I barely knew him, and he was far more equipped to defend himself than I was.

"Sure, maybe just for a little while? I'm pretty exhausted."

I wasn't exactly in a rush to spend time around a large group of people either, but I felt like I should make *some* attempt at getting to know my classmates.

"I won't keep you out too late." Marlen winked and started digging into his salad. "Finish eating, then we'll head over there. Leigh and Briallen are coming too."

We walked the short distance to the clearing together, where a large group of students had already started a roaring bonfire and were holding pitchers of ale. Marlen and Leigh went to fetch our drinks, while Briallen pointed out various students and made introductions that I promptly forgot.

Fortunately—or unfortunately—the mating pull I felt to Marlen was strong enough to render any weaker ones insignificant. I had noticed almost constant, slight twinges in my chest throughout the day when I had classes with unmated males, and I guessed it meant that I had some compatibility with them, but not enough to really catch my attention. Nothing like what I experienced with Marlen and Bryn, at any rate.

Marlen returned with ale for us, and our fingers brushed slightly as I took the pitcher from him. Even that infinitesimal amount of physical contact had me craving more.

I wanted to grab his shirt and yank him into me, to bury his face in my neck. I wanted him to *smell* like me. Curiously, I hadn't felt the urge to force

Bryn into submission. I wondered what it was about Marlen that brought out this dominant side of me. Maybe the surge of jealousy being directed my way from a few of the surrounding females. I didn't blame them really, Marlen was hot.

"Kelvyn!" Marlen shouted, getting the attention of a guy on the other side of the bonfire.

The man in question stalked over to us, irritation rising with every step until he stopped right in front of us. As soon as he spotted me, his irritation died and was replaced with a morbid curiosity that sent shivers down my spine.

I angled myself imperceptibly behind Marlen a little more, torn between standing my ground and getting the hell away from the dude throwing off all the creepy vibes. Marlen noticed my discomfort, his eyes scanning my face with his brow creased.

"Fi, this is my roommate, Kelvyn. Kel, this is Fi. She's new here," Marlen said slowly. I was grateful he kept my origin story vague.

"Fi as in Ffion?" Kelvyn asked, and I gave him a wary nod. "Pretty name. Welcome to the Academy." His emotions didn't feel malicious, but there was something off about his interest in me. It wasn't sexual, or even friendly, yet there was something intense about it.

"I'll be seeing you, Ffion." He gave me a long, assessing look before sauntering off.

"That was weird," Marlen frowned after his roommate. "He's a prickly bastard, but not so... odd, usually. Sorry, foxglove."

I hummed nonchalantly, unable to tell him about Kelvyn's bizarre interest in me without hinting at my abilities.

"Was it a mating pull? Did you feel a pull to him?" Marlen pressed.

"God, no!" I exclaimed in horror, making Marlen chuckle.

"Sorry, foxglove. I didn't mean to offend. Anyway, forget about Kelvyn. He's a fire affinity. Briallen and I have a theory that all fire affinities have asshole tendencies."

Thinking of my interactions with Bryn so far, I conceded that idea might have some merit.

We spent the next half hour with Leigh and Briallen, drinking our ale and laughing at Leigh's antics. As we listened to another one of his questionable jokes, I felt a sudden rush of panic from Marlen that made my head spin and my heart pound in my ears. Marlen looked determinedly at anything but the sultry redhead stalking over to him with a predatory glint in her eye. I willed myself to calm down, remembering how insane I'd been this morning with Aderyn, and she turned out to be his sister. Maybe this was another red-headed relative.

"Marlen," she purred, wrapping her long fingers around his upper arm and pushing her breasts against his chest. "I've been looking for you."

Ugh, definitely not a relative. Leigh and Briallen exchanged a wary look before discreetly disappearing into the crowd. *Thanks, guys.*

Fortunately for her fingers, Marlen extricated himself quickly from Red's grip and stepped back toward me, resting his hand lightly on my lower back. I had been about two seconds away from seeing if I could rip her fingers off using air magic. What I would give for Bryn's fire affinity right now, I bet I could do some serious damage with that.

What. Was. Happening. To. Me?

"Who is this?" Red snapped, narrowing her eyes at me.

Marlen went to open his mouth, but I got there first. I didn't need any man speaking for me—sexy fae or otherwise. "Fi. Who are you?"

She snorted and tossed her hair like it should have been obvious to me who she was. Maybe she was famous? Presumably they had famous people in Avalon. Something to ask Briallen about later.

"Corsen," she bit out, glaring at Marlen's arm that had disappeared behind my back. "Marlen, baby, what are you doing? Come, drink with me."

"Not going to happen, Corsen. You know what's going on here."

I guessed he was referring to the mating pull between us? People had been referring to it casually all day. It was par for the course amongst young fae, apparently.

She rolled her eyes. "Don't waste your time with this, Marlen," she sniffed, waving her hand dismissively at me. "You didn't have a problem coming to my bed two nights ago. Clearly, she's not enough for you."

Two nights ago?

I felt Marlen tense up next to me, his emotions becoming a tangled mess of panic, irritation, regret, and more than a bit of self-loathing.

"I didn't know Fi two nights ago. This changes everything, she changes everything. You know how this works, Corsen. There's no pull between you and me."

Corsen's cheeks matched her hair at this point, and I felt the teeniest bit bad at how this had played out. I mean, if he was sleeping with her a couple of *days* ago, it wasn't too much of a stretch for her to feel like she had some kind of claim to him.

She turned on her heel and stormed off while I stared into my pitcher of ale like it held the answers to all the questions in the universe.

This is precisely why I had told myself not to get involved with anyone, not to give in to the mating pull, and I was failing miserably after three days. I was already at a breaking point in my identity crisis—boy drama was a terrible development on so many levels.

I needed to get out of here.

I felt another rush of self-loathing from Marlen as he sighed and gave me a sad smile.

"You're going to run, huh?"

I was pretty sure I hadn't said that out loud. Aderyn had mentioned Marlen had a healing gift, definitely no mind-reading abilities as far as I knew. If anyone was likely to get those, it'd be me.

"It's what I would do," he explained at my confused expression. "The mating pull between us is strong; we're kindred souls. Chances are our decisions will overlap a lot of the time."

That sounded really nice, actually. It's a shame I'd never speak to him again.

"You're a powerful fae female, a rarity these days. You shouldn't settle for anyone. Make us work for it, foxglove." Marlen smiled gently, masking the insecurity he was feeling. "When we screw up, make us prove our worth as potential mates. And I for sure screwed up. I should have known she'd be here and kept you away from this mess."

His words calmed my ire. Still, I reminded myself that:

a) he had sex with another woman less than 48 hours ago, and

b) my freaky magic would only get stronger if I did actually take a mate.

It was stupid to put myself in this situation in the first place. The pull between us made me want to act on primal instinct rather than rational thought.

"That's excellent advice. I'm going to leave now. Please don't come to my cabin in the morning," I said in a low tone, the hurt in my voice obvious to even my own ears. "I'll see you around, Marlen."

I felt guilty ditching Briallen without a goodbye, but I knew it was for the best. If anyone ever found out about my abilities, at least she wouldn't get caught in the crossfire.

FFION

CHAPTER 10

I waited awkwardly near the commons, leaning against a tree and roughly braiding my hair for something to do with my hands. At moments like these, I really missed having a phone. Not because anyone had ever messaged me on it, but at least it had been something to occupy myself with when I was trying to be invisible.

As I waited, I vaguely monitored the emotions coming from the commons, noting the decreasing levels as the dinner rush passed. It was an old technique I'd relied on in my human life to avoid crowds, and it was coming in handy now. Plus, I had the bonus warning system of the mating pull, letting me know specifically *who* to avoid, even if it made me want to do the opposite.

Figuring the dining area was as quiet as it was going to get, I made my way around to the side door closest to the buffet table and slipped inside, releasing my half-finished braid so my curls sprung around my face in a messy shield. Moving as quickly as I could, I grabbed one of the giant leaves that students used for takeaway meals and made myself something that resembled a barley salad, with nuts for protein before wrapping it up.

Having successfully avoided anyone I knew at mealtime again, I ducked back out with my sad to-go meal, heading straight for one of the forest paths I'd gotten acquainted with over my past two weeks of self-imposed isolation. I still had Aderyn for company in class, but she didn't seem to speak to her brother or spend any time with him, so I greedily sucked up all the social interaction with her I could.

I was lonely enough as it was, I didn't want to give up Aderyn as well.

There was a spot in the trees I liked to take my meals at, sitting amongst the humongous roots with violet flowers blanketing the surrounding forest floor.

Huh. Two weeks, I thought, sitting back against the tree, unwrapping my salad and pulling a spoon out of my bag. I'd made a deal with Gwyneira to give the Academy two weeks, and it was already up. Despite the semi crushing loneliness, it had actually passed rather quickly. Probably because I'd thrown myself into lessons and avoiding Marlen, Bryn, Briallen and Leigh was a full-time job on top of that.

At least no one else in my classes was particularly interested in me. While I had felt faint mating pulls to other males I came across, they were easy enough to ignore, and I understood more every day what Briallen had meant by sensing the strength of compatibility.

I chewed for minutes on my bland barley salad, knowing that any one of the fae friends I'd made before abandoning them would have given me tips on how to make it taste better. Marlen was definitely trying to bump into me around the campus, and even Bryn seemed to pop up more and more each day, but a lifetime of foster care had prepared me perfectly for avoiding people.

I finished my meal and cleaned up, standing and brushing off my skirt. Not wanting to return to the crushing loneliness of my cabin, I shouldered my bag and began walking. These paths were familiar from my evenings of exploration, but I wanted to find a new one. This area of campus was free of treehouses and classrooms, but some of the plants seemed to be set up like herb gardens, and occasionally there were small storage huts interspersed among the trees.

It would be nice to have someone experienced at the Academy to ask, but the more I thought about it, the more convinced I was that giving in to the mating pull and getting to know Marlen would be an awful idea for both me and my magic. For all I knew, Marlen would bolt if he found out what my horrible invasive ability was, anyway. Bryn had hated it the second I'd told him about it.

I felt *terrible* avoiding Briallen, but I knew she was eager for me to spend more time with both Marlen and Bryn. Plus, I wasn't ready to tell her about my gift and the problems mating would bring. She was better off not knowing.

The paths branched off and I opted for the one I hadn't taken before, since I still had a couple of hours' daylight. I'd seen this one on previous walks and had always been curious about where it led. It was quieter than the others, so I'd be easier to spot if anyone was looking for me, but less likely to be stumbled upon by accident.

Branches and twigs snagged on my clothes as I made my way through the much narrower than expected dirt path through a tightly packed copse of trees, lined by the mysterious glittering wildflowers. The iridescent sheen that covered all the flowers here made me want to reach out and touch them, but I hesitated in case it was some kind of poison enticing me or warning me off. I admired them from a distance to be safe.

Albion's flowers really had nothing on Avalon's. My magic seemed to respond to the flowers too, or perhaps the trees. It was definitely something in nature that made my magic rise and swirl in my veins like it was saying hello.

The path grew steeper, but I gasped my way up, glad there was no one around to witness how embarrassingly out of breath I was.

Cardio. Must do some cardio.

Near the top of the incline, the path was lined with colorful stones as big as dinner plates. They were painted in elaborate detail to look like natural crystals. I wanted to reach down and run my fingers over them, but it seemed inappropriate; it looked like someone had put a lot of effort into painting them. It made me think of temples and offerings, and I wondered idly if that's what I was looking at.

There was a clearing at the top of the hill with some kind of giant marble arrangement. After hunching over with my hands on my knees for a few minutes to catch my breath, I took in the sight in front of me. Six slabs of bright white marble were arranged in a tight circle. Each slab was taller than me and as thick as a mattress. They sprouted out of the ground like they were naturally occurring.

I walked around the circle in awe. Something about the place resonated deep within my bones. Cautiously, I slid sideways through the small gap between two of the marble slabs and stood in the center of the cramped space.

The world around me went still. I couldn't hear the trees rustling or the birds singing or... anything. It felt like I was underwater. Some part of my brain reminded me that this was not normal, and I should probably get the hell out of here, but the most glorious sensation had taken me hostage. An invisible, warm, welcoming goo was reaching up from the ground and running up over my feet and all the way over my body. It wasn't sticky or suffocating; it was like a comforting caress.

My strange, blissful stasis lasted for what felt like minutes but could have been hours. By the time my head cleared enough for me to convince my feet to move, the sky had darkened and the temperature had dropped. Wrapping my arms tightly around my waist, I hurried back to my cabin, wondering what the hell had just happened to me.

I waited until there were no stragglers around the stairs leading up to my cabin and dashed up as quickly and quietly as possible, sneaking through the door and breathing a sigh of relief when no knock followed. Marlen had been hanging around the stairs and rope bridges near my cabin over the past couple of days, presumably waiting for me. My relief was short-lived.

Walking further into the room, I found my beautiful wooden wardrobe defiled in burn marks that spelled:

Heart pounding, I walked backward until I was leaning against the front door. Crap. What should I do now? I guess I should tell someone...? I'd spent my entire life avoiding authority figures. It felt weird to ask for help now.

At the same time, someone sneaking in here grossly violated my privacy, and I didn't want to stay in this room a second longer.

The decision was made for me with a loud knock right next to where my head was resting against the door. My breath caught, fear coursing through my veins. *Get it together, Fi!* It's not like whoever left this message would come back and politely knock on my door.

Shaking myself out of my terrified stupor, I focused on the visitor's emotions rather than my own. Nothing alarming.

"Ffion?" Gwyneira called through the wood, knocking again. "I was hoping I could speak to you."

I took a deep breath, keeping my head as clear as possible so I could focus on her intentions. Just in case.

Pulling the door open, I found that Gwyneira wasn't alone. A tall, distinguished man with salt and pepper hair and deep frown lines stood at her side. His hands were clasped behind his back, the picture of a gentleman. His strongest emotion was mild curiosity, nothing too concerning.

"Ffion, this is my mate, Mawrth," Gwyneira told me. "We were just leaving the campus for the evening, and I thought I would drop by. I wanted to request you attend another mentoring session tomorrow after your last class."

I nodded and made an affirmative noise in the back of my throat. My eyes flicked to the rope bridge behind Gwyneira and Mawrth, though I didn't know what I was looking for. An escape route, perhaps?

"You look rattled, Ffion? Is there something you're concerned about? May we come in?" Gwyneira asked as her gaze narrowed on my face. I hesitated for a second, but I couldn't really think of a reasonable excuse to turn the dean away.

"Um, of course," I murmured, stepping back and pulling the door open wider for them to enter.

Gwyneira strode purposefully into the cabin while Mawrth hung back in the doorway. She immediately spotted the message on the wardrobe.

"Ffion, when did this appear?"

"I found it a couple of minutes before you knocked on the door. It wasn't there this morning, and I've been out all day."

"Were you planning on mentioning it to me?" Gwyneira asked, her voice sounding far lighter than her emotions felt.

"Um, probably? I was just thinking about what I should do," I answered honestly, wishing for the millionth time that I could just outright lie. Gwyneira and Mawrth's concern was swirling around me, which wasn't helping; I really needed a dose of happiness to perk me up.

"Mawrth," Gwyneira said, turning to her mate. "Please fetch Bryn. Hopefully there is enough of a signature here for him to track their magic. I will stay with Ffion. I do not wish to leave her alone right now."

My stomach dropped. I could hardly say no, but I also had no desire to see Bryn. For all I knew, he could have been the one who left the message. He knew where I was from, which cabin was mine, and he loathed me.

It hadn't escaped my notice that they'd *burned* the message into my wardrobe. The only two people who knew the secret of my gift had fire affinities.

As we waited for Bryn, I contemplated whether the message was related to the weird sensation that rooted me to the ground surrounded by those slabs of marble. Was it some kind of magical ruse to give someone time to get into my room and do this? That didn't feel right somehow, but I wouldn't be heading back to visit those weird rocks any time soon.

After a few minutes, a magnetic tug in my chest let me know that Bryn was nearby. He stormed into the room with a face like thunder, his anger pulsing through my veins stronger than I'd ever felt, but it didn't seem like it was directed at me. He didn't acknowledge me at all while he moved around the wardrobe, running his hands through the air as if feeling for magic. It left a beautiful trail of glittering gold floating in his wake that was hypnotizing to watch.

Bryn continued throughout the whole cabin, and I could feel his frustration growing. "The only signature here is hers," he growled, still not looking at me. "But there is a… disturbance of some kind. Whoever did this must have masked themselves somehow, perhaps with an illusionist amulet." *Amulets?* I didn't realize magic artefacts were in play too. More things to look out for. More things I didn't understand.

"We can imbue natural crystals with small amounts of someone's gifted ability. Someone with an illusionist gift could transfer it to a crystal and sell it, for example. It is somewhat frowned upon to sell one's magic, but it is fairly commonplace."

Bryn snorted quietly at Gwyneira's explanation, and I guessed she was downplaying the whole selling magic thing, though it didn't sound so bad to me. Why shouldn't others enjoy useful magic like Marlen's healing gift if he was willing to share it? If I had a gift worth sharing, I wouldn't be averse to selling it. But I'd always been poor. It was becoming increasingly clear that most of the fae at the Academy were massive elitists.

As Gwyneira and Mawrth quietly discussed the possibilities between themselves, Bryn finally deigned to make eye contact, crossing the room until he was standing just a few inches in front of me.

"You okay, scout?"

I felt his concern swirling in my gut, very much directed at me, as well as the familiar heavy weight of Bryn's resentment. I again envied humans of their ability to lie. He may be acting civil now, but I still had no interest in baring my soul to Bryn.

"Not yet." I chuckled weakly. "Thank you for trying to track them down," I added awkwardly.

"Gwyneira asked me to," Bryn grumbled. I could almost see his walls coming back up. Confirming with Gwyneira that he was no longer needed, he turned on his heel and left without another word.

"Ffion, dear, I think it would be best if we moved you to another cabin. There is one at the other end of this cluster, currently unoccupied. Let us gather your things and move you there tonight. Please be assured that we will continue to investigate the matter. I am so sorry this happened."

I packed my things silently and followed Gwyneira to my new cabin, which was nearly a carbon copy of the last one. She left me to rest, but my mind was churning through tonight's events at warp speed. Between the weird moment with the rocks and the threatening message, I doubted I'd be getting any sleep tonight.

I sat cross-legged on my bed and attempted to study for my upcoming earth magic quiz. I'm not sure how much information I was actually retaining, but anything was better than tossing and turning in bed, being left with my own thoughts. A soft knock on the door nearly startled me out of my skin.

"Fi? It's Marlen..." he trailed off, and I waited to see if he'd say anything else. How had he even found my new room? There was a dull thud like he was resting his head against the door. "Maybe you're asleep. I know you've been avoiding me, foxglove. I get it. I just heard what happened tonight and wanted to check that you were doing okay."

The barrier I had been putting up between Marlen and I cracked a little at hearing the sadness in his voice and feeling his genuine care and concern. I crossed the room and opened the door, wishing I was wearing more than a plain sage linen shift and matching kimono-style robe.

"Do you want to come in?" I asked tiredly.

"Gods yes," he answered, already reverting to his usual playful self.

I rolled my eyes affectionately as I stood back for him to enter. We sat down at the two-person table, and I was grateful for the physical barrier between us. Right then, I was vulnerable and in the mood to tempt fate.

"Bryn told me about the message in your room. That's fucked up, foxglove. Any ideas who wrote it? Made any enemies in the past couple of weeks?"

"Bryn told you?" My eyebrows shot up. Bryn and Marlen weren't friendly as far as I knew. "Honestly, I thought it might have been him who wrote it.

I don't think anyone hates me more than he does."

Marlen snorted. "Bryn's an asshole, but he'd never do that to you. Why do you think he stormed over to my cabin in a huff? He was pissed I hadn't been looking out for you."

Awkward.

"I don't expect you or anyone else to look out for me, Marlen. I've been looking out for myself my whole life. I'm sorry that he said that to you. That was totally out of order."

"It really wasn't." Marlen gave me a sad smile. "If I was officially your suitor, then I would absolutely look out for you, and it would be my honor to do it. And I'd like nothing more. I know you're new to all of this, Fi, but I promise you there's no rush. We can keep things friendly, get to know one another."

I was finding it hard to stick to my guns when Marlen was right there in front of me, looking all rumpled and delicious, smelling like fresh pine and heaven. Avoiding him had been taxing for me, and it looked like it had been taxing for him too,

"Just friends," I said cautiously.

"Absolutely! Whatever I can do to be there for you, I want to do it." His eagerness brushed up against my skin like an overexcited puppy, and I cracked a small smile.

Marlen insisted on making tea for us and we sat at the table talking about nice, light topics for an hour. I had been so keyed up before he arrived; I thought I'd be up all night. A cup of tea and Marlen's safe, relaxing presence had my eyelids drooping.

I walked Marlen to the door, and he opened his arms to give me a hug.

"Friends hug," he said with a playful wink.

I didn't fight the mating pull as it drew me into his arms, burying my face in the crook of his neck and inhaling his soothing, woodsy scent. He was doing the same in my hair, arms wrapped tightly around my back as if he would never let me go.

I looked up into his eyes, and the pull between us was so pure and magnetic, I could barely have stopped myself if I wanted to. I leaned forward and gently pressed my lips to his—aware that friends absolutely did *not* kiss each other—and I was giving Marlen all kinds of mixed signals right now.

I was ready and very willing to take this kiss to the next level, but Marlen's lips stayed determinedly soft against me, tasting me gently with his tongue as his hands moved up to cup my face. It was sweet and romantic and a huge freaking tease, but I appreciated him not letting me get carried away 56 seconds after I said I only wanted to be his totally platonic buddy.

"Don't overthink it. It doesn't have to happen again until you're ready," he murmured softly in my ear as he pulled away, smiling at me with so much adoration my breath caught in my throat.

He gently stroked my face with his thumbs, gazing at me like I was something precious instead of the total imposter I felt like.

"I'll wait for you, foxglove. Sleep well."

I resumed sitting with Marlen, Leigh and Briallen at mealtimes over the next couple of days, and they politely didn't bring up the fact that I'd been avoiding them like the plague for the past week.

I hadn't forgotten about the message on my wardrobe, but with no leads to go on, I'd pushed it to the back of my mind so I could focus on mastering my magic. It felt like a screw you to whoever had left the message—I was here to stay because I had magic to learn. I would not be scared away.

'Home' wasn't Albion, anyway. How could that ever be home again when I knew Avalon existed? When I knew now what I'd been missing out on?

My bubble of peace popped when I went to leave my cabin for breakfast one morning and noticed a piece of paper had been slipped under the door.

GO HOME was written above a sketch of a woman with a mass of curly hair just like mine, curled up in the fetal position in a barred cage. My hands trembled as I stared at it. Not only did the messenger know where my new cabin was, but they'd also been right outside as I'd been sleeping and vulnerable.

Was it a student? How easy was it for someone outside the Academy to get on campus? There were male students on guard duty 24 hours a day, so it seemed unlikely that someone could sneak in twice without being noticed. I really didn't want to believe it was Bryn leaving me these messages, but a student seemed like the most likely suspect.

Gwyneira was the only other person who knew. Surely, she wouldn't have sold me out? She was the one who had warned me about what could happen if word got out about my empath abilities, there would be people who would try to keep me captive and use my magic for their own gain.

And then there was the picture. Was it a threat or a warning? Go home or be imprisoned? Or go home to avoid being imprisoned?

There were many reasons I hated my empath abilities, but they had given me good instincts about people and their intentions. Things were different in Avalon though, there was other magic at play. This was a whole new game, and I didn't know all the rules.

For the first time, I ignored the instincts that told me that Bryn and Gwyneira were trustworthy and decided not to mention the note to either of them. I hadn't grown up in foster care only to come out of it and rely on other people as an adult. I was the only person who truly had my own best interests at heart.

Pulling myself together, I hid the note in my satchel. Out of sight, out of mind. Taking several deep breaths, I headed straight for class, skipping breakfast so Marlen wouldn't see through my fragile facade. I wouldn't let whoever was sending me these messages get to me. This was the first time in my life I felt like I'd belonged somewhere. No one would take it away from me.

FFION

CHAPTER 11

Having avoided Marlen all day, I was looking forward to seeing him at dinner in a couple of hours. I went back to my cabin to shower and had a mini-heart attack when I saw yet another note slid under my door. I picked it up, heart in my throat, then breathed a sigh of relief when I saw it was from Gwyneira, asking me to go to her cabin for another mentoring session. I didn't know how I felt about Gwyneira yet, but at least it wasn't another drawing of me in a cage.

I freshened up as quickly as possible before making my way to her cabin, already uncomfortable with the secret I was keeping. My gut told me Gwyneira was trustworthy and that she would definitely want to know about the note, but she was also a powerful, 400-year-old fae. Who knew what she was really capable of doing? Maybe she had one of those freaky amulet things? Or maybe one of her three mates knew about my abilities and were behind the messages?

I chewed on my lower lip and talked myself into keeping quiet for the millionth time since I'd started down the route to her cabin, wishing I had someone I could talk to about this without endangering them. Someone I could trust implicitly.

"Ffion," Gwyneira greeted me with a warm smile at the door. "Come in, let us have tea. Today is an important day, you know, your two-week trial run is at an end."

With everything that had happened in the past few days, I had completely forgotten that this milestone was coming up. Not that it really mattered—after one week of seeing all the cool things I could do with air magic and eating three square meals a day, I was convinced that staying in Avalon was the right call.

I still missed eating meat and junk food, though. If I ever got my fae ass back to Albion, I planned to eat my bodyweight in fried chicken and beef burritos, magic be damned.

"I'm staying," I announced. "I'm really enjoying learning about my magic. I feel more... myself here than I ever did in Albion."

"Understandable. Your diet and environment here are much more conducive to your needs as a fae. Avalon will always be a much more comfortable place for you to reside." Gwyneira smiled kindly again, though the gesture had a kind of rehearsed feel. I guessed that if I had been around for 400 years, I'd perfect that polite, painted smile look too.

"Now that you are officially a student, I will ensure you receive the small stipend that all students get during their studies. I am sure you would appreciate the opportunity to add to your wardrobe, if nothing else," Gwyneira said as she passed me a small leather pouch that jingled with coins. "You'll be able to pick up your stipend every Monday at the administration building."

"Oh! That's an unexpected bonus. Are there shops here? I've never seen one." The idea of shopping lifted me out of my funk. I had gotten accustomed to all the linen and wool in my wardrobe, but I could definitely use a few brighter colors.

"There is a market town around an hour's carriage ride away, or a brief griffin flight. In a few weeks, they will hold the Avalon Fair on a field within walking distance of the campus. Merchants travel from all over the realm, it is a two-week event, and many fae look forward to it. Myself included," she said with a wink. Sometimes it was easy to forget she was 400-freaking-years old.

"Now, unfortunately, we must turn our attention to a less pleasant subject—extracting magic to create amulets. There is nothing wrong with choosing to imbue crystals with your magic, but those with rare gifts are at risk of having their magic being taken against their will."

Gwyneira gave me a pointed look and I felt my face fall. It had been a pleasant break from my funk while it lasted.

"I wish I did not have to tell you about this," Gwyneira continued softly, giving me an apologetic look. "Hunting others for their magic and stealing it for themselves is the worst of the fae."

"How exactly do they steal magic?" I asked with dread, not entirely sure I wanted to hear the answer.

"Blood. Certain crystals can be imbued with blood, creating an amulet that temporarily allows someone to use that fae's gift. Some fae imbue the crystals themselves and sell the amulets. Unfortunately, those with rare gifts are more likely to be hunted and kept captive so their blood can be drained regularly."

I was confident the blood had already drained from my face. It was the first time I'd really given any thought to what would happen if they had captured me. The goal had always been to never get caught in the first place.

Gwyneira hesitated before she continued. "The lure of blood magic can become difficult to resist when a fae starts down that path. Some forego the crystals and drink the blood directly from the vein." My stomach churned at the imagery. "It is a more concentrated dose, though it burns through the system just as quickly. Once they drink from the vein, there is no turning back. They will always feel called by the lure of blood, they cannot survive without it. We call them the dark fae. It is where the human myth of the vampire originates from," she added helpfully, as if to lighten the mood.

Unsure how to respond to what would probably be my future if anyone found out about my gift, I mechanically drank my tea without tasting it. If magic really was gifted by the gods, I had a bone to pick with them for landing me with this.

"You understand now why it is so important that we keep your gift a secret?" Gwyneira asked, and I nodded mutely, lips pursed. "You must be able to block out emotions in a crowd. You cannot risk drawing attention to yourself by becoming overwhelmed."

Gwyneira reached over and took the cup and saucer from my hands, placing them down on the table and staring at me. "I know I have painted a horrible picture, but I will never keep the truth from you, Ffion. For the rest of our session and all of our future sessions, we will work on strengthening your mental walls."

More determined than ever to master this, I spent the next thirty minutes in a meditation-like state, imagining constructing a forty-foot high wall of bricks piece-by-piece in my brain. Gwyneira projected her own emotions at me as powerfully as she could, the idea being they would bounce off the wall before I could feel them.

I didn't want to give up hope, but the exercise had failed miserably. I experienced each emotion as acutely as I always did. If anything, they were exacerbated by my own despair. I left Gwyneira to go to the commons for dinner, hopeful I would at least see Marlen and have some small distraction from this terrible day.

I was an emotional wreck at dinner. I sat with Leigh, Briallen and Marlen, but my mind was a million miles away, spiraling through a terrifying vortex of bloody crystals and vampire fae.

My grim mood hadn't gone unnoticed by Marlen. Every time I fidgeted uncomfortably in my seat or sighed under my breath, he'd give me a questioning look and press further into my side as if to physically offer me support. His concern swirled in my gut, and it was both comforting and unsettling to know he cared about me.

"Foxglove, do you want to go for an evening walk? Just the two of us?" Marlen asked, and I really wished at this moment that we had more subtle friends. Briallen and Leigh were wagging their eyebrows and winking all over the place.

"That sounds lovely, actually," I said, giving him a small smile.

I loved having Leigh and Briallen around. They unintentionally acted as chaperones when I was struggling to remember that I was supposed to be just friends with Marlen, but tonight I just needed him. It's like he read my mind.

We said our goodbyes and Marlen took my hand, interlacing his fingers through mine, which was definitely another strike in the *more than friends* column. Well, that and the kiss we'd shared that I'd semi pretended hadn't happened. Leading me out of the commons, we started down a narrow path to the stream that ran across one edge of the campus. Marlen walked purposefully to a secluded spot next to the stream, hidden by a beautiful, enormous willow tree.

Marlen settled back against the base of the tree, hiding us amongst the drooping branches, and pulled me down between his legs, with my back against his chest. I cringed a little—the position was definitely more than just friendly—but screw it, it had been a terrible day. I'd indulge just this once in the comfort he was offering me. I settled back and leaned my head against Marlen's shoulder, and as soon as I relaxed into his embrace, Marlen's happiness burst through me and buzzed over my skin.

"What's bothering you, foxglove?" Marlen breathed, his lips brushing against my hair. I tensed a little in his arms, thinking about what to tell him, and felt Marlen's insecurity crawl over my skin. Most of the time I hated my abilities, but I loved that I had this insight into Marlen that no one else did.

There were several things bothering me I could have told him about. Hiding my magic. Hating my magic. Fearing that someone already knew about my magic. Fearing whoever left those notes would resort to more drastic measures. Worrying about keeping him, Leigh and Briallen in the dark about my abilities... But I wasn't ready to talk about any of those things yet.

But there was one thing bothering me he could definitely help with...

"I guess I'm struggling a little with the mating pull," I said slowly. Marlen's insecurity felt like hundreds of snakes slithering over my skin, and I quickly grabbed his arms, pulling them tight around my waist to reassure him. "Probably not in the way you're thinking," I added.

"Okay... What exactly are you struggling with? I want to help you, Fi. I want to make this easier however I can, you know that."

Marlen gripped my chin lightly, guiding my head to the side so he could see my face, and I was glad there was only a paltry amount of moonlight filtering through the leaves to see by because my cheeks were flaming.

"Well, you know I have a powerful pull towards you and Bryn, and between the two of you, you're both around a lot, so I feel it all the time and..." I trailed off awkwardly. I knew the exact moment Marlen cottoned on to what I was saying. His lust exploded, an ache forming between my thighs, and his grin stretched broadly across his face. Marlen leaned forward until his lips were right at my ear, and I shuddered in anticipation.

"Are you feeling sexually frustrated, little foxglove?"

"*Yes*," I said hotly. "Every time I feel the mating pull, it gets me worked up, and I've spent more time than I care to admit either taking a cold shower or getting myself off lately."

I was briefly mortified that I'd admitted to Marlen that I'd been masturbating to thoughts of him and Bryn—I didn't even *like* Bryn—but I couldn't tell him I also felt *everyone else's* lust. This being an academy of young adults, there was lust every-freaking-where. It was also more potent when it was directed at me, and Marlen's desire for me destroyed my inhibitions on a daily basis.

Marlen made a low, growling sound in his chest that shot straight to my clit. "If you need to get off, foxglove, you come to me. And you'll come for me; I will make sure of it."

He ran his hands over my hips and down my thighs, rubbing circles over them with his thumbs, testing my response. I arched back into him, releasing a breathy sigh when I felt his erection rubbing against my ass.

"Say yes," he murmured in my ear.

"Yes. Oh, yes," I sighed. Marlen made a low sound of satisfaction as he gently pulled my dress above my hips, exposing my legs to the cool evening air.

I tipped my head back to capture his lips in a kiss that was far more X-rated than the sweet one we had shared a couple of nights ago. Where Marlen held back the other night, now he gave me everything. His tongue swept demandingly against the seam of my mouth, and I parted my lips eagerly, meeting him stroke for stroke. That same strange urge to *mark, own, take,* was riding me hard, and my teeth sunk into Marlen's lower lip before I realized what I was doing.

Marlen groaned in response, gripping me tighter. No one had ever kissed me like this before—it felt like he was trying to taste my very soul.

It was intoxicating, and I knew that my feelings toward Marlen would be a lot more complicated by the end of the night. I wasn't ready to officially pursue him as a mate and all that it entailed, but I couldn't stomach sharing him either. It was selfish to expect so much from him, and I hated myself for not being able to give him what he deserved.

As his mouth devoured mine, Marlen's stroking fingers worked their way up my thighs towards my panties, stroking me softly over the top of the thin linen fabric. I knew he'd be able to tell how damp they were from that touch alone—between him and Bryn, I basically walked around permanently wet these days.

"Foxglove," he murmured against my lips. "Let me taste you."

I felt my face heat along with every other part of my body. My previous sexual encounters had been pretty clinical—quickies in clubs, or occasionally in the library bathroom if I was lucky—oral had always felt way too intimate for what they were.

"I've never done that before," I replied shyly, feeling Marlen's lust and excitement spark up like a fireworks display.

"Then let me show you how good it feels. I'd be honored to be the first to taste you. I bet you taste like the heavens."

I could hardly say no to that. Marlen shifted out from behind me and gently laid me back, moving between my legs and bending them at the knee before leaning over my body to give me another toe-curling kiss, our tongues intertwining and hands pulling each other closer. Our movements were slow and intentional, and I got the impression that I wasn't the only one savoring this moment.

Marlen pulled back, pressing traveling kisses and nips down my neck, lavishing attention on my breasts before continuing down my belly to my aching pussy. It felt like more than just him getting me off to relieve some frustration. Marlen was worshiping my body like I was his own personal goddess.

I felt awkward just lying back, staring up at the willow tree, so I propped myself up on my elbows to watch as Marlen undid the lace-up sides of my panties, grinning up at me before lowering his head, tongue flicking out to swipe his lower lip as he gazed at my sex like he'd never seen anything so entrancing.

Holy mother of fairies, this was the sexiest thing I had ever seen.

Marlen's tongue slowly flattened against my folds, dragging upwards before brushing oh-so-lightly against my clit. My eyes rolled back, and I bit down on my lip to stop myself from crying out since we were out in the open and anyone could hear us. I'm pretty sure Marlen took my silence as a challenge. I felt his thrill of excitement as his tongue explored my pussy like he was an explorer visiting a foreign land for the first time. I *felt* the concentration he was trying to hold onto underneath his own raging lust as he cataloged each reaction, learning what got the strongest response from me.

"Right there!" I breathed, my entire body clenching in anticipation. How had I gone my whole *life* without this? I wanted oral every day.

Marlen listened, licking and sucking exactly where I told him to as he slid one long finger in my aching, needy pussy. I pressed my lips together to suppress the whine at how good it felt, how close I was, how much I needed *more.* But like he was reading my mind, Marlen added a second finger, increasing the pace of his movements. I gasped as his teeth scraped lightly over my tingling nerves before he soothed them with his tongue. His other hand had a firm grip on my inner thigh, fingers digging into my flesh, branding my skin.

Marlen found the perfect spot inside me with glorious precision, his fingers stroking and pumping over and over until it felt like there was molten lava swirling through my entire body. Plunging his fingers into me once more as he sucked lightly on my clit, my orgasm ripped through me like a hurricane, my back arching and toes curling into the grass. Crying out loudly enough for everyone within ten feet to hear me, I came riding his fingers, his mouth devouring me.

My head fell back on the grass as I panted wildly, struggling to catch my breath. Marlen, oozing satisfaction, held my eye while licking my arousal off his fingers. It was kind of filthy, and had me instantly ready for round two.

"You taste heavenly. Like honey and vanilla. Even better than I imagined, and I've imagined this a lot."

Marlen pulled himself up over my body and kissed me gently, his lips still shiny with my desire. I could taste myself on his tongue, which brought out a primal, possessive feeling in me like I'd never experienced before. I always wanted him to taste like me, to smell like me. I wanted to scratch him and bite him and leave my marks all over his skin, so everyone knew he was mine.

"I already want more. I won't ever be able to get enough of you," Marlen mumbled against my lips. Unsure how to respond, I buried my face in his neck, suddenly feeling too vulnerable and exposed to look him in the eye.

"Sorry, sorry. I didn't mean to freak you out with my affection," Marlen chuckled, guiding my chin back up to kiss me again.

"Thank you for being patient with me," I whispered.

"Always, foxglove," he replied with a soft smile. "Always."

FFION

CHAPTER 12

I woke up obscenely early to a persistent banging on my cabin door, well before the bells were due to chime, feeling both exhausted and still kind of tingly from that night.

"Fi! I know you're in there!"

"Briallen?" I climbed down from the loft hastily, wrapping a blanket around myself before shuffling my way over to the door and unbolting it and stepping back so she could come in. I'd gotten paranoid about locking the place up as tight as I could since both messages had been delivered to my cabin.

Briallen breezed in with a plate of breakfast food she must have snagged at the commons and immediately started stoking the fire to make us some tea. I don't know how she had so much energy at six am. I was still shuffling around like a corpse, contemplating whether it would be rude to just go back to bed and ignore her.

"So?" She spun around and pinned me with a look. "Tell me all about it!"

"All about what?"

"You and Marlen! You went for that 'walk' last night." She put 'walk' in air quotes and rolled her eyes as if it was the most absurd thing she'd ever heard. "Did you indulge in a little *try before you buy?*"

"Briallen!" I gasped. *This girl.* She seemed so sweet and innocent, but it was all just a cover for the gossiping nympho she was at heart. "We didn't have sex, if that's what you're asking. Though we did have fun," I mumbled, my face heating.

I wasn't sure I'd ever be able to adopt the cool-about-sex attitude of the fae.

Briallen squealed, her excitement buzzing intensely over my skin, and flung her arms around my neck. "Progress! This is so great. You two are so well matched. I can't wait until it's official."

"Marlen is wonderful. I'm fortunate to have a connection with someone like him," I replied vaguely, smiling at her enthusiasm.

I left out the part where I didn't think I could ever take things any further, because my gift was really a curse and I didn't want it to grow any stronger. She finished brewing the tea and set up breakfast for us on the little table while I dug around in my wardrobe for an outfit.

"Perhaps now that you're progressing things with Marlen, Bryn will get his act together too? I'm sure it grates on him seeing the two of you so happy together." Briallen looked at me conspiratorially, but I just laughed.

"No thanks. He and his mood swings can stay the hell away from me. I know he's your cousin and all but honestly, B. Brooding is only sexy to a point," I replied with a pointed look.

Also, he may be threatening me, but she probably didn't want to hear that.

She laughed, not in the least bit offended. "I totally get it, and I'm not pushing you to pursue him. Bryn's story is his to tell, but know that his parents had a strong mating pull and their story has a tragic ending. I think it's fear that keeps him away from you. He doesn't want to let himself feel the kind of connection that destroyed his family."

Even though we would never be together, the idea of him suffering made my chest ache. It could have been the mating pull dictating my response, but I wasn't entirely sure that was true. Maybe it was my own empathic nature. Or maybe I just had a hidden soft spot for the fire fae that I didn't like to acknowledge.

"No one knows better than me how hard he can be to put up with. But I'm also not giving up hope." Briallen winked, and we giggled our way through breakfast as she told me about her and Leigh's various sexcapades around campus, in case I needed to find a discrete spot in the future.

Thank the magical fae gods for girlfriends.

We packed up our breakfast and finished getting ready together before heading out to class. I had my first-year air mastery class first thing, and it had been the only thing giving me hope that I wasn't a complete waste of magical space. As the toxins from Albion had cleared from my system, Master Aures had allowed me to take part fully in class, and I had developed increasingly accurate control over my air magic. I could now easily control gusts of wind to push items away from me, and pull them back.

Marlen had mentioned that in the third year, we would use air to control our jumps from the tallest trees, and by fourth year I'd have enough control to create an air bubble around my head for breathing underwater. It was a great incentive to keep practicing.

The other elemental classes may as well have been theoretical for the amount of magic I produced in them. Not that anyone without an affinity for the element could ever do very much. They could at least grow and shrink candle flames, create whirlpools in their water basins, or bring flower buds into bloom. I had accomplished none of those milestones yet. It didn't look like I'd be graduating from the first-year class any time soon.

Feeling irritable after another pointless session of staring at my unmoving basin of water, my mood brightened considerably when I spotted Marlen heading over to me in the commons.

Now that I wasn't fighting the mating pull from Marlen; it felt like a comforting weight in my chest, rather than a knotted ache, as it still did whenever I saw Bryn. Mainly when I saw him with Saffir, which was more often than not. You'd think spending time with his girlfriend would perk him up, but he was more furious than ever these days. They seemed less touchy-feely now though, so maybe there was trouble in paradise?

Marlen greeted me with a kiss on the temple, immediately wrapping his arm around my shoulders. It was even harder now to be around each other without touching. Maybe because we'd taken things further last night? I wanted to blame it all on the mating pull, but Marlen was sexy as hell, and I wanted to touch him, mating pull be damned.

Now that my post-orgasm haze had well and truly faded, my guilt at going further with him without being honest about what he was getting himself into was eating me alive.

"Foxglove, you're thinking so hard, even I'm getting a headache," Marlen complained. "Come on, I told you I'd show you the library sometime, right? Let's head over there now. Then we can get some blackcurrant tea and turn that brain of yours off for a few minutes."

I grimaced at the thought of that ghastly tea, but Marlen's words had cheered me up a little. I would tell him everything. *Soon.*

The library was a stone, circular building that I must have walked past at least fifty times, but I'd assumed it was just another classroom since it was so small. The walls were lined with old books from floor to ceiling, and there were wooden shelves down the middle housing more rows of ancient tomes.

I was hoping for a *Beauty and the Beast* library moment and this... definitely was not it. But I was still excited to explore the books. Marlen must have noticed my disappointment. He gently turned me toward him, resting his hands on my shoulders.

"Not what you had in mind?" he asked slowly, a thread of vulnerability in his voice. I instantly felt guilty. He had been really thoughtful for bringing me here, and I was being an ungrateful brat about it.

"I'm sorry," I said quickly. "I'm excited, I promise. It's just that human libraries are huge, and I guess I was just expecting a bigger building is all. I can't wait to start reading though," I added with an apologetic wince.

Marlen gave me one of those warm, genuine smiles—the kind he only gave his sister and Leigh and Briallen, his two best friends. Everyone else got his cocksure, playboy grin. That one did spectacular things for my libido, but his honest-to-god smile turned me to mush.

"Books are rare in Avalon, foxglove. Paper is pretty scarce. This right here is probably the largest collection of books in one place in the entire realm," he explained.

Huh. I had noticed the absence of paper around campus, but never gave much thought to how that would affect book production. Did they even have printing presses in Avalon? How accessible was knowledge outside of the Academy walls? The thought sat uneasily with me. I loved the Academy, but it was clearly a place of privilege. I wasn't getting an accurate picture of Avalon or the fae by living here.

"I'm guessing we can't take the books away then," I mused, taking in the armchairs and little tables scattered throughout the cozy room.

"Gods, no," Marlen exclaimed in horror.

"Never mind," I muttered. "Human thing."

I grabbed a book on the history of elemental magic and settled myself into an armchair, ready to lose myself in the pages and relishing the feeling of doing something so familiar. Marlen grabbed a book and got comfortable in the armchair next to mine. His contentment wrapped around me like a blanket, and the realization that this was something we both enjoyed melted my heart to him just a little bit more.

Soon. I would tell him everything soon.

Marlen and Leigh were both on guard duty that night, so I invited Briallen back to my cabin to hang out since I knew she got lonely without Leigh around. I spotted Aderyn at dinner and asked her to join us too. I'd really been enjoying her company and wanted her and Briallen to get a chance to properly meet.

"So," Briallen began, clapping her hands together as we settled in on the floor of my cabin around the warm stove, leaning against the armchairs. "I think we should have a question-and-answer session for you, Fi. As a chance for you to get to learn about all things Avalon. You're learning a lot about magical theory and magical history, but the Academy doesn't cover the kind of general knowledge or popular culture that we learned as kids growing up here."

"That's an excellent idea," Aderyn agreed shyly. She was definitely less confident around Briallen than she was with just me. "Is there anything you've been particularly wondering about?"

"I'd like to learn more about the gods," I broached cautiously, remembering how sad Aderyn had felt the last time we discussed them.

"Really?" Briallen's eyebrows raised in surprise. "I guess I thought you'd want to find out about Avalon. You know, where to shop, sights to see, creatures to watch out for, that kind of thing."

"Er, let's definitely add 'creatures to watch out for' to our curriculum. Number two on the priority list? I really want to know more about where magic comes from." *And why some fae have so much and others so little*, I added silently.

"Don't worry," Aderyn reassured me. "You don't need to fear any of those creatures while you're on campus. It's why the male students do guard duty and take additional combat training."

It still seemed hella sexist to me, but fae had pretty rigid views of gender roles. There were also a lot more males than females, which I assumed played into it.

"Right, well, the gods are fairly mysterious, so I'll tell you what I can, but everyone has different ideas about them." Briallen shrugged.

"Everyone agrees that there are six gods: three male, three female. Their names are Aine, Cerridwen, Morgan, Eagan, Gawain, and Balfour. They're always depicted standing in a circle, holding hands with their eyes closed," Briallen explained, and Aderyn nodded in agreement. My mind drifted back to the tapestry of the six figures in white robes that hung on the wall in Gwyneria's cabin. Of course it depicted the gods. How had I not realized that before?

"Do they ever... visit? How is any of that known? Humans have gods too, but there isn't the same universal consensus about them that the fae have."

"Not just the fae, everyone in Avalon. The gods aren't fae. They're something other, far more powerful. Or they were..." Aderyn trailed off sadly.

"As for visiting, it's not straightforward. The gods commune with the spirits of deceased fae, and those with the gift of Second Sight can talk to spirits. They receive visions from them if the gods want them to see something," Briallen added.

"It's a powerful gift," Aderyn said thoughtfully. "Though it can make those who possess it pariahs of sorts. Many fae are fearful of those who can talk to spirits."

I pondered their words and decided I'd rather be an empath than see dead fae everywhere I went. Screw that. Especially if I had to *listen* to them. Emotions were quite enough to be dealing with.

"Aren't they hunted? For their gift?" I asked casually. Probably *too* casually. I'd mostly been a loner in my human life, and I was beginning to realize that my social skills were severely lacking.

"Never!" Briallen exclaimed. "The last thing a dark fae would want is to be reachable by the gods. The ability to communicate with spirits is powerful in its own way, but it isn't a power that can be easily exploited. That's the kind of power the hunters seek."

On second thought, maybe the talking-to-dead-fae thing wouldn't be so bad if it meant being left alone.

"So, the six gods are responsible for all the magic in Avalon, not just the fae. But fae magic is dying? What about everyone else's?" I asked.

"Only fae magic is dying," Briallen confirmed, her voice tinged with sadness. "The fae were once the most powerful race in Avalon, now we're probably the weakest. We're no match for goblin magic or mermaid powers now. Let alone the dragons."

"Um, okay, let's definitely schedule that magical creatures conversation for as soon as possible," I said, already planning another trip to the library in my head. "In my second week, I came across a circle of white marble slabs at the top of a hill in the forest. Is that a representation of the gods?"

"It's a temple," Aderyn replied, her voice heavy. "They used to be busy places. Fae would go to the temple to connect with the gods and thank them for their gifts. They're kind of a relic nowadays. The gods aren't there anymore, so the temples are empty."

It definitely hadn't felt empty when that strange magical sensation had engulfed me and held me hostage in the circle. I deliberated whether I should tell the girls about that, but decided against it. Probably best not to draw any extra attention to myself.

I would just add it to the increasingly extensive list of secrets I was already keeping.

And the even more extensive list of questions I had about this new life I'd stumbled into.

FFION

CHAPTER 13

Opening the door to my cabin after dinner the following night, I spotted another ominous piece of paper under my door and my heart sank to the floor. Whenever I allowed myself to start feeling comfortable here, one of these evil little reminders would appear, letting me know that I was putting myself in danger by staying.

With a heavy sigh, I dropped my satchel and picked up the note. Unlike the others, this one had no writing at all, just a drawing. It depicted the same curly-haired girl as the last picture, this time bound in chains and surrounded by small crystals. There were lines of ink running from her body to the crystals, and I realized with dread that it was meant to be my blood.

This was a depiction of what Gwyneira had said would happen if the hunters ever captured me. I'd be imprisoned and my magic bled out of me, stored in crystals.

I curled up in a ball on my bed, staring at the drawing, wondering who might have sent me this and why. My theory that one of the two people who knew about my ability had told a hunter seemed a bit weaker with this latest note. I thought the hunters were telling me to go home so they could get to me off campus, but why would they leave a depiction of what they would do to me?

My other theory that these messages were *warnings* seemed more and more likely.

Perhaps I would tell Gwyneira about the new notes soon. She'd been the one to explain all this to me, it seemed unlikely that she'd be behind the messages as well. No, if she thought I was safer in Albion, she had the opportunity to tell me one-on-one during our tutoring sessions. Sending anonymous threats didn't seem like her style.

That only left Bryn. I chewed on my lower lip, something in my gut urging me not to believe the worst of him. But he had told me I was trouble right from the moment he'd found out I was an empath. I constantly sensed anger from him directed at me, and it was getting worse rather than better. Plus, we had a powerful mating pull. Having me around was probably messing with his ability to feel other mating pulls since ours was dominant.

Maybe that was his motive? Use my fear of my empath abilities getting out to convince me to leave Avalon permanently. My head hurt from trying to figure it all out.

I stored the drawing at the bottom of my satchel with the other notes and went into the bathroom for a long, tepid shower. Gods, what I would give for Albion's plumbing on days like this.

With my forehead resting against the shower wall, I tried to think of how I could be proactive about this situation. I needed answers; not having all the information available to me was almost the worst part about all of this. One thing I was certain of was that these messages were linked to why I'd been dumped in Albion in the first place. If I could figure that out, then maybe I'd know why I was being pushed back there.

Maybe the answers to my current questions lay somewhere in my past.

"Ffion, please come in," Gwyneira greeted me, opening the door to her cabin. "I have tea for us."

I thought I'd drunk a lot of tea in my human life, but it was nothing compared to the amount fae drank.

"How are your lessons progressing?" Gwyneira asked, leading me into the sitting room. We sat side-by-side on the couch, and she leaned forward to pour the tea already set out for us on the coffee table.

I searched my brain for an answer, wishing I could just say 'fine' and be done with it, but the word got physically stuck in my throat.

"Slowly," I settled on eventually.

Gwyneira hummed, setting a teacup on a saucer and passing it to me. "To be expected, given how much you have to learn. Do not be discouraged."

I took a sip of my tea to avoid answering.

"Before we work on strengthening your mental defenses, is there anything else you wanted to discuss today?" I got the feeling that Gwyneira knew I was hiding things from her, but was giving me the chance to come to her when I was ready.

"Actually yes," I told her and felt her surprise.

"Oh?"

"I was hoping to learn more about my family, actually. Obviously I don't have much to go on, though I believe 'Ffion' was the first name my parents gave me. It was written on my arm when I was found outside the orphanage," I muttered the last part, embarrassed that they had left me on the side of the road like trash.

"All births and deaths are noted by the Fae Council in the Records Hall, around an hour's flight from here. You could check it to find a Ffion born twenty years ago. Are you hoping to reconnect with your family?" she asked hesitantly.

I could feel her concern. Maybe she was worried I would be disappointed? I snorted internally. Like I'd want to spend time with the people who left me on the side of the road in a whole different world.

"Not particularly. I suppose I'm just curious," I replied eventually. Not a lie, but not quite the whole truth. I had been spending a lot of time telling half-truths lately.

"Understandably so," Gwyneira said with a sad smile. "I know you want answers, but if you go to the Records Hall, you will need to sign in. I am not sure drawing the Council's attention to you would be wise until you have better control over your gift."

I searched for a hint of harmful intent in Gwyneira's emotions, but I only found genuine unease, rippling through my gut like a sickly wave of nausea.

"Perhaps you're right," I conceded. I wanted answers, but I wasn't in a rush to get put on any government lists either.

"Shall we work on your mental shields now? I think we should move on from the ineffectual brick-by-brick method. I want you to imagine a bubble around yourself instead. That visual may resonate more with you, given your air affinity."

An hour of visualizing a bubble of air surrounding me to keep the emotions at bay had resulted in an impromptu blast of air magic knocking over the teacups, but not a lot else. I had been so optimistic when I'd started the sessions with Gwyneira that I'd find a way to shut the emotions out. Now, I was resigning myself to the fact that this might be my life forever. I hadn't had a migraine since I'd arrived at the Academy, but the fear that I'd get overwhelmed by emotions in a crowd and everyone would realize I was an empath was crippling.

We said our goodbyes—Gwyneira contemplative and me subdued—and I made my way down the winding stairs to the forest floor where Marlen was waiting for me, leaning against a tree with his arms crossed.

His light, playful mood was an immediately soothing balm on my soul. When he opened his arms for me, I didn't hesitate to walk into them, resting my forehead against his collarbone and closing my eyes.

"Is everything okay, foxglove?" Marlen asked, wrapping his arms tightly around me. "I know you don't like to talk about these sessions with Gwyneira, but if you ever need to, you know I'm here."

He felt worried and confused, and I knew he assumed these tutoring sessions were about bringing me up to speed on Avalon. He was probably wondering why a simple history lesson had stressed me out so much.

"I know," I mumbled, inhaling his soothing pine scent one last time before extricating myself from his embrace. "Come on, let's head back. I'm starving."

"About that..." Marlen began. "I was hoping I could set up a little dinner date for the two of us in your cabin tonight? I'd offer mine, but Kelvyn is there, and he's a real asshole about having guests over. Perhaps you could hang out with Briallen for a bit beforehand while I get it ready?"

I had been pretty protective over my cabin with the messages and all, but I felt like I could trust Marlen alone in there, plus he was giving me his best puppy dog eyes and radiating hopefulness.

Besides, things had been heating up between us, and the way he spoke about the future made it clear he imagined me in it. This could be the perfect opportunity for me to tell him about my empath abilities. Hopefully he'd take it all in stride, not care at all that I had the worst gift, and we could celebrate. Ideally with several orgasms.

"Of course. Are you sure you don't want a hand setting up? I'll love it even if it isn't a surprise."

I leaned forward, pressing a light kiss on his lips before linking our hands together. I was finding it nearly impossible to be around him without somehow touching him.

"I know you would—you go far too easy on me, really. I'm trying to court you here. You should demand flowers and jewelry and dinner dates." Marlen winked, then leaned in until his lips grazed my ear. "And oral. You should demand that you come on my tongue at least once a day."

I snorted. "That would be going easy on you. You would enjoy that far too much."

"You wound me, foxglove," he said, feigning an arrow to the heart. "Maybe you're secretly making this hard on me after all."

I had spent an hour hanging out in Leigh and Briallen's cabin while Marlen prepared our dinner date. I had assumed, without ever asking, that Briallen had a female roommate. But apparently after the claiming marks appeared, bonded mates lived together. There were more bonded fae than not on campus, so it worried me a little that I hadn't realized that earlier.

Gods, no wonder the mysterious messenger had been able to get the jump on me three times now. My powers of observation were seriously lacking.

I made my way back to my cabin and kicked myself for not picking out a sexier outfit beforehand. I was in one of my shorter linen dresses, a thick woolen cardigan, no shoes, and I had pulled my hair into a thick braid tied with a strip of linen. It could have been worse, but I didn't really look like I'd tried, and I knew Marlen was inside, pulling out all the stops.

"Marlen? Can I come in now?"

"Of course, foxglove. I'm all ready for you."

Marlen pulled open the door and pulled me into his arms for a slow, seductive kiss before walking me to the table and pulling out a chair for me. It was all very gentlemanly, and it made me all gooey inside knowing that he had done all of this for me. The cabin smelled delicious, the rich aroma of spices coming from an earthenware pot on the table.

"It's lentil stew," he said, taking the chair opposite me and pulling the lid off the dish. "Nothing gourmet, but it's great comfort food. My mam makes it for us in winter. I know I get sick of the raw food at the commons, so I thought you might appreciate a hot meal."

He smiled across the table at me, and he looked so breathtakingly handsome in the candlelight that I nearly skipped the food in favor of dragging him straight to bed. But that couldn't happen until I'd been frank with him about my gift. I didn't want to lead him any further down this track under false pretenses.

"This looks incredible. Thank you for going to all this effort. It's like you read my mind—I have been missing hot food lately."

I spooned the stew into my bowl as Marlen poured us each a glass of what I assumed was red wine, though it had a distinct glittery quality to it I'd never seen in Albion.

"Fae wine," Marlen explained with a wink. "It's pretty potent. I'll only give you a little to start with."

"I'm sure it's delicious, but I wanted to talk to you about something, er, important." I cleared my throat uncomfortably. "It's probably best to do it with a clear head. I'll keep the glass. I may well need a swig or ten after we're done with this chat," I told the table, unable to meet Marlen's eyes.

"Fi? What is it?" he asked, radiating concern.

"Do you want to eat first, then talk?"

"I don't think I'll be able to focus on anything else now that you've brought it up, foxglove. You've really got me worried."

Gods, this fae was too sweet. I didn't want to ruin him with my burden.

"Okay, well, hopefully this chat goes well, then we can eat and discuss it and not ruin this lovely meal." I laughed nervously, then exhaled, willing myself to calm down. "You know I'm still on the fence about this whole mating thing," I started slowly.

"Believe me, I'm well aware," Marlen said wryly. He didn't feel angry though, just resigned.

"Right. Well, I'm still unsure about everything, but you've become so important to me. Whatever this is..." I trailed off awkwardly before concluding. "I don't want secrets between us, and this is kind of a big one. You should know what you're getting into with me."

I waited to feel his bitterness—I had just admitted to keeping a big secret from him and told him to his face I planned to keep stringing him along—but the bitterness never came, though. Marlen was still worried, but mostly curious, with a tiny glimmer of hopefulness I didn't quite understand.

This was why being around Marlen was so dangerous. I was always surrounded by cynicism and jaded emotions, but Marlen's soul was constantly joyful and bright. His was the kind of soul I could fall in love with.

"It's actually about my magic. You know I have an air affinity but I, um, also have a gifted ability. You never asked me if I did, and I never volunteered the information. I didn't mean to deceive you," I rushed out awkwardly.

Marlen's worry dissipated significantly, and I caught his amusement. "I'm not mad, foxglove. My magic wouldn't have called so strongly to yours if you'd only had an air affinity. After the message on your wardrobe, Bryn mentioned you had a gifted ability but said it was your story to tell, so I didn't push it."

That was surprisingly decent of Bryn. I filed that away for later consideration. Marlen smiled, reaching for my hand across the table. "Are you going to indulge me now? You've piqued my curiosity."

"I know," I sighed.

"You know?"

"I know I've piqued your curiosity. Just like I know you're not mad. And I know it worried you when I said I had something to tell you, and you thought it was funny when I said I didn't mean to deceive you. I know how you feel. How everyone feels."

I should have known there'd be no horror or disgust from him. That he wouldn't give me a petty nickname like Bryn had. There was definitely a wave of surprise, some awe, then a fresh wave of concern, but nothing that suggested Marlen wanted nothing more to do with me.

He let out a whoosh of breath. "Shit, Fi. Who else knows you're an empath?"

"You, Gwyneira, and Bryn."

His face darkened, and the sharp stab of jealousy I picked up when I said Bryn's name took me by surprise. Marlen often felt insecure, but I had never sensed jealousy from him before.

"You know Bryn collected me from Albion, right? He was the one who told me I was fae, and when I asked him about my abilities, he pieced together that I was an empath. Gwyneira made him swear not to tell anyone," I explained. Marlen's envy abated with a heavy sigh.

"Sorry, I don't know why I was jealous of that. I know you and Bryn have a difficult relationship at the best of times," he said with a sheepish smile. "I should be embarrassed that you've been able to read my emotions this whole time, but honestly, I've never tried to hide any of them from you anyway. That moment of jealousy might be the only thing I'm embarrassed about. I'm kind of excited you've been able to feel my lust this whole time." He waggled his eyebrows at me, and I rolled my eyes playfully.

"Yes, I can't doubt your level of attraction to me, don't worry about that.

I'm sorry I didn't tell you sooner. Gwyneira emphasized how important it was to keep this information on the down-low..."

"I'm glad you didn't tell me. It was smart of you to get to know me and assess whether I was worthy of your trust, Fi. Though I'm definitely freaking out a lot more about that message in your room now. I assumed it was Saffir or someone like her, someone jealous of your mating pull. This is so much worse. No wonder Bryn was freaking out."

I gave him a sheepish look. "I, um, haven't told anyone about this, but there were two more messages..."

Digging around in my satchel, I found the notes and passed them over to Marlen. "Both of them were slipped under my door in this cabin, one a couple of days after the wardrobe message, the other just yesterday."

Marlen was unnaturally still, even though his emotions were swirling like a whirlpool, too fast to accurately identify as he scanned each piece of paper.

"Please tell me Gwyneira knows about this?" Marlen asked, staring at me intently. I chewed on my bottom lip and looked at my hands. "Fi? You told her, right?"

"I know it sounds crazy. I get that she's the dean, and a big part of me trusts her, but I don't know... There are only two other people that know about my ability, and she's one of them. What if the threats are coming from her? Or someone she told?"

He let out a low whistle. "I get it. I'm not sure I agree with you—Gwyneira is basically revered by the whole fae world—but it makes sense to play your cards close to your chest until you're 100% sure who to trust. What about Bryn? Do you suspect him?"

I wrung my hands nervously in my lap. "I don't *want* to suspect him. He's always so furious around me since the moment I met him. He resents the strong pull between us. Maybe this is his way of getting me out of the way?"

"Maybe," Marlen hedged, but it didn't sound like he agreed with me.

He looked at me solemnly through his lashes. "Please promise me you'll be more careful, Fi. You've been taking a lot of risks, especially walking around campus alone. I need you to be safe. If anything were to happen to you..." he trailed off and gulped audibly. "Please, Fi. Let me help you. If you say no, I'll probably just follow you around like a stalker, anyway."

That made me smile. Gods, he was like a giant teddy bear. "I wouldn't want to make a stalker out of you. We'll figure out a plan that gives us both peace of mind." I laughed and brought his hand up from the table so I could gently kiss his fingertips.

Everything about how Marlen had handled this had been perfect. He was compassionate, didn't offer empty platitudes about how it would be okay, and the concern he showed about my safety made me feel warm and fuzzy inside. Even his brief spurt of jealousy had been kind of sexy.

I wasn't ready to admit it to him yet, I could barely admit it to myself, but I didn't think I'd be able to walk away from this handsome, playful, kind fae.

"Now that's out of the way, let's enjoy this amazing dinner you've prepared so we can move on to dessert."

FFION

CHAPTER 14

My relief at telling Marlen about my magic had me giddy. For the first time since I'd met him, I wasn't fighting the mating pull at all, and it was like someone had lifted a crushing burden off my shoulders. I reveled in the way the pull physically drew me to Marlen, the sensuality I was feeling, the feverish desire that had me squirming in my seat throughout dinner.

Without my secret holding me back, I knew I was flirtier than usual, touching him constantly throughout dinner. It was a side of me he'd never seen before, and it was definitely affecting him. I couldn't tell if it was all me or if the mating pull was driving us both insane with need, but everything about him was seducing me tonight.

Could fae go into heat? I felt like I was going into heat.

I could feel Marlen's desire like it was my own, tightening around my nipples and throbbing between my thighs. The double dose of his lust and mine was driving me crazy in the best possible way.

Marlen's desire was only second to the sense of pride he had been feeling since I told him about my magic, and I wished I had more insight into *why* he felt that way. My best guess is he was proud I trusted him? The thought made me feel all warm and fuzzy inside—an emotion that was entirely my own.

We worked together to clean up after dinner in the small basin. As we finished, I wrapped my arms around Marlen's waist from behind and rested my cheek against his back, pressing every inch of me against him, noticing that he was all firm lines in contrast to my soft curves. My hands slid slowly over the ridges of his abs, down to the bulge in his trousers, gently running them back and forth over his length.

Marlen exhaled a long breath. "Foxglove, what are you doing?"

"Just checking something," I mumbled into his back, smiling.

"What is it you're checking?" he asked, reaching his hands back and rubbing them down the outside of my thighs, pulling my body somehow closer to his.

I hummed in satisfaction, sliding around him and ducking under his arm so I was between him and the basin. Leaning up to his ear, I whispered, "I was checking to see if you're as turned on as I am right now."

Marlen ran his hands up my legs, under my dress, to cup a generous handful of my ass.

"And? What's the verdict? Surely you can *feel* just how much I want you," Marlen asked, raising an eyebrow at me.

He kept one hand on my ass, kneading it playfully, while moving the other between us so he could rub over my already damp panties. I was surprised at how comfortable I was at having his hands all over me.

"You're soaking," Marlen groaned, leaning his forehead against mine. "On the bed, Fi. I have to taste you."

I tipped my face up and bit down lightly on Marlen's lower lip, sucking it into my mouth. "Not this time. I have other plans for you tonight."

"Mm, and what might those be?" he asked cautiously, and I felt an ember of his hope spark in my chest.

"I want everything," I whispered breathily into his ear, lightly pushing him back towards the ladder and following him up to the bed.

I was *so* ready for this. Mentally and physically. I needed zero foreplay at this point. All I could think of throughout dinner is that there were no secrets between Marlen and me. Finally, we were free to take things to the next level. It was a weirdly massive turn-on.

Something about Marlen made me want to take the lead. Whenever I was with him, I had a burning desire to make him worship me, to possess his passion, to mark him and brand him to let everyone know he was mine.

Either I had a previously undiscovered dominant side, or it was a hang-up from the whole Corsen incident and knowing how recently he'd been with someone else. Just the thought made me want to leave a deep bite mark on his throat so everyone could see who he belonged to.

I crawled up the bed, attempting to look seductive and hoping I was pulling it off before straddling Marlen's hips and teasingly undoing the buttons on his shirt. He grinned up at me, tugging at the bottom of my dress. Tonight wasn't going to be slow. I had so much pent-up frustration to work off with this fae, and we had all night to explore the things we wanted to do to each other.

Hopefully, more than tonight.

I made quick work of our clothes and crawled to his side, angling my body over him and pulling my hair over one shoulder. With one last, hopefully seductive look, I wrapped my hand around his cock, pumping it gently as I leaned in to lick the forming bead of precum. He'd tasted me before, and turnabout is fair play. I hadn't ever given oral before—none of my past partners had ever made me want to—yet I'd been dying to try it on Marlen.

I worked his length slowly as I swirled my tongue around the head of his cock, experimenting with different angles and testing how he felt in my mouth, savoring the salty taste of him. Marlen gathered a handful of my hair and guided the back of my head gently to where he wanted me, groaning and making all kinds of delicious sounds that spurred me on. He was making those sounds because of me; I was having this effect on him. It made me feel... powerful.

I slowly moved down his shaft, taking him inch by inch into my mouth and marveling at the velvety smoothness of his cock. *This was much more fun than I thought it would be.* His lust was building in me, I felt how much he was enjoying this, felt his pleasure as if it was my own.

Just as I settled into a rhythm, Marlen tugged at my waist, encouraging me onto all fours. I moved willingly, sucking him as steadily as possible while angling myself so his fingers could slide between my thighs. He met no resistance as he slid two fingers into my aching pussy, pumping them to match my speed. *Gods, this is distracting.* I moaned around him and felt him increase his tempo, mercilessly plunging his fingers into me until I was a mewling mess.

Turned all the way on and needing more, I moved to straddle him. Letting him guide my hips, I sunk down inch by glorious inch, relishing the burning stretch of him filling me up. Either Marlen was supremely well endowed, or fae were just bigger in general because I had never felt anything like this before. I was *full*.

Taking a moment to adjust, I look up through a curtain of hair at Marlen's satisfied expression.

"This is quite the view, foxglove. I could get used to it," Marlen murmured, reaching up to cup my breasts, rolling and pinching my nipples between his thumb and forefinger. *Smug fae.*

Wanting to make sure he knew I was in charge, I lifted myself up and slammed down on him, relishing his groan of pleasure. He gripped my hips hard enough to bruise as I rode him hard, my nails raking lines into his chest and over his forearms. It was too much; I was too hot and too cold, pulling him closer and pushing him away. My body was wound so tight that if I didn't come soon, I might have actually died.

Marlen lifted his thumb to my mouth, and I sucked it deeply before he moved it down to work rough circles over my clit, sending me into a heart-stopping orgasm. My neighbors would probably hear, but I couldn't hold in the moan of relief if I wanted to. I *needed* this release, needed Marlen. I felt him tremble and still underneath me as he climaxed with one final thrust, growling out my name, hands still clamped on my hips as if he'd never let me go.

This was ten times better than when he made me come from his mouth alone. This was everything. I wanted at least three of these a day.

I collapsed against Marlen's chest, panting, sweating, and burning in all the right places. Marlen's arms banded tightly around me, pulling me up his chest for a slow, sweet kiss.

"You're incredible, foxglove," he whispered against my lips, and my heart swelled with affection for this man who knew my terrifying secret and accepted me regardless.

I moved next to him, cuddling up at his side with my ear against his chest and leg flung over his. Marlen's hand rested firmly on my hip, rubbing soothing patterns into my skin with his thumb. I'd never felt so at peace, even as I fought against my natural inclination to flee.

It might be awkward if I ran away from my own cabin.

"I know you haven't formally asked me to be your suitor, and maybe you don't see me that way yet," Marlen broached hesitantly. "But I want you to know you're it for me, foxglove. For what it's worth."

I moved my head back into the crook of his arm so I could meet his eyes. He looked down at me with so much adoration in his gaze that my cold, guarded heart skipped a beat. I'd sensed bouts of self-doubt from Marlen before, but I'd never seen him so visibly unsure.

"Though I doubt you'll have any competition for me," he added with a sly grin. "You marked me up pretty good."

He winked good-naturedly as he admired the lines I'd raked down his forearms, and my face heated. Fortunately, he didn't feel angry. If anything, he was exuding a smug sort of satisfaction that I'd never picked up on before.

"I'm sorry, I don't know what came over me," I admitted, blushing. "Maybe it's because of that night at the bonfire..."

He smiled reassuringly, as if I hadn't tried to rip his skin to ribbons with my nails. "It's normal, foxglove, if that's what you're worried about. Fae females are notoriously possessive over their suitors, marking them is one way they express that. After the claiming, the mating mark appears, which lessens those territorial urges."

Well, that was unfortunate since I still planned to put off anything to do with claiming for as long as physically possible. If ever. I deflected instead. "I guess fae males aren't possessive then? Because of the whole sharing thing?"

He tucked me closer into his side, one hand playing lazily with my curls as he pondered the question.

"Not at the beginning, I guess. After the claiming, we're very protective and wary of anyone outside our mating circle. Before we're bonded, we males are just doing our best to impress the girl, you know? We don't really have the right to be possessive yet." He smiled at me.

"That doesn't seem fair to me," I said, frowning at Marlen. "I don't want to be treated like some kind of goddess while doing nothing to woo you in return. You should expect me to impress you as well."

"That's not really the way it works here, foxglove. Particularly with a connection as strong as ours. You don't need to impress me. Our magic is compatible and we're kindred souls, I'd be crazy to let you go."

"I get that," I said slowly, not wanting to upset him. "It's just that everyone keeps saying that pursuing a mating pull is a choice. If you automatically pursue someone with a strong pull, it doesn't seem so much of a choice as an inevitably."

Marlen's insecurity was rising so quickly, I felt like I was drowning in it.

"All I mean is I want to be chosen for me, not because magic says it's a good idea, you know?" I added quickly, hoping to reassure him.

"Trust me, Fi, I choose you, for you, every day. Please don't be offended by me trying to impress you. It's a privilege for a male fae to get to demonstrate his worthiness. Even if I'm not officially your suitor." Marlen leaned down and sweetly kissed my temple. It still sounded kind of sexist to me, but I didn't want to upset him again.

"Between the two of us, it's not your worthiness that I'm worried about," I murmured.

Marlen chuckled. "I know you don't see it yet, foxglove, but you will. You've spent so long hiding your abilities and denying your nature that you don't recognize how amazing you really are. You deserve the world, Fi."

I tipped my head back to meet his lips again. I meant for it to be a sweet, gentle kiss, but it morphed into something much more. I was baring my soul through this kiss, telling Marlen all the things I felt but wasn't ready to say. He returned my passion in kind, reassuring me with every stroke of his tongue and nip of his teeth that he was mine, heart and soul, that he'd wait for me.

I vowed to myself to find out more about how mating would affect my magic and make an informed decision on the risk. I was losing the battle to keep Marlen at arm's length, and I wasn't sure I wanted to fight it anymore.

"Is there something you particularly wanted to discuss, Ffion? You seem distracted," Gwyneira asked kindly as I tried and failed for the hundredth time to erect a mental shield against Gwyneira's emotions.

I'd been keeping a close watch, but I still hadn't sensed anything concerning from her. My reasons for not telling her everything sounded weak, even to my own ears.

I could ask her about the impact of mating on my magic. It was a small leap of faith to confide that much in her, and I desperately hoped I wouldn't regret it. The guilt of constantly pushing Marlen away when I knew he wanted more was weighing heavily on me. In the week since we'd started having sex, the urge to claim him as my mate became so strong it was almost suffocating.

"I was curious about the impact of mating bonds on gifted abilities," I hedged cautiously. I hadn't explicitly stated that I was asking for me, but I'm sure Gwyneira figured it out. It was probably hard to pull the wool over the eyes of someone who had been around for 400 years.

Her eyes twinkled. "All of those with gifted abilities notice differences in their magic once they have completed a mating bond. It may be an increase in strength or an entirely new ability." She looked at me pointedly.

"You think it'll be the latter for me, I take it?" I muttered, my heart dropping.

"Not for the first bond, maybe not even for the second..." Gwyneira said cautiously. "From what I have read, only when an empath's mating circle is complete can they influence the emotions of crowds. Fully mated empaths were the most sought after," she added with an apologetic look. The most *hunted*.

"Ugh," I groaned petulantly, too disappointed to be embarrassed. "Sorry. I just really don't want to influence emotions. Experiencing them is more than enough to deal with."

Gwyneira chuckled at my outburst. "It is a powerful ability, one that was often abused when the empaths were still around. There was a time when all fae could erect mental shields, like the ones we have been working on, to prevent being influenced. It has been many centuries since we needed such a skill. While the myth of the empaths is still popular among the fae, much of the practical knowledge has been lost to time." She gave me a long look. "When you fully come into your abilities, you will be a coveted weapon if the information falls into the wrong hands."

I stared at her, at a loss for words. Why couldn't I get some telepathy skills instead? It'd be awesome if I could have silent chats with Marlen. We could really go to town on the dirty talk in public.

"So we know that will happen with the complete mating circle? Three mates?"

"Correct," Gwyneira gave me a tight smile. "However, as I understand it, you will develop some other abilities before that, perhaps influencing ones. You would have to physically touch someone to influence them, and it has to be done with intention. I imagine that one will appear with your second mate, provided you choose someone with powerful magic to balance it."

Well, that was reassuring, at least since I had no potential second suitors on the horizon. I sent a silent thanks to the gods that Bryn and I had no interest in each other. Well, aside from the part where he looked like an Adonis. That part interested me quite a lot.

"So, what do you think will happen if I have one mate?" I asked, giving up the pretense that this conversation was about anything other than me.

"I cannot say for certain, but the texts refer to empaths knowing the reason behind an emotion or understanding someone's general intentions. Correct me if I'm wrong, but your abilities at this stage just allow you to feel and know what others' emotions are, but not *why* they feel that way?"

"That's right," I agreed warily.

"My guess is your abilities will be sharpened with one mating bond if the magic is a strong enough match. I assume you would 'feel' emotions the same way you do, but you could examine them more closely if you wish. I do not think it would be exceedingly overwhelming."

Gwyneira was really trying to sell me on this. I wondered who she thought my potential mate was. She'd commented on the strong pull between Bryn and me before and probably assumed it was him.

It didn't sound like things would be that much worse with just one mate. If anything, it might make things *easier* if I could understand the emotions better. Not easier for people whose privacy I'd be getting all up in, but definitely easier for me. I'd spent my life giving things up because of my abilities. My education, my social life, my freedom to move around during the day. Why should I have to give up Marlen?

"We're almost out of time. Was there anything else you wanted to discuss today, Ffion?" Gwyneira asked, pulling me out of my musings.

"No, thank you. You've given me a lot to think about." I excused myself and hurried back towards the dorm. I had a sexy water fae to make things official with.

CHAPTER 15

Fi looked like she was deep in thought throughout dinner, but at least she didn't seem upset this time. It wasn't unusual for Fi to be withdrawn after her sessions with Gwyneira, but the occasional coy looks and flirty smiles were new. She sat next to me, leg pressed tightly against mine, occasionally trailing her fingers lightly up my inner thigh. I didn't know what was going on, but I wasn't going to risk questioning it. Not that she *wasn't* affectionate with me, especially since our date last week, but usually she was more reserved with other people around. She didn't even seem to care that Briallen was watching us with eyes as wide as saucers.

"Walk with me?" Fi asked sweetly as we all went to depart for our cabins.

"Always, foxglove."

"Could we take a brief detour tonight? To that spot by the stream? With the willow tree?"

I chuckled as she described it to me. That place would be burned into my memory for the rest of my life. Even now, I was having flashbacks of how good it felt to bury myself in her taste, her scent, the way her thighs had clamped around my head when she came...

"Now, what could be putting that smug smile on your face, Mr. Ferris?" Fi teased, wrapping an arm around my waist and throwing me a cheeky grin.

I laughed and threw my arm around her shoulders, tucking her in close to my side. "Just revisiting one of my favorite memories."

She released a tiny, adorable growl, and her nails dug into my side in warning. I must be messed up as hell because her possessiveness really did it for me.

"That memory better be of us. I've got big plans for you tonight, Marlen. I'd hate to put them on hold because I have to go kick some fae girl's ass."

I planted a firm kiss on her temple. "That spot is ours, foxglove, just for us. And you're the only girl that features in any of those kinds of favorite memories."

She visibly relaxed, then shook her head as if to clear away the jealousy. I chuckled and tightened my arm around her shoulders.

"I'm—"

"Nope, don't you dare apologize, Fi."

She smiled sheepishly. "I kind of feel like I'm going crazy," she murmured as we reached the stream and dropped onto the grass side-by-side.

"Not even a little," I assured her. "Though I can see why it would be weird for you, not having experienced this in Albion."

I hated that she doubted herself and her very normal reactions. However many times I had to reassure her that it was okay, I'd do it. Fi turned toward me, and I matched her position, sitting cross-legged facing each other, knees brushing.

"So, foxglove. Tell me more about these big plans you have for me," I said with a wink, trying to lighten the mood.

She'd been so confident and flirty a few minutes ago, but now she was chewing on her lip, staring down at her lap nervously.

"Fi? I kind of thought it would be good news. You seemed so excited on the way down here. Now I'm getting worried," I laughed nervously. I kept waiting for the moment when Fi would realize she was miles out of my league—it hadn't happened yet, but I'm sure it was coming. Finding out she had a powerful, formerly extinct gift had only heightened my insecurities.

Fi could have anyone she wanted, why would she choose me?

"I'm sorry, it is good news. I mean, I think it's good news. I hope you'll think it's good news. I don't want to assume anything. I've been so hot and cold with everything…" Fi babbled, like a total stranger. My Fi didn't babble.

I grabbed her ankles and pulled her legs forward, draping them over mine, then grabbed her hands in mine.

"Deep breath, foxglove."

"*Willyoubemysuitor*?" she mumbled, staring at our joined hands.

It took me a moment to unjumble the words and let them sink in, but once they did, I grinned from ear to ear like an overexcited kid. I knew she'd pick up my emotions, but I couldn't help torturing her a little. Fi was pretty hard to rattle, so this was a rare treat.

"Hmm. Could you repeat that? Maybe a little slower?"

She looked up and gave me a mock glare before pulling herself entirely into my lap and wrapping her legs around me.

"I said," she murmured, leaning forward until our lips were almost touching. "Will you be my suitor?"

She quietly enunciated each word against my mouth, her lips moving temptingly against mine.

"Yes," I breathed, capturing her lips with mine and showing her just how much I liked that idea. She moaned, and I pushed my tongue into her mouth, hands drifting down to cup her ass as she gouged nail marks into my shoulders. I only meant it to be a quick, celebratory kiss, but we both wanted—*needed*—more.

I slid one hand between us under her dress to stroke her over her panties, teasingly sliding my fingers under the fabric a little before pulling them away again. Fi started grinding against my hand, writhing in my lap until she was panting. Fuck that, I wasn't about to let her come in her panties. What a waste.

I reached under her dress to unlace her underwear and yanked them away, baring her to me. Fi returned the favor, tugging my cock from my trousers with fumbling movements, precum already beading at the tip because Fi decimated my self-control just by breathing.

I was already salivating, imagining her taste on my tongue as my hands moved below her thighs, ready to adjust our positions so I could devour her, but she moved before I could.

"Wait—" I began.

But I was too slow, Fi was already impaling herself on me in one swift movement, biting her lip as sank down.

I sucked in a breath at the surprise contact, worried for a second that I'd lose my cool and come instantly and Fi would call off this whole courtship before it even began.

"Are you okay? Does it hurt?" I asked her tightly because *fuck*, she felt so good, but I needed to check in on her. "I wanted to make you come on my tongue first."

Fi's eyes rolled back as she let out a long, breathy moan that had me swelling with pride because it was just for *me*. She always kept a cool, calm façade around others. She always held it together when everyone's emotions were battering her until she wanted to fall apart, but she never let them get the better of her. It was a heady feeling to know that I could make her lose control. If only for a moment, she could lose herself in the pleasure I gave her.

"It's good, I'm good," she breathed, rolling her hips gently, adjusting to my size. "I just needed you. Touch me."

Her hand was already grabbing at my wrist, yanking it upwards. Fi sucked my middle finger into her mouth with a lingering look that made my balls tighten as we met each other thrust for punishing thrust, and I pulled my finger free to circle her clit, cursing the awkward angle.

Fi didn't seem to mind, not when she was already so close. Her hips rolled against me in a broken rhythm as she careened towards her release, her nails digging into my shoulders to brace herself.

Idly, I wondered if I'd get in trouble for going to class shirtless to show off my new marks. These ones were special. These were my brand new courtship marks.

Fi leaned forward, capturing my lips, and we clung to each other almost desperately as we both found our peaks together, her walls milking me as I came harder than I ever had in my entire life.

I bundled my foxglove in closer and she immediately rested her forehead in the crook of my neck, a spot she favored. I held her close, softly stroking her back and savoring this moment. She'd picked *me* to be her suitor. A baker's son from a small-town, low-magic family. Someone with healing magic, decidedly less badass than many other gifts the gods could have bestowed.

My old insecurities reared their ugly heads, but Fi was there before they could take root, pressing lingering kisses to my lips and jaw, running soothing hands over my arms and chest. Her palms were firm against me, like she could physically push the vulnerability away if she tried hard enough.

It was kind of working.

Or maybe it was that Fi was wrapped around my body, putting her entire trust in me that made the less positive thoughts I had about myself fade into the background.

"That's better," Fi sighed dreamily. "Whatever you're thinking about now, keep doing that. You feel *wonderful*."

I held her tighter and silently vowed to do everything in my power to be the fae she deserved.

FFION

CHAPTER 16

Marlen stayed with me in my cabin that night. I'd always kicked him out before, worried that I would get too attached, but things felt so settled and amazing between us now. I couldn't imagine not having him next to me.

I woke up wrapped around him like a spider monkey, arms flung around his neck and leg all the way over his hip. Marlen's arm was wrapped around my waist. My thin singlet had ridden up overnight, and his fingers were resting on the sliver of skin. Embarrassed at my clingy position, I tried to extract myself without waking him up, but Marlen's grip around my waist tightened.

"Where do you think you're going, my little foxglove?" he rasped, his voice rough from sleep. I melted at his words. He'd never called me *his* before.

"I was just trying to give you some breathing room, I'm holding onto you pretty tight," I chuckled to cover my embarrassment. I'd never had a 'morning after' with someone before. *Should I offer him a cup of tea...?* Crap, I needed a handbook. I could ask Briallen for advice on handling these new milestones, but she'd probably just laugh until she wet herself.

"You're almost exactly where I want you, Fi," he murmured, hauling me up so I was laying over top of him, then sliding his hands up my ass underneath my loose sleeping shorts.

"I can work with this," I purred in what I hoped was a seductive voice, pushing myself up so I was straddling his hips and giving him the wake-up call we both wanted. Maybe this morning after thing wasn't so horrid after all.

After a very leisurely start to our morning, Marlen and I made our way to the commons together hand-in-hand. We'd been getting more touchy-feely around the grounds recently, but everything felt so much more significant now that we were official. No one was paying us any attention though, so I guess we didn't look any different from the outside.

Marlen and I headed over to the buffet and loaded up our plates with fruit, flatbread and hummus. He poured himself a blackcurrant tea and held the cup toward me in question, but I shook my head. I really was trying to get used to herbal tea, but nothing could replace my beloved coffee. We sat in our usual spot by the wall, beating Briallen and Leigh this morning. I allowed myself a few seconds to fantasize about bacon and eggs before shaking it off and tucking into my watermelon.

I was fine with it. Mostly.

I felt the pull that announced Bryn's presence, but did my best to shrug it off without acknowledging him. His avoidance had made his opinion on me pretty clear, and I wasn't about to pine after him just because our magic told us to. Briallen and Leigh waved as they came in a few minutes later, heading straight to the buffet to get their food before coming to join us. They were both looking a little rumpled and harried this morning, but satisfaction oozed off both of them. It looked like they had indulged in a morning quickie too. The thought made me giggle.

"Why are you so cheery this morning, Fi?" Briallen asked suspiciously, raising her brow at me. Leigh continued to shovel food into his mouth, totally oblivious. He was spectacularly bad at multitasking whenever there was food involved.

"Oh, you know. Just happy from waking up next to my suitor, I guess," I said with faux flippancy, tossing Marlen a smug grin.

"What?!" Briallen shrieked, and all three of us cringed at the noise. "It's official? Marlen is your suitor? This is really happening?"

Leigh chuckled, throwing his arm around his mate's shoulder. "So excited, my love. Are you living vicariously through Fi? Do we need to go on the hunt for a suitor of your own?"

Everyone else laughed, and I smiled, pretending that I was totally fine and not at all weirded out by that concept.

"Of course not. Well, not yet anyway. I just knew these two were such a perfect match though, I have been waiting for this moment for weeks, it's so romantic," Briallen sighed dreamily.

I shook off the sudden spike of anger coursing through me, doing my best to focus on Briallen's words.

"How do you even know it's romantic? I haven't told you how it happened yet," I asked, baffled. Honestly, it wasn't that romantic. I panic-asked Marlen to be my suitor. Then we screwed out in the open where anyone could have seen us. I didn't have any complaints, but 'romantic' wasn't the word I'd use to describe it.

"That doesn't matter," Briallen said, waving her hand impatiently. "It's about the whole will-they-won't-they of the past few weeks, and now you're finally together! That's the romantic part."

Leigh snorted into his bowl of oats. "It was more when-will-they rather than will-they-won't-they, but whatever makes you happy, my love." He smacked a kiss on her cheek and she rolled her eyes affectionately.

"Congratulations though and all," Leigh added. "I can't wait to see what your mating mark will be, something unique, I bet."

Before either of us could respond, there was a loud crash behind us. I whipped my head around in time to see Bryn's back as he stormed toward the exit, his chair lying on the ground where he'd shoved it back.

Well, that explained the rush of rage I'd been experiencing.

I turned back and quirked my brow at Briallen.

"What?" she asked innocently.

"You knew he was listening," I pointed out.

She shrugged, giving up the pretense. "He needed the push."

"I disagree, Briallen. There should be no pushing of any kind. It's a choice, that's what you told me," I argued.

She had the grace to look a little embarrassed. Her guilt clawed uncomfortably at my chest, and I rubbed my breastbone as discreetly as I could manage.

"You're right. I just… I know he wants you. Or at the very least is intrigued by you. But he won't even give himself the chance to get to *know* you because of his own hang-ups. If he would at least talk to you, I'd get off his back about it," Briallen said, exasperated.

"B, please promise me you'll let this go," I begged. "You're not doing either of us any favors by trying to force something to happen."

"Fine," Briallen reluctantly agreed. "I'll let it go for now."

Marlen rested his hand on my lower back, rubbing slow circles into my spine with his thumb and easing some of my tension. I chanced a sheepish look up at him from under my eyelashes, but he didn't seem bothered by the fact that we were talking about his friend hooking me up with her cousin.

I wondered how long it would take for me to be relaxed about this? Maybe by the time I reached my hundredth birthday? I shuddered involuntarily at the thought of getting so old, and Marlen gave me a questioning look.

"On that note," I said, standing and reaching for my satchel. "I'm going to head to my fire elemental class. Come with? I'm sure you want to see Aderyn," I asked, turning to Marlen.

A burst of his excitement fizzed over my skin and I could see the anticipation in his gaze. We waved goodbye to Leigh and Briallen, walking to the stone fire elemental building hand-in-hand where we found Aderyn sitting cross-legged on the ground, leaning against the building with her eyes closed and face tipped up to the morning sun. She rarely joined us for breakfast, saying that the solitude reminded her of the quiet mornings she spent alone in her family's bakery, preparing for the day.

Aderyn stood as we approached, greeting us with a smile. "Good morning, lovebirds," she teased.

Marlen gave her a broad grin, "It's a good morning indeed. I have to get to combat training. See you in a couple of hours," he said, turning to me. I expected him to kiss my hair or cheek like he usually did, but he wrapped his arms around my waist, hauling me up so my feet dangled off the ground and kissed me until I was seeing stars. Marlen gently put me back on my feet and tossed me a cheeky wink before walking off with a little extra swagger in his step.

Aderyn's surprise surged through my gut, but I barely felt it. There were three girls in my class who I'd seen making eyes at Marlen before, and their wave of jealousy tightened in my chest uncomfortably. As discreetly as I could, I took a deep calming breath to remind myself that the tightness in my chest wasn't real and the emotions weren't mine. *You're not actually going to have a heart attack outside your fire elemental class, Fi.*

"Anything you want to share?" Aderyn asked, quirking her brow at me, the corners of her mouth were tugging up in a faint, smug smile.

I snorted. "I'm sure you've figured it out. It's all, you know, official or whatever."

"Good," Aderyn said simply, making her way toward the class as the master arrived. Her satisfaction wrapped around me comfortingly, but she didn't make a big deal about it, which I was grateful for. Sometimes it felt like Aderyn was as intuitive to people's emotions as I was.

We sat ourselves down in our usual spot next to the wall, unlit candles and matches already set out on the desk in front of us. The master instructed us to light our candles and practice flame manipulation, as he did every lesson, before kicking his feet up on the desk and pulling out a book. Apparently we would spend the whole semester working with candles, and there was no guarantee we'd all have mastered them by the end, anyway. It all felt so pointless.

Aderyn was having intermittent success with her flame as usual while I lit my candle and glared at it. Why was I here? If I had an extra air mastery class in place of this pointless elemental class, I'd be much better off. Air was the only element that seemed to want to cooperate with me. Oxygen was more important than fire anyway, right?

Oxygen.

Holy shit, surely it couldn't be that easy?

My mind traveled back to a science lesson in high school where we'd learned about fire. The girl next to me had just broken up with her boyfriend and her heartbreak, as well as her friends' pity, had given me a stabbing headache. Even so, I remembered copying the teacher's diagram—The Fire Triangle. A fire needs heat, fuel, and oxygen to ignite.

Curious, I tapped into my familiar air magic, pulling it forward. It rushed through my veins like a comforting old friend, bringing a smile to my face. *How had I lived my entire life without it?* I cupped my hands around the candle flame and allowed my magic to swirl around it, to find the oxygen within the little flame and pull it toward me, laughing gleefully when the fire went out.

"Fi! You made that look so easy!" Aderyn accused, as if I'd been holding out on her this whole time.

"I just thought I'd try something different. I'm going to see if I can make it grow now," I replied, relighting the wick with a match.

Once it was burning, I cupped my hands around the flame again and let small amounts of air magic trickle out in tiny gusts, imagining a teeny set of fireplace bellows. Surely enough, the flame grew bigger and hotter, shooting up toward the ceiling.

"An impressive display of control, Miss Smith," the master commented curiously, wandering over to my desk. "This is your first successful attempt in this class, correct?"

Sensing his suspicion, I answered honestly, "I'm using air magic to manipulate the oxygen in the fire. I just wanted to see if it would work."

His eyebrows raised into his hairline. "Experienced air affinities can successfully manipulate flames using air, but no first-year student knows how to use magic that way."

"What do you mean? Fire needs oxygen. Take the oxygen away, the flame dies. Add more, it grows." I frowned at his accusatory glare.

"How did you know that?"

"From school…? Human school?" I replied, puzzled.

"We don't learn that kind of thing here, Fi," Aderyn interjected softly. "Our knowledge of the elements is based on their relationship to magic, not…"

"Science?" I supplied helpfully. Maybe my human education wouldn't be so useless here after all.

"I'll be telling Master Gwyneira about this," the master said with a final indignant huff before storming back to his desk.

I didn't care. I don't think I'd actually broken any rules by using air magic in this class, and even if I had, I wasn't really bothered about it.

If anything, I was excited to get back to my cabin and get a roaring fire going in my potbelly stove tonight. I could practically imagine my toasty toes now.

That thought kept me warm—pun intended—for the rest of the day.

Marlen stayed with me again that night because the idea of him *not* staying with me sent a panicky feeling through my chest. I was beginning to see why Briallen and Leigh had claimed each other within six weeks of meeting. Even though it was a huge, permanent step, the mating pull's urging grew more insistent every time I was around Marlen.

I woke up to the bells chiming, with Marlen spooning me, his arms wrapped tightly around my waist, his leg pinning mine to the mattress.

"Good morning, my little foxglove," Marlen murmured, pulling me back tightly, his erection rubbing temptingly against my ass. I wiggled a little before groaning.

"As much as I'd like a repeat of yesterday morning, I need to get up and shower," I said, sighing in disappointment.

"Is that so?" Marlen said in a low voice, right next to my ear. He rolled me forward, so I was lying on my front, running his hands over the top of my arms until he reached my hands and tangled our fingers together. His hips pressed me into the bed as he worked slow, languid kisses down the side of my neck.

I moaned softly, ready to say screw it and forgo the shower, when Marlen leaped over me off the bed and raced down the ladder.

"You snooze, you lose, foxglove!" Marlen called over his shoulder as he raced into the bathroom and closed the door behind him. I sat up in bed, stunned, as I heard Marlen turn the shower on.

A giggle escaped me. Did that just happen? Marlen had always been playful, but there was a new lightness to him now as we progressed our relationship. I had noticed fewer flashes of insecurity from him in the last two days as well.

I made my way down the ladder at a more leisurely pace than Marlen had, stripped, then wandered confidently into the bathroom without knocking. It definitely had the desired effect, Marlen paused, drinking me in from the tips of my toes to the top of my head. His eyes were filled with heat, and his cock was standing fully at attention. I gave him a smug grin.

"On second thought, let's share," Marlen purred, reaching out a hand to pull me in with him.

"I don't have any objections to that," I replied, sucking in a breath as the tepid water hit my skin. Marlen tugged me tight against him, my breasts pressing against his chest, and happily absorbed his body warmth. This lack-of-hot-water situation was a *lot* more bearable with someone else here with me.

"I can't decide whether to clean you up or get you dirty," Marlen said with a sultry grin, taking advantage of me leaning back to keep my messy bun out of the water by running his gaze down my front. "On second thought, dirty. Definitely dirty."

"Clean," I laughed, reaching for the bar of soap. "Definitely clean."

As tempting as it was, we didn't have time to play. Having Marlen's eyes on me was *addictive*, though. I hadn't intended to turn this into a whole *show*, but while I had his attention...

"Foxglove," Marlen groaned, his cock springing to attention as I ran the soap over my collarbone before oh-so-slowly moving down to my breasts.

"Gimme," he demanded, holding out his hand expectantly. "Let me do that."

"Nope," I replied as I snatched the soap out of his reach, more than a little smug at his reaction. "No touching. We need to get going, we have class today and if I don't eat, I won't accomplish anything." I frowned to myself. "Well, I'll accomplish less than the nothing that I usually accomplish."

"You'll get there, Fi. It just takes practice. In the meantime, let me take your mind off things." He had a wicked glint in his eye and before I could remind him that we really *did* need to get going, a swirling sensation at my nipple had me squeaking in surprise.

I looked down, startling when I realized the feeling was coming from a stream of water, twirling like a ribbon around one nipple before snaking across my chest to repeat the motion on the other side.

"This is a convenient way around the 'no touching' rule," I breathed, my body responding immediately to the sensation.

"Want me to stop?" Marlen asked, far too casually.

"I'm tempted to say 'yes' just to wipe the arrogant smirk off your face," I sassed, even as I arched my back towards him. "But no. Don't stop. I might hurt you if you do."

Marlen laughed, that damned ribbon of water trailing between my breasts and down my stomach before doing figure eights over my pelvis, infuriatingly close to where I wanted him.

"Now you're just showing off," I grumbled, twisting slightly to see if I could trick the water into aiming for my clit instead. Unfortunately, Marlen's reflexes were far too quick for that, his magic angling right along with me.

"A little," he admitted with a wink. "Spread your legs."

A shiver ran down my spine at the lazy command, especially coming from the usually laidback Marlen. Being around water really brought out his confidence.

I spread my legs wider, bracing one hand on the shower wall to steady myself as Marlen rewarded me with a dazzling smile, almost angelic compared to the devilish sensation he was causing between my thighs. The stream of water was so thick and steady, it felt like smooth cool fingers working relentlessly to stimulate my clit. I choked out a gasp, words escaping at me at how *good* the foreign sensation was.

"Remember, foxglove, we're in a hurry," Marlen all but sang, increasing the tempo. I wasn't prepared for the suddenness at which my orgasm hit me, and I gripped Marlen gratefully when he stepped forward to catch me as I sagged against him, my legs going weak.

"That was the most magical thing I've experienced since I got to Avalon," I admitted, struggling for breath. "Let's do that every morning."

After a longer shower than I had planned, I pulled out a collared navy, linen dress that fell to mid-thigh and had buttons all the way down it.

The dress had been a gift from Briallen. She claimed she didn't like dark-colored clothes, but I think she was also just sick of seeing me wearing Academy-issued outfits. This was the first thing I'd worn in the weeks I'd been here that was actually similar to my size and had buttons. Everything else had been a generic, baggy size that had to be wrapped tight and secured with ties or ribbons. One of these days, we'd take a shopping trip to a market town so I could pick some things out for myself.

The sleeves of the dress came to just past my elbows and I threw on my chunkiest, black knit cardigan over the top and a thick gray scarf. Today was the first day of winter and it certainly felt colder, though not nearly as cold as it got in London. Did it snow here? I was already on the fence about the whole no-shoes thing. There was no way I'd be forgoing shoes in the snow.

We stopped by Marlen's cabin so he could change into clean clothes. Fortunately, Creepy Kelvyn had already left for the day. Marlen emerged wearing his usual linen tunic-style top in dark green and dark gray loose pants, but he'd also added a thick light gray woolen jumper and dark gray beanie. I eyed it enviously, I really needed to go shopping.

As we approached the commons for breakfast, a large crowd was forming outside the entrance. Their emotions were a heightened jumble of confusion, apprehension, some amusement, and a few spots of malicious glee.

Marlen's grip tightened slightly on my hand as he led us through the crowd to see what had caught everyone's attention. My heart plummeted when I saw the words burned into the grass:

GO HOME FFION

Shit, this was not good. Whoever was trying to get rid of me was clearly upping their game.

The surrounding fae noticed my presence and whispers spread throughout the crowd, all jumbling together. They turned the focus of their pity, amusement, and apprehension directly to me, and a tidal wave of feeling crashed over me, threatening to drown me in the weight of their emotions. It hurt, *everywhere*. Every reaction I already struggled to process on a daily basis was multiplied, and my head spun with the effort of trying to separate what was theirs from mine. I stumbled slightly towards Marlen as black spots danced ominously across my vision. *Don't faint. Not here.*

"Shit, shit, shit," Marlen cursed softly, wrapping an arm around my waist to keep me upright. "We need to get you out of here."

We struggled through the crowd pressing in on us, volleying questions at me, for a few steps before I felt a second powerful mating pull yanking at my chest.

"Move!" Bryn barked, materializing in front of us. He led us out of the crowd, snapping at anyone blocking our path, flicking little fireballs at them that harmlessly fizzled out in front of their faces if they were too slow.

The pressure and dizziness eased as we got further away from the crowd.

By the time the three of us reached my cabin, my head felt like I'd been on a three-day bender. The pain had eased, but everything still felt fuzzy.

I fished out my key, passing it to Marlen with shaky fingers and pressing a palm to the wall to keep me upright as he let us in. Bryn stormed in behind us, slamming the door loud enough to make me wince. *Inconsiderate bastard.* Though I suppose it was nice of him to have helped us out back there.

I collapsed into an armchair while Marlen filled a glass with water, using his magic to freeze some ice cubes. I couldn't even get a decent read on Marlen's emotions. The force of Bryn's rage was so potent it sucked the rest of the feeling out of the room. It coursed through my aching veins, still recovering from the overload of a few minutes ago.

Bryn stalked over to me with a dangerous glint in his eye, leaning down with his hands on each arm of the chair, caging me in.

That bonfire scent was an unfair weapon when he was up this close.

"You don't seem all that surprised to hear from your mysterious messenger again, considering it's been weeks since that message on your wardrobe. Why is that, scout?" Bryn asked, his voice deceptively calm.

I attempted to blink away some of the fog in my brain and lifted my head to meet his gaze. He was closer than I expected—our noses were practically touching, and his warm breath fanned across my lips. His proximity made it incredibly hard to focus. Bryn and I had never been *this* close, there was barely an inch of space between our lips.

After a few seconds of intense eye contact, I realized Bryn was still waiting for my answer. I hesitated, not knowing how much to reveal. I couldn't understand why Bryn would have helped me if he was the one behind the messages, but I also never sensed concern from him about me. It was just anger, resentment, frustration and more anger. With an occasional dash of lust, followed quickly by even more anger.

"It's nothing you need to concern yourself with, Bryn."

I meant for it to sound stern and confident, but it came out as a breathy whisper, and I felt Bryn's lust before his fury doubled.

"Is that so?" he asked dangerously. "It seems like something I should very much concern myself with since Gwyneira herself asked me to track the messenger's magic. So, let me be very specific, Ffion. Have you received any other threatening messages between the one on the wardrobe and the one on the grass today?"

Shit, that was a difficult question to get around.

"I don't want to discuss it with you, Bryn." My voice broke slightly on his name. Bryn and I weren't friends or anywhere close to it, but I knew this conversation would end painfully for one or both of us, and I didn't relish that thought.

His eyes narrowed. "And why is that, Ffion?"

"I'm protecting myself," I whispered.

"You think I had something to do with this?" His tone was flat, but his eyes flashed with hurt. It was nothing to the sharp stab of pain I felt emanate from him. Those three words had caused an anguish in Bryn that was so acute it took my breath away.

Without waiting for me to respond or giving me a chance to explain, he turned on his heel and left. I felt a hot prickle of shame run down my spine, and I knew without a doubt that the emotion was all my own.

"Rest up, foxglove," Marlen murmured, pulling me to my feet and tugging me towards the ladder leading up to the bed we'd left only an hour earlier. "Whatever else is going on can wait until you're feeling better. It has to."

Usually, I appreciated Marlen's sweetness and patience with me, but today it only exacerbated my self-loathing. Why should I deserve his kindness when I'd made Bryn feel so wretched?

CHAPTER 17

I made my way to the edge of campus in a haze of anger, barely remembering the walk from Ffion's cabin to the base of the rocky mountain area that bordered the Academy on one side. With more aggression than was probably safe, I scaled the rocky incline, relishing the burn in my lungs and ache of my muscles. The physical pain was a good distraction from the mating pull that was twisting like a knife in my chest.

There were caves scattered throughout the hillside that were often used for practicing fire magic, and I was the only one who used the highest one. Maybe I could quite literally burn off my anger.

What the fuck was her problem? Was attacking my honor her way of punishing me for not pursuing the mating bond with her? Was this her twisted way of letting me know she wasn't interested in me either?

What the fuck did it even matter? *I* wasn't interested. I'd been clear about that. What did I care?

I was losing my mind.

Not since my parents had died fifteen years ago had I felt so conflicted. From the moment Briallen's family had taken me in, I vowed to never lose control like I had in the wake of what had happened with my parents.

That vow had been easy to keep until Ffion had shown up in Avalon and shattered the calm I had worked so hard to create in my life. The night I brought the little scout to Avalon, I spent hours in the caves, blasting my fire magic at anything and everything until I couldn't sustain it anymore.

It had helped, until I got to my cabin and found Briallen waiting outside for me, looking at me like I was a moron. I'd tried ignoring her while she yapped on about Ffion's positive attributes and waxed lyrical about the virtues of a strong mating pull. I'd always found her mate, Leigh, to be a bit of a fool, but Briallen would never see that. She was pretty rational most of the time, but the mating pull made fae stupid, because it was pure *instinct*.

An intense mating pull encouraged feelings of protectiveness and devotion, but I was determined to be stronger than my instincts. The stronger the pull, the worse it was. It was one of the many reasons I would never pursue the pull with Ffion. She'd already done more damage to my self-control than anyone or anything else in fifteen years.

No, trusting the mating pull blinded you to a person's flaws. My fathers let the strong mating pull to my mother dictate their choices, overlooking her mania and instability. I doubt they truly realized the extent of her issues until they woke up bound in the middle of the night with flames surrounding the bed and my mother laughing like she didn't have a care in the world.

I was four years old when I discovered my fire affinity. I pushed the wall of flames back as the house burned around me and barely escaped out the window, the sound of my mother's laughter ringing in my ears. It has haunted my nightmares ever since.

I wouldn't make the same mistake my fathers did. When I claimed my mate, it would be someone I could get to know objectively. Someone I could be sure was a suitable life partner. My magic wouldn't dictate my decision.

If Marlen Ferris was stupid enough to follow her around like a lost puppy while she scouted his emotions and everyone else's, that was his problem.

A healer. What good was a healing gift to Ffion? I knew he had a substantial water affinity too, but Ffion needed mates with offensive magic, not defensive. She was forever at risk with her rare empath abilities.

What was wrong with me? What did I care if she chose a weak mating circle? She thinks you're the one threatening her, idiot.

Marlen appeared to know about her ability now. He hadn't looked surprised when Ffion had been on the verge of fainting in the crowd, just concerned. It was on him if he wanted to put himself in danger by being with her, since I doubted this was the last threat she'd receive.

I threw increasingly large blasts of fire at the boulders along the mountain path. What a fucking nightmare. I'd never asked to have a strong mating pull to Ffion, I never wanted it. It felt like the gods were punishing me for something—maybe for not claiming Saffir before Ffion showed up. I wouldn't be experiencing the pull to Ffion if I was already mated. Except that idea didn't sit well with me either.

Before Ffion had arrived, I had been seriously considering pursuing Saffir, asking her to consider me as a suitor, regardless of our almost non-existent mating pull. She was from an influential family—her mother and one of her fathers were councilors. As an orphaned kid from a disgraced family, I could do a lot worse than Saffir as a mate.

But now, the faint pull to Saffir paled in comparison to what I felt with Ffion. Any other female would have immediately noticed my disinterest, but I doubt Saffir particularly cared whether there was a connection. She wanted magically powerful mates—whether she or her magic were suitable for them was an afterthought.

Then there was the other issue. No matter what tricks Saffir pulled, my cock was totally unmoved by the icy blonde, only coming to life when a mass of dark curls and luscious curves walked through the door. I hadn't even tried to get her into bed since Ffion had arrived in Avalon, and *that* was bothering Saffir.

The godsdamned mating pull was screwing with both my heads.

I slid down the rock wall in the cave, feeling a bit spent and slightly less enraged, but no less hurt. I'd known Ffion's secret for weeks and never said a thing to anyone. The gods knew I was a grumpy bastard most of the time, but I wasn't without honor. My honor was about all I had left after my mother destroyed our family's name. I wasn't about to sell Ffion, or any other fae, out to hunters who would keep her captive and drain her magic. The thought alone made me feel ill.

The mating pull was so distracting that I mostly avoided Ffion, but I'd helped her whenever Gwyneira had asked me to. I'd pushed Marlen back toward her when he needed encouragement, I monitored her from afar to make sure she hadn't done anything idiotic or gotten herself kidnapped. Just once or twice a day to check in. If anything, she should trust me *more* than Marlen, I doubt he'd done half as much to help her.

For a brief second, as we moved the crowd, we'd been on the same side, the three of us. It felt so easy to be around Ffion. Effortless in a way that it never was between me and Saffir. When Ffion had sat on that chair and I'd got up in her face, it had been a 50/50 chance whether I interrogated her or finally gave in and kissed her.

But then she all but told me she had to protect herself from *me,* and I remembered all the reasons why we were a terrible idea.

For fuck's sake, she wanted nothing to do with me. She was nothing to me. Why did I care about this?

Probably because I knew inherently that if the roles were reversed, I could trust her with my secret. The strength of the mating pull told us that we were kindred souls. If she didn't have integrity that matched my own, we wouldn't have such a powerful connection. That was why it stung that she didn't trust me.

Did I really come across as that much of an asshole?

Telling myself that this anger stemmed from my honor being questioned, I made my way back down the mountain to find Saffir with a new plan in mind. My cock still wasn't cooperating, but I could spend time with her. Try to find enough common interests to pursue something more serious with her.

Maybe I could make her *smile* or something. Maybe even laugh. The idea was sort of abhorrent, but maybe if I did, those laughs would drown out the persistent voice in my head telling me I was with the wrong female.

Step 1: Get Ffion out of my mind for good.

Step 2: Show her she meant as little to me as I clearly meant to her.

FFION

CHAPTER 18

Today was a total shitshow. I'd missed my morning classes to sleep off the hangover from the torrent of other people's emotions, pulled myself together enough to attend my afternoon classes, only to lose all the progress I'd made recovering from the empath overdose. I wished I could hide out for a few weeks until everyone forgot about this morning's incident—I'd never had so much emotion directed at me at once, and it was agony.

"I can just bring food to your cabin, you don't have to do this," Marlen said, not for the first time, as we made our way to the commons.

"I know, but I think I'd rather just get it over and done with. They'll lose interest if I don't show any reaction," I replied, squeezing his hand. I'd been gripping it like I might float away if I let go. "If it's too much, we can always sneak out, right?"

"Of course. Whenever you want." His attempt at a reassuring smile was grim.

As we neared the commons, I was relieved to see that the message in the grass had been cleaned up, presumably by someone with an earth affinity. There was no evidence it even existed except for the lingering stares and the stabbing feeling that lingered in my head.

All day, I'd been expecting a note from Gwyneira asking me to come and see her about the message, but I hadn't received anything. Did that mean

I was right to suspect her? Or was she just giving me space to process? My head throbbed even harder. What to do about Gwyneira would have to be tomorrow's problem.

Marlen snuck us into the commons using one of the back entrances and guided me to a table by the wall where Briallen and Leigh were already waiting for us with plates of food. They'd coordinated all of this, and I loved them for it. I'd never really had friends before—not for lack of trying—and I struggled to put into words how much all three of them meant to me.

I felt the second pull that usually indicated Bryn's presence, and my warm, fuzzy feelings dissipated instantly. Usually by the time I felt his presence, he was already halfway gone, which I doubted was coincidental. I felt terrible about our confrontation this morning, but my guilt had lessened over the day. It was mostly replaced with anger.

What right did Bryn have to demand answers from me, anyway? What right did he have to be mad at me for not trusting him when he had never given me a reason to? Yes, he brought me here, but that was an assignment he undertook on Gwyneira's orders, not an act of kindness. Yes, we felt a strong mating pull, but neither of us had ever acted on it or given any sign that we ever would. I didn't owe him anything. I regretted making him feel bad, but I didn't regret keeping him out of a loop he had no right to be in.

I chanced a look across the room where Bryn was leaning a little too casually against the wall, arms crossed with one leg propped up. He wasn't looking at me, but that felt intentional too, since he obviously knew I was here. His gaze followed Saffir's slender figure, slinking up to him in an indecently tight, short linen dress that I'm pretty sure was meant to be sleepwear. My eyes narrowed. What was he playing at? It all felt so... performative.

As Saffir got close to him, he reached out one hand to grab the back of her head, tangling into her hair and pulling her face forward to kiss her deeply. His other hand rested possessively on her lower back, and she gripped his shirt tight, pulling them closer together. Even in a crowded room, I felt the thrill of her conquest and the swell of her lust. It made my stomach turn.

Saffir and Bryn weren't a new thing, but that little show had absolutely been for my benefit. I just didn't understand why. I had never tried to pursue the mating bond with Bryn, so I shouldn't care what or who he did. I shouldn't care about his petty high school games.

I did, though. In spite of myself.

Why did he choose this way to hurt me?

Why did Bryn's cuts leave such deep scars?

Why, when Saffir's lust was so potent, didn't I sense any from Bryn?

As Bryn passed our table on his way to the buffet, Briallen's hand shot out to grip his arm, her knuckles turning white from the effort.

"What was that about?" she hissed, more venom in her tone than I'd ever heard. I could barely feel my heart splintering into a million pieces, Briallen's anger was so distracting. Why was I so heartbroken, anyway?

Bryn and I are not a thing.

"What was what about?" Bryn drawled lazily. His bored tone raised everyone else's ire, but I could sense his tension and bitterness. I wish I knew what they meant.

"That little display with Saffir!" Briallen whisper-shouted, her cheeks flushed with anger.

"Is there something wrong with me kissing the fae I'm courting? As I recall, Leigh couldn't keep his hands off you when he was your suitor, and I was polite enough not to complain about it," Bryn replied flatly, his jaw ticking.

"You're courting her now?" Briallen confirmed hoarsely as ice wrapped around my heart. I didn't know who the emotions belonged to, it was too numbing to pinpoint. Surely they weren't mine?

Unwilling to take part in this awful charade any longer, I stood up silently and made my way back through the exit, Marlen following behind me, unquestioning. I was starving, but it wasn't worth staying to eat. Bryn had brought a lot of attention to our table, and my head was aching. I'd probably be sick if I tried to force food down, anyway.

We walked back to the cabin in silence while I berated myself for my stupid feelings. Bryn wasn't mine to lose, he never had been. Just because we were kindred souls and our magic was trying to push us together didn't mean we were meant to be.

It didn't even mean we liked each other, because we absolutely didn't.

Ugh, had I not basically accused him of threatening me just a few hours ago? Obviously, that would have been the death knell in the relationship that never was.

I shook my head to clear my thoughts and gave Marlen a brief, reassuring smile to let him know I was okay.

Bryn had no right to be upset about my choices, and I had no right to be upset about his.

I'd slept like the dead in Marlen's arms, emotionally exhausted from the fucking nightmare that had been my day yesterday. Unwilling to risk another passive-aggressive showdown in the commons with Bryn, I'd chickened out and asked Marlen to grab food for me, eating it on my way to class.

My classmates were still giving off a strange mixture of emotions directed at me. Not enough to overwhelm my senses, but still definitely uncomfortable. Fortunately, notices had been put up around the campus yesterday afternoon announcing that students were invited to a masquerade ball that would take place in a few weeks to officially open the Avalon Fair, and that had taken the heat off of me. My mysterious drama was much less interesting than a ball.

As I entered the first-year air elemental class, Master Aures pulled me aside before I sat down.

"Ffion, I think you would be better suited for Master Drysi's second-year air class. Your control is coming along well, and the teaching assistant for Master Drysi's class has agreed to tutor you separately if they feel you need it."

"Oh, well, that's good news. Right?"

I had been enjoying my first-year air mastery class more than any of the others. It was nice to have one class where I felt like I was doing well instead of tossing weak, ineffective magic at everything.

"It's excellent news," she said with a reassuring smile, and I felt a hint of pride coming from her. "You are taking to air faster than we had expected, and now you are ready for a greater challenge. You should head to your new class now. It's right across the clearing."

At least I was one step closer to catching up with my age group. I rushed across the clearing to a similar open-air wooden building, not wanting to be any later than I already was. Master Drysi didn't seem surprised to see me, which was a relief. She was a statuesque, intimidating woman, with a severe black bob and crystalline blue eyes. Her outfit was like what the boys wore—loose, brown linen pants with a white tunic over top. Master Drysi was the first female I'd seen who didn't have long hair and wasn't wearing a dress. Maybe she was a warrior?

She had a warrior-kind of vibe and a no-nonsense disposition. I liked her immediately.

Two steps into the classroom and the now-familiar magnetic pull hit me right in my chest. I looked around, assuming Bryn or Marlen were here but confused as to why, when I realized the scent surrounding me wasn't Bryn's bonfire embers or Marlen's woodsy pine. It was a seductive icy smell, like the breeze off the mountain after a fresh snowfall, and it had me practically salivating. The drool situation wasn't helped when I saw who the scent belonged to.

His skin was a shade darker than mine—a rich brown that contrasted with his brilliant silver eyes. His hair was thick and black, cropped short on the sides with longer, messy pieces on top. My eyes drifted enviously to the cheekbones that were sharp enough to cut glass, before lowering to the dark stubble that looked more like an afterthought than Marlen's tidy scruff. Like he'd gotten so absorbed in his studies he'd just forgotten to shave. While he seemed studious and academic, I felt like there was a dangerous edge to him that perhaps not everyone saw. I hoped they didn't. I had an overwhelming urge to want that side of him all for myself.

His eyes cataloged every inch of me as I cataloged him, filled with heat but also assessing. I had been so absorbed in this feeling that I hadn't realized how close we were standing—we must have gravitated toward each other unconsciously.

"Ffion, this is my teaching assistant, Arthus Calder." Master Drysi's eyes twinkled with amusement. I guess Arthus and my response to each wasn't particularly subtle.

"Fi," I corrected absentmindedly.

Arthus' eyes never left mine. "Pleasure to meet you," he murmured softly, and the deep, silky timbre of his voice had my already overstimulated nerves firing up again. Blinking away some of my lusty haze, I focused on his emotions to get a read on him. The last thing I needed in my life was another Bryn.

Fortunately, Arthus was mostly experiencing a mixture of curiosity and lust, but he was also wound so tight, I could *feel* his self-control. I'd never experienced anything like it. He must be incredibly disciplined to maintain that level of control almost unconsciously. I was both relieved and disappointed when I didn't feel any excitement from him like I had from Marlen when we met. I didn't want this whole mating thing, anyway. Right? *Right.*

Each student had a small obstacle course of hoops and sticks set up in front of them, and Master Drysi piled the different items on a small tray, handing it to me before directing me to find an empty space to work.

Arthus stood like a silent sentry at my side, and while I wasn't entirely sure what to make of it, it made being the new kid in the class less terrifying to have someone standing next to me.

I made a beeline for the back of the room, setting my tray of objects down and trying to set up the obstacle course while surreptitiously studying the other students around me. I paused for a moment, unsure how to arrange the final hoop, and Arthus quietly leaned over to take the items from my hand, finishing the task.

He didn't touch me, not quite, but my body didn't get that memo. I had *goosebumps* from *nothing*.

Arthus stayed close to me throughout the air mastery class, steadfastly silent, but it didn't feel awkward, more like he was just quiet by nature. He continued to be careful not to make any kind of physical contact, even as he corrected my technique. But despite the lack of long-winded explanations or touch, I was weaving my feather pretty smoothly around the small obstacle course. I was a teeny bit proud of myself, even though upon further inspection, Master Drysi had given me less materials to build my course and it was definitely easier than what my classmates had.

She came to stand in front of my table as the lesson drew to a close, watching me work, and I felt her satisfaction like a warm hug.

"Excellent control, Ffion. Moving you up to the second-year class was the right call. However, I think you could benefit from some additional tutoring sessions with Arthus, at least for a few weeks, to ensure you're caught up with your fellow students. Perhaps twice a week?"

I looked to Arthus automatically. I didn't want him to be stuck with me if it made him uncomfortable. His face gave nothing away, but I felt a small wave of satisfaction roll off him that made my little affection-seeking heart light up.

"Of course. I would be happy to tutor Ffion." I smothered a grin as I agreed to the tutoring sessions because I really didn't need to be going around smiling like an idiot and scaring him off. I had a feeling I would often be trying to keep my cool around Arthus, and I made it my goal to use our tutoring sessions to crack a little of his composure.

"How was your air mastery class?" Marlen's voice startled me as he dropped into the seat next to me in the commons. I'd been so absorbed in my thoughts about Arthus that I hadn't felt him approach.

Don't panic.

"Oh, it was good. I'm in Master Drysi's second-year class now. They thought I was making good progress."

"That's brilliant news, little foxglove. I thought you would be happy about that? You seem nervous." He leaned in, wrapped an arm around my shoulders and planted an affectionate kiss on the tip of my nose.

"I'm not nervous…" I trailed off, not knowing the etiquette for telling one of my suitors I'd felt a mating pull as strong as his to someone else. Would Marlen be jealous? Did he know Arthus? I'd already met most of Marlen's friends around the Academy. Did they not know each other or worse, not like each other?

"What's on your mind, Fi? You know you can always talk to me," Marlen asked softly, his insecurity crawling unpleasantly up my skin. *Right, I guess we were doing this then.* Probably best to just rip the band-aid off.

"I felt a strong mating pull in my air class," I mumbled to my bowl of cold bean salad. "And it wasn't you or Bryn."

Still unable to make eye contact, I paid close attention to Marlen's emotions instead. I braced myself for anger or jealousy, but all I found was curiosity and a touch of excitement. *Weird. Fae were weird.*

"You can't just leave it there! Who was it? I hope I know him."

"Arthus. The teaching assistant," I replied, clearing my throat.

Marlen made a strangled sound, his rising excitement mixing in with his surprise.

"Really? Fi, that's amazing. Arthus only graduated last year, we were both students for the past three years. I don't really know him, but he never appeared to feel a mating pull towards anyone. Fae followed him around with stars in their eyes for years, but he's never shown an interest."

That made me feel all kinds of warm and fuzzy until I remembered that Arthus seemed kind of distant with me too. Maybe he just didn't want a mate? Or had whatever problem Bryn had?

"Isn't it, er, weird that he's… you know…" I trailed off, face flaming.

"That he's what?" Marlen asked, his confusion crashing through me like a wave of dizziness.

"A teaching assistant," I whispered, mortified.

"What?" Marlen blurted. "Why would that be weird?"

"Um, that's a huge deal where I'm from. He's part of the staff, it would be super frowned upon," I told Marlen, frowning. Why was he looking at me like I was the strange one here?

Marlen laughed, a proper belly-rubbing, keeling over kind of laugh. I was deeply unimpressed.

"Sorry, I thought you might have been joking. No?" He chuckled again, and some of my annoyance faded. It was impossible to stay mad at Marlen.

"Teaching assistants aren't really in authority positions here, only the masters are. Masters aren't eligible to teach unless they're fully mated, so that isn't really a problem," he explained. "The teaching assistants are usually graduates who were at the top of their classes and have an interest in pursuing teaching one day. When they're fully mated too."

"So, is it normal for teaching assistants to meet potential mates among the students? *Theoretically*," I added hastily, and Marlen gave me a knowing smile.

"Normal is probably not the right word. Most of the fae here meet their mates during their four years at the Academy. Arthus didn't for whatever reason, probably because he has strong magic and there wasn't a female on campus powerful enough to balance it until you came along," he said, shrugging like it wasn't a huge deal. "That's how it was for me anyway, and probably for Bryn, though he'll never admit it. Your magic is incredibly powerful, foxglove."

"Then Arthus has a gift too?"

"An exceptionally rare gift, he didn't mention it?" Marlen asked, his eyebrows shooting up.

"No? I mean, I know he has an air affinity, but we didn't talk about anything else. I figured if I asked him about his magic, he might ask about mine, and I definitely don't know him well enough to talk about that..."

"That's probably a good call, but Arthus' gift is well-known throughout the Academy. You'll definitely see it for yourself since they appear when he's frustrated or angry or experiencing any kind of heightened emotional state."

"They…?"

"His wings."

"He doesn't have wings," I said flatly, staring at Marlen. Surely my powers of observation weren't *that* lacking. "I'm sure I would have noticed that."

Marlen smiled indulgently, like I was the cutest thing he'd ever seen. "They're hidden most of the time. He retracts them when he's not using them to keep them safe. Fae wings are rare nowadays, and I'm sure he's been hunted for his before, they're worth a lot. There are fae who would kill him for them."

"That's awful," I muttered, knowing exactly how it felt to have rare and desirable magic. "Maybe that's why he hasn't pursued a mating pull before? He probably has some concerns about getting close to someone and making himself vulnerable. I'm not sure I would acknowledge the mating pull at all if everyone knew about my magic, I wouldn't trust that they were pursuing me for the right reasons." I could feel Marlen's insecurities slithering over my skin again. "I don't mean you, Marlen. I am pretty attuned to your emotions at this point, anyway. If you were duplicitous, I would have picked up on it."

"Thanks. I think?" he said drolly, but his mood improved. "Anyway, Arthus will probably be hard to get close to—*if* you intend to pursue him—but I think you'll find you have a lot in common once you get talking. When you're ready to tell him about your magic, I'm sure he'll understand the obstacles you're facing a lot better than I do."

"Well, fortunately for me, I have private tutoring sessions with him twice a week to get me up to speed on second-year air magic."

Marlen waggled his eyebrows, "I think you'll find that ends up being fortunate for both of you, little foxglove."

I laughed, feeling a lot more at ease about everything after Marlen's relaxed reaction to what I had assumed would be a huge bombshell. I guessed the whole multiple mates thing was normal here, but it still wasn't normal to *me*. I wanted to talk more about Marlen's expectations, but Leigh and Briallen joined us at the table before I could press the issue.

"How was your day?" Briallen asked cheerily.

"No more messages?" Leigh enquired around a mouthful of a mushroom wrap.

"Great, and no messages," I replied dutifully, not quite able to hide my smile of gratitude that they cared. "I got moved up to the second-year air mastery class, the masters think I'm making good progress with my air magic."

"That's wonderful, Fi!" Briallen's infectious excitement wrapped around me like a familiar blanket.

"Second-year with Master Drysi?" Leigh asked around another mouthful of mushrooms. I wrinkled my nose at him, and he swallowed, grinning at me.

"That's the one."

"I heard Arthus came back this year to assist for that class?" Leigh's question was directed at Marlen. I guessed it made sense for Leigh to know Arthus since they were both air affinities and only one year apart.

Marlen looked at me to respond, raising a brow in question. I appreciated him deferring to me; I wasn't ready to tell Leigh and Briallen about the mating pull I felt to Arthus yet. My gut told me to let Arthus take the lead.

"Arthus is the teaching assistant for that class," I responded vaguely, grateful when Briallen shifted the conversation to the upcoming masquerade ball before Leigh could follow up.

"What will you wear, Fi?" Briallen asked, tapping her fingers intently on the table as she gave it serious thought. "I think I might go as a unicorn, the whites and silvers will go well with my hair."

"Unicorns are badass," I agreed. A white and silver outfit *would* look awesome with her pink hair. "Is there a theme?"

"We always wear creature-themed costumes to masques—magical or non-magical, it doesn't matter," Marlen explained.

"Oh, that sounds fun. I guess we should schedule that shopping trip soon, B?"

"Most definitely," Briallen agreed. "For what it's worth, I vote for a dragon as your costume. Maybe a homage to fire will do it..." she muttered under her breath, but I chose to ignore her.

Hopefully Bryn and Saffir would complete their mating soon, otherwise Briallen would never let this go.

I ignored the hollow feeling in my chest that thought gave me as well.

FFION

CHAPTER 19

Marlen and Leigh were on guard duty together the following night, so Briallen, Aderyn and I planned a girls-only dinner in the commons, commandeering our usual table by the wall, as far away from the main dinner crowd as I could discreetly manage. There was still some lingering curiosity from the message on the grass, so I did my best to keep my head down, particularly in the commons.

We'd long since finished dinner and were relaxing at the table, exchanging stories and tasting different flavors of tea. They'd both noticed the face I pulled whenever Marlen brought me blackcurrant tea, and had made it their mission to find one I liked. So far, peppermint was winning. It was as close as I would get in Avalon to my beloved peppermint latte. We joked around as I sampled them all, but my laughter died on my tongue as Bryn and Saffir walked into the commons together, arms wrapped around each other.

I'd never had to actively avoid Bryn before. He'd always done a bang-up job of avoiding me. Unfortunately, now he seemed to pop up *everywhere*, making the mating pull in my chest go haywire. Each time I saw him, even if he was just walking by himself, all I could see was his hand on Saffir's ass, his grip on her hair, his mouth on hers. It made me feel stabby.

Rage always followed those feelings because why should I care what stupid Bryn did, anyway? After all, mating was a choice, as Briallen so often reminded me.

Briallen followed my gaze across the room and narrowed her eyes at her cousin. "Nope, this is an idiot-free night. Let's finish our tea in your cabin instead."

"I'm on board with that plan," I agreed, getting up from my seat.

I didn't want to run away, but removing myself from the situation was the best way to show Bryn that he wouldn't get a rise out of me. Besides, I would be less tempted to blast Saffir through a wall if I wasn't in the room. She had years more experience with magic than me and could probably drown me with her water affinity with a flick of her wrist.

Choice. Pursuing the mating pull was a choice. We'd both made our choices.

Briallen, Aderyn and I headed back to my cabin and tucked up on the floor in my cabin with cups of peppermint tea and knit blankets tucked around our legs while I lit the fire in the cast-iron stove and sent in small gusts of air magic to get it hot.

"Fi, didn't you want to know more about the other inhabitants of Avalon?" Briallen asked. "A lesson on magical creatures was high up on your priority list, wasn't it?"

"The little human girl in me really wants to know more about dragons and mermaids," I admitted as I reached for my satchel to pull out my slate board and pencil. These lessons about Avalon with Briallen and Aderyn may have been unofficial, but I didn't mess around when it came to knowledge. Knowing what else inhabited this realm seemed like critical information.

"What about unicorns?" Aderyn laughed.

"Are you screwing with me?" I asked seriously, and Aderyn frowned.

"Not at all. You didn't know we had unicorns in Avalon?" Briallen asked.

"You said you wanted a unicorn costume for the masquerade, but I assumed they were mythical creatures. How has no one mentioned this?" I exclaimed. I'd never been a horse girl, but I'd make an exception for a freaking *unicorn*.

Briallen snorted. "Well, they are super rare. Or maybe not so much rare as secretive? They live in remote areas and keep to themselves. They don't have an interest in making protection deals with fae like the griffins do."

"Okay, what about dragons?" I asked, furiously scribbling on my slate board as Briallen and Aderyn sipped on their tea.

"Dragons are shifters. They have a humanoid form, though much taller and bulkier than the average person. They have elemental magic too, though it's less refined than fae magic. But they can also shift into fifty-foot, element-breathing beasts, so it's best not to get on their bad side," Briallen explained. "They live in isolated mountain areas that are only accessible by flight. They also keep to themselves, but I think that's because they have a superiority complex."

I snorted at that. As if the fae didn't have a superiority complex.

"They have their own Dragon Council, but also sit on the Avalon Assembly, along with fae, mermaids, giants, goblins and centaurs. That's most races represented," Aderyn added.

"Goblins? What are they like?" I exclaimed.

Aderyn and Briallen both grimaced. "Fairly unpleasant to deal with, but they're mostly merchants, so you'll definitely come across them. They don't have elemental magic, but they're smarter than most."

"And what about the Assembly? What does it do?" I asked eagerly, getting excited about all the new topics I was adding to my research list.

"Keep the peace between the races, mostly. They resolve territorial disputes, monitor the portals, that kind of thing. The Councils are responsible for their own citizens, but the Assembly handles any crossovers. For example, the Fae Council would deal with disputes between fae and dole out punishment, but if a fae attacked a centaur, they would be tried by the Assembly and thrown into the dungeons. Or executed," Briallen said with a shrug, as if the death sentence was an everyday occurrence. Maybe it was.

"I've never been particularly interested in politics, but this is fascinating. If it wasn't so late, I'd ditch you both here and go to the library," I admitted.

"Good to know you value our company, Fi," Briallen said with a laugh.

"Maybe hold off on the obsessive research until tomorrow," Aderyn added with a wink. "But I'll leave you to analyze everything you've learned in peace, I need sleep."

"I second that," Briallen agreed, standing.

I walked them both to the door, and we hugged before exchanging goodnights. Girlfriends had been difficult for me to keep in my former life. Either I'd move away, or they'd get freaked out by my intuitive nature, or sick of my excuses when my migraines flared up. Having Briallen and Aderyn in my life eased an ache in me I hadn't realized was there.

I went to sleep with a smile on my face, grateful for the many amazing ways in which my life had changed, and dreaming about underwater fortresses and fire-breathing dragons.

I walked to my second-year air mastery class the next day, full of nervous excitement. I loved the challenge of pushing my magic and my control.

I'd always loved learning, but never really excelled. Spending hours with raging teenage human emotions battering at me gave me a migraine and no motivation to study.

I hadn't experienced migraines like that since I arrived in Avalon. Either the fae had less turbulent emotions or my magic was helping me, because I definitely wasn't making any progress with the mental shields that Gwyneira had me working on.

The other perk of my air mastery class was more time with Arthus, more time to get to know him, but also to explore my own unexpected reaction to him. Where I felt possessive and playful with Marlen—and furious around Bryn—Arthus had a dominating presence that made me want to roll over like a dog and let him rub my belly. There was a beast under all that self-control, and it felt like my subconscious was warning me not to challenge the biggest fish in the pond. I couldn't understand how I felt so assertive around Marlen and so submissive around Arthus. Maybe that's why I needed so many mates. Not for my magic, but for my sex drive and all my personalities.

In today's air mastery class, we were outside working on levitating heavy items. Apparently, it was a building block for when we could eventually use our air magic to make ourselves hover. I was giddy at the thought—it wasn't quite flying, but I'd take it.

It was fortunate we had to work up to it, because I'd have broken my neck by now if we started with our own bodies. I got my boulder into the air multiple times, but it landed with a deafening thump after a few seconds each time, and I winced imagining my body hitting the earth with that kind of impact.

Arthus appeared silently behind me, watching me work silently for a few minutes. Just his presence sent a wave of desire through me, the mating pull filling me with need.

"You're using your magic to pull the boulder up," he said in his low seductive voice, as his air magic swirled around the top of my dress, lightly tugging my already aching nipples upwards. I sucked in a breath at the unexpected sensation.

So... he was interested in me then? We probably should have exchanged more than a few words before diving into nipple play, but I wasn't necessarily mad about it.

"Your method is an impressive show of raw power, but you're burning magic and have less control. Channel your magic underneath the boulder, lifting it into the air, then creating a current underneath to hold it steady," Arthus murmured as his magic twined around my feet, moving gently up my legs brushing lightly against my panties before suddenly withdrawing. I bit down hard on my lip to stop myself from demanding he keep it up.

Holy air magic, Arthus did not play fair.

I looked up in time to catch his smug smirk as he walked away, leaving me a turned on, distracted, hot mess. My boulder didn't get off the ground for the rest of the lesson.

I had a break for lunch after my air-mastery class and I was feeling keyed up as hell. I paused on my way to the commons, contemplating whether I should pick up some food or just go back to my cabin to get myself off in the shower. I needed to get rid of some of this crazy tension. Godsdamn Arthus and his teasing.

Distracted by my dilemma, I didn't notice the mating pull until Marlen wrapped his arms around me from behind, squeezing my middle in greeting.

"What has you thinking so hard, my little foxglove?" he said into my hair where his face was buried, inhaling me as I drew in his pine scent.

I chewed on my lower lip, debating whether it was poor form to tell Marlen that another guy had got me worked up. Fae were all about the sex though, right? Surely it would be fine? Deciding that saying nothing might be better, I turned in his arms to face him and started pushing him back into the treeline. Marlen's brows raised, and his surprise skittered across my skin, even as he continued to let me move him where I wanted him. He was much stronger than me and could definitely have stopped us if he wanted to.

When we were a few feet from the main path and suitably hidden, I backed myself up against a tree and yanked Marlen towards me by the collar of his shirt. Winding my hand through his hair, I pulled his ear down to my mouth and gently bit his earlobe.

"I need to come," I breathed into his ear.

"*Gods*," Marlen choked out. "How ready are you?" he asked, hand already drifting under my dress to check for himself.

"So fucking ready," I said, swatting his hand away so I could yank my panties down. I wasn't going to waste any time, I was ready to go and already testing the limits of my exhibitionism.

Marlen quickly caught on, tugging his hard and ready cock out of his trousers and lifting one of my legs to wrap around his waist. I pulled my dress out of the way and he impaled me in one smooth movement as I bit down hard on his bicep to keep quiet, hoping my teeth would leave a mark through the fabric.

Marlen's grip tightened on my thigh, his other hand wrapping around the back of my head, tangling in my hair so he could pull me forward for a frenzied kiss. Our tongues battled as he roughly slammed into me, the bark scraping uncomfortably at my back, but it felt too good to stop.

I can't believe I thought I had a high sex drive before *I moved here.* I was insatiable now.

My hands pulled at Marlen's shirt, nails clawing at him, desperate for more, for everything. I leaned forward enough to suck on his neck, replacing the marks that had faded, and he rewarded me by pulling back further and slamming into me so hard I felt like I was seeing stars. I could feel him beginning to tense and wanting to get there with him, I sucked my finger into my mouth before reaching between us to rub circles around my clit, relishing the way Marlen's eyes widened and nostrils flared as he watched.

"You're so godsdamned sexy, foxglove," Marlen groaned.

"Less talking," I panted, throwing my head back against the tree trunk with a thud, my body wound so tight with need my limbs were trembling. "More fucking."

Marlen's grip tightened as he thrust into me harder, capturing my moans in a punishing kiss. I came so hard, my knees wobbled and my vision went black for a few seconds. Marlen never let me go, continuing to ride me hard through my spectacular orgasm until he found his own release, leaning his head in the crook of my neck as he spilled inside me.

"So," Marlen rasped, breathing hard against me. "Do you want to tell me what Arthus did in that air mastery class to get you so worked up?"

I laughed breathlessly because of course he had figured out why I was so turned on. There wasn't even a hint of jealousy from him either, just pure satisfaction. I inhaled deeply, trying to get enough oxygen in my lungs to respond when I noticed the second mating pull that had been burning in my chest, that I'd ignored in favor of chasing my orgasm.

Looking over Marlen's shoulder, I caught the briefest glimpse of blue-black hair as the second mating pull faded away.

How long had Bryn been standing there?

I approached my first tutoring session with Arthus the following night feeling more than a little apprehensive. The mating pull felt like it was twisting and coiling in my chest as I moved closer to the training area, eager to draw Arthus and me together.

Rationally, I remembered what Marlen had said about Arthus not getting close to anyone and how he had probably been hunted for his wings. Despite his flirting during class, I wasn't going to assume he wanted to get close to me. I had one hell of a crush on him, but if his teasing flirtation was as far as it ever went, I could live with that. I knew what it was like to have to take your gift into consideration when building relationships.

"Ffion, glad you could make it," Arthus said smoothly as soon as I entered the room.

Gods, his voice was like liquid sex. This would be harder than I thought. His burst of lust wasn't helping.

"Thank you for taking the time to tutor me. I imagine you have plenty of places you'd rather spend your evening," I replied, hoping I didn't sound as affected by him as I felt.

"I wouldn't be so sure about that."

The corner of Arthus' lip kicked up into the sexiest half-smile, and it took my breath away. He had a *dimple*. If he kept throwing dimples at me, I would have to track down Marlen again after my tutoring session. Was it weird to get turned on by one guy, then act on it with another? Maybe not for the fae, but it was still weird for me.

"Your control is impressive, given that you're new to all of this. However, by the second year, most air mastery students have greater precision, so that's what we'll be working on," Arthus explained, gathering materials from the storage cupboard at the front of the room.

I didn't sense any judgment from Arthus; he seemed like he genuinely wanted to help me get caught up. I watched with interest as he set up a small but elaborate obstacle course on the desk to float a feather through. The gaps were even closer than when Master Drysi set them up for me during class, and I raised a questioning brow at Arthus.

He smirked lazily at me, and I wondered how the same expression looked so tempting on Arthus and so infuriating on Bryn.

"I'm not interested in coddling you, Ffion. I have been tasked with bringing your skills up to the second-year level, and I intend to do so." I looked at him dubiously, and he gave me a reassuring smile. "For what it's worth, I am confident you will master this."

It was worth a lot actually, but it felt juvenile to admit that.

If my progress was slower than Arthus anticipated, he never let on. His emotions were calm and steady, and he was endlessly patient with me. After two hours of practice, I could guide the feather through the entire obstacle course using my air magic without dropping it. I had room for improvement—it definitely hit the sides a few times—but it was a step in the right direction.

"Let's take a break," Arthus announced, handing me a glass of water and I drank it down greedily before flopping onto the ground, rather ungracefully.

Arthus was definitely a taskmaster—I felt more wiped after two hours of training with him than I did after a full day of classes, because he didn't let me off the hook the way some of the masters did. He knew I was capable of more, and he was determined to get me there, which I respected him for. And maybe hated him for it a little too.

Arthus took a seat on the floor next to me. *Right* next to me. The mating pull did a little happy dance in my chest.

"So, the word on campus is that you grew up in Albion, and had no idea you were fae. That's an unusual background story," Arthus stated with zero preamble.

It probably should have rubbed me the wrong way the way he laid it all out there, but he delivered his statement with his usual factual calmness, and his emotions felt curious rather than judgmental.

"Was there a question in there?" I teased, and was rewarded with another one of those glorious little dimpled half-smiles.

"No," Arthus replied slowly. "I guess I'm trying to figure you out. Fae gossip, but it's rarely the full story." I felt a wave of bitterness emanating from him.

"Sounds like you're speaking from experience," I said cautiously. Arthus hadn't really given much away on a personal level yet, and while I didn't want to scare him off, I had hoped to get to know him better. Even though I wasn't interested in pursuing another mate. I mean, I'm pretty sure I wasn't.

99% sure.

67% sure.

"I'm sure you've heard things about me?" Arthus asked, arching an eyebrow.

"Uh, that you have wings?"

"And?" he pressed.

"And that you've never pursued a mating pull before? Which is totally understandable. It's a big deal, and I definitely hate the assumption that just because you feel a pull towards someone, you're obligated to explore it," I babbled nervously, my face feeling like it was on fire.

Why had I said that? Now it sounded like I was all 'mate with me, Arthus!' and *ugh*. The amusement I could feel from him wasn't helping, though at least he wasn't feeling abject terror at my weird forwardness and running for the hills. If he thought I was insane, he was polite enough to not mention it.

"Both are correct," Arthus replied eventually. "Having a rare gift like wings can be… taxing. I need to be on guard constantly to make sure I don't make myself vulnerable to people who would take advantage of me."

"I understand how that feels," I whispered, staring at the floor. His curiosity spiked sharply. "I'm not ready to talk about what my gift is just yet, but I can relate to having coveted magic. Trust becomes a rare commodity," I added under my breath, thinking of Bryn and Gwyneira and the lingering doubts I had about them.

"I've never felt a mating pull like the one I feel towards you, Fi." Arthus' use of my nickname sent a ripple of desire through me. "There have been times that I've felt a pull indicating compatible magic, but I've never felt the draw of a kindred soul before. It's intoxicating..." he trailed off, staring at me intently.

The combination of what he was feeling and I was feeling was a potent cocktail, making my head spin. Idly, I thought there might be something to this whole multiple mates thing at times like these. I could have used some of Marlen's levity right about now.

"You should know, Fi," Arthus began, his voice all smooth silk and unwavering confidence. "Control is essential to me. In *all* areas of my life. I have always assumed that my... preferences prevented my connection with other women. They may have had strong enough magic, but they weren't strong enough to handle me. But you are, aren't you Fi?" he murmured, leaning closer. I squirmed a little on the floor, starting to feel distinctly achy in all the best places. His heated gaze told me he clearly noticed my discomfort.

"You could be patient for me," he continued, voice barely above a whisper. "Wait for me. Take direction from me."

"I could do that," I replied breathily, barely recognizing my voice.

I really hoped we were talking about sex. Arthus was giving off lusty as hell vibes, but his words could technically be interpreted in multiple ways. My panties were soaked through, and my nipples were probably straining obviously against the fabric of my thin bra and linen dress. I'd never been submissive in the bedroom, but if Arthus wanted to tie me down and have his way with me, I'd be totally on board at this point.

I'd been leaning back with my hands splayed behind me on the floor, but before I could sit up to try hiding the evidence poking through my dress, swirls of Arthus' magic pinned my hands to the floor. He shot me that dimply smirk, his control of his air ability completely effortless, before releasing the invisible hold.

Oh yes, we had definitely been talking about sex.

"I know you could, but not yet. You're not ready for me yet," Arthus said in a low, seductive voice, his magic faintly tickling at my skin, the lightest tease. "And I'm not sure I'm ready for you yet either, Fi, but I'm working on it," he added with a sad smile.

"I understand," I replied quietly, the sharp twisting of the mating pull in my chest drawing me out of the fog of lust I'd been lost in.

We both stood, and Arthus reached out to stroke my hair again. "Goodnight, sweet Fi. Go find Marlen. I'm sure he will be more than willing to help you out with that ache you're feeling."

And with those parting words, he disappeared into the night, leaving me alone with my burning face and drenched panties.

CHAPTER 20

The weeks since Fi had entered my life had been some of the best I'd ever had. Not just because she was perfect for me and a godsdamned supernova in the bedroom, but because of how well she fit in with Leigh and Briallen, and how she'd brought my twin back to me.

Aderyn and I had always been close growing up. She'd been my best friend since the moment we opened our eyes, but since she'd been forced to attend the Academy a few years after me, things had been different. She'd always been careful not to be seen spending time with me and asked me not to advertise the fact we were related. It had upset me at the time, thinking she was ashamed of me, but after watching her from afar these past few months, I realized she was ashamed of *herself*. Of the fact that she, like most fae in Avalon, had no affinity and no gift.

That cut me far deeper than anything else could have.

Fi had brought Aderyn back into my life, probably without even realizing it. They'd hit it off straight away with the quiet, assessing nature that they shared, and mischievous sense of humor. They also had most of the same classes, so they spent plenty of time together. Her friendship with Fi seemed to give Aderyn the cover she needed to be seen hanging out with me around campus, though I thought it was stupid that she felt she needed one.

It also meant that Aderyn was getting to know Briallen better as well. B had become a significant fixture in my life via Leigh, and I really enjoyed her company and valued her opinion. Between Briallen and Aderyn, they'd done a great job getting Fi caught up on the kinds of things she wouldn't learn in her Academy classes. The kind of things we just *knew* from growing up here. It was good they'd taken the initiative to do it—not knowing all the answers was Fi's biggest pet peeve, but her independent nature often stopped her from asking for help.

Besides, Fi definitely wasn't asking for information about mating from me. I was grateful she had friends to discuss it with.

Today was a day off from classes, and I didn't have guard duty, so I planned an activity that would satisfy Fi's curiosity about Avalon, give me time with my sister, and double as a relaxing day out for all of us. I'd already asked everyone to meet me near the stables with spare clothes and snacks. I was pretty sure this would blow Fi's mind, but I was still nervous.

I felt like a kid with my first crush around my foxglove.

Our little ragtag group ambled over to meet me, and Fi's eyes sparkled with curiosity as she looked around the stables. This wasn't the kind of stable that housed horses; this was the home of the school griffins. It was an open-air structure, with a roof to protect the herd from poor weather, but the gates were always unlocked so the beasts were free to come and go as they pleased. Confining them would have been a grave insult to the creatures who *chose* to give the fae their allegiance.

They had the body, tail, and hind legs of a lion with the head and front talons of an eagle. They were at least as big as a carriage, though they could only carry two full-sized fae comfortably over long distances. They were also incredibly smart. They understood a lot of what we said, and could find places they'd visited before without direction.

Griffins were majestic beasts and had to be treated with the utmost respect; they weren't so much as kept by the school as offered sanctuary here in exchange for their services. Not all creatures in Avalon were as respectful of the griffins as the fae were. I was glad the Academy had made a deal with this herd. Avalon was big, and plenty of areas were only accessible by flying, including the secluded waterfall I was planning on taking us all to today.

"This is a griffin?" Fi breathed, sidling up next to me and staring at the tawny griffin I'd already asked to fly us today.

"Sure is, foxglove. They're something, right? Hop on." I lifted Fi around the waist and she scrambled, rather ungracefully, onto the waiting creature. He turned to give me a very fae-like *what the hell* face before ruffling his wings irritably. I smothered a smile at Fi's alarmed expression and boosted myself up behind her, nestling her in tight against my chest and wrapping my arms around her waist.

"A little warning next time, please?" Fi muttered, gripping my forearms while eyeing the griffin's feathers apprehensively, like she wasn't sure if she could touch them or not.

Once everyone was settled on their beasts—Leigh and Briallen on one, Aderyn flying solo—I gave Fi a quick squeeze and adjusted my bag, ready for takeoff.

"To the waterfall at the edge of dragon territory," I instructed the griffins, and all three inclined their heads in unison.

"Hold on, Fi," I told her cheerily. "Takeoff is the worst part." I leaned forward, curling my body over hers so I could gently grip the griffin between her legs, and moved Fi's hands to my thighs. The last thing we needed was to be thrown off at ten thousand feet because Fi yanked out a bunch of feathers.

"I'll wager you a kiss you scream during takeoff," I teased to ease some of her nerves.

"I'll wager you a kiss I don't. Either way, we both get what we want," she countered with a saucy grin, trying to hide the nerves in her eyes.

The griffin took off at a run, wings beating hard and buffeting our legs as the three took to the sky with us on their backs. It was the most efficient way to travel, but by far the least comfortable.

Fi's white-knuckled grip on my thighs would probably leave bruises, but I didn't mind. I *loved* wearing her marks. She didn't scream, but she squealed in delight as our griffin swooped and then leveled out, gliding high above the brilliant forest and glittering meadows below.

We soared through the sky and I stared at Avalon below us, trying to see it through Fi's eyes. She stared so hard at everything, hardly blinking, memorizing each detail. I knew she'd be taking this flight as seriously as a class or a textbook—Fi never let an opportunity to gain knowledge pass her by.

"Aren't you scared at all, foxglove? I think my heart stopped the first time I rode a griffin," I called over the sound of the rushing wind, grimacing at the memory.

"Oh, I'm terrified. However, I trust that you have this under control. Right?"

Cute.

"Your faith in me is heartwarming and entirely misplaced," I told her honestly. "This is my first two-person trip, it is sort of terrifying."

"Marlen!" she shrieked, her nails digging into my thighs.

"We'll probably be fine. The griffins are amazing. They won't drop us unless they want to. Besides, we're almost there," I said, pointing at the mountain ranges ahead and an enormous waterfall that dominated a clearing in the trees.

"Not that I don't love this idea, because I absolutely do, but isn't swimming more of a summer activity?" Fi called back teasingly, not releasing her vice-like grip on my legs.

"So much faith in my flying skills and so little faith in my date-planning skills." I shook my head even though she couldn't see me. "The mountain is dragon territory, dragonfire burns in the mountains year-round and warms the water. It isn't like a hot spring, but it's comfortable enough to swim in winter. Plus, there's never anyone here this time of year."

The griffin began its descent and Fi leaned so far back into me it was like she was trying to embed herself in my skin. I curled myself around her and enjoyed this moment where Fi was depending on me. I knew she trusted me, but she didn't *rely* on me. I didn't take it personally though, I would be the mate to comfort her and make her laugh. Hopefully she'd find someone for her mating circle who she felt comfortable turning to for guidance.

Arthus would be the ideal choice if they could open up to each other. Fi had barely been able to keep her hands off me since their tutoring session the other night. I was definitely reaping the rewards of his seduction.

We landed gracefully; the griffin cantering to a halt a few feet from the pool of water. The other two landed quickly behind us. Leigh and Briallen looked unaffected, but Aderyn was looking a little green. Traveling by griffin was a luxury only the wealthy could afford, my sister and I hadn't done it until we'd arrived at the Academy.

Dismounting the griffin, Fi made a beeline for the waterfall, just like I thought she would.

There was a gigantic pool at the bottom of the falls, perfect for swimming, and rocky paths to climb to the top. The entire area was lush and green and relaxing. It was the ideal place to escape to when life at the Academy became too much.

Satisfied the griffins were making themselves comfortable nearby, I walked up behind Fi and wrapped my arms around her shoulders, resting my chin on her forehead, relishing the way her body melted into my touch.

Every moment we spent together, Fi became more relaxed around me and let me in a little more. She was used to doing everything on her own, and I never took for granted the chances she gave me to show her she could lean on me, because I knew each one was a tough concession on her part.

"I've never seen a waterfall in real life," Fi breathed, staring at the rushing water in awe.

"What do you think, foxglove? Wishing you had some sweet water magic right about now?" Fi laughed, the sound warming my soul.

"Why would I want that?" she asked, gesturing at the waterfall. "The water is already here."

"But you can't do fun things like this," I curled a finger, beckoning a stream of liquid towards me, then directed it square between Leigh's eyes. He swore loudly as he attempted to swat it away, before using a gust of air magic to deflect it, narrowing his eyes at me playfully.

"It's on, Ferris. You just started a battle that you can't win."

I scoffed, shucking my shirt and wading into the pool wearing only my shorts. "Bring it on. I'm literally in my element." I spread my arms to gesture at the water around me and tossed him a wink.

I turned back to the edge where Fi was waiting and preened a little when I noticed her gaze was firmly locked on my chest. She shot me a challenging glare before oh-so-slowly lifting her dress over her head, seductive gaze firmly caught in mine.

Gods, I was glad Aderyn was distracted exploring her surroundings. I really didn't need my twin to see me eye fucking my girl.

Fi stood at the edge of the water in a skimpy dark blue linen bra, tied tightly behind her neck and around her back, and matching underwear, laced up the sides. It was just the standard, Academy-issued underclothes for fae females, but it looked like it had been designed just for her.

She waded slowly into the water, skimming the surface with her fingers, seemingly marveling at how warm it was. As she got close, I tugged her into my arms, reveling in the feeling of her bare skin against mine.

I wondered if she'd be open to adopting a no-clothes rule whenever we were in her cabin.

"That was mean, foxglove," I murmured, my lips grazing the shell of her ear. "Now I have a hard-on, and my sister is here."

Fi laughed lightly, pulling my hips tightly against hers and rubbing herself discreetly against the bulge that my wet shorts were doing a poor job of hiding. "Guess we'll just have to wait until we're back at the Academy to do something about it then, hm?"

"Not a fucking chance," I breathed, summoning a wave of water to scoop us up and speed us through the waterfall to the hidden spot behind it. Fi squealed, clinging onto me tightly but laughing in delight. It seriously took a lot to shake this girl.

I boosted Fi onto the ledge and used my magic to reinforce the curtain of water behind us, cocooning us in our own little oasis. Unfortunately, it wasn't soundproof. I could hear Leigh and Briallen's laughter follow us through.

"My, my, it appears I've got you all to myself, Mr. Ferris," Fi laughed as she pulled me to stand between her legs. With her sitting up on the ledge, we were at eye-level. Level in all the right places, in fact. Fi lazily licked a line from the base of my neck to my ear before nipping at my earlobe. *Gods*, this girl.

"So, what shall I do with you?" she murmured.

"Anything you want," I breathed hoarsely, her hand moving down to stroke my painfully hard cock over my wet shorts.

I groaned as she pulled her hand away but perked up when she moved it to unlace her underwear.

"You do owe me a kiss since I didn't scream when the griffin took off, but I don't believe we specified where that kiss would be." Fi winked, tugging her underwear off, so she was bare from the waist down. *Gods yes*, I could work with this. "Best make it quick, we've got company," she added huskily.

I dropped to my knees in the shallow water without hesitation, ignoring the slight pain from the impact of my legs on the rocks. I *needed* to taste her. It was like a compulsion at this point. Nothing tastes as good as she did.

She moved with me as I pulled her long, tanned legs over my shoulders, and draped on my back, leaving her beautifully exposed for me. The view was even better when I parted her with my thumbs, flattening my tongue against her folds and slowly licking up to her clit. Fi's head dropped back against the rock wall behind her as she sighed, a long, breathy moan that I felt through my entire body to the tip of my cock.

I could write a thesis on giving Fi pleasure. I had all of her hot spots memorized. I knew she liked it when I started slow and steady, before increasing my tempo and moving my tongue slightly to the left where she was most sensitive. I knew she liked it when I dug my fingers into her soft thighs, and I knew she was close when her nails raked impatiently over my scalp.

Just as I felt her tense and squirm, her hand reaching down to grab me, I yanked my cock free of my shorts and dropped her legs back to the ledge so

I could stand, sinking deeply into her and smiling into her neck as her walls clenched tightly. Fi came around me, biting down hard on my shoulder to hold in a scream, then breathing out my name as reverently as a prayer.

I gripped her ass, pulling her closer to me as she wrapped her legs around my waist, meeting me thrust for thrust. If sneaking off together hadn't given away what we were doing, the gouge marks Fi was leaving on my back and shoulders definitely would.

I was happy that swimming gave me an excuse to show them off. My craving for claiming marks grew stronger every day—I wanted the world to know I was hers.

Our mouths met in a frantic tangle of tongues and knocking teeth as if no matter how close we got, it wasn't enough. The mating pull was drawing us dangerously closer together, encouraging us to seal the bond.

Not yet. She's not ready yet.

With a punishing bite to my lip that had me groaning, Fi found her release again, arching her back and thrusting her breasts towards my face, her expression euphoric. Taking a nipple into my mouth and enjoying her drawn-out moan, I followed quickly behind her, growling out her name. We rested our foreheads against each other's, both searching the other's eyes for a long moment.

"That was... intense," Fi hedged, still clinging tightly to my shoulders.

"It's the mating pull, encouraging us to claim one another now that we've grown closer." Fi's eyes widened a fraction in panic, and I moved my hand to cup her jaw, stroking my thumb across her cheek. "Hey, it's okay. We don't have to act on it, foxglove. We're moving at your pace, remember?"

"Snail's pace," she said apologetically, though she had nothing to apologize for. The decision was big and permanent, and no matter how much I *wanted* it, I knew it couldn't be rushed. Not when everything about our world was new to her.

"Right!" Leigh yelled, bursting our bubble of serenity. "Unless you two are actually having your mating ceremony in there, do you mind coming out and joining us?"

It totally killed the moment, but the bright smile Fi was fighting made it worth it.

"You're monopolizing Fi's time, ye' selfish bastard," Leigh added. *Prick.*

Fi laughed, already reaching for her underwear. "Come on then, before Leigh loses his patience and follows us in here."

"I'm wounded that you have so little faith in my magic, foxglove," I told her, feigning an arrow to the heart. "No one is getting through that water without my say so."

I leaned forward, so my mouth was right next to her ear and bent to lace up her underwear, pressing my healing magic into her skin to heal the scrapes from the rocks. "I'm not about to let just anyone see you like this. Practically naked and on display for me. Though I'll make an exception if Arthus ever wants to join us," I murmured, loving the way her breath hitched. Oh, she *definitely* liked that idea.

As we made our way back to the group hand-in-hand, I thought about telling Fi that I'd be okay sharing with Bryn too if he ever pulled his head out of his ass long enough to become her third mate, but I didn't think she was ready to hear it yet.

Even if those two were an inevitable conclusion, they were the only ones too stubborn to see it.

FFION

CHAPTER 21

As soon as Marlen and I waded back into the main pool on weak legs, a strong gust of air magic blasted us apart and I landed on my ass in the shallows.

"Dude!" I exclaimed, glaring at Leigh.

"For your own safety, Fi!" Leigh called back, grinning like mad as he gusted air magic at Marlen over and over each time he tried to stand. Marlen laughed, using his own magic to create an enormous globe of water that he shot at Leigh.

Leigh grinned in anticipation, getting ready to block the ball of water when vines shot out of the ground below him, binding his hands and feet. Marlen's ball of water exploded above Leigh's head, leaving a confused, spluttering air fae in its wake.

"Briallen!" Leigh yelled in mock outrage. "What did you do that for?!"

"Sorry, my love," Briallen said sheepishly, retracting the vines. "I just wanted to see how that would play out." She shrugged, tossing Leigh a mischievous grin.

Between the three of them and Aderyn who was sitting on the rocks watching, their amusement tickled my skin so strongly, I had to resist the urge to squirm. Instead I dove into the water, trying to distract myself from the strange sensation on my skin.

When I broke the surface again, Marlen gave me a knowing smile before resuming his attack on Leigh. It was such a relief to have someone know my secret. Someone I could be my whole self around.

I spent the next half hour in and out of the water to distract myself from the boys' rambunctious emotions. When Briallen joined their games again, I swam over to the rocks where Aderyn was sunbathing.

"Do you fancy climbing to the top?" I asked her, eager to have a breather from the excitement.

"Sure," Aderyn agreed. She was such a soothing person to be around with her endlessly calm emotional state. It was like constantly floating down a lazy river when I was focused on her emotions.

With an embarrassing amount of effort, we both reached the top of the rocks, panting for breath and slightly red in the face. I was relieved that I wasn't the only one out of shape. The boys all did mandatory combat training, and I'd yet to meet one who wasn't fit. Female fae had it easy, which still seemed unfair to me.

Aderyn and I settled in beside each other, perched on the rocks by the waterfall with our legs dangling over the edge. Briallen and Leigh had teamed up against Marlen, trying to dunk him in the water, but they were still at a disadvantage when Marlen was surrounded by his affinity. He turned the wall of water he'd been using as a shield on them with a laugh, making the griffins nearby bristle with irritation as water flooded the ground.

Aderyn smiled sadly as she watched it all unfold, the melancholy edge to her emotions making my throat feel tight. I'd caught flashes of sadness from her in the past, but it was more potent than usual today.

"Are you okay?" I asked her cautiously. "You seem a little down today."

"You're so intuitive," Aderyn said after a beat, turning that sad smile on me. I laughed nervously, looking anywhere but her face.

"Perhaps I'm just in a reflective mood today," Aderyn hedged eventually. "You know I'm not really supposed to be here? At the Academy?"

"Of course you are," I said immediately, frowning as I twisted to look at her. "Or you wouldn't be here."

Another tight smile that barely disguised her sadness. "Twins are pretty rare among the fae. Did you know that?"

I shook my head, though now that she'd brought it up, I *hadn't* met any other twins since I'd arrived in Avalon.

"Marlen and I have an older brother and sister. They have mates now, have their own families... We don't really have much to do with them, but that's normal for a fae family. With each child, it's like starting over again from scratch because it's been fifty years since the last one," Aderyn explained.

Marlen and Aderyn had always seemed like siblings to me—the way I thought of siblings in the human world—but every other fae I'd met seemed like an only child. For all intents and purposes, they kind of were, I supposed.

"Okay..." I said slowly. "But what does that have to do with you being at the Academy?"

"Our older siblings didn't pay us much attention, until Marlen's affinity began to manifest. We were about five when we realized he had remarkable control over water. Our elemental abilities—the ones all fae have—don't usually manifest until we're 18, but strong affinities show up much earlier, as does gifted magic. There hasn't been anyone with an affinity in our family for generations."

She took a deep, steadying breath while I kept silent, waiting for her to collect her thoughts. The laughter from down below felt at odds with the serious conversation we were having up here.

"Our parents are bakers. Did Marlen tell you that?" Aderyn asked. I nodded. "When we were 13, my dad had an accident at the bakery. He had terrible burns all the way up his arm. I think he'd probably been drinking. Don't get me wrong, he's a good man, but the drink... He struggles sometimes."

She seemed uncomfortable to have revealed so much, and I patted her back awkwardly to try comforting her. "I'm not judging," I reassured her.

Aderyn swallowed thickly before she continued. "My older siblings came home to help out and Marlen was so distraught seeing dad's arm. He touched the burn almost instinctively, and that's when he discovered his healing gift."

I felt her happiness. It was obviously a good memory for her.

"There was no question that Marlen would attend the Academy of Avalon when we came of age—everyone with gifted abilities comes here. My plan was to work with my parents like my older siblings had until I was mated. Then my mates and I would figure things out from there," Aderyn finished with a shrug, though I felt her longing for that future.

"But you came here instead?" I prompted, sensing she wasn't sure how to proceed.

"Not by choice. My older brother is quite vindictive. My theory is that he was trying to find a way to get Marlen *out* of the Academy, and instead stumbled upon a way to get me *in*. There's some obscure rule about siblings of current students, if they're an eligible age, being given a place at the Academy automatically. It must have been a rule designed to keep multiples together, but there are so few of us, it's barely used."

"Okay," I said slowly, trying to make sense of the timeline.

"It was only a few months ago that my oldest brother found the loophole and contacted Gwyneira on my behalf," Aderyn said bitterly, the resentment rolling off her. "I had been working at the shop pretty happily for the past three years. Then I got a letter out of the blue from Gwyneira, apologizing profusely for the oversight and insisting I start my first year in the fall. My eldest brother was only too happy to take the credit, and my parents wouldn't have dreamed of turning down an opportunity like this. So here I am."

"Is it so bad here?" I asked curiously. I enjoyed life at the Academy, but I didn't have many positive memories to compare it to. Perhaps if I'd been happy before all of this, I wouldn't have been so inclined to jump into a vat of mystery goop just because a cute, grumpy guy suggested it.

Aderyn sighed, her conflicted emotions rolling off her and written all over her face. "I'm grateful to learn more about magic. Most weak fae like me don't get the chance. And I enjoy seeing Marlen, even though I don't want people to know we're twins and asking questions about why I'm so far behind. Fortunately, 'Ferris' is a common surname," she said with a hollow laugh.

"There's something else," I hedged. I could feel something was causing her pain.

She blew out a long breath, staring out over the treetops. "I haven't felt the mating pull at all since I came here. I'm by far the lowest on the food chain, it's not surprising that my minimal magic isn't a match for anyone at the Academy."

My heart broke, feeling her loneliness and the burden of rejection she was carrying around. Maybe I'd been a bit of brat complaining about the several intense mating pulls I'd been feeling.

"The village my parents are from is tiny, there weren't many eligible fae there. I had planned to travel this year to meet people. There's still the Avalon Fair, it's going to be in a field a short walk away from the campus. Lots of people meet their mates there." Her bright smile didn't match the hopelessness she was feeling.

I reached over and squeezed her hand. "What if you do and he's from some far-off land? Will you leave?" I selfishly wanted her to stay, but I understood why she'd want to go.

Aderyn shrugged. "Would you? There's a high chance you'll discover another strong connection there, you know." She elbowed me lightly and grinned.

I blanched. "I have enough, so I seriously hope not. I definitely wouldn't leave the Academy though. I totally get that it might not be right for you," I added hastily. "I just think this is where I'm supposed to be right now."

Aderyn laughed, not offended in the least. "Like you'd ever plan your future around a man. You're the most independent female fae I've ever met. Most females with as much magic as you would have at least three suitors on the go, swapping them out when stronger mating pulls came along. Even Gwyneira kept her mates on a long leash for a couple of years, so the rumors say, not letting them get too close so she was able to put off claiming."

"I guess that's the human side of me showing," I muttered uncomfortably. Not that I'd ever want a rotating harem of male lovers. But between the threats I was keeping to myself, the mating pull driving Marlen and me crazy, and the tension between Bryn and me, I wondered if my independent streak had been causing more problems than it solved.

"Aderyn! Fi!" Marlen called. "Get down here, I need allies. These two don't fight fair."

"Come on," Aderyn said, carefully climbing back over the ledge. "I've moped long enough. Let's go have fun."

I entered the water elemental class arm-in-arm with Aderyn, and we sat in our usual spot on the outer edge of the room. Since our waterfall trip a couple of days ago, something had settled in our friendship. Or it had on her end at least, because she'd confessed something to me that had been weighing on her mind.

I was still keeping all my secrets.

We sat down at the bench and I sighed loudly, fully prepared for another pointless, unproductive lesson spent staring at my unmoving basin of water.

Aderyn looked over at my mopey face and chuckled. "It's not going to get any easier if you don't even try, you know."

"I *am* trying," I huffed, staring down at the still basin. "It's just that nothing ever happens."

Why couldn't I crack this? Gwyneira had asked me to try gaining control over the other elements *without* using my air affinity to help me as I had in my fire class, and I'd made zero progress since then. I'd spent my entire life being the worst student because my head hurt too much to concentrate, and it made me angry that I was failing here, even without the migraines.

The master lounged in his seat at the front of the class, occasionally taking a lazy look around the room but otherwise leaving us to it. I couldn't even remember his name; we had so little to do with him. I suppose it must be infuriating for him as a water affinity to try to teach fae with no water inclinations.

I stared at the basin of water, willing it to move and silently commanding my air magic to stay put when it gusted through my veins to come to my aid. Idly, I wondered if Marlen's water magic felt like water in his veins since my magic always felt like a controlled breeze. I tried to imagine cool liquid trickling down my arms instead, running down to my fingertips, until the tiniest ripple ran through the basin of water.

"Aderyn! Did you see that?" I exclaimed. I imagined the watery feeling again, and the surface gave another weak ripple.

"You did it, Fi! Well done, Marlen is going to be so excited that you manipulated his element," Aderyn said with a beaming smile that I couldn't help but return.

Finally. I was finally making some progress towards becoming a fully-fledged fae. For my efforts, the master looked over and gave me a curt nod. *Ah well, can't win 'em all.* I still wasn't going to bother learning his name.

I didn't get a chance to tell Marlen about my development during the day, and I had to go to a tutoring session with Arthus directly after my last class, so I made Aderyn promise to tell Marlen at dinner. I hoped it made him happy since he was stuck on guard duty tonight and probably needed a little pick-me-up.

I entered the air mastery room just as Arthus finished setting up the obstacle course for tonight's tutoring session. It looked the same as last time, and I was mildly disappointed we'd be doing the same thing yet again. I'd gotten quite good at controlling my feather's movements.

"Good evening, Fi," he murmured in his low, silky voice. It never ceased to amaze me the way my body responded to his voice alone. There was a fluttering in my lower stomach just from those three words, and I was more than a little embarrassed at how easily he got me going.

He made me feel *needy*, and knowing how needy I felt both humiliated me and made me want him more.

"Good evening," I replied breathily, before clearing my throat and trying to pull myself together. Arthus smirked knowingly.

"How was your day?"

"Good, actually. I made some progress in my water elemental class. I've never made anything happen in that class, so it was a pretty big moment for me," I rambled, setting my satchel down on an empty table and moving to join him.

"That is an achievement worth celebrating," Arthus said without a trace of sarcasm. "In many ways, it is easier for fae with no affinity to manipulate the elements than it is for fae who have strong affinities. Our specialization element takes over, distracts us."

Of course we would have this conversation *after* I'd figured out that I needed to set aside the sensation of air in my veins and try to imagine something else.

"That's what I figured out today, finally. Hopefully, I can replicate it for earth and fire now," I said absently, pondering whether I needed to imagine dirt in my veins for earth magic. Something to ask Briallen about—she was the only earth affinity I was friendly with.

"So, more feather obstacles today?" I asked brightly, careful to keep the disappointment out of my voice. I must not have succeeded as Arthus quirked a brow at me and I felt his amusement.

"Don't worry, Fi. I won't let you get bored. Today, you'll be completing the obstacle course multiple times over as fast as you can," Arthus said, and I rolled my eyes internally. *Easy peasy.* "However, you'll be switching the item you float through each time. You can start with the feather if you like," Arthus added smugly. He laid out a row of small items that would easily fit through the obstacle course, but they were all different sizes and weights.

Right, slightly more of a challenge then.

Arthus positioned himself directly behind me so he could watch me work over my shoulder. I absently pulled my mass of curls over one shoulder and was immediately met by the feel of his warm breath skittering across my neck, making me suck in a startled breath.

This is probably part of the challenge, I thought wryly to myself. Arthus wanted me to complete the course with him standing right behind me, tempting me with his icy scent and close proximity.

The feather went through the obstacle course without incident, but when I attempted the course again with a small rock, I knocked half of the course over within a few seconds. Arthus chuckled, highlighting just how little space there was between us.

"Not as easy as you thought, hm? Maybe you need a strong hand to guide you," he murmured, and I felt the effect of his words in my panties instantly, even as my face heated.

Hands shaking, I reassembled the delicate wooden course before attempting to float the marble through it. This time, I couldn't even get the marble into the first hoop; it either fell short or shot rapidly into the air. Apparently, my newfound precision was exclusive to feathers; with anything heavier, I was out of my depth. I growled in frustration as the marble landed with a thump again. It felt like I was always taking one step forward and two steps back.

Arthus leaned in until his lips were right at my ear. "Close your eyes, Fi. Take a deep breath. I know you can do this, I would never push you past your limits."

He was definitely talking about more than magic, and it was distracting as hell, but his words did have the desired effect of calming me down enough that I could focus and start over.

We practiced for an hour, and I made good progress with the strip of fabric, the marble, and the leaves. The small rock and lump of amethyst were a total bust, though. A selfish part of me was glad I hadn't mastered them since it would mean more tutoring sessions with Arthus, but the non-idiotic part of my brain reminded me that I didn't need to fail a class to spend time with a boy, and I should really get my shit together.

I helped Arthus pack away the obstacle course, our fingers occasionally brushing together and sending the most delicious rush of sensations over my skin—a mixture of his emotional response and my own reaction, blending seamlessly together. There was such a thrill at each point of contact because Arthus wasn't generous with his touch. Every movement was controlled and deliberate, and it made me appreciate those little brushes we had all the more.

As I went to leave, Arthus stepped in front of me, standing closer than usual, and I tipped my head back to look at him. Fae seemed to be attractive in general, and I'd definitely been attracted to all three guys I'd felt a strong mating pull to, but Arthus was particularly beautiful. Everything about his face was sharp and angular, and with his lean build and pointed fae ears, he was everything I'd imagined a fairy prince would be in my childish daydreams.

Moving with his signature slow-paced control, Arthus picked up a lock of my hair, wrapping it around his finger the way he'd done before. He searched my face for something, though I wasn't sure what he was looking for, and with him standing so close, I was too vulnerable to control what he saw. Eventually, I felt a hint of his satisfaction, and he released my hair slowly, the curl springing back into place.

"Goodnight, Fi," he murmured, breaking the silence we'd descended into.

"Goodnight, Arthus," I breathed quietly, hating that this peaceful moment was over, even though it meant I could go find Marlen, who I'd missed all day. Each interaction with Arthus felt like a stolen one, and I could never get enough of them.

I grabbed my bag off the table and let myself out of the classroom, forcing one foot in front of the other before I went back in there and did something embarrassing like throw myself at Arthus. I'd already put significantly less fight into avoiding the mating pull with him than I had with Marlen. It was as if giving into Marlen had opened the floodgates—while the idea of having *more* mates, *more* magic was terrifying—I didn't *want* to fight my connection with Arthus. I didn't want to run and hide and avoid him, the way I'd tried to do with Marlen.

The way I'd do forever with Bryn.

Maybe I should just tell Arthus about my magic? I wasn't worried about him selling me out to the hunters—if anyone had a reason to avoid them as much as I did, it was Arthus. If I was honest with myself, I *wanted* to tell him about my gift. I wanted to talk to someone who understood the fear that came when your gift was also your curse.

Mind made up, I went to track down Marlen and tell him about what I planned to do.

CHAPTER 22

This beautiful fae was going to ruin me. I hadn't been able to stop thinking about Fi since our last tutoring session—the way she swayed toward me when I stood behind her, and the way she'd bared her neck to me without even thinking about it. The two nights since I'd only been able to sleep after jerking myself raw at the fucking *thought* of her.

I'd teased her into a frenzy during today's air mastery class, but Fi barely faltered. Never complained, never whined for more, just took everything I threw at her. I'd been testing her the whole time. I wasn't accustomed to letting myself get close to others, not when I carried such value on my back, but Fi had made me *want* it. I'd all but given up on ever finding a mate before she came along, but the pull of kindred souls was irresistible.

When I'd tested her to see if she could handle my particular flavor of intimacy, I should have known before I began that she'd pass with flying colors.

I'd expected Fi to vanish after class, most likely to find Marlen Ferris to take care of her pent-up sexual frustrations. Instead, she approached me, looking uncharacteristically serious as her hands twisted nervously in front of her.

"Are you free right now?" Fi asked, chewing on her lip. Unconsciously, I reached out and tugged her lip away from her teeth, soothing the worried skin with my thumb.

Like silk.

She immediately relaxed into my touch, releasing a breathy sigh. It was the first time I'd touched her skin, and I struggled to pull my hand away. Her lips were soft, her warm breath on the tip of my thumb felt like it traveled over my entire body.

"I am," I confirmed, forcing my hand to my side and inclining my head curiously. Fi hadn't ever made any kind of move on me. She subconsciously seemed to defer to my commanding nature, letting me take the lead in all of our interactions.

Fi shook her slightly, refocusing her thoughts. "I wanted to talk to you about my gift. I know I said I wasn't ready to discuss it before, but I think I am now. Could we talk in my cabin? Marlen is waiting there too."

"Of course," I agreed easily, following her out of the classroom and across the campus, ignoring the inquiring glances we were getting from other students. Fi had said she knew what it was like to have a coveted gift, maybe she wanted advice on dealing with it? This felt like an important step, whatever it was. She was trusting me, and I wanted her trust.

Fi let us into her cabin, and Marlen crossed the room to greet her with a gentle kiss. Gods, I wished I could kiss her like that.

"Arthus," Marlen greeted me with a warm smile. I'd always liked him, he was friendly but not *overly* friendly, and seemed to get along with mostly everyone at the Academy. I could see why Fi had chosen him.

"Marlen," I returned, inclining my head toward him in greeting as I pulled the cabin door closed and took a seat in the armchair Fi indicated. She followed suit, sitting in the chair next to me, and we angled ourselves toward each other, our knees almost touching.

Marlen pulled out one of the wooden dining chairs and sat facing us, maintaining a small amount of distance. His presence seemed to be comforting for Fi, but he was giving her space to lead the conversation. They really were a good match.

"So," I broached when Fi continued gnawing on her lip and staring at her hands. "You wanted to talk to me about your gift?"

"I, um, well..." she hesitated before taking a deep steadying breath and pulling her thoughts together. "Screw it, I'll just be direct. I'm an empath."

An empath...

A fucking *empath?*

The gods were laughing at me, at all of us.

The empaths were meant to be extinct.

My panic was so acute, it ate away at the edges of my vision. It wasn't just panic, it was fear. Fear for Fi. Fear that I would lead the hunters right to her. Fear that news of her gift would get out and her life would be in danger.

Gods, this was not the time for me to lose my shit. I didn't speak for a few minutes while wrangling my terror under control. How could this be happening? Was this why Fi had been kept away from Avalon for so long?

Clear my mind. I am in control. Deep breath. Keep my anger in check.

I looked up to see Fi's crestfallen face tipped down, staring at her hands wringing together in her lap. Of course. She could feel my reaction. I was screwing this all up.

"Who knows?" I rasped.

"You, Marlen, Bryn, and Gwyneira."

I laughed bitterly. "That's three fae too many, Fi. You know what could happen if this information fell into the wrong hands, right? Your life would be over. The hunters would come for you, you would be held captive and drained of your blood repeatedly until you had none left. Amulets with empath magic would be worth a fortune..." I muttered, my control over my emotions slipping again.

Fury was rising, coursing through my veins, the muscles in my back were straining from the effort of keeping my wings back. The idea of someone hurting her...

"Rein it in! You're hurting her," Marlen snapped, his tone harsher than I'd ever heard it.

My eyes shot to Fi's as she clenched her jaw tight, trying to disguise how much pain my out-of-control feelings were causing her, and I could *see* the moment where my painful anger morphed into a heavy regret. I was handling this all wrong. She'd trusted me with this, and I had shown exactly why empaths couldn't trust anyone.

"I'm sorry, Fi," I whispered, my voice hoarse. She wouldn't even look at me. "I'm so very sorry."

I stood up and left without looking back, ignoring Marlen's furious gaze as it burned into me until I was out the door. I needed to pull myself together. I couldn't stay there knowing I was making her miserable, not even able to pull my own thoughts together.

The mating pull had led me to the one fae at the Academy with magic more rare and coveted than my own. *Gods, this was a mess.* My wings were significantly harder to hide than Fi's empath ability. Being seen with me could put a target on her head, and she couldn't afford the extra attention.

Hurrying through students until I got to the edge of campus, I pulled off my shirt and tied it around my waist before releasing my wings and shooting up into the treetops. At least there I could have space to think, to breathe. I had put enough physical distance between Fi and me that the mating pull had all but disappeared, but I couldn't escape the memory of her devastated face.

Furious at myself, I took off into the air above the tree canopy, feeling as though Fi's hurt-filled amber were following me into the sky. It wasn't safe for me to land until I calmed down enough to retract my wings, or I'd risk someone trying to subdue me to cut them off. It wouldn't have been the first time.

Yet another reason Fi and I could never be together.

Gods, I'd had such high hopes when I first felt a powerful pull towards her that day. The more I got to know her, the more hopeful I'd become. Few powerful fae females could give up control, even for their own pleasure, but Fi would. I could see it in the way she moved around me, the way she'd unconsciously expose her nape or throat to me.

I'd observed her with Marlen from a distance, more than I cared to admit to, and she never acted that way around him. If anything, the little minx had a little dominant streak with Marlen, scratching and biting him liberally. I couldn't believe such a female could be a perfect fit for both of us, but I'd seen how comfortable they were together. There was no doubt that their pull was as strong as Fi's and mine.

My back muscles began to ache from exertion, unused to flying after rarely risking it, so I headed towards a high point of the mountainous area on the edge of campus. Landing on a ledge where I had a good view of anyone approaching my spot, I sat on the ground overlooking the Academy.

I'd only been sitting there for a few minutes when I heard someone exiting one of the caves, heading towards me. I eyed the ledge warily. They weren't making any attempt to sneak up on me, but they might have been lulling me into a false sense of security.

I was both surprised and completely unsurprised when Bryn Edan appeared. He watched Fi as closely as I did, but from much further away. We weren't particularly friendly—the guy had a reputation—and I wasn't sure I'd ever spoken to him before.

Bryn approached carefully with his hands up, like he was nearing a wild animal. I didn't think he'd attack me—he was honorable enough to work with Gwyneira for the Academy—but I still appreciated him leaving ample space between us when he sat down.

We both looked down over the campus, Bryn lazily drawing small fireballs into his palm and extinguishing them mindlessly, while I idly admired the control he had over his fire magic.

"She told you then? About her gift?"

In my moment of panic, I hadn't asked Fi *why* Bryn knew about her gift. My eyes flicked to his face, assessing his expression. He and Fi exchanged heated glances and angry glares, but I'd never seen them converse. Were they being pulled to each other as well? Why were they both fighting it so hard?

"Yes," I said cautiously, in case he'd discovered Fi's secret against her will.

He snorted at the suspicion written all over my face. "I tracked Ffion to Albion at Gwyneria's request. She thought she was a human, and didn't even believe magic was real. When I told her about what she was, she mentioned her ability to feel emotions."

"You brought her back to Avalon?" I confirmed.

"I did."

"You knew before anyone," I murmured, wondering about the strange dynamic they had now. I doubted he'd been the most compassionate when delivering the life-changing news about what Fi was.

"Yep," Bryn said, popping the 'p'. We sat in silence. It wasn't awkward, but I also didn't really know what to say. Why was he here? Last I heard, he was courting Saffir Castell.

"You're an idiot to run, you know," Bryn remarked.

"Excuse me?" Gods, I'd heard Bryn was insufferably rude but the rumors didn't do his obnoxious attitude justice.

"You think you're doing the right thing, that you're somehow keeping Ffion safe by ignoring the pull, but she needs you. She didn't grow up here. She barely understands anything about our world. As soon as she arrived, Gwyneira freaked her out about the danger she was in because of her magic," Bryn explained flatly, staring out at the campus. "No one will hold Marlen captive for his healing magic. He doesn't get it. But you do. She needs *you*."

Bryn's tone was unfeeling, but I wasn't fooled. He wouldn't be here talking to me if he didn't care.

"What's your excuse then?" I challenged. "You must feel a powerful pull towards each other, I've seen the way she looks at you. And you're always staring at her when you think she's not looking."

He turned his head and glared at me. "You're hiding up here because you think you're doing right by her. I'm only pointing out that you're not. I have no interest in avoiding her for her own safety or any other noble-but-stupid reason."

"Then why *are* you avoiding her?" I pressed, noticing that he didn't say he had no interest in her. That was an untruth he couldn't tell.

"It's not your concern, wings. Besides, I'm courting someone else." He stood, taking a few steps back towards the cave before pausing and turning back to me. "Ffion has already received at least two threats. I'm convinced there's been more, but she won't tell me about them because she suspects I might be responsible for them," he added bitterly.

Two threats? About her gift? Who of the people that she'd told had betrayed her?

"Pursue her or not. It's your decision, but if I find out you've told anyone about her gift, I will come after you myself," Bryn threatened, vanishing back into the caves.

Fuck.

He was an asshole, but he was probably right about this. Fi hadn't asked me to come and talk to her about pursuing the mating bond, she'd asked to talk to me about her gift. If she'd told me because she needed my help, then I had utterly failed her.

I flew back to the tree canopy above my cabin, landing among the branches, finally calm enough to retract my wings. Gwyneira had given me an isolated cabin without a roommate because of the dangers of me being vulnerable around people I didn't know. The only secluded cabins were the ones for mates, so I currently enjoyed having the vast space all to myself. Though there would be plenty of room for Fi and Marlen to move in if we ever got to that point.

I shook my head to clear my thoughts. *One thing at a time.*

Grabbing a slate board and pencil, I sketched out everything I knew about Fi's schedule and the times I had observed her walking around on her own. Those days were at an end. I wanted to make Fi mine, but more importantly, I would ensure her safety if it was the last thing I did.

FFION

CHAPTER 23

Marlen had been plying me with cups of peppermint tea and backrubs, despite my pleas for him to break out the extra-potent fae wine since Arthus bailed. He was determined to keep me sober for some reason, which was the last thing I felt like being.

The humiliation of rejection was too much to bear.

I dropped my head into my hands, choking back the sobs I refused to let out. *What had I been thinking telling him?* Marlen had taken the news about what I was well, but he was clearly the exception, not the rule. Arthus obviously felt the same way about empaths that Bryn did.

"Stop," Marlen ordered, lifting me out of the chair so he could sit in it, then pulling me back down onto his lap and wrapping his arms tightly around me. "Don't write him off just yet. I'm confident he just needs a little while to process things."

"You're wrong," I rasped, relenting and letting a couple of tears fall.

"I don't think I am. You have a powerful pull to Arthus. You're kindred souls. You ran away from me when you needed some time to think, remember?" Marlen pointed out. I did remember, but it was rude of him to be rational about it when I felt so shitty.

It was two hours after Arthus had fled that we heard a knock on the door. I paused at the sink where I'd been polishing the already clean counter for something to do with my hands, and Marlen turned to give me a very pointed, smug smile.

"Didn't I tell you? He just needed a moment to process. Like you did."

I rolled my eyes at him, drying my wet hands. "First of all, you don't even know that's him. Second, he might be knocking on the door to tell me he never wants to see me again."

"It's him, and he's not," Marlen replied absentmindedly as he went to answer the door.

Feeling suddenly unsteady, I took a seat at the small dining table, clasping my hands to hide the shaking. For a long moment, Marlen stood in the doorway so I could only just make out Arthus' form around him, and the two of them had some kind of stare off. Silent conversation? No idea, I was busy taking deep breaths and discreetly wiping under my eyes, hoping it wasn't obvious that I'd been crying.

Arthus must have passed whatever test Marlen was conducting, as he stood aside to let Arthus through. He was wearing a different shirt to what he'd left in, and it looked like he'd yanked it on haphazardly— his hair was a disheveled mess too, far more so than usual. Gods help me, if he'd been screwing some girl for the past couple of hours while I sat here bawling over him, I'd mount his testicles on my wall.

Arthus lowered himself into the seat across from me without saying a word. his intense gaze boring into my soul. His emotions felt... settled. Like he'd been through a raging storm, but had reined it in. I didn't know what to make of it.

Marlen leaned against the wall, quietly observing as the silence between Arthus and me stretched on and on. Rationally, I knew I should have said something, but something about Arthus seemed to demand my submission, so I waited for him to speak. He was pretty frugal with words at the best of times.

Arthus sighed. "I shouldn't have run."

"I would have," I replied quietly.

Marlen gave me an encouraging nod from over Arthus' shoulder, then slid quietly out the door, evidently confident that I would be okay here without him.

"I didn't run because I find your magic abhorrent or anything like that, Fi," Arthus said sharply. "I'm worried about putting you in more danger. My gift is common knowledge here at the Academy, and the hunters are always looking for an opportunity. I couldn't live with myself if they took you to get to me, especially if they found out about your gift. My wings are rare, but empaths are myth."

I felt his sincerity—his concern for me swirled uncomfortably in my gut—but his words were basically a breakup letter, and tears pricked at the back of my eyes. Gods, I would not cry in front of him. That would really be the cherry on top of my mortification cake.

"Stand up," Arthus commanded in the low, sultry voice he used to flirt with me.

Say what now?

As if my legs had a mind of their own, I stood and stepped to the side of the table. He mirrored me, standing so close I could feel his breath fanning across my face. His hands were at his sides, and he felt so close yet maddeningly far away.

What was this? How did we get here? It would hardly be the first time I'd been wondering where a conversation with Arthus was going, though.

"Ask me to be your suitor," Arthus murmured. From Marlen, those words would have been a request, but with Arthus they sounded more like a command.

"Why?" I challenged him, straightening my shoulders. "Are you going to say no?"

He scoffed lightly. "I'm not going to say no, sweetheart. Now ask me. And I'll punish you for your insubordination later."

He gave me a sultry smirk, and my knees wobbled a little. That was a dangerous look.

"Will you be my suitor?" I asked obediently. He continued to look at me expectantly. "Uh, please?"

Another dangerous, panty-melting smirk. Dimples on point. *Oh my stars.* "Yes."

Arthus wound his hand through my hair to cup the back of my head and pulled me forward to *finally* kiss me. All the flirting, all the foreplay, had led us to this moment that I had begun to think would never happen.

It was worth waiting for.

Arthus kissed me like he owned me, one hand tangled in my hair with the other gripping my jaw while my palms rested lightly on his stomach. My lips parted for him automatically, an embarrassingly needy sound escaping me as his tongue swept against mine.

Arthus dominated and took and possessed, and I *loved* it.

I could give my control over to Arthus, and he would protect it with his life, giving me the freedom to just feel for myself for once. It didn't feel better or worse than what I had with Marlen—rather it felt like a different part of my soul was being nurtured. I needed both.

I was definitely eager to take this make-out session to the next level, but Arthus pulled back, still holding my head firm as he stared at my swollen lips. I could feel him reigning in his lust, tightening the leash on his emotions.

"Not yet, sweetheart. Soon," he promised, dropping another light kiss on my lips. "There's something important I need to finish working on, I'll come see you later."

Disappointed, I leaned into him and sucked his lower lip into my mouth. Another rush of his lust ran through me before Arthus pulled his emotions in tight again. I didn't even know that kind of control was possible. I don't think he was doing it to hide himself from me. It wasn't for my benefit, but his own.

"Until later, Fi," he murmured against my lips.

That evening, I sat in our usual corner spot in the commons with Marlen, Briallen, Leigh, and Aderyn. I was happy with the result of my conversation with Arthus, but the entire exchange left me emotionally exhausted and more than a little confused since we'd started kissing instead of talking about anything. *What happens now?* Marlen and I were already so close that nothing much changed when he became my suitor, but Arthus was a whole different story.

Would I still just see him in class and tutoring sessions? How was this actually going to work?

I was picking unenthusiastically at my raw mushroom salad, mulling that over, when I felt the mating pull encourage my eyes to the door.

I expected to see Bryn, who often made an appearance in the commons with Saffir hot on his heels. I definitely did *not* expect to see Arthus striding purposefully over to our table, leaving a trail of open mouths and wide-eyed stares in his wake. I'd never seen Arthus in the commons before. I'd barely even seen him outside of the classroom.

He swung by the salad bar and loaded up a plate with eyes on him the whole way before approaching our table. As he got closer, Marlen moved down the bench, pulling me closer to him so there was room on my other side for Arthus. He lowered himself onto the seat, throwing me a tiny, smug half-smile before starting on his own salad without saying a word.

My friends stared at him, and I could feel their disbelief rolling off them, and something akin to awe radiating from Aderyn. I quirked a brow at her slack-jawed expression, and she blushed red, clamping her mouth shut and staring down at her plate.

Marlen's amusement grew as he watched his star-struck sister. "Aderyn has been obsessed with fae wings since she was a little girl. She's got a serious case of hero-worship going on right now," he whispered. I stifled a smile, not wanting Aderyn to feel any more embarrassed than she already was.

Arthus didn't reach for me or touch me affectionately the way Marlen always did in public. However, his leg pressed tightly against mine, and our pinkies brushed together a little too often to be coincidental. It was small and discreet, but coming from Arthus it felt like he was making a huge statement about our relationship. That must have been how everyone else was taking it too—there was a suffocating wave of surprise, disbelief, and more than a little jealousy coming my way.

I tensed as the emotions started to become overwhelming, and Marlen wrapped his arm tightly around my waist, nuzzling my neck comfortingly.

"Focus on me, sweetheart," Arthus instructed under his breath, leaning to talk in my ear. "Just me. Drown out the noise."

I tipped my head down, hiding my face behind a curtain of hair and closed my eyes. Working to isolate Arthus' emotions from the rest of the crowd, I focused on his steady calmness and his ironclad resolve to stay in control.

Arthus was a liferaft in a turbulent sea of emotion, and I clung to it with everything I had, keeping my eyes scrunched shut until the impending migraine retreated. I gave myself a few more minutes before opening my eyes and meeting Arthus' concerned gaze.

"Better?" he asked softly.

"Much," I breathed, staring at him in wonder. Several meditation sessions with Gwyneira focused on building mental walls hadn't achieved results. Yet Arthus had figured out in seconds that it wasn't a wall I needed, but an anchor. How had he known?

"Instinct," he breathed, replying to the unspoken question in my gaze. Leigh cleared his throat loudly, and the spell was broken. Looking around the table, I found three confused faces staring back at me. Crap, I wouldn't be able to keep my gift a secret from my friends much longer. It got harder and harder to hide each day.

I gave them an apologetic look and scrambled for a topic to break the tension. Hopefully they'd play along for a while longer. The commons were definitely not the location to be having *that* conversation.

Arthus arched a brow, looking around the silent table. "Is your dinner conversation always this stimulating, or is this all on my account?" he asked lightly.

Leigh snorted, and I felt some tension at the table dissipate. "You're a bit intimidating," Leigh replied honestly, and Briallen elbowed him.

"So, how do you and Fi know each other?" Briallen asked casually while shooting me a glare that promised we'd be discussing this new development later. I hadn't mentioned Arthus to my friends because I wasn't sure he'd be comfortable with me telling people about us.

"I'm her suitor," Arthus responded smoothly, without an ounce of hesitation. *Huh*, maybe I'd read him wrong after all.

Leigh let out a low whistle. "Both your suitors have gifted abilities, Fi? Quite the circle you're forming there."

"She's not done. She'll have three for sure. There's still time for Bryn to get his act together," Briallen muttered.

"B!" I hissed, face flaming. Speaking of the devil, Bryn had just walked through the door, and I looked up in time to see his hard glare on our table. Our eyes collided, and for a second I thought I saw a flash of something that looked like hurt, but it was gone the next instant. There were too many people in the room for me to get a clear read of his emotions. Even though he had just entered the commons, presumably to get dinner, Bryn turned on his heel and stormed out. *Confusing fae.*

I shrugged off the weird moment and focused my attention on the five people in front of me who had quickly become a significant part of my life over the past few weeks. I'd never had a group of friends before, and I was more grateful than they could know for their friendship.

We finished up dinner then Marlen, Arthus, and I seemed to naturally gravitate out of the commons together. Having them walking on either side of me felt like a little slice of heaven. Could I be selfish enough to pursue claiming them as mates despite the problems it might present for my magic?

Would the mating pull even give me a choice? As we walked, Marlen's hand gripped mine tightly, and the idea of not being able to touch him seemed insane to me. How much of that was me and how much was the mating pull?

"There was something I'd like to discuss with you both, if you have a moment," Arthus enquired politely. He was much more reserved around Marlen than he was when it was just me. There were zero sexy air magic tricks happening right now.

"I'm free," I said a little hopefully, looking to Marlen. It felt so good being around both of them, I didn't want to go back to my cabin yet. Even if Marlen would have probably come with me.

"Sure," Marlen smiled at me. I should have known. He never really denied me anything.

I was beginning to understand what Briallen had meant about different mates balancing you in different ways. Marlen was my teddy bear who would let me get away with murder, but I could already tell that wasn't how the dynamic between Arthus and me would go. If Bryn and I had pursued the mating pull, I knew without a doubt he wouldn't let me get away with anything.

That was probably the one thing I liked most about him. It was a pity about the rest of his personality.

"Let's go to my cabin. Fewer ears around," Arthus added quietly, drawing me out of my reverie before striding off ahead. I exchanged a glance with Marlen before pulling him along after Arthus.

Arthus' cabin was *much* nicer than mine. Not to bitch about it because I genuinely liked my space, and I was grateful I didn't have to share it, but holy hell, this one was way cooler.

"How'd you wrangle a circle cabin?" Marlen asked with a low whistle.

"A what?" I asked him.

"It's a cabin for mates, they're more spacious and have enough furniture for three people. And just the one bed, though it's much bigger," Marlen added with a wink that made my face flush. It was too soon for *that* conversation.

"I've had it since I was a student. Everyone knows about my gift, so it isn't exactly safe for me to have a roommate," Arthus answered with a shrug. "Speaking of safety, I'd like to talk to you about your schedule, Fi. Specifically, all the times I've noticed you walking between classes on your own. That is a dangerous risk to take, given the two threats you've already received," he continued, and I stared at him.

"Er, first of all, have you been watching me around the campus? I... don't know how I feel about that. And what do you know about the threats?

Only one was public," I said suspiciously. Had I read Arthus completely wrong?

"I've hardly been following you," Arthus replied dismissively. "You've been going out of your way to walk past the air mastery classroom, have you not? The mating pull is constantly drawing us together."

That didn't sound as creepy as following me around, and he had a very valid point about me hanging around outside the air mastery classroom.

"As for the threats, Bryn told me you'd received two, and he thought there may be more, but you wouldn't tell him because he's on your list of suspects?" Arthus raised his eyebrow at me in a way that made me feel distinctly judged.

"I don't know," I sighed, rubbing my temples. "I'm just being cautious, just in case. I know that upsets him, though I don't really understand why. He doesn't even like me."

A potent tickling sensation told me both Marlen and Arthus were amused by that idea.

"What?" I asked them accusingly, crossing my arms and giving them each my best glower.

"I don't know Bryn well, sweetheart, but I doubt he would have threatened me to keep your gift a secret if he didn't like you, much less call me an idiot for running away from you," Arthus said with a light chuckle.

"He did those things?" I asked, baffled. "Maybe it's the mating pull driving him to protect me or something. Remember, I would be able to tell if he had feelings for me. Empath, remember?"

"You've spent most of your life trying to avoid other people's emotions, foxglove. I'm not sure you would be able to tell with Bryn. It might not be as obvious as you expect it to be," Marlen countered gently.

"Okay, let's move on from this topic and never discuss it again," I muttered irritably. "What were you saying about my schedule, Arthus?" Arthus gave me a long look, but thankfully he let the subject drop.

"I can tell you're resistant to the idea of relying on other people, but can you at least allow the two of us to escort you on campus until we know where the threats are coming from?" Arthus asked.

I huffed a sigh, but I could feel both Arthus and Marlen's genuine concern, and Arthus didn't even know about the two drawings of me in a cage yet.

"Okay, sure. You two can escort me around like bodyguards until we figure out who is sending the notes," I conceded.

"That's our girl," Arthus murmured into my ear, kissing me lightly on the temple.

Oh my, those three words had a serious effect on my libido. Arthus definitely noticed, tilting my chin gently towards him and stroking his thumb over my cheekbone. I knew my stare was bordering on longing and I should have tried to regain some cool points, but I just wanted him so much I totally lost my head being in close proximity.

"Soon, sweetheart."

He smirked. *Soon?* That infuriating word again. I resisted the urge to growl at him as Marlen wrapped his arms around my waist from behind me.

"All in good time, foxglove. Let's head back to your cabin, I'll take care of you," he purred in my ear, giving my hips a light squeeze. I don't know what I expected to happen, but I was definitely surprised when Marlen threw Arthus a cheeky wink and Arthus chuckled softly in response. How was this my life?

I was not thrilled at leaving Arthus behind, but at least I was bringing my sexy water fae home with me.

FFION

CHAPTER 24

"I hired a carriage for us tomorrow," Briallen said casually as all six of us ate dinner together for the second time.

"Why?" I asked, my tone laced with suspicion. "Where are we going?"

"Where indeed, my love?" Leigh enquired, his voice deceptively calm considering the tension he was feeling. "Marlen and I are both on guard duty tomorrow."

Marlen's concern swirled through my gut, and I reached over to give his hand a comforting squeeze.

"Don't be mad," Briallen pleaded. "Fi hasn't visited Inver yet. She only owns Academy-issued clothing, and we both need dresses for the masquerade. I'm so desperate to take her shopping!"

Leigh's resolve crumbled into dust when confronted with Briallen's pout. I don't think I'd ever seen him say no to her.

"What's Inver?" I asked, turning to face Arthus.

"A market town, around an hour's carriage ride from here. It's shorter by flight, but that would limit the amount of stuff you can bring back," he replied, cocking a brow at Briallen who flushed as pink as her hair. "I can accompany them tomorrow," Arthus added, and both Marlen and Leigh's relief was palpable.

"Do you not have guard duty?" I wondered aloud, frowning as I realized again that I didn't know all that much about my mysterious air fae.

"Not anymore, sweetheart. That's just for the students," Arthus said softly.

"That seems unfair," I muttered.

Marlen shrugged. "It's how we earn our keep around here. The Academy isn't as well-funded as it once was. Not enough magic to keep the population up."

"Swear you'll stick with Arthus the whole day, B. I mean it. I don't like you going out without me," Leigh interjected, still fixated on tomorrow's shopping trip.

"I swear," Briallen said honestly, gripping his hand.

"Aderyn, are you coming with us?" I asked. She had been even quieter than usual tonight.

"I'm going to sit this one out, I hope that's okay," Aderyn responded shyly, and I felt a strange awkward embarrassment emanating from both her and Marlen. I frowned up at him, but his look clearly said *not now*, so I let it drop. I trusted that he'd talk to me when he was ready.

Briallen's rising excitement made it hard to focus on anything else after that. It buzzed over my skin like a swarm of bees. I smiled at her giddiness, I could think of worse ways to spend my day than shopping with Briallen and Arthus. Besides, I'd been meaning to learn more about Avalon, and this was the perfect opportunity.

The journey to Inver was beautiful. I hadn't been in a carriage since that first night I arrived in Avalon, so I was glad I had another opportunity to see the realm from the ground. The view was mostly trees and a couple of rolling meadows again, but I still hadn't gotten used to the majestic beauty of Avalon, or the sense of peace it provided me.

The Academy grounds must be seriously isolated, because we traveled for a long time before I sensed other souls around us. As we approached Inver, the forest became sparser, and cottages were interspersed increasingly closer together. We crossed an arched stone bridge over a little river to get to the town, then exited the carriage where it would wait for us outside the gates.

The town was walled the whole way around, with an arched entryway that held a large metal grate that could be dropped to keep the citizens in. Or the intruders out. Whatever. We passed through on foot, and I was immediately struck by how different Inver was from the Academy. There were no dirt paths or treehouses here—Inver was all cobbled streets lined by tall, interconnected stone buildings. It looked like the ground floor of each building was a shop or workspace, with housing above them.

I looked around in awe, but keenly felt the loss of the grass beneath my feet. There was an uncomfortable tightness in my veins that made me think my discomfort wasn't emotional, but magical. My *magic* didn't like being away from nature.

"Inver is a market town for the entire realm, not just fae," Arthus said, taking pity on my confused face. "More and more fae live within the city walls now though. Without an affinity element, the need isn't as pressing to live amongst nature. Goblins don't care about being close to nature, and they make up most of the population here."

As we followed the winding path into the town, the streets became more crowded, and stalls littered the pavement. It became apparent pretty quickly that there were more species than just fae here. Toward the hub of the market, the goblins definitely outnumbered everyone else.

A vain part of me was grateful I was a fae, not a goblin. Aesthetically, they were... not great to look at. Their noses were more like a short elephant trunk that hung down over their blubbery, downturned mouths. All of them had shifty, beady eyes that glittered black, contrasting with their pale leathery skin. Goblins kind of reminded me of blobfish, if blobfish had spindly arms and legs.

A hard elbow to the ribs from Briallen made me realize I was staring. I wasn't exactly being subtle either, and the goblins were a good couple of feet shorter than me, so my perusal had been pretty obvious. Cringing at myself, I forced my eyes upwards, focusing on the stalls instead.

Some rows had more permanent-looking stalls, with canvas coverings and makeshift wooden displays for the wares, while others looked like they'd just parked up their cart of goods for the day wherever they could find a spot.

One of the carts was manned by two centaurs. They were beautiful and majestic—basically the polar opposite of the goblins—with the head, torso, and arms of a human, while their lower half was the body of a horse.

The female centaur had smooth, dark skin that seamlessly blended into a rich ebony horse coat. Her long black hair was as straight and silky as her tail, both swished elegantly as she moved. She wore a brown leathery-looking bikini top to preserve her modesty, but nothing else, and her face was the most beautiful I'd ever seen, with high, angular cheekbones and dark almond-shaped eyes. Her male companion was just as stunning, with pale skin and thick chestnut hair that matched his coat.

I had about a million questions on the tip of my tongue, but Arthus silenced me with a wary, knowing look.

"Some visitors to Inver have more sensitive hearing than we do. Best save the questions for later," he whispered, leaning in close, and I nodded to let him know I'd heard him.

Briallen didn't have time for my questions, anyway. She powered through the crowd, parting it with ease until we came to a dressmaker's shop, marked by a wooden sign with an engraving of a needle and thread hanging above the window. Briallen tugged me through the door, and I snagged Arthus' hand to make sure I didn't lose him. I felt a brief flash of his surprise, probably because I never initiated physical contact with Arthus.

There were racks on racks of dresses all throughout the store, and Briallen explained that we could choose the design we wanted, and the tailor would make them to our sizes and send them to us on campus. It felt indulgent to spend my stipend on clothes when I probably had enough Academy-issued things to go on, but I also really wanted a few things for myself. The meager supplies I'd brought with me from Albion were basically a disintegrated mess now—as Bryn warned me they would be—and I needed a dress for the masque. My Academy wardrobe definitely had not come with a gown.

I drifted over to the wall of evening dresses and felt Arthus step up close behind me, inches from my back.

"You know, Marlen and I talked about it this morning and we both like you in red," he mused in his deep, sexy voice, breath hot on my ear. Arthus' gently circled my wrist and lifted my hand, guiding it until my fingers brushed over a beautiful, deep red ball gown.

It was made of linen, like all of my other clothes, but it looked and felt infinitely more luxurious than anything else I owned. I didn't have a great view of it on the rack, but the bodice looked quite skimpy while the skirt was made up of asymmetrical layers that gave it a full, fluffy effect. It was very striking.

"I'll try it on," I promised, my voice breathy. Gods, all Arthus had done was touch my *wrist*, and I was a hot, panting mess. He'd better stop with this you're-not-ready-Fi bullshit soon, I was losing my mind.

In the end, I bought the red gown and an emerald linen long sleeve top and maxi skirt combo that seemed to be a popular winter fashion trend. We stopped at some roadside stalls, and I picked up a plum-colored woolen beanie with matching gloves, and an enormous scarf that could have doubled as a blanket in a plaid-type pattern, donning all three straight away because I definitely was not warm enough in my wrap dress and cardigan.

On our way back toward the city gates, something must have caught Arthus' eye as he directed Briallen and me to stand with our backs to the wall so he could keep an eye on us at all times while he went to talk to a stallholder.

"Briallen?" I asked, and she hummed in response, distracted by admiring the silver leaf brooch she'd just purchased.

"My feet are freaking *freezing*."

"What?" She looked up in surprise.

"My feet! Why don't fae wear shoes? It's winter," I said, trying and failing to keep the whine out of my voice. Briallen burst out laughing.

"We use the connection to nature to support our magic. You can get by without it, but it always feels... odd. You're not feeling that now? Being in the town?" she asked curiously.

"I mean, I guess so. I just... Do you all just get used to having cold feet all the time? It's seriously uncomfortable," I replied, already feeling resigned to a life of frigid toes.

"I suppose we're just used to it. I have leather riding boots I use sometimes in winter if I'm flying and it's freezing out, or if I'm visiting somewhere snowy. It doesn't feel right though, so I don't use them much. Did you want to get some while we're here?"

I sighed, not wanting to be the odd-fae-out on campus by wearing shoes. "No, it's fine. I'll guess I'll just have to toughen up."

Arthus returned then, one hand behind his back and the slightest hint of nervous energy rolling off him, skittering down my spine.

"I have something for you," he said slowly, and Briallen politely took an interest in a nearby fruit stall to give us an illusion of privacy.

"You didn't have to get me anything," I told him sincerely, even as my excitement bubbled up, threatening to overflow. No one had ever gotten me anything before. I'd been given donated presents each Christmas, but they were always purchased by an anonymous stranger for a Girl, Aged X, not for me in particular.

"I wanted to," Arthus responded honestly as he held out his hand to show me the gift he'd chosen just for me.

It was a deep green swirling stone that had been cut into a rough triangular shape with polished edges. Threaded through the top of the stone was a long silver chain. *Silver like Arthus' eyes. Deep swirling green like Marlen's eyes...*

"Green and silver, to represent each of your suitors," Arthus confirmed my unspoken theory, and I felt myself tearing up a little.

He lifted the chain over my head as I undid my scarf and pulled my curls out of the way so he could put it on me. The chain was long, letting the stone sit in my cleavage, and I sort of loved that I could hide it. It was too personal to share with the world.

"I love it, thank you," I whispered, gently stroking Arthus' face, never sure how he'd receive my touch. Arthus' relief spilled through me, and he leaned into my hand for the briefest second. My heart melted that he would let me touch him like this—I doubted many people had gotten the privilege.

I wrapped myself up in my scarf again, then we grabbed Briallen and headed back through the crowd to the city walls. Arthus walked close enough to me that our hands brushed together—from him that was a huge amount of physical contact in public. We sat close to each other the whole carriage ride back to the Academy as Briallen listed all the other market towns within a few hours' flight or ride that we had to visit.

For a moment, I felt like the normal young human woman I'd always wanted to be, hanging out with her boyfriend and best friend after a day of shopping. But the moment passed, and I was glad for it. I was fae. I had two boyfriends—suitors—whatever. I had multiple friends. My life was so much richer than what I could have ever dreamed for myself back in Albion.

I leaned slightly more into Arthus and smiled like a goofball as I listened to Briallen making plans for us. Blasting Kayden out of a window had been the best thing I'd ever done.

✕✕

As I undressed that night to pull on my pajamas, Marlen's hand shot out and he gently grabbed the pendant around my neck. I was startled, not sure how he'd feel about me wearing a gift from Arthus even though Arthus had considered Marlen when he chose it.

"Um, Arthus got it for me. It has silver for him and green for you, see?" I said awkwardly, pointing them out like he couldn't clearly see the only two colors of the pendant for himself.

I didn't sense any jealousy from Marlen, but his insecurity crawled over my skin and his sadness constricted my throat.

"Marlen?" I asked cautiously. "Does it bother you that Arthus got this for me?"

"Not at all, foxglove," Marlen replied instantly, shaking his head. "I'm just a little upset that I can't do things like that for you. You deserve beautiful things like this," he added sadly.

"Do you really think I care about things like that? I grew up with nothing," I chastised. I gripped his chin, forcing him to look at me. "It was really lovely of Arthus to get this for me, but I don't expect gifts from either of you. I haven't got you anything."

Some of Marlen's insecurity eased. "Aderyn didn't come shopping with you because we both send most of our stipends home to our parents," he admitted. "Our family is one of the poorer families at the Academy, so the coin really helps them…"

"You need to stop feeling bad right this instant, Marlen Ferris," I commanded. "That is incredibly sweet and generous of the two of you to do that for your family. I wouldn't care if you were from the poorest family in all of Avalon, your riches are soul-deep."

I startled as an emotion I'd never felt before wrapped around my heart, spreading like fireworks to every nerve in my body. It felt warm, tingly, fluttery, light but heavy at the same time. It wasn't like the usual affection Marlen felt for me. This was something… *more*.

It was probably something I should unpack… later. I wasn't ready to analyze this sensation or what it meant for us just yet.

Marlen leaned forward to capture my lips in a deep, intoxicating kiss. I felt his hand move toward his belt and hoped this kiss was leading to even more fun places, but he pulled away and I realized he'd been reaching for the dagger he kept in a scabbard that hung from his belt. I watched with fascination and a small degree of apprehension as Marlen sliced the pad of his index finger and squeezed until blood welled up.

"Um, Marlen? What are you doing?"

He grinned, pinching the stone of my necklace in one hand, and bringing his bloody finger up to it with his other. The blood didn't smear over the stone like I expected it to—it seemed to absorb straight into it like the stone was sucking the liquid off his skin. The pendant briefly glowed a bluish hue before returning to its rich, swirly green tones. It felt different afterwards though... It felt like Marlen.

"What did you do?" I breathed.

"I don't think it was a coincidence that of all the green crystals Arthus could have chosen, he picked malachite. It's the best crystal to absorb healing magic. Now you have some healing magic, enough to heal a minor injury or tide you over if it was something more serious. If you use it up, I can give you some more. You'll always have some of my healing gift with you now, foxglove," Marlen said, his pride evident in his voice.

I pulled his head down into the crook of my shoulder and hugged his head tightly as his arms wrapped around my waist. I didn't think it was a coincidence that Arthus had chosen that either, and I made a mental note to figure out how best to show him my gratitude. If it involved him tying me down and having his way with me, so much the better.

We had another day off from classes and I was eager to get away from campus for a few hours. I felt like I saw Saffir's smug smile everywhere I went, and it was doing terrible things to my blood pressure. I wasn't even sure if she *was* smug, or if I was projecting. She'd never actually spoken to me and I was always too enraged when she was around to separate my emotions from hers.

When Marlen had suggested a walk to the field where the vast Avalon Fair would be held in a few days, I'd jumped at it. Apparently, there would be all kinds of inhabitants from every corner of the realm in attendance, and watching them set up was a great chance to people watch. Fae watch? Creature watch? Whatever.

Arthus had volunteered to accompany us, and walking through the forest with my two suitors felt surreal. Marlen had my hand tucked in the crook of his arm, guiding me around logs and rocks, while Arthus walked close by and told me all about the unique birds and plants only found in Avalon. He was still physically keeping his distance in public, but the fact that he was here, just hanging out with us, felt like a huge step forward.

We paused to look at a for-sure-magical orange bird perched on a branch above us—it was as big as a turkey, but flitted from branch to branch as if it were no bigger than a sparrow. Maybe my human science knowledge wasn't so helpful here, because that bird for *sure* defied the laws on physics.

I was about to ask Arthus, but a powerful blast of air magic hit from out of nowhere, forcing all three of us apart. I landed heavily on all fours, gasping in surprise, scrambling to get up and see where it had come from.

"Fi!" Marlen yelled, sounding panicked. I opened my mouth to reassure him that I was fine, but before I could I was being dragged upright, my hands quickly bound behind me.

I opened my mouth to shout, but the air vanished from my lungs and I choked at the lack of oxygen, before suddenly it was back and I was sucking down air like I'd never get enough of it.

Well, that was a neat and terrifying trick. Not sure I'd be asking Master Drysi about that one.

I saw the griffin in front of me for a split second before I was all but thrown on its back, one bulky body in front of me and another behind, keeping me in place as the griffin took off on foot, leaping into the sky as Marlen and Arthus yelled behind us.

My heart dropped to my feet from my position, lying sideways over the griffin's back, half dangling off the side. I was staring down at the ground as it grew further and further away, and I would *absolutely* die if the captor situated behind me let go of his grip on my bound wrists.

I tried to calm myself down enough to get a read on their emotions and was startled to find both of them feeling determined and perhaps a little protective? Of what, me? Now that I was focusing on it, I realized the man holding onto me was being careful not to hurt me. However, his emotions held a touch of resentment that the man in front of me didn't have.

It... wasn't how I expected kidnappers to feel.

A tugging in my chest pulled my gaze below us, where Arthus had lost his shirt and was gaining on the griffin, his glorious fae wings on display. They looked like enormous butterfly wings, spanning a couple of feet either side of him, reaching to his knees and above his head. The edges of his wings and the veining down the middle were an inky black, but the center was the same brilliant mixture of steely gray and silver as his eyes.

I was still panicking, but I was no longer afraid. Not really. Not when even from this vantage point, I could see the look in Arthus' eyes that promised he would never give up.

And then promised retribution.

ARTHUS

CHAPTER 25

Faster. I had to move *faster.*

My wings beat furiously behind me, the muscles in my back aching with exertion. It had been idiotic to not stretch my wings more often, to not *use* the gift the gods had given me. Now when it mattered, when Fi needed me, I was worried they were going to fail at any moment and drop me out of the sky.

I wouldn't even catch myself with my magic. I had a gust ready to go, trained on the airspace underneath Fi since the males who'd snatched her had unceremoniously slung her sideways over the griffin, and only their grip was keeping her in place.

My chest tightened at her precarious position. Fi had a deep well of her own magic to draw from, but she was inexperienced, and her hands were bound behind her. I wasn't sure she would be able to catch herself if the worst happened and she fell.

Hurry the fuck up, Marlen. We need backup from the Academy.

I only hoped that wherever they were taking her, it wasn't so far that Marlen wouldn't be able to find us when he brought help.

The griffin faltered slightly and I sucked in a terrified breath, forcing my wings to move faster. Three adult fae bodies was a lot of weight for one griffin to carry, and it wasn't showing any sign of descending soon. Where the hell were they going?

I dodged the blast of air that one of Fi's captors sent at me, but they were too far away to do any real damage, and their magic was no match for mine anyway. Still, I couldn't risk retaliating while Fi was in such a precarious position.

The male tried again as the griffin began its descent, and I realized they were trying to lose me before they reached their final location. A field of wildflowers spread out, centered around a pond that glittered an unnaturally bright shade of silvery blue.

The portal! They were taking her to the portal.

Fuck.

FFION

CHAPTER 26

It felt like we'd been in the air for hours, but I doubted the griffin could have carried three adult fae for that long. Only when we landed with a thump that made my whole body fly into the air for a moment did I realize I'd been here before. This was the meadow where Bryn and I had arrived via the portal. Were they going to take me back through it? Were these men responsible for hiding me in Albion in the first place?

I twisted and strained my neck, trying to search the skies for Arthus, but with my wrists bound, I was too off-balance to look up.

Should I scream? Fight? I felt uncomfortably vulnerable in this position, and I didn't want to risk the griffin bucking me off onto the ground.

Surprisingly, my captors were gentle as they carefully helped off the griffin right next to the pond where the portal to Albion was. My wrists were still tied, and someone's air magic swirled at my ankles, keeping my feet suctioned to one spot on the ground. They clearly didn't trust me not to run, which was a smart call, even if their gentleness had taken me off-guard.

The griffin hung back, and both men stayed close to me, crowding into my space, but they didn't seem to be threatening me. I'd never been kidnapped before, but I assumed the captors would have ill intentions. These two were feeling a confusing combination of relief, sadness, resolve, and yearning.

"I'm Galvyn Laisren," said the man who had been in front of me, directing the griffin. Both men had fairer skin than me, but Galvyn had distinctive amber eyes with gold flecks that looked a lot like the glimpses of mine I'd seen... "You once called me Father."

Well, okay. Family reunion it is.

"This is Attie Laisren. You used to call him Papa." Attie, who had been carefully holding on to me throughout the flight, tipped his chin to me in greeting. He gazed at my face, and I felt so much sadness bursting from him I felt like I was drowning in it.

"Ah, okay. I'm Ffion?"

I didn't mean for it to come out as a question, but the realization that perhaps 'Ffion' was not the name I was born with hit me mid-sentence. It was written on my arm when I was found outside the orphanage, but I didn't know who wrote it.

"We know lass, we named you. Ffion Laisren." A hint of Galvyn's amusement tickled behind my ears, though his face gave nothing away. This guy would give Bryn a run for his money in the blank expression department.

"Your mother wrote your name on your arm when she transported you to Albion." There was no amusement from Attie, just a tinge of bitter resentment on top of his despair.

For the second time today, I was hit with a large gust of air magic. Galvyn and Attie went flying in opposite directions, landing sprawled out along the grass. I stumbled as the magic that had been pinning my ankles suddenly released me, but powerful arms instantly circled my waist, keeping me upright and pulling me into a hard chest.

I inhaled Arthus' fresh, icy scent as if I were taking my last breaths. Galvyn and Attie didn't seem like they were planning on hurting me, but they definitely felt determined to get me out of here and I wasn't ready to leave, not ever. Arthus' wings curved around us in a protective embrace, the tips of them trailing lightly over the fabric of my shirt, making me shiver. He immediately reached his arms around me to untie the binds on my wrists, throwing them to the ground in disgust.

"Can't say I think much of your choice of suitor, daughter," Galvyn grumbled, brushing debris off his clothes as he stood. "I would have never been so disrespectful when I met your grandfather."

Fortunately, Arthus had the presence of mind to respond because I was totally speechless at his casual use of the word 'daughter' and the mention of a grandfather I didn't know I had.

"Yes, well, I imagine you didn't meet him right after he'd kidnapped your girl," Arthus drawled, unperturbed.

His bored tone didn't reflect the white-hot fury he was experiencing. It was coursing through my veins and making it hard for me to look at the situation objectively. I rubbed my temples and tried to clear my head. Gods, all I wanted was a walk off-campus with my two suitors. This entire afternoon had really gone to shit.

My dads—*what the actual hell*—made their way back to each other's side, standing with arms crossed and identical scowls on their faces. They didn't seem like they were going to attack, though my mind was so clouded by Arthus' rage that it was hard to tell.

"Give me a minute," I said to them, holding a finger up with more confidence than I felt. I turned in Arthus' arms, acutely aware that this was our first cuddle, and it was happening in front of my two pissed off fathers, right after they'd kidnapped me.

"Arthus," I cooed in my most soothing voice, standing on tiptoes so I could speak into his ear and balancing my hands against his chest. The small amount of contact seemed to break him out of the haze of anger he was in, at least a little. He looked away from my fathers down to my face, scanning for any sign of injury. "I'm okay, and I want to hear what they have to say. I *need* to hear it. Please, Arthus, calm down for me. I can't focus when you're this angry."

His demeanor immediately changed, his shame prickling down my spine. I knew it bothered Arthus when he lost control; he had been so upset with himself when he stormed out of my cabin a few days ago. Now that his rage had cleared, I took a deep breath and leaned forward to give him a quick, reassuring peck on the lips. I never wanted him to feel ashamed of his emotions.

"Thank you," I murmured against his lips, turning in his arms to face my dads again.

My plural dads.

Logically, I had assumed that my birth family would look like this once I learned about the whole mating circle concept, but actually *seeing* two dads standing in front me was still confronting.

"Attie, Galvyn, this is Arthus, one of my suitors. Arthus, these are my fathers, apparently. Attie and Galvyn Laisren. I'm hoping they were just about to tell me why they've brought me to the portal," I said warily.

"To return you to Albion, of course," Galvyn scoffed.

"Fi isn't going anywhere," Arthus growled, the rumbling from his chest traveling through my back where I was still held tight against him. The distinct tug of two more mating pulls drawing closer

"Would you prefer her dead in Avalon or alive in Albion?" Attie snapped.

"I've spent 17 years watching over her in Albion, glamouring her, keeping her safe. She was never supposed to come back here," Galvyn gritted out, glaring at Arthus.

She was standing right here, feeling increasingly irritated. *Men.*

"Ah, so it was you then," Bryn said, strolling out from a copse of trees at the edge of the meadow next to an uncharacteristically pissed off Marlen. *How the hell had they gotten here?* "You're the illusionist. That's how she had such a strong glamour, and why I couldn't track the magic from her wardrobe."

My heart dropped at the now obvious realization that Bryn had nothing to do with those messages, guilt churning uncomfortably in my gut.

"How were you getting on campus?" Marlen asked conversationally, his body language tense. It was a strange feeling—Marlen's fear chilling the blood in my veins while Bryn's anger cut through it like lava. It didn't feel as painful as it should've, though.

They were trying to keep their emotions in check for me.

Bryn and Marlen circled around us so they were standing on either side of me, and it was quite the show of unity considering the four of us had never spent any time together.

"*Three* suitors, daughter?" Galvyn asked, raising a judgmental eyebrow at me.

I registered Bryn and Marlen's surprise at that last word, they must not have overheard that revelation.

"Two," I rasped awkwardly. Bryn's irritation chafed uncomfortably against my skin, but what was he expecting me to say? He was literally courting someone else.

There was a beat of silence, and I could have sworn Bryn muttered "*for now*" under his breath.

"How were you getting on campus?" Marlen asked again, irritation seeping into his tone.

"We weren't. Your roommate passed the messages on for us," Attie replied, cutting Marlen an annoyed look.

"Kelvyn?" Marlen confirmed, surprise spiking in all three guys.

"Nothing personal. We know his parents, and knew he was at the Academy. He did it for the coin," Galvyn said with a shrug.

It all made total sense now, in hindsight. The messages on the wardrobe and the grass had both been burned in, and Kelvyn had a fire affinity. He'd be able to track my whereabouts easily by following Marlen, and he'd been creepy as all get out when we met, assessing me like I was a project. Or a job. Which I guess is all I was to him.

"You gave him a cloaking amulet," Bryn guessed.

"I have an illusion gift," Galvyn confirmed. "Though not a powerful one. I mated with your mother for love, not for magic. My abilities never grew because her magic wasn't strong enough to balance them."

My mother? Parents who loved each other? I blinked back the tears that burned behind my eyes. This was really not the time for me to lose it. As if they could sense my distress, Marlen and Bryn moved in closer at my sides and Arthus' arms tightened around my waist. I drew strength from their support, allowing myself a moment to indulge in the comfort they were offering me.

"Is she here...?" I asked hesitantly, dreading the answer when Galvyn and Attie's combined heartbreak clawed agonizingly at my chest.

"Your mother, Rhedyn, took you to Albion to keep you safe. She wanted to keep you away from Avalon and those who would capture you for your abilities. Those same fae killed her for hiding you. You can't be here, Ffion. We're taking you back."

The Unwanted Challenge

"LIFE SHRINKS OR EXPANDS IN
PROPORTION TO ONE'S COURAGE."
- ANAIS NIN

ARTHUS

CHAPTER 27

"I'm not going back to Albion," Fi announced in a surprisingly steady voice, considering how she was trembling in my arms. Marlen and Bryn flanked us on either side as we faced off against Fi's fathers, Galvyn and Attie.

Fathers and kidnappers. *Who didn't dream of reuniting with their long-lost parents after seventeen years by way of abduction?* I thought drily.

"This is my home now. Besides, I couldn't leave the guys behind..." Fi continued, trailing off awkwardly. Probably because of Bryn's presence next to her. He wasn't one of "the guys", not really.

I was squeezing Fi so tightly I was surprised she hadn't complained. She tucked one arm into the crook of Marlen's elbow and she pulled him close so that we were a little unit of three, huddled together.

Bryn shot us a brief scowl before refocusing his attention on Fi's dads. I wasn't even sure how he had ended up at the portal with us. I assumed Marlen had grabbed him and used his tracking magic to find Fi, so I supposed I couldn't really complain about Bryn's presence.

"They won't be able to protect you, daughter," Galvyn said softly.

He'd been an obnoxious prick to us, but he clearly adored Fi. I imagined that was making things harder on her, rather than easier.

"You think we would have sent you away if there'd been any other option?" Attie added bitterly. "The gods cursed you with this gift and as your parents, we have done everything within our power to keep you safe all these years. Or was your mother's sacrifice for nothing?"

I knew going into this that courting Fi would involve being a combination of lover and bodyguard, but I hadn't expected to fend off attacks from her own family, well-intentioned as they may have been.

Fi's spine straightened, her muscles no longer trembling though still taut with tension. I was glad to see some of her fire returning. Meeting her dads and finding out about her mother had to be overwhelming, but Fi would never let anyone else dictate her path. Especially not the family that had left her behind.

"Thank you for all you've done for me, and I'm sorry that you've suffered," she began stiffly. "That being said, I'm no longer a child and the responsibility of protecting myself falls to *me* now. You'll have to excuse me if I don't eagerly rush to follow your orders. The only threats I've had to endure since I moved here came from *you*."

Both Galvyn and Attie reeled back as if she'd hit them, somehow surprised that Fi was upset that they had tried to frighten her into going back to Albion. I forced myself to take another deep, calming breath before I let my anger get the better of me again. I didn't want to pain Fi with my rage again. Besides, at this rate I would never get my wings to retract.

"Don't be foolish, you need—" Attie snapped, but Bryn's warning growl cut him off. Flames licked at one hand, swirling around his wrist like they were just itching to get to the target of his anger.

"Bryn," Fi said softly, grabbing his non-flaming hand in hers and giving it a squeeze. The shock of her touch seemed to shake him out of the depths of his rage. "They're still my fathers."

He scowled, but extinguished the flames nonetheless.

"I know what I need, but thank you for your concern," Fi said firmly, turning her attention back to her fathers. I'd never heard her sweet, soft voice filled with so much conviction. To their credit, they didn't argue with her. They both gave her long, assessing looks, arms crossed and clearly displeased.

"Don't trust anyone you're not mated to, and avoid the Council. Whatever happens now is on you, kid," Attie said despondently.

From where I was standing behind her, I could see Fi's eyelashes batting furiously, probably blinking away tears. She was independent and full of fire, but she must have imagined what her birth family was like at least once or twice in her life, and I doubt these two grumpy assholes were what she expected.

"I'd like to leave now," Fi demanded softly, so only the three of us could hear her.

"Are you sure, foxglove?" Marlen whispered, sounding as surprised as I felt. Yes, they had kidnapped her, but I still thought she'd be interested in learning a bit more about the family she'd been separated from her entire life.

"Yes." Fi's tone brooked no room for argument.

Before she'd even answered, Bryn was moving toward the copse of trees they'd entered through, presumably where they'd left the griffins they flew here on. Fi moved to follow him, and I quickly tucked her under my arm, covering her back with one of my wings. She gave her dads one last lingering look over her shoulder before moving toward the trees, walking in silence until the woods hid us from their view.

Bryn was already leading the griffins towards a small clearing where they could take off from, his entire demeanor stiff with tension.

"You okay, foxglove?" Marlen asked sympathetically, his fingers intertwining with hers.

I admired the easy touch between the two of them. I'd spent my life keeping people at arm's length in case they tried to take my wings, so it was difficult for me to be physically affectionate with Fi. This whole incident with her dads was the most physical contact we'd ever had.

"She's pissed off," Bryn grunted from up ahead of us.

"I am," Fi agreed, shooting Bryn an annoyed glance from under her lashes. "Did they really think that was the right approach to helping me?

Send anonymous threatening messages for months, then kidnap me? What kind of alpha male bullshit is that?"

She rolled her eyes, huffing irritably.

"Don't lump us all together, Fi. The three of us all agree it was idiotic," I murmured into her hair, relishing the feel of holding her safe in my arms.

"Come on, we need to get back to the Academy before Gwyneira sends out a search party," Bryn announced, both griffins ready and waiting for us.

I sighed, my wings ruffling in irritation. "I'm going to fly back next to you. I need to burn off some of this anger or my wings won't retract."

Even that admission of weakness was difficult, but there was no judgment in Fi's eyes.

"Okay," Fi gave me a sad smile and reached tentatively up to cup my cheek. "Thank you for coming for me," she added in a whisper meant just for my ears.

"Don't thank me for that, sweetheart. I'll always follow you," I turned my head so I could kiss the palm of her hand, then stepped back so she could climb on the griffin.

"Foxglove?" Marlen called with uncertainty, looking a little sheepish.

"What is it?" she immediately moved to comfort him, but he gave her a reassuring smile.

"Would you be okay flying with Bryn? You know I'm not used to flying two-person, and I'm barely able to focus on keeping myself safe in the air right now. Bryn is one of the most experienced fliers in the Academy."

Marlen was clearly apologetic at asking her to fly with Bryn, but there was a hopeful glint in his eye that I'm sure was reflected in mine as well. Although Bryn was keeping up his ridiculous pretense of courting someone else, he and Fi were perhaps the best suited out of all of us. Unfortunately, it meant they were both as stubborn as each other as well. Whenever they got past their issues and finally came together, it would be explosive.

"Oh," Fi replied awkwardly, glancing at Bryn's stoic face. She paused for a moment, but whatever emotions she sensed from him must have been enough to convince her that she'd be okay. Or that *he'd* be okay. I wasn't sure who we needed to be most worried about.

Fi approached the griffin that Bryn was standing next to and with no preamble, he grabbed her around the waist and hoisted her up onto the beast. The physical contact from Bryn seemed to have alarmed her more than mounting the griffin.

Marlen climbed onto his griffin more carefully, and I followed as the two creatures took off into the skies. I had a brief moment of envy at the power of their wings—my muscles were burning from the flight over here, but my wings grew tauter at the idea of retracting them. They responded defensively to threats and my high emotions, and until I had myself back under control, I wouldn't be able to draw them in.

I kept a close eye on Fi as we flew, noting that Bryn's arms were wrapped tightly around her waist, and she was leaning back slightly into his embrace. It was probably because Fi wasn't used to griffin flight—and was perhaps a little traumatized by the one she'd taken here—but she also wouldn't have pressed her vulnerable back against just anyone.

There was something there, even if they weren't willing to admit it. I was surprised at myself that I didn't feel jealous—just glad that Fi was safe and comfortable.

I doubted Saffir Castell would feel as charitable if she saw the two of them right now. The sooner Bryn dropped his pointless charade of a relationship with her, the better off we'd all be.

The griffins landed next to the stables at the Academy and I followed not far behind with a lot less grace than usual, every muscle in my back burning. The flight had done its job though—I was finally calm enough to retract my wings.

My shirt hung off me in tatters where my wings had burst out before I had a chance to remove it.

I was contemplating how wise it was to walk through the Academy shirtless when Marlen sidled up next to me. "Let me heal your back muscles," he said quietly. "I know they're bothering you."

I grunted in agreement, uncomfortable with the idea of anyone touching me. I had to have a good relationship with Marlen, though, if I wanted me and Fi to work. Reluctantly, I held up my forearm, and Marlen gave me an approving smile as he rested his palm on my skin, letting warm healing magic flood my body, easing all my aches and pains.

He was a convenient fae to have around.

Gwyneira and two of her mates, Derwyn and Cadfan, burst into the clearing as Marlen pulled his hand away, making all of us tense.

"Ffion? Are you okay? Are you hurt?" she asked breathlessly, gripping Fi's shoulders tightly and examining her for any signs of injury. "My magic alerted me that you were in danger."

Of course, Gwyneira's guardian magic would have picked up on Fi's distress. No wonder Bryn was eager to get Fi back to the Academy—his tracking ability meant he worked closely with Gwyneira to find students in need of assistance to attend the Academy. He'd been the one to go to Albion and retrieve Fi in the first place.

"I'm fine," Fi assured Gwyneira, though her smile was small and shaky. My wings itched to come back out, to defend her from anything that would upset her, even threats that had already passed. "Can we talk somewhere?" Fi asked uneasily, glancing around the open clearing.

"Of course, let us return to my cabin." Gwyneira leveled us all with a sweeping gaze before turning and striding purposefully through the forest.

Fi moved immediately toward Marlen, gripping his hand tightly before giving me a questioning look. I nodded once and took off after Gwyneira. The three of us really did work together seamlessly. Marlen offered Fi warmth and comfort, while I could take the lead when she was unsure. In the background, Bryn cursed softly before crashing along the path behind us.

We made our way to Gwyneira's cabin in silence, each lost in our own thoughts, and for the first time, I felt an almost desperate urge to claim Fi as my mate. Even when I'd wanted a partner, I'd never particularly craved the mating *bond* before, but right now I'd do just about anything for the peek into Fi's psyche that the bond would give me.

Gods, I thought my family was dysfunctional. They had nothing on the Laisrens.

We all piled into Gwyneira's sitting room, Marlen and I flanking Fi on the small sofa with Gwyneira and Bryn taking the armchairs opposite. Derwyn disappeared into the kitchen, and I heard the familiar clang of a kettle on cast-iron. Cadfan stood like a sentinel at the door, watching over his mate.

"Ffion? What happened, dear?" Gwyneira asked, eyes soft with genuine concern, which surprised me.

Gwyneira was a compassionate fae and dean, but usually distant and reserved with her students. The other guys must have been thinking the same thing, judging by their expressions.

"Well, I met my dads," Fi answered cautiously. "They, uh, kidnapped me... They wanted me to go back to Albion, they don't think it's safe for me here."

Gwyneira pursed her lips. "They think Albion is safer for you than Avalon?"

"They hid me there in the first place. My mother died getting me there," Fi choked out, and Marlen immediately wrapped an arm around her shoulders. "They told me to stay away from the Council. My fathers kept me safe there all these years..." she trailed off, looking a little overwhelmed before staring up at me beseechingly.

"One of Fi's fathers, Galvyn Laisren, has an illusionist gift. He was regularly traveling to Albion to reapply Fi's glamour without her knowledge. They were responsible for the messages that had been left for Fi here at the Academy. He supplied the student who was leaving them with a cloaking amulet." I laid out the details as factually as possible, keeping my emotions in check for Fi's sake.

I couldn't think about that prick Kelvyn right now or my wings would reappear, then I'd fly straight to his cabin and chuck him out of a window. His fire affinity wouldn't do him any good then.

Gwyneira's eyes flashed dangerously. "We will come back to that student in a moment. Ffion, how many messages were left for you in total?"

"Four," she told the floor, squirming uncomfortably in her seat like a naughty child. Four was news to me too. I glanced over her head at Marlen who gave me an apologetic look, not looking surprised in the least.

It was strangely comforting, knowing that. At least Fi had told *someone*, and Marlen had been around her a lot longer than I had.

"I should have told you about the notes," Fi said guiltily. "I'm not used to trusting other people."

Bryn's expression morphed from furious concern to ice cold resentment. He stood abruptly, glared at Fi and stormed out of the cabin. Gwyneira's raised eyebrows followed his journey.

"We fire fae are passionate about the safety of those we care about," she said lightly. Fi snorted quietly. "While I understand your concerns, Ffion, this was a security issue, and it is important that those are brought to my attention." Gwyneira's tone was firm, but her eyes were kind.

It was evident she had a soft spot for Fi, and it made me a little nervous. Perhaps it was my greedy nature when it came to Fi, but I didn't like the idea of anyone who didn't have a strong mating pull or at least a solid *friendship* with her being so invested in her life.

"I'm sorry," Fi mumbled, thoroughly chastised. "It won't happen again."

Gwyneira nodded, seemingly satisfied with Fi's apology. "I imagine the three of you have much to discuss. In the meantime, I will see what I can find out about the Laisren family without drawing any attention to you from the Council."

"I would appreciate that, thank you." Fi gave Gwyneira a watery smile and I could tell it was time to go. The unexpected appearance of her family in Fi's life had shaken her usually unflappable calm, and she needed some time to process it.

"Thank you, Master Gwyneira," I said, standing up, followed quickly by Fi and Marlen. "We'll be sure to inform you of any updates in the future."

Gwyneira nodded and the three of us made our way out to the forest path to return to campus. Fi needed Marlen and me right now.

FFION

CHAPTER 28

"Let's regroup at my cabin," Arthus announced. "Fewer ears around," he added.

"Good plan, but I have guard duty tonight," Marlen said, shooting me an apologetic glance. "I'd feel much better knowing you were staying with Arthus, foxglove. I've never been so scared in my life."

"If that's okay," I said hesitantly, looking at Arthus. It was probably an unnecessary confirmation since I could feel his satisfaction at that idea. It felt a bit intrusive just barging in and staying with him like that, but I doubted either of them would be comfortable with me staying on my own any time soon.

Honestly? *Same.* The idea of being alone at that moment was terrifying.

"I'd love to stay with you," I told Arthus shyly, tucking my arm into the crook of Marlen's elbow, cuddling closer into him. Now that I was out of imminent danger, Arthus had returned to his usual hands-off routine, but I didn't mind. I could feel how settled his emotions were compared to the sheer rage he had experienced back at the portal.

The physical contact had helped Arthus calm down, and I was glad I could do that for him. It seemed like such an insignificant gesture, considering how he'd taken off like a bat out of hell to follow me when he thought I was in danger.

We piled into Arthus' cabin, and he immediately got to work building the fire and brewing tea. Fae and their tea. One of my old foster mums drank about six cups of English Breakfast a day and I'd thought *she* had problems. Since arriving in Avalon, I probably had double that some days.

The size of Arthus' cabin caught my attention again—it was so much larger than mine. His was a circle cabin, designed for students with multiple mates. As it was slightly further away from the campus, he was safer here. It had a two-person couch and an armchair instead of the two armchairs my cabin had, a three-seater table and just one platform, accessible by ladder, with a generously-sized bed on it. I couldn't look at the bed without blushing, so I kept my eyes firmly at ground-level.

I curled up at one end of the couch, tucking my knees under my chin and wrapping my arms around them. It was a self-soothing mechanism, how I'd always sat at night in my foster homes when I needed a hug but didn't have anyone in my life to give me one.

Marlen immediately moved to my side, pulling my legs over his lap and running his hands up and down them. I really didn't want to cry, but it was such a comforting gesture and the reminder I needed to realize that I didn't have to get through bad days on my own anymore.

"Talk to us, foxglove," Marlen urged.

"I don't even know where to begin," I said with a sigh. "When I arrived in Avalon and found out what I was, I had no desire to track down my family. They left me on the side of the road like a sack of trash. Why would I want to get to know those people? Then, as I realized they probably had their reasons for ditching me in Albion, I was curious about what those reasons were, so I wanted to talk to them about it."

"And now that you've met them?" Arthus prompted.

"I suppose I'm a little disappointed," I said with a hollow laugh. "More than a little. I wasn't expecting some kind of joyous, tearful reunion, but kidnapping me, tying me up and trying to kick me back out of the realm were definitely *below* my expectations."

It was a kick in the teeth to the little girl inside of me who always hoped her parents would come back for her. They did come back, but they were assholes.

Sorry, inner child. We're probably not going to be having family game nights any time soon.

"Seeing my dads face-to-face... it made me feel a little resentful about all the things I've missed out on?" I continued, unable to hold the flow of words back now that I'd gotten started. "Especially when Galvyn said he mated with my mother for love, despite the fact she wasn't a strong match for his magic. They loved each other, but I spent my childhood completely unloved. It kind of blows."

"You've got a new family now, foxglove," Marlen said gently, leaning forward to brush his lips against my temple. "It doesn't make up for the years you spent on your own, and you have every right to be angry about how you grew up. Just don't let that anger consume you. Don't let it detract from the happiness ahead of you."

Arthus began pouring the tea and Marlen gently shifted my legs off him, standing up. I missed the warmth of his body immediately.

"I'm sorry, Fi. I need to get to my post for guard duty tonight. If I could get out of it..." he trailed off guiltily.

"I'm okay, don't feel guilty." I gave him a reassuring smile, leaning up to kiss him lightly, very much aware that Arthus was still in the room.

"Come back here when you're finished," Arthus instructed and Marlen gave him a quick nod before departing. *Huh.* Apparently I wasn't the only one susceptible to Arthus' bossiness.

Arthus took Marlen's spot next to me on the couch, bringing over two cups of sage tea—his personal favorite. I did my best to keep my features neutral. Sage tea was effing *gross.*

"Shall we talk about something else?" Arthus asked politely, and I suppressed a giggle. Comforting an upset woman was clearly not Arthus' strong suit. He was probably missing Marlen already.

"Can you tell me about your family?" I asked hesitantly. This thing between Arthus and I had moved at lightspeed, and while it felt incredibly right with no regrets on my part, I also realized I knew very little about him.

"Sure, sweetheart," Arthus said with a small smile, but I felt a wave of sadness. "I have one older brother, he lives near my parents near *Garrán Naofa*, the sacred grove. My parents all work at the main temple there. They're very... devout."

"That bothers you," I surmised, tucking my foot up under my knee and wriggling back into the couch cushions.

"My wings first appeared when I was three. My parents were thrilled that the gods had given me such a rare gift. As I got older and more aware of the danger my wings put me in, I became resentful of the gods for cursing me with them. My parents don't understand that. To them, any emotion towards the gods other than gratitude is sacrilege."

"They're not going to like me then," I muttered. Gratitude was the last thing I felt for the gods.

"I think they'll adore you. A rare gift, a strong pull between us... they'll take those as signs of a union blessed by the gods." His tone was light, but I could feel his bitterness.

"Have you told them about me?"

"I don't write many letters, for my own security. Nor should you," Arthus added, shooting me a warning look.

I snorted. "You don't need to worry about that, I don't have anyone I could write to. I might have been inclined to keep in touch with my dads, if they hadn't tried kidnapping me."

"You don't want to get to know them? They didn't make a great first impression, but your safety has clearly been a priority for them over all these years," he suggested, as if he hadn't been borderline feral with rage directed entirely at them just a couple of hours ago.

Did I want to get to know them? Not really. Or right *now*, at least. Their efforts at keeping me safe had dehumanized me in their eyes—I wasn't their daughter with a mind and goals of mine, I was a *thing* to them now. An object that required protection.

"Not any time soon," I said eventually. "Maybe one day, when they're ready to start seeing me as an individual rather than a job. *Maybe*."

Arthus reached along the back of the couch and ran his fingers through my hair, gently detangling my curls as he contemplated my words.

"Do you disagree...?" I asked tentatively after he'd been silent for a long while, his emotions swirling all over the place.

"Not at all, sweetheart," Arthus replied, surprised at my question. "If anything, I was thinking about applying your theory to my own parents. Giving us both space until they see me as an individual rather than a vessel for the gods."

I was the teensiest bit disappointed. I had wanted to meet them, and Marlen's parents too. Someday.

"We'll meet them first," Arthus reassured me, correctly identifying the source of my melancholy. I blushed at being caught out. It was objectively *way* too soon to be thinking about meeting the parents.

"Come on," Arthus said, standing and pulling me to my feet. "You need to eat."

"I don't want to go out. I might see the others, and I'm not ready to tell them about my disastrous family reunion quite yet," I groaned petulantly.

"It's late. The commons is nearly closed for the night, so I doubt there will be anyone there. We'll grab some food and come back here to eat it," Arthus replied firmly, all sexy bossiness. "Besides, you'll need your strength for later."

"Why?" I asked, instantly perking up. "What's later?"

"Your first sleepover with me," Arthus replied with a seductive smirk before striding out the door, leaving me scrambling to catch up.

If anything could improve my crappy day, it would be Arthus' many promises of 'soon' finally coming to fruition.

We sat at the three-person table in Arthus' cabin eating the small collection of scraps we'd managed to forage from the buffet table in the commons.

There wasn't a lot left at the end of the day, but we had been able to scrape together enough to make wraps followed by a dessert of watermelon slices.

"Shower, if you like. I'll find you something to sleep in," Arthus announced. He hadn't hinted at anything other than sleep since before we went to get dinner, but I had the feeling he liked keeping me hanging in suspense.

"Okay," I agreed. A shower sounded really nice, actually. Even if it was only lukewarm.

The soap in Arthus' shower was different from the Academy-issued one I used, he must have bought his own. It smelled like cucumber and melon— fresh and delicious like him. A primal part of me liked having the smell of him on my skin.

That cavewoman part of me did a little happy jig when I noticed Arthus had left me one of his own shirts to wear. It was creamy linen that laced up around the collar and fell midway down my thighs. I went commando underneath because I had zero desire to put on worn panties.

Arthus was already in bed, lying back against the pillows with his arms folded behind his head, staring up at the stars through the skylight. He didn't have a shirt on, and my mouth watered a little at the sight of his bronzed, muscular chest. Arthus wasn't bulky, his muscles were lean but cut, every ridge was defined. I wanted to trace them with my tongue.

He looked over as I ascended the ladder, his eyes filled with heat.

"I like seeing you in my shirt, sweetheart," Arthus said in a low, husky voice.

"I like wearing your shirt," I replied, aiming for playful but sounding breathy and more than a little desperate instead. Gods, one day I would be able to keep my cool around Arthus.

I climbed into the bed next to him, all too aware of how close he was, how good he smelled, how potent his lust for me was as it coursed through my system. Maybe I *should* have worn panties.

"I want to make you mine, Fi," Arthus murmured, leaning over to capture my chin between his thumb and forefinger, sucking gently on my lower lip. "But if you'd prefer to go straight to sleep, then tell me. I won't push you.

"I want to be yours," I whispered against his lips. I felt more than saw his smile, but it was a brief moment of playfulness before Arthus went into full sexy boss mode. And I obeyed every command.

"Lie back, hands above your head. Spread your legs. Don't. Move."

He unlaced the top of the shirt, pulling it apart enough for him to get a generous view of my cleavage, but he didn't pull it all the way down my arms. If I had fire magic, I'd have burned it off myself.

Arthus was the ultimate tease. He repeatedly pulled aside my shirt, stroking and licking my skin before moving the fabric back into place. Sometimes he'd follow his tongue with a soft gust of his air magic. I'd wanted a distraction after today, and it didn't get much more distracting than this. The whole thing was unhurried and maddening, I was going insane with want, but I didn't dare say anything in case he stopped.

Gods, I waited too long to risk ruining this now. I'd wanted Arthus from the moment I met him.

He planted soft kisses up my legs, and I expected him to stop and tease me some more, but instead, he pushed two fingers into my wet and aching pussy. The shock of the intrusion rode the perfect line of pleasure and pain that had me arching my back off the bed, gasping loudly.

"Oh dear," Arthus murmured as his magical fingers stilled. "Remember what I said when we started, sweetheart?"

"Don't move," I panted, forcing my limbs to still. "I swear I won't do it again. Gods, please don't stop."

He hummed, a low, seductive sound. "What to do?"

Arthus removed his fingers slowly and licked them thoroughly. It was sexy as hell, and I kind of wanted to cry. I needed to come so badly my brain was short-circuiting, heightening my emotional response.

Arthus flipped me over roughly, lifting my hips in the air as he situated himself behind me. I propped myself up on my forearms and looked back at him over my shoulder. I should've been embarrassed—I was seriously on display right now—but Arthus' face showed nothing but raw lust.

He let his hand slide down over the curve of my ass and down my outer thigh before dragging it back up between my legs, his thumb just brushing where I wanted him most. I bit down hard on my lip to focus on not squirming.

After a few more tantalizing strokes over my ass and thighs, Arthus' hand came down with a swift crack on my ass that had me gasping. He rubbed the spot where he'd just spanked me, soothing the sting, and the whole sensation sent delicious flutterings straight to my core.

So, it turns out I'm into spanking.

Alternating sides, he spanked me five more times, each time following up the slap with a gentle touch. My pussy clenched tightly around nothing, and I was on the verge of begging.

Did he want me to beg? I didn't hate the idea.

I was learning a lot about myself tonight.

"You liked that, didn't you, sweetheart? So pretty, seeing my handprints on you. If I touch you right now, will I find you soaking and aching for me?" Arthus asked casually.

"*Yes,*" I all but cried. "Please, *please*, I need you."

"Well, when you ask me so nicely," he chuckled. He wound one hand through my hair, wrapping it tightly around his fist while his other hand firmly rested in the center of my back, gently pushing me down into the mattress.

That's all the warning he gave me before thrusting his cock into me until our hips were flush. I let out a muffled scream into the bedding, my back arching against his hand at the sudden invasion. *Holy fucking fae.*

Arthus' hand moved from my lower back to my hip, his grip firm enough to leave bruises from his fingers. I kind of hoped there would be, Arthus seemed like he would get a kick out of making his mark on me, the same way I did when I marked Marlen.

I scrambled to hold onto the sheets while Arthus relentlessly fucked me into the mattress, entirely in control. Trusting him to lead, I basked in the sensation of letting go and giving myself and my pleasure completely over to him. I made noises I didn't even recognize, not a trace of self-consciousness in sight.

Arthus reached around me to stimulate my clit, and I went off like a rocket. Every inch of me was alive and tingling with sensation, my brain floating away from my blissed-out body until there was nothing but Arthus and me, the way our bodies connected.

He extended my orgasm without reprieve, constantly stimulating me and never letting up until my screams became hoarse whispers while he found his release, filling me, *marking* me.

"You're so tight, sweetheart, you're strangling me," he panted, hips stilling. "You feel so fucking perfect."

Arthus pulled out, and I collapsed onto my stomach with a satisfied groan, clamping my thighs together so I didn't make a mess on the sheets. Arthus snorted and lay down next to me, pulling me into his side. Despite the explosive sex we'd just shared, this felt a lot more intimate. I doubted Arthus usually hung around for post-coital snuggles.

He planted a kiss on my shoulder blade that made me feel all warm and fuzzy inside. "I'm going to get a washcloth, okay?"

I was half asleep by the time he returned to help me clean up and I passed out curled up into Arthus' side, safe and sated. When I woke up some time later, Marlen's arms were banded tightly around my waist and his face was buried in my hair.

Whatever unresolved feelings I had towards my fathers and what their revelations meant for my future could wait until tomorrow.

I wasn't going to let anything intrude on the perfection of this moment.

CHAPTER 29

After our failed attempt to walk through the Avalon Fair site a couple of days ago, I was surprised when Fi requested we try again, though I shouldn't have been. If Fi was anything, it was insatiably curious.

We both had early classes, which meant there was plenty of time for us to go in the afternoon. Unfortunately, it also meant Arthus couldn't join us as he had to work. He was adamantly against Fi going off campus without the two of us, but she must have worked some kind of voodoo sex magic on him that convinced him to cave.

I know Arthus thought he was in control when it came to Fi, but she called the shots with him as much as she did with me. Just in a more roundabout way.

Besides, her dads weren't about to pull the same stunt twice, right? Maybe I was giving them too much credit. Their decision to just grab her and try forcing her through the portal back to Albion was ludicrous. Still, I got a small amount of comfort knowing it had come from a place of genuine concern.

Fi was practically vibrating with excitement as we entered what would soon become the fairgrounds. The fair itself didn't start for a few days, but there were merchants from every corner of the realm here already, setting up their stalls and preparing their wares. I was getting motion sickness just watching Fi's eyes dart around to take everything in.

A large, emerald green dragon flew overhead and Fi's eyes went round, her jaw dropping as she tracked its progress through the sky. She was like a kid on Solstice Day. It was infectious—I felt like I was seeing everything with fresh eyes along with her.

"A dragon!" she squealed. "Marlen, did you see?"

Fi tugged at my arm to get my attention, in case I'd missed the 50-foot beast that had just flown over us. I grinned at her enthusiasm.

"Sort of hard to miss, foxglove. Did you see the color?" Fi nodded. "Earth dragon. Dragon magic is rooted in the elements the same way fae magic is. Blue dragon for water, a red dragon for fire, a silver dragon for air, and a green dragon for earth. Each flight has one of each element, plus the leader—the black dragon—who has control of all four elements."

"Wow," Fi said in awe, still scanning the sky for more dragons. "Is a flight of dragons a family? Are they all related?"

I laughed. "Not so much. You know they're shifters, right? Their dragons don't appear until they're of age, then the magic draws the flight together. Each consists of five males. Most probably don't know each other before their dragons surface."

"What about girl dragons?" Fi asked, puzzled.

"Much like the fae, dragons share," I said with a wink, enjoying her blush. "Once the males of the flight come together, they're called to their mate. Her dragon will be gold and smaller than the male dragons. They're quite secretive about their females, but from what we know, they don't have elemental magic. They look after the children, guard the hoard, and have some healing abilities. They're mostly nurturers."

Fi hummed under her breath, frowning slightly, and I chuckled.

"If you think Arthus is an alpha male, he's got nothing on dragon shifters. Their mate is lucky if she leaves the den," I told her as we made our way down one of the rows of stalls. Fi gave me a withering look that just dared any of us to try that shit on her, and I grinned back.

It was a shame that none of the goods were set up in the stalls yet, but

Fi was far more interested in the stallholders than what they were selling anyway. I discreetly elbowed her when she gaped at a large wooden tub of water where a merman was lounging comfortably and barking directions at the fae who were setting up his stall. Merpeople were notoriously temperamental, so it was best not to get on their bad side.

Fi immediately looked away, blinking like she couldn't quite believe what she'd just seen with her own eyes, and we completed our loop of the grounds.

"The sun is setting," I sighed, looking up at the streaks of pink and gold in the sky. "We should probably head back now... Just in case."

Despite knowing that Fi's dads hadn't intended to hurt her and were actually just trying to keep her safe, I couldn't help replaying the moment they'd snatched her away from us in my mind. The terror I'd felt would stick with me for a long time, and being off campus only made it worse.

Arthus was probably having a coronary knowing we had left the campus without him.

"I know you're right," Fi said, looking longingly at another tub being assembled for a mermaid. "There's just so much to see. We're definitely going to come back for the fair, right?"

"As often as we can get away from lessons," I promised her, linking our fingers together and leading her back through the forest path that led to the campus. Even before I knew about Fi, I'd been looking forward to the fair. The Academy could feel very insulated sometimes.

I entered Fi's cabin behind her and was momentarily distracted when she bent over to retrieve something on the floor. Gods, that *ass*. But then I realized she was holding a piece of paper in her hand and my heart dropped.

"What is it, foxglove? What does it say?"

"It's a note from Gwyneira," Fi replied, her voice filled with relief. Theoretically, she shouldn't be getting any more notes now that we'd met her dads and knew where they were coming from, but the whole thing had made her jittery nonetheless. "I think she just wants to check on me after the whole my-asshole-dads-kidnapped-me debacle. She said to come over whenever," Fi added, moving to grab her shawl that she'd just dropped and headed straight back out.

Fi gave me a hesitant look as my panic spiked at the idea of being separated from her. The mating pull was writhing uncomfortably in my chest, demanding I keep her in my sights, whispering *claim her* on repeat in my head and in my heart.

One look at Fi's face told me she was facing the same dilemma.

There was a reason that fae didn't usually wait so long to have their claiming ceremony after they felt a strong mating pull.

"Do you want to come with me?" Fi asked hesitantly.

"Gods, yes," I groaned in relief. I had promised that this relationship would happen at Fi's pace—and I meant it—but resisting the urge to ask for more was growing harder every day.

"Thank the gods," she muttered, probably not intending for me to hear. It made me grin a little that she at least felt as strongly about me as I did about her.

I grabbed her hand as we headed out of the cabin and made our way down the staircase that wound around the tree trunk to the forest path that led to Gwyneira's cabin, suppressing a groan at how good the skin-to-skin contact felt. We'd only been physically separated for about ten *minutes*. It was definitely getting worse.

Fi knew the short walk through the forest to Gwyneira's cabin better than I did—the dean never had any interest in me except for when Aderyn had been brought to the Academy. Fi knocked on the door, still gripping my hand as if I'd float away from her, and Gwyneira greeted us with a bemused expression, leading us into the sitting room for tea.

"Mr. Ferris, I was not expecting your company. Sit, please. I will go fetch a third cup," she said, hustling us into the room before departing for the kitchen. Fi moved closer to me on the couch, resting our linked hands on my thigh and leaning in tightly to my side.

Gwyneira seemed to consider us for a moment before she busied herself preparing the tea.

"Ffion, I wanted to ensure you were feeling okay after the incident with your fathers. Now, I am wondering if there is something else we should perhaps discuss," Gwyneira said, giving our hands a pointed look.

"Sorry?" Fi's confusion was written all over her face, and I squeezed her fingers in encouragement.

"You are putting off the mating bond, and it is causing you both discomfort," Gwyneira stated bluntly.

"Ah, well, I didn't know exactly what was happening, but that sounds about right..." Fi trailed off, looking to me for support.

"All of this is new to Fi. Our courtship and claiming is happening on a timeline she's comfortable with," I explained, stroking the back of Fi's hand as her cheeks flushed, her brows drawing down. I didn't want her to feel like was holding things up for me, but that was probably exactly where her mind had gone.

"Ffion, if this is about your magic, I would urge you to face your fears head-on," Gwyneira said sternly. "The changes will likely be minimal with your first mate, and if anything, your increased abilities may be vital in keeping you safe in the future. For example, if you had the ability to influence emotions with touch, you could distract someone long enough to get away if they grabbed you. The situation with your fathers may have gone very differently if you had more tools at your disposal to fight back with."

The passion in Gwyneira's voice startled me, I'd only ever heard her sound calm and even keeled. It was nice that she felt so strongly about Fi's safety, but kind of weird at the same time. I wasn't as naturally suspicious as Fi, but I got the feeling there was something Gwyneira wasn't telling us.

"I don't want to claim Marlen just to level up my magic," Fi argued. "That's not a good reason to mate with someone for life."

I hid a grin behind my teacup at Fi's unshakeable moral compass. I wanted to claim her as my mate because I *loved* her, but I hadn't told her that yet. Mostly because if she sensed the love I had for her, she hadn't mentioned it, and that made me nervous.

What if she didn't feel the same way?

What if it was just the mating pull encouraging her to be around me? Had she finally realized she was way too good for me?

"Besides, the situation with my dads turned out fine. It was basically a misunderstanding..." Fi trailed off with a shrug.

Gwyneira gave her a reproving look. "They may not have meant you harm, but there is no guarantee that you will not come to harm in the future. Regardless of whether or not you choose to pursue claiming Marlen, I am enrolling you into some higher-level courses so you can protect yourself better in the future."

Both Fi and I perked up at that. She was always excited to learn something new, and I was happy with anything that meant she was better protected.

"Let's start with the second-year potions class. You will need to build up potion-making skills before you can move on to offensive and defensive potions," Gwyneira continued. "Once we have a tutor available to assist you, you will be enrolled in the senior combat classes as well."

"That's for third- and fourth-years, Fi. You'd be in that class with me," I told her excitedly. "And Bryn."

She gave me a skeptical look, but nodded. "Physical activity isn't really my thing, but some self-defense skills sound like a good idea."

"Agreed," Gwyneira said with a firm nod. "That's all I wanted to discuss with you for today, Ffion. Please consider what I said earlier," she added, giving me a pointed glance. "We will postpone any further mentoring sessions about your gift until we get a better idea of your abilities and how they will develop."

We said our goodbyes to Gwyneira and headed back to campus, walking hand-in-hand. I could practically hear her brain whirring, she was thinking so hard.

I pulled her to a stop facing me, grabbing her other hand and holding them both tightly. Maybe words of love and reassurance were what she needed from me? My old insecurities about coming from a poor, low-magic family flooded through me and Fi immediately took a step closer, getting into my personal space.

"What is it?" she asked, concern written all over her face. I sighed, *why am I being such a coward about this?* This was Fi, I could tell her anything.

"I love you," I blurted out, staring at our hands.

Fi pulled one of her hands free, and rejection hit me like a hurricane.

"Hey, hey, none of that," she chastised softly, gripping my chin between her thumb and forefinger and forcing me to meet her gaze. "I love *you*, Marlen Ferris. Stop doubting yourself, because I don't doubt you. The way you feel about me blows me away, I don't feel like I deserve love as pure and heartfelt as yours, but I'm selfish so I'm going to take it anyway."

"You love me?" I confirmed skeptically, barely hearing anything she'd said after those three words. She couldn't lie, but I still struggled to believe it could be true.

Fi could have *anyone*.

"I love you," she agreed, threading her hands around the back of my head and tangling her fingers through my hair.

I pulled her in close, arms banding tightly around her waist. She smelled like vanilla and wildflowers and paradise, and the idea that maybe I'd get to keep her, that I'd get to inhale her delicious scent and hold her body in my arms and grow old with her was too good to be true.

"Marlen, let's do the claiming ceremony," Fi whispered.

"There's no rush. We can live with the discomfort of the mating pull. I want us to seal the bond, I want you forever, but I didn't tell you how I felt to push you into this decision. I just needed you to know," I murmured against her temple.

"I want to do the claiming ceremony, Marlen. I want to claim you. You're mine," Fi insisted.

I pulled my head back so I could look into her eyes and found only fierce determination blazing back at me.

"I'm yours anyway, Fi. But I'm not going to argue with you. Let's make it official." I grinned at her. Were we actually doing this? Was this really going to happen?

"Then it's settled. Should we go do it now? What do we have to do?" Fi bounced slightly on her toes, clearly excited and totally in the dark about what a mating ceremony entailed. Apparently, Briallen and Aderyn hadn't gotten around to explaining the specifics to her just yet. I laughed at her enthusiasm.

"Give me a day to set it up, foxglove. It'll just be the two of us, but we'll be going off campus, probably at sunset. Is that okay?"

"Oh, of course," she said sheepishly. "What happens? Do I need to do anything?"

"Not for the claiming, let me take care of all that. You should probably mention it to Arthus beforehand though, as a courtesy."

"I agree," Fi murmured pensively, probably worried about his reaction. She shouldn't be, Arthus would be fine with it. Maybe a smidge jealous, but mostly happy for us. Bryn might be another story, but he was courting Saffir and didn't have much of a say in it regardless of his obvious feelings for Fi.

"Come on," I said, grabbing Fi's hand and tugging her back to campus. "Let's go to the commons, I'm craving beetroot salad."

"Words I will never say," Fi promised with a laugh.

I'd been pretty secretive about the mating ceremony, which I knew drove Fi crazy, but the ceremonies were usually planned by the male, and I wanted to be able to surprise her, just this once. I'd told her to meet me by the stables and dress warmly, but that was all the information I had given her.

Fi had tried questioning Arthus about mating ceremonies too, but he enjoyed watching her sweat even more than I did. I was glad Fi had brought him into it, it was a good distraction for him—he was happy for us, but I definitely noticed a flash of jealousy in his eyes.

If I noticed it, Fi definitely sensed it. She hadn't said anything, but my bet was she'd go out of her way to do something special for him in the next few days to show him how she really felt about him. Their urge to claim each other wasn't as strong as ours was since they hadn't been holding off for as long, but they had grown close quickly, so it must have been riding them at least a little bit.

"There you are," I greeted Fi cheerily as she approached the griffin stables. I was already waiting next to the safest looking griffin I could find—a majestic, tawny one—with a satchel stuffed to the brim with treats and a rolled-up blanket secured on top.

"Hi, I missed you," she said immediately, going up on her tiptoes to place a light kiss on my lips. Her words caused some of the constant undercurrent of self-doubt that threatened to drag me down to ease.

"I miss you every second we're apart," I admitted. "Are you certain you want to go through with this?"

"Completely certain," Fi said with resolve, looking expectantly between me and the griffin as she waited for me to boost her up.

I helped her up, noting the slightly panicked look on Fi's face as the griffin jostled beneath her and trying to hide my own nerves. It was windy today, and I still wasn't overly comfortable flying two-person. I'd felt much better when she was securely held in Bryn's arms the other day as we flew back from the portal, even if their relationship was rocky at the best of times.

"Ready to fly?" I asked Fi quietly, and she shot me a reassuring smile over her shoulder and nodded her head. "To the waterfall at the edge of dragon territory," I announced in a louder voice, for the griffin's benefit.

The griffin ran a few feet before launching into the sky, and I promptly remembered all the reasons why I was jealous of Arthus' wings. The view was phenomenal up here, but flying on a griffin was seriously uncomfortable.

I could see Fi consciously trying to keep her grip on the griffin's feathers loose and not strangle it with her legs. I rested my hands securely on her upper thighs, my body curved protectively over Fi's to protect her from the strong winds.

Note to self: get Arthus to teach Fi how to make some kind of comfy air bubble for griffin travel.

Fortunately, even with the rough winds, we were at the waterfall within half an hour. The griffin landed near the pool of water and shot us an irritable glare as we dismounted, ruffling his windblown feathers and grooming himself. *Herself?* I wasn't exactly game to check.

Despite the less-than-ideal trip over here and our shared dislike of griffin travel, a sense of calm and rightness washed over me as I stared at the waterfall we had all to ourselves.

Whatever happened after tonight, Fi would be mine and I would be hers, and no one could ever take that away from us.

FFION

CHAPTER 30

No one had told me much about what to expect tonight, and my heart skipped a beat as nervous anticipation ran through me. I'd asked Briallen about mating ceremonies, but her only advice had been to "wear cute panties," so I wasn't getting much of any help from her.

Well, that wasn't strictly true. I wore my prettiest pale pink lace-up panties, just in case.

"Ready for this, foxglove?" Marlen murmured in my ear as he wound our fingers together, a thread of vulnerability in his voice. He was trying to be calm and steady, and I knew he felt excited, but he was nervous as well. It only made me love him more.

"So ready," I said confidently, and I meant it. In general, once I made a decision, I stuck to it. And after last night's confessional with Marlen and a get-your-shit-together pep talk from Gwyneira, I was feeling good about this.

"Good," he said quietly with an almost boyish smile.

Why had I put this off again? This felt like the most natural thing in the world.

"Come on, we're going to the cave behind the falls where we went last time, but we'll take the dry route this time," Marlen explained, tugging me along with his hand.

The sun was setting as we carefully picked our way along the pool's edge to the base of the cliff where the waterfall crashed into the basin. My heart was full remembering the fun day we'd spent here together with our friends. I loved this place. I couldn't think of a more perfect location to claim our forever together.

Marlen guided me over some rocks until we got to the thick cascade of water, holding his hands steadily in front of him for a moment before making a motion like he was pulling open a curtain. The waterfall parted, making a gap as large as a door.

"That's a neat trick," I breathed, following Marlen into the rapidly darkening cave, and he chuckled as he let the gap fall closed behind us.

'Cave' was a fairly generous term for the space—it was more like a ledge, but it was wide enough for us to sit comfortably, at least. The ceiling was too low for us to stand, so we both ducked our heads as Marlen rolled out a blanket for us to sit on, before pulling out some candles, matches, snacks wrapped in leaves and a bottle of fae wine from his satchel.

It was a cold evening, but the love and adoration emanating from Marlen wrapped around me like a warm, safe cocoon.

"My, you were prepared," I exclaimed, admiring his haul. I hadn't really given much thought to how the claiming ceremony would play out before yesterday. I assumed there'd be some kind of wedding-like vow, then sex. This was much more romantic.

"I wanted it to be special," Marlen said shyly, lighting the candles and setting them out around us in a loose circle. The candlelight flickered off the rock walls, casting the cold cave in a warm, inviting glow and dancing off the sheet of water on our other side.

We arranged ourselves sitting opposite one another on the blanket, legs crossed. It was reminiscent of the position we'd been in when I asked Marlen to be my suitor, and the little flicker of happiness that I felt running through him made me think he was remembering the same thing.

"What do we do now?" I asked nervously.

"We take turns saying the vow, then we'll seal the bond." Marlen's cheeky wink cleared up what that entailed. "That's pretty much all we have to do. Our mating marks will show up after that."

Crap, I'd totally forgotten about the mating marks. I hoped ours were good. Remembering Briallen's half-finished mark reminded me that I'd only be getting a third of my mark today.

"I don't know the vow, is it a specific set of words?" I asked.

Why hadn't Briallen told me about this? I should have researched mating ceremonies at the library. This is what I got for spontaneously committing to someone for life with only 24 hours' notice.

Marlen watched me as he pulled out a worn scrap of black leather from his pocket and carefully unfolded it. Squinting at it in the low light of the cave, I realized there were tiny letters embossed on the material, and I moved one of the candles closer so I could read it.

"This is a Calder family heirloom," Marlen explained with a smile.

"This is from Arthus?" I exclaimed. Given his bout of jealousy, it was a surprisingly supportive gesture.

"It is. I think he's hoping you'll use it with him next," Marlen added with an impish grin. If he kept up with the sweet gestures like this, I was sure I would. "Okay, I'll start. I think we should use your birth name for this too, your fae name. Is that okay, foxglove?"

Feeling a little overcome with emotion and not trusting myself to speak, I gave him a mute nod.

Marlen gave me a reassuring smile and grabbed my hand with one of his own. He held the small rectangle of leather in the other hand, low to the ground so he could see it by candlelight.

"I, Marlen Ferris, take you, Ffion Laisren, to be my bonded mate. I pledge you my love, my magic, my loyalty, and my devotion. I vow from this day forward to put the needs of you and our mating circle first, forsaking all others."

The words struck a chord deep within my soul. I felt the mating pull solidifying, moving and twisting in my chest, reforming into something more permanent. Something that would be part of me until the end of my days.

It was so much more than I expected. More powerful. More all-encompassing. More *everything*.

Marlen gave me an encouraging smile, and I took a deep breath before reaching for the piece of leather and repeating the vow back to him.

"I, Ffion Laisren, take you, Marlen Ferris, to be my bonded mate. I pledge you my love, my magic, my loyalty, and my devotion. I vow from this day forward to put the needs of you and our mating circle first, forsaking all others."

Marlen had a look of wonder on his face that made me think he was experiencing the same settling sensation in his chest that I just had. I was so overwhelmed by my own feelings, I couldn't separate them enough to get a read on his.

Gods, he looked good in candlelight. The golden light made his green eyes glow, and his dark red hair shone like fire.

"Now what?" I asked breathily, admiring this pretty mate of mine.

"Now, we consummate our union," Marlen said with a seductive grin, his eyes as heated on me as I'm sure mine were on him. "Apparently we'll feel our magic moving between us, solidifying the bond."

"Cool," I managed to get out before grabbing Marlen by the front of his shirt and yanking him towards me, capturing his lips in a frenzied kiss.

I don't know if it was the magic, the weight of the commitment we'd just made to each other, or just the *love* I had for Marlen, but I felt like I'd die if he wasn't inside me within the next few minutes.

We pulled at each other's clothes, desperate to get them out of the way and not caring if they ripped in the process. Finally, with nothing separating us, I climbed onto Marlen's lap, grinding against his hard length and moaning as he took my nipple into his mouth, swirling his tongue in teasing circles as his hand moved between my legs.

I swatted it impatiently out of the way—it wasn't his fingers I wanted—but Marlen grinned unrepentantly, pulling my wrist out of the way before teasing my clit lightly with one finger.

"I want to make sure you're ready for me, foxglove," Marlen insisted as I ground down on his hand, forgetting my objections. This was good, too. I could work with this.

I sunk my teeth into my lower lip, steadying myself by gripping his shoulders. I didn't even need to look to know that I was gouging marks into his skin again, but I could feel how much Marlen liked it. Two fingers teased at my entrance before finally pushing upwards, and my hand shot down to grip his wrist, keeping him in place so I could stimulate my clit against the palm of his hand. I was moving shamelessly, chasing my release, *needing* to come.

Marlen's fingers pressed against that sensitive spot inside me as I rolled my hips, and despite my desperate movements, the orgasm that built slowly and unfurled through my body took me by surprise.

I sucked in a surprised breath, stilling and letting the bliss wash through me, vaguely aware of Marlen withdrawing his hand and gripping my hips. Drunk on love and orgasms, I let him guide me up on my knees as he lined his cock up at my entrance, before sinking down with an indecently wanton moan.

For a moment, I didn't move. I could barely even breathe. Wherever our skin touched, magic rippled between us, rawer and more tangible than I'd ever experienced it.

Marlen's grip tightened on my hips, and I gripped his shoulders as our lips found each other's once again. We groaned simultaneously at the feeling of magic rolling over our lips and tongues like tiny sparks, bursting and tingling against each nerve. Our hands roamed everywhere, unable to get enough of the fizzing sensation between us.

My hips rolled against his, Marlen thrusting from below me, but our movements were smaller than usual, not willing to break the skin-to-skin contact for anything. We exploded at the same time in an orgasm so intense I would remember it until my dying day. Each nerve ending felt like it was wrapped in a warm layer of magic that tingled before dissipating. *Remaking me.* I wasn't the same as I was before, I never would be. Not when Marlen's soul was so thoroughly intertwined with my own.

I luxuriated in the sensation until my brain floated back down into my body. I was surprised to find my head was resting against Marlen's shoulder and his head was resting on mine like we'd been physically unable to support our own body weight.

We pulled apart panting, staring into each other's faces and taking in the new sensation of being bonded. The mating pull was gone, and in its place was something that felt much more permanent. When I concentrated on the bond, it felt like cool water, smooth and inviting.

Drawing the bond to me, I could feel everything Marlen was feeling. It was far more intimate than my empath abilities; it was like I could see into his psyche. It was mind-blowing and terrifying and awe-inspiring and *everything*.

I was quietly glad that it seemed to be something I had to consciously reach for rather than something I would be feeling 24/7. I had enough feelings to deal with already.

Marlen caught me and gave me a mischievous grin before I felt a strange pulse of... love? It felt like Marlen had told me he loved me without saying the words. He laughed at my confused face.

"Try it," he insisted.

"Try what? I don't even know what that was."

"Just... think of an emotion you want to send me and sort of shove it at the bond," he explained unhelpfully. I really hoped Marlen didn't have dreams of teaching at the Academy one day.

I furrowed my brow and focused on isolating that feeling of pure love that I felt for Marlen and imagined channeling it through the watery bond in my chest.

Gods, the smile that lit up his face could have melted even the hardest of hearts.

"Love you too, foxglove," he whispered, leaning forward to brush his lips against mine.

There was a bizarre sensation in my left wrist—not quite painful, but *odd*—and Marlen and I both flinched at the impact of it before holding our wrists up in front of us. Marlen smiled as the mating mark began to manifest on his skin, burned into place by magic.

I frowned down at mine. It was a single, thin, black diagonal line sloping from my inner wrist, about an inch long. It was nice as far as lines went, but I kind of had higher expectations for the mark that was going to be permanently embedded on my skin.

Marlen laughed. "I love being able to feel your emotions, Fi. It really evens the playing field."

He extended his arm for me to examine, and I admired the beautiful lines that had appeared on his skin. It looked like two X's next to each other, connected so they formed a diamond in the middle. It was simple but striking. I held my wrist up next to his to compare. The single line matched one of the strokes that made up Marlen's mark, but there were three yet to appear.

Marlen cupped my face, running his thumb over my cheekbone gently. "Foxglove, I hate to break it to you, but you're definitely going to have four mates."

I groaned, squeezing my eyes shut. Of course, my magic would be all *ta-da! You didn't even want three mates, have a bonus extra too!*

"Are you sure?" I asked, opening one eye to look at him.

Marlen smiled, a little brighter than his smile had been before our ceremony. "Your rune appears one stroke at a time as you take each mate. The symbol is determined by your magic, not ours." He held out his wrist again. "This is the end result. It's made up of four lines and you only got one today."

He leaned forward to gently kiss my forehead, probably feeling my panic spiking.

"But I don't *want* four mates," I whined, not caring how sullen I sounded. I'd *barely* gotten my head around the idea of dating both Marlen and Arthus at once!

"No one is going to make you do anything you don't want to do, Fi."

Marlen gave me an unusually serious look. "You don't have to take four, you'll just constantly feel the mating pull if there's a gap in your mating circle. And your magic won't grow stronger without a balance, but I doubt that bothers you." He grinned.

"Not even a little bit," I confirmed. I clambered off Marlen's lap, awkwardly realizing we were still *very* intimately connected. He chuckled, and I snuggled into his side, draping my legs over his lap as I pulled my dress back on.

Marlen tucked the leather vows away in his satchel, found his own clothes, and pulled out the bottle of fae wine and some fruit for us to snack on. The rush of the waterfall blocked out the outside world, so it felt like we were the only fae in Avalon tucked away in here together.

"Do you want to know what it means?" Marlen asked curiously, his gaze flicking from the mark on his wrist to my face.

"The mating mark?" I asked, surprised. "Sure. I never thought much about the meanings. You said my magic determined them?"

"No one really understands the reason behind the rune that appears, just that it seems to fit that mating circle perfectly."

"So, what does ours mean?" I asked warily.

I sensed his hesitation. "Remember, the meanings are complex, it isn't always obvious the message they're trying to convey," Marlen said slowly. "I'm not great with remembering runes and symbols, but this one has always been one of my favorites. Maybe I always felt connected with it."

Well, that was kind of sweet, even though I had a *very* bad feeling based on his obvious discomfort.

"It symbolizes sacrifice. Leaving behind something old to create something new," Marlen said eventually.

Of course, it meant sacrifice. Of course it wasn't just a pretty tattoo that meant eternal happiness or endless orgasms.

Though, sacrifice and new beginnings weren't necessarily bad, right? I'd left Albion for my life here in Avalon. I'd left behind my fear of my magic growing stronger to bond with Marlen, and I would likely do it again to bond with Arthus.

But those things were hardly sacrifices, I reminded myself. Nothing I'd given up had been truly difficult to part with. I had a feeling it wouldn't be that easy.

"It can also indicate fertility, so maybe your magic is trying to tell us you'll get the Ferris twin gene?" Marlen continued when I didn't reply, throwing me a wink.

"Don't even joke about that," I countered playfully, elbowing him in the ribs. "I almost prefer the sacrifice idea."

We spent a couple of hours holed up in the cave, drinking wine and talking about everything under the sun. Conversation was always easy between Marlen and I. The only time we were silent together was when our mouths were otherwise occupied.

Strangely, I hadn't noticed any change in how my empath gift worked. Gwyneira had said I'd be able to dig deeper into the why behind people's emotions after I'd taken my first mate, but when I hesitantly tried to explore the overwhelming satisfaction I was feeling from Marlen, nothing happened.

I flagged it as something to experiment with later on someone I wasn't mated to. I could look into Marlen's soul via the bond, so maybe that canceled out my empath abilities.

"Come on, foxglove. We'll already be flying back in the dark. If I don't get you back soon, Arthus will hunt us down and drag us back himself."

Since I didn't have a roommate, it made sense for Marlen to move into my cabin. We had to go to the administration office and show them our mating marks like they were proof of identification or something before we got the go-ahead to officially move in together, and I'd surprised myself at how relaxed I was about the idea of permanently sharing my space. After I'd aged out of group care, I'd been pretty adamant that I'd never share a bedroom with anyone again.

I'd made an exception for Marlen.

We'd spent every night together since Marlen had become my suitor, anyway—Marlen had *no* desire to be anywhere near Kelvyn—so it seemed like a kind of pointless administrative exercise to officially move in, but whatever.

A rapid knock on the door preceded Arthus' entrance, and I picked up his happiness, lust, and affection when he saw me, as well as the tiniest flash of envy when he saw Marlen putting his clothes in the wardrobe.

He'd greeted us warmly when Marlen and I arrived back on campus after our claiming ceremony, and if he'd been feeling insecure at all, his surprise that I'd only received one-fourth of my mating mark instead of one-third as expected had overshadowed it.

"You know, Marlen," Arthus said conversationally, looking around the cabin. "I don't think we've done a very good job at showing Fi the benefits of having multiple mates."

I looked over my shoulder in time to catch Marlen's mischievous grin. "We have been rather negligent in that area, haven't we?"

I didn't *think* they'd planned this, but sometimes they were so in sync, it was genuinely hard to tell.

Marlen dropped the shirt he was in the process of hanging up and climbed up the ladder to the bed without further ado, and I blinked at his back.

"Come along, sweetheart," Arthus said in a low voice, filled with amusement. He swatted me lightly on the ass to get me moving.

"What? Is this seriously happening right now?" I asked, confused by our abrupt switch from unpacking to ménage à trois.

"Oh, it's happening," Marlen called down from his spot lounging on the bed.

I mean, I wasn't going to say *no*…

I climbed up the ladder with Arthus following close behind me, and the predatory glint in both their gazes sent zings of heat everywhere, causing an ache to form between my thighs just from seeing the way they watched me.

They looked at me like I was the most desirable woman they'd ever seen.

Marlen was laying back languidly against the pillows, one hand behind his head, watching me. I crawled onto the bed, kneeling between his outstretched legs.

"Lose the clothes, sweetheart," Arthus instructed quietly from somewhere behind me.

I pulled my dress over my head then slowly unlaced my bra and panties, never breaking eye contact with Marlen. A small smile pulled at his lips as he watched my amateur strip show and began removing his own clothes.

"Move closer. Your mate can't reach you," Arthus whispered in my ear, maddeningly close but not actually touching me. I followed his directions obediently, shuffling forward on my knees until I was right in front of Marlen, balancing my hands on his firm chest and leaning down to kiss him.

Arthus moved up behind me, his hands trailing deliciously slowly down my back, cupping my ass then down the backs of my thighs before moving back up again. The slow, gentle sensations coming from both in front and behind of me were an exquisite kind of torture.

Marlen's lips explored mine, his thumbs brushing teasingly at my overly stimulated nipples, but it wasn't enough. I needed more, immediately, or I'd die of orgasm deprivation.

But I didn't make the rules.

Arthus gripped my hips, tugging me back towards him so I was bent over Marlen. His fingers ran slowly over my back entrance as he leaned forward enough to graze the shell of my ear with his teeth. "Soon, sweetheart, I'll have you here too. While you're riding Marlen."

He nipped lightly at my earlobe and just the thought of having them at the same time brought forth a gush of arousal that coated my inner thighs. I'd probably be embarrassed about it if I could have thought straight.

Arthus moved his fingers lower, brushing through the wetness, and I could practically feel his arrogant smirk. "You like that idea."

His fingers found my pussy from behind as Marlen's hands shifted lower. Arthus knocked my legs further apart from behind, spreading me wide open while Marlen's fingers found my clit, and I sucked in a breath at the feeling of multiple hands on me. It was utterly taboo to my human sensibilities, and yet it felt so incredibly *right*.

I forced my brain to be quiet, focusing on just feeling as Arthus savagely pumped his fingers into me from behind, my breath coming in needy pants as Marlen picked up his pace while I writhed between them. My muscles were clenching in no time, squeezing Arthus' fingers as I gouged nail marks into Marlen's chest, rolling my lips together to muffle my moans.

I collapsed against Marlen's chest, fairly confident I was about to meet the gods in person when a torturously delicious lick through my folds from behind brought me back to the present with a surprised squeak.

"Did you think we were done, sweetheart?" Arthus murmured.

"Gods, I hope not," I panted, writhing in anticipation, already wanting more.

"Hands and knees, Fi," he commanded, and I obeyed without question. Whatever it was he had in mind, I was game.

"Time to show me what you can do with that pretty little mouth of yours," Arthus said, as he and Marlen swapped places so Arthus could kneel in front of me. I licked my lips in anticipation.

Gods, I was like a dog in heat. At that moment, I decided I was okay with that.

Marlen moved behind me, his touch along my back gentle and caressing. It was all a ruse, though. I knew he'd fuck me like a demon when it came down to it, like he always did.

He didn't disappoint, plunging into me desperately from behind, making my eyes roll back for a moment before I recovered. To make up for it, I gave Arthus my best sex kitten eyes as I took as much of him into my mouth as I could. His fingers threaded through my hair and I maintained eye contact as I let him take control, the two of them working in tandem to bring me to heights of pleasure I didn't even know were possible.

I felt taken, owned, possessed in the best possible way. I wanted to give them everything because I knew they'd always give me all of themselves in return.

"Last chance to pull back, sweetheart," Arthus grunted, but I swallowed him deeper, choking slightly. He made a low, rumbly sound of approval that set me off again and we both came together, his release coating my throat, branding me.

"Fuck!" Marlen choked out. "You're milking me, foxglove." He let out a strangled groan as he followed us into oblivion, all three of us gasping for breath and covered in a slick sheen of sweat. We collapsed next to each other, me tangled between them, limbs everywhere.

"You're incredible, you know that?" Marlen whispered into my hair as my eyes drifted shut. He was wrong, though. They were the incredible ones.

Every difficult step in my journey so far, every challenge I had yet to face, I would be able to face head-on knowing I had these two in my life.

FFION

CHAPTER 31

After an incredibly invigorating wakeup call from both Marlen and Arthus, I kicked them out for the day so Briallen and I could use my cabin to get ready for tonight's masquerade.

I thought I'd struggle with the whole multiple-guys-in-my-bed situation, but apparently my inhibitions vanished in the portal to Avalon along with my glamour. Waking up sandwiched between two solid blocks of muscle had felt like the most comforting, natural thing in the world. It was like we were meant to be there together.

Marlen and Arthus had given me the rundown of what to expect at the ball between orgasms. Apparently, animals—both mythical and otherwise—were the go-to costume theme of choice for masquerades in Avalon. Marlen and Arthus had both voted I go as a phoenix, claiming I'd risen from the ashes of my life in Albion and my disappointing parents.

I didn't object, since my tanned skin looked hella good in phoenix colors, but I did begin to regret my costume choice when Briallen joked about how me dressing as a firebird was basically leaving Bryn a calling card.

Whatever. He was with Saffir. It didn't matter what he thought of my outfit.

The red linen ball gown Arthus had helped me pick out in Inver was the most beautiful thing I'd ever owned. The skirt was made of pieces of linen, cut asymmetrically at random to create a full, fluffy skirt that reminded me of feathers. The bodice was fitted, held up with thin straps and dipped down low at the back. It was both the sexiest and most princessy dress I'd ever worn, and I loved it.

Briallen and I had purchased plain masks and painted them throughout the week—mine in reds and golds with feathers and hers with white and silver for her unicorn-inspired costume. Her dress was fitted and sleeveless, flaring out at the knees, and made of a bright white linen that contrasted perfectly with her dusky pink hair. She'd pulled it up into a long, straight ponytail reminiscent of a unicorn's tail.

Briallen pinned my curls back from my face so they cascaded down my back like a waterfall. I didn't have a mirror—apparently they were luxury items here, but I felt beautiful.

"Now for the finishing touch," Briallen announced, pulling out a small lidded earthenware bowl. "Fairy dust." She winked at me.

"What now?" I raised an eyebrow. I was going to be seriously pissed if I'd been living here for months and no one had told me about Tinkerbelle-style magic fairy dust.

She laughed. "Well, that's what humans call it, we call it *O'r Blodau*. The flowers in Avalon produce it—it doesn't have magical properties or anything, it just makes things pretty and sparkly. Wealthy fae use it all the time, but it's kind of pricey so I save it for special occasions."

She dipped a small brush in the pot of iridescent powder and started dusting the bodice of my dress and top pieces of my skirt, fading it out as she moved down.

Once she'd finished, my previously plain dress shimmered like it had been designed that way. She brushed a coat of fairy dust over my mask before we tackled her outfit. It had been so much fun getting ready together, and the only thing that could have made it better would be Aderyn's presence, but she insisted that balls weren't for her. Marlen thought it was more likely that she couldn't afford the dress, but she would have been mortally offended if anyone offered to help her out with it.

Arthus, Marlen and Leigh came to the cabin to collect us shortly after. My dates had coordinated in dark dress clothes with eagle masks, and they looked *good*.

Arthus' black hair blended into the black feathers of his mask, and his silver eyes practically glowed in contrast. With his sharp jaw and five o'clock shadow visible below the mask, he was the very definition of 'tall, dark and handsome.'

Marlen's dark red hair made him look like an eagle in flames. His emerald green eyes twinkled as he took me in from head to toe, his desire evident. He was a little taller than Arthus and built like a swimmer.

The two of them looked good enough to eat.

Or to eat me. I was definitely bookmarking that thought for later.

They kind of looked like they wanted to eat me too. Devour me, in fact.

"Exquisite," Arthus murmured. Marlen didn't even speak, he didn't have to with the feelings of pure desire he was shoving through the bond at me.

"You both look really good too," I breathed.

A loud *smack* broke me out of my reverie, and I snorted as Briallen rubbed her ass, shooting Leigh an affectionate grin that promised she'd get him back for it later.

The Academy was providing carriages to transport us to the field where the masquerade was being held, just off-campus next to the fairground, so our little group made our way there, taking in everyone's costumes as we went. The anonymity the masks offered was *delightful*. Between the excitement everyone was feeling and the fact that there were no emotions directed straight at me, I felt almost drunk on my empath abilities.

Marlen and Arthus stood on either side of me as we waited for our carriage, my head leaning against Arthus' shoulder while Marlen's arm was wrapped around my waist. I felt the familiar, strong mating pull that always signaled Bryn's presence tugging me backward, but despite my best attempts to resist, I couldn't help but look.

I twisted to rest my cheek against Arthus' arm as my gaze connected with the prickly fire fae looming behind me. He was standing closer than I expected, in a fiery-red dragon-inspired mask that contrasted with his inky blue-black hair and made his sapphire blue eyes glow.

Those same eyes lingered just a beat too long on my lips, the generous amount of back my dress showed off, and the curve of my waist to be friendly. I felt his powerful surge of lust before he smothered it with his usual blend of irritation and anger.

Neither of us said a word, but when the carriage arrived, Bryn silently took the fourth spot next to Arthus and stared resolutely out the window. Marlen and Arthus exchanged a look as their amusement spiked.

Marlen grabbed my hand and linked our fingers together, rubbing circles on the back of my hand with his thumb. He had probably checked the bond and felt my confusion and irritation. Bryn was such a mindfuck.

Shouldn't he be sitting with his girlfriend?

Deep down—*very* deep down—I felt a bit sorry for him. The mating pull was probably messing with his head the same way it messed with mine, and it was probably frustrating as hell for him.

The carriage brought us to the edge of a clearing where lights had been strung through the surrounding trees and a group of musicians played ethereal folk music. The night was clear and the moon shone brightly over the revelers, all drinking and dancing and laughing, elaborate masks and costumes sparkling in the moonlight.

While I never forgot that I was in a different realm, there was something incredibly fairy-like about the ball. It felt like something out of a dream.

I exited the carriage quickly—eager to escape the awkwardness that was Bryn and I—but as soon as I got out of the carriage, I found my feet taking me towards the dance floor of their own volition.

If I'd been paying attention, I would have noticed the mating pull tugging in my chest, but all I could concentrate on was finding the source of that delicious cinnamon and cloves smell that had my mouth watering and my nipples hardening.

"Fuck," Bryn groaned behind me, sounding like he was a million miles away. "It's happening again."

I kept following the mating pull, right into the arms of an obscenely handsome behemoth of a man who seamlessly spun me onto the dance floor. My mate, suitor, and Bryn all stood nearby, watching as the mystery man who smelled like heaven gently moved us in time to the music, his enormous hands encircling my waist.

Unconsciously, my own hands drifted up to his neck as I stared into his purple eyes, mesmerized. They were a deep amethyst color, unlike anything I'd ever seen before. His dark brown hair was short and neat and under his black jaguar mask, I could see his strong jaw that was covered by a thick but well-maintained beard and full, kissable lips. He looked older than me and my guys, perhaps in his mid-20s, though it was impossible to tell with the fae. He was built like a mountain too, with broad shoulders and bulky muscles concealed under a tailored, expensive-looking outfit.

"I feel like I've waited forever for you, cariad," he murmured.

"*Carr-ee-ard*?" I sounded out, my voice coming out far breathier than I had intended. "My name is Fi. Ffion. Fi."

Ugh, I was stuttering like I'd never spoken to a man before instead of a woman who had just had a godsdamned threesome last night.

He smiled as though I'd done something really adorable. "*Cariad* is a term of endearment, like darling. It's such a pleasure to meet you Fi. My name is Eamon."

Gods, his emotions were giving me a contact high. He wasn't cautious or holding back; I felt his unbridled affection for me—a total stranger—and honestly, it did wonders for my ego. Fuck Bryn and his games. This guy liked me after a minute of dancing and a few words of conversation.

I realized I was still staring like a lunatic and blinked a couple of times to clear my head and looked back at my guys. Bryn still hung around like a bad smell, scowling.

"Your mate and two suitors? Will you introduce me?"

"How did you know that?" I asked, startled. "I mean, Bryn isn't my suitor. Arthus is, though. Marlen and I are bonded."

"I'm surprised that he isn't your suitor, I can see a strong bond between you so clearly, though it's a little fractured in places."

"You can see bonds?" I gaped at him, suddenly aware that while we had stopped dancing, his hands were still around my waist while mine rested on his shoulders.

"I have the gift of Second Sight," Eamon replied with a rueful smile.

I racked my brain trying to remember everything I'd heard about Second Sight. Wasn't that the talking-to-dead-fae thing Briallen and Aderyn had mentioned? There was clearly more to it than that if Eamon could see bonds too.

He was apprehensive now, watching me as though I would bolt. I gave him a shy smile, tugging on his arm to get him to follow as I moved back toward my guys and Bryn. As we walked, Eamon's hand came to rest lightly on my exposed lower back.

He was relieved. Was he used to people running away when they found out about his gift? That was awful.

And relatable. But still awful.

I analyzed my own feelings, surprised at how I was reacting underneath the constant bombardment of everyone else's emotions.

The mating pull had brought out different aspects of me with each of the guys so far—a territorial side with Marlen, a submissive side with Arthus, and the fiery passion that ignited whenever I was around Bryn. So far, I wanted to preen in Eamon's presence, to wallow in his undivided attention, to let him worship me.

Gods, at this rate I was going to develop a serious personality crisis.

"Eamon, this is my mate Marlen, my suitor Arthus, and Bryn. Guys, this is Eamon." I gestured awkwardly between the four of them. This multiple boyfriends business should really have come with an instruction manual.

"Shall we find a table? I'd like to get to know you all," Eamon suggested politely.

Arthus and Marlen nodded, their expressions carefully neutral, but I could feel their curiosity. Bryn, as per usual, felt outright hostile and it was written all over his face. I rolled my eyes.

"Shouldn't you go find Saffir?" I hissed at him under my breath as the other three turned toward the edge of the dancefloor which was lined with seating.

"No." Bryn cut me a quick look, and I felt the briefest flash of his pain and confusion before he took off after the other guys. If I lived until I was Gwyneira's age, I still wouldn't understand him.

Marlen waited patiently for me to catch up, hand outstretched to take mine.

"Is this weird?" I asked him softly.

"Not at all. It's exciting in a way," he replied with a chuckle.

I reached for the cool, watery mating bond in my chest to reassure myself that Marlen really was okay with this. I found him curious about Eamon, genuinely interested in getting to know him, and excited for me. I also picked up a note of worry for my safety, which had been a constant presence ever since the surprise visit from my dads.

I hadn't felt any insecurity from Marlen since we officially claimed each other, and I loved knowing he felt confident about us. Hopefully it would stay that way if I took a second mate.

Just in case. Just keeping my options open.

We found a round table big enough for the five of us, and I took a seat between Marlen and Eamon. The guys began removing their masks and I followed suit, carefully untying the ribbons secured behind my head and setting the mask down on the table before getting distracted by Eamon's face.

His features were chiseled and defined like Arthus', but in a more rugged, masculine way. Combined with his full but well-kept beard and massive size, everything about him screamed masculine.

Eamon flagged down a server to bring us pitchers of ale and I took a deep swig of my drink, my nerves getting the better of me. Marlen reached over and squeezed my thigh under the table.

"So, I assume by 'Eamon', you mean Eamon Adair, sole heir to the Adair Estate since your parents never had a daughter, feared for your Second

Sight and relationship with the spirits?" Bryn asked in his most assholish voice from across the table.

I take back every thought I ever had about feeling sorry for him.

Eamon's face fell slightly, and I felt a rush of his worry. I gave Bryn my best *shut the hell up* face before returning my attention to Eamon.

"Ignore him," I instructed, making Bryn bristle with irritation. *Good.* "Tell me about yourself."

"He's not wrong," Eamon began. "I am Eamon Adair, I do have the gift of Second Sight. Some people fear me because of that." His emotions were resigned and a little melancholy.

"No one is a fan of my gift either, myself included, so don't worry about that," I replied cheerfully. Bryn rolled his eyes while Marlen and Arthus shot me amused glances.

"You're not afraid?" Eamon asked curiously.

"She doesn't know to be afraid. She doesn't know what Second Sight is," Bryn interjected, and I did my best not to snarl at him like a feral dog.

"I do know what Second Sight is." *Mostly.* "And no, I am not afraid. Bryn, don't you have somewhere else you'd rather be?"

"Not particularly," he said with an infuriating shrug.

Eamon looked between us with an amused expression. "I see now why the bond between you is so strong yet so fractured."

I gave him a disbelieving look, but didn't say anything because I really didn't have an answer for that.

"Well then, we can probably wrap this conversation up since Ffion only has two gaps in her mating circle," Bryn snapped.

"You are literally *courting someone else*," I hissed at him across the table. Had he forgotten about Saffir? What was happening right now?

"Actually, Fi has three gaps," Marlen announced with a gleeful grin, moving my wrist to the table and flipping it up to show my incomplete mating mark before pulling up his sleeve to show his own.

"What the fuck? You claimed him? When?" Bryn demanded, though his angry tone didn't match the flood of relief that he was feeling.

I scowled at him. "Two days ago."

Eamon was going to think we were all bonkers, sitting here arguing amongst ourselves. *Way to make a good first impression, guys.*

"Now that that's been cleared up, perhaps we could all give Fi and Eamon the opportunity to talk?" Arthus interjected drolly, taking control of the situation and giving Bryn a warning look.

"Yes, let's do that," I agreed, bobbing my head. "Eamon, I would love to hear more about your gift."

"Of course. What do you know about Second Sight?" Eamon asked gently.

"I was raised in Albion, so not a lot. Something about talking to spirits and the gods?" I hedged. I felt Eamon's surprise at my admission that I'd been raised in Albion, but he didn't pry.

"The spirits visit me, yes. Or I can travel to their realm, though that is much less comfortable. Sometimes their messages come directly from the gods, other times they're personal," he explained, that slightly wary look coming back into his eyes again. That was okay. I wasn't going to run, and he'd realize that for himself.

"Okay," I said slowly. It definitely didn't sound as bad as I'd thought when Briallen and Aderyn first told me about it. I'd imagined Second Sight meant seeing dead spirits everywhere, just hanging about. The way Eamon described it, it was more intermittent than that.

"Second Sight is the sight of the soul. That's why I can see bonds, souls tainted by darkness, and souls as pure as light," Eamon said, giving me a soft pointed smile that made my cheeks flush. Out of the corner of my periphery, I noticed Bryn rolling his eyes.

Who doesn't want to be told they have a pure-as-light soul? If it was a line, it was a freaking good one, and fae couldn't lie.

"He can also see through glamours and illusions. She'll find that interesting," Bryn added helpfully in his most dismissive tone. As much as he irritated me, Bryn had understood my curiosity and the kinds of questions I'd asked from the moment I met him. Another thing I didn't like to reflect too hard on.

Maybe Bryn was reading too much into my phoenix-inspired outfit. Godsdamned Briallen, putting the calling card idea into my head.

Between the new, powerful mating pull to Eamon and Bryn's focused attention on me, tonight was proving to be a little overwhelming. I'd only just claimed Marlen two days ago after all, and my relationship with Arthus was still fairly new, especially the intimate side of it. All these fae males vying for my attention were making my head spin.

Fortunately, Marlen picked up my slack on the conversation front so I could have a momentary breather. This evening had gotten a whole lot more complicated than I'd planned.

CHAPTER 32

What am I doing?

I knew I was acting like a fucking moron, and yet I couldn't seem to stop. The mating pull dragged me more insistently than ever to Ffion's side, even though I *knew* Saffir was around here somewhere, quite possibly planning my death for abandoning her.

I needed to find her. I was acting like a prick. Saffir didn't deserve it.

It was just the bond between Ffion and Marlen making my pull to her go crazy. Reminding me that if I wanted a chance with her, I was running out of time.

My eyes landed on Eamon, leaning in to tuck a lock of Ffion's hair behind her ear. She gazed up at him, all big amber eyes and soft smiles that had never been directed my way, and the lack of time on my side felt like it shrunk right before my eyes.

But I didn't want that. Right?

Right.

Courting Saffir had seemed like an easy choice when Ffion had insulted my honor, but having seen firsthand the lengths her fathers had gone to, I could bitterly admit that it made sense for her to be suspicious of a fire fae who knew about her gift.

I didn't like it, and I wasn't about to tell her that, but it made sense.

"Would you like to dance?" Eamon asked, all politeness and upper crust mannerisms. My aunt and uncles, Briallen's parents, were fairly wealthy and I'd grown up with more than most when they took me in, but *nothing* like what the Adair family had.

"I'd love to," Ffion replied, beaming at him as she stood, Marlen and Arthus immediately rising to their feet when she did. They were all wrapped around her little finger, all entangled in her web, drunk on the intoxication of a strong mating pull.

It would be so easy for me to give in too.

I forced my body to stay in my chair, grabbing my tankard of ale and downing the warm liquid in one swig, refusing to make eye contact with any of them.

Marlen and Arthus thought I would change my mind, it was written all over their faces. If anything, their amused expressions made me *more* determined not to. Even if I did, Ffion's was already made up.

We had stubbornness in common. That was the kindred soul part of our mating pull, I was sure of it.

Once they'd disappeared into the crowd on the dancefloor, the persistent yanking in my chest eased slightly, and I made myself move further away, circling around the revelers until I spotted Saffir, glittering in emerald as she stood talking to Corsen.

Nothing. I felt absolutely nothing. She was a beautiful fae, flawlessly put together, and a few weeks ago I'd have been trying to hide my erection in public at seeing her look like that.

Yet now, nothing.

Swallowing thickly, I wound through the crowd, securing my mask in place as I stopped in front of her.

She'd foregone the mask in favor of elaborate face paint that moved as she pursed her lips, but Saffir wasn't the type to make a huge scene even if she was angry.

"There you are," she said stiffly as Corsen glared at me through the slits of her fox mask.

"Here I am," I replied gruffly. There was no point offering an explanation, I didn't have a good one.

And I physically couldn't apologize for keeping her waiting, because I wasn't sorry. I was *glad* I'd witnessed the moment when Ffion and Eamon met, and I didn't know what that made me except for a heartless bastard.

That I definitely was.

"Better late than never," Saffir sighed, not quite able to hide her disappointment. "The least you can do is get me a drink, Bryn."

I nodded stiffly, because she was right. That really was the *least* I could do. I linked our arms together, leading her towards the bar, the mating pull writhing and objecting the entire way.

FFION

CHAPTER 33

Idanced for so long that Marlen had to use his healing magic to ease the pain in my feet. I couldn't stop, between my three partners I was having far too much fun—twirling playfully with Marlen, being subtly seduced by Arthus, and being revered by Eamon. He danced with me as though I was a queen and he was my noble knight, showing me off to the court and pushing me into the limelight.

It was a heady feeling. Eamon could do terrible things for my ego just by looking at me like that.

Halfway through the night, I noticed a flustered Saffir and a tense-looking Bryn lingering nearby. She was gripping Bryn's forearm tightly and whispering furiously in his ear, glancing around like she was worried she might be overheard. Bryn inclined his head towards her but never took his eyes off me where I was firmly ensconced in Eamon's muscled arms. I didn't take my eyes off him either, despite knowing I should.

Bryn was not only taken, but he was also a health hazard that I should have been staying far away from for my own sanity.

Eventually, Saffir coaxed him out onto the dancefloor with her. Her dress was made of slinky emerald silk that clung tightly to her body and probably cost four of mine, and her icy blonde hair was wound around her head in an elaborate braid. Instead of a mask, she had painted a glittering green snake coiling up her collarbone and neck, ending at her cheek.

I bit back all the spiteful snake jokes I wanted to make because really, Saffir hadn't done anything to me. It wasn't her fault Bryn liked her more than me.

Looking at her lithe figure in that drop-dead gorgeous dress, I thought I might like her more than me too.

The sun was starting to peek through the gaps in the trees by the time the masquerade was coming to an end. Even with Marlen's magic, my feet were crying out for a break and my face ached from smiling so much, but I wouldn't have changed a thing. I didn't think I'd ever been so happy in my entire *life*. Marlen, Arthus, Eamon and I walked back through the forest together, deliriously tired and grinning like lunatics.

"This is where I must leave you, cariad," Eamon said softly as we approached a fork in the forest path. We moved to the side so the other exhausted Academy residents could shuffle their way past, yawning and leaning on each other as they went with their masks dangling from their fingers.

"I'd really like to explore the Fair tomorrow after class, around four pm. Maybe I could meet you?" I suggested, cringing internally at the eagerness in my voice. Marlen sent a wave of reassurance through our bond that warmed me from the inside out.

"I would like that very much," Eamon assured me.

He gently took my hand and brushed his lips lightly over my knuckles. It was chaste and brief and innocent, but I felt it *everywhere*. I was bereft from the moment Eamon broke physical contact, giving me a rueful smile as he backed towards the other path before striding away into the early morning light.

"You like him," Marlen teased quietly, linking my arm through his. I immediately leaned my weary body into him, giving one lingering look at Eamon's back before following Arthus towards the campus.

"I like him," I agreed. It wasn't like I could hide anything from Marlen anyway.

Where was the young woman who arrived in Avalon, adamantly against having any mates? Where was the young woman who led Marlen on a merry dance trying to keep him at arm's length? Was I embracing this part of my fae life or just resigning myself to it?

All I knew for sure was that once the idea of having multiple mates had felt impossible, and now it felt inevitable.

If only the Avalon Fair was an everyday occurrence, I thought dreamily as we emerged from the forest in front of the expansive fairgrounds. It was like my shopping trip to Inver, but on steroids, for three amazing days straight.

It would be even better if classes were canceled—I wanted to explore the stalls, learn more about Avalon, and buy a few more items of clothing that I was sorely lacking, but I'd be lying if I said that seeing Eamon wasn't a big draw either.

He looked even more handsome by daylight, waiting against a tree in a dark linen shirt and trousers with a pale gray knit sweater over his top. From a distance, he looked quite unapproachable, but the moment he saw me, his entire face lit up.

I fairly swooned, which was a touch embarrassing as Marlen was monitoring the bond like a hawk and couldn't even pretend to not be amused.

"Fi," Eamon said, closing the small distance between us and leaning down to kiss my cheek. "You look even more beautiful in the daytime."

"I was just thinking the same thing about you," I replied before my brain caught up with my mouth.

Playing it cool, I was not.

Eamon's incredible amethyst eyes sparkled, a warm delicious feeling spreading through my body that was all him. Arthus and Marlen politely hung back as I took Eamon's arm, hoping he was prepared for the six million questions I would end up asking him about each stall.

We stopped right at the entry to the fairgrounds because he insisted on buying me roasted chestnuts to snack on, and I idly contemplated having a claiming ceremony with him on the spot.

"Did you have to travel far to get here today?" I asked Eamon as I devoured the chestnuts. My head was feeling a tad tender after the lack of sleep and all the ale I drank at the masquerade, despite Marlen's healing last night. Food helped and the chestnuts were good, but not entirely cutting it.

Gods, what I'd do for a greasy cheeseburger and fries right now.

"A short walk. I still own the home I lived in just off campus when I was a student at the Academy. It's about a twenty-minute walk from the edge of campus," Eamon explained casually. Cool, no big deal, he just owned a whole house to live in while he studied.

If I didn't believe he was rich before, I certainly did now.

"Where do you usually live? Where do you work?"

"My family owns properties all over Avalon, mostly used for growing fruit and vegetables. I travel between them and handle the administration from wherever I am at the time. I don't have to travel as much as I do... it's a technique I employ to avoid my mother." He gave me a wry smile, but I could sense the honesty in his words. He really didn't like spending too much time around her.

"I've only ever spent time at the Academy, the fairgrounds, and I went shopping in Inver once. I didn't get to travel in Albion either, so I'm really hoping I get to explore more of Avalon one day. Where's your favorite house?"

"I have one in the northern Outer Isles that I am particularly fond of. The Outer Isles are beautiful, they're a series of small islands that circle the edges of the realm. They're isolated and mostly left alone by the Councils and Assembly, so it's peaceful there. Less posturing and politics than on the mainland."

Eamon had a wistful, dreamy look in his eye that made me eager to see the Outer Isles for myself. He was such a giant, muscly teddy bear. I wanted to snuggle him.

We talked more about the fair and Eamon's travels through the realm as we wandered leisurely amongst the stalls. He described the big wooden ships he used to travel to the Outer Isles in such detail that I could almost feel the planks swaying under my feet and the salty ocean breeze in my hair.

Maybe I could live there after graduation if the inhabitants were left mostly to themselves? The idea of keeping my gift a secret for the rest of my life filled me with dread, but Eamon had given me a healthy dose of wanderlust on top of the regular lust I was experiencing around him. He was so good-looking, yet so shy about it. I wanted to get to know him better so I could shower him in compliments and build up his self-confidence. He was great—a total catch—and it was crazy to me that he didn't recognize that.

Eventually, he excused himself apologetically to get back to his place, as he still had a few letters to send before the end of the day. I didn't mind—it seemed like he had quite an important job, and hanging out with college kids in the middle of the day probably wasn't his top priority.

We bumped into Aderyn outside a small stall selling crochet goods, manned by a fae so old she made Gwyneira look like a spring chicken. We must have stood outside her stand talking for too long, as her irritation started to chafe painfully against my arms. I was desperate to spend as much time at the fair as possible, but the number of people was overwhelming my empath senses. Most of my limbs had gone numb an hour ago and my head was throbbing.

The combination of fae and non-fae at the fair didn't help—I felt fae emotions more deeply, but non-fae emotions sort of pushed up against my periphery in a way that was far more irritating.

It had been a lot easier to deal with at the masquerade, which I attributed mostly to the alcohol, both theirs and mine. *Maybe I should take up day drinking around crowds?*

"Foxglove," Marlen murmured disapprovingly behind me as I insisted Aderyn and I tackle the next row of stalls together. "You need to rest."

I could see him practically telling Arthus with his eyes that I was overdoing it. *Traitor.* At that moment, I wished for nothing more than the ability to turn my freaking gift off so I could enjoy an afternoon out in public with my friend.

And holy fucking fae, it worked!

The sensations weren't completely gone, but they were so muted I barely noticed them. The lightest tingling sensation in my arms, a brush of something down my spine, an awareness of feeling in my chest... They were so toned down I couldn't determine what I was even experiencing. It was glorious.

For a long moment, I just stood there reveling in my own excitement.

Not someone else's excitement. Mine. *All* mine. I pulled Marlen and Arthus aside as discreetly as I could in my slightly manic state while Aderyn was distracted looking at some hideous copper trinkets.

"I turned it off. My ability! I wished it would go away, and it did!" I whisper-shouted at them.

"I can assure you, wishing had nothing to do with it," Arthus responded drily. "Try to *turn it on* again."

He emphasized the three words with raised eyebrows, silently communicating with his disbelief that magic wasn't an on/off thing.

I huffed a little because I was really enjoying the solitude of my own emotions, but curiosity got the better of me. I took a deep breath and concentrated on allowing the emotions around me in. Immediately my bones felt heavy, and my shoulders dropped at the weight of it all.

"Turn it off again," Marlen whispered urgently. "You look so uncomfortable, foxglove. Even I can feel it weighing on you."

"You can't turn magic on and off," Arthus muttered irritably.

"Maybe we can refer to it as muting and unmuting?" I suggested, rolling my shoulders now that I had successfully blocked the emotions out again. This was a freaking game changer.

"Slightly less offensive," Arthus conceded with a nod. "That must be the new element of your ability since mating with Marlen. Greater control."

I'd take it. If all my mating level-ups were as innocuous as that, I'd go four-for-four without even questioning it. Somehow, I didn't think I'd be that lucky.

"You know I think you guys are the cutest circle in the making or whatever, but I was kind of hoping Fi and I would get a chance to hang out?" Aderyn drawled from somewhere behind me.

"Guess we're not in a rush to leave after all," I sang, shooting my guys a mischievous grin, because they were 110% over shopping. I only needed another half hour or so. I was a kind mistress.

We started down another row of stalls that seemed to be mostly food-related. I was eyeing up an exotic-looking juice stall and so enamored with my new muting ability that I didn't notice Aderyn wandering off. If I hadn't muted my gift, I would have sensed the abrupt shift in her mood. As it was, it took a few minutes for me to realize she wasn't standing next to me.

I scanned the crowd only to find Aderyn looking adoringly into the eyes of a man that must have been a stallholder, based on the apron he was wearing. His attention was entirely on Aderyn as he tentatively raised his hand and gently pushed her hair back behind her ear. Marlen made a low rumbly noise in his chest next to me.

"Shush you," I chided. "Aderyn hasn't felt the mating pull the entire time she's been at the Academy, and she was really upset about it. This is an amazing thing for her."

"She's my sister!" he replied, horrified.

"All the more reason for you to be happy for her. The *happiest*, in fact," I lectured.

"Let me get to know him before I decide that," Marlen grumbled, and Arthus made a manly grunting sound that I assumed was an agreement.

Aderyn and her mystery man were already wandering off together towards a small tea stand at the end of the aisle, and I snagged Marlen's hand before he could march off after them. Aderyn would never be able to get to know him with her brother hanging around like a bad smell.

We took three seats on the opposite side of the stall so Marlen could surreptitiously spy on her instead. Mystery Man had a rugged, sexy highlander look about him with an almost wild red beard and windblown hair. They looked beautiful together—like a throwback couple from the moors of Scotland or something. I really hoped he wasn't an asshole, but I assumed he wouldn't be if he and Aderyn felt a strong mating pull.

She was one of the kindest souls I'd ever met.

We headed back to campus that afternoon and I looped my arm through Aderyn's as we headed into our fire elemental class. We had moved on from growing and extinguishing candle flames to working on heat control. Each of us had small pots of water hanging over a little flame in a cast-iron bowl on the desk in front of us. The idea was to bring the water to boil, then cool it down again by controlling the fire.

I pulled Aderyn down into our usual seats and semi wondered if I'd grabbed the wrong person when she started giggling. A proper schoolgirl giggle. Aderyn was always cool and collected. She must be seriously smitten.

"So?" I asked eagerly. "Tell me about him! Is he nice? Do we like him? Can I call off your rabid brother?"

"What? Gods, tell Marlen to stay out of it! His name is Lachlan," she said with a dreamy sigh. "He's a shoemaker, from a small village on the outskirts of the Black Forest."

I was still playing with muting my ability, but I could see the guilt all over her face.

"What aren't you telling me, Aderyn?" I asked, already knowing where she was going with this and dreading what she was going to say.

I really needed to get a map of Avalon.

"It's a few days away by carriage ride... It's a coastal village. Almost as far as you can go in Avalon, except for the Outer Isles."

I blew out a long breath, because I always expected Aderyn to leave as soon as the opportunity arose. She wasn't happy here.

"Have you made a decision already?"

"No, no, of course not," she replied hastily. "We just met. Even fae don't move that fast, Fi. But I guess we'll see where it goes. It's a strong mating pull, we're kindred souls." Aderyn's whole face softened, and her eyes were brighter than I'd ever seen them.

I leaned across the desk and squeezed her hand. "I'm happy for you, seriously. I'll always support you, whatever decision you make. But if you decide to move thousands of miles away, I'm not going to be the one to tell your brother."

"I wouldn't do that to you, sis," Aderyn said with a laugh, and my heart exploded into a million happy butterflies at the endearment. "Come on, let's boil some water."

The following day, we met Eamon for a picnic at the fairgrounds and to enjoy the second day of the fair instead of eating lunch in the commons. Marlen had class, but Briallen and Leigh tagged along with Arthus and me.

"Eamon Adair, I can't believe it," Briallen whispered, leaning in close to gossip with me as we made our way through the crowd. "His family is insanely rich, you know?"

"I've heard," I replied drily. It's not like it was a *bad* thing that he was rich, but it wasn't the massive highlight for me that Briallen thought it was. Rich people came with expectations.

"And an older man," Briallen giggled.

"I haven't actually asked him how old he is," I told her, frowning. "He can't be that much older, right? Otherwise he'd be mated by now."

"I think he's about 40. Definitely old to be unmated, but his gift is kind of terrifying," Briallen replied thoughtfully, and I shot her a sharp glance out of the corner of my eye. Aside from the fact that I hated people judging Eamon for his gift, I was also wary of Briallen's response since she didn't know about my gift yet either. What if she thought I was terrifying once she found out?

At the very least, she'd probably be pissed that I'd been spying on her emotions the whole time I'd known her, even if I couldn't help it. I'm sure it's how I would feel if the roles were reversed.

I decided to shelve the revelation that Eamon was twenty years older than me for now. Maybe it didn't have to matter? I liked Eamon, I could deal with the age gap if he could.

Besides, we were theoretically going to live for *hundreds* of years, so what difference did twenty make?

The extended lifespan concept was still a bit overwhelming if I thought too hard about it.

We all grabbed food from different stalls and sat down on the grass under a large oak tree on some blankets we'd brought with us. It was too cold for a picnic really, but we all huddled close together and lit a fire in a miniature cast iron cauldron Leigh had brought along.

Arthus and Leigh got into a debate about the Academy's air masters with Briallen chipping in from time to time, so I had plenty of opportunities to quietly talk to Eamon. We got along so well, it felt like we'd known each other for a lifetime. It helped that he looked at me like I hung the moon, and the feelings I sensed from him bordered on adoration.

I hadn't told him about my magic, but I had shared that I'd grown up in Albion because my fathers were worried my gift would put me in danger. I even told him about how my dads and I had recently reconnected of sorts, and that they were massively disappointing.

"I can't even imagine not growing up around my family, cariad," Eamon said softly. His eyes were filled with emotion, but I could sense that it was empathy rather than pity. "My parents are very involved in my life—*too* involved. They've been around for a while, so they've seen a lot. My mother and two fathers are all approaching their 400th birthdays."

I blinked at him in silence for a few seconds because lordy, that was freaking old. What did one even *do* for 400 years? Surely life got dull eventually.

"Do you have any older siblings?" I finally asked, remembering that it was polite to respond to people when they spoke to you.

"No," he grimaced. "Centuries of trying, and they were only successful on my mother's last opportunity to have a child. Unfortunately for them, they got a boy."

"Unfortunately?"

"Fae society is matriarchal, as I'm sure you've noticed," Eamon said, cutting me a glance out of the corner of his eye. "When I claim my mate, I will take her name. The main branch of the Adair family will end with me." He shrugged like he didn't care either way.

"That doesn't bother you?" I asked curiously.

It seemed a little old-fashioned to me, but it's not like I had any kind of family legacy to speak of, or a strong attachment to my surname so I couldn't really judge. Marlen had taken my surname, and hearing him say 'Marlen Smith' always made me giggle. It sounded absurdly human and out of place here, but we didn't want to draw unwanted attention by using 'Laisren', my fae surname.

"It doesn't particularly bother me. There are perks that come with a name like Adair, don't get me wrong, but there are also a lot of expectations. I wouldn't mind losing those."

Eamon smiled as I nibbled thoughtfully on my vegetable pot pie. I was glad Eamon was more progressive than his parents, however the reminder that he came from a rich, fancy family had freaked me out a bit.

I was still finding my feet when it came to living among the fae—rubbing shoulders with their elite seemed like a surefire way to make myself miserable. But wasn't that what Eamon meant by having expectations on him? I didn't want to judge him just because his family was rich, just like I hoped he didn't judge me because I wasn't.

He seemed eager to drop the subject of his parents, so we moved on to safer topics like potion making, which Eamon apparently had quite the knack for, and cooking, one of his passions. He was genuinely fascinated with anything I had to say, and so surprised when I asked him questions in return that I got the impression people tended to admire him from a distance.

"We should head back to campus, sweetheart," Arthus interrupted softly, shooting me an apologetic look. I knew he had tutoring sessions he had to prepare for and couldn't just babysit me all afternoon.

"You're right," I sighed. "Will I see you tomorrow?" I asked, turning my attention back to Eamon.

"If you'd like to," he replied with a heartbreaking smile.

"I would. I've got a full day of classes, but perhaps we could meet for drinks in the evening? I'm told it's Solstice Eve tomorrow," I added.

"That is worth celebrating," Eamon agreed. "Until tomorrow, cariad."

He leaned forward to place a chaste kiss on my cheek, and his beard scraped deliciously over my skin.

"Until tomorrow," I parroted as Arthus led me back to campus.

Gods, I was in over my head with all of these handsome fae men. At this rate, I'd be acquiring the powerful emotion-influencing magic in no time.

FFION

CHAPTER 34

After our classes, Marlen, Arthus and I made our way back to the fairgrounds in the evening to meet Eamon for a drink in the tent bar on the last day of the fair. I had been so excited to see him, I'd barely been able to concentrate in class, which was practically unheard of. It was the eve of Winter Solstice—which was sort of Christmas-esque from my limited understanding?—and the day before a short break from classes. It felt like half the Academy had turned out at the fairgrounds.

Part of my excitement was definitely down to the upcoming two weeks off from classes. As much as I enjoyed them, a break to just do *nothing* sounded glorious.

Most students would be returning home tonight to spend the Solstice with their families, including our friends. Aderyn had left for home as soon as our final class finished. She was excited to bring home news that Marlen had claimed his mate, but disappointed to say goodbye-for-now to Lachlan. I had semi-expected Marlen to go home with her, but apparently we were kind of joined at the hip after the whole claiming thing. Marlen explained it would be physically uncomfortable for us to be separated for more than a few days.

After only having myself for company since I was a toddler, I selfishly loved the fact that he couldn't escape me for too long.

Leigh and Briallen had gone back to her parents' place in Northgales. I'd wanted to ask her if Bryn was going there too since he was raised by her family, but I didn't want to give Briallen any more ammunition for her Bryn-and-Fi ship.

Marlen, Arthus and I navigated around the crowd to an enormous tent that had been erected at the center of the grounds. It was the size of a big top, with temporary bars set up inside and wooden benches and barrels scattered around to sit on. The bar stations were mostly staffed by low-magic fae, but there were all manner of creatures drinking and enjoying themselves in the tent.

Gods, I was glad I could turn off my gift for a while now. This place would be hell on my senses if I couldn't.

It was early enough in the evening for it to be a pleasant place to sit and chat, though I knew that in a few hours it would get pretty rowdy here. There was a centaur band that had played live music after dark each night, and it was pure carnage after that.

Eamon was already waiting for us when we got there, with pitchers of ale for the boys and mulled fae wine for me. It was a Solstice specialty that Eamon had insisted I try, and I'd immediately fallen in love with it. It was filled with berries and oranges and cinnamon sticks, and it smelled like happiness in a cup.

And a little like Eamon, though I wasn't about to admit that out loud.

"Hello!" I greeted Eamon excitedly, dropping down onto the bench next to him while Arthus and Marlen sat on the other side of the table. Being close to Eamon felt like the most natural thing in the world. The mating pull felt warm and snuggly in my chest.

As always, he looked at me like I was the last cherry on his ice cream sundae, and that heated gaze never diminished when he saw me hanging all over Marlen or discreetly flirting with Arthus. If anything, it grew hotter. *Eamon might have a voyeuristic side.*

"How was your day, cariad?" Eamon asked, angling his body toward me and leaning in close like he was genuinely interested in hearing what I had to say as he pushed the goblet toward me.

"Fine," I said with a shrug. "Better now. Yours?"

"Better now," he agreed.

"I'm looking forward to having a few days off from classes. It feels like I've been going non-stop since I arrived in Avalon."

"What will you do with your time off?" Eamon asked, the corner of his mouth tipping up slightly into an almost-smile. If it wasn't for Marlen and Leigh, I'd think all fae men were broody assholes who didn't know how to smile.

Speaking of broody assholes...

"Marlen, Arthus, Eamon... Scout." Bryn pulled up a stool at the end of our table, sitting himself down with a pitcher of ale like he'd been invited all along. I cocked a questioning brow at him and he mimicked my expression, but didn't say anything.

Okay then.

"Bryn, good to see you," Marlen said jovially, giving him a manly thump on the back. "I thought you'd be en route to Northgales by now."

Nice of Marlen to tell me that Bryn was going home with Leigh and Briallen. Not that I *cared*, I was just nosy. Marlen should know that.

Bryn shrugged. "I'll fly there tomorrow morning and fly back after the feast. It gets a little crowded at home over winter break, I prefer the quiet of the campus."

It annoyed me how similar he and I were.

"What about you? Where are you spending the Solstice?" he asked curiously, looking around the table.

"We'll be on campus," Marlen answered easily. "Neither Arthus nor I are particularly fussed about visiting our families and Fi's dads are pricks so..."

I snorted. *Don't pull any punches on my account, love.*

"You could come to my house," Eamon offered. "It'll just be me there. My mother and fathers live at the main estate, and I have no desire to suffer through the Solstice with them if I don't have to."

"You wouldn't mind?" I asked hesitantly. I wanted to spend some time with Eamon without the hordes of people around.

Plus, I was dying to see his place.

"I would love it," he assured me, his face softening. I wasn't going to risk using my ability in a room this crowded, but I got the feeling he was underselling it. It would mean a lot to Eamon for us to spend the Solstice with him.

I chanced a glance at Marlen and Arthus, who both looked like they were waiting for me to make the call either way.

"Okay," I said brightly. "That'd be great."

Eamon's relief was palpable. Bryn shot me a brief scowl, but perked up a lot faster than usual. Maybe the happy Solstice Eve vibes were affecting him.

"What does the Solstice entail, anyway? Aside from the feast?" I asked.

Four incredulous faces looked back at me, and I guess that's what I'd look like if a grown-ass human woman asked me what Christmas was.

"The feast is the major part of the day—breaking bread together, exchanging small gifts, that sort of thing," Eamon responded, recovering faster than the rest of the guys. He was more suave than the others— somehow he looked as at home here in this rowdy tent bar as I imagined he would look at a high society event with a glass of champagne.

"Oh? When were you going to mention the getting-each-other gifts part to me?" I asked, giving Marlen and Arthus a withering glare. They both had the grace to look a little sheepish, which was adorable on Marlen and unnerving on my usually stoic Arthus.

Bryn snorted. "I don't know about Arthus, but I'm sure that mating mark Marlen is wearing is the greatest gift you could give him," he said in such a serious, no-bullshit tone that I had to look away.

I didn't know how to handle Nice Bryn.

Where was his girlfriend, anyway? Bryn was a shitty suitor.

Marlen's grin was downright smug. "Well put, Bryn."

"Some families have other traditions too," Eamon said, breaking the awkward moment. I gave him a grateful smile.

"Such as? What do your families do?" I asked, looking around the table.

"Mine watched the sunset over the temple," Arthus offered.

"We're early risers because of the bakery. We'd watch the sunrise together over the fields," Marlen added, smiling softly at the memory.

"It's the shortest day of the year, I'm sure we can manage both," I said with a casual shrug, and they both gave me indulgent smiles. It made me feel like a goddess when they looked at me like that.

I cocked a questioning brow at Bryn to see if he'd continue the most-words-in-one-conversation streak he was currently on.

"There's a long history of fire affinities in my family. We light candles at our ancestors' tombs to honor them on the Solstice," he said, maintaining eye contact and giving me a look that clearly said *challenge accepted*.

"That's really nice," I said a little wistfully. Maybe I could light a candle for the mother who lost her life protecting me. Hopefully she hadn't been as much of a dick as her mates were.

"I suppose," Bryn replied stiffly, and I remembered Briallen telling me he'd gone to live with her after his parents had died. If we ever got past our own bullshit, maybe we could talk about that together.

We drank and talked a little more before the crowd in the tent became too intense to maintain a conversation. The five of us walked out together, and I didn't let myself reflect on how right it felt to be around them.

I farewelled Eamon with an affectionate hug at the fork in the forest path before heading back to the campus with the others. Bryn was heading straight to the stables to fly home, and I noticed him shoving something into Marlen's hand before he turned to me and paused.

The silence extended as we stood in front of each other, the air heavy with expectation.

I got the impression that Bryn wanted me to prove something to him, but I couldn't for the life of me work out what that was. Maybe I was reading too much into it, but it felt like sometimes he pushed me to stake my claim. It was like he wanted me to declare that he was mine.

But he couldn't be mine, because he was hers.

At the end of the day, he was courting Saffir, and it would always circle back to that. If he thought I was going to pursue anything with him while he was involved with someone else—or even own up to the fact that my feelings were more complicated than platonic—he didn't know me at all.

"Happy Solstice, Bryn," I said quietly. His eyes scanned mine, searching for answers I didn't have.

"You too, scout. *Bendithion*."

I planned to be a thoughtful mate and wake us all up to watch the sunrise, keeping Marlen's family tradition alive. Instead, I overslept and woke up with the usual morning bells and the first rays of sunlight already filtering through the cabin.

"I'm sorry," I groaned into Marlen's chest where my head was resting. "I really wanted us to watch the sunrise together. You should consider getting alarm clocks in Avalon."

Marlen chuckled and Arthus' amusement tickled behind my ears. He was lying on my other side, as close as he could be without snuggling.

Arthus wasn't really a snuggler, but I was okay with that.

"It's fine, foxglove. It's not like I enjoyed getting up in the dark to work at the bakery. Our tradition can be watching the sunset. It's at a much more hospitable hour," Marlen said cheerfully.

"*Bendithion*, sweetheart," Arthus murmured into my hair.

"What does that mean? Bryn said it yesterday."

"Did he?" Marlen asked, surprised. "He doesn't strike me as the devout type."

"It's an old-fashioned phrase that the fae say on the Solstice. It means 'blessings'. Like may the gods bless us during the dark, cold winter," Arthus explained. "Since magic started to disappear, the greeting has gone out of style. Not with my family, obviously."

"*Ben-dee-theon*," I told Arthus over my shoulder as I twisted back to kiss him, hoping I didn't butcher the pronunciation too badly.

"Yes, yes, blessings all around. Now get that sexy ass in the shower," Marlen said, playfully tapping my ass where his hand rested on it. "The sooner we're ready to go, the sooner we can head over to Eamon's fancy house. I know you've been obsessing over what it looks like."

I snorted. "And you haven't?"

"Oh, I definitely have. I wonder how big his bed is?" Marlen pondered, waggling his eyebrows at me.

"Shower, both of you," Arthus ordered, rolling onto his stomach and pulling the pillow over his head like our antics were just too much for him to deal with in the morning.

Marlen laughed, dragging me off the mattress by my ankle while I shrieked and Arthus groaned as if he was being tortured. It was better than any Christmas morning I'd had as a kid by far.

Woah.

Seriously *woah.*

Eamon's "house" was a godsdamned tree palace. It made our cabin back at the Academy look like the treehouse equivalent of an outhouse.

Eamon's tree-mansion was a series of four interconnected cabins that seamlessly wound their way through a cluster of trees. Each cabin looked sort of hexagonal in shape and had a small turret with windows in the center of the thatched roofs. The whole structure was built on a platform, surrounded by a railing of polished branches, with enough room for two people to walk side-by-side around the whole thing.

The three of us made our way up the winding staircase that led to one of the two central cabins, the one with a beautifully carved wooden door.

If this was Eamon's *student* accommodations, what was his family estate like?

Arthus knocked firmly on the door as I threaded my fingers through Marlen's, feeling a fresh wave of insecurity now that we were here. I'd grown up in group foster homes for the most part—so this was nicer than anything I'd ever been in.

My insecurities faded when Eamon opened the door, beaming at me like I was the best Solstice gift he could ask for.

"Come in, please," he said, standing back from the door to let us in.

We walked into a cozy living room. There was a fire roaring in a carved clay fireplace against one wall and comfortable furnishings filling out the room. The small turret in the center of the roof had glass panes all around it, and combined with the large picture windows on the front and back walls of the room, the whole space was bathed in soft light.

The furnishings were simple and masculine—a beige couch with a sheepskin rug hung over the back and two forest green armchairs. There were some large navy cushions on the floor and an entire bookshelf on one wall. It was tiny compared to the number of books humans had, but there were still at least forty books on there, and this wasn't even Eamon's primary residence.

"Would you like a tour?" Eamon asked, his amusement cutting through my gawking. I felt my face heat.

"I didn't mean to stare. I haven't seen any houses in Avalon except at the Academy. This is a lot bigger," I told the woven jute rug at my feet. I swear the poor girl vibes were radiating off me so heavily I could see them in the air.

"All the more reason to stare, cariad. Explore to your heart's content, I promise you I don't mind. We should move into the kitchen anyway, I have mulled wine on the stove," Eamon said amicably, gently cupping my elbow and leading me through a wooden archway to another cabin that served as the kitchen and dining area.

It was simple, with a polished wood counter and cupboards along one wall, following the hexagonal shape of the room. There was an enormous tin sink set into the counter, and a huge cast-iron oven and stove top built into the corner. The structure encasing the stove looked like whitewashed clay, with built-in storage shelves filled with cut firewood.

Marlen gave a low whistle as he and Arthus joined us in the kitchen and looked around the room. He and Arthus moved to the enormous farmhouse table that dominated the rest of the room and dropped into chairs next to each other.

"Nice place," Marlen commented lightly, admiring the enormous stove in the corner.

"Thank you," Eamon replied, busying himself with taking the mulled wine off the heat and setting out earthenware mugs for us to drink from. I knew I'd forever associate Eamon's natural cinnamon and cloves smell with mulled wine and the Solstice after being in his home.

I awkwardly hovered next to the counter as he poured our drinks and helped him carry them over to the table, wanting to feel useful since we were taking advantage of his hospitality at such short notice.

Eamon's eyes crinkled as he sat down next to me across from Marlen and Arthus. I think he sensed my discomfort and was being extra sweet to put me at ease. Marlen was sending waves of reassurance through the mating bond every few minutes and combined with a few sips of wine, I finally started to relax and enjoy myself.

There were definitely worse ways to spend a day than tucked away in Eamon's warm home with three kind, supportive, sexy-as-hell guys.

CHAPTER 35

Fi was a goddess among fae in my eyes. And I'd received visions from the actual gods before, so I knew what I was talking about.

The graceful way she moved, the throaty quality of her laugh, the way her amber eyes lit up when something sparked her curiosity...

Everything about her called to me.

At 43 years old, I had completed all four years at the Academy of Avalon and traveled throughout the realm, yet I'd never encountered a kindred soul before. I had experienced the mating pull whenever a female fae's magic called to me, but their souls never did.

They couldn't be a kindred soul if they were terrified of me. For all the riches the Adair family came with, no one wanted a mate plagued by spirits.

I could spoil Fi. Buy her beautiful things, show her my houses all around the realm, feed and clothe her in the finest Avalon had to offer. Fi would never have to worry about coin again if I was her mate, but none of that would matter to her if she feared me. Even though she wasn't the kind of fae to value material goods over her own happiness, part of me was waiting for that moment of terror to set in. I was holding my feelings back as much as I could, not letting myself get too attached, because I was waiting for the moment when my abilities scared her and she ran into the arms of a safer choice.

I needed to find a way to introduce her to my abilities without frightening her. Maybe if I could ease her into the world of Second Sight, she wouldn't immediately bolt in the other direction.

Preparing the Solstice feast with Fi, Marlen and Arthus was a kind of domestic bliss I never thought I'd experience. Fi's soft laughter filled up every cold corner of this large, impersonal house. It had been my living quarters while I studied at the Academy, but it never felt truly home to me until the three of them walked through the door.

Fi and I stood side by side in the kitchen, chopping up the vegetables for the mushroom and leek pie while Marlen kneaded the dough for the bread like he'd done it a million times. Arthus sat at the table, gutting the pumpkin that would be stuffed with mushrooms, wild rice and cranberries before going into the oven to roast.

It was all traditional fae Solstice fare, the kind I'd eaten every year growing up, but I'd never looked forward to it so much. All of it was new to Fi, who'd barely had a hot meal since she arrived in Avalon, and her curiosity about everything made me feel a sense of childlike excitement.

I hope she enjoyed the honey cakes I made for dessert earlier in the day. I really wanted her to like them.

We finished preparing the food and putting them into cast iron pots where they would cook in and around the wood-fire stove. Fi questioned every part of the process and regaled us with descriptions of human cooking contraptions.

We all gathered at the table with more cups of mulled wine while the aroma of the Solstice feast filled the room. Usually, I wouldn't make so much but Fi liked it, so I'd kept a pot of it on the stove all day. Arthus and I sat on one side of the table, with Fi and Marlen opposite.

"Shall we give Fi our gifts now?" Marlen asked with all the excitement of a small puppy. His enthusiasm was rubbing off on me. I'd never particularly cared for the Solstice, it was just another boring ritual spent with my boring parents.

Fi groaned. "You're all getting an IOU on the present front. If you wanted a gift today, you should have given me more notice." She gave Arthus and Marlen a dirty look, but it didn't have any real fire behind it.

My mother would have flayed her mates alive for such an infraction.

Marlen pulled a small item wrapped in cloth from the pouch hanging off his belt and gave Fi a sheepish look. "Remember, you said my riches were soul deep. You said that."

She laughed—the sexiest, throatiest sound that made my pants uncomfortably tight. "I'll love it, no matter what it is, because you gave it to me."

She took the item from his hand and unwrapped a carved wooden figurine. She held it up to examine it and I could just make out a pair of fae wings on a flat platform, with intricate lines and patterns carved into the wood.

"I didn't study Arthus' very closely, but they're based on his," Marlen said shyly. Fi leaned over and kissed him hard, pulling away to whisper a thank you against his lips.

"I love it, I'm going to keep it next to the bed," she announced, lovingly stroking the little figurine.

Arthus smirked, clearly smug at how enamored she was by wings. He leaned over the table and handed Fi his gift. She gave him a grateful smile and unwrapped a silver brooch as big as her palm. It was an oval shape, and I could just make out the stem of foxgloves in the middle of the design.

"For your shawl. You always complain it doesn't stay in place," he grunted, and I smirked a little, seeing the usually unflappable Arthus out of his element. Fi blinked away the tears she refused to let fall. In the few days I'd spent with her, it had become clear she didn't like showing weakness.

"Thank you, that is so sweet," she replied hoarsely. She looked on the verge of panicking, so I handed my gift over to distract her. Fi clearly wasn't used to being shown kindness. That would have to change.

She looked between me and the larger gift curiously. It wasn't particularly elaborate, I'd happily spend my entire fortune on Fi, but I got the feeling that expensive gifts would only make her uncomfortable.

Fi carefully unwrapped the fabric, revealing the carved wooden hand mirror within. It was a simple circular shape with a long wooden handle, no intricate carvings or inlaid stones like my mother's mirrors. Nevertheless, it was a luxury item and Fi was clearly thrilled with it.

"Thank you," she breathed, staring at her reflection, entranced. "This is the first time I've properly seen my reflection without a glamour. There aren't any mirrors in my cabin. My eyes are so different," she murmured, blinking.

"They're beautiful," I assured her. Amber was my new favorite crystal.

"And my skin! It's so glowy," she cooed, turning her face from side to side. "Probably all the vegetables."

"You'd trade in your glowy skin for some terrible human food in a heartbeat," Marlen said with a snort, and Fi shrugged, not disagreeing.

"Huh, I really do look a lot like my father," Fi mused sadly.

"Oh, you have one more gift, foxglove," Marlen said hurriedly before she could sink too deep into her own head, pulling a small rectangular package out of his pouch.

Fi looked at him curiously before gingerly setting the mirror aside to take the gift from him. She opened it and stared. It was a tiny pocketbook with a worn leather cover that read *A Guide to Unicorns*. Even small books were expensive, so it was a generous gift.

Fi ran her finger down the leather cover and gaped at Marlen. "Not me," he said with a rueful smile. "It's from Bryn."

"What!?" she practically shrieked, making Arthus and I both wince.

"He got me a book? Do you think Briallen told him I wanted to learn about unicorns? Why would he give me this?" Fi said quietly to herself as she gently ran her fingers over the worn leather cover. "I better add a fourth IOU to my list."

After a leisurely, delicious dinner, the four of us had sat in a row on the floor of the narrow wraparound porch to watch the sun setting through the trees. It was one of the most tranquil moments I had ever experienced, and I never wanted it to end.

As the sun sank below the horizon, so did my mood. It was too easy to let myself believe that there was a future in this, that maybe I'd earn a spot in Fi's mating circle one day, but I needed to remember that this was all temporary.

It would only last for as long as it took for Fi to see my ability firsthand.

"Could you give us a moment?" Fi asked Marlen and Arthus. She must have noticed my despondent mood, and that only made me feel worse.

Marlen and Arthus immediately went back into the house as Fi moved closer to me, angling her body to face mine and leaning her shoulder against the wall of the house.

"Want to tell me what's bothering you?" she asked, cocking a challenging eyebrow at me. *Not really.* I had a feeling she wouldn't let me off that easily though.

"I keep finding myself getting caught up in the fantasy of this," I admitted, gesturing between her and I. "You'll see my gift soon enough and realize you deserve someone less... frightening."

Fi gave me a long, searching look. I wasn't used to anyone looking at me like they wanted to see into my soul. Especially females. Usually, our interactions had a single objective and occurred under the cover of darkness.

Anyone who knew about my gift tended to avoid eye contact. Probably worried they'd see the spirits of their dead fae relatives reflected in my eyes.

"You don't have to put me up on a pedestal, you know," Fi stated flatly. *Yes, I do.*

"What do you mean?"

"You know exactly what I mean," Fi countered mildly.

I sighed and ran a hand through my hair, looking everywhere except into the all-knowing eyes of the beautiful fae next to me.

"My gift will frighten you. Maybe it doesn't now, but it will, eventually."

Fi scoffed like it was the most absurd thing she'd ever heard.

"Believe me, cariad, I wish it wouldn't. I've never felt a connection like this before—most fae fear me. It will be hard to lose you when you see my gift for yourself and run."

Fi moved to kneel in front of me and ran her hands up the side of my face, tangling them in my hair and pulling my head backward so I was looking up at her. She leaned down and placed an affectionate kiss on the tip of my nose. My heart clenched at the unexpectedly sweet gesture.

No one had ever touched me like this.

"I'm an empath," she said softly, retaining her hold on my head so I couldn't break eye contact.

"I know," I replied in a low voice.

"What? How?" Fi startled, pulling back. I felt the loss of her warmth instantly.

"The spirits told me. I can see that you've been touched directly by the gods' magic, I asked them how it was possible," I explained hurriedly, worried that I had upset her. "I didn't mean to pry, cariad. I've never seen someone with the gods' magic directly on them before."

"It's okay." Fi sighed, but gave me a reassuring smile. "I was worried you'd heard it from someone else. Someone, er, alive," she added awkwardly, and I chuckled. "I don't know what you mean about the gods' magic though," Fi added with a frown, sitting back on her heels.

"You don't?" My eyebrows shot up as I peered at her confused face. "You've been sanctified by the gods. I'm surprised you don't remember, it's supposed to be quite a memorable experience. Pleasurable even."

"Holy shit," Fi whispered, her eyes going wide.

At least my gift was coming in useful for a change.

"Marlen! Arthus!" Fi called, her voice higher and more panicky than usual. She moved to stand up, but I pulled her down next to me instead, wrapping my arms around her shoulders.

It seemed like the right thing to do. I didn't have much experience comforting people.

"What is it, foxglove?" Marlen asked as he and Arthus rushed out onto the porch. Arthus remained standing, always on guard, but Marlen dropped to his knees in front of Fi, linking their hands where hers rested in her lap.

Fi shook her head in disbelief. "I can't believe I forgot about that weird moment with the marble slabs."

"Fi?" Arthus prompted impatiently, eager to fix whatever it was that was distressing her.

"That night when I got the first message, the one on my wardrobe. I'd just come from the temple, or at least I'm pretty sure it was the temple. Six big white slabs of marble in a circle?"

"The temple," Arthus confirmed with a nod.

"Right. Well, I'd stumbled upon it by accident, and it felt like it was calling to me or something, so I stood in the middle of the circle and... I don't even know how to explain it. It felt weird. *Good* weird, but I couldn't move for ages..." she trailed off, looking at me helplessly.

It made both my ego and another part of me swell that she looked to me for help. I wasn't proud of it.

"You think Fi's been sanctified?" Arthus asked sharply, interpreting my silence. Marlen's eyes went as wide as saucers.

"I know she's been sanctified," I confirmed. "The spirits told me, and I can see the gods' magic on her."

"They told him I'm an empath too. No secrets among the dead, apparently," Fi said drily. I grimaced. There were none indeed.

"Oh well, we're all friends here," Marlen said cheerfully, and Arthus shot him a wry look. *Oil and water, those two.* "You really never thought to mention the temple thing, foxglove?"

"I didn't know it was a temple at the time," she said, shooting him a baleful look. "Besides, I've had a lot going on. Now, can someone please explain this whole sanctification thing?"

Marlen's arm swept grandly between Arthus and I. Between his upbringing and my gift, we'd be able to give Fi all the answers on almost anything relating to the gods.

"A sanctification is how the gods mark you for a mission or a purpose," Arthus began slowly. "Whatever your mission is, it has been sanctified—

legitimized—by the divine."

Fi's brow furrowed in confusion. "First of all, I don't want that. Any of that. Second of all, I don't know anything about any mission from the gods. They didn't tell me that when I was in the warm, gooey, happy magic at the temple."

Marlen snorted.

"I have a feeling your mission will become clear soon enough," I muttered. Knowing my luck, Fi would receive a message from the gods via me and would be so freaked out I'd never see her again.

I should have known this was all too good to be true. When the spirits encouraged me to go to the masquerade and I immediately felt the strong pull to Fi, I thought they'd been on my side for once.

In all likelihood, the gods were using me as a conduit to communicate with Fi. If that was the case, I'd enjoy every second of her company for as long as I had it. If I never met another kindred soul in my life, I would always have the memory of my time with Fi to carry me through the next few lonely centuries.

Fi gave me a sharp look. "Okay, now that we've got that cleared up, mind if Eamon and I have a couple more minutes out here? We'll be in soon," she said to Marlen and Arthus. They looked at her curiously before heading back inside.

She really did have us all wrapped around her little finger.

Fi clambered onto my lap so she was straddling me and draped her arms loosely over my shoulders. "I don't give a shit about other fae being scared of your ability, Eamon. I'm not. So, are you going to be my suitor or not?"

I stared at her coy expression in silence for a moment, scarcely believing this moment was actually happening. *Get it together, Adair. Don't screw this up now.*

"I'll take you for as long as you'll have me, cariad," I promised.

After that, nothing else mattered because Fi's mouth was on mine and her hands were in my hair and it was godsdamned everything. Everything. She fit me like a glove, her soft body molded perfectly against me, her mouth felt like it was designed to kiss mine.

I couldn't have stopped myself from hardening underneath her if I'd tried. She was every temptation I'd ever had wrapped into one perfect package. Fi rolled her hips against me, clearly noticing my excitement, and I groaned into her mouth. Fucking gods, I would never get enough of her.

We stayed locked in each other's embrace, exploring each other's mouths for what felt like hours. Eventually, we broke apart and Fi giggled. "Marlen just sent me a pulse of impatience through our bond."

I tipped my head up to lightly brush my lips over her jaw. "Let's not keep them waiting. It's dark. Will you guys stay here tonight?"

"Can we?" she asked, surprised, pulling back to look into my eyes.

"I wouldn't have it any other way, cariad," I said softly, entranced by her exquisite face and the innocence in her eyes that didn't match the sensuality of her movements.

"Then I'd love to," Fi said with a giddy grin. "Let's go ask the guys."

She stood up and reached out her hand to help me up. I snorted and stood up on my own, I probably weighed two of her. She laughed, not offended in the least, and took my hand to lead me into the house.

I'd follow her anywhere.

FFION

CHAPTER 36

I must have died and gone to fae heaven. That was the only explanation for the blanket of solid muscle that I was wrapped up in. I was tightly ensconced in Marlen's arms, with Eamon's hand on my hip and legs tangled in mine from his spot behind me. Arthus lay on Marlen's other side, and I reached a little further over Marlen's chest so I could brush Arthus' bicep with my fingertips.

Fae. Heaven.

Marlen chuckled sleepily from underneath me. "Enjoying yourself, foxglove?"

"So much," I told him seriously, not in the least bit embarrassed that I'd been caught.

Eamon stretched a little behind me and I felt his hard-on brush against my ass before he quickly moved away. His entirely unnecessary embarrassment warmed my cheeks, so I rolled over to plant a kiss on his jaw to let him know that I wasn't bothered.

The total opposite of bothered, if anything.

Eamon tangled his hands in my hair and gave me a firm kiss on the forehead in return. "I'm going to make us some breakfast, get up whenever you're ready."

I stretched out like a lazy kitten into the space Eamon vacated, luxuriating in the feel of his fancy sheets against my skin. The Academy-issued stuff was fine, but these sheets were next level. I was halfway to orgasm just from rolling around on them.

There was only one bedroom in the house, and it was accessed via the living room and had a bathroom in an attached cabin on the other side. The bed was weirdly huge in proportion to the room, and it had comfortably slept all four of us last night.

The guys hadn't even blinked at sleeping in the same bed, which made me question everything I thought I knew about men. The human boys at the group home I grew up in would rather sleep on the floor than share beds most of the time.

Aside from the large bed, there was a set of drawers and a carved wooden wardrobe in the room. Currently, the heavy forest green velvet drapes were drawn around the windows and the room was almost pitch black.

Arthus and Marlen were both breathing steadily again, drifting back to sleep, so I carefully got out of bed and went through to the bathroom to freshen up before helping Eamon with breakfast. I eyed the sunken circular bathtub in the middle of the floor enviously.

Maybe Eamon got proper hot water in his house? After months of tepid showers, I'd consider trading a kidney for a hot bath.

By the time I reached the kitchen, Eamon already had a large pot of porridge going on the stove. He hadn't put a shirt on yet and I admired the subtle ripples of his muscular back as he stirred the porridge and stoked the fire.

It really should be illegal to have a *back* that's sexy enough to make me contemplate stripping off right here in the kitchen.

"Let me help," I offered, my voice a breathy rasp.

Eamon's eyes ran up from the thick woolen socks on my feet, pausing on the stretch of thigh showing underneath the shirt I'd borrowed from him to sleep in. My hair was pulled up in a messy bun and my face was probably splotchy from sleep, but Eamon looked at me like he was genuinely contemplating having *me* for breakfast.

"Sure," he replied eventually, swallowing thickly. "You could cut some fruit, if you like."

I moved to the counter, pulling out a knife and cutting an assortment of fruit to go with the porridge while Eamon finished cooking. The sky was growing lighter outside, bringing the sound of birdsong with it, and it was all so... normal. *Domestic.* I was just a normal woman, making breakfast with my boyfriend for ourselves and my other two boyfriends, who were crashed out in the bed we'd all shared last night.

Just a totally normal, lazy morning.

The noise must have roused Arthus and Marlen as they shuffled in not long afterwards and helped us lay out the breakfast on the table. They hadn't put on shirts either, and between the three of them, I was guzzling peppermint tea like it was going out of fashion because my mouth was hella dry.

"Thirsty?" Arthus asked lightly, cocking his brow at me.

So thirsty. So much thirst.

"Something like that," I replied diplomatically, raising my cup to him. He gave me a knowing smirk.

"What's the plan today?" Marlen asked, loading up his bowl of porridge with berries.

"Don't feel that you need to rush back to the Academy. You're all welcome to stay for as long as you like," Eamon said with an adorably tentative smile.

"Do we need to rush back?" I asked, glancing between Marlen and Arthus, who both shook their heads. "Then I'd love to hang out with you more," I told Eamon decisively.

If you want to not get dressed all day, that would be fine too.

We ate slowly and cleaned up together, the picture of domestic harem bliss. Marlen and Arthus moved into the living room to admire Eamon's book collection while he and I got dressed to cut some firewood outside.

By which I mean he cut the firewood and I perved on him from my spot at the bottom of the stairs, tugging my shawl tightly around me to keep out the chilly wind.

"Do you like staying at this house?" I asked Eamon curiously as he balanced the next log on the stump to cut.

Eamon paused to consider his answer. "I like it far more now than I did when I was a student," he said, shooting me a wry smile. "Better company."

"What are your other houses like?"

"Ground level, mostly. Bigger. This is the only house I've ever purchased for myself, the other ones belong to my family. What was your house in Albion like?"

"I lived in a boarding house, so I mostly just stayed in my bedroom. It was fine. Have you ever been to Albion? Humans don't really live in trees, you know," I babbled, feeling embarrassed about my humble beginnings again. It was stupid, I'd only ever sensed curiosity and interest from Eamon about my past. The insecurities were entirely of my own making.

Eamon lifted the ax above his head and swung it down gracefully, splitting the log with ease. He'd unfortunately opted to put on a shirt, but it was loose and half unbuttoned, showing off a generous amount of muscular chest. The thin sleeves whipped around his biceps as he moved, and he'd rolled the ends up, displaying his tanned, corded forearms.

Gods, he was easy on the eyes.

"Fae don't like to clear trees for housing, it's seen as disrespecting the natural environment. Hence all the treehouses," Eamon explained with a shrug. "It's a bit hypocritical—there are a million other ways we disrespect our environment—but I guess it's a tradition at this point."

"I'd really like to see one of your other houses sometime," I told him shyly. I didn't want to pressure him or come across like a full-on stalker, but I was desperate to learn more about his life and visit the amazing places he went to.

"I'd like that too, cariad," Eamon replied with a smile so hopeful that it made my breath catch in my throat.

We spent another day and night at Eamon's place before Marlen, Arthus and I headed back to the Academy. Eamon had to spend a couple of days traveling to check on one of his other properties, and I was secretly sulking a bit about having to leave him, but it seemed rude to Marlen and Arthus to admit that, so I didn't say anything.

Except Marlen and I were bonded, and apparently that meant I couldn't hide anything from him. He figured it out within five minutes of leaving Eamon's place.

Strangely, I didn't have any desire to reach for my bond with Marlen and try to get a read on him. Maybe it was a lifetime of being bombarded with other people's emotions, but I loved being able to mute my ability and just chill in my own head with nothing but my own company. I loved Marlen, but I was happy to see his feelings play out in his words and actions rather than taking a sneak peek into his psyche.

Arthus had disappeared to the air mastery classroom to plan his tutoring sessions for after winter break, so I dragged Marlen to the library for an afternoon of shared solitary reading time.

The library was dead during the break since there were barely any students on the campus. The elderly librarian was tucked up in a rocking chair she'd brought in from somewhere with a knit blanket over her knees, looking half asleep. Maybe Gwyneira would hire me one day, because that librarian looked like she was living my dream.

Marlen snagged a military history tome before dropping unceremoniously into an armchair near the window. I perused the shelves slowly, not entirely sure what I was looking for. The problem with knowing *nothing* is that *everything* was interesting, but I was also flying blind on where to begin.

I wanted to get better at manipulating elements other than air, but there weren't a lot of books on that. It was something you had to just *feel*. I also wanted to know more about the dark fae, but there didn't seem to be any books specifically about them in the library. Were they so rare they weren't worth writing about, or were books about them censored? Strange.

I ran my fingers over the worn leather spines until one caught my eye—
The Gods: Winning their Favor and Incurring their Wrath.

Interesting. Not that I needed any more favor from the gods, but knowing what *not* to do would probably be a sensible idea.

I gently pulled the book down from the shelf and curled up in the armchair next to Marlen, tucking my feet underneath my body.

A large part of the book was devoted to where various temples were located around Avalon and what kind of rituals should be performed at the temples to appease the gods. I mostly skimmed those bits since Arthus was a walking encyclopedia of temple-related information. What fascinated me was the author's thinly veiled criticism towards the fae sprinkled throughout the book.

I already knew the gods weren't dead like Aderyn had suggested—I doubted I would have been sanctified if they were dead—but the way most fae talked about the gods was like they had forsaken the fae. Given up on them. For... reasons.

The author in this book was far more critical of the fae's role in their own demise. The fae weren't losing their magic because of the gods' oversight, but because they were being *punished*.

Based on the warnings I'd got about what would happen to me if knowledge of my gift got into the wrong hands, that seemed like an obvious conclusion to me. Too many fae had gotten greedy, and the gods were taking away their magic bit-by-bit to set them straight.

Was the author of this book really in the minority with that opinion? For the hundredth time, I wondered if I was getting the full picture here at the Academy where almost everyone was full to the brim with magic, and I'd wasted my opportunity to talk to low-magic fae at the fair because I'd spent all my time mooning over Eamon. Maybe Marlen would be willing to take me on a trip to visit his parents and stay in the village he grew up in?

I needed answers, and I wasn't going to find them within the Academy's privileged walls.

Lost in my thoughts about the gods, I barely noticed when Marlen and

Arthus swapped babysitting duties en route to the cabin. Marlen headed over to the arena to work out, since apparently he'd slacked off enough during the break, and Arthus led me back to the cabin to relax.

"Sweetheart? You're very quiet. Did you not want Marlen to go?" Arthus asked quietly. A tightening in my chest and an uncomfortable slithering sensation alerted me to Arthus' jealousy.

It was gone as quickly as it came, and I decided not to call him out on it. Yet.

"It's not that at all. I was just thinking about a book I was reading," I replied, giving him a reassuring smile as Arthus took the key from me and unlocked the cabin.

Arthus had never needed reassurance from me before, not really. Not in the way that Marlen did with his insecurities about his background or Eamon did with his fear of rejection.

He gestured for me to enter and closed the door behind me. We both stood in the doorway removing our winter layers and hanging them on the hooks next to the door.

"Good. I have plans for us tonight and I'd hate to put them on hold because you're missing Marlen," he replied, running his fingers lightly over my collarbone and up my neck. I tipped my head back to give him better access, feeling goosebumps rise everywhere he touched.

"What kind of plans?" I asked breathily.

"Want to play?" Arthus asked in his silky sex voice.

Yes, please.

"Okay," I responded with as much chill as I could muster. I kind of wanted to salivate all over him.

"Good. Upstairs, sweetheart. On the bed," Arthus ordered, and I happily complied. He followed me up the ladder a few seconds later with his satchel slung over his shoulder.

"Trust me?" he asked, a little less confident than he had been just moments before. His nervousness skittered down the back of my neck.

"Always," I assured him.

He reached into his satchel and pulled out a long length of rope. I watched him curiously.

"Still trust me?"

"So far, so good," I replied, though I was the teeniest bit nervous. Arthus moved to the center of the bed and threw one end of the rope up over the ceiling beam, which was about four feet above us.

He beckoned me over to where he was waiting with the rope, and I had a fairly good idea of where he was going with this. My core clenched in anticipation.

"Strip," he commanded. I pulled my dress off while giving him my best bedroom eyes.

Once I was naked, I kneeled underneath the rope and Arthus began binding my wrists together above my head. The fact that he was fully dressed while tying me up naked sent another gush of arousal through me. Everything about this felt... bad, illicit. Fucking hot.

"You say 'stop' and I'll stop," Arthus promised before leaning forward and capturing my lips in a ferocious kiss that left me panting.

He pulled away, and I swayed after him like I was under his spell, my lips swollen and tingling from his attention. Arthus smirked again, flashing me his dimple before moving back completely to undress. I stared unashamedly at all that smooth bronze skin and taut, defined muscles on display.

He took his time moving around me—kissing and sucking every inch of my body except the parts I very much wanted him to kiss and suck. I knew he was testing me, seeing if I could be good and wait patiently. I wasn't about to risk saying anything now—*surely*, he'd cave soon. His lust was burning through my veins, blending with my own need, and for once I had no desire to mute my ability. I wanted to feel every second of this.

"So patient for me, sweetheart," Arthus murmured approvingly, his lips brushing against the soft skin of my throat.

Just when I thought he was going to start his torture all over again, he looked up at me with an excited gleam in his eye, full of filthy promise. Without giving me a moment to process what that look meant, Arthus gripped the back of my thighs, lifting my legs up from my kneeling position to wrap around him.

With one more swift movement he'd hefted me up so my legs were wrapped around his head and his face was buried in my pussy. I held on tightly to the ropes and leaned my body weight back. My muscles would probably hate me for this acrobatic shit later, but holy hell was it worth it right now.

Arthus' tongue was made for sin. I wanted to watch the master at work, but I couldn't keep my eyes open, too overwhelmed with sensation. My head tipped back and the feeling of my long hair tickling my back, my body suspended in the air, and the rope rubbing against my wrists made my pussy clench in anticipation. This was too fantastical to be my life.

With one more punishing suck on my clit, my body exploded into ecstasy, my thighs clamping tightly around Arthus' head. I didn't know where he began and I ended. I didn't know anything except how good this feeling was.

Arthus gave me a moment to recover before he lowered me back down to wrap my legs around his waist. He plunged his cock into me mercilessly, his tight grip on my ass both supporting my weight and moving me along his length.

I didn't even try to fight him. I moved where he wanted me to move and let him own every second of my pleasure.

"Come for me, sweetheart. I can feel your muscles clenching around me, I know you're ready. Come," Arthus demanded, and by the gods, I did exactly what he asked. Liquid heat caressed every bit of my body. My vision was a hazy mess of blurred shapes and bright stars.

Groaning my name, Arthus found his release, stilling inside of me and tightening his grip on my thighs. We stayed locked together, catching our breaths for a long moment before Arthus recovered enough to lower my legs to the mattress and untie my wrists.

I collapsed on the bed and was relieved when Arthus followed suit, pulling me closer to his side. He didn't have the same compulsion for intimacy after sex that Marlen did, so I appreciated his efforts all the more because I knew they were just for me.

We lay staring up at the stars through the skylight for a while, Arthus' hand loosely playing with my hair while mine drew light circles on his chest. I needed a moment to build up the courage for the conversation I wanted to have with him.

"There was something I wanted to talk to you about," I said finally, propping up on one elbow so I could look down at Arthus. He folded his hands behind his head, making the muscles in his arms bulge deliciously.

I was tempted to let myself get distracted by his fine as hell body and not have this conversation, but I knew it was necessary even if it might be awkward.

"What's that, sweetheart?" Arthus drawled, looking mildly amused with me blatantly checking him out. I shook my head slightly to clear my wayward thoughts.

"Us. Specifically, the bouts of jealousy you've been having around Marlen lately." I raised a questioning brow at Arthus, who tipped his head back to stare out of the skylight above us and blew out a long breath.

"I'm jealous that you've claimed him as your mate, even though I have no right to be. You've been with Marlen longer and even if you hadn't, it would still be wrong of me to pressure you into a decision," Arthus said carefully.

"That's not how this works," I retorted, exasperated with having this conversation over and over again with each of the guys. "Or it's not how it works with me, anyway. I'm not some kind of queen who makes all the decisions here. If you think we're moving too fast or too slow or whatever, then we discuss it together." I gave him my sternest I-mean-business face.

"Are you trying to give me orders, Ms. Laisren?" Arthus asked, his voice slipping into that dangerous, seductive tone he always used when he wanted to get into my panties.

It was working. My nipples were painfully tight, and my vagina was ready to party despite being out for the count with a sex hangover about two minutes ago.

"You don't want to experiment with that dynamic?" I teased. "I bet you'd look good all tied up."

Arthus snorted. "I'm going to paint your ass red for that comment."

"Promises, promises." I winked and leaned down to kiss his pectoral. I'd never be tying Arthus up—of that I was certain—but the fact that he was comfortable with this gentle, affectionate contact was huge progress.

"Alright, I'd like to discuss taking our relationship to the next level," Arthus said, as if he was humoring me by having an adult conversation about our future.

Fae males were something else.

"I'm open to the idea of a claiming ceremony, if that's what you're saying," I told him quietly, staring down at the sheets. I was 90% sure that's where he was going with this conversation, but I'd still be mortified if I was wrong.

Arthus' arms banded around me as he suddenly hauled me up onto his chest. We were practically nose-to-nose, his stare intent on my face, searching for something in my expression.

"Do you mean that, Fi? You can't say something like that if you're not serious."

"I wouldn't say it if I didn't mean it," I assured him.

I knew I was being spontaneous, but I didn't question my commitment to him for a second. From the moment I'd met Arthus, I followed him around like a little lost puppy, totally enamored. I'd been smitten with him from the beginning, trusted him from the beginning, and he'd never let me down. I knew that trust didn't come easily for Arthus, and I hoped one day I could be that person for him if I wasn't already.

"Well, okay then," he said softly, his voice filled with more emotion than I'd ever heard from him.

"Soon? Before the end of winter break?"

"Anything you want, sweetheart." He leaned up to capture my lips in the sweetest kiss we'd ever shared—no power play, no games, just the two of us agreeing that this thing between us was for keeps.

FFION

CHAPTER 37

It had only been a couple of days since we'd last seen Eamon, but it felt like *forever*. Marlen, Arthus and I were walking to his place to spend the night there, celebrating New Year's Eve, just the four of us.

There were plenty of parties happening on campus, but even with my ability to mute my empath senses, I wasn't really a party girl. Maybe too many years of not being around crowds had put me off the idea entirely.

Eamon ushered us into the house out of the cold just as the first snowflakes began to fall outside. I gave him a quick kiss then dragged him over to the window, mesmerized as dainty white snowflakes floated lazily to the ground.

Eamon stood behind me, wrapping his thick arms around my middle and resting his chin on the top of my head. He was a freaking giant.

"Do you enjoy the snow, cariad?" he asked softly.

"It's much prettier here than where I grew up. This is the first time I've really appreciated it," I admitted. Snow in London equaled public transport going to shit and gray sludge all over the pavement. It was a lot more picturesque out here in the middle of a forest.

"I'm sorry to say it won't get much heavier than this. This region of Avalon is too warm for snow to settle on the ground for long," Eamon said forlornly, and I felt his genuine remorse. If it were in his power, I'm sure he'd have the entire forest blanketed in knee-deep snow, just to make me happy.

He was both a sweetheart and an overachiever like that.

I turned in his arms and placed a soft kiss against his lips. "This is almost perfect. We just need a drink in hand to sip and enjoy the view," I added teasingly. He smiled and led me by the hand into the kitchen where Marlen and Arthus had made themselves entirely at home with mugs of ale.

I was torn between being impressed at how comfortable they were and feeling like I had errant children whose horrible manners I needed to apologize for.

I didn't sense any annoyance from Eamon, though. Just… satisfaction? It was a hard-to-identify emotion, but it definitely felt on the warm, fuzzy side of things. He opened a bottle of fae wine for him and I to share, leaving Marlen and Arthus to their ales. Eventually, Eamon produced the most beautiful pack of cards I had ever seen, and the guys schooled me in every card game known to fae.

The drinks had been flowing without us paying much attention, and we were all pretty happily buzzed after a couple of hours. I'd never felt safe enough to truly let go and lose control in Albion, so getting drunk was a weird and novel experience. The four of us were standing in the kitchen, making drinks and laughing at Marlen and I as the clock approached midnight.

"To books! And paper! Beautiful, sexy paper," I announced as I raised my goblet, my voice a little more slurred than I'd intended.

"No, no, that's a terrible one," Marlen replied, shaking his head. "I'll come up with a better one. Um, to…snow? The snow is so nice. Like cold water. I love water."

Marlen flicked his fingers at me, and a few droplets of water landed in my hair to illustrate his point.

"I'm not toasting to water," I said somberly, shaking my head. "Air is a much cooler affinity. Maybe the best one. Or fire. Fire is badass."

"I'll be sure to let Bryn know," Arthus said drily, raising an amused eyebrow at me. My face felt weirdly hot and tight. Too much alcohol for me.

"Okay, okay, it's nearly midnight. Let's get serious here. To Fi's beautiful orgasms, long may they continue. Long. Like they go on for ages. It's incredible, honestly," Marlen said, tilting his drink toward me in appreciation, and I burst out laughing. Even Arthus and Eamon smiled a little at that one. Arthus didn't roll his eyes once.

We clinked our goblets just as the clock struck midnight and tipped our drinks back simultaneously.

I was still giggling from Marlen's toast, but my laughter died in my throat as Eamon's face suddenly went blank and his eyes fell shut.

"Eamon?" I lightly shook his shoulder. "Eamon? What's happening?"

Arthus and Marlen appeared on either side of me like a sexy dominant devil on one shoulder and a light-hearted cuddly angel on the other.

"Sweetheart, I think he's communing with the spirits," Arthus said softly, resting his hand lightly at the base of my back to calm me down. Marlen reached forward to grab my hand and gave my fingers a gentle squeeze. The buzz from my wine seemed to drain straight out of my body, leaving me stone-cold sober and more than a little freaked out.

After a few terrifying seconds, Eamon's eyes opened, but there wasn't a trace of the beautiful rich violet I loved to lose myself in. His pupils had disappeared completely, and the irises of his eyes were a cloudy gray that seemed to shift and swirl the more I looked at them.

It was beautiful, in a horrifying kind of way.

"Sanctified Empath. The darkness will come for you. Do not lose faith. The gods have plans for you."

Eamon's usually raspy voice was low and hoarse, sending a shiver down my spine. His emotional state felt fine though, so I wondered if he even knew this was happening.

He blinked as though he was trying to get dust out of his eyes and shook his head slightly. When he raised his head to look at the three of us, his eyes were back to their brilliant amethyst hue.

"Do you, um, remember what happened?" I asked cautiously. Eamon gave me a wary smile even as he took a small step back from me. His despair constricted painfully in my throat, and I was reaching for him even as he tried to get away.

"I do. Do not worry about me, cariad. I am far more worried about you."

I noticed out of the corner of my eye that the guys were exchanging loaded looks above my head and let out a long sigh. Why couldn't we just have one night of frivolous drunken fun? *Thanks, gods.*

"I don't even know which part scares me more. This abstract darkness that is supposedly coming for me or the fact that the gods have plans for me specifically. Neither of those sounds great," I muttered to no one in particular.

Before he could run any further, I leaned forward to grip Eamon's shirt, holding him in place. This was the first time I had really seen his gift in action, and while it caught me by surprise, it didn't scare me. He could no more control which ability the gods "blessed" him with than I could, and seeing it firsthand didn't change the way I felt about him.

Eamon looked down at where my hands held tightly to his shirt and I felt the smallest embers of his hope flaring in my chest, burning through his suffocating despair.

I looked him in the eye, wanting him to see the sincerity in my face. "I am not afraid of you or your gift, Eamon Adair. You cut that crap out right now."

Marlen chuckled next to me, and I felt Arthus' amusement. "Don't even think about wallowing," Marlen added. "Fi doesn't tolerate it."

I blushed slightly at his teasing tone but did my best to give Eamon a stern, don't-mess-with-me face. He rewarded me with a soft, genuine smile that made his already handsome face glow. He looked younger when he smiled like that, almost boyish. Gods, I wanted to see that happiness on his face every second of every day.

"Thank you, cariad," he said softly, leaning forward to kiss my forehead, but I tipped my head up and pulled him down by his shirt to my lips instead.

"I'm going to go outside for a moment," Eamon said softly, giving me a weak smile as he extricated himself from my grip, making a beeline for the door.

I allowed him five minutes of wallowing in his insecurities before I followed him out onto the porch outside the living room. The view out here was so freaking magical, I couldn't believe he lived here. It wasn't even his full-time house.

Eamon was leaning back against the wall next to the window, staring up at the sky, and I gently pushed the door closed behind me so we could have some privacy before sliding down the wall next to him and curling up against his side. I could feel his tension, but he still reached an arm around me and pulled me closer, as if any distance between us was too much.

"I'm not going to run," I assured him when he remained silent. "If anything, you're running. I'm chasing you right now," I chided, and Eamon chuckled.

"Very true, cariad. I can't say I thought I'd ever run from you. You feel too good to be true, I'm waiting for the gods to take it all away," Eamon admitted reluctantly.

"Haven't you heard? The gods like me. I'm sanctified," I teased, climbing onto his lap so I could straddle his legs just like I had when I'd basically ordered him to become my suitor. The mating pull writhed and strained in my chest, begging me to get closer.

I leaned forward to capture Eamon's lips in a light kiss, but his hands caught my ass in a tight grip, pulling me closer as his mouth devoured mine.

"You sure you're not going anywhere?" he rasped between kisses.

"Show me how much you want me to stay," I countered, panting a little and squirming uncomfortably on his lap as the ache between my thighs grew.

My hands were everywhere. Eamon was broad as hell and built like a mountain. He made me feel like the dainty little flower that I definitely wasn't.

In the back of my mind, I realized we were about to screw outside in the snow in the middle of the night, but I couldn't move away, couldn't stop for even a minute. We'd just have to keep each other warm.

Eamon's hands had shifted under my dress to unlace my panties but he left my dress, shawl, and thigh-high socks on, probably concerned for my comfort. His enormous hands ran up and down my inner thighs, his thumbs brushing just shy of my pussy before moving away again.

"Don't tease," I moaned in protest, and he gave me a surprisingly cocky smirk.

"I want to take my time with you, cariad, but I don't want you to freeze to death either," he admitted.

"We can do this again. Tonight, even. Touch me," I all but begged, or maybe commanded.

Eamon let out a low growl as he ran his hands up my thighs again, this time letting his thumbs go higher, feeling the wetness that was already gathering between my legs. I sighed in ecstasy, leaning back on my hands so my heaving chest was thrust out, all of me exposed and wanting.

It was dark outside but the light from the fire and candles was streaming out through the window next to us, putting a spotlight on me for him. He continued to tease me with his thumbs a little longer and I was giving him one hell of a view. I'd gotten the impression before that Eamon was a very, er, visual person. His eyes always darkened with lust when he saw me kissing or touching Marlen or Arthus. The laser focus of his eyes on my pussy as he worked me slowly was all the confirmation I needed.

One of Eamon's thumbs roughly circled my clit while he slid two thick digits inside of me and I nearly came on the spot. The combination of the feeling of his hands on me, how wantonly on display I was for him and his lascivious gaze had my skin heating and core tightening.

I rode his hands, desperately chasing my release, and came with a muffled scream that Marlen and Arthus definitely heard. My head fell back, and I stared up at the stars as snowflakes caught in my hair, chest heaving.

"That was—"

"Perfect, you are perfect," Eamon interjected. I tilted my head back down and his lust-filled eyes were concentrated solely on me.

"—just the beginning. I need more," I said hoarsely. "I want all of you."

"You have me," Eamon assured me. He removed his hand from my thigh to unlace his trousers and pull out his —

Holy crap, was that even going to fit?

Eamon was tall, broad-shouldered, muscly, and fucking huge everywhere.

I stared at his cock wide-eyed for a second before shifting my weight forwards and lining him up with my entrance. To hell with more foreplay. I wasn't 100% sure he was going to fit, but I was really eager to try, I bet it'd feel amazing.

Eamon's breathing was labored as I lowered myself down, slowly easing him into me, biting down so hard on my lower lip I was sure I would draw blood. His upper body was tense with the effort of holding himself still and letting me go at my own pace.

"Cariad, you feel amazing," he said in a strangled voice as I took more and more of him. "So godsdamned *tight*, so wet. Shit, I'm not going to last long at this rate."

I laughed. "Good, neither am I. Your cock is a freaking monster. In a good way. A good monster."

Finally, he was fully sheathed, and I held still for a moment to adjust to his significant size. Eamon's hands cupped my ass, kneading my cheeks and making me squirm. The second I did, we both groaned at the friction.

I gripped Eamon's shoulders tightly for balance and lifted up on my knees before slowly sinking down again. Generally I was a fan of hard and fast, but I wanted to savor this moment, ushering in the new year while riding my newest suitor out in the snow.

When I was with him like this, the warning from the gods didn't exist. There was no darkness coming for me, just a beautiful life filled with light and goodness. Eamon's eyes were hazy as he watched me move, thrusting his hips upwards to meet mine. His lust fueled mine, mixing into a cocktail of want.

I leaned forward to capture his lips in a deep, exploratory kiss. A kiss that felt like a promise of more to come.

Eamon's thumb moved back to the apex of my thighs, and he watched avidly as he circled my clit, biting his lower lip in the sexiest way as he admired his handiwork. *Literally*. His burst of additional lust sent me over the edge again and my nails dug in tightly to his shoulders as I cried out, barely able to keep myself upright as my whole body went boneless.

Eamon drew out my orgasm for what felt like hours, wringing every ounce of pleasure out of my body before he found his own release. I slumped forward and rested my head on his shoulder with his arms loosely wrapped around me.

Honestly, I was semi-regretting not having this little moment on a bed because it wasn't the most comfortable, and my knees were starting to hurt where they were digging into the decking, but mostly it was beautiful and magical and everything I ever wanted.

After a few minutes of snuggling, the door banged open and Arthus strode out, irritation written all over his face.

"I'm really happy for you both." *He says, looking furious.* "But you need to get Fi inside right now before she catches her death out here in the snow."

I muffled a laugh against Eamon's shoulder. "I'm fine, but yes, we will be right in." Arthus stormed back in the house, and I gave Eamon a kiss to assuage the guilt he was feeling.

"Ignore him—he's immensely overprotective and out of practice using his words with other living creatures. Honestly, I have no idea how he tutors people. Let's go inside and resume this cuddlefest by the fire."

We woke up in the bed the following morning in a tangled mess of limbs, just like we had the morning after the Winter Solstice. We'd only slept—I didn't think I was quite ready for intimacy with all three of them, and they seemed to realize that—but being around them was the most refreshing sleep I ever got.

"Cariad, I hope this isn't overstepping, but I stopped at a market town when I was visiting that other property..." Eamon trailed off, running his hand through his hair awkwardly.

"Okay...?"

"There are some clothes in the wardrobe for you. Not that I don't like your regular clothes," he added hastily. "I just thought maybe you'd like some more? There's some more suitable for winter too."

My already full heart swelled. "That is so sweet of you, thank you." I leaned over to give him a soft kiss before wriggling out of the tangled mass of limbs to the wardrobe. About a third of which was taken up by women's clothes now.

It made me a little bit weepy.

I picked out a green dress that was tailored pretty well to my size and buttoned up the front. It had three-quarter length sleeves and the circular skirt fell to just below my knees. Most importantly, it was made of a thick wool-blend type of fabric that was much warmer than the linen dresses I had been making do with.

After a leisurely breakfast, we decided that all four of us should talk to Gwyneira as a group about the sanctification at the temple and the warning from the spirits. I didn't want a repeat of the telling off she gave me for not mentioning the other notes—deserved as it was—and she may have some useful insight. Surely you didn't live until age 400 without learning a thing or two.

Eamon knew Gwyneira well from his time at the Academy so I was glad he was coming along. We were all technically adults, but Eamon seemed more adult than the rest of us. He was older, and between his business-like demeanor and Arthus' commanding nature, it took some pressure off me to make all the decisions.

It was a novelty having people to rely on. I wasn't entirely comfortable with it just yet, but I was making progress.

We walked through the forest together, taking a path that skirted around the campus to get to Gwyneira's isolated cabin. I alternated between walking arm-in-arm with Eamon and getting a piggyback ride from Marlen. I sensed he was feeling a little bit physically neglected now that he had to share my affections with Eamon. Arthus wasn't a touchy-feely person, so Marlen had always been the exclusive recipient of my casual touches. I needed to make sure they both felt equally valued.

Maybe there was a *How To Keep Your Harem Happy* guidebook in the library. I could use a little extra guidance.

Gwyneira welcomed us into her cabin with a questioning look. "Mr. Adair? This is a welcome surprise."

"Master Gwyneira, always a pleasure to see you. I imagine you'll see more of me now as I'm courting Ffion," he explained succinctly without taking his eyes off me.

"Well, how wonderful! Come in, let us have tea," Gwyneira said, ushering us into the sitting room. I sat in between Marlen and Eamon on the couch while Arthus stood behind us, hovering above me like a sexy, brooding guardian angel.

"To what do I owe the pleasure of this visit?" Gwyneira asked lightly.

I glanced at Eamon, hoping he'd explain. I didn't like asking any of them to speak for me, but I was in way over my head with spirit stuff.

"The gods have taken an interest in Fi," Eamon began, picking his words carefully. "She has been sanctified at the temple on campus. Last night, the spirits visited and told us the gods had plans for her and that she shouldn't lose faith when the darkness came for her."

I didn't need my ability to see how taken off guard Gwyneira was. She gave me a long, concerned look that was distinctly maternal, and I questioned again why I hadn't just trusted her with the notes. She had always been so compassionate towards me.

"I suspected the sanctification," she admitted.

"You did?" I asked, immediately rescinding my *why didn't I just trust her judgment* moment.

"Just a suspicion," she said placatingly. "I went to the temple to make an offering to the gods, and the place felt pregnant with magic, both yours and divine. I wondered then if you had been sanctified, but I thought you would ask me about it during our mentoring sessions. It is supposed to be quite a distinctive experience," Gwyneira continued.

"Right. It happened the same night as the message on my wardrobe, I guess I got distracted," I muttered, embarrassed that I'd just dismissed the weird sensation almost as soon as it happened. Everything had been so new and foreign that I hadn't been able to differentiate between *routine-weird* and *weird-weird*.

"The warning from the spirits is alarming. Both that they referred to 'the darkness' coming for you—dark fae, most likely—but also the fact that they warned you personally. It is rare for the gods to share visions of the future with us," she explained, wringing her hands in a nervous gesture I'd never seen from the usually unflappable Gwyneira.

"You need to be with one of us at all times, sweetheart," Arthus said in a low voice.

"Us or Bryn, he wouldn't let anything happen to her," Marlen added confidently, and Arthus made a small noise of agreement in the back of his throat.

I wasn't as confident in their assessment of Bryn. I didn't think he'd deliberately let anyone hurt me, but I wasn't confident he'd go out of his way to stop them either. Why would he? He had his own girl to worry about.

"I will expedite my request for an additional combat instructor. You need to be able to defend yourself as well," Gwyneira said with a cutting look at all three men.

You tell 'em, Gwyneira! Fae girl power!

"I agree, I'd like to be able to defend myself too," I added primly, ignoring the assorted grumbles from the three muscle heads surrounding me.

"Then it is agreed. Your focus after winter break will be building your defenses," Gwyneira decreed with an approving nod.

Hopefully, it would be enough.

CHAPTER 38

The mountain pass where I wanted to take Fi for the claiming ceremony was around an hour's flight from the Academy. The griffins would take us about halfway up the mountain, then we would hike another thirty minutes or so to get to the spot I had in mind. It was a gap between two mountains that caught a cross breeze, the perfect place for two air affinities to seal a bond.

Fi flew with me on the griffin while Marlen took his own. He'd agreed to come with us for Fi's safety since we were traveling so far from campus, but he was going to wait with the griffins lower down on the mountain. It was important that the claiming ceremony was a moment between just the two of us, since everything else going forwards would happen as part of the mating circle.

It was still a little surreal to think of. *I* would be part of a mating circle. I'd get to keep Fi for as long as we lived. It was a gift beyond measure.

Fi and Marlen said their goodbyes after dismounting the griffins and he made himself comfortable sitting on the ground, tossing me a reassuring grin as Fi and I started up the path. Fortunately, it wasn't too steep—my Fi did *not* enjoy physical activity outside of the bedroom. If she got too tired, I'd fly her up the rest of the way.

"Before we start walking, I want to give you these," I said gruffly, handing

Fi a bundle of fabric. She eyed it curiously before gingerly unwrapping the layers.

"Boots!" she squealed, amber eyes lighting up with excitement.

"There are socks in there for you too," I told her as I pulled my own socks and worn leather boots out of my bag and began putting them on. The loss of connection to the earth diminished our magic, but making Fi walk up a rocky mountain with the remnants of snowfall on it wasn't my kind of sadism.

I liked pleasure with my pain.

Fi dropped to the ground and pulled up the knee-high gray wool socks before lovingly stroking the boots for a few moments. They were a simple dark brown, made of soft leather that came up to her ankles and secured with laces.

"They're a perfect fit," she noted, surprised.

"Marlen measured your feet while you slept," I told her with an unapologetic shrug.

"I'm going to pretend that's romantic," Fi laughed.

"They were made by Lachlan, Aderyn's suitor. Almost suitor. Whatever," I muttered, clearing my throat. I should have made Marlen give them to her. He was better at this sort of thing.

"Aw, I love that. I'll have to tell her how talented he is, though I hope he's made her some shoes now that he's courting her. That's like plus *ten* suitor points right there," Fi said cheekily as she finally finished lacing the boots and allowed me to pull her up.

"Good to know. Come on, let's get going. We need to be back down here before dark."

We walked side-by-side in comfortable silence. I was lost in my own thoughts. The fae side of me, driven by instinct and the mating pull, felt that Fi and I claiming each other was right, natural, perfect. The rational side of my brain told me that I didn't deserve this yet, not even close.

I'd been Fi's suitor for just over three *weeks*. Marlen had spent at least a couple of *months* getting to know her. This was incredibly fast to make a decision I'd have to live with for the rest of my long life.

Was it even a decision, though?

When it came down to it, there was nothing in this realm or any other that could separate me from Fi. That moment of pure, unbridled terror when her fathers snatched her from right next to me had sealed our fate. I would never let her go.

We reached the spot I had in mind and Fi looked around in awe as she caught her breath, a small smile lighting up her features. *Gods, she was so beautiful.* I put my satchel down on the ground and cast an air bubble around us to keep the cold wind at bay.

"One thing before we begin, sweetheart," I said, smirking at her.

"What's that?" she asked suspiciously, no doubt sensing my intentions.

"Lose the panties."

She barked a startled laugh but did as she was told, reaching under her dress to pull them down slowly over her shapely legs and over the boots, never breaking eye contact. *Little vixen.*

I held my hand out for her to pass them over and she did so with a tiny eye roll, failing to suppress a smile when I tucked them into the front pocket of my shirt for safekeeping.

"Ready?" I confirmed, and Fi nodded.

Seeing the pure emotion shining from Fi's eyes, she seemed as prepared for this moment as I did. She wasn't one for pretty words or bold declarations of love. Fi showed her love through the loyalty she willingly gave us, the trust she placed in us, the unwavering support and comfort she offered us.

I wasn't one for pretty words either, but in my soul, I knew I loved her. I'd do anything for her, follow her anywhere, give up the wings on my back just to keep her safe.

I pulled out the worn piece of leather with the embossed claiming vows on it, running my thumb over the words that so many fae before me had uttered. When my mother had passed this heirloom onto me before I departed for the Academy as a first-year student, I had pocketed it without a second glance. The temptation of a kindred soul seemed too far-fetched to even consider.

I was glad I hadn't settled. Fi was worth waiting for.

"Okay, sweetheart. You know how this works now. I'll go first, then you repeat the vow back to me," I said softly, staring into Fi's soulful amber eyes. She looked a little jittery, but I suspected it was more excitement than nerves.

Gods, I couldn't wait until the bond was in place so I could have some insight into her feelings.

"I'm ready," she replied with a firm nod, and I allowed myself a small smile.

"I, Arthus Calder, take you, Ffion Laisren, to be my bonded mate. I pledge you my love, my magic, my loyalty, and my devotion. I vow from this day forward to put the needs of you and our mating circle first, forsaking all others."

I kept my eyes on Fi as the mating pull in my chest twisted and turned like a slow-moving tornado, moving into place and imprinting forever on my soul.

Without a second's hesitation, Fi took the scrap of leather from my hand and repeated the vow back to me.

"I, Ffion Laisren, take you, Arthus Calder, to be my bonded mate. I pledge you my love, my magic, my loyalty, and my devotion. I vow from this day forward to put the needs of you and our mating circle first, forsaking all others."

Fi's eyes closed in ecstasy and I gave her a moment to adjust to the sensation of the bond settling into place before sliding my hand around the back of her head and pulling her to me for a long, heated kiss.

Every part of my body burned to be closer to her, to have her skin on mine, her taste on my tongue. I needed her. *Now.* Five minutes ago.

I guided her back against the ridge, having just enough presence of mind to maintain the air shield around us so the wind didn't bother her. Pinning her against the wall with my hips, I pulled her wrists above her head and held them there with one hand while the other drifted up to her thigh, hiking her dress up with it.

I allowed myself a quick mental pat on the back for getting her to ditch the panties beforehand.

Fi's breasts heaved against my chest, nipples straining through the thin dress, breath coming in short pants. I wasn't the only one feeling the dire need to consummate the bond. My aching cock twitched at the thought.

I need to be inside her.

My hand teased up in the inside of Fi's thigh as I continued to kiss her punishingly. I groaned when I felt her arousal coating her thighs and she bucked against my hand.

"Patience, sweetheart," I told her, sounding far more relaxed than I felt before delivering a hard nip to her bottom lip.

Fi let out a growl as threatening as a kitten's. "We're bonded Arthus, I can feel how much you need me. Don't give me that *patience* crap."

I smirked against her mouth. *Minx.* Though perhaps she was right, it wasn't fair to tease now. Not when the fresh bond was driving us to finish the claiming ceremony, making both of us ache.

Yanking my cock free of my pants, I roughly shoved her dress out of the way, dropping my hold on her wrists so I could pick her up and hold her against the mountain face. Fi wrapped her legs tight around my waist and dug her hands into my shoulders. I dropped the air shield so I could use my magic to support her weight, relishing her gasp of astonishment as she felt the rushing wind swirling beneath her.

Unable to hold off any longer, I thrust into her warm, wet pussy and we both groaned in relief. *Home.* That's what she felt like. Our magic instantly flared between us, sparking along our skin like fireflies of ecstasy.

Nothing had ever felt this good. It didn't even matter that I was barely dominating this exchange. Everything about it was perfect.

I drove into Fi over and over, relishing the feel of her writhing and the sounds of her incoherent moaning, losing herself in pleasure. Her hands worked their way under the collar of my shirt until her palms were on my bare skin and we both exhaled loudly as magic sparked there too.

Fi's head tipped back against the rock wall, and I immediately latched my lips onto her smooth, unblemished throat, leaving a love bite that would last for weeks and scraping my teeth over the juncture of her shoulder and neck. Her nails dug into my chest in return, biting into the skin hard enough to draw blood.

Usually, I hated females marking me, but this was *my* female. She could brand me every day of my life and I'd wear her marks with pride.

Fi tightened around me, and I leaned forward to kiss her again, exploring her mouth with my tongue and sending her over the edge.

I gave her a moment to catch her breath before lowering her feet to the ground and flipping her around, bending her over as her arms leaned against the rockface for support. Fi looked back at me over her shoulder, lips parted, eyes hazy with lust, dress bunched at the waist with her ass in the air.

She was the most beautiful thing I had ever seen.

I ran my fingers down her ass to the tight little bud I know she hadn't shared with anyone yet, and she gasped slightly as my fingers circled her back entrance.

"You can't have two mates and be a virgin here, sweetheart," I murmured. Fi bit her lip nervously, her muscles tense. I delivered a swift slap on her perfect ass cheek with my other hand and relished her wanton moan. Her desire for a dash of pain on top of her pleasure made my cock ache for her. "Tell me yes."

I ran my fingers through her slick juices, coating my cock as a lubricant and rubbing the head against her ass while my other hand reached around her front to play with her clit, making her squirm and wriggle against me.

"*Yes,*" she breathed. My brave little mate.

As quickly as I could, I leaned down to flip open my bag, grabbing the small bottle of oil I'd brought as lubrication just in case. I applied it generously to my cock, stroking my shaft a few times before coating my fingers and massaging her back entrance until she relaxed enough for me to push one finger in.

Fi sucked in a breath, pausing for a moment before rolling her hips experimentally, her fingers working in a steady rhythm to stimulate her clit. Forcing myself to be patient, I gently worked in a second finger, scissoring and stretching her muscles so she could take me.

"More," Fi gasped. "I want more. I'm ready."

"So brave," I murmured approvingly, withdrawing my fingers and replacing them with my cock. I pushed forward slowly, keeping up a steady stream of comforting words while encouraging her to relax and let me in. She was so fucking tight I doubted I'd last more than two minutes. Fi's gasps turned into needy mewls and pants as I pushed myself in further, inch by inch until I was fully sheathed inside her.

My little goddess.

My grip on Fi's hips was hard enough to bruise, but her hand continued to work furiously between her thighs, both of us desperate to wring another orgasm from her overstimulated body before I came undone. Our magic flickered frantically between us, increasing every sensation until we were both delirious with need.

Fi screamed my name as everything clenched around me and her nails gouged into the rock she was so desperately clinging to with one hand. With one final thrust I followed after her, feeling like I was branding her in a primordial way, taking the last vestiges of her virginity.

It could have been seconds or minutes before we both regained our senses, her forehead resting on her forearm and my arms gripping her waist tightly, both of us breathing heavily.

I pulled out gently, smug at the mess I'd made of her, and spun Fi in my arms, pulling her to me for a tight embrace. I usually hated losing control, but my connection to Fi made me feel like the best kind of out of control—barely tethered to the world, floating in the clouds, burning up with desire kind of out of control.

Fi trailed one of her hands across my chest and up the side of my neck to softly cup my jaw.

"I love you, Arthus."

She smiled at me with complete adoration in her eyes, and I choked back the foreign lump that rose in my throat.

"I love you too, Ffion," I finally replied hoarsely and was rewarded with a dazzling smile that lit up every inch of Fi's face.

I gently kissed her temple and cursed myself for not bringing a spare cloth or something with me, but if Fi was bothered, she didn't let on, yanking her panties out of my pocket with a playful smile and using them to clean up as best she could. I rolled out the blanket on the ground of the little alcove, sheltered somewhat from the strong winds, then pulled her down to sit between my legs. She winced slightly as her ass hit the ground, and I hid my grin by grabbing a bottle of fae wine for us to drink.

Hesitantly, I felt for the mating bond in my chest and drew it towards me. Fi's soul was laid bare for me, everything that made her who she was on display.

It was awe-inspiring, terrifying and humbling all at once to have that kind of connection to her. And for her to be able to see everything that made up me.

Including all the dark and ugly parts.

I caught a glimpse of Fi's overwhelming happiness before I was distracted by the tingling in my wrist.

"Ooh, it's happening," Fi squealed, looking at her own wrist where a single black line was appearing, combining with the mark she'd received from Marlen to form an X. I watched in awe as the distinctive XX rune—connected to create a diamond in the middle—appeared on my own wrist.

I took several deep breaths to get my emotions under control and keep my wings contained. For once, it wasn't anger but excitement that made the muscles in my back twitch.

I was going to throw away all my long-sleeved shirts. I wanted my mark to be always visible.

Fi sighed happily as we shared a drink together, her sitting between my legs and resting her head contentedly back against my shoulder. I'd never felt so close to a person before, but loving Fi was the best kind of vulnerability.

As the sun began to set in the distance, I packed up our belongings and took Fi's hand to guide her back down the mountain. She winced slightly as she walked, and I felt like a total asshole for not thinking this through. Of course she would be feeling a little tender after our rough claiming ceremony.

Fortunately, as soon as we got halfway down the mountain to where Marlen was waiting with the griffins, he came over and cradled her face in his hands, releasing healing magic that flowed through her entire body. I didn't know if he'd checked his bond with Fi and sensed her discomfort, or if he'd just assumed I'd been rough with her.

It was probably the latter. He'd got quite a kick out of healing the rope burns on her wrists a couple of days ago.

We flew back to the Academy with Fi in my arms again, and I kept my sleeve rolled up so I could look at my fresh mating mark throughout the trip. It was comforting to have a visual reminder of our bond on my skin.

As we landed outside the stables, Bryn stormed past us with a face like thunder as the three of us dismounted.

"He's mad we didn't tell him we were going off-campus," Fi murmured. There was half a second's silence before she looked at Marlen and me with wide eyes. "How did I know that?"

"Your ability is changing, sweetheart," I said as Marlen wrapped an arm around her shoulders. We were both holding our breath, waiting for Fi to break down.

Eventually she let out a long breath and nodded her head. "Could be worse, I suppose. Come on, I'm starving."

FFION

CHAPTER 39

Winter break was over, which was disappointing, but I woke up on the first morning back feeling like a giddy kid, anyway. *Today is my first potions class!* I was going to learn to make freaking potions.

Aside from how objectively cool that was, potions was my first real equal opportunity subject at the Academy. It didn't matter how much or how little magic you could wield, potion-making required concentration and attention to detail in order to get it right. I'd frantically read through a couple of books at the library and talked to both Marlen and Arthus about what to expect. I had high hopes that maybe I could kick ass at this.

Maybe.

The potions class was held in a small stone building at the very edge of the campus. There were no glass panes in the windows—wooden shutters had been thrown open to ventilate the entire room—and it was chillier here than any other classroom, though the multitude of fires that would be burning once class got underway would probably warm it up.

There were six long stone benches with wooden stools at each place, and each student had a small cast iron cauldron—*a real-life freaking cauldron*—some knives, a mortar and pestle, a couple of ladles, and matches to light the fire underneath the cauldron.

There were only about fifteen people in the class, but they were all second-years. Unfortunately for me, the only people I recognized were Saffir—who Bryn was supposedly courting—and Corsen, the girl who had been sleeping with Marlen before I arrived at the Academy. *Awesome.*

I took a seat at the back of the room by myself. I was here to make kickass potions, not friends.

Saffir ignored me completely, which I was totally fine with, but I repeatedly caught Corsen glaring at me with poison in her gaze. I'd gotten in the habit of muting my empath ability during classes, but I dropped my wall temporarily to see what Corsen's deal was. Her anger coursed hot through my veins and resentment crushed my lungs. I quickly pulled my defenses back into place before anyone saw my discomfort.

Was she really that upset about me claiming Marlen? Sure, they'd been sleeping together—*don't dwell on that Fi*—but that was months ago and as far as I'd heard, they hadn't had anything to do with each other since then. There hadn't even been a mating pull between them, so her reaction seemed doubly odd.

Whatever. *Not my circus, not my monkeys.*

"Quiet down," Master Cadha called out over the din. She was a small, rounded woman with mousy brown hair and a ruddy complexion, but she had a distinct don't mess with me aura that I was taking seriously. There was a hard woman under that soft, cat lady exterior.

"The potion we are going to be brewing today is an effective antidote to most kinds of venomous bites. We will be working on it intermittently over the next few weeks and should any of you brew an effective batch, I will help you bottle it in small vials which you can carry on your person.

"It will take five weeks to complete, and it would be very disappointing if all that work was in vain, so I highly recommend you concentrate on following the directions exactly," she continued.

We took turns gathering supplies from her desk and I busied myself grinding eggshells with my mortar and pestle. After obsessively scraping at the powder every few minutes to weigh it on the scales, I began to accept that potion making wasn't going to be my strong suit after all.

Why had I thought it would be? I didn't have the patience for *baking*.

I spent the remainder of the lesson cutting three roots of ginger into perfectly even slices and grinding a cockle shell into a fine powder. My hands were cramped and achy, but there was something oddly satisfying about doing manual work after so many lessons on elemental magic.

At the end of class, I tidied up my workstation and gathered my things to head toward my fire elemental class when Corsen stopped in front of my table and slammed her hand down next to my cauldron.

"What is your issue with me?" she demanded, glaring daggers at me.

"*My* issue?" I asked incredulously. "I don't have an issue with you. You're the one confronting me."

Corsen faltered for a moment before regaining her composure. "You haven't said anything to me directly, but you know what you did."

"I genuinely don't," I replied, exasperated with this conversation. This class would have been so much better if Aderyn was here too, but this was a second-year class that Gwyneira had enrolled me in ahead of schedule. It didn't look like I'd be making friends among the second-year students any time soon.

"You keep going after my guys!" she hissed, taking me off guard.

Marlen, sure. Not that I went after him per se, but I could sort of see where she was coming from. But I didn't think we had any other overlaps.

Ugh, I hoped not.

"You're going to need to be more specific," I told her calmly. "Is this about me taking Marlen as my mate?"

"Whatever, I'm over him. But you went after him and then you sent your suitor after Kelvyn as soon as he and I started sleeping together, so don't act innocent with me."

Corsen stormed through the exit with Saffir trailing after her, looking bored with the entire conversation.

Kelvyn? The guy my dads commissioned to leave me those messages? She said 'suitor'. Corsen definitely knew that Marlen was my mate, but it was possible she hadn't heard about Arthus and me yet.

"What did you do?" I grumbled under my breath, packing up the rest of my things and heading out of the classroom.

Marlen met me after class and walked me to the commons for dinner. We both loaded up on chickpea salad at the buffet table before joining Arthus, Leigh, Briallen, and Aderyn at the table.

I tucked into my salad, momentarily forgetting about Corsen's dramatics in potions class in lieu of filling my stomach until she and Kelvyn walked past our table and shot matching glares my way.

"Arthus," I asked in a sickly-sweet voice that put him and Marlen immediately on guard.

"Someone's in trouble," Briallen said in a singsong voice as she clapped her hands gleefully from across the table.

"Yes, sweetheart?" Arthus asked, looking mildly amused.

"Care to explain why Corsen accused me of setting my 'suitor' on her new man? She already knew Marlen and I had the claiming ceremony, and I highly doubt Eamon has ever spoken to her, so she must mean you."

"Who's her new man?" Marlen asked curiously, and I instinctually shot him a death glare.

He held his hands up in surrender and met my green-eyed monster with a roguish grin. Apparently, I wasn't as over him sleeping with her as I thought.

"Kelvyn," I gritted out.

"I did take it upon myself to have words with him," Arthus said, not apologetic in the least.

"What kind of words?"

"The kind of words that left no room for interpretation," he replied with a shrug, eyes narrowed on me.

"I give up," I sighed, flinging my hands in the air in defeat. "Please refrain from threatening people on my behalf in future."

"I'll let you know about it beforehand," Arthus conceded, as if that was an entirely reasonable compromise. Marlen and Leigh sniggered, so I decided to quit while I was semi ahead.

"You have a break after lunch, right, sweetheart? I had a tutoring session scheduled, but they canceled. Want to move yours up so you can take the evening off?" Arthus asked in a conciliatory tone.

"I suppose that is an acceptable way for you to make things up to me," I sniffed, though I wasn't *that* upset. Kelvyn was a dickhead, and I appreciated Arthus telling him to stay away from me so I didn't have to do it.

We said our goodbyes after lunch and headed to the air mastery classroom together. Our tutoring sessions had always been pretty steamy, but they'd gotten a lot more fun now that Arthus had let his dark side out to play.

He was still an attentive teacher, but between exercises he would send a tiny flutter of wind up my thigh, under my dress or to swirl around my wrists or ankles like a bind, or tug at my hair. It was sexy as hell, the things he could make air magic do.

Until Gwyneira showed up, the most effective cockblock in Avalon.

She strode into the classroom looking weirdly out of place on her own campus, then I realized how rarely I saw her outside her cabin. Her floor-length navy cloak and long black dress swished around her ankles as she made her way past the tables to the front of the classroom where we were practicing, and her waist-length silver hair was braided today, draped over one shoulder. I had to stifle a giggle. She wouldn't have looked entirely out of place with a broomstick and pointed hat.

"Forgive me for interrupting. The senior students are in combat training right now, so I thought it may be beneficial for you to go and observe their lesson." She gave me a loaded look. "I have also secured a new teaching assistant in that class that I would like to introduce you to. His name is Enfys. I am hoping he will tutor you, if you are comfortable with it."

Arthus tensed a little next to me, and I felt his wariness at the idea of me spending time with anyone else one-on-one so soon after I had been snatched out from under his and Marlen's noses.

"Of course, your mates are welcome to accompany you to all of your tutoring sessions," Gwyneira added with a pointed look at Arthus. Evidently, you didn't need any fancy emotion reading abilities to sense Arthus' discomfort.

He nodded gratefully, sticking close to my side as the three of us made our way to the clearing where the third and fourth years were practicing. To my surprise, I could see Marlen and Bryn sparring and even *laughing* together in the distance.

What fresh body-snatching hell was this?

I'd never seen Bryn laugh at anything. I wasn't even sure I'd ever seen him *smile*. To confirm my suspicions, as soon as I got close enough for him to sense my presence, he closed up like a clam again. *Prickly fae.*

They both lowered the swords they were practicing with and came over to meet me, looking sweaty, disheveled and distractingly sexy.

"Foxglove! This is a nice surprise." Marlen cupped my cheek and gave me a sweet peck on the lips while Bryn scowled into the distance.

"I wanted Ffion to observe the combat class today to give her a goal to work towards," Gwyneira said, returning with a tall, handsome blonde in tow. "And I wanted to introduce her to Enfys Owen, our new combat teaching assistant. It is my hope that he will be able to provide her with additional instruction."

Enfys was tall and lean, but all muscle, with pale blonde hair he kept short and neat, and icy blue eyes. He was beautiful in an untouchable sort of way, and looked like the consummate soldier.

I had been so distracted by my two mate bonds and the overwhelming pull I felt to Bryn that I hadn't noticed the significant pull between Enfys and I. It was weaker than what I'd felt for any of my guys—including Bryn, who was very much *not* mine—but still a lot stronger than what I felt to most unmated males on campus.

Enfys stepped forward, reaching out to shake my hand. I unmuted my abilities and sensed he was quite enamored with me. Curious as well, with a hint of lust.

"It's nice to meet you, Ffion," he said in a low, steady voice. His lips quirked slightly, and I got the feeling that this was the equivalent of a toothy grin for him. He didn't strike me as the kind of guy who gave a lot away.

"It's nice to meet you too, Enfys." I shook his hand and offered him a polite smile.

Bryn's irritation surged like a tsunami, and I glanced back at him over my shoulder. His emotions were running wild, but his expression stayed carefully blank.

Marlen and Arthus hovered close by. I could feel their curiosity, but also a fierce protectiveness I hadn't noticed when I met Eamon. They were probably monitoring the bond and feeding off my uncertainty.

"Is one of these gentlemen your mate?" Enfys enquired, surveying the wall of muscle that surrounded me on three sides.

"Two of them actually," I said, motioning toward the two at my sides. "Marlen and Arthus."

I felt his surprise. "And you still feel the mating pull? You must be a powerful fae." I felt a twinge of admiration from him that made me wary.

Bryn snorted derisively behind me. "She is."

I was surprised he said anything, and I didn't quite know what to make of it, but I was glad he didn't elaborate. I wasn't keen on everyone knowing I had strong enough magic for four mates just yet.

Enfys' eyebrows raised slightly as he took Bryn in. "And you are?"

"Bryn Edan."

He didn't add any detail of who he was to me, and I didn't offer any. What would I even say?

This is Bryn, a perpetual thorn in my side and star of my most pornographic dreams.

Also, he's seeing someone.

I felt a trickle of amusement from Gwyneira, who I had totally forgotten was standing there, observing all of this awkwardness. She winked at me when she caught my eye, and I wondered if she enjoyed the romantic drama among the students more than she let on. She was 400 years old, after all. You gotta get your kicks somewhere.

"Ffion, why don't you and Arthus find a spot to observe from while you three continue training? After the session, you can establish Ffion's availability for tutoring," Gwyneira suggested.

Grateful for her timely intervention, I offered Enfys a small, awkward smile and grabbed Arthus' hand, tugging him to the edge of the training field, doing my best to ignore Enfys' warm gaze and Bryn's furious scowl throughout the remainder of the training session.

He was probably a nice guy, but Enfys just became another complication I *really* didn't need.

My relief at the training session drawing to a close was short-lived as Enfys made his way over to the sidelines where Arthus and I were waiting for Marlen to put his weapons away and clean up.

"Ffion, do you have a free moment? I was going to head to the commons for some tea. Perhaps you could accompany me?"

Enfys' manner of speech was so formal and stilted, he sounded more like Gwyneira than any of the younger fae I'd met. Briefly, I wondered if he was a lot older than he looked, but I doubted he'd be unmated if that was the case.

Arthus' stare was burning a hole into the side of my head, but he sent a wave of reassurance through the bond, assuring me that he'd support whatever I wanted to do.

"Sure, that sounds nice," I replied hesitantly after some deliberation. I wasn't dying to spend time with Enfys, but I couldn't really think of a good reason to get out of it either. It was just tea, and it would probably pay to get to know him since I'd be spending more time with him as my combat tutor.

"Wonderful. We can establish your training schedule at the same time," Enfys said jovially.

Marlen strolled over at that moment, and we made our way towards the commons, my guys peppering Enfys with questions along the way.

It didn't escape my notice that Bryn was only ever a few feet behind us.

From Marlen and Arthus' questions, I gathered that Enfys was 22, had a fire affinity and some kind of gifted combat magic, and hadn't attended any type of academy but had instead done all of his training through the

Council where he'd worked as an Enforcer since he was 18.

"The Council has loaned me to the Academy for a few months. Their objective is for me to find suitable new recruits who are close to graduation and would be a good fit for a career at the Council," Enfys explained. Arthus made a noncommittal noise in the back of his throat, and Marlen shot me a concerned glance out of the corner of his eye.

"Do you enjoy working for the Council?" I asked mildly, working hard to keep the suspicion out of my voice. It's not like I had concrete evidence that they were bad—just my dads' word—but that had been enough to make me nervous.

"Of course," Enfys replied, giving me a confused look. "Why wouldn't I? They are the elite of the fae world, the very best of all the fae. It is an honor to be considered worthy of a place in their organization."

Gods. He spoke of them with such hero-worship in his voice that the hairs on the back of my neck rose.

We walked into the commons and the four of us headed over to the drinks table to make tea. Not two minutes after we sat down at a table large enough for all of us, Bryn pulled a chair over and planted it between Marlen and Arthus, who were sitting kitty-corner to each other. Enfys sat opposite me, eyeing Bryn warily.

"Shall we discuss a training schedule, Fi? May I call you Fi? I noticed your friends do. I am so looking forward to getting to know you better."

"Er, of course," I replied awkwardly, blinking at him. "Perhaps once a week for training? I'm free tomorrow at four pm."

I didn't love the idea of combat lessons with Enfys—he came on a little strong and I didn't need the extra complication—but I did want to learn to fight. I figured I could deal with politely rebuffing Enfys if it meant learning how to defend myself if the mysterious darkness did, in fact, come for me.

"Excellent. I will meet you outside the commons and accompany you to the arena."

Marlen, Arthus and Bryn all bristled at Enfys' tone, but he didn't seem to notice, his attention now firmly on his cup of tea.

I bristled too, but internally. Because, unlike those three, I understood the art of subtlety.

"Sure. Thank you for taking the time to help me with this," I responded politely.

"It is my absolute pleasure," he replied gallantly.

Crap, this could all go very badly very quickly if I didn't tread lightly. I wasn't interested in Enfys at all romantically so I didn't want to lead him on, but I had to be agreeable enough to not draw any extra attention to myself. What if he caught wind of my gift and alerted the Council? *Crap, crap, crap!*

I thought Gwyneira was on my side. Why the hell had she set me up with a Council lackey?

CHAPTER 40

Enfys Owen was an obnoxious prick, and I hated him.

He swaggered around the Academy like he owned the place, ignoring anyone who he didn't deem worthy of his attention. Unfortunately for all of us, Ffion made the cut. He popped up everywhere she was, valiantly making a show of carrying her satchel for her, opening doors, and pulling out her chair.

It made her uncomfortable. Even from a distance, I could see her uneasiness around him. Ffion hated people doing things for her, whether she asked them to or not. She may not have grown up knowing she was fae, but a fae's sense of pride was innate.

I was hovering in the shadows of the arena like a fucking stalker, waiting for their first combat tutoring session to begin. I wasn't strictly stalking her—Arthus had asked me to keep an eye on them since both he and Marlen were busy with classes, but he'd probably intended for me to make my presence known.

I had in a way—Ffion would feel the mating pull and know I was here. It was her decision if I stayed hidden or not.

They entered through one of the tunnels and I sank down in my seat behind a column, watching Enfys lightly gripping Fi's elbow to guide her into the arena like she was a godsdamned moron who hadn't been to the arena before this fucker ever showed up on campus.

Why did she allow it? If I tried that kind of shit with her, she'd probably break my nose.

As she came close enough for our mating pull to register, her eyes shot up to where I was hiding in the stands. Her eyes scanned the shadows, and I could have sworn the corner of her mouth twitched in amusement, not that Enfys noticed. He was too busy pontificating on the virtues of working for the Council, probably.

Enfys left Ffion in the center of the arena while he set up targets, and I could hear their conversation clearly as they called to each other across the enclosed space.

"What will we be doing?" she asked curiously.

"As an air affinity, you are fortunate to be able to call upon an air shield that will protect you from elemental attacks from all three of the other elements. Air affinities tend to have weaker offensive magic, but their defensive capabilities are by far the best," Enfys called back.

It irritated me that his assessment was so spot on.

"I'm fine with concentrating on defensive magic," Ffion assured him, and I sniggered under my breath. A warrior, Ffion was not. She was a scholar if anything, judging by the amount of time she spent in the library.

"Excellent, we will spend half of each session working on your air shield, and the other half on weapons training."

Ffion nodded, but I could see the doubt written all over her face from here. She'd probably never handled a weapon in her life. That kind of thing was frowned up in Albion, from what my memory serves.

"I am going to demonstrate my fire shield now, and I would like you to try to copy my movements as best you can," Enfys called smugly over his shoulder as he put some more distance between him and Ffion.

At least he wasn't going to accidentally set her on fire. Small mercies, I suppose.

Enfys conjured an admittedly impressive fire shield and barked instructions to Ffion on how to emulate it with her air magic.

I rolled my eyes at the absurdity of a fire affinity trying to teach an air affinity how to create an air shield. Fire shields were walls of flames, created at a reasonable distance away from the body so we didn't burn ourselves. Basically, the exact opposite of air shields, which curved protectively around the wielder, closer to their form.

Ffion was trying to copy Enfys' movements, resulting in a weak and ineffective wall of air that wouldn't defend shit. *Must tell Arthus that he needs to train her in creating proper air shields...*

They continued on this pointless track for another twenty minutes until I contemplated having a nap to stave off the headache that was building behind my eyes.

Fortunately, they switched to archery before I could nod off. Enfys was clearly more comfortable with weapons training than elemental magic—his combat gift meant he could attack and defend instinctively—but he was barely paying Ffion any attention as he hit bullseye after bullseye.

When he used his magic to light the tip of his arrow on fire and hit the bullseye, I rolled my eyes so hard I think I may have pulled a muscle.

Fucker was just here to show off.

Standing close together, I couldn't hear their conversation, but I'd bet coin that Ffion's teeth were gritted with irritation.

Considering all he'd done was roughly show her how to hold the bow and notch the arrow, she wasn't doing terribly. Her arrows were going wide of the target, but they weren't falling short, which was a good start.

Enfys strolled leisurely off to the targets to collect the arrows while Ffion glared at his back, dropping the bow to her side.

"Not to worry, Fi. It will come easier with practice. You shouldn't need these skills anyway, your mating circle will be there to protect you," Enfys called out in what he probably thought was a reassuring tone, puffing out his chest slightly.

It only aggravated Ffion. Her shoulders tensed, and I could see how tightly her jaw was clenched from here. Marlen and Arthus were right next to her when her dads showed up, yet they blasted them apart and snatched her from under their noses. Ffion knew as well as the rest of us that she needed to be able to defend herself, not rely on the males in her life to do it for her.

Even if that idea annoyed those aforementioned males.

"Shall we go to the commons for an early dinner?" Enfys asked chivalrously, offering Ffion his arm. I huffed a silent laugh at the theatrics.

"I think I'm just going to stay and practice a little longer. You go on ahead," she replied, her eyes flicking subtly to the shadows where I was hidden.

"Are you sure?" Enfys asked with a frown.

"Very. Please go on ahead. I'll see you later," she added sweetly, softening the rejection. She was being too polite, if anything. Fae females held a lot more power when it came to courting, and Ffion was more powerful than most.

If she'd grown up here, she'd have probably developed the arrogance to go along with it.

"Alright," Enfys said slowly, clearly unhappy with this turn of events. He briskly made his way to the exit, and Ffion watched his back as he walked along the path toward the main campus while I picked my way through the stands, dropping over the arena wall to join her.

Ffion picked up another arrow, her eyes still on Enfys' retreating figure, barely visible at the end of the tunnel.

"Checking to make sure he actually leaves?" I asked casually, sauntering over to her.

"Maybe I was pining after him," she snapped. She couldn't help herself when it came to me—I brought out a monster in her, and I'm pretty sure she brought out a monster in me too.

"I guess we'll never know," I replied with a chuckle.

She definitely was not pining after him.

Ignoring me, Ffion notched the arrow, ready to keep practicing without Enfys' help. I circled her, assessing her terrible form. What had he even been teaching her? She watched me warily out of the corner of her eye as I prowled around her like a predator eyeing up their prey.

"You're putting too much weight on the balls of your feet," I told Ffion lightly. She huffed irritably, but shifted her weight nonetheless.

Surprised she'd actually listened to me, I moved in closer, lightly touching her hand gripping the bow to adjust the angle slightly. Everywhere our skin touched felt like it was on fire, and I found it difficult to keep my breathing even. *Gods, her skin is so soft.* My fingers trailed up her arm to loosen her locked elbow slightly before I dragged them up to her shoulders and pushed them down slightly to relax them.

My fingers lingered on her shoulder for a second too long to be friendly, but she didn't push me away.

"Try now," I rasped, enjoying the way Ffion's breath hitched slightly. *At least she was as affected by me as I was by her,* I thought bitterly. Then I remembered I was supposed to be courting someone else and took a healthy step back. Ffion let the arrow fly, and it embedded itself on the outer edge of the target.

I almost grinned at the slow, smug smile that overtook her face. Gods she was fucking beautiful, but not mine to admire.

"That was shit," I commented lightly.

"Piss off, Bryn. That's the first time I hit the target and I'm going to enjoy my success with or without your approval," she replied haughtily.

"Without, then," I said with a smirk, enjoying the way her eyes narrowed in irritation. "Come on, your mates will be waiting for you."

I tried to tell myself that my renewed obsession was because I'd barely seen Ffion or her mates over winter break. I'd just get my fix and go back to normal. Throughout the break, I'd hardly even felt the mating pull, so I assumed she was off campus, probably staying with Eamon Adair, which weirdly didn't grate me as much as her hanging around Enfys did.

Probably because I'd met Eamon a couple of times now and found he was a decent, respectable fae who practically worshiped the ground Ffion walked on. She could do worse.

Enfys was worse.

Like I'd summoned him with my thoughts, he and Ffion appeared from around the corner, deep in conversation, or he was at least. Ffion's expression was mildly interested at best, but that seemed to be good enough for Enfys.

I only glimpsed them for a couple of seconds before they disappeared into the commons together and I blew out a long breath.

What was happening to me?

My protective instincts over this fae had been going crazy from the moment Marlen grabbed me and dragged me to the stables, insisting I track Ffion's magical signature because she'd been taken. I hadn't experienced fear like that since I had woken up in my childhood bed with my house burning down around me. It was the kind of fear that gripped every part of me and turned my blood cold in my veins.

Then we'd flown back to the Academy with Ffion in my arms on the back of the griffin, and nothing else mattered more to me at that moment. But then Ffion apologized to Gwyneira for not trusting her and didn't say shit to me about how she'd suspected me of planting those fucking notes in the first place. At that point, whatever bridges we'd started building fell apart again.

The least she could do is apologize, but she'd never brought it up again. It was like she'd completely forgotten that she'd insulted my integrity.

Inherently, I knew I'd probably die of old age before Ffion apologized. She was my equal in both pride and stubbornness.

All of this drama, all of these emotions for a girl I wasn't even courting. Technically I was still Saffir's suitor—not that I'd put much effort into it. I hadn't even slept with her since Ffion arrived in Avalon, my dick would remove itself from my body in protest if I tried.

I ground my teeth, hating to admit even to myself that I'd fucked up. Committing to something as serious as a courtship while I was in a blind rage had not been my best idea, but every time I'd tried to talk to Saffir one-on-one about our relationship, she found an excuse to either get away from me or drag someone else into the conversation. I didn't want to be the kind of asshole that strung a girl along, but that's exactly who I'd become.

It was fucking disgraceful, and I had no one to blame but myself.

I pushed off the tree and started towards Saffir's cabin. I had some time before my next class, so I would try to talk to her again. Maybe if I spent some more time with her, it would give me some answers about where this relationship was heading. It should have been a no-brainer—the courtship with Saffir had been everything I'd ever wanted. She fit into the *plan*.

1. Find a fae female who I could get to know objectively—without a strong mating pull clouding my judgment—from a reputable family

2. Graduate at top of my class from the Academy

3. Use my credentials from the Academy and contacts from my well-connected mate to secure a respectable career

4. Distance myself as much as possible from the fucking disaster that had been my parents

That had been the plan from the beginning. Was deviating from it even an option? Why was I even considering it?

Gods, I was going to end up like my fathers at this rate.

It didn't take me long to get there, and I stood outside Saffir's cabin door brimming with irritation. I could sense her magical signature in there, but after two minutes of knocking she was still feigning absence. She was definitely avoiding me intentionally, but why? It was fucking *infuriating*.

"Ew, I did not need to see my cousin going for an early morning hookup," Briallen called out from behind me, almost making me smile. She may be my cousin, but she felt more like a twin sister most of the time.

I smirked at her expression, but her nose wrinkled in disgust. "You're in luck, I wasn't. Do you have some free time now? I haven't seen you much lately."

"Sure, want to get some tea?" she asked curiously, her gaze narrowed on me suspiciously. My cousin was my favorite fae in the world, but I never asked to spend time with her. I should have. Briallen was the only person

I knew who always had my back, and I owed her more than scraps of my attention.

"Let's go," I called over my shoulder, already heading to the commons. She huffed as she ran to catch up with me.

"What's going on, Bryn?"

"Can I not spend time with my favorite cousin without the interrogation?"

"I'm the only cousin you speak to, and no." She was still a little behind me, struggling to keep up with my long strides, but I didn't need to see her face to know she was rolling her eyes. "Is this about Enfys Owen?"

I stopped in my tracks to look at her. "What about him? Has something happened? Is he courting her?"

Briallen gave me a mischievous grin that clearly told me I had played right into her hands. I didn't even care.

"No, of course not. I think Fi is just humoring him, being polite, you know?" *No, she never humors me*, I thought wryly. Then again, I guessed I hadn't given her much reason to.

Ffion didn't fit in the *plan*.

"No, you probably don't know. You're never polite," Briallen continued cheerily.

"I definitely wouldn't be polite to a pompous ass like him," I muttered.

"That is an apt description," Briallen agreed with a giggle.

We arrived in the commons, and I didn't feel an overpowering mating pull, so Ffion must have already left. Briallen and I headed over to the drinks table to make tea. I went straight for my favorite—dandelion—while Briallen made herself a cup of peppermint.

"Peppermint?" I asked her with a questioning brow. That was new.

"It's Fi's favorite, I've been drinking it more lately. It's grown on me," she replied with a nonchalant shrug. The pointed look she was giving me said she was trying to tell me something.

I guessed it couldn't hurt to know what Ffion's favorite tea was. I filed that information away for later. It seemed like my life was determined to be tangled up with hers in some capacity, no matter what I did.

We took our cups and found a quiet table next to the wall. The commons were still fairly empty, fae always felt sluggish after being with their families over the break.

"You had a strong mating pull with Leigh, right?" I asked Briallen, looking out over the room instead of meeting her eyes.

"I did," she agreed. "Kindred souls, compatible magic, the works. Knowing how that feels, knowing how great Leigh and I are together now, I would never settle for anything less."

"Even if you met someone from a prestigious family? Or someone particularly well connected?"

Briallen gave me an exasperated sigh. "To answer the question you're really asking, I would choose Fi over Saffir if I was you—even if Saffir comes with wealth and fancy connections and Fi has neither. Life is long if you're unhappy, Bryn."

She gave me a stern look, and I grimaced at being told off by my usually exuberant cousin.

"A strong mating pull isn't a guarantee of future happiness," I reminded her, thinking of my unfortunate parents. Maybe if my fathers hadn't been blinded by the strong mating pull they felt towards my mother, they would have realized she was unbalanced and gotten away from her before she burned them alive.

Though Ffion wouldn't be like that. Would she? She seemed fine. More stable than me, if I was being honest with myself.

Briallen sighed. "What happened with your parents was a tragedy, Bryn, but it was by no means normal. From what my parents have told me, there was no indication that your mother was having issues with her mental health until just a few months before the... incident."

My aunt and uncles had told me as much before. I had always struggled with that idea, though. It was almost easier to process that my mother had been deteriorating for a long time and it had been ignored than stomach the idea that she flipped and killed her mates, almost taking her only child out in the process.

That idea was fucking terrifying. Was it hereditary? What if it happened to me one day? Gods, maybe I should stay away from Ffion for her safety rather than mine.

"For all you know, Saffir could do something terrible fifty years down the track too," Briallen continued when I said nothing. "You can't predict terrible events using the mating pull, Bryn, but it is a good indicator of potential future happiness in a relationship."

I nodded and pretended to take an intense interest in my tea. There were two clear paths ahead of me, and I'd never felt so indecisive in all my life. The only thing I knew for certain is that I couldn't carry on the way I was going, or I'd bury myself too deep in this clusterfuck to get out of it.

FFION

CHAPTER 41

In the week since winter break had finished, the three of us had moved into Arthus' cabin together since it was designed for a mating circle, and conveniently in a less populated part of the campus. I woke every morning firmly ensconced between the two of them, and it never failed to make my heart beat a little faster.

How was this my life?

No matter how tedious my potions lessons were or how infuriatingly futile my combat lessons with Enfys turned out, my nights were bliss.

The only thing that was missing was Eamon, as well as some quality girl time. Briallen, Aderyn and I hadn't had a chance for a girls' night since winter break, and I vowed to set one up as soon as possible. I knew Aderyn had been writing letters to her shoemaker beau, and I was dying to hear how it was going between them.

I made the longer walk back to the new cabin with Enfys after class, since the guys took my safety seriously, it was rare that I was ever on my own these days. In addition to Marlen and Arthus' constant supervision, Enfys seemed to pop up out of nowhere to escort me between classes while Bryn silently shadowed me from a distance.

With Marlen guarding the campus gates tonight and Arthus still tutoring, they'd reluctantly asked Enfys to walk me home, and he'd been scarily ecstatic about the opportunity.

"I really hope you'll consider a career with the Council one day, Fi." I'd all but tuned out Enfys' chatter on our walk, but that bit managed to catch my attention.

"Sorry?" I asked, blinking stupidly at him.

"I'm here as a recruiter," Enfys explained slowly, his tone dripping with condescension. He probably didn't even realize he was doing it.

"Of course," I replied with a tight smile. "How could I forget?"

We reached the cabin door, and I turned to Enfys on the stoop to say goodnight. He was looking at me expectantly, like I'd invite him in, but something about the idea made me feel uncomfortable. I didn't want him in our space.

"Er, well thank you for walking me back," I said hesitantly. "Goodnight, Enfys."

It felt like my heart sank to my stomach as I sensed his disappointment, and I immediately muted my gift before I panicked and invited him in just because his emotions were affecting me.

It sucked that he was sad and all, but the more time I spent muting my gift, the more I realized that I shouldn't take on the responsibility of everyone else's feelings. I had my own shit to deal with.

"Goodnight, Fi," Enfys replied politely, his lips pressed flat. I let myself into the cabin with a sigh of relief, almost slipping on a note that had been pushed under the door.

Meet me at the big oak tree near the fire training area after sundown. I need to talk to you.

From,
Bryn

I stared at it for a long moment, not entirely sure what to think. In some ways, things between Bryn and I had improved recently. We'd been getting along a little better, and he didn't seem so aggravated around me. Probably since I'd stopped suspecting him of threatening me.

Ugh, I probably owed him an apology for that. On the one hand, he'd always been an asshole to me and quite frankly, we weren't even friends, so I didn't owe him any kind of explanation. On the other, he had been nicer lately, and I appreciated him looking out for me when Marlen and Arthus weren't able to. Maybe I should swallow my pride and at least say sorry for assuming the worst about him. I'd be pretty pissed if someone made that kind of assumption about me.

Bryn had definitely been testier since Enfys had shown up, but not with me. Whenever both of them were around, I felt like I was drowning in the distrust Bryn had of him. Was that what he wanted to talk to me about? It made sense in a way, since Enfys had become something of a shadow to me ever since we met at the Academy.

Not that any of that should matter because, as I had to keep reminding myself, Bryn was courting Saffir. Maybe they had finally decided to go ahead with their claiming ceremony, and he was just giving me a friendly heads up. Not that Bryn was ever friendly, so that would be weird. And while he wasn't mine, the thought of him and Saffir claiming each other made me feel queasy.

Sundown was rapidly approaching. Marlen was on guard duty already, so at least he'd be nearby if Bryn and I ended up screaming obscenities at each other at the edge of campus. Arthus was still tutoring, but he wouldn't be too far away. I'd leave him the note so he would know where to find me.

Screw it. I may as well go and hear him out. I'd been more cautious about my own safety since the whole kidnapped-by-my-dads incident, but fae couldn't forge notes—part of the whole no-lying deal—and I trusted Bryn, as did Marlen and Arthus.

I refastened my dark gray cloak with my silver foxglove brooch and left the note on the table for Arthus to find.

Steeling myself as I left the cabin, I resolved that Bryn and I would either take a step forward together tonight or finish this awkward dance we'd been doing for good.

It didn't take me long to find the large oak tree near the fire training area. I wasn't as familiar with this part of the campus—it was where the fire affinities trained—but it was beautiful in a medieval kind of way. All of the structures in this part of the campus were made of stone and there were fires burning *everywhere*—in sconces, firepits, and even small candles in glass bowls. Despite the dark sky overhead, the area felt well-lit and comfortable, and I could see some fire affinity students in the distance still practicing their magic.

I leaned against the tree facing the campus, idly wondering what was taking Bryn so long since it wasn't like he could lose me, and I couldn't feel the mating pull yet. Maybe it was some kind of power move to make me wait for him.

Hearing a rustle behind me, I turned my head as a hand shot out from behind me and clasped over my mouth while another hand shoved a soaked piece of fabric over my nose. Before I had a chance to scream or bite or cast an air shield or do anything, my body succumbed to the darkness.

Sensation returned slowly and painfully. I came to in some kind of mossy cave, shackled to the wall.

Disoriented, I tried to conjure my air magic to rip the shackles off the wall or bust out of the cuffs, but my magic felt trapped somehow. Like it was stuck under my skin and straining to get out. *Shit, the cuffs must have some kind of magic blocking ability.* That explained why I felt so drained and terrible. Well, that and the whole drugged and kidnapped thing.

How did I even get here? I was leaning against a tree next to the fire training area...

Bryn! Bryn. I'd been waiting for him. He'd asked me to meet him. Unwittingly, I felt tears well behind my closed lids. Shit, I never cried. Bryn wasn't my mate or my suitor, but the connection we felt had been so strong—perhaps the strongest of all my mating pulls.

I had naively assumed that pull and the protective urges he'd shown towards me would be enough to keep my secret safe with him. After all, Bryn was the first to find out about my gift, and he hadn't sold me out yet.

Until now.

I wracked my brain for an alternative, but he *had* to have written that note. Unless another fae named 'Bryn' had written it, since fae couldn't forge signatures. Gods, I hoped that this was all just a terrible coincidence and Bryn had been running late to meet me when someone saw the opportunity to seize me and went for it. I supposed I'd find out soon enough, whenever my captors decided to reveal themselves.

Taking a deep breath, I took stock of my surroundings and recited to myself what I did know to help keep myself calm.

The cave was a circular shape, around 5ft either way, and was lit by a single flaming torch too far away for me to reach. The walls were rock with patches of moss growing through the cracks in places, and the floor was hard dirt. Next to the torch was an enormous boulder that appeared to be blocking the entrance. I couldn't see any other way to get in or out.

The chains had enough slack for me to reach the bowl of water and a dry hunk of bread that had been left next to me on the floor, but there was no way in fae hell I was touching those. They'd already dosed me with some kind of poison to get me here, I wasn't going to risk consuming anything else they gave me.

I was still wearing my wrap dress and heavy shawl secured by my foxglove brooch. *I could use the pin to stab someone, I guess.* That would definitely have to be a last resort option. It wouldn't do enough damage to buy me much escape time.

My head and my heart were hurting. Cursing my stupidity in going out to that godsdamned tree on my own in the first place, I gave myself a teeny mental pat on the back for at least leaving the note on the table for Arthus. Then I was struck by a crippling wave of insecurity and paranoia, because what if Marlen and Arthus decided I wasn't worth saving? I'd really brought them nothing but trouble since the moment I barreled into their lives.

I mean, the sex was amazing, but I'm pretty sure they'd be able to find someone else to have filthy, mind-blowing threesomes with if I died.

Faes mated for life, but what if one of them died? Were mates replaceable then? I'd never asked because it wasn't something I wanted to think too much about. My dads didn't mention finding a new mate, and they seemed heartbroken when they talked about my mother.

Great, now I was actually crying.

Hearing a scratching noise followed by some rustling, I quickly wiped my tears, schooled my features and stood as best I could with my shackled ankles. *Game face on, Fi. Don't let 'em see you sweat.*

The large boulder rolled slowly into the cave, precariously close to where I had just been sitting. Great. Apparently I had to add 'getting flattened' to my list of concerns. Two figures moved into the cave, one of them using earth magic to roll the boulder back into place, sealing the entrance behind them.

These bastards were lucky I hadn't figured out how to get these cuffs off yet or I'd be trying that snatch-the-air-from-their-lungs trick Attie tried on me. Except I wouldn't stop until they turned blue.

Concentrating on my captors, I decided one was a male and one a female, though it was hard to tell at first behind the creepy-as-hell masks they wore. They were bird masks, made of gold, shaped sort of like a crow with black feathers sticking out the top back over their hairline. The masks covered the entire top half of their faces, but I could clearly see their mouths. They had black, shapeless robes on that hid the rest of them.

Of course I've been captured by some kind of weird cult. Just my luck.

Fortunately, the shackles didn't seem to be affecting my empath gift. The emotions coming from the male were by far the most potent. He was so power-hungry, he practically reeked of greed.

The female's emotions were more conflicted. There was definitely determination to achieve a goal, as well as a distaste for me and a healthy dose of apprehensiveness about what she was doing. She'd definitely be the one I would try to soften up, because there wasn't a hope in this realm or any other that the creepy dude was letting me go.

One thing I was confident of based on the way their emotions were impacting me was that they were fae.

"Ffion Laisren," the male announced in an absurdly pleasant tone, like we were two old friends bumping into each other on the street. I glared at him, not trusting myself to speak yet. How the hell did he know my birth name?

"I have wondered about you for many years since your naughty mother smuggled you to Albion. She wouldn't tell us what your gift was, you know? I knew it must be something rare and interesting if she was bothering to hide you." The man circled closer to me and I felt distinctly like prey. "But you'll tell us, won't you? You're a good girl."

Gross.

"If I'm such a good girl, why am I chained up in a cave?" I asked drolly, my voice coming out as a rasp.

"A mere precautionary measure, I'm sure we can do away with these savage restraints once you prove your loyalty. I'd hate to see you stuck in these accommodations any longer than necessary," he said with a manic glint in his eye, gesturing at the dank cave he'd trapped me in.

It was disturbing to realize that he believed every word he spoke to be true.

"What is your gift?" the female barked suddenly from her spot near the mouth of the cave. I didn't even need my gift to be able to tell that she wanted to get the hell out of here.

I shrugged, wishing again that I could just lie. Gods, humans didn't appreciate their ability to lie their way out of terrible situations.

"Now, now, Ffion. Let's not make this any more difficult than it needs to be," the male sang in an eerie voice as he pulled a silver dagger out of the sheath that hung around his belt and twirled it absentmindedly between his fingers. This *had* to be the darkness the spirits had warned me about. This guy was insane.

"I'm certainly not going to make it easy," I sniped back. The mask hid everything except his gleeful smile. He looked like I'd just given him a priceless gift.

"Oh good, I do love it when they scream," he called over his shoulder to the irritated female—his mate?—as he approached me. She shot vines out of the ground that held my already weak muscles in place as the male pulled a small dish out of the pocket of his robe and approached with his dagger held high.

The more I struggled, the tighter the vines became until I could barely move an inch. He stopped right in front of my face, lifting the dagger and drawing it swiftly across my cheek. In my head, I'd planned to show him no pain, but *fuck that hurt*. I whimpered slightly as he lifted the dish to my face and let the blood pool.

He was only a couple of inches from me, his breath fanning over my injured cheek in a way that made me feel distinctly violated.

"What a fun little mystery this is, Ffion. Thank you for the entertainment," he whispered, still grinning like a demonic clown.

If I had any saliva in my mouth, I might have spit on him. It wouldn't have helped the situation, but it might have made me feel a little better.

"We shall be back once I have tested your blood to find a compatible crystal. Do try to think about your childish behavior in the meantime, Ffion," he called over his shoulder as he and the female left. The vines receded as the boulder moved back into place, trapping me alone in the dark cave once again.

I curled myself into a ball on the ground, closed my eyes, and sobbed.

BRYN

CHAPTER 42

The day before...

I laid in bed, staring up at the skylight above me as I formed small fireballs in the palm of my hand and extinguished them again. The morning bells had just rung, but I'd been lying awake for what felt like hours.

What a fucking joke of a week—nothing was going right. The mating pull was so incessant that I could swear Ffion's vanilla and wildflowers scent was following me around campus. Plus, that dickhead Enfys had bested me in yesterday's training session, and I had no doubt that the deep gash he'd inflicted on my shoulder during sword fighting practice was entirely intentional. I'd been lucky that Marlen was around to heal it.

Despite trying to avoid Ffion since our impromptu archery lesson, it hadn't lessened the draw I felt to her. She was my personal temptation, all sinful curves and curious amber eyes. Being close to her without being able to *have* her was like waving a lit match next to dry tinder, hoping it didn't catch fire and burn the fucking world down.

The other disadvantage of me staying away was that it seemed to bring Enfys closer, and I *hated* seeing him around Ffion. Hated it on a bone-deep level. I'd never experienced that kind of reaction seeing her with Marlen or Arthus, or even Eamon, even though he was rich and should've been a total snob. Maybe because I knew the mating pull she felt to them was as strong as the one she felt to me? I knew she didn't feel so strongly about Enfys, and they clearly weren't well suited. The idea of her settling for him didn't sit well with me.

Or maybe it was just that Eamon was a sure thing and Enfys was encroaching on that final position in Ffion's mating circle.

I didn't know why I was fighting it anymore. *If* I was even fighting it anymore. Ffion had proven herself time and time again. She was a powerful fae, a worthy mate and sexy as sin.

The conversation with Briallen had replayed itself over and over in my head, and while I still thought there was more risk associated with a stronger mating pull... How could I settle for anything less, knowing Ffion existed? How could I stand by and let *her* settle for anything less, knowing we were such a perfect match?

I groaned and ran my hand over my face. *Fuck, I needed to make it clear to Saffir that we were done.* Ffion would never take me seriously until Saffir was out of the picture. I couldn't take *myself* seriously either. I'd handled this whole thing badly from the very beginning.

Casting a glance at the clock on the wall, I figured I had enough time to talk to Saffir before grabbing some breakfast. I blew out a long breath as I pulled on my jacket and scarf. This was going to be uncomfortable.

Saffir's cabin was only a few minutes' walk from mine. I knocked on her door, but again she didn't bother answering despite the fact that I could feel her magic inside. She was still avoiding seeing me one-on-one, and I had a feeling it was because she knew this talk was coming. I grabbed a small scrap of paper from the precious collection I kept in my satchel and scrawled:

Meet me at the big oak tree near the fire training area after sundown. I need to talk to you.
From,
Bryn

I kept the wording intentionally vague in case her gossipy roommate,

Corsen, spotted the note first. At least the oak tree would be a private enough spot to talk because I definitely didn't want to have this conversation in front of Corsen. The whole Academy would hear about it within the hour if she overheard. Sliding the note under their door, I headed down to the commons for breakfast. With any luck, I'd get a glimpse of my curly-haired siren while I was down there.

I spotted Fi around campus a few times that day, but Saffir did an excellent job avoiding me. *Fine, it was fine.* We'd talk after sundown. It didn't matter if she avoided me all day. With just a couple of hours to go, I headed for the commons to grab dinner first, running into Briallen at the buffet in the commons as I assembled my avocado, strawberry and spinach salad.

"Trouble in paradise?" she asked sweetly, though her eyes were hopeful.

"Good evening to you too, little cousin," I responded. "I have no idea what you're talking about."

Briallen frowned. "Saffir? Going back to her parents' estate this morning? Corsen is telling everyone who will listen that Saffir got some kind of note from you, burst into tears and rushed off campus."

I looked at her, puzzled. Saffir was taking this harder than I thought she would, and we hadn't even talked yet.

"Gwyneira was furious," Briallen continued. "Saffir skipped all of her classes and didn't even tell the administration when she left campus, but you know her parents are hotshot Councilors, so there wasn't anything Gwyneira could do."

I only half-listened as Briallen followed me to a table and relayed all the gossip she'd heard about it throughout the day.

Saffir had never professed any deep feelings toward me and while I had a powerful gifted ability, my family name was tarnished. We both knew— had *always* known—that I really wasn't much of a catch for the daughter of two Councilors, but Saffir wasn't the type to rush off in tears. Something about the whole situation didn't sit right with me.

Briallen left me to it when Leigh showed up, knowing better than to try to get me to socialize when I was so deep in my thoughts. I hung around the commons, reading and hoping for a fix of my Ffion addiction to get me through this nightmare of a day, but she never showed.

She was probably in the middle of a screaming orgasm with one or both of her mates, lucky bastards.

As sundown approached, I made my way to the oak tree and waited to see if Saffir would come back tonight and meet me as requested. After fifteen minutes, I reached out with my tracking magic and couldn't find her presence on campus. Annoyed, I stormed back to my cabin to sleep off my rage. Why was she making this so difficult? Why couldn't she just step up and face me?

Ffion would have faced me. She wasn't afraid of anything.

I'd sleep on it. Tomorrow, come what may, I was going to pull Saffir aside for that chat.

Another frustrating day where shit remained unresolved, and I was more pissed off than ever. I laid in bed, contemplating how best to force Saffir to confront me.

She'd reappeared on campus with her dragon of a mother earlier in the day. Apparently, Councilwoman Castell had come along to smooth things over with Gwyneira, who was furious at Saffir for fleeing the campus and ditching her classes.

I didn't want to talk to Saffir with her mother around, but after she left, Saffir went straight to her cabin and I definitely wasn't going to talk to her in front of Corsen.

Unable to sort shit out with her, I'd spent even more time than usual hovering around Ffion like a fucking lost puppy. Feeling the mating pull gave me a sense of reassurance I'd never gotten anywhere else. It meant Ffion was nearby. It meant she was safe.

I was such a sap.

Thank the gods my roommate had guard duty tonight. If he thought I was an asshole normally, I was practically feral tonight.

"Bryn! Open up right now or I will blast this door down!"

Arthus' roar startled me out of bed as he pounded on the door. He and Marlen must have shown up abruptly for my magic not to have picked up on them. Then my stomach dropped as I realized Ffion wasn't with them. I reached across the campus with my tracking magic as I often did to check in on her, panic spiking in my chest when I didn't pick up her signature.

"Where's Ffion?" I snapped, yanking the door open.

Arthus' fist connected with my jaw hard enough to send me sprawling.

"What the fuck, Arthus!?" I yelled, pushing up to my feet and taking a step back in case he swung for me again.

Arthus was a pillar of rage—his dark silver wings had ripped through his shirt and his breathing was heavy. Marlen didn't look much calmer, which was alarming since Marlen was usually the most relaxed fae I'd ever met.

"What the fuck indeed," Arthus fumed as he stalked forward, shoving a piece of paper into my chest. I snatched it out of his hand, irritated with his attitude, but as soon as I looked down at the innocuous message I'd left for Saffir in my hand, my stomach pooled with dread.

"Where is Fi?" Marlen's voice was hoarse with emotion. "Eamon is on his way. If it's coin you want, he'll pay you double. Please, Bryn, just tell us where she is."

"I don't know where she is. This note wasn't for her," I rasped. Which means I knew where to start looking. "I'll track Ffion. Wherever she is, I will find her."

"Who was it for?" Arthus seethed.

"Saffir," I choked out. "I left this for her yesterday, she never showed when I asked her to meet. She went home to her parents."

"Her parents who sit on the Council," Marlen whispered, looking stricken. "Shit, Fi's dads were right."

Marlen and Arthus exchanged a long glance, seemingly having some kind of silent conversation that had jealousy surging uncomfortably in my gut. I wanted to be part of that. I wanted to be on Ffion's team, not on the outside.

"Fine. We believe you," Arthus said eventually, and I rolled my eyes internally, it's not like I could lie even if I wanted to. "But until we're positive you aren't working with them, we won't be keeping you in the loop," he added coolly, snatching the note back from where I was holding it loosely between my fingers.

Marlen gave me an apologetic look. "Arthus, we need to get back to the cabin, Eamon will be here any minute."

"You'll tell us if you know anything, I assume?" Arthus said, giving me an assessing look.

"Of course. I'll be talking to Saffir about this straight away," I responded, equally cold. First the notes, now this. I was getting a little sick of these accusations when I'd only ever had Ffion's back.

Arthus barked a laugh. "You're the one courting her, do what you like. You've already chosen your side."

Marlen and Arthus left without another word and I stood rooted to the spot, icy fear coating my veins while my gut churned with regret.

The evidence all pointed to Saffir's family being involved in some way.

Whichever way I looked at the situation, it was my fault. *My fucking fault.* Whatever Ffion was going through right now was on me.

Saffir Castell was a dead fae walking. I just had to figure out a way to get information out of her without her tipping off her parents.

CHAPTER 43

I raced along the dark forest path behind Leigh with my heart in my throat. He'd shown up, banging on my door and shouting that Fi was missing, so we'd taken off in a sprint back to the Academy grounds together.

I'd never been more grateful for keeping a house so close to the Academy.

We made the twenty-minute journey to campus in ten as Leigh led me to the cabin that Fi shared with Marlen and Arthus.

Lucky bastards.

Not the time, Eamon.

Leigh swung the door open without knocking before dismissing himself to go check on his own hysterical mate. I walked in to find a shirtless Arthus pacing, his wings flicking out behind him like they had a mind of their own and were as agitated as the fae they were attached to.

Marlen sat at the dining table, elbows resting on the table holding his head in his hands. He looked like a broken man.

"What happened?" I asked Arthus without any preamble.

Arthus spoke as he paced, eyes darting around the room, seemingly unable to stay still. "Fi is missing. Marlen was on guard duty and I was tutoring a student. I got back here at nine pm and Fi was gone."

My throat constricted painfully.

"There was a note on the table from Bryn asking to meet him at the fire training area to *talk*." Arthus practically spat out the last word, and my brows furrowed in thought. I hadn't spent as much time around Bryn as these two, but he seemed like a nice enough guy. Grumpy, but well-intentioned.

I could *see* the threads of a bond between him and Fi.

"I assume you've already spoken to him?"

"He says the note was for Saffir Castell, as in daughter of the Castell Councilors. Swears he doesn't know where she is," Arthus clipped out.

"I believe him. He had nothing to do with this. You'll feel the same way once you've calmed down," Marlen said morosely, lifting his head out of his hands briefly.

I wanted to ask more questions, but Gwyneira swept into the room at that moment with one of her mates, Cadfan, and a young male fae. His icy blonde hair matched his cold blue eyes, and he had an arrogant tilt to his mouth that I recognized from my high society upbringing. He immediately raised my hackles up.

Gwyneira's mouth was set into a firm line as she gave me a curt nod in greeting.

"Mr. Adair." I inclined my head respectfully in response. "This is Enfys Owen. He is Ffion's combat instructor, currently on loan to the Academy from the Council. He has a combat gift which may be useful in retrieving Ffion, though I desperately hope it does not come to that."

"Even if my gift is not required, I care for Fi and hope to be her mate someday. I will be helping regardless," Enfys announced, and I caught the wary glance Marlen and Arthus exchanged out of the corner of my eye.

"Cadfan and I will reach out to some of the contacts we use to retrieve students in need of assistance. My magic notified me that Ffion was in danger, but whoever took her must have put a cloaking amulet on her almost instantly, I cannot get a read on her now. I will let you know if I hear anything." Gwyneira gave us a sympathetic look before leaving with Cadfan.

Enfys immediately strode across the room toward me with his hand outstretched. "Enfys Owen, and you are?"

Gods, he certainly didn't want for confidence. I took his outstretched hand and gave it a firm shake. "Eamon Adair, Fi's suitor."

His expression soured instantly, and he gave me a long appraising glance. "Adair, was it?"

"Unimportant," Arthus snapped. "We need to question Bryn again."

"Agreed," Marlen said forlornly from his spot at the table. "We should have brought him with us after we talked to him."

"No need," Enfys interjected, waving his hand as if he were swatting away an annoying bug. "I will reach out to my connections at the Council, we'll have this all resolved by sunrise."

My eyes narrowed at the insinuation that Fi's disappearance was simply an easily resolved blip.

"But Bryn—,"

"Is an insufferable ass to both Fi and everyone else he comes into contact with, we do not need his input. The Council employs skilled trackers of their own," Enfys said dismissively, cutting Marlen off.

I did not like to think ill of my cariad's judgment, but was Fi serious about this guy?

"Right, I'm going to send word to my Council contacts. I'll see you gentlemen in the morning," Enfys said confidently before striding out.

There was a moment of stunned silence between the three of us before Marlen groaned loudly.

"By the gods, I hate that fae."

I snorted and Arthus' lips twitched in amusement.

"So, what's the actual plan?" Marlen asked, looking to Arthus for direction.

"I don't feel comfortable with him contacting the Council, but I don't know how to stop him without drawing attention to Fi's gift," Arthus admitted, the strain of not having a clear course of action written all over his face.

"If I may," I interjected. "I've only met Bryn a couple of times, but I'm confident that if he has a lead, he will follow it to the bitter end, with or without our prompting." Marlen and Arthus both nodded in agreement. "In the meantime, I suggest we return to my estate and I will call on the spirits to help find Fi." I hesitated a second before pushing on. "You are both welcome to stay at my place for as long as you wish. If Fi was taken from the grounds, perhaps this isn't the safest place to be."

Marlen gave Arthus a pointed look—his wings always put him at risk. Under the kind of emotional stress he was experiencing, it would be a while before he was able to retract them.

Arthus nodded thoughtfully. "If you're sure it's not an imposition."

"Not at all. I will need one of you to anchor me when I contact the spirits, anyway. It's more difficult when I'm the one trying to reach them, rather than the other way around."

"Then let's go. Pack light, Marlen. I'll fly and meet you there. The sooner we contact the spirits, the sooner we can get some answers."

Hopefully, the spirits would be on my side and this cursed gift would come in useful for a change.

The moment we were back at my house, Arthus busied himself setting up candles in the shape of a pentagon on the floor, large enough for two of us to stand in. I worked in the kitchen, preparing bundles of herbs as offerings to burn—bay leaves, dandelion and lemongrass, while Marlen laid on a rug in the living room and stared forlornly at the beams on the ceiling.

We reconvened in the living room once we had everything set up, and without hesitation Arthus stepped into the candlelight with me and took my hands. He'd need to hold them throughout the ceremony to anchor me to the mortal plane. Generally, spirits crossed into my realm, not the other way round. If he let go, I might not have been able to return.

It was a good thing I trusted Arthus, and that his upbringing had clearly trained him well for these kinds of rituals.

Marlen placed the first bundle of herbs in an earthenware bowl, struck a match and dropped it on top before slumping back down to the floor. This particular blend was a peace offering, signifying to the spirits that we had pure intentions.

I took in a lungful of the pungent burning smell and closed my eyes. Thoughts of Fi swirled chaotically in my head, and I'd never found it so difficult to clear my thoughts before. But I forced myself to focus on finding a state of calm, letting the world around me fall away. When I could no longer hear the rustling of the trees, the crackling of the burning herbs or Arthus' even breaths, I opened my eyes.

My soul always rematerialized in a small forest clearing in the spirit plane, no matter where I left from. Everything was hazy here, wispy and insubstantial. The trees around me looked like shadows of the trees found in Avalon.

Within seconds, hordes of spirits began to drift through the trees towards me.

"I mean you no harm," I called out unnecessarily. They would have been able to sense if I had any malicious intentions.

"What is your business here, gifted fae?" A disembodied voice called out. Like all spirits, his voice was echoey.

"His future mate has been taken, he seeks her location," another, more feminine voice replied.

The spirits referring to Fi as my future mate bode extremely well for me, but now was not the time to focus on that happy piece of news.

"Do you know her location?" I asked loudly, in the general direction of where the feminine voice had come from.

"I have been following the Sanctified Empath at the behest of the gods. Where she has gone, the spirits cannot follow," the eerie voice replied.

"If we learn anything new, we shall visit you, gifted one. Return to your plane," the first voice interjected, and I felt my soul spinning uncomfortably through the void before I had a chance to object. I slammed back into my body and opened my eyes to find both Arthus and Marlen's alarmed stares locked on me.

"That looked a lot more painful than I thought it would be," Marlen said lightly, sitting up from his spot on the floor. Arthus released my hands and began to move the candles from the floor to the safety of the nearby tables.

I collapsed onto the couch, exhausted. "It's only painful when they kick me out. They said where she's gone, the spirits cannot follow."

"Cannot follow? Where can't they go?" Marlen pondered out loud.

"Nowhere good," I sighed. "The Council and Assembly buildings—including the dungeons—are all warded against uninvited visitors, spirits included. Wealthy fae usually use similar wards for their properties, if they can afford it..."

"The Castells are both Councilors and wealthy. The note was given to their daughter. I think it's a pretty safe bet we know who took her, we just don't know where they're keeping her," Arthus surmised grimly.

"I'm not well acquainted with them, but I know they have multiple properties," I added, rubbing my temples.

All three of us had matching glum expressions. Fi was no use to anyone who would exploit her magic if she was dead, but there was a whole list of other awful things that could happen to her short of death.

Compared to many of those things, death would be a kindness.

Hold on, cariad. Wherever you are, we haven't forgotten you. We will come for you.

The three of us returned to campus the next morning to talk to Gwyneira and see what Enfys had heard from his Council contacts. Both Marlen and Arthus were discreetly rubbing their chest from time to time, Fi's absence was already causing them some small physical pain, and I wasn't sure how long it would be before that ache became unbearable.

Mated fae were not meant to be parted for long.

We got a few strange looks as we passed through the campus, and I wasn't sure if it was because of my presence or if news of Fi's disappearance had leaked out.

"Marlen!" A young, weaselly looking guy ran up to us, making both

Marlen and Arthus tense up. The guy gave Arthus a wide berth and spoke directly to Marlen. "Look, I don't mean any harm. I heard Ffion was taken, and I knew you don't like her dads, but I promise you they're good guys, they'll want to know about this so they can help find her," he explained.

"This is Kelvyn," Marlen told me, giving Kelvyn a wary glance. "He was my roommate. He left Fi notes telling her to go home to Albion on behalf of the fathers she has no recollection of."

Kelvyn's face flushed in genuine shame. "Her fathers are friends of my family."

"Maybe we should talk to them?" I suggested, directing my question to Marlen and Arthus in a low voice. "Fi told me that her dads kept her hidden all these years, they're guaranteed allies at least." Arthus gave me a curt nod.

"Where can we find the Laisrens? We'll talk to them ourselves," he snapped at Kelvyn, who immediately rattled off a location in Eastland. It was over an hour's flight, but worth it to get some information.

Arthus dismissed Kelvyn as though he were an errand boy, and the guy jumped about a foot in the air before running off. I raised a questioning brow at Arthus.

"I taught him a little lesson about what happens when you fuck with our girl," Arthus said, completely unapologetic.

We didn't see Enfys around—which no one seemed upset about—or Bryn, which was a bit more disappointing. Gwyneira's mate, Mawrth, told us she was off-site following up leads of her own. So, in the absence of any other plan, we decided to pay Fi's dads a visit.

Marlen clutched at his chest the entire way to the stables. We had to get some answers now, before he and Arthus were too weak to do so.

The griffins landed outside a small stone cottage on the edge of an apple orchard where Kelvyn told us Fi's fathers lived.

Had they always lived here? Is this where Fi was born? She would have had an idyllic childhood here, playing in the orchard, climbing the trees, learning about her magic... Instead, she'd been cast out on her own in a foreign realm, not knowing about who or what she was.

It soured my opinion of her fathers, and I hadn't even met them yet.

Arthus marched up to the wooden door and banged hard on the brass lion head knocker. His shoulders rolled continually and his back twitched. It was probably taking every ounce of his self-control to keep his wings retracted.

The door swung open to reveal a gruff, burly man on the other side who easily filled the entire door frame. He had unruly auburn hair and amber eyes, the exact same shade as my cariad's. While Fi's were always bright with curiosity, her father's were narrowed in suspicion.

"Where is my daughter?" he barked, glaring coldly at Marlen and Arthus.

"She was taken," Arthus snapped, though I noticed the way his head bowed slightly in shame.

Her father's face fell, pain written over every feature. "You'd better come in then," he rasped, standing back to let us through.

We walked into a hallway with doors leading off to either side and followed him through an archway at the end of the corridor. It led to a small, tidy kitchen with a scratched wooden dining table and four chairs in the middle of the room. Marlen, Arthus and I took seats around the table silently, taking in the space around us.

Fi's dad must have been a fire affinity. He ignored us as he built a roaring fire in the potbelly stove, shuffling around morosely as he made some tea. It was strange he hadn't immediately started interrogating us, but as I watched the slow, despairing way he moved around the kitchen, I realized he'd already given up.

It didn't matter the circumstances. As far as he was concerned, Fi was gone and never coming back.

Fuck. That.

As he poured the sage tea, another man walked through the kitchen door with a basket full of vegetables, pausing on the threshold to take in the scene.

"Who are you?" he asked me curiously. He was thinner than the other man, with thick black hair, dark gray eyes, and a cold, distant expression.

"Eamon Adair," I replied politely. "I'm courting your daughter. And your name?"

"Attie Laisren," he said, looking questioningly at the man handing us cups of tea.

"I'm Galvyn," the other male grunted for my benefit before turning to Attie, eyes filled with pain. "They took her."

Attie sighed, placing the basket of vegetables down on the bench before going to pour his own cup of tea. Galvyn joined us, laying his elbows on the table and head in his hands.

"You see now why we wanted to get her out of here?" he mumbled to no one in particular.

"Sure. But you were still wrong," Marlen replied lightly, and both Arthus and I looked at him in surprise. He was the least confrontational among the three of us.

Galvyn looked up to glare at Marlen, a feral gleam in his eye.

"I see why you did it, but hiding isn't the solution. The solution is making Avalon safe for her. For anyone with coveted gifts," he continued, his eyes flicking to Arthus. "We're not giving up on her. We're going to bring her back. Whatever it takes."

"Whatever it takes," Arthus agreed.

"She's sanctified, you know," I added conversationally, sensing that her fathers needed something to cling on to. Both Galvyn's and Attie's heads whipped up to look at me. "The gods chose her. They warned us that the darkness would come for her, but they also told us they have plans for her."

"How do you know this?" Attie asked desperately, with a flicker of hope in his eyes.

"I have the gift of Second Sight. The spirits came to me a few weeks ago to warn Fi."

"Galvyn, she's sanctified," Attie whispered in awe. "We knew she was special when we realized she was an empath. She was just a wee lass, but as soon as she could talk, she told us about everyone else's emotions. She was so compassionate too, always wanting to help those who were suffering."

"This isn't what we wanted for her," Galvyn said hoarsely. "None of it. We were so happy when she was born–our first child, a *daughter*, a gift from the gods. We wanted her to have a happy, simple life. Gifted magic would've been a nice bonus, something common like my illusions. Nothing that would paint a target on her back."

"But we have hope now, don't you see?" Attie challenged, giving Galvyn a hard look. "The gods themselves chose her. She may yet have a happy future. Here! In Avalon."

"With her mates," Marlen added, his wrist outstretched. Arthus copied his movement and my jealousy flared that they bore her marks.

I wanted that with her. I wanted *everything* with her.

"Some mates you are if you couldn't keep her safe," Galvyn muttered.

"They could say the same about us. Rhedyn is dead," Attie retorted and Galvyn reeled back as if he'd struck him.

"I hate to bring up such a painful memory, but we need to ask you about that," Arthus interjected. "If there's a connection between whoever has Fi now and the fae that hurt your mate when she took Fi to Albion, we need to know."

"Murdered our mate," Galvyn corrected, and Arthus winced slightly.

"You warned us about the Council the last time we saw you," Marlen prompted.

"The portals were harder to travel through without permission back then. Nowadays, there are other means..." Attie trailed off, then shook his head slightly. "Anyway, back then we smuggled Rhedyn and Ffion through, but the Council noticed. We had been standing watch at this end so we weren't pursued, but they picked up Rhedyn's magical signature. She was taken into custody as soon as she set foot back on Avalon soil."

She emerged from portal lake, golden brown curls hidden under the dark heavy cloak she'd worn into the human realm, her small daughter hidden beneath it, cradled in her arms.

Rhedyn sniffed, stifling the sobs of agony she wanted to let out. A memory potion given to her child with wide trusting eyes, a simple note on the girl's arm so she wouldn't forget the name she'd been given—because a fae's name was sacred—and that was it. At least Galvyn's glamour would hold long enough until he was able to make another trip to Albion to create another.

It took everything in her not to turn around and go back. To snatch her only child away from the human orphanage and bring her back to Avalon where she belonged. But she wouldn't be safe here, not with the terrible gift the gods had bestowed on her. An innocent child. Her mere existence made her a target.

Too late. Too late, anyway.

Ffion had drunk the memory altering potion Attie had spent a small fortune to acquire. She wouldn't remember her own parents now.

"Rhedyn Laisren."

She spun around, so lost in her grief that she hadn't been paying attention to her surroundings. Two well-dressed males wearing Fae Council insignia stood waiting, hands clasped in front of them, feet spread. Ready to give chase should she run.

"You have been summoned by the Council."

And so, it began.

She fought against the Councilors. She screamed when they tried to torture the secret from her lips. She held on when the absence of the mating bond threatened to tear her apart from the inside.

It wasn't enough. It would never be enough to keep her daughter safe, because they knew Rhedyn's name. They knew her name, and it had only taken a trip to the Records Hall to find Ffion's birth record for them to know precisely who she had been hiding, even if they didn't know why she'd been hidden.

They would never know why. She would never tell them. Galvyn and Attie may never speak a word again after she died, and she could feel that dreaded moment drawing closer each second. She knew in her heart that her mates would never say anything either.

So long as their child stayed hidden, stayed away, she would survive.

Stay in Albion, Ffion, she wished with everything she had left in her. There

"We were in agony," Galvyn continued, staring at the table. "You'll start to feel it soon too, the absence of the mating bond. After a few days, it's almost unbearable. We couldn't help her, we couldn't even move and we didn't know where she was."

"Just when we thought it couldn't get any more painful, it did. The pain disappeared entirely. It just vanished. That's when we knew she had died. There's a hollowness now, an empty cavity in our chests where the bond should be," Attie finished, rubbing at his chest.

"How do you know for certain it was the Council that killed her?" I asked, leaning forwards. Both Marlen and Arthus looked stricken, probably already feeling the strain of separation from their mate.

"One of them sent a note, the smug bastard," Galvyn spat. "Saying they'd tortured Rhedyn, but she had never broken. And if Ffion Laisren ever returned to Avalon, they'd make it their mission to find out her secret. I guess they got her name from the birth records. There was no name on the note, just a picture of a bird's mask. The Council was the last to have Rhedyn in custody though, it must have been one of them."

Arthus, Marlen and I exchanged worried glances. "So, they might not have taken Fi because they knew she was an empath," I said slowly.

"They took her because they found out her real name and they're hoping she has a rare gift," Arthus concluded. "Why else would she have been hidden in the first place?"

"They'll bleed her until they figure it out," Galvyn whispered, his enormous frame hunched over the table. "They'll bleed her and try every crystal under the sun until they find the one that holds her gift."

"We need to get back to the Academy," Arthus ordered grimly. "We need to let Gwyneira know about this and track down Bryn. If he's the one who let slip about Fi's last name, I'm going to take out some of this pent-up rage on his face."

FFION

CHAPTER 44

I had no idea how much time had passed.

The cave was always dark, unless my jailors came to visit and lit the torch for a while. Food was practically non-existent and appeared at random. There was nothing to give me any sense of routine or the passage of time.

For the past, however many days—weeks?—I'd been here, I'd had a few small chunks of dry bread and just enough water to keep me alive.

Even that small amount of water was enough to make the place reek of piss and made me want to heave up my meager bread rations.

My arms, legs, hands and feet were all covered in dried blood from the multiple knife wounds that covered my body where the male abductor had bled me. It would only take a drop of my blood into the malachite healing crystal imbued with Marlen's magic around my neck to heal me, but I was saving it. Just in case the madman's dagger hit an artery or something.

Gods, how was this my new normal? Hoping the cuts from the knife I was regularly prodded with weren't fatal. Things had taken a spectacular nosedive for me.

Aside from the multitude of wounds and my generally terrible condition, there was a burning ache in my chest where I usually felt the mating bonds to Marlen and Arthus. It was so painful it kept me awake while I tried to sleep my way through this waking nightmare.

For the first time, I regretted taking Marlen and Arthus as my mates—not because I didn't love them, but because I *did*. More than life. I hated the idea that they were in this kind of pain too.

They'd have been so much better off if I'd never come to Avalon.

With each minute that passed, the endless darkness pressed in on me more and more, and the control I had to stop my thoughts spiraling into despair was slipping away. Physically, things weren't going great for me. But mentally? The cave was only the first layer of my prison, my mind was the second.

The only faint silver lining was that my captors still hadn't worked out what my gift was. While I sensed the female's fury at my refusal to tell them and her irritation at how long it was taking to find out, the male was practically vibrating with a sick sense of excitement at every failed attempt. The greater the challenge, the greater the likelihood that my ability was rare and worth pursuing.

He reminded me of the Mad Hatter. He'd stroll in wearing his creepy gold bird mask and robes like it was the most normal thing in the world, and his emotions always bordered on gleeful, so I had taken to muting my ability in his presence because his buoyant jubilation filled up my chest like a balloon.

It was repulsive. I didn't want to feel joy here. His happiness made my skin crawl.

When he wasn't around, I'd unmute my abilities because, in my more lucid moments, I felt like I wasn't entirely alone in my imprisonment. There definitely wasn't anyone else in the cave with me, but it kind of felt like there were others nearby.

Other *whats*, I wasn't exactly sure, because they sure as hell weren't fae.

When I lived in Albion, I experienced human emotions like waves lapping at my body. I could feel them, but they were separate from me. The same thing happened when I visited Inver, or when I went to the masquerade. I could feel the emotions of the non-fae inhabitants of Avalon, but they didn't sit on my skin or soak into my bones the way fae emotions did.

There were moments when I felt waves of despair and loneliness lapping at the edges of my consciousness, but I couldn't tell if they really did belong to other prisoners or if I was just slowly losing my grip on reality. Maybe my brain was reenacting some of my experiences among humans as a way of distracting me from the trauma?

Not knowing what was real and what wasn't was agony. Darkness, isolation and torture had warped my mind so much that I began to wonder if there was even any point trying to escape. What good would I be now? I was broken.

Where the fuck were the gods now?

In a twisted way, I almost looked forward to when the madman showed up to slice me to ribbons and collect my blood. The pain was the only indicator that I was still alive, not floating aimlessly through purgatory, waiting for judgment day.

At the edge of my consciousness, I felt someone else's loneliness and heartbreak lapping at my skin, echoing the loss I felt being away from the people I loved. I selfishly took a small amount of comfort in knowing that I wasn't entirely alone, and I hoped that the sensations I was experiencing didn't just exist in my head.

Another day.

Well, I'm pretty sure it was another day.

I laid face down on the floor of the gods forsaken cave, wishing for the sweet, merciful relief of death.

The scraping sound of the boulder moving broke me out of my wallowing temporarily. My fight was gone, though. I stayed where I was, lying on the dirt floor, turning my head slightly so I could face my captors.

The male sauntered in, smug as can be, with the female fidgeting uncomfortably behind him. He took one look at me lying on the floor and laughed gleefully. "It suits you, you know. Laying in the dirt at my feet."

"One day, I will take away everything you care about and leave you an empty husk of a fae," I promised flatly, staring at the hem of his robes.

"I doubt that," he replied cheerily. "Especially now that I know your secret, little empath. Worry not, you will live out the rest of your days under my protection. You'll be safe with me."

Crap. Nothing good was going to come out of him finding out I was an empath. I didn't even have the energy to roll my eyes at his delusions anymore.

"Kyanite," he continued to ramble as I willed myself to be literally anywhere but here. Maybe I could crack teleportation if I concentrated hard enough. "That is the crystal that allows me to channel your gift."

He threw a rough chunk of blue crystal on the ground in front of my face and I stared at it, entranced in spite of myself. It was a sea blue color with streaks of white that reminded me of crashing waves. If he had put me in front of a lineup of crystals, I'd have been able to pick this one out of the pack without even looking. It had a comforting, familiar energy that called to me.

The man leaned over me and hooked his arms under my armpits, roughly yanking me back into a sitting position against the wall. I bit down hard enough on my lip to draw blood, but a small scream of agony escaped anyway. I hated giving him the satisfaction.

"You know," he began conversationally. "If you'd had some boring or useless ability, we'd have wiped your memory and let you go."

He was crouching down in front of me where I leaned against the wall, my head tipped back to hold it up. He was so close I could feel his breath on my neck as he spoke, yet he delivered his creepy speech as casually as if we were old acquaintances who had just bumped into each other at the supermarket.

Apparently, all of my years of human books and television had given me unrealistic expectations of villains. This guy's brand of sadism wasn't menacing or diabolical. It was delivered with a playful wink and a cheeky grin.

"An empath, though," he mused. "An empath we can use. Which is wonderful for all of us, as we can do away with these uncomfortable masks. They were a simple precautionary measure, I'm sure you understand. Now that we know what you are, we can tell you all about ourselves and really get to know each other. Since you'll be staying, after all."

The female hesitated for a moment, but she removed the creepy mask at the same time as him nonetheless.

I didn't recognize either of them, but I didn't really know anyone outside the Academy either. They looked older and had a refined air about them that screamed wealth. They looked disappointingly normal, in fact. The female's icy blonde hair and navy-blue eyes looked familiar, though I couldn't place where I recognized them.

He had light brown hair with streaks of silver through it, and the coldest black eyes I'd ever seen. He was conventionally handsome—in a slimy kind of way—but upon closer inspection his eyes practically screamed *sociopath*.

"You don't recognize us?" he asked lightly. "I think my daughter looks rather like her mother. Fortunately for all of us, my mate is beautiful, is she not?"

I took a closer look at the woman. The only fae female I knew with white-blonde hair and navy eyes was...

Saffir Castell.

Godsdamnit, Bryn! I'd been trying not to think about him the whole time I was here. His name on the note had been a smoking gun, but I couldn't conclusively say he'd sold me out, so I did my best to force those thoughts from my mind. Until now. I couldn't ignore the fact that I was being imprisoned by his girlfriend's parents. Bile rose in my throat, but I choked it back down.

Not now, Fi.

"Ah, I see the recognition in your eyes. You do know our Saffir!"

He seemed delighted at this, clapping his hands together excitedly. Briallen had mentioned that a couple of Saffir's parents were on the Council. Surely not this guy? He seemed like he had several screws loose.

Crap, my dads had been very specific about avoiding the Council.

Double crap, I didn't want anyone exploiting my abilities, but corrupt Councilors would be extra bad. For the fae in general, not just me.

"It's rude to ignore us, you know," the male continued. "My name is Glendower Castell, this is my mate Evalina."

She squirmed a little with discomfort at me knowing about their true identities. *Good.*

"Well, that's probably enough of an introduction for now. We'll have a lifetime to really get to know one another. Now we have established what you can do, let's get on with the extraction."

What a civilized way of saying *I'm going to slice you open and bleed you dry now.*

"I didn't take enough last time evidently, since I wasn't able to influence anyone," he muttered thoughtfully, an almost manic gleam in his eye.

It wouldn't matter if he took every last drop of my blood in my body, he'd never be able to influence anyone because *I* couldn't influence anyone. I couldn't achieve that level of magic without a complete mating circle, and I was only halfway there.

Should I tell him that?

As Glendower pulled out his dagger, my mind flitted through all of the possibilities, and I decided to say nothing. Maybe he'd think I was just a particularly weak empath and leave me alone? It was a naïve hope, but the idea of telling this creep anything about me or my mates—current or future—made my stomach turn.

Could he force me to take more mates if he realized that's what was missing? He must have seen the mating mark on my wrist when he was bleeding me, but the lighting was limited in here. Maybe he'd assumed it was complete? Surely I couldn't be coerced into a claiming ceremony. I'd never willingly say the vows.

Just the thought sent another wave of agony through my chest. *Gods, what I would do to see Marlen and Arthus right now.* Eamon too—he may not have officially been mine, but he felt like he should be. If I ever got out of this cave, I was going to tell him that. It was selfish, given what I was putting my other mates through right now, but I didn't have the presence of mind to be selfless right then.

I just wanted them.

Glendower moved in closer next to me, dagger in one hand and blood collection bowl in the other. Vines sprung out of the ground to immobilize me, courtesy of his she-devil mate. They needn't have bothered; I was too weak to fight back anyway.

As Glendower dug the blade into my side, tearing through the fabric of my dress until he dug into my skin and slid the blade down towards my hip, I closed my eyes and imagined my happy place.

Waking up in Eamon's bed the morning after Winter Solstice, sprawled across Marlen and reaching over him just enough to brush Arthus' bicep with my fingertips, Eamon wrapped around me from behind.

For a brief moment, my idiotic brain flashed an image of Bryn's face when he told me my mating mark was the greatest gift I could have given Marlen. The sincerity in his eyes when he said that, the gentle sensuous curve of his lip that for once wasn't mocking or sarcastic.

But I shook that thought away and focused on the three handsome fae men in my life who I knew beyond a shadow of a doubt hadn't betrayed me. The sounds of my own screams lulled me into unconsciousness.

By the time I woke up, I was alone again with a fresh new wound in my side. It was by far the deepest he'd ever cut me and the most blood he'd collected at one time. I closed my eyes to stop the world spinning and took a deep breath of the putrid cave air. There was another lump of bread next to me and some fresh water, but I couldn't stomach the thought of either.

I willed my mind to send me back into the oblivious state of unconsciousness, but there was too much going on in my brain for me to switch off. Knowing that Saffir's family were responsible—and therefore Bryn—had thrown me for a loop, and I resented them even more for making me think about it.

Why couldn't they have just stayed anonymous? I didn't want to think about how I'd gotten here when I had no way of getting out. If I was going to live out the rest of my life in captivity, I'd rather take a mental vacation from reality, thank you very much.

I hated Saffir for her part in all of this, but I couldn't help pitying her for having these two as parents. Evalina's other two mates had appeared occasionally to top up my water or toss me a lump of old bread, but their emotions didn't feel nearly as twisted as Glendower. They mostly looked at me with a strange mixture of pity and revulsion, but they were obviously twisted enough to go along with all of this, so their pity didn't mean anything.

Between their passive acceptance, Glendower's special brand of crazy and Evalina's outright hostility, it was no wonder why Saffir's personality was about as warm as an igloo.

And then there was Bryn.

Betrayal sliced through me like a burning knife in the back as his beautiful face and mocking smirk popped into my mind.

Nope, not ready yet. A time would come when I was ready to think about him, but it was not now. Now was the time to forget.

MARLEN

CHAPTER 45

Fifteen days.

Fifteen days since the love of my life had been taken from us. Fifteen days she had been suffering somewhere alone. Every second was agony. It felt like fifteen years.

Arthus and I were less than useless—we'd been laid up on the enormous bed in Eamon's room for the past few days, hunched up under the covers, clutching at our chests where our mating bonds burned like a searing, excruciating brand on our souls, pressing and twisting and distorting.

Fi needed us, and we couldn't even get out of bed.

Two days after Fi's disappearance, the absent bond started to grow uncomfortable. Five days later, it became painful. From day ten, it had become an acute agony. I'd tried using my healing gift on both Arthus and I, but it didn't work. Our ailments were in our souls, not our bodies, and they couldn't be healed by magic.

When the pain had gotten too much to bear, we stayed at Eamon's house around the clock. It felt safer here than at the Academy, and although we were a burden, I think Eamon liked having us close by. Arthus and I had each other—Eamon would have been alone if we'd stayed on campus. He hadn't even questioned going to Gwyneira on our behalf and telling her we needed time off.

She had been more than understanding. It was a universal fact that the strain of being far away from one's mate was crippling, and the idea that Fi was suffering this same agony somewhere *alone* broke my heart.

We were pretty confident that Saffir's parents had taken her, but we had no idea where she was being kept or how to get her out even if we did find her. We were practically considered infants in the fae world. We wouldn't stand a chance taking on a Councilor. Besides, we were no good at all to Fi if we got ourselves arrested.

Our cautious hopefulness in the beginning had morphed into quiet hopelessness. We wouldn't ever give up looking for her, but the odds were increasingly stacked against us.

Also, being bedridden put us at a massive disadvantage.

Eamon sat at the foot of the bed like he did most mornings, sifting through letters. He had hired several fae detectives he trusted to investigate both Saffir's family and the other Councilors, and he maintained correspondence with Gwyneira now that Arthus and I couldn't. By the way he threw the papers aside and ran his hand over his face, I assumed he'd had as much success today as he'd had every other day. Zero. Zilch. Nada.

Enfys hadn't given up his search for Fi either, which was unfortunate. He seemed to take it as a personal affront that he hadn't found her within the twelve-hour window he'd set for himself. Enfys was insistent that the Council would be the best resource for finding Fi, but none of us felt comfortable divulging what we knew about Saffir's parents, lest he try to get us arrested for treason. When it came to the Council, the guy was a zealot.

Since we'd stopped going to the campus, Enfys had taken to coming here instead to update us, which irked me to no end. Eamon's house felt like a home to us, to our mating circle. Eamon may not have been officially part of it yet, but he was in every other way. The moments we'd spent here on the Solstice and New Year's Eve were sacred memories. I didn't think Fi would want Enfys to be here, his attention had always made her a little uncomfortable.

Enfys had gone to Saffir's father who told him to exclude Bryn Edan from all conversations in relation to the search for Fi, which meant Enfys had ordered *us* not talk to Bryn. It rubbed me the wrong way and must have set Arthus' teeth on edge—no one gave him orders, but Glendower Castell insisted Bryn had 'acted dishonorably towards his daughter and was to be watched around female fae' or something.

Glendower was a fae like the rest of us. He couldn't lie, and Bryn *had* acted dishonorably throughout his courtship to Saffir. He'd gone into it for all the wrong reasons and persisted with it even when his head and the mating pull were leading him towards Fi.

In the condition we were in, we weren't able to go visit Bryn anyway, so in a sense we *were* obeying Enfys' orders. However, everything he'd said about the Councilor both confirmed our suspicions and confirmed Bryn's innocence, otherwise why would Glendower bother warning Enfys away from him? Too bad that none of us trusted Enfys enough to share that with him though.

"You two need more food," Eamon muttered as he stood, looking over both of us worriedly. Poor bloke had been playing nursemaid, chef, detective and landowner, plus he was dealing with his own feelings about Fi's disappearance.

Before he turned to go, his features slackened and eyes fell closed. He stood in front of us, as still as a statue for a few moments until his eyes reopened, dominated by the creepy swirly clouds that indicated the presence of the spirits.

"Where the Sanctified Empath is, the spirits cannot go."

The words came from Eamon's mouth, but the eerie voice sounded disembodied and totally different from his own.

Like every day, we waited for more information. Like every day, the spirits said nothing further. Eamon's eyes drifted closed and he shook his head before opening his usual purple eyes again.

The same thing every day, some fucking help they are," he muttered. "I'll get you both some soup."

He returned with two bowls of soup on a tray that had the whole house smelling like pumpkin. Eamon sat on the edge of the bed and spoon-fed us each a few bites before we were strong enough to feed ourselves.

Fi better claim this guy, he'd seen way too much of Arthus and I to let him walk away now. I mean, he'd literally bathed us the other day.

Fucking. Mortifying.

Given Enfys' hate-on for Bryn, I was surprised when Eamon led him into the bedroom later that afternoon. Eamon knew Bryn the least out of all of us, so I figured he'd be the most likely to follow Enfys' orders.

"Gods, this is much worse than I thought," Bryn muttered, looking at the sorry state of Arthus and I. His condescending tone was belied by the worry written all over his face.

"Any success tracking her?" Arthus gritted out, clutching his chest so tightly his knuckles were turning white. He was a stronger fae than me, I couldn't speak at all.

"None," Bryn replied grimly, sitting on the edge of the bed next to Eamon. "I convinced Saffir to go and search her family estate—every room—but she didn't find any evidence of Ffion there."

He sighed, tipping his head back to look up at the ceiling as if the answers to all our problems would suddenly appear there.

"Saffir admitted she threw the note away at her parents' house and her mother was very insistent about escorting her back to campus the next day, so I'm guessing Evalina Castell planted it. For what it's worth, I believe Saffir when she says she knew nothing about it," Bryn added.

"The Castells have many properties, they could be holding Fi off of the main estate," Eamon suggested.

Bryn ran his hands through his disheveled hair and huffed out a sigh. He wasn't in the same kind of agony that Arthus and I were experiencing, but I'd never seen him look so distraught either. His usually bright blue eyes were dull and shadowed with dark circles, so I doubted he'd slept much more than we had.

"Unlikely," Bryn argued. "They want her blood, so they'll keep her close enough to access it regularly. Besides, you told me yourself that wherever she's being held is warded against spirits. I doubt they've bothered to ward any except for the main estate they conduct Council business from. It would raise questions about what they were hiding if they warded all of them."

Huh, I guess Eamon had confided in Bryn more than we realized. I wasn't mad about it because seriously, fuck Enfys and the high horse he rode in on.

Eamon scrubbed his hand over his face. His beard was getting long. All of us needed a shave.

"I have people discreetly checking the Castell's registered properties for wards and illusions. I assume this is why Councilor Castell explicitly told Enfys to leave you out of his search for Fi—he assumed you'd put the pieces together," he pointed out, giving Bryn a wry smile. "Our options for getting her out of a wealthy Councilor's heavily guarded property on our own are slim. I think our best option is to spread the word to the wider fae community that Fi was separated from her mates against her will. No fae would stand for the Council acting like that. They'd be afraid that their mates might be taken next."

My gut churned uneasily. I wasn't averse to some mild treason to get my girl back, but I didn't want to plant her smack bang in the middle of a revolution either. By the look on Bryn's face, he wasn't entirely comfortable with that idea himself.

"Exposing them is a risk," Bryn hedged. "They might just kill her if they think she's too much trouble. Find an excuse to explain away the death and then it's their word against ours."

"True," Eamon replied dejectedly. "Fi's fathers certainly never got any justice for their mate."

"We need a way through the wards, I know in my gut that she's on the main estate. I'm going to monitor the edges of the property, see if I can see anyone coming or going that might be of use to us," Bryn replied. "I'll get

Saffir to visit her parents again and take another look around. We're no longer together, but she feels guilty, so she'll help."

So, all it took for Bryn to see sense was for the girl he was courting to inadvertently be responsible for the kidnapping of the girl he actually wanted to be with.

Progress, I guess?

"Okay," Eamon agreed slowly. "We'll focus on finding a way onto the estate to check for ourselves. For all we know, he could have a whole prison somewhere on the property with gifted fae in it. Somewhere Saffir wouldn't think to look."

"There's not even any point in me giving Saffir a tracking amulet. She doesn't have Ffion's magical signature to follow," Bryn muttered dejectedly.

"That reminds me," Eamon said abruptly to Bryn, striding over to collect something from the dresser. I could just make out him handing over a long silver chain with two crystals hanging off it that I'd completely forgotten about.

"What is this?" Bryn asked cautiously as Eamon dropped it into his hand.

"Amethyst and malachite," Eamon replied. "Healing magic from Marlen, Second Sight from me. It's not the easiest ability to share, but you'll be able to see through glamours and weak illusions temporarily when you blood it."

"Thank you," Bryn said in a hoarse voice, staring down at the crystals in his hand.

"You're most welcome," Eamon said with a small smile. "We know you want to find her as much as the rest of us."

"I do. Shit, I should go. I memorized Enfys's signature so I could track his movements. He's nearby," Bryn said irritably, glaring out the window.

He stood and gave Arthus and I another concerned glance where we lay on the bed.

"I won't give up," Bryn promised, so quietly I wasn't sure if he meant for us to hear him or not. Eamon escorted him out and some of the weight sitting heavily on my heart lifted.

Bryn was still looking for Fi.

Bryn would keep looking for Fi.

Despite being an emotionally stunted grouchy asshole, if anyone cared about Fi as much as Arthus, Eamon and I did, it was Bryn.

Hopefully, wherever Fi was, she knew that. Given the fact that she'd gone to meet him and then been kidnapped... It was asking a lot of her to have that kind of faith in him.

A couple of minutes after Bryn had disappeared through the front door, Enfys' monotone voice echoed through the house.

"Hello? Gentlemen? Are you around?"

Arthus and I managed to flash each other matching eye rolls between waves of pain. Where else would we be? We hadn't moved in days.

Eamon's low voice carried through the house as he spoke in a clipped tone to Enfys. Eamon entered the room alone shortly after.

"I don't feel comfortable bringing him in here," Eamon admitted quietly, and I managed to nod my head slightly in agreement. The bedroom that mates shared was a sanctuary. It felt wrong to bring someone like him in here. Someone not suitable for our mating circle.

"Do you want to try to come out to the sitting room?" he asked hesitantly. Arthus and I both managed to grit out a "no" and Eamon gave us a sharp nod in agreement. He'd handle Enfys. We could rely on Eamon, he'd proven that to us time and time again over these past couple of weeks.

I just hoped we could rely on Bryn.

ENFYS

CHAPTER 46

I gritted my teeth, swallowing my anger as I discussed the updates on Fi's disappearance with Eamon. I had *specifically* told them to stay away from Bryn, yet I saw him leaving here not five minutes before I arrived.

How hard was it to follow simple instructions? I had been following them just fine.

"Mr. Owen," Councilor Castell greeted me enthusiastically, pulling me into his office at the Council administrative building and clapping me soundly on the shoulder. "Good to see you. Join me for a glass of wine."

Gods, this was an honor beyond my wildest dreams. I followed him gladly, sitting in the chair in front of his desk while he poured the wine at a small bar in the corner of the room. He strolled languidly toward me, handing me the glass before tipping his to me in a toast. I copied the gesture, wondering what I had done to deserve this privilege.

Perhaps it was for my training work at the Academy? It would be logical for Gwyneira to pass on to the Council how I was excelling.

"Now, Enfys—if I may be so forward as to use your first name, though I think we shall be friends—I am told you are here to enquire about a missing student?" the Councilor asked, sitting on the chair next to me in front of his desk instead of the grand chair behind it.

"Yes," I said eventually, clearing my throat. I hadn't expected such a warm

reception, and I had allowed it to distract me. *Focus, Enfys—this is not the time to make a poor impression.* "Ffion Smith, a student at the Academy has been reported missing. Her mates suspect foul play, possibly the involvement of a Mr. Bryn Edan."

Councilor Castell looked at me intently, leaning casually back in his chair with his wine glass dangling loosely from his fingers. It was a deceptively relaxed pose—my combat magic swirled through me, identifying his weak points and possible attacks subconsciously. His muscles were coiled tight and though he was leaning back in the chair, his spine was rigid and ready to move.

No wonder he had achieved a position on the Council. This was not a man to be trifled with.

"My youngest daughter, Saffir, is familiar with Mr. Bryn Edan. Poor girl, she has no gifted ability. Such a disappointment to us..." he trailed off wistfully, and I shifted uncomfortably in my chair at the blunt description of his daughter.

"Where was I? Ah, Mr. Edan. His dealings with my daughter have been a touch dishonorable, I'm afraid. I will investigate him personally in regard to Miss... what did you say her surname was?"

"Smith," I supplied.

"As you say. Anyway, I shall talk to Mr. Edan myself. I recommend that you and anyone else searching for Miss. Smith exclude Mr. Edan. Given his history with female fae, keeping him away from your friend would probably suit you better, would it not?"

It would suit me much better, as a matter of fact...

One of our illustrious Councilors had taken time out of his day to warn me about Bryn. Who were any of us to ignore such a great man?

Eamon Adair may be rich, but all of his wealth was inherited. He was no one of consequence. He hadn't even offered me a cup of tea upon arrival. Clearly, money couldn't buy manners.

"Where are the other two?" I asked in a clipped tone, wanting to update them all on my findings as quickly as possible so I could get back to more productive activities.

"Indisposed," Eamon snapped, his tone as impatient as mine.

"Right, you can relay the information to them then. I visited the Councilors yesterday to make inquiries on Fi's behalf."

I waited outside the imposing oak double doors and took a deep breath to calm myself. I had requested an audience with the five Councilors who supervised the Enforcers unit that I belonged to, hoping they would allocate resources to Fi's disappearance after I made my case.

"Enfys Owen, enter," a disembodied voice called through the door. I pushed open the double doors and walked into the surprisingly small meeting room. The five Councilors sat around a round wooden table, each with a secretary sat in a chair behind them taking notes.

"Please, sit," one of the Councilors said graciously, gesturing at the empty seat next to him.

"Councilors, thank you for meeting with me and on such short notice," I began, honored beyond measure to be sitting at this prestigious table.

"Not at all," the elderly man next to me replied. His hair was a shocking white and his features were wizened with age. He looked at least 500 and a day. "You have an excellent track record as an Enforcer and have never called upon us before. We were curious as to what you needed."

"A friend of mine—my future mate, I hope," I explained, making a couple of secretaries giggle. "She was taken, two weeks ago now. Her mates and I are very distressed."

"Of course, of course. Her name?" The question came from an elderly female Councilor sitting opposite me, dressed in multiple layers of garish purple.

"Ffion Smith."

"Ffion, you say? There have been rumors in the Council building that a Ffion recently appeared with an empath gift, can you believe it? The last name wasn't Smith though..." the elderly female replied thoughtfully.

"They did not have any news on her location, but one of the Councilors mentioned she'd heard rumors of an empath named 'Ffion' being discovered recently. An impossibility, I'm sure," I relayed to Eamon, eyes narrowed.

I waited for his denial, but none came. There wasn't even a flicker of surprise on his face.

"Fi... Fi is the empath?" I confirmed, stunned. It was common knowledge that empaths had been hunted into extinction centuries ago by dark fae.

Eamon gave me a cool, assessing look but said nothing, which was confirmation in itself. Excitement bloomed in my chest at the thought of my future mate having such a rare and powerful gift. Of course, it was aggravating that no one had told me, but the thrill of her power, her *potential*, overruled that.

Once we'd found her, I would be sure to take her to the Council and make introductions—they would be instantly taken with her. She could easily have a future as a Councilor herself—fae would travel from across the realm to see an empath in the flesh.

I would explain to Fi when I found her my disappointment that she hadn't confided in me, and I was confident she would then be more forthcoming in the future. Fi was a very reasonable female. It was one of the things I liked most about her.

I stood to leave, and Eamon followed suit. Clearly, we were both eager to end this conversation. He wasn't necessarily my competition to become one of Fi's mates—I'd seen her mating mark and she had enough magic for both of us, which made sense now that I knew what her gift was—but I didn't trust him either. Particularly since I'd seen Bryn leaving his house. Eamon might try to convince Fi that Bryn was a better choice.

I was confident Fi would see through that delusion.

"You do remember what I told you about talking to Bryn?" I asked, pausing and looking over my shoulder to narrow my gaze on Eamon.

"I do," Eamon replied smoothly, not breaking eye contact.

"That advice came from a Councilor, you'd do well to heed it," I sneered, losing patience with his arrogance.

"Noted," Eamon responded, moving to the door and holding it open for me. Fine, if he wasn't going to listen to me, I'd take it up with Bryn directly. He needed to be reminded of his place.

I walked out without saying goodbye and stormed back to the campus in a rage. My fire magic had been burning hot in my veins in the two weeks since Fi's disappearance. *Weeks*. How was it possible that we hadn't found her yet? Even *with* the Council allocating resources, we had no leads, and between the four of us, rescuing Fi should have been a cakewalk.

Eamon would be able to see through any illusions if he got close enough to them. I could fight my way through whoever was guarding her. Arthus could fly Fi to safety. Marlen could heal any injuries she'd sustained.

Strategically, I had it all planned out, yet we had no idea where she was or who had taken her. That plan was obsolete now anyway—Marlen and Arthus were too weak from the absence of the mating bond to be of any assistance.

Supposedly, Bryn had tracking magic. If he actually cared about Fi—if he was actually looking for her—he'd have found her already. Not that any of the Council trackers had either, but they didn't have the vested interest in her that Bryn supposedly had.

The other three may buy Bryn's innocence regarding the note, but I didn't. I wasn't there when they interrogated him, they probably didn't ask the right questions. The Councilor had said Bryn acted 'dishonorably' towards his daughter. What did that mean? What kind of schemes was Bryn pulling on unsuspecting female fae? Those were the kinds of answers we needed.

The more I thought about it, the more I felt I needed to talk to Bryn myself. Not just about the note either. I wanted to make it crystal clear what my intentions were with Fi and where his place in the fae world was.

I knocked on the door to Bryn's cabin, hoping he was there alone. I preferred to have this conversation privately.

Not that I thought I was doing anything wrong, but it may not reflect well on my Council position to stoop to delivering such a message.

Fortunately, the gods were on my side—Bryn opened the door and immediately went to slam it shut, but my combat magic kicked in, moving my muscles without conscious thought to block the closing door and barrel inside past a fuming Bryn.

He kicked the door shut and glared at me as though he could kill me with his eyes alone.

"I don't recall requesting a visit, Owen," Bryn drawled, crossing his arms over his chest and doing his best to look unaffected.

I snorted. "I don't take requests from disgraced fae like you, Edan."

"Get out," he snarled.

"No. I've got a few things I'd like to discuss with you first. Starting with that note. I don't believe whatever you said to Marlen and Arthus to trick them into thinking you weren't involved—"

"Fuck off, I don't answer to you, Owen. Ffion's actual claimed mates know I wasn't involved, I'm not going to waste my breath trying to convince a wannabe suitor like you."

"Watch it, Edan. I could make your life very difficult," I growled. *Disrespectful little prick.*

"You're already making my life difficult," Bryn snorted.

"Oh? Scared of a little competition?" I taunted.

"You're no competition," he retorted, and I knew I'd hit a sore spot. He was worried Fi would pick me over him as her final mate.

Good, he should be. She would definitely pick me.

"You know, one of my fathers was a Council Enforcer before me," I said casually. "I remember him coming home one day and telling me how one of the oldest fae houses had tragically tarnished their family name. A fire that killed an entire mating circle, deliberately set by the matron. And a child who should have been dead, but got lucky."

Bryn was vibrating with rage, but I was going to see this conversation through to the end. It's not like he could best me in a fight anyway.

"My father was called in to clean up the aftermath. He witnessed the raging little orphan standing in the middle of the forest, cursing the gods," I continued.

"Get. Out."

"I'll leave when I'm done, orphan. Your own mother tried to kill you. You're not good enough for a rarity like an empath," I snapped, registering the surprise on Bryn's face when I mentioned Fi's gift. Was that because he already knew or because he didn't?

No matter, everyone would know soon enough. A gift as special as Fi's deserved to be shared.

"The Calders are a devout line, famous in the temples. The Adairs are some of the wealthiest fae in Avalon. Marlen was an unfortunate mistake that can be attributed to her first mating and a lack of proper guidance. There's no room for a failed fae like you, Edan. Even if your pull to Fi is stronger than mine—which I doubt because you're too bitter to even be capable of meaningful connections—she deserves better than you. I will work with her existing mates and suitor to get her back. Once she is back, you will stay away from her. I'll only tell you this once."

Satisfied my words had hit their mark, I stormed past him and slammed the door behind me.

Fae were ruthless. Fae valued power and reputation. Fae fought for what they wanted. I was twice the fae Bryn would ever be.

FFION

CHAPTER 47

When Glendower barged into the cave practically shaking with anticipation, I knew this time was going to be different. He usually swaggered in like his dick was too big to walk like a normal person, but today he was all urgency and something a lot more dangerous.

He lit the torch on the wall and yanked it out of its sconce, bringing it alarmingly close to my body.

Please don't set me on fire. That really was the last thing I needed.

Fortunately, that didn't seem to be his plan. Unfortunately, he snatched up my left wrist and held it close to the flame to examine my mating mark.

"Of course," he muttered, a strange combination of exasperated and gleeful. "You need access to more magic. How could I not have considered this earlier? Then your blood will be perfect. Perfect, powerful blood."

He dropped my wrist and busied himself unlocking the shackles from the wall, hissing in discomfort whenever he had to touch the magic-blocking metal. The skin around my ankles felt raw and tender where they had been cuffed. My wrists were still bound, but the chain connecting me to the wall had been disconnected.

If I wasn't almost dead, I'd have tried to make a run for it, but there was no chance. I was exhausted, in pain, and not even entirely sure I could *stand*.

"Come along," Glendower announced, gripping my forearm tightly and yanking me to my feet. My ankles screamed with protest at every ounce of weight I put on them, and Glendower huffed impatiently when I tripped over my feet.

Walk. You have to walk.

I hated that I was too weak to get away. It felt like the opportunity was right within my reach, and yet so incredibly far away all at once.

"You will be pleased to know that I am taking you to a ball tonight, aren't you a lucky girl? I shall find you more mates—strong mates—and they will claim you and your magic will be unmatched. I will have to ensure they don't get any ideas about keeping you, of course. That would be most inconvenient for me. Occasional visits to keep your magic strong will do. And I'll find those other two you've claimed, I'm sure I'll be able to find accommodations for them as suitable as yours," he muttered to himself with a deranged chuckle.

Please, gods, keep Marlen and Arthus safe. If nothing else, don't let them get hurt because they loved me.

I was dragged roughly through the small side entrance of a massive mansion. The hallways we walked through—or that I stumbled through, rather—were stone and lined by flaming candles in sconces. It was too nice to be a dungeon at least. Maybe it was some kind of servant's quarters?

Gods, all that time trapped in a cave and I was probably only a hundred yards from a giant house filled with fae, though I doubted anyone here would have been willing to help me. The most dominant emotion I could sense here was fear. I tried to block it out, but I was too frail to mute it properly. My own already weak limbs trembled from how afraid everyone else felt.

Glendower shoved me roughly through a doorway and I cried out as my palms and kneecaps crashed into the unforgiving stone floor, but he was already roughly flipping me over. To my surprise, he unlocked the cuffs around my wrists, ripping them unceremoniously off me before turning to leave. The door slammed shut behind him and I heard the scraping of a key in a lock.

From my vantage point on the floor, I could see a small cot bed in the corner with a frayed blanket, as well as a toilet, a small basin, and an empty stone fireplace. The only exit was the same door Glendower had just locked behind him, and there were no windows. It was basically a five-star hotel compared to where I had been staying, but I knew nothing good was going to come of my upgraded accommodations.

I was a pig that was being fattened before being led to slaughter. No wonder he had no need to bother with the cuffs anymore.

There was no one around to see me, so I allowed myself to wallow in my misery, each injury hurting tenfold from the short journey to the house. With tears streaming down my face, I crawled onto the cot and curled up in the fetal position. The scrap of blanket didn't cover my legs, but it was better than no blanket at all.

Eventually, I cried myself to sleep. Every so often I'd wake up screaming, coated in a sheen of sweat and blissfully unable to recall the nightmare I'd been having.

It was probably about torture. I wouldn't forget the torture for as long as I lived, however long that would be.

I wasn't sure how long I slept on and off for, but the creaky opening of the heavy wooden door roused me some time later.

Glendower entered—his face a mask of benevolence that hid the gleeful anticipation for whatever he'd got hidden up his sleeve.

I was too exhausted to care. Too raw, too hurt, too bone tired.

Following Glendower was his daughter, Saffir Castell. I couldn't say I ever thought I'd see *this* bitch again. I assumed she'd wash her hands after all this messy business once she'd done her part to get me off campus, too busy solidifying her claiming bond with Bryn to bother with her parents' prisoner.

Saffir stood a foot behind her father with an enormous swathe of silky maroon fabric draped over her arm and a carefully blank face. I expected to feel some kind of sick sense of triumph or glee from her. Instead, I picked up surprise at seeing me that quickly morphed into horror at the state of me.

Surprise? Had she not known what her parents were doing to me? How was that possible? Perhaps they'd kept the details vague.

"Get her ready. She needs to be presentable enough to attend the Councilors Ball tonight. I assume you can manage such a simple task," Glendower said, his tone dripping with condescension. It was quite possible he had more affection for *me* than his own daughter.

"Yes, father," Saffir answered obediently, moving aside so Glendower could leave the room. He pulled the door shut behind him, but didn't lock it.

Saffir waited a few moments as his footsteps receded down the hallway before dropping the dress, rushing over to the cot and dropping to her knees next to me.

"Ffion, I'm so sorry," she breathed, startling me. "I swear I didn't know. I searched every inch of this house for you, just like Bryn asked. I even searched in this room. I don't understand how I missed you."

"Cave," was all I could manage, and I wasn't sure she even understood me. The word felt like it had been clawed from my throat with a razor.

Bryn asked her to look for me? Did he write the note to lure me out, then regret his actions and send Saffir to make amends? Why did she say she didn't know I was here then? Maybe if my head didn't feel like it'd been put through a meat grinder, I'd have been able to make sense of all this.

"They kept you in a *cave*?" she whispered, horrified.

Saffir reached out and paused hesitantly before pushing a lock of filthy, matted hair away from my face. "I'm going to have to get you ready for this ball, my father can't catch on that I'm helping you. As soon as I get back to the Academy, I'll find Bryn. He'll come for you, I'm sure of it."

I felt an overwhelming sense of loss from Saffir when she thought of him. Whatever was going on, it had cost Saffir her relationship with Bryn. The tiniest ember of hope flickered in my chest—maybe Bryn hadn't betrayed me after all?

Saffir moved to the basin and grabbed a mug from beside it, filling it with water using her magic. She lifted me into a sitting position against the wall with disturbing ease considering we were basically the same size. I must have lost a lot of weight. Saffir held the cup against my lips to drink and the icy cold water felt heavenly against my raw throat. All the screaming had made me hoarse, if not worse. I'd be surprised if I hadn't done permanent damage to my vocal cords.

"I'm going to have a tub brought in so you can bathe and get you some tea and broth from the kitchens," Saffir said softly, and I managed a small nod in acknowledgment.

She left with a torn look, returning shortly after with a maid who gave me a terrified glance before building a fire in the small fireplace. Another couple of servants lugged in a large metal tub and placed it in front of the fire, where Saffir proceeded to fill it with her magic.

The first maid returned again with a tray of broth and ginger tea, which Saffir took before ushering her out. After giving the ratty cot bed a distasteful look, she sat down next to me and spooned some of the warm broth into my mouth, nodding encouragingly as I parted my lips. *Hungry*. I was so hungry.

And humiliated.

Glendower had mentioned altering memories. Hopefully I could get my hands on some kind of memory-wiping amulet because I would dearly love to wipe this event from both of our minds.

Even the light broth made my stomach contract painfully, and I eventually shook my head slightly to let her know I was done. I blinked back a fresh wave of tears at the idea that I couldn't even manage to eat *soup*. If I did get out of this, what kind of shape was I going to be in? I didn't want my mates to have to nurse me the way Saffir was nursing me right now.

She checked the temperature of the bath and grimaced slightly. "It isn't as warm as I'd like, but we don't have much time," Saffir said apologetically as she tipped a small bottle of oil into the water. Lavender, by the smell of it.

Saffir whispered apologies over and over again as she helped me stand, brought me over to the bath and stripped me out of the ragged remnants of my cloak and dress. She carefully removed the foxglove brooch that had been holding my cloak together and put it to the side. It made my heart warm to see it. I'd run my fingers over the cool metal more times than I could count to draw comfort from my memory of the Winter Solstice.

Her kindness combined with my mortification at being seen like this was overwhelming me. I choked back more tears, not wanting this situation to get even more embarrassing.

I should really be focusing on how close to death's door I was instead of how naked and damaged I was in front of some random girl from school whose parents abducted me.

Pride, thy name is Ffion.

Being naked really was the least of my concerns, I still had to get into this freaking tub somehow, and I could barely move my muscles. In the end, I decided Saffir seemed like she wasn't going to let me drown so I took a deep, ragged breath and flopped myself into the tub, sighing in relief when she immediately reached into the water and yanked my head above the surface.

"Gods! Are you suicidal?" she shrieked.

"A little," I croaked hoarsely. If this was going to be my life for the next 400-and-something years, I'd rather be dead.

Saffir blanched, quickly busying herself by washing my hair with lavender-scented soap and tackling the matted curls with a wooden comb. I closed my eyes and tipped my head back against the edge of the tub. The tepid water felt heavenly, even if it was rapidly turning pink as the blood washed off my skin.

Saffir grabbed my hand where a small scrape from when I'd fallen on the floor was still bleeding. She looked at it for a long moment before quickly grabbing my necklace and pressing the bleeding wound against the malachite crystal.

"You need healing," she whispered apologetically.

As soon as my blood hit the crystal, Marlen's healing magic skittered across my skin like a thousand warm, friendly butterflies. I sighed in ecstasy as my bleeding wounds knitted themselves closed and some of the pain eased.

After a few minutes, I opened my eyes and inspected my arms. They were crisscrossed with faint white scars, but nothing was bleeding anymore. Unfortunately, the lack of other injuries brought my attention to the acute agony of the absent mating bonds that still lingered in my chest.

Saffir lifted the chain with the now empty malachite crystal on it over my head. "I'm going to take this and your brooch back to the Academy, okay? You won't be able to wear them with the dress, I'll keep them safe for you."

I nodded mutely, getting a little teary-eyed.

Saffir grabbed a washcloth and helped get all the dried blood and dirt off my skin. Eventually, the water was unsalvageable, and she used her magic to pull it out of the tub and deposit it in the basin across the room. She refilled the tub partway with cold water so I could rinse off the last of the dirt before helping me out and wrapping me in a towel.

"I know attending this ball is probably the last thing you feel like doing, but it will be the best opportunity to get help. I don't know what my father has planned, but he has a flair for the dramatic and loves attention, so I doubt it's going to be anything good..." she trailed off, gently patting my hair dry and taming my curls. I felt like a freaking corpse, and I doubt I looked much better.

"Mates," I croaked. "He wants to complete my mating circle to increase my magic."

If she was going to get help, and her intentions felt genuine, then I wanted them to know exactly what they would be walking into.

Saffir helped me stand, balancing me against the wall so she could stuff my uncooperative limbs into the maroon silk gown. She apologized for the lack of undergarments, but I didn't have it in me to care. The dress covered the important bits anyway.

The gown was full length and incredibly tight until midway down to my knees before flaring out, mermaid-style. Saffir laced up the corset-style back for me, and I was almost glad for the uncomfortable boning in the bodice since it felt like the only thing holding me up. There were no straps, and I was acutely aware of how on display my scarred arms were.

Surely that would be a warning sign to other people at this ball? Even if I felt a super-strong mating pull, wouldn't they run in the opposite direction at the sight of me? Unless the circles Glendower ran in were as depraved as he was. He'd called it the Councilors Ball, but I didn't have a lot of faith in the Council anymore.

Saffir lowered me back into a seated position on the cot and moved behind me to twist my hair into a low bun, securing it with a length of silk ribbon that matched the dress. When she was finished, she crouched in front of me on the floor and rested her hand on my arm.

"I'm going to sneak out now. I don't want to risk my father forcing me to take a memory altering potion or I won't be able to get help for you," she said quietly, looking at my face intently. I gave her a small nod to show I'd heard her.

Saffir huffed a breath and looked around the room awkwardly. "Look, I wanted Bryn as one of my mates. He's powerful and has gifted magic. My parents have always been really disappointed that I don't have a gifted ability, so I thought maybe if I had gifted mates, it would help them get over it..." she trailed off, and for the first time I felt more than just pity at her shitty parents. I felt enraged on Saffir's behalf.

"Anyway, it was obvious that Bryn and you had a strong mating pull, and I should have just cut my losses and found someone else. I barely have a pull to him at all, and it's really not like me to settle for being someone's second choice. It doesn't matter, we're over now. He ended things, rightly so." She gave me a sad smile. "I'm going to fix this, and hopefully one day you can forgive me for the part I played in it."

"Which was?" I croaked, not really wanting to use my energy on speaking but needing to know exactly how she'd contributed to this.

"I asked my parents to get Bryn a Council internship to make him stay with me. Sweeten the deal or whatever. I came home and, well, I was ranting,

I suppose. Kelvyn told Corsen and me what your real surname is. I usually don't confide in my parents, but I mentioned that Bryn was distracted by a new girl from Albion who wasn't even using her real name. When I said 'Ffion Laisren', my dad got this horrible look on his face..."

"Unintentional, then," I rasped.

"Of course," Saffir said, nodding vigorously. "I stupidly threw the note from Bryn away and my mother planted it in your cabin when she insisted on bringing me back to campus. I should have known there was something weird going on. She never wants to spend time with me."

The bitterness Saffir was feeling coated my tongue like iron.

"I'm not the nicest fae or whatever," Saffir said quietly, looking at the floor. "I know I'm not, but I'm not evil, Ffion."

I believed her, even without her words. I could feel the horror Saffir was feeling, the despair that had taken over the moment she saw me here. Her actions had set off this whole chain of events, but not by design.

She stood and gave me a lingering look, torn between wanting to get help and not wanting to leave me alone. It was sweet. Maybe we could be friends one day.

As long as she ditched her crazy family.

"Go," I whispered, attempting a weak smile that probably looked more like a grimace.

Saffir gave me a curt nod and slipped quietly out of the room. I slumped back against the wall, unable to hold myself up any longer but mindful not to destroy Saffir's hard work in making me presentable. It was nice to feel clean again. It gave me a miniscule amount of hope.

Even if she didn't go and find Bryn, I still wanted Saffir gone before her asshole father got back. Especially if he did shit like give her memory altering potions. What a monster.

It was really making me reconsider my relationship with my own fathers—maybe I'd been too harsh on them? They'd been trying to protect me from this exact situation. I was going to reevaluate a lot of my life choices if I ever got out of this place.

I must have eventually dozed off sitting against the wall, because I awoke with a start when the heavy wooden door banged open and Glendower stormed in.

"Where is my daughter?" he barked, all traces of *Mad-Hatter-meets-The-Joker* Glendower gone.

"I don't know," I croaked out. She *could* have been anywhere between here and the Academy, but I didn't technically know for sure, so it wasn't a lie.

"Useless, disappointment of a child," he muttered under his breath before running his eyes over me in a lecherous, appraising sweep. "My, my, don't you clean up nicely, my little empath?"

He stalked over to me and offered me his hand gallantly while I glared at the offensive appendage and didn't move. That was the hand he used to wield his dagger, to hurt me, to drain my magic. If he thought I was going to be amiable about this mess, he was sorely mistaken.

Glendower sighed and gave me a grossly paternal look of disappointment. He reached down and wrapped his hands around my forearms, lifting me roughly onto my feet.

"You will behave, my little empath. If not for your own benefit, then for your mates'. I will be collecting them as soon as possible, and their stay here will be as comfortable or uncomfortable as you make it," he threatened, effectively cutting off my rebellion at the knees.

I felt his triumph as he watched the fight seep out of me.

"Now, a glamour, I think," he said, clapping his hands like a kid in a candy shop and completely reverting to his demented ways. "You'll never attract new mates looking as haggard as you are. Such a pity."

I felt his magic slide over me, covering my hair and every inch of my skin. It felt slimy and foreign, but I fought back the urge to shake out my limbs to try to get it off. I held up my arm and saw that my skin was completely flawless, not a scar in sight. *Bastard.* I'd be walking around this stupid ball in agony, covered in the evidence of my torture, and no one would be any the wiser.

It was a special kind of cruelty. That was Glendower's whole thing.

"Come along, we'll be taking the carriage. Don't say I don't treat you, my little empath," Glendower sang, forcefully yanking me out of the room by the crook of my elbow.

Please don't let me down, Saffir.

BRYN

CHAPTER 48

I paced the length of the cabin for the millionth time. The one-month anniversary of Ffion's disappearance had come and gone, and we were no closer to finding her than we were the day she was taken.

Word about Ffion's disappearance had spread around campus, and the mood at the Academy was decidedly bleak. Even if she wasn't particularly well known by most of the students, the idea of anyone being snatched from the grounds was terrifying. In addition to the search, I'd been putting in extra hours on guard duty like all the other male students.

I had tracking magic for fuck's sake! Why had the gods gifted me with this ability if I couldn't track one of the few people in this entire realm I actually gave a damn about?

The most frustrating thing was, I knew in my bones that Ffion was on Saffir's family estate where the Councilors lived full time. Saffir had been completely cooperative—she'd visited their estate to search for information herself. She'd sworn that she'd checked every room in their gaudy mansion and hadn't found a trace of Ffion, which didn't make sense. She *had* to be there.

I'd gone to the border of the property myself and found nothing—an illusion hid the entire thing, but I couldn't sense any magic behind it. Unfortunately, the chances of me getting an invitation from her parents to cross the threshold were basically zero since I'd ended things with Saffir.

Even if I was able to lie, I couldn't have pretended to be interested in Saffir if I tried, even if only to appease her psychotic parents. Not anymore. Saffir wasn't the fae I wanted.

Briallen sat morosely in an armchair in the corner of my cabin, staring unseeingly at the fire. She'd taken to hanging out here a lot since Ffion's disappearance, and I wasn't sure if it was for my benefit or hers. She was definitely missing her friend, but she'd always seen right through my front when it came to Ffion.

"Please, Bryn. Just tell me what her gift is," Briallen beseeched softly, still staring at the fire.

"It's not my secret to tell," I replied, same as always.

"It's why she's missing, though. I always knew she had a gift, I hoped she would confide in me, but she never did."

"For your own protection," I told her sharply. I wasn't in the mood to coddle Briallen right now. Whatever emotional turmoil she was dealing with was nothing compared to whatever Ffion was experiencing.

"Enfys has been more of a raging asshole lately. Storming around the campus like he owns the damn place. Has he said anything to you?" Briallen asked quietly, picking up on my irritation with her pity party and changing the subject.

"Not since he showed up here a couple of weeks ago telling me I was a disgraced orphan, not good enough for Ffion, and warning me to stay away," I muttered.

She'd picked the only topic of conversation that could piss me off more.

"What?!" Briallen shrieked. "What the hell, Bryn?! You'd better not listen to him."

"Which part?" I asked wryly.

"All of it! Especially the staying-away-from-Fi part though. You are not doing that shit anymore. She'll come back, we'll get her back. And once that happens, you two are going to live happily ever after whether you like it or not. I am going to make it happen," Briallen fumed.

"That's not how mating works," I reminded her lightly, though her little rant had lifted my spirits slightly. "If it makes you feel any better—which it won't—Enfys isn't a fan of your buddy, Marlen, either. Said Ffion claiming him was a mistake, but she didn't know any better because he was her first mate."

"That *asshole*," she seethed. "Council Enforcer or not, I will make him regret saying those things about either of you."

"Don't make promises you can't keep, cousin."

I'd basically set my cousin on Enfys by relaying that to her, and she was vicious as hell when she wanted to be. I didn't feel remotely bad about it.

"I don't," Briallen snapped, and my face twitched in amusement. I kept my grin locked down, not wanting her to turn that vengeful energy on me. "In fact, I'm going to find Aderyn right now and come up with a revenge plan. She'll be furious that Enfys said that about her brother."

Briallen stood and swept imperiously out of the room, on a pointless mission that was sure to fail—Enfys was a godsdamned *Enforcer*—but at least it gave her a sense of purpose. She'd been drifting around aimlessly ever since Ffion was taken.

I wanted to go check on Marlen and Arthus again, but Enfys was hanging around Eamon's place like a fucking guard dog. Gods I hated that fae. I almost wouldn't care if Ffion didn't choose me, as long as she didn't choose him.

Almost.

It was infuriating to think that he probably could get an invitation to the Castell's estate since he practically kissed the ground the Councilors' walked on, but Eamon, Arthus, Marlen and I had agreed not to confide in Enfys because his Council-worship made him too much of a liability. He may claim he cared for Ffion and wanted her as a mate, but we couldn't be confident of where his loyalties really were if the Councilors put him in a difficult position.

I contemplated going to visit the guys anyway and sneaking around Enfys, but before I could decide, I felt Saffir's magic as she approached my door, hesitating for a long moment before knocking. Saffir hadn't flirted with me or tried anything at all since I ended our courtship, and while she'd tried to help find Ffion, that didn't mean I trusted her.

If Ffion thought I was responsible for that fucking note and her subsequent abduction, I'd make Saffir's life miserable.

I pulled the door open and moved back to sit at the small table. Understanding that was all the invitation she was getting, Saffir followed me in, her pale blonde hair disheveled, and face filled with worry.

"She's there. At my parents' estate," Saffir whispered.

"What?!" I all but exploded, jumping out of the chair. "You said you checked everywhere!"

"I did, Bryn, calm the fuck down," she snapped, her regular sullen personality returning. "She was only moved into the house today. She's been kept in a hidden cave somewhere on the property, I have no idea where."

"A cave?" I choked, dropping back into the chair. "How is she?"

I had to ask, even though I knew it wouldn't be good. Marlen and Arthus were in terrible shape, and Ffion had undoubtedly endured a lot worse.

Saffir's usually aloof gaze was full of sympathy. "It was bad, Bryn. When I found her, she was in a heap on a dirty cot, shackled with magic-blocking cuffs, covered in blood." Saffir's voice was hoarse with raw emotion. "My father demanded I clean her up. She had a malachite with healing magic, so I made her blood the amulet which closed her wounds, and I bathed her, got her some broth..."

Saffir closed her eyes for a moment, holding back tears. When she opened them, they were filled with icy determination. "My father wanted me to prepare her for a ball tonight. He sent for me this morning to come home specifically to bring back a dress. It's a Councilor's Ball, so it'll be held at the old Oberon Hall on the Eastland-Northgales border."

"Why would he take her to a ball?" I asked, genuinely confused. I didn't know much about kidnapping, but bringing your captor out for a night on the town seemed odd.

"Ffion suspects that he's trying to find mates for her, so that her magic reaches its full potential or whatever." I took a deep breath to keep the fire magic roaring through my veins at bay. "I think he may want to draw attention to her somehow. When he walked me to the room she was in, he was muttering about how grateful she would be for his *protection*." Saffir practically spat the last word out.

"He's going to paint a target on her back," I murmured to myself.

If word got out that Ffion was an empath, her anonymity would be gone. Glendower would have a legitimate reason as a Councilor to guard her for her own safety.

Cunning bastard.

"You have to get her out, Bryn. The ball is your best shot, it's a public venue so there are no illusions to shield it. And I promised her you'd come for her," Saffir added guiltily.

"Does she know the note was for you?" I asked harshly, already moving towards the wardrobe to find something suitable for a ball.

"She does," Saffir confirmed. "I explained everything."

"And she knows you and I are done? Forever? Never, ever going to happen?"

Saffir winced, and I knew it was harsh, but I needed her to understand we were done as much as I needed Ffion to understand that Saffir and I were no more.

"Yes," she said sadly. "I told her that too."

"Good," I replied, pulling out my best dark trousers, shirt, and waistcoat that I'd worn to the masquerade a few weeks ago. I allowed myself a moment to remember how beautiful Ffion had looked as a phoenix, the smooth expanse of her skin visible in her backless dress... I was going to get her back tonight, come hell or high water.

"Be careful," Saffir whispered, and I gave her a curt nod before she left. Just seeing her face was a reminder that Ffion was in this whole situation because of me.

I dressed and headed to my cousin's cabin first. Fortunately, Leigh opened the door as Briallen wasn't back from harassing Aderyn yet. I'd rather have this conversation without her around—she'd probably try to tag along.

"Can you get a message to Eamon, Arthus and Marlen?" I asked Leigh brusquely, wasting no time on pleasantries.

"Of course," he responded immediately, giving me his full attention.

"I know where Ffion is, I'm going to get her tonight. There's an Academy-owned safehouse halfway between her location and the campus. She can rest there overnight and I'll make sure we're not being tailed. I'll deliver her to Eamon's house tomorrow morning so long as we aren't being followed. Tell them our suspicions were correct," I added, already moving toward the stables. Leigh narrowed his eyes but didn't ask any questions as we parted ways.

It was a three-hour flight to Oberon Hall where the ball was being held. Hopefully, I'd get there early enough for the griffin to have a decent rest before I got Ffion out of there and flew another couple of hours to the safehouse. It wasn't my most well-thought-out plan, but time was of the essence.

So long as I got Ffion out of there, I'd figure the rest out.

I hovered in the shadows of the large stone hall the ball was being held in, watching the wealthy elite of the fae world with disgust as they drank expensive wine and mingled.

Oberon Hall was both ancient and ostentatious. The walls were the same traditional stone as they had always been, but somewhere along the way patterned marble floors had replaced the wood, and simple wooden torches became wrought-iron chandeliers that cast the room in golden candlelight.

The arched ceiling was supported by intricate beams that ran the length of the room, with sculptures of ancient fae lounging amongst the rafters. The wings of the sculptures were painted every shade under the sun and flecked with gold leaf, and they were renowned throughout Avalon for their detail and beauty.

They were probably the gaudiest things I'd ever seen.

My family was once welcome in these circles, until my mother's tragic breakdown. I was glad for the ostracization—I didn't want to spend any time with these assholes. Enfys' insults about my disgraced family had only solidified my opinion of them.

I'd glamoured my hair a dark blonde and my eyes green, to throw off anyone who might recognize me, planning to stay hidden as much as possible. But if Glendower spotted me, I'd be out on my ass in seconds.

There was a small, raised platform, around four feet high, in the center of the room where a couple of fae were currently performing on the flute and harp. I positioned myself nearby, figuring that if Glendower were going to make a scene, that's where he'd do it.

My best bet for a distraction was a controlled but significant fire. There'd be water affinities here who could counter it, but the element of surprise would be on my side. I only needed a couple of minutes to grab Ffion and get the hell out of here.

It was a plan, albeit one that was full of holes. It would have been great to have the other guys here for backup, but Eamon was the only one strong enough to help, but he was by far the most recognizable of all of us to this crowd. I wasn't sure he would be able to create a glamour strong enough to hide the fact that he was the Adair heir, not around this hierarchy-obsessed crowd.

I scanned the room, my gaze catching on a ceiling-height wooden partition that blocked the entrance to the bathrooms from the main ballroom—it was the perfect fire hazard. It was also at the opposite end of the room from the kitchens, which would be our best escape route. Now, all I needed was the girl.

Come on, scout. Where are you?

I was beginning to lose hope in Saffir's tipoff when I felt the mating pull yanking at my chest, pulling my attention to the main doors. Of course that fucker Glendower would wait to make a dramatic entrance.

A few moments later, they entered together—surprisingly without the rest of Glendower's mating circle. My heart leaped to my throat seeing

Ffion shuffling in, clutching her captor's arm to keep herself upright.

That was one of Saffir's fathers holding onto her.

This is my fault. My fucking fault.

Ffion was clearly in pain from the extended absence of her mating bonds, but aside from that she didn't look as terrible as I'd expected her to look after a month in captivity. Saffir had implied that Ffion had suffered a lot, but the only evidence I could see of physical maltreatment was the loose fit of her dress. Fi's luscious curves had all but vanished in a month, they obviously hadn't been feeding her properly. The thought made bile rise in my throat.

Bryn, you fucking moron. He has an illusion gift!

Cursing quietly under my breath, I discreetly unsheathed my dagger and ran the pad of my thumb along it before pressing the wound to the amethyst pendant around my neck. Thank the gods that Eamon thought ahead.

With the glamour out of the way, it was easy to see what Saffir had been talking about. My stomach churned and my fists were clenched so tightly that my nails were cutting into my palms.

Ffion's usually rich, bronze skin had taken on a grayish tinge, her eyes were glassy and surrounded by dark shadows, and the dress wasn't just *loose*, it was hanging off her. Her *bones* were protruding out of her skin, for fuck's sake.

But the thing that had my fire magic coursing through my veins like lava was the litany of scars that marred her once-perfect skin. They were everywhere that I could see—all along her arms, over the top of her hands, along her collarbone, her neck, even on her face. Shame prickled over my entire body.

My fault. My fucking fault.

The bastard glamoured her to cover up the scars he inflicted and the pitiful state she was in. Ffion was in so much pain she couldn't walk unassisted, and he had perversely used that as a way to have her on his arm like she was his fucking date.

I wanted to destroy him. I wanted to rip his arm off where it touched hers, to peel his smile off his smug fucking face.

I wanted his blood.

With restraint I didn't know I possessed, I pulled my fiery magic back through my veins, tamping down my bloodlust for the time being. I didn't have a hope of getting Ffion out of here safely if I attacked a Councilor in a room full of witnesses.

The mating bond writhed in my chest and my fingers itched to reach out and touch her. I wasn't even sure if Ffion would be able to sense my presence with the agony she was in, but for a brief heart-stopping moment, her eyes flicked up and scanned the crowd as if she was searching for someone. My heart jumped into my throat.

Hold on, scout. Just a little bit longer.

The crowd parted for Glendower and what was clearly his prisoner, like he was the king of the fucking fae. No one seemed surprised in the slightest to see a malnourished female on his arm, barely keeping herself upright. Clearly the rot in the Council ran deeper than the guys and I had assumed.

Glendower half-dragged Ffion through the room to the platform where the musicians had quickly gathered their equipment and scurried out of his way, and it took everything in me to hang back as Ffion stumbled on the stairs.

Patience. I had to have patience.

If Glendower was ever going to release his grip on her, it would be when they were on the stage and he was hamming it up for the crowd.

I moved purposefully through the crowd like I belonged there, positioning myself next to the wooden partition. I'd have to move quickly and discreetly once I started the fire—getting arrested was not part of my plan tonight—but being so close to Ffion was all the motivation I needed.

There was no way I was leaving this room without her.

FFION

CHAPTER 49

He was here for me, I could feel it. His distinctive scent of bonfire embers wrapped around me like a comforting blanket.

Glendower had a firm grip on my elbow as he stood on the platform, angled slightly in front of me so he could commandeer the attention of his adoring fans. I edged myself as far back on the platform as I could while he was still holding onto me, hoping the ground would open up and swallow me whole.

This room was incredibly intimidating, I'd never been anywhere like it before. The marble floor was so shiny I'd been able to see my glamoured reflection in it, and the circular wrought iron chandeliers that hung from the ceiling were as big as truck tires.

I had muted my abilities with my meager energy reserves, but there was at least a hundred fae in this room and their attention was very much on me. It didn't give me a crippling migraine like it would have once upon a time, but I definitely felt dizzy. I attempted to focus on what Glendower was saying but black spots were blurring my vision, and everything sounded so far away...

"Young Ffion Laisren here is an empath!" Glendower announced, plunging me back into the present with a sense of dawning horror. He just godsdamned *announced* it! Like it was nothing. Like I hadn't worked my whole life to keep this part of me a secret. Anonymity, gone. Outed me, just like that.

Bastard. Cruel, awful bastard of a fae.

Before the crowd had time to react, fire exploded up a nearby wall, licking the ceiling yet carefully missing several fae standing right next to it.

This was no natural fire.

Glendower released my elbow in surprise, and I felt the mating pull grow stronger. He was on the move.

An almost uncomfortably hot hand wrapped around my ankle, pulling me back off the platform. I landed against a strong chest, warm arms banded around my waist. I squealed in surprise, but I wasn't scared. I knew that strong pull, those hands that felt like fire, that glorious bonfire scent could only belong to one person.

A blonde-haired Bryn set me back on my feet, gripping my hand tightly as he maneuvered us through the throngs of confused fae. The crowd had moved, allowing the water affinities to put out the fire, but the confusion was already wearing off. I didn't dare look back at Glendower. I was too scared to *breathe* until we were free of the crowd.

Bryn's movements were sure as he led us through a kitchen area packed with waitstaff and into the trees behind the building. A beautiful tawny griffin stood tall, waiting for us.

I let out a shaky breath of relief, even knowing we were quite literally not out of the woods yet. The night air was cool, and I smelled nothing but Bryn's scent and the trees—how long had it been since I hadn't been sitting in my own filth in an enclosed space? How long had it been since I could breathe in fresh air and see the stars above me?

How long had it *been*?

Bryn still hadn't said anything, and from the tight set of his jaw, it looked like he wasn't going to any time soon. It didn't bother me—I barely had the energy to stand, let alone speak, and he was clearly busy concentrating on getting us out of here.

He gave my fitted dress an agitated look before flicking his fingers ever so slightly. I sucked in a breath as flames appeared at the hem, running up the fabric in trails and burning the material clean away until the dress stopped just above my knees, leaving me in a borderline indecent mini dress. I'd felt the warmth of the fire against my skin, but nowhere had it burned me.

Under different circumstances, I might have appreciated how sexy it was that he could burn my clothes right off my body.

Bryn encouraged me closer to the griffin, glancing back over his shoulder the whole time, before boosting me up onto the beast. While I was able to straddle it with my newly shortened dress, there was now nothing borderline about how indecent it was, and I tugged at it fruitlessly, silently cursing my lack of underwear. Modesty aside, the feathered back of the creature was not a comfortable place to sit with a bare butt. Bryn climbed up easily behind me, wrapping his arms tightly around my waist and wordlessly communicating to the griffin to take to the sky.

Bryn could have loosened his grip once the griffin leveled out, but if anything his grip tightened, his forehead falling forward to rest on the back of my neck. His skin was so warm, it was just shy of uncomfortable, but as I dropped my empath guard and took in what he was feeling, I knew the body heat was a heightened emotional response.

The relief rolling off him was *palpable*, though it was mixed with a healthy dose of fear that I could definitely relate to.

I hesitated for a moment, not knowing how to respond to this Bryn who was so unlike my Bryn. *No, not my Bryn*. Regular Bryn. But I couldn't overlook the fact that he had come for me, even if he hated me. Or just resented me. I wasn't sure anymore.

Risking his rejection, I reached one hand behind his head to tangle my fingers in his curly locks, holding him close for a moment before resting both hands atop his on my stomach. Something in this moment felt pivotal. Like we were standing on the precipice of something important, something that would set our path forever.

Bryn exhaled in relief, the skin-to-skin contact instantly soothing us both.

I could sense how guilty he felt, but I didn't want to dive too deeply into his emotions to find out why. If he wanted to tell me, then he would.

"I saw Saffir earlier, she brought me this dress for tonight." Bryn made a strangled noise in his throat behind me, and I felt his rush of anger run through my veins. "She explained about the note," I continued. "I know you had nothing to do with it."

"But you suspected I did before you talked to her," he deduced. I felt his sting of hurt all the way down to my bones. I thought about deflecting, but isn't that what Bryn and I always did? We deflected and pushed each other away and hurt one another. I didn't want to play that game anymore.

"I didn't want to," I told him honestly. "I couldn't figure out the note without your involvement but... it didn't sit right with me, the idea of you being involved."

He was still hurt, but there was another rush of relief at my words. I wasn't going to apologize for being suspicious—Bryn and I had a complicated relationship at the best of times, and part of having my gift meant I couldn't afford to be blind in my trust.

Deep down, Bryn knew that too.

"Ffion," he began in a low voice. "I wouldn't. I would never do that to you. I know we haven't always..." he trailed off as his discomfort grew.

"I know," I whispered, tilting my head back and planting a chaste, grateful kiss on his cheek. "Thank you for coming for me."

"Always," Bryn promised.

There was the briefest flash of an impossibly tender emotion, but I shook it off. My head was a mess, I was probably seeing and feeling things that weren't there. I needed rest. And water. And my mates.

We flew for what felt like hours, with me drifting in and out of consciousness along the way. Bryn must have been using his magic to keep his body running hot, because it felt like I was wrapped in the best kind of fiery blanket. Safer and warmer than I had in a long time, I let my eyes drift closed.

Eventually, the griffin began its descent into a small clearing in an expansive forest. I knew immediately that this wasn't the forest surrounding the Academy—the trees here were taller and skinnier, with no lower branches at all, and the very air around us felt thinner. It had been too dark to see anything from the air, but I suspected we were up a mountain.

We landed below a tiny treehouse, nestled snugly in the canopy high above us. Bryn practically dragged me off the griffin, who proceeded to make itself comfortable at the base of the trees while I made the slow and agonizing climb up the narrow staircase.

Bryn kept his arm wrapped securely around my waist to support me up the stairs before leaving me at the threshold so he could check out the cabin first, his glittery gold magic trailing over surfaces as he investigated them. Was this his place? It seemed unlikely, given how thoroughly he was checking it.

Eventually, he gestured for me to enter and I hobbled into the tiny cabin, feeling increasingly weak but not wanting to ask him for help. He'd done so much for me already.

Plus, I was both proud and stubborn in equal measure. I could admit that.

Bryn dropped his glamour as he moved about the room, continuing to look for whatever he was looking for. I felt a warm comforting rush seeing his inky blue-black hair and sapphire eyes again.

Safe. I was safe.

For how long, I was less certain.

The cabin was small and basic, but it looked comfortable and well maintained, and I wasn't about to be fussy after being chained up in that cave. There was a bed with a large trunk at the end of it, a potbelly stove in a tiny kitchen, and a door that presumably led to a bathroom. Bryn used his fire magic to light candles as he moved throughout the room. The cabin was strangely bare of windows—the door I was standing in seemed to be the only way in or out.

Bryn finished checking the bathroom and turned back to me, faltering slightly as he took in the state of me. He only hesitated for a moment before striding over and scooping me up bridal-style, holding me close to his chest. His warm body was an inferno, cutting through the bitter cold that had been embedded in my bones from the moment I woke up in that cave.

Bryn deposited me gently onto the bed as if I was fragile as glass. For once, I set my pride aside. I felt fragile.

"What is this place?" I whispered, struggling to keep my eyes open.

Bryn moved to the stove, using his magic to get the fire going before setting the kettle on it to boil. "Safehouse. Just for tonight, to make sure we weren't followed. Besides, you need to recover. It's still at least an hour's flight to campus."

He returned to my side with a glass of water and a jar of preserved peaches that he twisted open. He disappeared and dug out a loose dress and a blanket from a chest at the end of the bed.

"Your mates and Eamon knew I was coming for you, they're expecting you tomorrow morning," he grunted, almost adorably out of his element.

I pulled the blanket over myself, teeth chattering, knowing I needed to get out of this butchered dress but too sore to move. Bryn continued to fuss around me, brewing tea and looking through the cupboard for more food.

He walked back over a second later, pulling something over his head. I squinted a little and realized it was a chain with a green crystal and a purple crystal hanging off it. Bryn lowered it carefully over my head where it hung low between my breasts. Carefully, he withdrew his dagger from its sheath, and I flinched back instinctively.

If I never saw another dagger again in my life, I'd be completely okay with that.

"I just need to cut your finger a little to activate the healing malachite," he told me slowly, as if he was talking to a wild animal. "Would you prefer to do it yourself?"

I shook my head and held out my hand. I was shaking so much, I'd probably take off my whole finger if I tried.

Bryn took my cold shaking hand into his warm steady one. His hands were large and engulfed mine as he wrapped his fingers around my palm. *Safe. Bryn was safe.* He took the dagger and carefully pricked the tip of my finger as lightly as he could before setting the blade aside and pressing the bleeding wound to the crystal around my neck.

I felt the rush of Marlen's magic immediately. The crystal I'd used earlier had staunched the bleeding, but this second dose seemed to work a bit deeper—I could feel my wounds knitting together under my skin.

It was pleasant and unpleasant all at once. The pain was easing, but there was a distinct ickiness to the way the magic squirmed under my skin.

I laid back against the pillows to let the crystal do its thing while Bryn busied himself at the stove.

"Dandelion tea," Bryn announced, bringing over a steaming cup for me. "I know you prefer peppermint, but there isn't any here. Dandelion is my favorite, hopefully you like it..." he trailed off awkwardly and I gave him a small grateful smile as I wrapped my hands around the hot mug. For the first time, I really didn't miss coffee.

Dandelion tea wasn't as good as peppermint, but it would probably be my second choice.

How had Bryn even known peppermint was my favorite?

"Are Marlen and Arthus okay?" I rasped, desperation bleeding into my tone. My vocal cords felt much better, though I still sounded like I'd smoked a pack a day for the last hundred years.

"As well as can be expected with the extended absence from their mate. They haven't left Eamon's place, he's been looking after them." That wasn't entirely surprising, Eamon was a saint. I'm glad they had each other.

"How long was I gone?" I asked, needing to know, but dreading the answer all the same.

"Just over a month," Bryn replied, his mouth set in a grim line. "We suspected the Castells had you, but we didn't know exactly where or how to get you out safely."

We sat in silence after that as we drank our tea together, but it was companionable rather than awkward. It was the silence of two people who had just experienced something enormous together and needed a moment to figure out how to process it and move forward.

My secret was out, and my anonymity was toast, Glendower had ensured that. I'd also disappeared from right under his nose, and I doubted he was going to let that slide. Whatever happened from here, my quiet introduction to the world of magic and the fae was over.

The absence of the mating bond ached in my chest, but the healing crystal had healed my remaining wounds enough for me to get myself to the bathroom and at least wash my face.

I hobbled back into the room and sat on the edge of the bed, too exhausted to even attempt unlacing the corset back of the dress. It'd be a bitch to get out of, even if I wasn't half dead.

I cleared my throat awkwardly. "Could you help me change?" I asked the polished wooden floor.

Bryn didn't say anything, but he moved behind me on the bed and began to slowly unlace the scrap of a gown. The tips of his fingers felt like heaven against my skin, the mating pull to Bryn flaring hotter than ever and easing some of the agony in my chest.

Once he'd unlaced the dress, he pulled it out carefully from under my ass and tugged it over my head. Without prompting, he pulled the loose beige dress over my head, and I shoved my arms into the elbow-length sleeves.

"This is not how I imagined undressing you for the first time, scout," Bryn murmured quietly behind me, gently smoothing the dress down over my hips and making my breath catch.

"You've imagined undressing me?" I asked hoarsely, instantly mourning the loss of his touch when he pulled his hands away.

He snorted. "You know I have. Don't pretend you haven't had similar thoughts about me." I could practically hear the arrogant smirk in his voice, but for once it didn't irritate me. The teasing banter was a pleasant distraction from the less-than-pleasant circumstances.

I huffed an approximation of a laugh before shuffling slowly back towards the headboard, and Bryn helped me slide under the blankets, arranging the pillows around my head. He really was a fantastic nurse, even if his bedside manner was a little on the brooding, grouchy side.

He went to move away, but I reached out to snag his hand, wincing at the pain the sudden movement had caused me.

"Please stay. It hurts less, with you..." I sighed in relief when he didn't make me explain. He climbed under the blankets and instantly pulled me into his arms so we were facing each other, and I decided there would be plenty of time to be mortified about begging him to stay with me tomorrow.

A long moment passed where we just stared at each other as if we were both too afraid to move and shatter this fragile moment of perfect peace between us.

"I really want to kiss you," he said finally, putting into words the emotion I'd already been picking up from him.

There was no going back from this.

And yet...

"Then kiss me," I whispered, semi wondering if I'd lost my mind back in that cave.

He leaned in and I used what was left of my strength to meet him halfway, because Bryn and I would *always* meet halfway. We were the most similar out of all my guys, the most equally matched, and the most volatile.

His lips met mine in a kiss that wasn't the demanding, consuming fire I expected. It was soft, careful, *loving* even. It warmed the corners of my body and soul that had been cold and empty since the moment Glendower had snatched me away from the Academy.

It was perfect. Heartbreakingly so.

"Sleep, scout. I'll keep you safe," Bryn whispered, his lips still a hair's breadth away from mine. I closed my eyes and gave myself over to sleep, safe in Bryn's arms and the knowledge he'd take on the whole godsdamned Council like a vengeful warrior of fire and death if they came for me.

I woke up in some kind of furnace. There was a bright light burning through my eyelids, sweat coating my skin, and I wriggled a little to get away from it, finding instead that I was in a bed with strong, warm arms tightening around my middle.

Not a furnace. *Bryn.*

Slowly, I forced my eyes open and tipped my head back against his shoulder. He was looking down at me already, dark shadows circling his tired eyes.

"Did you sleep?" I croaked, cringing at the raw sound my damaged vocal cords made.

"Couldn't," he replied. "Needed to be alert in case we were followed. I should have stayed guard outside."

My heart dropped, and I quickly muted my ability, not wanting to know how Bryn really felt about staying in the bed with me last night after I'd practically begged him to. My humiliation was more than complete as it was.

I shuffled away from him, and Bryn frowned but eventually let me go. His contact on my skin had given me a happy buzz that dulled some of the ache of Marlen and Arthus' absence, which hit me in full force now. But I'd regained just enough of my pride not to crawl right back into Bryn's arms.

"I don't think we've been followed. We should leave for Eamon's house now, while it's still early. Your mates are probably getting impatient."

I nodded mutely in agreement, lumbering towards the bathroom to freshen up as best I could before the long and probably harrowing griffin ride we had ahead of us.

Not long. Not long now and I'd be back with my mates.

CHAPTER 50

Ihad managed to shift Marlen and Arthus to the couch in the living room in anticipation of Fi's arrival this morning. I already knew Bryn had successfully got her out—the spirits had visited and told us she was in safe hands. I'd never felt so relieved in all my life.

Bryn was a godsdamned hero. We'd never be able to repay him for bringing Fi home to us.

Enfys' presence in the armchair opposite where Marlen and Arthus were slumped put a slight damper on things, but I was hoping he'd be too concerned about maintaining his perfect attendance record at the Academy to hang around. The spirits hadn't told me anything about Fi's condition, but I doubted it would be good after over a month in captivity. She wouldn't like Enfys buzzing around when she was feeling vulnerable.

I wasn't entirely sure she'd want me around either. I loved Fi, I knew that without a shadow of a doubt, but I wasn't her mate, and I didn't know how she truly felt about me. If she'd be more comfortable without me here, I'd gladly give her the deed to this house. She could have it forever as far as I was concerned.

The other issue with Enfys being here was that we couldn't talk freely. I didn't feel comfortable discussing anything about Fi in front of him. He was so in love with the Council it was a wonder he hadn't tried to have a claiming ceremony with them.

I paced back and forth in front of the door while Enfys tapped his foot irritatingly on the floor from his spot in the armchair. Marlen and Arthus were leaning against each other on the couch, but they looked more alert than they had in days, their eyes both glued to the door. I could see the exact moment Fi grew closer, both of them exhaled matching sighs of relief. A minute or two later, the mating pull twinged in my own chest.

Finally, she was back where she was meant to be.

Enfys jumped to his feet as I pulled open the door. Bryn stood at the threshold, carrying my beautiful girl huddled in his arms. She clung to his shirt like a lifeline, though she offered me a weak smile when she saw me.

"Hello," she whispered. She'd had quite a husky voice before, but now it was barely a hoarse rasp. I swallowed the lump that rose up in my throat.

"Hello, cariad. I have missed you so much," I told her softly, standing back to let Bryn pass.

Fi looked frail. Her face was gaunt and the legs that poked out under the loose beige dress and Bryn's coat she was wearing were bony and scarred. *Scarred.* What had she been through?

Bryn nodded at me as he strode through the room to gently place Fi on the couch between her two mates. The three of them gravitated toward each other like magnets, tears streaming down Fi's face as she clung to them like she would never let them go.

I hoped one day she would cling to me like that. I was a little jealous she didn't.

What kind of asshole did that make me, being jealous right now?

"Foxglove," Marlen croaked into her hair, nuzzling the back of her neck. I'd nearly forgotten what his voice sounded like.

"I love you, I love you, I love you," Fi whispered through her tears, constantly moving to try to get closer to them. Arthus moved his hand to firmly grip the nape of her neck and he leaned his forehead against hers, capturing her gaze. She stilled immediately in his possessive hold.

"We love you too, sweetheart. And we are never letting you out of our sights again," Arthus promised sternly. Fi let out a strangled sounding giggle and seemed surprised at the noise. I doubt she'd had much to laugh about lately.

Enfys cleared his throat pompously like he was about to herald his own announcement. "Fi, so glad to see you're back and well."

Bryn and I shot him matching incredulous glances. In what world did Fi look *well*? A strong breeze would knock her over.

"Cariad, do you want some food? I made you soup," I asked her gently, and she rewarded me with a tiny nod and smile. All three of them were already looking healthier. Their skin was less grayish and their eyes more lucid.

I moved into the kitchen and served a small bowlful of pea soup from the pot on the stove I'd made in preparation for her arrival. Marlen and Arthus had only been able to keep down soup these past few days, and I figured it would be easier on her stomach if she hadn't been fed well. I hadn't expected her to look quite that malnourished. *Maybe I should make a broth...*

In the end, I couldn't stay in the kitchen a moment longer once I heard Enfys telling Fi about all the things he had done to aid her retrieval. Bryn had done it without any of us. If we'd listened to Enfys and left Bryn out of the loop, she would probably still be missing.

I moved back into the living room and kneeled in front of the couch. I dipped the spoon into the thick green soup and held it up to her lips. "May I?"

Fi nodded tiredly. It went against all her instincts to be coddled, but we both knew she needed it. Just this once.

"Unfortunately, I have a class to teach shortly, so I will have to leave you to it, Fi," Enfys announced. Fi gave him a startled glance like she wasn't quite sure what to make of him.

"Thank you for helping with the search," she told him uncertainly, her eyes flicking between Bryn and me for guidance.

"Of course, Fi. It was nothing. I will come back later to check on you," Enfys said with a smooth smile before departing. I could have sworn I heard her tiny sigh of relief.

"I should go. Give you some privacy," Bryn said flatly, but his eyes were trained on Fi and full of longing. Surprisingly, her expression reflected his feelings.

"You don't have to," she said softly, and he almost smiled.

"I need to update Gwyneira, let her know you're safe. You'll need a few days off to recover, I can arrange that with her."

Fi's face softened even more. "You'll come back? Later?"

"I will," he promised. He gave me a stern look that said *take care of her or else* before he left, and I looked down to hide my grin. If there was one silver lining to this disaster, it was how Bryn and Fi were finally acknowledging their feelings for each other.

Which also meant she wouldn't claim that fuckwit Enfys as a mate. So, two silver linings.

Fi, Marlen and Arthus spent most of the day as a sleeping pile of tangled limbs. First on the couch, then later on the bed when they got too uncomfortable. The physical contact obviously did them a world of good. By the end of the day, Marlen and Arthus looked almost back to normal just from having her nearby.

I made them all a vegetable broth and freshly baked bread for dinner, which the guys inhaled but Fi only picked at. Just the effort of eating dinner had drained her energy reserves, and she had put off taking a hot bath until tomorrow. I tossed and turned restlessly until Arthus insisted I take his spot next to Fi in the middle of the night. Finally, I fell asleep with my beautiful cariad in my arms, exactly where she was supposed to be.

Two days of rest, regular meals, closeness to her mates, and basically anything else I could provide her. Two days dedicated to recovery. Two days in which it had become crystal clear that the Fi who was taken from us was not the same girl who returned. Maybe she never would be again.

From what I knew of Fi's life before she came to Avalon, she'd never had it easy. Whatever she had experienced in the last month had been infinitely worse, and any chance she thought she had of finding peace and happiness in Avalon was probably gone.

Fi had lost her innocence. Her expressions were more guarded, her opinions jaded. That almost childlike curiosity about how everything worked had disappeared.

Seeing her like this was agony for all of us. Marlen had healed her physical wounds, and being close to her mates again had eased the aching pain in her chest. Her voice was still raspy, despite Marlen's daily healing attempts on her vocal cords, and her diet was mostly liquid. Anything too heavy made her feel ill.

Mentally, Fi was a mess. Aside from confirming that the Castells had taken her and kept her prisoner in a cave—*a fucking cave*—on their estate, Fi had said very little about her ordeal and we hadn't pushed her to share.

I doubted Fi was going to tell us the full story without all of us here. Bryn included.

From the scars she had shown up with, we could deduce that she'd been bled multiple times—probably with a dagger by the looks she gave the ones we all wore on our belts. The chafing around her wrists and ankles indicated magic-binding shackles, and she'd clearly been starved. Plus, there was a fear of the dark that she didn't have before, though a month in a cave would do that to anyone.

I'd run Fi another steaming hot bath that Marlen joined her for so he could use his healing magic on her scarred skin. Maybe she'd open up to him about how she'd got the scars, if it was just the two of them. Marlen had always been Fi's greatest source of comfort.

Arthus sat at the kitchen table, nursing a cup of sage tea while I made a lentil stew for dinner. Seeing Fi's tiny frame and sunken cheeks sent pains through my chest. *She needed more food.* Food I could manage.

I'd barely stopped moving since she got back, yet it felt like nothing was enough. Until Fi was entirely whole and healthy again, nothing would be enough.

"Go to her," Arthus said quietly, observing me over his cup of tea.

"Sorry?"

"Help her out of the bath. You need alone time with her as much as Marlen and I do," he replied.

"I appreciate the thought, but you know that's not strictly true. She hasn't claimed me," I stated, trying to keep the dejection out of my voice.

"Then think of it as her needing alone time with you. Specifically you, in fact."

"There is nothing I can offer her that you or Marlen can't," I argued, not entirely sure where he was going with this.

"Wrong," Arthus countered. "Fi needs to feel good. She needs to indulge in a little escapism. She *wants* intimacy. But she's not emotionally ready for the kind of playful dominance she has with Marlen, and she's certainly not physically or emotionally ready for the kind of intimacy that she and I have..." Arthus muttered sadly.

"She will be," I assured him. "Give her time."

"Of course," Arthus said sharply, his eyes swinging to mine. "Whatever Fi wants. Her needs come first, which is why she needs you. She needs your brand of adoration. She needs to feel safe. You give her that."

Did I? That's how I wanted Fi to feel around me—worshiped, adored, protected, cherished, but we hadn't discussed our feelings for one another. We'd never had the opportunity.

I gave Arthus a curt nod and moved through the interconnected rooms to the bathroom at the end of the house, collecting some clean clothes for her on the way. Fi's soft voice called for me to come in before I even knocked, the mating pull alerting her to my presence.

"Are you okay? Do you need help to get out?" I asked gently, entering the bathroom slowly, giving her plenty of time to cover up if she wanted to.

"Please," she replied with a much brighter smile than she'd had a couple of hours ago, still submerged in the water.

I moved to the counter to set down the clothes while Marlen heaved himself out of the sunken tub, wrapping a towel around himself and moving toward the bedroom to dress. He shot me a reassuring smile before leaving me alone with Fi.

He and Arthus were unnervingly in-sync sometimes. I wondered if I would be like that with them if Fi ever chose to bestow her mating mark on me.

I gently lifted Fi's far-too-light body from the tub and wrapped a towel tightly around her, melting a little at the way she easily clung to me. Without clothes, Fi's frail frame was starkly evident. Her skin had regained some of its color and the scars had all but gone, courtesy of Marlen's healing gift now that he was mostly back to full strength, but she'd lost a lot of weight and muscle tone in the month she'd been gone.

Fi moved towards the counter where I'd left her clothes but ignored them to turn around to face me, looking like a combination of heavenly innocence and sinful desire. The mating pull writhed uncomfortably in my chest, insisting that I go to her, touch her, make her mine.

I could fight it. I was a gentleman. I'd never take more from Fi than what she offered me.

But the look in her eyes said *take*, loud and clear.

"Cariad," I whispered, my voice coming out strained.

"Come here," she breathed.

I obeyed like a man possessed. Our lips met in a kiss that was gentle yet demanding—both of us demanding Fi's pleasure. She needed it. I needed to provide it for her.

Her lips parted on a needy groan, and I swept my tongue into her mouth, tasting every inch of her. I wanted to feel every inch of her, have her wrapped around my body, lost in ecstasy, but she wasn't ready for that yet.

Instead, I pulled the towel away from her body and lifted her gently onto the edge of the counter, never breaking our kiss. My hands ran gently over the top of her thighs and if I had any doubts about whether or not she was ready for this, they disappeared once my hands reached the apex of her thighs, parting her slowly.

She was definitely ready for this. Already slick for me, head thrown back, chest heaving as she waited for more.

I wasn't about to make my girl wait.

I dropped to my knees, peppering light kisses and teasing licks up her inner thighs, relishing her breathy sighs and quiet moans. The jasmine oil from the bath still clung to her skin, mixing in with her natural vanilla and wildflowers scent.

Fi squirmed impatiently on the counter, seeking friction, and I chuckled before pressing my tongue flat against her and licking a slow line up to her clit, my fingers dimpling her thighs as I held her wide for me.

I wanted Fi to feel like a goddess, so I worshiped her. I kneeled on the floor at her feet and worshiped at her altar with my lips, teeth, and tongue. Her hands gripped my hair tightly, pulling me close and pushing me away at the same time while she writhed restlessly, chasing her release.

As much as I savored the taste of her on my tongue, the feel of her, the scent of her, this wasn't about teasing her or drawing out her pleasure. This was about making her feel good. I waited until I could feel her right on the edge before plunging two fingers into her pussy, pumping them steadily until she was clenching around me, gasping out *my* name.

The territorial part of me was preening with satisfaction—nothing made me happier than watching my cariad fall apart. Fi's eyes were closed, her teeth sinking into her lower lip, completely lost in a world of bliss. If I thought orgasms were the cure to her problems, I'd give her ten a day.

It might be worth a shot.

Fi slowly floated back to the present, giving me a lazy smile, her eyes still half-closed. I grinned, lifting her gently off the counter so I could reach the clothes I'd brought in for her. She didn't protest as I dressed her in a sage-colored sleep top and shorts, with a thick woolen cream cardigan and matching thigh-high socks to keep her warm. Fi was definitely getting better at accepting our help, some of the time at least.

I went to lead her out of the bathroom, but she snagged me by the hand and pulled me back to stand in front of her, giving me a long, assessing look.

"I think we should talk about your jealousy," she started hesitantly. "I've noticed you experiencing it quite a bit these past two days."

"It's awful, I know, and I'm sorry. I have been jealous of Marlen and Arthus, and their bond with you," I admitted sheepishly. "I wasn't jealous of the pain—I'm no masochist—but of the connection that they have. Of the fact that they had a physical manifestation of the mental anguish we were all feeling."

This conversation was a risk. I was laying my heart on the line in the hopes Fi didn't stomp all over it and squash it under her perfect feet.

"What are you not saying?" she asked slowly, moving closer to me and linking our hands in front of us, tangling our fingers together.

I let out a long breath and looked her in the eye so I could see her reaction. "I'm saying that I want you. Today, forever, and every moment in between. I'm saying I will take every ounce of the pain for the pleasure that being your mate brings."

Fi's grip on my fingers tightened and her lips parted ever so slightly, but I pushed on before I could lose my nerve. "Before everything happened, I was already beginning to suspect I couldn't live without you. The last month confirmed those suspicions—"

"Yes," Fi interrupted loudly, blushing slightly. "Yes, to all of it. Yes, to forever."

I tugged her towards me by her hands and caught her against my chest, wrapping my arms around her shoulders as hers snaked around my waist. I breathed in Fi's addictive scent, burying my face in her curls. I wanted to make up for every moment Fi had been imprisoned.

"Foxglove?" Marlen asked from the doorway, clearing his throat. "Sorry to interrupt, but I have to go in for guard duty. I haven't been in weeks and Leigh's been pulling doubles to cover for me. Even Kelvyn covered for me a couple of times. He felt bad about blowing your cover and getting you kidnapped," Marlen added with a characteristic lack of tact.

Fi shot me an apologetic smile before sauntering over to Marlen. I loved watching them interact—Marlen brought out a lightness in her that no one else did.

Though, a little of that was me, wasn't it? I'd brought some lightness into her life this afternoon too.

As soon as she got close enough, she jumped on him and wrapped her legs around his waist. He laughed, grabbing her ass to hold her up. My cock stirred in my trousers again, seeing his hands on her.

She leaned down, whispering something I couldn't make out into Marlen's ear before capturing his lips in a languid, sultry kiss. Gods, between that and giving Fi some much-needed relief, I was due for an ice-cold shower.

MARLEN

CHAPTER 51

While I doubted I'd ever feel completely *good* about the Academy grounds now—not after Fi had been snatched up from right under our noses—I did feel a small sense of satisfaction when it came into view after spending so long looking at the walls of Eamon's cabin. I wouldn't have been comfortable leaving Fi before tonight, but she was in better spirits now than she had been since she'd come back.

I guessed that quality time with Eamon had been much needed.

I wasn't jealous, not really. There was no doubt in my mind that Eamon was in love with Fi, and he'd stepped back so Arthus and I could reaffirm our mating bonds. He'd needed time with her too, and Fi had absolutely needed time with him.

She got something from him that she didn't from Arthus and I. Her mating circle was shaping up to be a good one, a balanced one. Knowing how afraid she'd been of the whole mating concept in the beginning, I was incredibly proud of my girl. My mate.

"Marlen!"

I barely registered my sister's red hair before she was slamming into me, flinging her arms around my neck. I hugged her back, holding her a little tighter than usual, overcome with emotion.

While I would have been comfortable with my twin visiting us, I knew

Arthus would have struggled, and I didn't want to put him through that. He'd kept to himself his whole life because of his wings, just being around *me* was enough stress for him.

"Are you okay?" Aderyn asked, pulling back and gripping my upper arms, her eyes watery. "Is Fi okay? Briallen said she was back, but that you weren't ready for visitors yet."

"I'm sorry," I told her with a grimace, pulling free of her grip and draping my arm over her shoulders so I could tug her along with me to where I'd been stationed for guard duty. "We've needed some time, just us. Fi... well, it was a rough experience. I'll let her tell you when she's ready."

Aderyn nodded approvingly, ducking out from under my arm as we approached a group of students. I guessed we were still doing the I-don't-know-him thing in public.

"Is there anything I can do?" she asked.

"Keep our parents distracted?" I asked hopefully. I loved my folks, but they lived a quiet life in the country surrounded by low-magic fae. They would never admit it, but they were a little afraid of *my* gift. Fi's would terrify them.

Aderyn shot me a reproving look. "Fortunately for you, they're plenty distracted with my courtship. They quite like the idea of having a cobbler in the family." I opened my mouth to apologize at how uninvolved I'd been in Aderyn's life, but she waved me off before I could start. "You've got enough going on, Marlen, and there isn't much to say. It's going well."

She looked off into the distance with a slightly dreamy smile on her face, and I felt a pang in my chest even though I was happy for her. Aderyn had never asked for this life, but I'd still miss her when she left it behind.

"Well, I'd still like to hear about it when things calm down a little, and I know Fi would too," I told Aderyn. "Unfortunately, I have to head for guard duty now. I've been slacking off these past few weeks."

"Hardly," Aderyn scoffed. "No one would have expected you to do guard duty under those circumstances. Shall I bring you a snack from the commons?"

I wasn't about to say no to that. While I was grateful to Eamon for making nutritious foods for Fi that were gentle enough for her stomach, if I never saw another bowl of soup in my life it would be too soon.

"I'd appreciate that," I replied, pulling her into a hug before she could protest. She grumbled as she pulled away, glancing around to make sure we hadn't been seen before heading down the path that led back to the main campus.

I climbed the ladder that led to the treetop outpost I was assigned to that day, watching over the forest that bordered the southern edge of the Academy.

The moment I got to the top rung, Leigh appeared suddenly dragging me up the rest of the way with a relieved laugh, hauling me in for a one-armed hug. "I never thought I'd miss your pretty face, Marlen."

"Settle down, would you? I'm a happily mated male," I laughed, clapping him on the back before pulling away to look around, finding no one else up here with us. "Surely you're not on duty with me tonight? You're well overdue for a break after covering my shifts."

"Eh, what with Fi vanishing right from campus, Gwyneira has upped all of our guard duty hours anyway. I'm glad I'm stationed with you. I did a couple of shifts with Bryn and I was worried that he'd set me on fire if I so much as breathed too loudly."

I snorted, taking my position on one side of the platform while Leigh settled into the other. It wasn't much—just a stool and a telescope affixed to the sidewall at each station so we could keep an eye on things. There was a bell above us to be rung in case of emergency, which would set off a chain reaction along the watchtowers.

The extra shifts seemed rather pointless to me. The Castells had been welcomed onto campus, the bells would have never been sounded for their presence. I couldn't tell Leigh that, though. Not without Fi's permission for a start, but we also needed to be mindful of Gwyneira's wishes. The Castells were a powerful enemy.

Leigh sighed. "You're not going to say anything then? I figure it's all a bit hush-hush, but I was hoping you'd give me something to go on. Some explanation of why this all happened."

"I was just thinking how I wished I could tell you," I said with a wry smile. "There's a lot of players on the chessboard, and I risk upsetting the balance if I aggravate one."

Gods, I was relieved that Fi had taken Arthus as her mate. I was not much for all this strategy business, and I was more than happy to leave the decision making to him and Eamon.

"So long as you're all safe now, I don't care," Leigh said with a decisive nod before turning his attention back to the telescope.

I couldn't respond to that because we weren't. Glendower's retaliation was a matter of 'if', not 'when'.

I turned my attention to my telescope, taking care with my search and smiling to myself as Leigh sang a bawdy tune under his breath that he wouldn't dare utter in Briallen's presence.

"Do you have any regrets?" Leigh asked suddenly, startling me.

"About Fi?" I said incredulously.

Leigh had the grace to look sheepish. "It's just that B and I really pushed for you to get together. I hate to think we forced you into a decision—"

"No one forced me into anything," I interjected. "I'm a grown male, if I hadn't liked Fi I wouldn't have pursued her no matter how much pressure you and Briallen put on me. I could never regret Fi, no matter how many challenges are thrown at us. I knew she was it for me from the moment I laid eyes on her."

I couldn't quite keep the sharp edge out of my voice, despite knowing Leigh's question came from a place of concern. My relationship with Fi meant more to me than anything in the world, and I wouldn't have it questioned.

"Good," Leigh said firmly, though his smile was a little sad. "For what it's worth, both Briallen and I feel you're strongly suited for each other. The gods themselves couldn't have made a better match. May they be on your side through whatever troubles lie in your path."

FFION

CHAPTER 52

I was on day three of being holed up in bed at Eamon's house. I could barely even recognize myself, this cowardly fae who didn't want to leave the house. A fae who was content to lie in bed all day instead of going to class.

Physically, I probably could have made it. Marlen, Arthus and I had spent the bulk of the last two days snuggling, relishing the feeling of skin-to-skin contact as our fractured mating bonds repaired themselves. Marlen had used his healing magic on me repeatedly, and there was no external evidence that Glendower's dagger had ever touched me. Between Marlen's magic and Eamon's devoted attention, I had gained back a small amount of weight and was feeling much more energetic.

The problem was that the better I felt physically, the more I deteriorated mentally. The pain had distracted me from the memories, but now they felt like they were crashing in on me from every side.

After the first night back, when I'd woken up in complete darkness screaming to be let out, we slept with the curtains open. If I could see the moonlight and the glittering stars outside, it helped center me faster, reassuring me that I wasn't in the cave any longer.

The second morning, I'd managed to get up for breakfast but flinched so hard when Marlen reached for the dagger hanging from his belt that I fell off the chair. They started warning me before they used their daggers after that.

Fortunately, none of them looked at me like a basket case for being terrified of things that hadn't phased me in the least before.

Before. That's how it felt. There was a *Before Fi* and an *After Fi*, and we were all trying to figure out how to deal with After Fi. Myself included.

The guys were waiting patiently for me to tell them about everything that happened, and I needed to be honest with myself about what I'd been through, not let my terror silence me. But I wasn't there yet. The first time I tried to tell them about the details, I'd thrown up. Now I stopped talking when I felt the bile rise in my throat.

The next time we're all together, Bryn too, I'll tell them the whole story, I vowed to myself.

I dragged myself into the kitchen and dropped down at the table between Marlen and Arthus. They looked basically back to normal—with the exception of the gauntness in their cheeks from lack of food and the extra scruff they were sporting around their jaws—and were both catching up on Academy work while Eamon prepared lunch. He'd nursed all three of us back to health, no questions asked, no complaints.

After knowing how much agony Marlen and Arthus were in while I was imprisoned in that cave, I wasn't sure if I could face claiming another mate again. Being back solidified the love I felt for Eamon the whole time I was gone, which was why I wanted to protect him from the kind of pain the three of us had gone through by never claiming him, but I knew that wasn't going to fly with him.

Eamon acquiesced to me on almost everything, but he wouldn't let me keep him away for his own protection. He wanted forever, and I wasn't strong enough to deny that I wanted that too.

My musing was interrupted by a knock on the door. I wasn't altogether surprised—between Gwyneira, Bryn, and Enfys, we'd had a steady stream of visitors. I'd mostly stayed in bed while they were here, letting the guys handle the socializing.

I extended my abilities to assess our visitor as Eamon wiped his hands and went to answer the door. Concern for my welfare and a curiosity as to how I was adjusting. *Definitely Gwyneira.*

My newfound, entirely justified paranoia had made me quite good at determining who someone was by emotions alone.

Enfys' emotions were always edged with a confidence that bordered on arrogance. Even without the mating pull, I could identify Bryn by his constant sense of crushing guilt.

I shuffled into the kitchen and dropped into a chair just as Eamon led Gwyneira into the room.

"Ffion, Arthus, Marlen," Gwyneira greeted us warmly, nodding at each of us in turn. "You are all looking much healthier today, I am glad to see."

"Tea?" Eamon enquired politely, ever the host.

"Please," Gwyneira said with a small smile, taking a seat opposite me.

"Any word from the Council? Or the Castells specifically?" Arthus asked sharply, getting straight to the point.

"No," Gwyneira sighed. "Though I suspected that would be the case. I put the word out that Ffion was back at the Academy. It would be difficult for the Council to justify removing her, even if they claimed it was for her own safety. The Academy is supposed to be a safe place for gifted fae. It is the only school for them, after all."

"So, it'll be more obvious if something happens to me now?" I confirmed. The three guys make an assortment of distressed sounds in the back of their throats, and I realized I probably could have worded that more tactfully.

"Yes, that is the idea," Gwyneira said sadly. "Anonymity is no longer an option, so I suggest embracing your role as a public figure. Your notoriety will act as your first line of defense."

I slumped over the table, resting my cheek against my forearms. So much for my dream of moving to the Outer Isles with my mates and living in isolated bliss for the rest of my days. Preferably on a beach.

Godsdamn Glendower! I'd gotten away from him, but he was still torturing me from afar.

Gwyneira gave me a long, searching look. "Eamon, perhaps a visit to the Adair ancestral home would be nice for all of you? It is well warded, is it not? And the grounds are extensive..."

My ears perked up at extensive grounds. Eamon's treehouse was far larger than the cave I'd been trapped in, but it still felt suffocating, and I couldn't wander around the surrounding forest as it wasn't warded. I wanted to be outside, with no walls imprisoning me.

"Are you sure it's wise for us to travel right now? It's only a two hours flight, but we can't be sure Fi's not being watched," Eamon asked nervously, pacing back and forth in front of the table.

"I do not think they would be so bold as to try anything while Ffion is with the three of you—they made sure to get her alone last time," Gwyneira pointed out.

I swallowed the lump that rose in my throat and fought off the tremors of fear threatening to overtake my body. I didn't want to think about that night and my too-stupid-to-live moment where I'd gone out to the edge of campus by myself. *Fucking moronic.*

"I suggest we call in an illusionist. Fi needs a cloaking amulet to hide her magical signature, and a strong glamour. At least while we're in the air," Arthus clipped, eyebrows drawn down. "But a few days away would probably do us all some good."

"Agreed," Eamon said with a firm nod.

"I will arrange it, give me a day to get everything in order," Gwyneira confirmed, rising regally from her seat and giving us a sweeping look. Her eyes softened as they landed on me and I knew I probably looked terrible, hunched over the table with my head in my hands.

"Ffion, I am deeply ashamed both that you were taken from the Academy grounds and that I wasn't able to find you. Know that I will do everything in my power to make it up to you," she said sadly, leaving before I had a chance to formulate any response.

I was angry—*so* angry, all the time—but not at Gwyneira. She didn't have to earn my forgiveness because there was nothing to forgive. Neither did

Bryn, despite the enormous guilt he was carrying around.

Glendower was the primary target of my wrath, followed closely by Evalina. I wouldn't let myself lose sight of who really deserved my enmity in all of this.

I was lying in bed the following day when I heard the knock on the door that I assumed was Gwyneira returning with the arrangements for us to travel to Eamon's family estate. I wandered absentmindedly into the living room where the guys were already waiting, feeling a bit out of it since I hadn't had my usual mid-morning nap yet.

I expected to sense Gwyneira's usual matronly concern, but I also felt an intense rush of someone else's joy and relief a second before they scooped me off my feet.

No. Two someones.

My fathers, Galvyn and Attie, were on either side of me. Galvyn was giving me a bear hug that perfectly matched his grizzly bear persona. Attie stood at my side, running a shaky hand over my hair and whispering how happy he was to see me.

Maybe it was the genuine parental love I was feeling—an entirely new sensation when it was directed at me—or maybe it was because I'd spent so much time thinking about how they'd been right all along, how they'd only ever tried to protect me.

Whatever it was, I wasn't in the mood to fight with them. I wrapped my arms around Galvyn's neck, buried my face in his shoulder and *sobbed.* After a minute, he put me down and Attie wrapped his arms around my shoulders, resting his chin on the top of my head and rocking me side to side, shushing me gently. I wondered if he'd done that when I was a baby, and the thought made me cry harder.

Whatever issues I'd had with my fathers in the past evaporated at that moment. Their fear hung thick in the air, mingled with their joy and relief. I'd been captured by the same psycho who'd tortured and killed my mother.

No wonder they were so frightened.

"Good to have you back, kid," Attie said softly, and I sniffled a bit more.

I was surprised at how emotional I was feeling. It was more than just their reassuring presence after a shitty ordeal. This was the reunion I'd always dreamed of in my head if I ever got to meet my parents. I'd imagined that it would be tearful and joyous, and when they hugged me, it would feel like they never wanted to let me go.

It was exactly this.

Basically, the total opposite of our first meeting, but I could let bygones be bygones at this point.

Eventually, I extricated myself and took a step back where three sets of hands reached for me at the same time. I could feel my mates' distress at how upset I was and their need to physically comfort me. I sent Marlen and Arthus a wave of reassurance through our bonds to ease their worry and gave Eamon's hand a firm squeeze.

"Come, let's sit," Eamon said finally, gesturing at the chairs. Gwyneira and Attie took the armchairs, Galvyn stood leaning against the wall, and my three guys squeezed onto the couch. I was firmly ensconced in Marlen's arms, perched on his lap. Eamon's hand reached out to rest on my thigh.

"Ffion, as you know, your father Galvyn is an illusionist. He has prepared a cloaking amulet for you to hide your magical signature." Gwyneira handed me a silver chain with two polished lumps of a black crystal hanging from it.

"One for the journey there, one for the way back," Gwyneira explained.

"It's black tourmaline," Galvyn added gruffly, watching me intently as I studied the crystal. I gave him a small smile and his expression softened instantly. It was difficult to see his mouth behind his bushy beard, but his eyes crinkled slightly at the edges, and it made me want to hug him again.

"Go pack, sweetheart," Arthus said softly. "Your father can put a glamour on you before we leave, something more intricate than what you can manage on your own." I nodded, not really knowing what he was talking about because as far as I knew, I couldn't put any kind of glamour on myself.

I moved into the bedroom and grabbed my school satchel—the only bag I owned—and roughly shoved some undergarments and a couple of dresses from the wardrobe into it. I doubted we'd be gone for very long. I did have to go back to class, eventually.

We hadn't got around to replacing my one shawl yet, so I pulled on one of Eamon's wool coats instead. It was probably super expensive, but I doubted he'd care about me borrowing it. After a moment's hesitation, I added some thick wool socks and the leather boots Arthus had given me before our claiming ceremony. Two hours in the sky in this cold weather with bare feet was a recipe for disaster.

As I reentered the living room, I took a moment to absorb the absurdity of the situation in front of me. In human terms, my two dads, my two husbands, my boyfriend, and my school dean were all sitting around, chatting cordially and having a cup of tea.

This was... not exactly how I had imagined my future when I was growing up.

Marlen came to stand at my side while Eamon and Arthus took their turn packing bags.

"Ready for your glamour, foxglove?"

"I guess so," I muttered, trying to block the memories of Glendower glamouring my scars from my mind.

"Don't worry, we'll teach you how to do it yourself at Eamon's place," Marlen said cheerily, squinting for a moment until his emerald green eyes turned blue. I blinked in surprise while Marlen grinned like a little kid. Had he always been able to do that?

Galvyn stood in front of me, his expression was unreadable but his eyes seemed warm and kind. "It won't hurt, daughter."

"I know," I assured him. "Though I am curious as to how you glamoured me for years in Albion without me realizing."

"In your sleep," he grunted, looking a little sheepish.

"That is so freaking creepy," I deadpanned, giving him a reproachful look. One of these days I was going to have a very long chat with my fathers about boundaries.

"Sorry about that," he replied gruffly. "Right, shall we?"

The old Adair estate was beautiful. Eamon explained that his parents rarely stayed here because it wasn't as grand as their newer properties, but I loved it. The house itself was like an overgrown cottage, entirely made of pale gray stone that was barely visible underneath the greenery that grew up the walls. It was two stories high, with a thatched roof and enormous chimneys at either end of the property.

Inside, the exterior stone walls were exposed, and I ran my hands over them every chance I got, marveling at how many fae must have passed through these rooms over the centuries. The floors were whitewashed wood, and the ceilings were low with exposed beams running lengthwise along each room.

The estate was located at the base of a small mountain range that could be seen from the back of the property. There were extensive vineyards on the other three sides that were manned by workers during the day. It felt very exposed, but I'd been assured that the house itself was well warded. We could only get through the ward at the gate with Eamon escorting us.

"Cariad, the vineyard manager has been trying to get me here to take a look at some issues on the property for months. Will you be okay if I go talk to him now? I'd prefer to get it out of the way so I can give you my full attention for the rest of the time we're here," Eamon asked regretfully.

"Of course," I assured him, reaching for his hand to give it a reassuring squeeze. "You have spent so much time looking after the three of us lately, you must have things you need to catch up on."

"Nothing that couldn't wait," Eamon said with a shrug. I was sure his employees would disagree with that. "If you follow the path outside from the kitchen, you'll find a hot spring at the edge of the wards. It's ancient, and is supposed to have healing properties. Perhaps the three of you could relax there this afternoon?"

Hells yes, I'd never been in a hot spring before.

"Ah, there's that beautiful smile I've missed so much," Eamon murmured, running his thumb over my jaw.

"I'm sorry," I whispered.

"You have nothing to be sorry about, cariad. Go, enjoy your afternoon. I will visit the cellar and we can have some wine from the vineyard with our dinner."

Did I really have to go back to the Academy? The idea of being a kept woman and staying here forever was really growing on me.

"Let's go find those hot springs," Marlen said cheerfully, grabbing my hand and tugging me along behind him. I giggled and all three of them gave me indulgent looks.

Arthus followed along behind us as Marlen pulled me impatiently between the raised garden beds and ancient knotted trees to the bottom of the garden. It was easy to find the hot spring from the steam rising off the surface of it. It was an oval shape, probably only wide enough to just fit the three of us, but that's all we needed. There were rocks surrounding the pool and just enough surrounding trees to give us the illusion of privacy.

"Gods, yes. I am all about this," Marlen said with a cheeky grin, stripping off his clothes without a second's hesitation and lowering himself into the water. He let out a long, low groan that acted as a wake-up alarm to my libido.

Fuck, he looked delicious.

Either Arthus was monitoring our bond, or my desire was written all over my face. He gave me a knowing smirk while slowly pulling off his shirt.

"Strip, sweetheart."

I obeyed. I hadn't been ready for this, for the *everything* that my mates demanded of me, even though I usually craved it.

I'm ready now.

Naked, I perched on the rocks and dipped my feet into the water first. The heat felt so good—it was the first day of spring, but the air was still chilly. Marlen extended his arms towards me and I went willingly, letting him guide me into the water since I couldn't see the bottom. I stuck to the edge of the pool where there was a rocky ledge I could stand on while he moved into the middle, the water coming up to his chin.

Arthus lowered himself into the water next to me, a mischievous glint in his eye. Despite that look, he made no move to touch me or give me instructions. I checked his bond first, pulling the airy strand in my sternum towards me, then Marlen's liquidy bond afterward.

I was definitely going to have to take the lead here, because neither of them wanted to push me into something I wasn't ready for. My chest swelled with affection for these two vastly different, incredibly caring fae.

Knowing that Arthus would probably have a heart attack if I tried to take the lead with him, I crooked my finger and beckoned Marlen over to me.

"Hello foxglove," Marlen said smugly, swimming over in one smooth movement and stopping right in front of me. His affinity was so obvious when he was in the water, he really looked like he was meant to be there rather than on land.

"Hi there," I said coyly, doing my best flirty smile. I wrapped my arms around Marlen's neck and my legs around his waist, enjoying the way he sucked in a breath at feeling my naked body against his. "Carry me?"

"Anything the lady wants," he replied, a little hoarsely. I buried my face against his neck and grinned, listening to his heart thundering in his chest.

"Bring her here," Arthus commanded softly, in his most dangerously seductive voice. Apparently that voice worked on Marlen too. He walked with me in his arms until my back hit Arthus' chest.

"Fi sandwich," Marlen announced with a grin, and I giggled. His ability to say the unsexiest thing possible without breaking the mood was a trait I really admired.

Arthus' hands slid around to my front until he was cupping my breasts in his hands. They felt heavy and achy, desperate to be touched. I leaned my head back into the crook of his shoulder and wriggled down against Marlen, grinding against his hard-on, frantically seeking friction.

Surprisingly, the water wasn't getting in the way of my movements. I blushed at the thought that Marlen was manipulating it away from our nether regions on purpose, even if it was a nifty trick.

"Do you need to come, sweetheart?" Arthus murmured, his lips pressed to the shell of my ear, pinching and rolling my nipples between his fingers.

"Yes," I breathed. Gods, I'd missed them. I'd missed *this*. "I need to come."

"Ask nicely," Arthus chuckled like the shithead he was.

I squirmed harder against Marlen and tried to decide if I was too proud to beg for orgasms.

Nope, definitely not.

"Please," I managed to gasp out. Marlen's fingers were there the moment the word was out of my mouth, massaging my clit with a surprising amount of pressure, giving away just how much he was craving me. After a moment, he slid two fingers inside me, finding that sensitive spot with unerring precision and pumping steadily, still keeping the water away below the surface.

Arthus slipped a hand of his own down to work my clit, his teeth raking along the side of my neck and over my shoulder.

"Beautiful," he murmured, making me melt a little further into him.

"You're so close, Fi," Marlen said approvingly, picking up his pace as I clenched around him.

"I want you in me," I breathed, nudging him with my heel. I *needed* that feeling of connection, that togetherness after so long apart.

Marlen didn't make me wait, thrusting into me so suddenly that the air left my lungs. He gripped my thighs as he plowed into me relentlessly, the surface water rippling and splashing all around us.

"Don't come yet, sweetheart. Wait until I give you permission," Arthus ordered.

"I can't," I whined, clawing at Marlen's forearms.

"Wait," Arthus commanded again, entirely in his element now that he was bossing me around again. I bit down hard on my lip to distract myself, riding the perfect line between pleasure and pain, knowing the payoff would be worth it.

Arthus moved faster, working his fingers in frantic circles around my clit until I was almost delirious with the need to let go.

"Now," he whispered in my ear, and I exploded. My muscles seized, and I let out a moan so loud and full of relief that I was sure most of the vineyard heard me. Marlen groaned my name as he found his climax, his movements stuttering to a stop as he gripped me hard enough to leave bruises, panting hard.

I tipped my head back against Arthus' shoulder and he banded one arm around my waist to prop me up, the other hand running gently over my hair as I floated lazily back to reality.

"Feel better?" Arthus asked, his voice filled with amusement.

I hummed absentmindedly, too content in their arms to speak or open my eyes.

I think the hot spring just became my favorite part of the Adair estate.

CHAPTER 53

"Edan."

While his greeting was curt, Arthus approaching me in the commons at all took me by surprise. Even though I'd been going to Eamon's to check on Ffion via her mates, it wasn't like Arthus and I spent a lot of time together.

"Is Ffion okay?" I asked, instantly on guard.

"Fi's fine, but we need a favor. She's at the old Adair Estate in Northgales with Eamon. Marlen was supposed to be their escort back to campus, but his masters are flipping out at how many classes he's been missing, and I have to tutor this afternoon. Could you fly over there and escort them back?"

I could. I didn't have any more classes that day. I didn't know how I felt about playing babysitter, though.

Nothing was ever straightforward when it came to Ffion. I wanted her, but I didn't deserve her, not after what she'd been through. Not after everything that had transpired between us.

Worse still, she *knew* how I felt about her every time I was in her presence, despite my best attempts to cover it up.

"If not, I'll have to ask Enfys instead," Arthus continued casually, immediately raising my hackles. *Low blow.*

"Fine," I gritted out. It's not like the area wasn't familiar to me, Briallen's family who I'd grown up with were based in Northgales. I could fly there with my eyes closed.

"Great, they're expecting you around five pm. Well, they're expecting Marlen, but you get the idea. Thanks," Arthus said with an almost smile before wandering off.

I could admit to myself that seeing Ffion with Arthus gave me hope for the two of us. It's not like he was the warm and fuzzy type, yet she still seemed to like him well enough.

He hadn't gotten her locked up in a cave for a month.

The thought left a bitter taste in my mouth, and I finished up my food unenthusiastically before heading back to my cabin to change into my flying clothes. Suitably dressed, I went to the stables to find a griffin who would make the two-hour flight to Northgales.

What were they thinking, taking Ffion so far off campus only a week after she'd escaped the Castells? She'd probably be safe on the property, but the flying between the locations was risky. Anyone could snatch her out of the sky if they knew where she was.

I mounted a sturdy looking brown griffin and instructed him to take me to the old Adair estate in Northgales—it was their ancestral home and a famous spot. Unfortunately, the long flight gave me time to reflect on what a fuck up I was and how I should be staying as far away from Ffion as possible.

My head had been a total mess over the past week. Seeing Ffion was painful, but staying away from her was godsdamned agony. I'd visited Eamon's house three times, and each time they'd told me I was welcome to go into the bedroom where Ffion was resting.

Each time I hadn't been able to face her.

Every time I got close enough to feel the mating pull, all I could think was *my fault.*

I had talked to the guys at length about how she was doing, and got constant updates on her recovery.

The gauntness in her cheeks and loose fit of her clothes? *My fault.*

The way her eyes flit around the room, constantly scanning for threats? *My fault.*

The way she flinched whenever any of them reached for their dagger? *My fault.*

The way she could barely eat more than a few bites at each meal? *My fault.*

It was all my fault. My fucking fault.

I chose to get involved with Saffir even when I knew deep down that I didn't want a future with her. I pulled away from her because my feelings for Ffion were growing and that was the catalyst that set off the chain of fucking disasters that left Ffion shackled and tortured in a godsdamned cave for over a month.

I thought I should have stayed far away from her, let her be around people who were safer for her than me. Even that sanctimonious prick Enfys would have been a better choice. He'd never gotten her kidnapped before.

Yet every time I stayed away, a gnawing ache would grow in my chest, almost like I could feel the absence of the mating bond, even though Ffion and I hadn't claimed each other. So, despite my best intentions, I found myself gravitating towards Eamon's house just to check on her. A couple of times I'd found myself on the path to his house without even realizing where I was heading and had to force myself to turn back.

She didn't need me.

I didn't deserve her.

I couldn't let her go.

The time had come for me to let go of my hang-ups about having a strong mating pull in a relationship, but taking the first step was excruciating. I wasn't used to owning my mistakes, and I'd definitely made plenty with Ffion.

I could grovel and apologize—I was sure Leigh could give me some tips on how, Briallen was a godsdamned taskmaster—but I doubted Ffion wanted that. She'd find it awkward and get all uncomfortable. As much as I wanted her squirming for me, that wasn't quite the kind of squirming I had in mind.

I'd just have to prove to her that I could be who she needed me to be and hope she'd be open to seeing it. However long it took.

I landed outside the warded area and rang the bell on the outer wall to let them know I was here. They weren't expecting Marlen until a bit later, but I wanted to give the griffin enough time to rest before the flight back.

And I wanted to make sure Ffion was okay being so far away from campus. My fire magic flickered, responding to my rising stress levels.

Eamon came out to the gate and raised his eyebrows when he saw me, but didn't question me showing up in Marlen's place.

"Fi's in the kitchen. Go on ahead if you like, I'll show the griffin to the stables," he offered. I gave him a nod and followed the cobbled path to the large stone house, forcing my magic to be still. Even the warded section of the grounds was extensive—Ffion was probably thrilled she could spend so much time outside.

My pace quickened as I felt the mating pull guiding me, and I strode into the kitchen to find Ffion perched on a stool at the island, sipping from a teacup.

"This is a surprise," she said lightly, cocking a brow at me.

It took me a moment to respond, I was so overwhelmed with relief at seeing her. The scars were gone, her eyes were brighter and her skin healthier. She still looked too thin and the dark shadows under her eyes were concerning but compared to the frail girl I'd placed on the couch between Marlen and Arthus a week ago, she'd come a long way.

"Marlen has missed a lot of classes and needed to make them up. I had the afternoon off," I said by way of an explanation. Ffion hummed noncommittally, probably realizing there was a little more to it than that.

"Tea?" she asked.

"Sure, thanks."

Eamon joined us as Ffion poured me a cup of peppermint tea and we moved to the dining table.

"We were just practicing my glamour before you showed up," Ffion said, looking at me over her teacup.

"Oh?" I asked stupidly. I had about a million other questions I wanted to ask her, mostly about how she was feeling, but I couldn't get them out.

"I want pink hair like Briallen, but the best I can get is a weird, maroon-y color," she grumbled. I smirked, shaking my head slightly and focusing on the exact hue of my cousin's odd hair until I knew mine was the same dark, dusty pink. Ffion gaped at me.

"Show off," she muttered. "It kind of suits you. You look like a sexy marshmallow."

I snorted, shaking off the glamour. I didn't know what a marshmallow was, but she'd called me sexy and that was all I could really focus on.

Ffion stroked her hair repeatedly, scrunching up her nose adorably in concentration. When the fuck did I start thinking of things as adorable? Gods, this girl had my balls in her pocket.

Sure enough, her hair morphed into an odd maroon color with streaks of pastel pink running through it.

"You did better that time," Eamon commented lightly as he sipped his tea. "There's some actual pink in there."

Ffion stood and wandered over to the mirror on the wall to inspect her handiwork. She barked a laugh before shaking the glamour off. "Maybe pink is too ambitious."

"Remember, it's easier to envision a glamour once you've seen it on yourself before. Try to recreate the short, black hair your father glamoured on you for the journey over here," Eamon suggested, smiling at her like a lovesick pup.

"Are you expecting company?" I asked sharply, sitting up straighter in my chair as I felt three new magical signatures approach the warded area.

"No," Eamon replied before looking up as the bells next to the door chimed, letting us know that someone had entered the warded inner sanctum of the property.

My eyes darted between Ffion and the door, wondering how quickly I could get her out of here and which would be the safest route to take.

Eamon cursed under his breath. "Most likely my parents, though I have no idea what they'd be doing here. Cariad, grab your cloaking amulet and put on your best glamour, you need to go with Bryn."

Ffion was a smart girl. She probably knew logically that Eamon was doing this for her own safety, but her expression shuttered like he'd just rejected her.

"Oh, cariad," Eamon groaned, grabbing her face and planting a kiss on her forehead. "Don't look at me like that. It's just that my parents are friendly with some of the Councilors. I don't want them seeing you."

"Cry about it in the air, scout. We've got to move," I told her unsympathetically. It worked. Ffion snapped out of her funk and threw me a dirty look as she hurried into the bedroom to grab her things.

In the few minutes it had taken her to grab the essentials, Eamon had already headed out the front of the estate to run interference. I grabbed the satchel out of Ffion's hand and shouldered it, leading her by the elbow out a side door into the garden.

I was feeling fucking tense and desperate to get Ffion out of here, but I kept my touch on her arm gentle. The last thing I wanted was to frighten her or give her flashbacks of being manhandled by Saffir's parents.

Fi told me to follow the cobblestone path that wound through ancient trees and patches of wildflowers to the stables, and I left Ffion outside while I found a griffin who was up for flying the two-hour journey.

I emerged with a hardy-looking gray dappled griffin and fought back a smile as a black-haired, dark-eyed Ffion greeted me. She'd put up the same glamour that her dad had put on her in Albion—minus the height and ear changes—and the strange familiarity of it hit me like an arrow to the chest.

Gods, how much trouble would I have saved us both if I'd handled that first meeting between us differently? I shook my head. No use dwelling on that now.

It wasn't the strongest glamour, but it might throw people off from a distance at least. My lips twitched in amusement and Ffion gave me an exasperated look.

"Shut up," she said with no real conviction.

"Wasn't going to say anything," I replied, amused. Such a petulant little thing. "Don't forget your cloaking amulet."

"Right," Ffion sighed, pulling the tourmaline pendant out of her satchel and dropping it around her neck.

Blood. She needs to blood it. A part of me I long thought dead ached at the thought.

"May I?" she asked warily, gesturing at the dagger sheathed at my hip while simultaneously glaring at it like it had offended her and all of her ancestors.

I held her gaze as I unclipped the entire sheath, presenting it to her laid flat across my palms. Maybe if she had control over pulling the knife out, it wouldn't scare her so much. Ffion's eyes were watery as she gave me a grateful nod, taking the sheath from my hands.

Gods, please don't cry. My guilt was crushing me already, and I wasn't entirely sure what to do with a crying fae.

Ffion pulled the dagger out slowly and calmly pressed the blade to the pad of her thumb. She pushed the wound to the crystal at her neck, looking much more relaxed about the process than I expected.

"Good," I said, my tracking gift reaching through the air towards her and finding nothing. "Can't sense you at all. Come on, let's get going."

I boosted her onto the griffin and swung her satchel across my body before following her up. My arms were wrapped tightly around Ffion's middle, and I cursed myself for not bringing her some warmer clothes to wear for the flight. As the griffin took to the air, I focused on pulling my fire magic to the surface, heating up my skin to keep Ffion warm.

She shuffled further back against me and threw up an air shield to protect us from the worst of the wind—it wasn't perfect, but she'd obviously been practicing. I smiled to myself against the back of her head. We made a pretty good team.

"So," Ffion began as the griffin leveled out. "Want to tell me why you were avoiding me all of last week?”

“I wasn’t avoiding you, I visited Eamon’s house three times,” I retorted.

She snorted. “You didn’t see me once, and I know the guys were happy to bring you into the bedroom.”

I tried to tamp down the rising tide of guilt before Ffion’s empath ability picked up on it, but of course she was too quick for me. “Oh, it’s that misplaced guilt thing again. I thought I was just a really bad kisser.”

I let out a strangled laugh that surprised both of us. Honestly, I don’t remember the last time I’d found something genuinely funny.

“Your kissing isn’t the issue, scout,” I muttered.

“It’s a long flight back, Bryn. We have plenty of time to discuss your issues,” she sang. “We’re just going to set the guilt thing aside though, because the Castell’s actions are their fault and theirs alone. It was really only a matter of time before my past caught up with me. Besides, it was Kelvyn that let slip to Saffir about my surname, not you.”

“Why are you pushing this? What is it that you want from me?” I asked begrudgingly. Ffion didn’t say anything for a long moment. Long enough to make me nervous.

Why wasn’t she saying anything? My nerves morphed into irritation, and she chuckled.

“Chill out, grumpy. I’m thinking.” She sighed dramatically, making my lips twitch. “Okay, I’m just going to lay it all out there and hope you’re not going to be an asshole about this. I want you. I think you want me too. But I wasn’t your first choice and that fucking hurts. So, if we’re going to do this, you need to show me that you genuinely want me for me, not just because you can’t be bothered to resist our strong mating pull anymore.”

I opened my mouth before closing it again, surprised at how candid she’d been and needing a moment to collect my thoughts. “Fine. That’s fair. But you’ve got to be open to seeing it.”

“What is that supposed to mean?” Turning her head back so her eyes snapped to mine, filled with that passionate fire that I felt *every-fucking-where.*

"I've spent this past month trying to find you, working with your mates to track you down, collecting you myself." I kept my voice low and even, all too aware of Ffion's perception of me as a hothead.

"Those could have been actions borne of guilt or a sense of obligation. You can't deny you've been struggling with guilt over me being taken— even if it was unnecessary," Ffion replied mildly.

"What about that kiss? What about you sleeping in my arms that night? You're right that I felt guilty about you being taken, but that's not why I kissed you. That's not why I stayed with you instead of standing guard outside the cabin like I should have," I countered, and some of her tension ebbed away.

"Fair point," Ffion conceded. "I knew you before I met anyone else in Avalon, yet I know you the least. Let's just start there, okay?"

"Okay," I agreed because she was right. I had greedily absorbed every piece of information I could find out about her, but we'd barely spent any time actually conversing.

I knew from talking to the others that Ffion had been napping a lot while she recovered and she'd evidently hit her limit because not long after that, she swayed slightly in my arms, her head drooping forward. I guided Ffion's head back against my shoulder and tightened my grip around her waist, doing my best to ignore the weird tightening in my gut as she relaxed into me.

"Sleep, scout. I won't let you fall," I murmured softly into her ear. She shuddered slightly and I willed my cock to behave.

"Or push me off?" she confirmed sleepily.

"Or push you off," I agreed, smiling against her temple. Even practically comatose, she still wanted to argue with me, never willing to let me have the last word.

I'd rather jump off myself at ten thousand feet than let anything happen to Ffion, but I wasn't going to tell her that. I'd prove my feelings, so there was no doubt in her mind or mine about just how much she meant to me.

FFION

CHAPTER 54

Ten days after Bryn had rescued me from that ballroom, I decided it was time to get a sense of normalcy back in my life and return to classes.

Arthus, Marlen and I decided to head onto campus early so I could spend some time with Leigh, Briallen and Aderyn. The guys had seen them around campus but hadn't invited them to the house because my friends didn't know about my ability or where I'd been for the past month, but that was all going to change tonight.

Word was going to spread if it hadn't started already. I didn't want them to hear about my gift from someone else.

And I didn't want to keep the truth from them any longer.

As I walked into the commons for breakfast with Marlen and Arthus flanking me and Bryn at my back, I'd never been more grateful for the ability to mute my empath perceptions. There were plenty of people staring after my extended absence, and I was sure I'd be curled up in a ball on the floor if I hadn't been able to block out the responses.

"Fi!" Briallen screeched, launching herself at me in a blur of pink hair.

I stopped so suddenly that Bryn walked into my back. His hands lingered on my hips for a long moment, steadying me as Briallen flung her arms around my neck.

I returned her hug with equal enthusiasm, squeezing tight enough to make her cough before I eased off. There had been days where I thought I'd never see her again.

"We were so worried, Fi," she sniffed into my hair.

"Ain't that the truth. You must have quite the tale to tell, Fi," Leigh added, standing by the table. Aderyn hovered next to him, relief-filled eyes fixed on me.

Enfys had joined our table this morning, and I found myself oddly disappointed by his presence. Marlen and Arthus must have been monitoring the bond pretty closely, both shooting me concerned glances at my change in mood.

"I do. Tonight? Meet us in our cabin before dinner? It's the last night we have it, we're moving off-campus to Eamon's place," I said, gesturing at Marlen, Arthus, and me as we got ourselves settled around the large table and Marlen disappeared to get food for the two of us.

Briallen's eyebrows shot up into her hair and my cheeks probably looked like they were on fire. "We *do* have a lot to catch up on."

Out of the corner of my eye, I noticed Enfys shoot Bryn a venomous look that made the hair on the back of my neck stand up. Bryn was sitting diagonally from me, and I had a clear view of his carefully neutral expression—if he caught Enfys' glare, he wasn't responding to it. I had to assume he hadn't seen it because Bryn never *not* responded to anything.

I silently vowed to keep a closer eye on Enfys. He'd been nothing but kind to *me*, but that didn't mean he was always kind. If I hadn't been worried about the potential migraine, I'd have taken a closer look at his emotions.

"Your place tonight, then," Briallen said with a clap.

"You're not hurt, are you Fi?" Aderyn asked softly and Briallen's face filled with guilt for not thinking of it.

"I'm okay," I told Aderyn, shooting Briallen a reassuring smile. "Really."

Bryn gave me his best *really?* face, but fortunately didn't say anything. It was hard to tell with him whether he'd cooperate or not—he was kind of a renegade at the best of times.

I felt a weight lift off my shoulders at the thought of clearing the air tonight. Secrets were a heavy burden to bear, and I'd been carrying them around long enough.

We all piled into the cabin that evening, getting comfy on the floor around the stove. Bryn had set a roaring fire going, keeping away the chill that could still be felt on the air in the evenings.

Over the course of the last week and a bit, I'd told the guys a little about my forced stay in Glendower's cave of horrors. They'd worked out he was the most likely culprit, so that didn't come as a surprise to them, but I'd glossed over some of the details of what actually happened because I hated upsetting them.

Marlen and Arthus were monitoring the bonds between us almost constantly at the moment. Every time I started to get upset or think too much about what happened, one of them would scoop me up in their arms and distract me from my misery.

We couldn't put it off any longer, though. It was time. I wasn't sure about including Enfys in this conversation, but his feelings towards me had always been caring and protective. I'd just have to keep my particularly explicit rants about the Council to myself for the time being.

"I'm not sure where to begin," I said, shooting an unsure glance at Arthus, who gave a single reassuring nod. He was my passionate protector, my angel of vengeance. He was forever trying to keep me safe—even when the dangers were only in my memories.

None of this story was going to make sense if Leigh, Briallen and Aderyn didn't know about my gift. I blew out a long breath, releasing the years of secrecy and shame with it.

"I'm an empath. That's my gifted ability."

Briallen and Aderyn both gasped quietly, while Leigh gaped at me like a fish.

"Well, that would explain the kidnapping," Leigh muttered,

uncharacteristically serious. "Someone found out about your gift?"

"Yes and no. To cut a long story short: my parents hid me in Albion when I was a toddler. My dads found out I was back in Avalon and got Kelvyn Kneath to leave those messages for me—they're friends with Kelvyn's family, so he knew my birth name was Ffion Laisren."

I took a deep breath and Briallen laid a hand on Leigh's thigh when he looked like he was going to interrupt.

"Anyway, Arthus, um, had words with Kelvyn about the notes. I guess he was upset, he was complaining about me to Corsen and Saffir and he told them my real last name."

Everyone's faces darkened at the mention of Saffir, and I employed a little of my blocking ability to mute the anger.

"Anyway, Bryn left a note asking her to meet him to talk and Saffir panicked, then went back to her parents to try to get them to offer Bryn a Council internship so he would stay with her."

I chanced a look at Bryn, whose mouth was set in a firm line. I'd meant it when I told him his guilt was misplaced, but I don't think he was quite ready to let go of it yet.

"That day Saffir bolted from the campus? And showed up the following day with her Councilor mother?" Briallen clarified.

"Right. Evalina Castell. She planted the note in my cabin to get me to the edge of campus, under the guise of meeting Bryn," I continued, but Leigh cut me off.

"The Councilor abducted you?" he choked and Enfys made a strange, strangled sound.

"*Councilors*, plural. Evalina Castell planted the note and assisted, but it was definitely Glendower Castell's plan. He was the one I dealt with, mostly..." I said, trailing off.

I chanced a glance at Enfys, who sat as still as a statue, the furthest away from the group. His usually stoic face was tight with tension, his knuckles white where his hands gripped the legs of his trousers.

He looked like his foundations were crumbling beneath me, and although he wasn't my favorite fae, I felt pity for him.

"Wait, so they knew you were an empath based on your last name?" Aderyn interjected, confusion written all over her face.

"No. Glendower Castell intercepted my mother when she hid me in Albion seventeen years ago. They knew my name was Ffion Laisren and assumed I was being hidden because I had a gift worth stealing," I said with a hopeless shrug. The scales had been tipped against me long before I'd come to the Academy.

"What happened to your mother?" Aderyn asked softly.

"He killed her," I replied, my voice cracking. I took a deep steadying breath, but I couldn't suppress the regret that arose every time I thought of the mother who'd given birth to me and died keeping me safe. The regret that I never knew her, that I couldn't even remember her.

"Gods, so they captured you and interrogated you?" Leigh asked, looking a little green. I muted my abilities completely, their fear and panic starting to overwhelm me. Arthus gave me an approving nod.

"I wouldn't tell them, but Glendower Castell is not a patient fae," I said with a bitter laugh. "He bled me constantly, trying different crystals until he figured out that he could read emotions with imbued kyanite."

Marlen's healing had made the scars all but vanish on the outside, but I could still feel every cut on the inside.

"How'd you escape?" Briallen whispered. Leigh wrapped his arm around her and pulled her close as tears welled in her eyes.

I looked at Bryn to see if he wanted to take over, and he inclined his head. I was a little shocked he hadn't told Briallen already, but then he'd never sought any kind of glory for coming to my rescue.

"Saffir approached me," Bryn said flatly. "She said she'd been called home because her parents wanted to borrow a dress from her. When she arrived, she discovered the dress was for Ffion, who was locked in the servant's quarters."

I looked at the floor, unable to make eye contact with anyone and see the pity on their faces. It was too *raw*. Marlen moved behind me, shifting me to sit between his legs and wrapping his arms around my waist, and I clung to his arms like a lifeline.

It didn't seem like a good time to tell them that I'd actually been kept in a dirt cave and the servant's quarters were a freaking luxury in comparison.

"Glendower Castell has a strong illusion gift—their whole estate is cloaked at all times. He keeps crystals at the perimeter of the property and regularly tops them up so it can't be seen," Bryn explained. That part was news to me. No wonder the guys hadn't been able to find me. "Glendower took Ffion to a Council Ball, that's why he needed a dress for her. He introduced her to the room and told them about her ability, presumably so he could keep her under the guise of protecting her. With Saffir's tip-off, I snuck into the venue, caused a distraction during Glendower's speech, grabbed Ffion and ran."

Bryn delivered this all nonchalantly, like he hadn't saved my life all on his own at great risk to his own personal safety. I lifted the block on my abilities and felt the echoes of his fear from that night. He had been so scared he would be too late.

"Bryn was amazing, he saved my life," I said sternly, giving him a long look. I felt a hot surge of anger from Enfys directed at Bryn—anger that he was here, anger that he'd gone after me.

Had I read this really wrong? Was he reporting back to Glendower?

Marlen and Arthus sent waves of comfort through the bond simultaneously, and I relaxed back into Marlen's embrace. I was going to get to the bottom of this, but I'd catch more flies with honey than vinegar. Better keep up my sweet facade with Enfys for the time being.

But I wouldn't say anything about any future plans or protective measures we were taking in front of Enfys, just in case.

Briallen extricated herself from Leigh's embrace to give Bryn an affectionate one-armed hug. "Proud of you, cousin," she said teasingly. Bryn rolled his eyes, but the corner of his lip twitched ever so slightly. That was basically a full-on belly laugh by Bryn's standards.

"Anyway, that's basically the full story. Glendower Castell announced my gift at that ball, so the secret is out now I suppose."

"Shit, Fi. You do realize life as you know it is over, right?" Leigh asked bluntly as Briallen jabbed him sharply in the ribs.

"Unfortunately, yes. I do realize that," I replied with a sad smile. "Starting with moving permanently into Eamon's place, so let's get packing because I am one hundred percent finished with this depressing chat."

Marlen chuckled lightly behind me. "You heard the lady, let's get it done."

We all stood and Enfys tipped his chin at me from his spot by the wall, summoning me to talk with him.

I was not a great fan of being summoned, but I figured I could let it go this one time. Enfys looked like his whole world had been turned inside out.

"Enfys," I greeted him quietly with a tentative smile.

"I didn't know," he gritted out, looking past me at the fireplace. "I was going to him, asking for help to find you, and the whole time he managed to deceive me. I had no inkling that he even knew who you were, let alone that he was responsible."

"He's been around a lot longer than you, Enfys. Besides, he's a politician. He knows how to get what he wants." I unmuted my gift and was surprised at the potency of Enfys' shame as it ran down my spine. It was the first time I'd experienced Enfys' emotions without the tinge of arrogance that usually accompanied them.

"He cannot be allowed to get away with it," Enfys said suddenly, meeting my gaze for the first time. "The Council exists to protect fae. He is a disgrace."

"He is," I agreed. "But a very powerful one."

"I shall leave you now, Fi, to be with your close friends." I heard the undercurrent of pain in his voice, but I didn't have it in me to insist he stay yet. I needed to know more about where his loyalties really were.

He gave me a tight smile and left without a goodbye, though I noticed the glare he shot Bryn on the way past. Whatever their issue was, Bryn clearly wasn't too worried about it. He rolled his eyes and continued lounging on the armchair, not helping with any packing in the slightest.

Briallen meandered over to me, and we hung back as our mates busied themselves packing the final items and talking, giving us the illusion of privacy.

"Things seem to have improved between you and Bryn?" Briallen said hopefully.

"Well, he did save my life," I replied with a wry smile.

"You know what I mean," she huffed impatiently. "It's more than that. You look at him differently."

I knew she was right, but I didn't know how to vocalize what that meant or how I actually felt yet. The truce between us was new and tenuous. I focused on tidying the small kitchen cupboard to distract myself, and Briallen gave me a knowing smile.

In some ways, I thought Bryn had been right to call me out on my shit. His only crime was being a grumpy bastard, and even that was understandable considering how my appearance in his life had screwed up every plan he'd made for himself. He hadn't owed me friendship or anything more than that.

On the other hand, I couldn't help the pull between us any more than he could. I wasn't excusing him taking his anger out on me, but a few snippy comments and a bad temper weren't insurmountable obstacles to overcome in time. Besides, I'd been quietly assuming the worst of him and blaming him when things went wrong from almost the moment we met, even though he'd always been on my side.

He'd gone out of his way to help me lately and although my feelings for him had changed, I'd never taken the idea of an 'us' seriously. Neither of us had.

It was... complicated. We'd woven a tangled web of anger and assumptions and sexual tension that neither of us knew how to unravel.

"Hey, B..." I started, unsure what I really wanted to ask her. "What do you think of Enfys? Not as a suitor, just as a person," I added hastily, not wanting her to think I was measuring him against Bryn. I wasn't, really. I didn't know where things were going with Bryn, but when it came down to it, Enfys would never hold a candle to the feelings Bryn provoked in me even on his worst day.

Briallen's sunny face darkened, and I felt her anger course through my veins, startling me. Briallen was never truly angry.

"He was a real asshole to Bryn when you were gone, you know? Told Bryn that he wasn't good enough for you because Bryn's parents disgraced their family name. Even said Marlen wasn't good enough for you because of his family, but it could be attributed to an unfortunate first choice," she relayed bitterly.

"What the hell? Why has no one mentioned this to me?" I seethed. I was definitely glad I hadn't pushed for him to stay now.

"I don't think Bryn told anyone except me, he vented to me in a moment of frustration. He wouldn't tell you because he's embarrassed about it, but I think you deserve to know."

"I'm glad you told me," I told her sincerely, shaking my head lightly when Marlen and Arthus looked up, still monitoring the bond closely.

"Always. Aderyn and I were in the midst of plotting our revenge when we got the news that Bryn had found you. We'll make sure you're there for the next discussion," Briallen told me seriously.

I pulled her into a hug, shaking with laughter and wiping away the tears that had sprung to my eyes. If your friends weren't prepared to exact vengeance on your behalf against boys who slighted you, were they even really your friends?

We finished packing up our belongings—most of which belonged to Marlen and Arthus, since I had acquired very little in my time spent here— and were getting ready to leave when Eamon arrived at the cabin with Gwyneira and one of her mates in tow.

"Come on, ladies," Leigh called out. "Aderyn, we'll walk you back to your cabin."

Aderyn and Briallen both gave me quick hugs as they left, bowing their heads in deference to Gwyneira as they went past. *Huh. Maybe I should start doing that?* Gwyneira glided into the room, leaving Mawrth by the door, as Eamon strode in after her, moving behind me and wrapping his arms around my waist.

"I missed you, cariad," he murmured into my hair. I squeezed his hands and gave Gwyneira a small smile.

"Everything okay?" I asked her, weirded out that she'd made a house call.

"I am told that Glendower and Evalina Castell have been attending Council meetings and events as normal, so no change in behavior to report," she said grimly.

There was such a loud cacophony of male growling sounds that I looked around the room in alarm.

"Sorry, foxglove," Marlen muttered with a quiet chuckle. "We all sort of want to murder them."

"No 'sort of' about it," Arthus added with another menacing growl. His temper rivaled Bryn's, he just had better control over it. Most of the time.

"Yes, well, that would be highly inadvisable given their prominence in not just the fae community, but throughout all of Avalon. Both of them have served on the Avalon Assembly at one point or another. They are highly visible and well respected," Gwyneira said drily, as if my mates hadn't just been casually advertising their murderous appetites.

"So, what can we do?" I asked, looking around the room at all these wonderful people who were offering me their support without conditions. This slightly ragtag group was the family I never knew I needed.

"Lie low. Travel between the campus and your new home with one of your mates," Gwyneira said with a regretful smile. "Most importantly, make time to visit the temple again, Ffion. The gods sanctified you, they chose you. It is imperative that you find out why."

With everything else going on, I had pushed all thoughts about the gods and their supposed plans for me to the back of my mind. It wasn't like I needed the extra stress. I'd be quite happy to go back to how everything was before—spending my days in class and my nights tangled up with my mates, getting very little sleep in the best way.

But of course it couldn't have been that simple.

I was hit with a double dose of love and support through my mating bonds as Marlen and Arthus noticed the melancholy direction my thoughts had taken, while Eamon's arms tightened a fraction around my middle. I gave them a weak smile in return.

"I think I need to sleep on all of this. You're right though, I should go back to the temple. Try to figure out what it is the gods want. Maybe their goals will align with mine."

AKA, fuck shit up for Glendower and Evalina.

"I hope so," Gwyneira said with a sad smile.

ARTHUS

CHAPTER 55

Fi had been in a contemplative mood since our talk with Gwyneira last night. Both Marlen and I were checking the bond constantly to see how she was doing, waiting for the moment when she slipped back into that state of darkness she had existed in almost constantly since Bryn found her.

Surprisingly, talking about her ordeal last night and Gwyneira's reminder that the gods had something bigger planned for her seemed to have lifted Fi's spirits. The burden of keeping them to herself must have been bigger than Marlen and I had realized.

The three of us arrived in the commons at the height of the lunch hour when most of the tables were taken. It was a relief that Fi could mute her ability now—a couple of months ago, sitting in a crowded room like this would have been agony for her.

She'd come so far in so many ways since she'd moved to Avalon. She'd suffered far more than anyone should in an entire lifetime, but she'd grown immensely as well.

I just hoped she didn't regret coming here. I never *felt* that from her, but Fi had done her best to hide her darkest feelings from us since she'd come back, wanting to shield us from the pain we would have gladly taken as our own.

We grabbed our plates of food but could only find a two-person table. Without hesitation, Marlen pulled Fi onto his lap and I took the chair opposite, relishing the sound of her giggles. Considering everything she'd been through, she was coping well, but she rarely laughed anymore. Fi had lost the lightness and innocence she'd arrived in Avalon with, and we all blamed ourselves for it in different ways.

I should have been there to protect her.

Or maybe I shouldn't have been such a selfish bastard when her dads tried to send her back to Albion. Maybe I should have let her go.

Fi picked at the selection of vegetables and hummus on her plate unenthusiastically—her appetite still wasn't back to normal yet. Bryn strolled into the room and pulled a chair over to our table, making her eyes light up with interest.

"Scout," Bryn said by way of greeting, tipping his chin to acknowledge Marlen and me. I'd take his gruffness over Enfys' arrogance any day. Bryn didn't bother getting his own plate, he just helped himself to Fi's leftovers. She didn't so much as blink. I knew sending him to collect her from Eamon's estate would pay off.

"Maybe I should start calling you 'stalker' because of your tracking magic," Fi mused, giving Bryn a glare that held no real heat.

"Be my guest," Bryn replied cockily. He probably liked the idea of her having a special nickname just for him, even if it was meant to be insulting.

"Stalker it is," Fi announced.

Before Bryn could reply, Saffir cautiously approached our table, ignoring the borderline feral glare Bryn was giving her. Marlen's arms tightened around Fi's waist, but I reached for our bond to check her response and found nothing alarming. Fi was almost *happy* to see Saffir.

"Ffion," Saffir began softly. "I'm glad to see you back at the Academy."

"It's good to be back," Fi responded with a genuine smile.

"Are you two friends now?" Bryn asked, his tone dripping with disdain. Fi gave him a censuring look.

"Saffir has seen me naked, obviously we're friends now," Fi deadpanned.

Marlen and Bryn both tensed, but I knew Fi was making light of the situation to distract herself from the emotions she wasn't ready to confront yet. I sent a wave of reassurance through the bond and Fi gave me a wobbly smile.

"Here are the things I was looking after for you," Saffir said softly, handing over a small, wrapped package. "If you need anything, I'm around. Even if you just want to talk."

Saffir gave Fi a meaningful look. I wouldn't be surprised if Fi took her up on the offer. Saffir was the only one who had seen the conditions Fi had been kept in.

"One more thing," Saffir added hesitantly. "Word is spreading about the ball. About who you are... What you are."

"I figured it would. Thanks for the warning," Fi said with a shrug, feigning an indifference she didn't feel. Saffir gave her a respectful nod before departing for her own table.

"I vote we start going by 'Laisren' now," Fi sighed, staring out the window at the trees beyond. "Everyone knows, or they'll find out soon enough. We may as well end the charade. Besides, 'Smith' is a weirdly human name that I have no real connection to anyway."

"Ffion, Marlen and Arthus Laisren," Marlen pronounced. "I like it."

Bryn shot him an icy glare that I'd bet my left wing was borne of jealousy. His time would come. All he had to do was ignore his natural instincts to fuck everything up for himself.

We farewelled Marlen at the Academy before he left for guard duty, and I walked Fi home. The second we walked into the house, Fi was in Eamon's arms. It was hard on both of them being separated during the day, so Marlen and I made sure to give them lots of time together in the evenings.

Eamon pulled Fi onto an armchair, so she sat sideways across his lap. Her hands cradled his neck as she alternated between peppering his face with kisses and leaning her forehead against his.

"How was your day?" Eamon asked, paying rapt attention to Fi's response.

"Fine," she said vaguely. "We decided to go by 'Laisren' now, since word of my appearance at the ball is spreading."

"Speaking of that," he began, kissing her shoulder. "I received a letter from my mother today. She did some digging and found out I had hired some investigators to search for a 'Ffion'. She realized straight away that the mystery Ffion I was searching for and the empath Ffion she heard about at a Council ball are one and the same," he said with a grimace.

"She wasn't best pleased, I take it?" Fi confirmed, scrunching up her nose.

"She hasn't been pleased with anything I've done since the moment I was born," Eamon replied with a shrug, looking genuinely indifferent. "If the Council weren't after you, she'd probably be almost impressed. But as it stands she enjoys being in the Council's good graces, so she's no ally of ours."

"I'm sorry," Fi said sheepishly.

"Please, cariad, do not apologize for my mother's greed. If she cared half as much for me as she did for power, we wouldn't be having this conversation," Eamon assured her.

I did my best to repress my own concerns, not wanting to add to Fi's stress when she was finally relaxing in Eamon's arms. The stress was there, though, a constant looming presence. I rolled my neck to try release some of the tension that never quite left me.

Another enemy. Another player on the board to be aware of. Gwyneira believed that notoriety was Fi's first line of defense, but all I saw was an increasingly long list of fae who knew more about us than we knew about them, and that we somehow had to avoid.

After a light supper, we moved into the living area, Fi wanting to be close to the door as she waited for Marlen to finish guard duty. Fi and I sat on the couch opposite Eamon in the armchair as we relaxed with books from his small library, the firelight casting shadows over the walls of the treehouse.

It was a cozy kind of domesticity I hadn't been sure I would ever have, and

I was grateful for it.

Fi must have been feeling a lot better—she'd been shooting Eamon flirty looks all throughout supper and giving me coy glances through lowered lashes, finding ways to bare her neck to me in clear invitation. I sat on the couch with a raging hard on, wondering if Eamon would be comfortable joining in. Marlen and I often shared intimacy with Fi, but Eamon had only been with her alone so far.

Only one way to find out.

I caught his eye, and he must have seen something in my expression because he immediately sat up, setting his book aside to pay attention.

"Sweetheart, give Eamon your panties," I said mildly, returning my gaze to my book as if I wasn't particularly bothered either way. I couldn't help the little smile that tugged at the corner of my lips though. Especially when Fi startled for a brief second and stared intently at me.

I reached for the bond in my chest and felt Fi's lust and curiosity. Definitely on board, and ready to play.

Fi stood slowly and pulled her sleep shorts then her panties down her legs, bending over and giving Eamon a generous view of her cleavage, keeping eye contact with him the whole time. If I wasn't hard enough to hammer nails before, I was after that.

She made her way over to Eamon, hips swinging, and dropped the panties coyly in his lap before turning back to me and waiting expectantly for more instructions. *Gods, she is perfect.* Behind her, Eamon smiled slowly, his eyes alight with excitement. He probably hadn't seen this side of her before.

I smirked at her. "Lose the rest of the clothes while you're at it."

She didn't even blink, pulling the cardigan off, then her sleep top, unlacing her bra, then oh so slowly peeling the thigh high socks down before dropping them to the ground.

"Come here."

Fi instantly moved forwards, no hesitation in her face as she stood between my legs without a stitch of clothing on. My beautiful, confident mate. I lightly pushed her hips to turn her to face Eamon and moved my legs together before pulling her back onto my lap. Fi stilled for a second until I gently parted her legs and dropped them on either side of mine. She was completely spread eagle in front of Eamon, presenting him with a *glorious* view. My cock ached in my trousers, and I had no doubt Fi could feel it beneath her.

I ran my hands up and down the inside of Fi's thighs, gently brushing her pussy with my thumbs before moving my hands away again. She gave a breathy sigh and tipped her head back against my shoulder, trusting me to take her where she needed to go.

"Eyes on Eamon, sweetheart. Until I tell you otherwise, you know the rules."

I teased her entrance with my middle finger, collecting her arousal before drawing it up to her clit as Fi writhed encouragingly against me.

The combination of Fi staring at Eamon while I worked slow circles around her clit, building up until her movements were frantic had Eamon roughly yanking his dick out of his trousers and fisting it desperately. Fi watched him hungrily, the bond between us practically pulsating with lust. I could see her eyeing up his cock out of the corner of my eye as her tongue darted out to lick her lower lip.

"Soon, sweetheart. If you're good," I murmured, making them both groan.

I collected more of Fi's arousal, nipping and sucking at her neck, my leisurely movements at odds with the way she desperately writhed against my hand. She was *drenched*, eager, needy for us. Gods, this fae was fucking perfect for me. For *us*.

I slipped two fingers inside her clenching pussy, using the palm of my hand to roughly stimulate her clit, my movements picking up pace. Fi gasped, bucking harder as she chased her release while Eamon's eyes never left my hand.

I knew that fucker liked to watch.

Fi's channel fluttered around me, and I could feel that she was right on the verge of an orgasm when her eyes rolled back. I immediately removed my hand and delivered a swift slap right on her pussy.

"Eyes on Eamon."

Eamon's eyebrows darted up. He hadn't seen this side of her sensuality and was probably questioning how she was going to react. The wanton moan Fi gave told him she wasn't upset in the least. Her eyes met his again and hers were filled with so much filthy promise, I almost came on the spot.

I slid my fingers back inside her, my thrusts rough and demanding until Fi was crying out in ecstasy, bucking against my hand and reaching up behind my head to pull at my hair. *Fuck this*, I was going to come in my trousers like a teenager at this rate.

One handed, I undid my trousers and Fi lifted herself just enough for me to pull them down. Without any further warning, I pulled her back down onto my lap and plunged my cock into her, sucking in a breath at how godsdamn *good* she felt. Every time with her was like the first. Every time felt like a miracle. I fucked her roughly from underneath, forgetting all my plans to put on a slow seductive show, and pulling Fi's hands back behind my head when she tried to touch herself.

"Perhaps if you ask Eamon nicely, he'll help you with that," I grunted.

"Please, please, Eamon. I need you, please."

No fae could say no to that. Eamon stood and moved towards the couch, looking more unsure than I'd ever seen him. He definitely hadn't shared before.

"No need to be shy, Eamon. Fi isn't," I added with a smirk as she panted on my lap.

With that, he dropped to his knees and rested his hands on Fi's thighs, alternating between licking and rubbing her as I fucked her into another screaming orgasm.

"I think she can handle a little more, don't you, Eamon? Why don't you lie on the couch and we'll give her what she really wants."

Not about to question his luck, Eamon stripped and laid back on the couch so Fi could crawl over him. She stared at him hungrily before reaching down and lining up his cock with her entrance. She sunk down slowly, and his eyes rolled back in ecstasy as she took every inch of him.

And there were a lot of inches.

It absolutely took her longer to work his giant dick into her pussy, but Fi was nothing if not determined. I checked the bond again, finding only desire and need.

"Stay still," I purred in Fi's ear, disappearing into the bedroom to get some lubricant. I emerged and Fi was leaning forward over Eamon, her hands splayed on his chest as he reached up to capture her lips in a deep kiss, biting her lower lip as she moved away.

I kneeled behind Fi on the couch and her breath hitched as I massaged the oil over her back entrance, preparing her for me. I pressed in one finger, then two, scissoring and stretching while Fi made the most delightful muffled, needy sounds.

She wiggled impatiently and I chuckled, withdrawing my fingers before pushing my cock slowly into her as patiently as I could. Through her thin wall, I could feel Eamon holding himself still inside her. She was so godsdamned *tight* I could barely fit, and I let out a choked breath at the sensation.

Once I was fully seated, Eamon and I began to move in tandem as our beautiful Fi held on tight enough to Eamon's chest to leave gouge marks. I bet he'd find some excuse to go shirtless later just to show them off.

Right as she neared the edge, the front door opened and Marlen came in. He dropped his satchel and stared at us from the entryway, a mixture of shock and awe on his face before he broke into an amused grin on his face.

"Well, that explains what was going on with the bond. I miss all the good stuff," he whined. Fi gave him a saucy wink and beckoned him over.

"You haven't missed out yet," she said, licking her lips.

"Go on, M. Don't leave our girl wanting," I added with a smirk. Fi was so brave, so adventurous, if she wanted this, there was nothing we would deny her.

Marlen strolled over and dropped his pants, revealing his cock already standing at attention. Fi pulled him closer and swallowed him deeply without any preamble, too lost in the throes of her own passion for foreplay.

Eamon and I began to move again as Marlen sighed in relief. Over Fi's shoulder, I could see the hunger in Eamon's eyes as he watched Marlen's cock going in and out of her luscious mouth. Watching them together sent him over the edge.

Fi immediately clenched around me, moaning and writhing through another orgasm as I slammed into her once more with a groan and followed. A few more pumps and Marlen finished in her mouth, Fi greedily sucking down every drop.

Looking slightly delirious and perfectly messy, Fi slumped forward on Eamon's chest, and he wrapped his arms tightly around her. My beautiful, blissed-out sweetheart. I loved her so much it physically hurt.

Marlen and I pulled back and got ourselves half-dressed before Marlen disappeared, returning with a wet washcloth. He cleaned Fi off with only a few embarrassed protests from her before giving Eamon a wink as he left them to cuddle on the couch. I decided to shower and give them some alone time. She was in good hands. No one was better at nurturing Fi than Eamon, and they needed time together after that experience.

I emerged half an hour later, showered and dressed, just as Marlen was setting out cups of tea for each of us. Fi had dressed in a short linen nightdress and matching gown and was curled up against Eamon's side on the couch. I really needed to thank him one of these days for all the sexy additions to Fi's wardrobe.

"So that was a fun distraction and all, but we really should talk about what Gwyneira said last night," Fi said, raising a challenging brow and looking at Marlen and I on the armchairs facing her to see if we were going to object.

We both shook our heads. I enjoyed it whenever Fi tried to take charge—it was a challenge to see if I could control my natural urge to take over.

Fi opened her mouth to speak just as Eamon's features slackened and his arm dropped from her shoulders.

"It's the spirits, sweetheart," I reassured Fi when she startled. The spirits had visited Eamon most days while Fi had been missing, so Marlen and I had gotten used to these episodes.

Eamon's eyes closed for a moment. When he opened them, his irises were a swirling cloud of gray.

"Sanctified Empath. You have faced many trials and will face many more. The gods have tasked you to be the fae's Keeper of Balance. Restore the balance between light and dark. Allow those in hiding to find their way home. Show that the fae are worthy of their blessings."

"What? What does that mean?" Fi asked in a panicked voice, gripping tightly to Eamon's shoulders.

"Restore the light. Bring them home, Sanctified Empath. Make the fae worthy. Keeper of Balance," the spirit reiterated before Eamon gave a large shudder and closed his eyes. When he opened them again, his purple irises were back.

"What does that mean?" Fi wailed. "Is this a save the world thing? Am I the naïve, inexperienced heroine that is somehow supposed to save the world?" she babbled, getting increasingly agitated.

"They don't want you to save the world, cariad," Eamon assured her. "They want you to redeem the fae."

the Reluctant Keeper

> "SHE CONQUERED HER
> DEMONS AND WORE HER SCARS
> LIKE WINGS."
> - ATTICUS POETRY

FFION

CHAPTER 56

Gods, I love the stars here in Avalon. The night sky was a brilliant blend of inky blue and dusky violet, and there were so many stars it looked like someone had thrown a silver glitter bomb at the sky. London didn't have stars like these, or none that you could see anyway, not through the haze and light pollution that such a big city produced.

For the first time, I missed it.

My life in London—or Albion, the human realm, as the fae called it—had been monotonous and unfulfilling, but it was simple. I worked the pre-dawn cleaning shift at a corporate building. I avoided people for the most part, but would head out for a night on the town when my sexual frustration became too uncomfortable. I read a lot of books—some of which contributed to my sexual frustration.

It had been a lonely life, but there had been very little riding on my shoulders in those days. The only person I had to look out for was myself, completely unlike the life I had now. Now I had the weight of the fae on me, their future and their access to magic had somehow become my responsibility.

Because the gods had chosen me.

I read books about *The Chosen One*. I didn't want to *be* the chosen one. I didn't know how to be a chosen one. Half the time I felt like I still needed adult supervision to make sure I ate properly and went to bed at a reasonable hour. I wasn't cut out for mysterious divine missions and carrying the weight of the world on my shoulders. I had barely scratched the surface of what it even was to be fae and what my magic could do. Nearly anyone else would have been better suited to this task.

The gods chose wrong.

I was sitting alone on the narrow wraparound porch that surrounded Eamon's treehouse, reflecting. My rust-colored linen dress wasn't warm enough to be sitting outside in, but I needed a minute to clear my head. I knew Marlen, Arthus and Eamon were watching me obsessively through the windows, but they'd at least given me the illusion of space since the spirits dropped into Eamon's body an hour ago and informed us of the mission the gods had for me.

"Sanctified Empath. You have faced many trials, and will face many more. The gods have tasked you to be the fae's Keeper of Balance. Restore the balance between light and dark. Allow those in hiding to find their way home. Show that the fae are worthy of their blessings."

Basically, a lot of words that didn't mean anything to me. I didn't know what a 'Keeper of Balance' was or how one went about restoring the balance between light and dark magic. I had no idea where those supposedly in hiding were.

As for showing the gods that the fae were worthy of their blessings... I wasn't 100% convinced that they were. That was a sentiment that was difficult to admit out loud, even to my more-than-understanding mates.

How was I supposed to fight for the fae when I wasn't sure they were worth fighting for? Maybe a couple of months ago, I wouldn't have questioned it. I would have done what I was asked because it would have seemed like the right thing to do, and I was a rule follower at heart. But that was *before*. My experience with Glendower and Evalina Castell, and my brief encounter with other Councilors I was forced to meet at the ball, had significantly diminished my opinion of the fae.

There was a very large, vocal part of me that said *fuck 'em*. Let them lose their magic. Let those who had been given so much and still weren't satisfied see how it felt to be a low-magic fae.

The tug of the mating pull in my chest alerted me to Bryn's presence before the crunching of leaves under his feet did. He made his way up the stairs and dropped to the floor next to me, leaning against the wall of Eamon's treehouse. I glanced at him out of the corner of my eye, the candlelight shining through the windows illuminating his sharp, angular features. His hair was the same inky midnight blue as the night sky, and I could make out flashes of his sapphire blue eyes as he stared ahead of him, joining in my silence.

He really was a beautiful fae.

Beautiful, and complicated. Though I could hardly judge on that front. I'd been given a mission by the gods via a dead fae who had dropped into my boyfriend's body.

I was complicated too.

"What are you doing here?" I asked him quietly. We had cleared the air between us and agreed to move forwards, but I still wasn't all that clear on what that meant for us. *How* did we move forward? Marlen, Arthus and Eamon had all been so forward in their own ways, I guessed I'd just sit back and wait for Bryn to do his thing too.

"I'm not entirely sure why I'm here," Bryn replied honestly, lazily creating fireballs in the palm of his hand and letting them fizzle out. "I just had a feeling I should be here. Since I've found you sitting out here by yourself looking like the world is caving in on you, my intuition must have been dead on."

There was an arrogant tilt to his mouth and I rolled my eyes, my mood lifting slightly. He was still a smug asshole, but I liked that about him. Bryn always said exactly what he meant.

"We got a message from the gods tonight, via Eamon," I told him, staring at my legs stretched out in front of me, leading to my bare feet. Fae rarely wore shoes—it interfered with our connection to the elements and our magic—but it never ceased to feel strange to me, especially in this cool weather.

Bryn sat up a little straighter, and I could feel his gaze boring into the side of my head. "And? What did they tell you?"

"That the gods want me to be the 'Keeper of Balance', whatever that means. Somehow restore the balance between light and dark. Help the fae out of hiding. That sort of thing." I waved my hand absently and heaved a sigh. It sounded so much worse out loud.

"Fuck," Bryn breathed.

"Yep. *Fuck.*"

Fuck, indeed. Fuck everything.

My eyes were still trained on my outstretched legs and I heard a quiet thud as Bryn's head fell back against the cabin wall.

"I'm guessing they didn't tell you how to do any of that," he said wryly. In that moment, I found I was glad he was the one I was sitting out here with, discussing these things. Bryn wasn't awed by the gods, he wasn't really awed by anyone.

"They did not," I confirmed. "That would be far too easy."

The mating pull writhed in my chest, encouraging me to draw comfort from Bryn. To touch him.

To stake my claim.

I wasn't feeling quite that bold, though. Instead, I shuffled over slightly, so our shoulders brushed against one another, and I felt Bryn's surprise like a surge in my gut. He wasn't upset at all though, so I took it as a win and leaned in a little further. It was like resting against a furnace. Glorious.

The door opened, spilling light out onto the porch. "Sweetheart, come inside. I know it's a lot to process, but we need to discuss this," Arthus called, his voice tight with impatience. "You too, Edan."

Bryn acknowledged Arthus with a tilt of his head and stood up, reaching out his hand to help me. I took it and let the soothing waves of comfort that emanated from a happy mating pull relax me a little. We made our way along the narrow porch into the house, Bryn never once letting go of my hand.

We'd kissed once, only once, but somehow this felt more intimate.

All three guys greeted Bryn warmly, not surprised in the least that he'd just shown up out of nowhere. I released his hand as Marlen snagged my waist and pulled me down into his lap, so I wriggled back against his chest, sinking into his firm, lean body and reaching back to push his dark red hair off his forehead.

Marlen leaned into my touch, giving me a sad smile as he scanned my face. His searching gaze wasn't necessary, I doubted he'd stopped monitoring the bond since the spirits' pronouncement.

"I take it Fi's filled you in?" Arthus asked curtly as the rest of the guys took their seats around the room.

Arthus sat in the forest green armchair opposite me, his messy black hair flopping over his brilliant silver eyes. His gift from the gods was a rare pair of fae wings that he usually kept retracted so as not to attract the attention of hunters who would happily cut them off to make a profit. He always struggled to keep them hidden when his emotions were running high and I could see him rolling his shoulders now, fighting his instincts.

"She did," Bryn replied, casually flicking a ball of fire at the hearth of the white curved clay fireplace, making it flare to life.

"Cariad? Talk to us," Eamon pleaded quietly, his amethyst eyes trained on me, looking a little forlorn. He was an enormous man, built like a bodybuilder, yet so incredibly sweet and sensitive. Both Arthus and Marlen were my mates and could determine my general mental state through our bond, but Eamon was only my suitor—he wouldn't have that insight until we'd officially claimed one another.

Which would probably happen sooner rather than later because I was head over heels for this kind, nurturing gentle giant of a fae.

"I don't even know where to begin," I admitted, drawing absent shapes on Marlen's forearm with my fingers. "Was this always in the cards for me? Is that why I was given this empath gift in the first place? It feels like... like my life was never really my own. I'm just a tool in the gods' bigger plans."

"We all are, in a way," Marlen said from behind me, and I felt him shrug.

"There were many times where I envied my family's lack of magic. The idea of the gods favoring me was intimidating. Why me, you know?"

Oh, I knew. Even before I'd known what my ability to sense emotions meant or why I had it, I'd wondered *why me.*

"If they give out gifts because they favor us, how come assholes like the Castells get it?" I asked bitterly.

"One theory my parents endorse is that it's the gods' way of testing them, seeing how they'll use the power they're given," Arthus suggested. His parents were hotshot priests at the oldest temple in Avalon, so I guessed they'd know.

"I'm not sure I like these gods enough to do their bidding," I grumbled. Bryn snorted at Eamon's alarmed expression.

"You probably shouldn't make a habit of sacrilege," Arthus commented lightly, though he didn't look overly concerned. His own relationship with the gods was difficult because of his wings. We both knew what it was to feel like our gift was more of a curse.

"It's kind of a lot to dump on a person though, right?" I protested.

"You still have a choice, cariad," Eamon soothed, scrubbing a hand down his thick dark brown beard. "But the gods chose you, so you'll have a better chance at creating change than anyone else because they've offered you their support."

I snuggled into Marlen as I mulled over Eamon's words, annoyed that they'd made a crack in my resolve. On the one hand, saving the fae from themselves didn't feel like my responsibility. On the other hand, restoring the balance between light and dark potentially worked well into my plans for vengeance against the Castells.

Two birds, one stone…

"Do you want to discuss this with Gwyneira? We could go see her tomorrow morning," Eamon suggested cautiously, looking closely at my expression.

"I know this is a huge deal, but do you think maybe we could just mull it over between the five of us for a couple of days? As soon as I tell Gwyneira, it will turn into this huge thing."

I chewed nervously on my bottom lip, hoping they weren't going to push the issue. I'd only just gotten out of captivity at the Councilor's house, couldn't I catch a freaking break? Maybe have a holiday?

"Two days to process seems reasonable," Arthus conceded, challenging the other guys to contest him with a warning glance. "You need sleep, sweetheart. I can feel your exhaustion." Arthus tapped his sternum where the mating bond sat, giving me a disapproving look.

"You staying?" Arthus asked, turning to Bryn. Bryn looked questioningly at me, brow raised.

"Stay," I said firmly. I wasn't ready to say goodbye to him yet, and I could sense his reluctance to leave. Bryn nodded and said nothing, but the rush of his relief spilled through my body like a warm, relaxing wave.

How was every interaction with Bryn somehow not much and everything at the same time?

There was no awkwardness as the five of us got ready and slid into the enormous bed together. It felt so right, so natural, it was almost mundane.

Marlen and Eamon being the most touchy-feely of my guys always slept next to me. Bryn didn't even question it, just laid down on Eamon's other side while Arthus laid down on Marlen's other side like he always did.

Strange. Good, but strange.

The four of them fell asleep easily while I lay awake, staring at the ceiling and reflecting on the past few hours. Eventually I let the calming sound of their steady breathing lull me into an uneasy sleep, plagued by dreams of destitute fae and vengeful gods.

Waking up sandwiched between Marlen and Eamon, with Arthus and Bryn on either side of them, was not nearly as weird as I thought it would've been.

It was still a little weird, but maybe 10% weird instead of 98% weird like I expected.

Eamon was up first, making us all breakfast while the rest of us got ready for the day, and Marlen's naturally chatty nature meant there were no awkward silences.

Despite that, I still escaped the room by claiming the bathroom first. While Bryn had been the one to break me out after a month of imprisonment and had definitely seen me at my worst, I still felt weird about him seeing me so disheveled first thing in the morning.

I quickly braided my thick, curly hair over one shoulder and secured it with a navy linen ribbon, splashed my face with some cold water and pinched my cheeks for color. I really missed makeup sometimes. Checking my reflection in the hand mirror Eamon had given me for Winter Solstice still hadn't gotten old. Here in Avalon, without the glamour my father had been applying, I was taller, with smooth caramel-colored fae skin and pointed ears. My eyes had transformed from a flat dark brown to a vibrant amber, and my black hair was now a dark brown mixed with light honey-colored streaks.

No one looking at me now would mistake me for a human.

I pulled on a simple short-sleeve navy shift dress and joined the guys in the kitchen, where the *alarmingly mundane* trend continued over breakfast.

Eamon made us all mashed banana and egg pancakes that all the guys loved, and I kind of thought tasted like baby food. I slathered mine in honey because if they weren't fluffy, they should at least be syrupy.

Arthus and Bryn gave me matching grossed out faces before topping their pancakes with pecans and even more bananas. No wonder they were both so surly. They needed more sweetness in their life.

Eamon interrupted the sounds of everyone eating from time to time to make sure we didn't need anything, and Marlen spent all of breakfast looking between Bryn and I like he was watching a tennis match. He leaned forward on his elbows, eyes alight with mischief, grinning like an absolute lunatic. His picture should really be in the dictionary, listed under 'obvious'.

Maybe it should have bothered me more that they were all so blatantly rooting for Team Bryn In The Harem, but it weirdly didn't. I knew that if I ever unequivocally said I wasn't interested in pursuing him, none of them would force the issue.

Bryn pulled me aside after breakfast on his way to the front door. His grip around my elbow was light as he led me away from the others, giving us a moment of semi privacy. The constant warmth of Bryn's palms never failed to surprise me, his fire magic always so close to the surface. It was comforting.

"My aunt and uncles are visiting campus today, I need to head back," Bryn said, dropping his hand from my arm a little slower than necessary. His deep blue eyes scanned mine, looking for something in my expression that I wasn't sure I was giving.

"Oh yeah, of course," I agreed, nodding awkwardly because I wasn't sure what level of goodbye we were at yet. *Hug? Friendly wave? Handshake?*

We'd made out one time, and had an awkward chat about things progressing naturally, but we never really discussed what that meant for our relationship on a day-to-day level.

A handshake was definitely overkill, we slept in the same bed last night.
Maybe a hug.
Was Bryn a hugger?

Before I had the chance to overthink myself into a coma, Bryn stepped into my space and smacked a firm kiss onto my temple before walking out the door.

The spot where his lips touched my skin felt warm. As did the rest of my face from the blush that had undoubtedly taken over.

Get it together, Fi! You had a foursome, you can't be blushing over forehead kisses.

"See you at the bonfire," Bryn called over his shoulder without turning around.

I lingered for a moment, watching him walk away and feeling a sense of calm satisfaction I rarely got after my interactions with Bryn. Maybe it was a temporary truce, but I hoped it meant we were finally moving forward. I smiled to myself like an idiot as I wandered back into the kitchen to pour myself more peppermint tea.

Wait, what bonfire?

CHAPTER 57

I snagged Fi's arm as she entered the kitchen, pulling her back against my chest, wrapping my arms around her shoulders. Some of the happy high she'd been on with Bryn was wearing off, and I needed to find a way to preserve it. My mate just couldn't seem to catch a break at the moment.

"Don't think about the gods or their mission or anything heavy today, foxglove. Tonight is about celebrating, so we're going to celebrate," I encouraged, giving her shoulders a squeeze.

"I assume this is the bonfire Bryn mentioned. What are we celebrating?" she asked, tipping her head back so she could meet my eyes and giving me a wary look. "This better not be another thing where I'm supposed to buy gifts and you haven't told me," she grumbled, shooting me a reproachful look.

We had screwed up there, I could admit that.

"No gifts for Spring Equinox," I assured her with a chuckle. "Just a big bonfire on campus and plenty of ale."

"He's leaving out a significant religious element, but yes, that is the general idea," Arthus added drily from his spot at the dining table, not looking up from his book.

Fi narrowed her eyes at me. "The gods are kind-of on my shit list right now, so you'd better expand on those religious elements real quick."

"Fi!" Eamon choked out as he prepared a tray of peppermint tea and honey cakes. He knew honey cakes always cheered Fi up, the big softie. "You shouldn't talk about the gods like that, cariad."

"Like what? Like they're ruining my life, sending me on save-the-fae missions I want nothing to do with?"

Fi's fiery response, the bitterness in her tone, was actually reassuring. She'd mostly been a mix of sad, thoughtful or hopeless since Bryn had delivered her back to us after her month-long torture at the hands of the Castells.

Anger was an improvement. At least she was feeling *something*.

"Come on, let's do something fun today," I suggested, grabbing her hand to try and pull her towards the living area.

"What did you have in mind?" she asked suspiciously, playfully pushing me off so she could pour herself another cup of tea.

"Sexy bath?" I asked hopefully. "Sexy game of cards? Sexy reading on the couch together?"

Fi rolled her eyes as she tried to suppress a smile. "You have such a one track mind."

"So… Which one was it? Lady's choice." I spread my arms magnanimously and fought back a grin.

"Sexy bath," Fi called over her shoulder, already heading towards the bathroom with her cup of tea in hand. I shot Eamon and Arthus a triumphant grin as they smirked at me before jogging to catch up with our girl.

If Fi wanted a distraction, that was my job. I was the fun mate. Fun, I could do.

By silent agreement, Eamon, Arthus and I had all gone out of our way to distract Fi throughout the day. She practiced air shields with Arthus, baked honey cakes with Eamon, played cards with me, and finished each activity with an orgasm.

By the time we left to go to the bonfire, Eamon had to carry her on his back half the way there because Fi was still boneless from spending an hour with her legs slung over Eamon's shoulders with his face buried between her thighs.

It wasn't just a matter of distracting her from last night's bombshell—we also wanted her to relax so she wouldn't think too hard about attending an event on campus with the whole school and half their families there. After a lifetime avoiding crowds, Fi was still skittish around them, and even more so now due to her newfound and entirely unwanted fame.

The damage may have been done, but we could find ways to make Fi as comfortable as possible in spite of the Castells and their schemes.

As we approached the clearing on campus where the bonfire was being built, I reached for the bond and felt the moment when Fi muted her abilities. The curiosity around her disappearance that the other students felt, and suspicion of her empath gift now that word had spread was really affecting her. It had taken the shine off the Academy she'd come to love so much, and I hated it.

Fi had felt like something 'other' her entire life. She should have felt like she belonged here.

The pyre was stacked high with wood ready for Gwyneira to arrive and thank the gods before setting it alight. Fi's fingers linked through mine and she stuck close as she took it all in, examining our surroundings while carefully avoiding eye contact with the nosy fae who weren't trying to hide their stares. There were definitely some who wanted to ask about her empath gift, but Arthus was on Fi's other side giving them his best *fuck off* face, and he was a mean-looking bastard when he wanted to be.

He had nothing on Bryn, who had appeared out of nowhere and was protecting our flank, looking like he might set someone on fire for glancing at Fi the wrong way.

Like his sexual frustration, fear, even love, Bryn dealt with his guilt through rage. Not that he needed to feel guilty about Fi's kidnapping—not even Saffir, whose parents had taken Fi, didn't deserve to feel guilty about it. The blame belonged solely to Glendower and Evalina Castell.

We picked a spot near the back of the crowd with Eamon standing sentry close by. He didn't look out of place being here since a lot of friends and families took advantage of the Spring Equinox celebration to visit the campus. It was obvious through the bond how much Fi enjoyed having him near.

"So, now what?" Fi asked, analyzing the pyre in the distance as her natural curiosity outweighed the wariness at being around a crowd.

"Gwyneira will show up, either she or someone else will say a few words, light the fire, some other fire stuff…" I told her with an impatient wave of my hand. I craned my neck, scanning the crowd for the barrels of ale. The ceremony stuff was boring as fuck.

"By *say a few words* he means 'give a dedication to the gods'. And by *some other fire stuff* he means 'burn offerings of special herbs to ask the gods for fertility and a good harvest,'" Arthus added drolly.

"Semantics." I shrugged. "More importantly, I've spotted the ale. I'll go get us some pitchers."

"Stay," Bryn ordered, the bossy bastard. "I'll go."

"I'll give you a hand," Eamon offered.

I wasn't about to argue with them. Besides, I had a feeling this was Bryn's form of wooing. Hopefully Fi was into 'awkward and grumpy', because I really felt like Bryn was the right fit for our mating circle. His natural pessimism was perfect considering the powerful enemies Fi had, but they would both need to push through their emotional barriers to get there and I wasn't convinced it was going to happen yet.

They returned ten minutes later with a pitcher of ale for each of us, and Fi gave Bryn a grateful smile before discreetly wrinkling her nose as she sipped the ale. Eamon had spoiled her with all that fancy fae wine.

A flash of pink barreling towards us caught my attention a second before Briallen came to a stop in front of us, panting with exertion, clutching Leigh's hand in one of hers and a mystery fae's in the other. I gave him an assessing once-over—Briallen was a good friend of mine, after all—but her cousin walked right up into New Guy's personal space and quickly blocked my view.

"B," Bryn drawled with a menacing intensity. "Who's this you're dragging around?"

"This is Hagan," she replied breathily, staring adoringly up at him. "He's my new suitor."

"What? When did you guys meet?" Fi asked, her voice filled with surprise as she leaned forward to grab Bryn's arm and yank him out of the way.

Hagan had bronze skin, short, thick brown hair and eerily pale green eyes. He was basically the opposite of Briallen with her porcelain skin, dusky pink hair and dark brown eyes.

"About half an hour ago," Briallen replied dreamily. "He's visiting a friend at the Academy for the Equinox."

Fi's eyebrows shot up to her hairline, but she wisely said nothing. Briallen was a romantic at heart and the most impulsive person I'd ever met. She also wasn't afraid to shank a fae who disagreed with her.

I liked my mate un-shanked.

"You don't waste time," Fi eventually commented lightly, looking slightly at a loss for words.

"When you know, you know," Briallen replied cheerily. Hagan blushed a little, wrapping his arm tightly around her shoulders.

I shot a glance at my best friend, but Leigh didn't look worried, though he was sticking close to Briallen's other side. So long as Leigh was around, Briallen was safe. He'd never let anything happen to his mate.

Before Fi had to come up with another awkwardly polite response, the crowd parted for Gwyneira. "Shoot, we need to get back to my parents," Briallen whispered, waving at us before grabbing her guys' hands and dragging them back through the crowd.

Fi stared after them, looking a little baffled after experiencing Hurricane Briallen, and I fought the urge to laugh, considering this was supposed to be the serious part of the night.

Gwyneira glided past where we were standing wearing traditional Equinox garb—a long white linen gown with floaty sleeves, no shoes, her waist length hair unbraided with a laurel wreath on her head.

Fi looked impressed by the display of piousness, but if she'd unmuted her ability, she'd have sensed the crowd's discomfort. The Spring Equinox was, above all, a celebration of fertility. The dedication was traditionally given by a female approaching a window of fertility, which Gwyneira was many years past. For her to continue to insist on doing the dedication each year... It came across as a little arrogant.

Gwyneira reached the pyre and turned to address the crowd with her three mates fanned out around her.

"My fellow fae," she called out. "Thank you for joining us at the Academy of Avalon for this year's Spring Equinox celebration." She paused for a moment, allowing a few weak cheers and a smattering of applause.

Awkward.

"We give thanks to the gods for the generosity of their bounty and ask that it continues for the following harvest. May our lands and our people be blessed with fertility, this year and every year, by our kind and benevolent deities."

Gwyneira gave the crowd a once-over. Her expression was serene, but the gesture was domineering. Whatever she saw must have satisfied her— without looking back, she flicked a ball of fire from her fingers over her shoulder, sending the pyre up into a tower of flames. Fi gasped lightly next to me, suitably impressed.

"Now we drink," I announced with a small shake of my head, happy the theatrics were over and done with.

Arthus lifted his pitcher in agreement, giving me a loaded look as he took a swig. If *I* noticed Gwyneira was being a little high-handed, Arthus definitely noticed. He was all about the ceremonial shit.

We drank and listened to the music as a band of fiddle players took up their instruments for a while before the first of the mating circles approached the pyre to make their offerings. Fi watched with interest as the groups would approach, bow their heads, then throw bundles of herbs on the roaring fire. Her eyes lit up in recognition as Master Cadha, the potions master, and her three mates approached the bonfire with their offerings.

"Cornflower, mint, coriander, and blackberry leaves," Bryn muttered quietly, answering Fi's unasked question. She shot a glance at him out of the corner of her eye.

"Not to worry, foxglove. We've got a few decades before we need to worry about that," I added cheerfully. Fi's first fertile window wouldn't be for another thirty years.

"I most definitely was not worried," she retorted, looking appalled. I grinned and smacked a wet kiss on her cheek. I loved teasing her.

Also, I was possibly drunk. A *little* drunk. Just a bit drunk.

Fi jabbed me in the ribs and I doubled over slightly just as Aderyn approached with her new suitor, Lachlan.

Godsdamn it, now I looked weak in front of my sister's new man. Fi's smug expression told me she was thinking the same thing.

"Hello," Aderyn began shyly. She hated being the center of attention. "This is my suitor, Lachlan. Lachlan, this is... everyone."

I stepped forward because fuck off Bryn; it was my turn to Alpha Male all over the show.

"I'm Marlen, Aderyn's twin," I announced, holding out my hand for him to shake and squeezing his fingers a teeny bit harder than necessary. He didn't flinch. That was one point for him in my book.

"If you're done with the posturing," Fi drawled, bumping me out of the way with her hip and giving me an admonishing look. "I'm Fi, Marlen's mate."

She made the rest of the introductions and Aderyn smiled at her gratefully while being sure to glare at me.

"Addie's told me much about you all," Lachlan said with a nervous smile.

Addie? I used to call her that when we were kids to rile her up and would often end up with bruises for my troubles. Apparently she didn't mind it nowadays, judging by the lovesick smile she was giving him.

"So how are things going between you and *Addie*?" I asked conversationally. Obviously not conversationally enough since my sister sent me a death glare and Fi grabbed my hand, pulling me into the crowd.

"We're getting more drinks!" she called over her shoulder before giving me a reprimanding look. "Can you take it down several notches, please?" she hissed.

"I'm just getting to know him," I protested.

"Ah no, you're having a metaphorical dick measuring competition is what you're doing. I get that she's your twin and she's always been a consistent presence in your life, but this is maybe the first time Aderyn's ever had something for herself. Even her place at the Academy was forced on her." Fi stopped pulling me along and turned to face me. "You have the opportunity to make this experience really pleasant or really unpleasant for her. Choose wisely."

Suitably scolded, I trailed Fi over to the barrels to refill our pitchers. I still didn't love the idea of some guy hanging around my twin, but I didn't want to tarnish Aderyn's courtship—especially since my sister had always made such an effort with Fi.

Begrudgingly, I ordered pitchers of ale for the two of them as well. Fi helped me carry them back, grinning from ear to ear.

"Here," I grunted, shoving a pitcher at Lachlan. "Peace offering." He smiled graciously and pretended not to notice Bryn, Eamon and Arthus smirking at me triumphantly from behind Fi.

"Tell me about this village you're from," I said with a sigh.

"It's called Dubris, it's right on the edge of the Black Forest. There's a port a few miles away that sails for the Outer Isles, so it's a popular thoroughfare. Only two hundred fae live there," Lachlan mumbled, watching Aderyn's face carefully. He was probably worried she wouldn't find it impressive, given that she was attending Avalon's premier Academy.

"Our childhood village would have only been half that size, right Aderyn? And very isolated," I added, trying to help her out. Her expression softened, and she shot me a teensy smile.

"Oh yes, it was tiny. I've always wanted to see the Black Forest, I've heard it's a popular hideout for unicorns."

"No way," Fi gasped. "What's the protocol on tracking down unicorns? Seeing one in real life is topping my list of life goals right now."

"Your priorities are incredibly concerning, sweetheart," Arthus muttered, clearly thinking of the sacred mission she was doing her best to ignore.

"That's one of your more terrible ideas," Bryn told Fi lightly, not in the least concerned if he was insulting her. "Unicorns can do plenty of damage with those horns if you piss them off."

"Noted," Fi said drily, scowling at Bryn before turning the full force of her dazzling smile on me. "I'll bring my healer with me," she added affectionately, patting my chest.

She was distracted from teasing by the clearing of a throat behind her, and we all turned in unison to find Enfys standing a few feet away, a non-threatening distance that he was making a show of maintaining.

"Hello Fi, how are you?" he asked stiffly, his gaze darting uncomfortably around the rest of us. I didn't like the guy—no one would tell me exactly what he'd said about me that had angered Fi so much, but I was guessing it wasn't good. To be fair to him, he'd seemed genuinely surprised to find out that the Councilors he held so dear had been the ones who captured Fi.

If he betrayed her now that he knew the truth, I'd have to kill him for sure though.

"I'm getting by," Fi said through a forced smile. *Bet she was wishing she could lie right now.* "How have you been?"

"Fine, fine," he replied, absently waving his hand as if he was swatting away an annoying bug. "I'll be taking some days off from the Academy this week. I, uh, was very troubled by the information you shared a few days ago. I would like to investigate it further and see what can be done," Enfys added vaguely, aware of the distinct possibility our conversation was being listened to.

"Really?" Fi asked, her eyebrows shooting up. Enfys looked at her like he wanted to say more, perhaps pull her aside to chat, but before he had a chance Bryn was there guiding him away.

"Walk with me," he commanded, his tone brooking no argument. Either

Bryn would find out what Enfys had planned or he'd set Enfys on fire for threatening him while Fi was missing. I was reasonably okay with either option.

"The attention is getting a little much," Fi mumbled, looking between Arthus, Eamon and I. She'd been distracted by Briallen and Aderyn, but the stares and whispers directed her way had been incessant from the moment we arrived.

"I agree," Arthus said, rolling his shoulders in the way that indicated he was trying to keep his wings contained. "Let's get out of here."

We said our goodbyes to Aderyn and Lachlan before quietly slipping into the treeline and walking through the undergrowth for a while until we got back to the main path. I wasn't optimistic that Fi's newfound fame was going anywhere so if we couldn't outlast it; we would have to figure out a better way to live with it.

FFION

CHAPTER 58

I woke up feeling a little hungover and a lot unexcited about the prospect of a full day of classes. I used to love my magic classes, but based on the amount of attention directed my way at last night's bonfire, my anonymity had long since disappeared and the enjoyment of my classes along with it.

And that was without them knowing the gods had made me some kind of champion for the fae.

I couldn't imagine that was going to *improve* my situation.

I groaned loudly as I rolled over onto my stomach, yanking my pillow over my head. I had about thirty seconds of peace before Arthus' hand wrapped around my ankle, tugging me down the mattress. I yelped, attempting to land a kick on him with my free foot, but he quickly flipped me onto my back and pinned my wrists and ankles with his air magic.

He was being more gentle than usual, the magic would have been easy enough for me to break through, and I appreciated him for it. Even though I was feeling good about it, it was bright in here and I could see Arthus, which helped.

In fact, it was all kinds of sexy, but I didn't think that was the direction he was going. This time, anyway.

"It'll be fine, sweetheart."

"You absolutely do not know that," I argued, throwing my head back against the mattress and staring up at the ceiling as Arthus released me.

"Between Marlen and me, you won't ever be alone between classes. Aderyn will stick to your side like glue during class," Arthus stated, laying out the facts in a way that usually calmed me down.

"My first class is potions, I don't have any friends in that class," I countered. Aderyn was in all my first-year classes but potions was a second-year course, so I was on my own.

I felt a brief flash of Arthus' panic and immediately regretted my complaining. It went against all of his instincts to let me out of his sight—he'd probably been trying to reassure himself all morning, and I'd just made his panic worse.

"Ignore me, it probably will be fine. I doubt anything terrible will happen to me in class," I backpedaled, shuffling back on the bed so I could move around him and head into the attached bathroom for a shower.

Arthus snorted, unconvinced. "I appreciate your effort, sweetheart. I'll put on some tea for you," he called over his shoulder, striding out of the bedroom.

I cranked up the shower, grateful for the hot water Eamon had in his cabin, and rested my forehead against the cool tiles.

What's happening to me? I'd been alone my whole life. I'd grown up in foster care, never settling in one place because I either creeped families out with my strange sense of intuition, or the constant migraines I got from sensory overload made me too difficult to look after.

When did I get so dependent on other people? I'd gotten so complacent about having the guys around that going to class by myself was freaking me out.

That was entirely unacceptable. I rolled my shoulders back and submerged myself under the shower water, trying to wash my insecurities away. *Find your lady balls, Fi. You can do this!*

My bravado had entirely worn off by the time we reached campus and I entered the airy stone potions classroom with a sense of impending doom, hoping that Arthus and Marlen weren't monitoring the bond, even though

I knew they totally were.

I took my usual seat at the center stool of the bench at the back of the classroom, doing my best to ignore the mixture of curiosity, suspicion and awe my classmates were feeling. It was like a thick tar coating my insides, and while it would have been a lot more pleasant to mute my ability, I needed it as a warning system. If anyone's intentions were malicious, my gift would tell me.

Gods, I'd become so dependent on the guys watching my back that I'd actually forgotten how uncomfortable a large rush of emotions could be.

I gritted my teeth against the discomfort and waited until everyone else had collected the poison antidotes we had all been working on from the storage cupboard before going to get the one that had been assigned to me. Master Cadha had given me a spare base potion that she'd already started, but it still put me a couple of weeks behind the rest of the class after my extended *absence*.

I returned to my station to find a resolved Saffir and a resentful Corsen setting their things up on either side of me.

Great.

"Hello," I said awkwardly, setting the heavy cauldron down on the bench in front of me with a thunk.

"Good morning, Ffion," Saffir replied, almost cheerfully. Her demeanor was as cool as her icy blonde hair, but her emotions felt warm and pleasant.

"Hi," Corsen grunted, giving me a dirty look. She'd been involved with Marlen before I arrived at the Academy, and I still had some residual weird feelings about it, much to my annoyance. Between losing Marlen and Arthus scolding her new man for messing with me, I definitely wasn't Corsen's favorite fae either.

Corsen's emotions were resentful—she was clearly only sitting here at Saffir's behest—but I didn't pick up any ill will necessarily. We weren't going to braid each other's hair any time soon, but she didn't want to harm me either.

"How's your poison antidote coming along?" Saffir asked conversationally, as if we sat together in class every day. "Mine looks more dove gray than slate gray, I think," she added, peering into her cauldron.

"Ah, I missed a lot of class, so I'm starting mine from scratch," I muttered quietly, not wanting to draw attention to it. Saffir's overwhelming wave of guilt was suffocating.

"Not your fault, Saffir," I murmured, leaning towards her under the guise of reaching for my ingredients so Corsen wouldn't hear. Saffir shot me a disbelieving look out of the corner of her eye, but said nothing.

I sighed quietly as Saffir and Corsen started grating ginseng root into their cauldrons. My potion wasn't anywhere near that stage and as tempted as I was to rush to catch up, I'd probably just screw up the measurements and have to start over anyway. Again.

At least I'm here now. I'm back at the Academy. I'm safe and healthy. I repeated everything positive about my life in my head like a mantra, using it to keep myself calm in an emotionally turbulent room.

"Try this knife," Corsen muttered, sliding her knife across the bench to me. I'd been trying to finely slice my valerian root, but the dull blade was butchering it.

"Thanks," I replied quietly, her knife sliding through the root like it was butter. Immediately, my mood improved. It was hardly a grand gesture of friendship, but in a room full of people that seemed to either fear or suspect me of influencing their emotions, I'd take what I could get.

Honestly, it's not like I'd be sitting here, marinating in their mistrust if I was manipulating their emotions. Morons.

Halfway through the lesson, we set aside our antidote potions to brew and started on a simple poultice for bruising and swelling instead. My spirits lifted considerably now that we were all working on the same thing, and most of my classmates were too focused on getting it right to pay any attention to me.

"I told my father Bryn is pursuing you now," Saffir whispered, leaning across the bench under the guise of inspecting my ingredients.

"What? *How?* That's not true," I hissed back. Fae couldn't lie.

"Yes it is," Saffir replied with an eye roll. "He's always at your side when you're on campus, and he watches you even more obviously than he did before. Plus, he looked like he'd cook anyone who tried to speak to you last night."

Huh. Maybe that was Bryn's version of pursuing me. He wasn't exactly good with his words.

"Why'd you tell your father that?" I asked quietly, shuffling my stool closer to Saffir and ignoring Corsen's dirty look.

"I have to be careful what I say. I want to help you, but he can't catch on. So I told him Bryn was pursuing you and that I'd "keep an eye" on you. He assumed I was still mad about Bryn and that I would be on his side."

"And you're not?" I challenged, narrowing my eyes as I assessed her. I'd felt Saffir's genuine horror and distress when she'd found me imprisoned at her parents' place, as well as her guilt and remorse every time I'd seen her since. That didn't necessarily cancel out her loyalty to her parents though.

"Stay behind after class," she breathed, shooting a nervous look at Corsen out of the corner of her eye. I nodded subtly. Corsen was making a show of dragging her stool closer to where Saffir and I were huddled, obviously fed up with our rudeness. Fair enough, really. We were being a little impolite.

I was so impatient for the lesson to end to figure out what Saffir had in mind that I definitely chopped my plantain leaves too roughly and the horse chestnut seed extract was a write-off, but Saffir's offer of help had me all kinds of distracted.

If Saffir was willing to go against her family because they were in the wrong, wasn't that a demonstration of the fae deserving magic? Maybe I could fulfill the gods' remit without some huge gesture. Maybe I could just convince individuals to step in when they saw wrongdoing, and that would be enough?

I could already imagine Arthus' judgy eye roll if I suggested that plan to him.

After Master Cadha dismissed us all, I packed up my equipment as slowly as physically possible and pretended not to eavesdrop as Saffir made her excuses and promised to meet up with Corsen later.

Master Cadha locked all the potions and ingredients away in the long cupboards along the wall and gave us a funny look as we hung around the bench but didn't say anything as she left us to it. The classrooms were always unlocked for tutoring sessions throughout the day anyway.

"What did you want to talk about?" I asked quietly as soon as we were alone. Marlen was going to meet me outside, and if I didn't head out soon, I was sure he would barge in.

"I don't want my parents to do to someone else what they did to you," Saffir said, pushing her shoulders back and looking me in the eye. "I could help you expose them somehow. They're Councilors, they should be made an example of."

"Are you sure about this?" I asked carefully. "I mean, I totally agree, but they're your parents."

"My older siblings both have gifted magic. I don't and it's always made my relationship with my parents... strained. I *do* love them, but that's all the more reason to do this, isn't it?"

"Is it?"

"Of course. Fae who steal magic and imbue crystals are only ever one step away from drinking it directly from the vein and going dark. There's no coming back from that," Saffir said forlornly, shaking her head. Her pain was genuine, and I struggled under the weight of it.

"Make a deal with me," I sighed, hoping I wasn't leaping headfirst into a huge mistake. "Swear that you'll help me see your parents punished for kidnapping and torturing me, and that you'll never double cross me."

I held out my hand and Saffir took it without a second's hesitation, to my great surprise.

"I swear it."

I hadn't made a deal with a fae since I'd arrived in Avalon and made Gwyneira promise that I could leave the Academy if I wanted to, but I'd never forget the strange sensation that felt like a gong being struck in my chest once a deal was made though. *So weird.*

I didn't feel as triumphant as I thought I would, having gotten Saffir to agree to work against her parents. At best, I felt a grim sense of satisfaction. Mostly I felt sorry for her. Revenge wouldn't be sweet for Saffir.

By the time we arrived back at the cabin, Eamon had already finished up his administrative tasks for the day for the properties he managed, and was rolling out the pasta dough he had made for our dinner.

Handmade. Pasta.

I was going to claim this fae so hard he wouldn't know what hit him.

Marlen and Arthus had discreetly disappeared to other parts of the cabin, both with convenient excuses for leaving Eamon and I alone. They knew how much I missed him after being on campus all day.

"So," I began casually, in a surprisingly optimistic mood after my conversation with Saffir. "Did you have a specific place in mind for our claiming ceremony?"

Eamon's hands stilled on the rolling pin as he looked across the kitchen island at me, eyebrows lost somewhere in his hairline.

"It's just that when I was recovering here after the whole imprisonment debacle, you said you wanted me *today, forever, and every moment in between.* I kind of thought a claiming ceremony was where this was headed."

I could sense his excitement, but I kept my face impassive. Eamon worshiped me like a goddess, and I sometimes wondered if his indulgence brought out the worst in me. His adoration made me kind of bratty.

Luckily, I had my other mates for balance.

"Of course that's what I want, cariad," Eamon said softly, looking at me like I was a gift sent from the heavens especially for him.

"Well then, let's do it. Where did you have in mind?"

"There's a spot by the stream on the Old Adair Estate, under an enormous oak tree. It's a place I've always found peaceful, I'd like to share it with you," he said hesitantly. "It's probably not as impressive as the places Arthus and Marlen chose—"

"I don't care about that," I interjected. "If it's special to you, then it's special to me. It sounds perfect."

"Okay then," he replied with a soft smile.

"Next time we're at the Estate, then?" I asked hopefully. Honestly, I'd do it sooner, but I'd missed over a month of classes already and I couldn't afford to miss any more. I didn't *want* to miss any more. I hated being behind.

"I'm looking forward to it, cariad."

"Me too. Now teach me how to make pasta," I demanded, standing on tiptoes to kiss him on the cheek, his beard tickling my skin.

"What's going on, sweetheart?" Arthus asked as he strode into the kitchen with Marlen trailing curiously behind him. "I was checking on you through the bond."

"At least you don't try to hide your snooping," I teased. "Eamon and I were just discussing the details of our claiming ceremony."

"Is that so?" Arthus murmured, looking between the two of us with one eyebrow raised.

"Next trip to the Old Adair Estate, it's happening," I said decisively. Marlen beamed with just as much excitement as I was feeling.

"Good," Arthus pronounced.

"Good," I agreed. "Now, roll up your sleeves you two. We're having a family pasta-making night."

Arthus did not roll up his sleeves on command to help us make pasta—*spoilsport*—but he did clean up the kitchen after dinner while Eamon, Marlen and I curled up in the living room in front of the fire playing cards.

"He's on guard duty tonight," Marlen said casually as my eyes flitted to the front door for the millionth time.

"Who?" I asked unconvincingly, clearing my throat.

Marlen snorted at my attempt to play coy. "A certain moody fire fae, who else?"

I rolled my eyes affectionately, even though he was totally right. Since

Bryn had stayed over a couple of nights ago, I kept expecting him to come back. It made me uneasy that he hadn't.

Did his time with the rest of us make him realize this wasn't what he wanted? He'd been pursuing Saffir who didn't have gifted magic that needed lots of mates to balance—she would only end up with two. For all I knew, that might have been *why* he was pursuing her. I doubted a five-way relationship was for everyone...

"You two really need to talk this thing out, foxglove," Marlen said quietly, giving me a searching look. "You both take a step forward, avoid talking about what it means, then take two steps back again."

I gave Marlen an appraising look because while he was basically dead on, I hadn't expected that assessment to come from him—Eamon was the quiet observer of all of us. Marlen had spent the most time with Bryn out of all the guys though, since Briallen was Bryn's cousin and Briallen's mate was Marlen's best friend.

"You're right," I sighed, collecting up the cards to reshuffle them.

Arthus entered the room at that moment with a tray of chamomile tea, distracting me from my confusing thoughts of Bryn.

"Oh, I made a deal with Saffir today," I announced.

"What? Why?" Eamon looked at me like I'd lost my mind, which didn't bode well since he was the most empathetic of the three of them.

"She swore to help me see her parents pay for what they did, and promised she'd never double cross me." I shrugged. *Still seems like a good deal to me.* "What happens if she does?"

"You mean if she breaks the deal?" Marlen clarified, and I nodded.

"It's believed that the gods curse you with misfortune," Eamon said slowly. "It's hard to say whether that really is the case or not, but fae who break deals do seem to experience an inordinate amount of bad luck until they prove themselves trustworthy again."

"Even the fae who believe the gods are dead don't make deals they can't honor," Marlen added. "No one wants to risk it. I'm more intrigued that you wanted to make the deal in the first place, though. Does this mean the denial stage is coming to an end?"

"My thirst for vengeance is entirely separate from whatever-the-fuck the gods think they have planned for me," I sniffed because no, the denial stage was absolutely not at an end.

"Sweetheart," Arthus broached gently, like I was a wild animal about to bolt. "I think it might be time to tell Gwyneira about what the gods said. I know you're trying to pretend this isn't happening, but Gwyneira might have some useful insight or at least an idea of where to begin."

"I'm really not in a rush to do anything about the message, but I suppose getting Gwyneira's opinion couldn't hurt," I agreed reluctantly. "At least I had one last day of normalcy," I added wistfully.

"Finish your tea and I'll run you a bath," Marlen suggested. "Don't think about it tonight, we'll go see Gwyneira in the morning."

FFION

CHAPTER 59

I woke up with my face buried in the crook of Eamon's neck, and Marlen plastered to my back, listening to Arthus' soft breathing on Marlen's other side. This was usually my happy place, but there was a heavy knot of dread sitting in my gut.

Telling Gwyneira about the message made it real. She'd want to talk about it. Maybe make plans. *Act* on it.

Gods, I really didn't want to do this.

I snuck out of bed before the guys woke up, grabbing a blanket from the sofa before letting myself outside. Sliding down against the wall of the cabin and covering my legs with the blanket, I watched as the first rays of sun began to slowly filter through the trees, enjoying my last moments of peace before I started getting pushed around like a chess piece on a playing board I didn't fully understand.

Eventually, Eamon joined me, handing me a cup of steaming hot peppermint tea.

"I'll come with you today to campus, cariad. I want to be there when you talk to Gwyneira," he said, sitting down next to me.

"I'd like that."

"Do you want to ask Bryn to come too?" Eamon asked, giving me a searching look.

Why couldn't the gods give me an instruction manual on Bryn?

I hummed under my breath. "It seems like he should be there, since he already knows what's going on."

"And you want him there," Eamon guessed.

"And I want him there," I agreed, clutching my tea close to my face and letting the steam warm my skin. "What do you think Gwyneira will want me to do?"

Eamon looked out at the forest thoughtfully. "She has always been one of the more devout fae. So many others have given up on the gods as magic began to disappear, but Gwyneira's faith has never wavered."

Great.

"So she's not going to just let this go is what you're saying."

"I imagine she'll push you to act. Perhaps make a public statement of some kind," Eamon hedged.

"Not happening," I countered instantly. "I have no interest in becoming some kind of figurehead, and if that's her idea she can shove it. If I'm going to take up this mantle, it'll be a stealth mission."

"That's a nice idea," Eamon said absently, clearly not believing it was possible, but not wanting to upset me by pointing that out.

"Okay, I'm going to find my most badass outfit and do my hair."

"Why?" Eamon asked, baffled.

"It's my armor," I replied with a shrug. I wanted to look and feel like I was in control of my destiny, not like I was a conduit for the gods' plans. Which was exactly how I felt.

I eventually settled on a long-sleeved fitted indigo dress that fell to my knees and pulled my mass of curly hair up into a high bun, secured with a matching ribbon. It wasn't leather and thigh-high boots, but it was probably the fae version of a power suit.

I skipped breakfast, eager to get this over and done with. Eamon waited on the outskirts of the campus, near the path to Gwyneira's forest—so we didn't draw attention to ourselves walking through the students as a big group—while Arthus and Marlen escorted me to Bryn's cabin.

This was a good idea, right?

Right.

I knocked nervously, never really sure how he was going to receive me. I sensed the moment he felt the mating pull, followed by surprise, then a rush of muted happiness. I lived for those flashes of genuine emotion from Bryn that helped me remember he wasn't as indifferent as he liked to appear.

"Scout," he greeted me, pulling open the door and leaning against the door jamb. He was only wearing a loose pair of drawstring sleep pants and I forced myself to maintain eye contact instead of creeping a view of his chest like a perv.

I mean, a two second scan was probably socially acceptable.

Gods, he'd been hiding some sleek muscles under those loose shirts he wore.

Focus, Fi!

"Er, we were just on our way to see Gwyneira and tell her about, you know," I mumbled, feeling flustered and not wanting our conversation to be overheard. "Do you want to come with us?"

I felt his flicker of surprise at being asked before he quickly smothered it with forced apathy. "Sure, give me a minute."

He retreated into his cabin and emerged fully dressed a couple of minutes later, much to my disappointment. Marlen shoved a forceful pulse of amusement through our bond, and I cut him a glare as we made our way to the path where Eamon was waiting for us. He and Bryn greeted each other cordially, and Bryn seemed fine with Marlen and Arthus, so maybe my fear that my large mating circle would put him off was unfounded after all.

We didn't talk much on the way to Gwyneira's cabin. All four guys were too busy watching me like I was a flight risk.

I blew out a long breath as we stood on Gwyneira's stoop while Arthus knocked loudly on the cabin door. Her mate, Cadfan, answered a few minutes later with Gwyneira standing close behind him.

"Ffion? Is everything okay?" she asked, frowning at me.

"For the most part. We got a bit more clarity around what the gods are expecting of me. We thought you'd like to know."

"Of course! Come in, come in."

Gwyneira ushered us through to the sitting room, her excitement buzzing over my skin. She wasn't reading the room very well—the five of us were all in varying states of melancholy.

"What did the gods say? Did they send a message through you?" she asked, directing the second question at Eamon, who nodded grimly.

"They said... the gods want me to be the fae's Keeper of Balance, and restore the balance between light and dark. And, um, bring those in hiding back home. And to show that the fae are worthy of the gifts," I recited tiredly. It sounded like *so* much when I listed it all at once.

I just wanted to go to magic school and do fun harem stuff.

"The gods have chosen you to show that the fae are worthy of magic?" Gwyneira confirmed with an indecipherable look on her face.

I'd muted my abilities unconsciously, but I turned them on to scan Gwyneira's emotions. There was a determination for me to succeed in my mission, but there was an edge to it... a ruthlessness I never expected from her. It was discomfiting, and my nerves immediately put Marlen and Arthus on edge.

Gwyneira's gaze cut to Bryn. "Are you and Ffion courting?"

Bryn's split second of hesitation before he answered felt like an hour of silence. Why was she putting him on the spot like this?

"No."

The word hung awkwardly in the air, and I didn't know why it was so painful to hear. We *weren't* courting. We'd never discussed that kind of commitment.

Gwyneira hummed under her breath, giving Bryn an unreadable look before her gaze shifted to me. "Ffion and Marlen Laisren, you are hereby expelled from the Academy of Avalon. Arthus Laisren, you are hereby fired from your position at the Academy of Avalon. The three of you have one hour to collect your belongings and leave the premises."

There was a couple of seconds of stunned silence before Arthus rumbled out a dangerously low, "*What?*"

"There is nothing more important than this task. You cannot afford any distractions," Gwyneira clipped, already wringing her hands impatiently like we were taking too long to leave.

"Isn't that my decision?" I gritted out, muting my abilities again as the combined force of all four guys' fury coursed through me painfully.

"The gods have made this decision for you," Gwyneira replied with a censuring look. "Are you so arrogant as to think you know better?"

Arrogant?

With that I jumped to my feet, outrage making me bolder than usual. "The gods haven't tasked me with saving the fae from some villainous enemy. They've tasked me with saving them from *themselves*. The arrogance of the *fae* is what got them into this situation."

Marlen and Eamon stood on either side of me, reaching for me at the same time to calm me down. Marlen threaded his fingers through mine, while Eamon rested a heavy hand on my nape.

"Have you been sanctified, Master Gwyneira?" Arthus asked coolly, his tone scarily detached. "Have the gods ever communicated with you directly?"

"No," she replied, eyes narrowed on Arthus.

"And yet you presume to know more about their plans for Fi than the Keeper of Balance herself? It isn't Fi who suffers from an overabundance of arrogance."

Shots fired.

So smoothly it must have looked choreographed, the five of us turned and left, briskly walking down the forest path toward the campus in silent agreement not to discuss anything until we'd put some distance between us and Gwyneira.

Arrogant. Expelled. The two words kept floating around my head on repeat. Who knew that with my empath abilities, I could read someone so wrong?

Marlen and Eamon kept their strong comforting holds on me while Arthus stormed ahead and Bryn watched our backs.

Arthus stopped abruptly when we were a few feet from the campus and turned to face us, his expression grim. "Are you okay, sweetheart?"

He knew I wasn't, but he was trying to comfort me in his own awkward way.

"Not even a little. What do we do now?"

"Head back to the house for now," Eamon suggested, his brow creased with worry. "Pack what we need and head to the Old Adair Estate. It's more secure."

Arthus grunted in agreement while Marlen gave my hand a quick squeeze. I looked over my shoulder to find a stony-faced Bryn staring into the distance. His emotions were a volatile cocktail of rage and despair, but I was too emotionally spent to offer him any words of comfort.

I could give him a hug though.

Breaking away from Marlen and Eamon, I closed the distance between Bryn and I. Before he had a chance to say something irritating as a defense mechanism, I slid my arms around his waist and rested my head against his chest.

He hadn't asked to be put in this position any more than I had.

Bryn always felt so warm, like his fire magic was ready and raring to go. He blew out a long breath before wrapping his arms around my shoulders and leaning his head against mine.

I felt the barest hint of something sweet, potent, and undefinable before Bryn pulled away, erecting his metaphorical wall of anger again, and I felt the loss instantly—both the physical contact and the raw emotional connection.

"I'll be seeing you, scout," he murmured, leaning forward to brush his lips against my temple. With a curt nod to the guys, he continued past us down the path to campus.

"Well, I guess that answers my next question," I said with a weak laugh to cover up my disappointment.

Arthus snorted. "I doubt he meant that in a figurative sense, sweetheart, don't worry about it. Come on, let's say goodbye to your friends."

We headed straight for Leigh and Briallen's cabin since it was early enough that they probably hadn't left for breakfast yet, and Marlen agreed to meet us there after he'd tracked down Aderyn. Eamon linked his arm through mine as we followed Arthus through the campus and I was glad for his support, because I felt like I was wading through molasses.

In all the scenarios I'd run through in my head, I'd never imagined Gwyneira kicking us off campus. How was I supposed to tackle this absurd mission I'd been given when I barely even knew how to use my magic? If anyone needed to be at the Academy right now, it was me.

Gwyneira was old as dirt and theoretically wise, but I couldn't help feeling like she'd made the wrong call here.

Arthus rapped his knuckles impatiently on Leigh and Briallen's door, clearly eager to get me off campus now that he knew we weren't welcome here. Leigh answered, looking disheveled and half-asleep just as Marlen and Aderyn joined us at the door.

"Gods, what are you lot doing here so early?" Leigh asked, eyes widening as he took us all in.

"Let us in, would you?" Marlen called from the back of the group. "We need to talk and we haven't got much time."

Leigh stepped back to let us in just as Briallen emerged from the bathroom tying her robe into place.

"Should I put the kettle on?" she asked hesitantly, looking around at all of us.

"No time," Arthus responded grimly before giving me a pointed look to get talking.

"We're leaving, Gwyneira just kicked us out of the Academy."

"What?!" Briallen shrieked. "Why? You haven't done anything wrong!"

"What's going on?" Leigh asked, looking at Marlen.

"No, we haven't done anything wrong," I assured Briallen, appreciating that she'd immediately jumped to our defense. "Gwyneira would just prefer I focus on my mission from the gods than my education," I said diplomatically, impressing myself given how salty I was feeling about the whole thing. Briallen had a bit of a temper and I didn't want her doing anything stupid in the name of avenging our honor or something.

"And what mission is that?" Leigh asked curiously, but with a heavy side of 'I'm not really sure I want to know'.

"Redeem the fae, restore the balance of light and dark magic, etc," I said, waving my hand absently. We didn't really have the time to get into it right now, and I wasn't that jazzed about discussing it again.

"Right," Briallen said, looking dazed. "That's... something."

"Aderyn?" I asked, turning towards Marlen's twin. She'd been silent this whole time, but nervous energy was pouring off her in waves and I didn't need my ability to sense that.

"I was going to find the perfect time to tell you, but seeing as you're leaving..." she sighed, shooting her brother an anxious glance.

"You're going to claim Lachlan?" I guessed. Aderyn's cheeks flushed, and I tried to suppress my grin. A grin that grew wider when Marlen made a weird rumbly sound in his chest behind me.

"Be happy for me," Aderyn ordered, glaring at her brother. "I have never been anything but happy for you and Fi."

I pulled the watery bond in my chest toward me and got a sense of Marlen's internal struggle—his desire to protect her clashed with his relief at her finding happiness. Plus, he'd only recently got his sister back in his life after they'd been separated when he came to the Academy, and he worried he was losing her all over again.

I gave Aderyn a reassuring smile. "He's happy for you, really. He's just going to miss you. Trust me, I can tell." I winked at her and tapped lightly on my chest where I could feel the mating bond.

"I can't wait for that," Aderyn said with an envious sigh.

"You'll have it soon by the sounds of it," Marlen groused.

"A good thing too," I added, reaching for Aderyn and pulling her into a hug. She wasn't the most touchy feely person, but she responded instantly, wrapping her arms around my waist and giving me a squeeze.

"My turn," Briallen announced, tugging at my elbow. I laughed as I let her pull me into a hug too. "I'm going to miss you, Fi. Promise you'll keep in touch," she whispered.

"I promise," I assured her. "Promise you won't do anything stupid."

Leigh laughed as he pulled me into a one-armed hug. "She won't agree to that, Fi, and you know it. Take care of my boy here," he added, reaching across to ruffle Marlen's hair good-naturedly.

"I always do," I replied primly.

"Come on, sweetheart. We need to get off the Academy grounds before Gwyneira has us escorted off like criminals," Arthus grumbled from near the door where he was waiting impatiently, arms crossed.

"We'll see you soon. Somehow," I said with a little wave, letting Marlen link his fingers through mine and tug me towards the door.

My heart was heavy as we made our way through the campus for the last time. This was the first place that had truly felt like home to me, and I was being forced to give it up to pursue some heaven-sent mission I didn't want.

Why me? I asked the gods silently. *What did I do to make you saddle me with this task?*

ARTHUS

CHAPTER 60

The four of us walked back through the forest to Eamon's cabin in silence, each lost in our own thoughts. Each trying to process what had just happened.

Kicked out.

I'd spent four years at the Academy as a student—the top air affinity student, no less—and the pride I'd felt at being asked to stay on as a teaching assistant had only been surpassed by the pride I felt when Fi claimed me as her mate. The Academy had represented freedom to me—a chance to get away from my parents and their suffocating insistence that every difficulty I'd ever faced was a gift from the gods in disguise. Attending the Academy had been the opportunity to set my own course in life.

Gwyneira had snatched it all away with a few words and a shrug of her shoulders.

My rage felt like a slow-moving hurricane whirling through my veins. I hoped Fi was muting her abilities because my emotions were a wreck and would undoubtedly cause her great discomfort, and I couldn't even calm down enough to reach for our bond to check. She was walking arm-in-arm with Marlen just ahead of me and I knew he'd be soothing her. He and Eamon were her go-to's when she needed comfort. My job was to keep us all safe and on course, even though I no longer knew what that course was.

I wasn't just enraged that we'd been unceremoniously booted from the Academy, though that had hurt my pride. The realization that Gwyneira's interest in Fi had always been a cover for her ulterior motives is what had me truly furious. Maybe she had been genuinely interested in helping Fi manage her empath gift in the very beginning, but as soon as Gwyneira suspected the gods were interested in Fi, that's what drove her actions.

How had I not seen that earlier? I'd made myself Fi's self-appointed guardian when I first became her suitor, yet I had failed her time and time again. If I wasn't already mated to her, I'd consider leaving so she could find someone better. Someone actually able to keep her safe.

No, I wouldn't. I was too selfish to let her go.

Once we arrived back at the cabin, Eamon threw himself into action, filling up two trunks with books, clothes, and any food we could transport.

"I'll fly to Inver and get us a couple of carriages," I grunted, still struggling to keep my emotions in check. The short flight there and the hour-long carriage ride back would help me burn off some steam.

Fucking Gwyneira. Our abrupt expulsion meant we didn't even have access to the school griffins to fly us to Northgales. It would be at least a full day of travel by carriage ride, and we'd need to stop somewhere overnight.

"Is it safe for you to go alone? Won't someone see your wings?" Fi asked nervously, chewing on her bottom lip. My anger dissipated almost instantly, replaced by the need to reassure her. I stepped in close so I could run my fingers down the side of her face, her skin was as soft as petals and cool to touch from the wind.

"I'll be careful, sweetheart. I'll land in the tree canopy and retract my wings before climbing down. I've done it plenty of times," I assured her.

"How long will you be?"

"I'll return with the carriages—so no more than a couple of hours—then we can leave for Northgales. It's a long trip by carriage ride, so dress comfortably and don't forget your glamour," I warned her. I leaned down and brushed a light kiss against her lips and clapped Marlen's shoulder on my way out.

Once I was on the top of the steps, I pulled off my shirt and tied it around my waist so I could let my wings out. They rustled impatiently behind me, eager to get into the sky and feel the rush of the wind beneath them. It truly felt like they had a mind of their own sometimes, especially when my emotions were high. I embraced the sensation and took to the air with a jump, hoping I could leave my vengeful thoughts on the ground.

What now?

I hated feeling like things were out of my control, and right now every plan I had was falling apart. Fi had only had access to magic for five months, she *needed* the Academy. How was she supposed to carry out this quest from the gods if she couldn't effectively use her magic? Expelling her was absurd.

I growled at my own defeatist attitude. Fi didn't need the Academy, she had us. I had been tutoring her with her air affinity, I would merely increase our tutoring sessions and set a stricter curriculum for her. Marlen and Eamon could help her learn about water and earth elemental magic, respectively. Eamon was good with potions as well. He could help Fi prepare some offensive and defensive ones that hopefully she'd never need to use.

Once Fi and Bryn got their shit together, he could tutor her in fire elemental magic, combat, and even how to fly a griffin on her own.

I wasn't about to be grateful to Gwyneira for taking the decision out of our hands, but we could choose to see this as an opportunity for Fi's education, rather than a catastrophic setback.

No more sulking, I promised myself as I landed in the tree canopy in a quiet part of the forest. I'd visited Inver hundreds of times while I'd attended the Academy and never had a problem getting in and out without my wings being seen.

I pulled my shirt on and crept along the branches, moving from tree to tree until I was confident that there was no one around, then dropped to the forest floor to walk the rest of the way to the walled town. The carriages for hire were all lined up outside the walls, and I doubted it would take long to find a couple who were willing to travel a couple of days to Northgales.

Coin was coin, after all.

I slipped easily into the crowd, branching off as we approached the city gate to wander along the row of carriages.

"...*an empath they've been saying, at the Academy of Avalon.*"

"...*only an hour from Inver? An empath? I thought they were extinct...*"

I rolled my shoulders and cracked my neck, desperately trying to keep my fear and agitation in check so my wings wouldn't snap out again. There was never any doubt that news of Fi's existence would spread after Glendower announced her presence to the elite at the Council ball. The fact that it had become gossip for the commoners who frequented Inver was slightly more alarming, though. This wasn't the sort of place that fancy Councilors and their ilk frequented.

I shouldn't have been surprised, really. Fi was the first empath in centuries. Of course that's all anyone in the realm would want to talk about.

I approached two carriage drivers who were chatting among themselves, leaning against their respective carriages. They seemed to be well acquainted, which would make for a more pleasant trip for all of us. If they were talking to each other, they'd hopefully leave us alone.

They both straightened as I approached, and I inclined my head in greeting. "I'm looking for two carriages for a trip to Northgales, one to carry four people, one to carry luggage. I'll pay extra for your discretion," I added.

"How much extra?" the short, balding one asked, stepping forward. His lack of hair emphasized the pointed tips of his ears, and I idly thought that Fi would get a kick out of that. It had been months since she arrived in Avalon, and her fascination with fae ears still hadn't worn off.

"If you'd be willing to strike a deal, I'll double it."

Their eyes glimmered excitedly, and I could admit that life was much easier with the Adair fortune at our disposal.

"Would we be doing anything illegal?" the wiry one with graying black hair asked. He didn't sound entirely averse to the idea either way.

"Nothing illegal," I assured them.

They exchanged a look, then the bald one shrugged. "I could use the coin, and it's been many moons since my last trip to Northgales. May as well. You'll pay for our bed and supper tonight, though."

"Fine. Let's go pick up the other passengers, we'll strike the deal once we're away from the town."

I gave them directions to get back to Eamon's cabin and climbed into the back of one of the carriages. It wasn't a lot, but I felt like I'd regained some level of control after Gwyneira had thrown our plans completely off course.

Fi, Eamon and Marlen were waiting on the porch with the trunks when I arrived back with the drivers. I'd made them pull over halfway along the forest path to the cabin to strike a deal for their silence, so we were all ready to get on the road.

Fi had glamoured her hair and eyes black and had clearly made an attempt at straightening out her distinctive curls. It wasn't much of a disguise—and without a cloaking amulet to cover her magical signature she'd be pretty exposed on the open road, which didn't sit well with me—but our options were limited. Hopefully the fact that as far as anyone knew, we were still at the Academy would work in our favor.

The drivers loaded the trunks into one carriage, and we all piled into the other. Fi opted to share a bench with Eamon since he took up the most room and she took up the least, and if she was cramped, she didn't seem to mind. She draped her legs over Eamon's lap and he ran his enormous hands up and down her calves, his adoring smiles occasionally slipping into worried frowns when Fi wasn't looking.

"Get comfortable," I sighed. "It's eight hours to Vinovia where we'll stop for the night, and the horses will need breaks on the way."

"I am comfortable," Fi replied cheerfully, snuggling closer into Eamon. I didn't need to check the bond to know the cheerfulness was forced, but if Fi wanted to pretend she was fine with how today went, I wasn't going to push her.

Not yet, anyway.

Around an hour into the journey, Fi drifted off, her head resting against Eamon's shoulder, and it was dark out by the time we reached the small tavern in Vinovia where we'd be spending the night, and we were all sick of the sight of each other. I was less sick of the sight of Fi than I was of Marlen and Eamon, but we all needed a little breathing room after hours cooped up in a tiny carriage together.

Eamon approached the manager to organize a room for us and one for the drivers while I ordered food for everyone. Marlen and Fi wandered around the tavern, stretching their legs and taking in the paintings and knickknacks that had probably been hanging on the walls for centuries.

I remembered suddenly how little Fi had seen of Avalon. This was her first trip to a regular, small town tavern. Inver was mostly home to goblins, but Vinovia was a fae town, and this was Fi's first real introduction to *regular* fae, not the exceptional crowd at the Academy.

Eventually we all converged at a corner booth and a server brought us bowls of thick vegetable stew and fresh bread. Our drivers sat close by, tucking into their own dinner, keeping to themselves.

Marlen groaned as he ate his first mouthful of stew, and the look of sheer bliss on his face broke the tension among us. It had been a long day, and food helped.

"So we're staying here tonight," Fi began, ripping apart a chunk of bread to dip in her stew. "How long will it take to get to the Estate tomorrow?"

"We'll be traveling the entire day," Eamon replied with a grimace. He looked admirably comfortable for a wealthy fae who probably hadn't spent a great deal of time in taverns in his youth.

Fi's nose scrunched up in distaste. "Well, I certainly appreciate griffin travel a lot more now."

"Did you see the notices posted around the village by the Council this afternoon?" The low voices of the table next to us carried, and all four of us stiffened slightly in our seats at the mention of the Council.

"Aye. Glendower Castell's announcement that he'd be taking personal responsibility for a little empath at the Academy of Avalon," the second man grunted, sounding distinctly unimpressed. "I didn't think much of him wanting reports if she's seen off campus. Since when were fae not free to travel as they please? Rare gift or not. I feel sorry for the poor lass."

I was listening to the two men's conversation, but my eyes were trained intently on Fi as a silky black ripple ran over her hair. She was nervous and trying to strengthen her glamour, but I gave her a hard look in warning to stop. The last thing we needed was her drawing attention to herself by disguising her appearance in plain sight.

"I thought much the same," the first man replied thoughtfully. "Makes you wonder what they're thinking over there at the Council. What will they do next? Start locking up gifted fae to keep their magic safe?"

"Safe or under their control?" the second man mumbled as his associate frantically shushed him, eyes darting around the room. *Smart man.* That kind of talk could get a fae in trouble should the wrong ears pick it up.

Eamon gave me a thoughtful look across the table, and I knew we were both wondering if there was something here. If these seeds of discord could be sown into something more between the fae and the Council. Fi had buried her face into Marlen's bicep, probably trying to concoct the exact opposite plan. She thought she could fulfill the gods' plans for her while keeping herself hidden away, but I was confident that wasn't possible.

If we pulled this mission off, all of Avalon would know of Ffion Laisren, Sanctified Empath, Keeper of Balance, Redeemer of the Fae.

"I don't feel very hungry anymore," Fi said quietly, pushing her stew around her plate.

"Come on, sweetheart. Let's go up to the room and I'll run you a bath." I stood, reaching my hand out towards her. Marlen gave Fi a sad smile and Eamon nodded his head reassuringly as she stood and slid her hand into mine, looking at the floor so her hair fell in a curtain in front of her face.

I led her through a hallway at the back of the tavern and up a narrow set of wooden stairs to where the rooms were. Our room was designed for mating circles, so the bed took up most of the space, but it'd still be a squeeze. Only powerful fae females had more than two mates, and they didn't usually frequent taverns like this, it wasn't designed for four of us. The furnishings were old and a little dusty, but they'd be fine for the night.

Off the bedroom was a bathroom with a generously sized bathtub taking up most of the room. I left Fi in the bedroom to shake off her glamour and get undressed while I ran the bath as hot as I could.

I intended to be a gentleman and not look when Fi entered the bathroom naked, but she planted herself right in front of me and looked up at me with big doe eyes that I could never say no to.

So much for being in control. It was all an illusion when it came to my mate anyway. I was only as in control as she allowed me to be. Her acquiescence was a gift, not a right.

"Come in with me?" she asked sweetly.

"Are you sure, sweetheart? I ran it for you, I want you to relax."

"I'll relax better if you're in there with me," Fi replied coyly, tugging at my shirt.

Fuck it, I wasn't about to argue with her. I quickly undressed as Fi lowered herself into the tub, and the combination of breathy sighs and low moans she made as she settled in the water immediately went to my cock, the evidence of her effect on me very clear when I removed my pants. Fi gave me a small, cheeky smile as she scooted forward so I could slip in the tub behind her, and I wouldn't have been surprised in the least if she'd put on that show just for me. My little minx. I pulled her back against my chest and wrapped one arm around her waist, the other resting on her upper thigh.

"Thank you," Fi murmured, nestling back against me. It was surprisingly nice—usually she only did this kind of cuddling with Eamon or Marlen. "This is exactly what I needed."

"I can help you relax a little more if you'd like," I suggested in a low voice, my hand drifting from her upper thigh to in-between her legs, running my fingers lightly over her skin. It wasn't my usual style of intimacy, but I found myself relaxing my rules around Fi. I didn't *need* to maintain physical distance with her—she didn't want me for my wings. She wanted me for me.

Fi said nothing, but her legs parted ever so slightly as her head tipped back against my shoulder with a breathy sigh. I pulled the bond in my chest towards me and felt her need for a distraction, for a bit of escapism. All the things she was too shy to ask for out loud, but *needed.*

I could manage that.

Dropping light kisses up and down the side of her neck, I began drawing lazy teasing circles around her clit just the way she liked. Fi tipped her head to the side, giving me better access. I could tell she wanted to squirm, to buck against my hand and take what she wanted, but she inherently knew that I wasn't going to concede that much even though this was meant to be relaxing rather than play. I'd get there when I was ready.

My other hand slid up over her soft stomach to cup her full breast, kneading it and toying with her nipple until I could feel her muscles turn rigid from the effort of keeping her body still.

I rewarded her patience by slipping two fingers inside her, grinding the heel of my palm against her clit and humming in approval at how wet she was. I checked the bond again, using it to pace the precise movements of my fingers that brought her the most pleasure and picking up the pace until Fi was delirious with need, twisting from side-to-side and writhing against me.

"Now, sweetheart," I growled low in her ear, loving the way she completely let go on command. Her nails sunk into my thighs, deep enough to leave marks, and I hurriedly clapped one hand over her mouth as she lost control. I loved the sounds she made as she came, but I didn't want to share them with the entire tavern.

Pulling my fingers free, I wrapped my arms around her, holding her securely against me as she floated back down to reality, stroking her skin soothingly to help her come down rather than winding her back up. Fi leaned back to meet my mouth in a slow, sensual kiss and I felt the gratitude that was pouring from her lips. She really was such a sweetheart. *My* sweetheart.

"Come on, let's wash up and get you in bed. We've got a long day tomorrow."

FFION

CHAPTER 61

I'd never been so happy to stand on solid ground. My butt was numb from the last few hours of sitting in that carriage and as much as I loved Eamon, he was a gigantic fae and took up all the room.

It was late by the time we arrived at the Estate and unloaded the trunks. The Old Adair Estate was an oversized stone cottage, two stories high with three large bedrooms. The living room, dining room and kitchen were all one big open space, with an enormous stone fireplace dominating one wall and low wooden beams running lengthwise across the ceiling. The walls were all exposed brick, and the floors were worn wood. It had belonged to the Adair family for thousands of years and must have seen some incredible things in its time.

Marlen and Arthus dragged the luggage inside while Eamon and I made up the enormous bed in his room. The master bedroom upstairs was reserved for his parents even though they rarely visited this house. They preferred the newer estates—ones that had staff and full-time cooks—to this almost quaint, ancient cottage on the edge of a vineyard. Fortunately, the bed in Eamon's room was still comfortable enough for all of us, especially compared to the tavern bed we'd shared last night.

Despite the late hour, none of us were ready to go to bed. We'd been cooped up all day and had spent a lot of the trip napping since there was nothing else to do in the carriage. Eamon lit the enormous stove in the kitchen to make us all some tea while Marlen and I sprawled out on the white sofa and Arthus sat in the matching armchair, looking as dignified and unruffled as ever.

"So, what's the plan?" Marlen asked cheerfully, as if we hadn't been expelled from school and were now in hiding at Eamon's most secure property until we figured out how to fulfill the gods' mission.

No biggie. Just a regular day in the Life of Fi.

"Any ideas?" I shot back. I was entirely reliant on them for information, I barely knew *anything* about this world in the grand scheme of things. Not for the first time, I wondered how I was possibly the best choice for this 'mission'.

"We could interfere with Glendower Castell's next attempt to keep his Council seat somehow?" Marlen suggested half-heartedly.

"That won't be enough," Arthus disagreed, shaking his head. "Aside from the fact that we know from the ball the Castells aren't the only rotten ones on the Council, it won't fulfill the brief from the gods to restore the balance between dark and light..."

"Or bring the other fae out of hiding," I added grimly. That part was almost the most daunting. Was I supposed to go on some kind of find-the-fae treasure hunt? Where were they hiding? No one had mentioned hiding fae before.

"We need a whole new Council, at the very least," Eamon agreed.

"How do you beat an enemy who has a big stick?" I mused. After a moment, I realized they were all staring at me and enjoyed their confused reactions to my human analogy.

Silence.

"It's a metaphorical stick," I eventually added, taking pity on them. Arthus rolled his eyes, but he was almost smiling.

"Go on, cariad," Eamon said with an indulgent look. I really wished I'd spent less time in Albion reading werewolf smut and more time reading *The Art of War*. Then maybe I could get them to take my battle plans more seriously.

"We need a bigger stick," I told them confidently.

"Right..." Arthus drawled. "Any specific ideas on what that metaphorical stick might be?"

"Obviously." I rolled my eyes. So little faith. Even though I didn't entirely know if what I was talking about was possible, so maybe it was deserved. "The Assembly."

The stunned silence that met me was tinged with admiration, and I was more than a little offended by it.

"The Assembly would be furious to know of the corruption within the Fae Council... The councils are supposed to be the pinnacle of each society," Eamon mused, rubbing his beard.

"And they'd be concerned about the fae representatives within the Assembly itself," Marlen added thoughtfully. "Whether those Assembly members are complicit, how involved they are..."

Arthus was quiet. Probably miffed I'd come up with this badass plan, not him.

"It's more than that." I hesitated. I'd never told them about the foreign presence I could sometimes sense near the cave, sometimes wondering if I'd imagined it entirely.

"What aren't you telling us, Fi?" Arthus asked, looking studiously at me. At least that broke him out of his sulking.

"I wasn't in the best state, mentally, in the cave," I began, uncomfortable with bringing that time up again. Marlen immediately dragged my legs up over his lap, rubbing soothing circles into my skin. "I'd have these moments though, where I swore I could sense someone else's emotions nearby. Someone who was as desolate as me. Someone... not fae."

"Another prisoner?" Arthus clarified. "A non-fae prisoner?"

I nodded my head.

"We need to contact Brently," Eamon blurted out, sitting forward in his chair. "I'll write to him immediately and invite him to the vineyard."

"Who is Brently?" I asked, confused.

"He's an investigator I tried to hire to track you. When I said I wanted him to watch the Castell property, he said he couldn't take the job because he had a conflict of interest."

"As in, he worked for the Castells?" I asked, trying to figure out why Eamon would want to meet with him.

"That was my first thought, so I had him followed," Eamon said with an entirely unapologetic shrug. "I found out he was meeting with dragons and left it at that, figuring it wasn't relevant to you."

"Surely if the Castells were keeping a dragon captive, the dragon community would have rained death down on them already?" Marlen said dubiously. "Dragons are brutal, and there's no way they'd stand for one of their own being abused by a fae."

"I assume dragons can't see past fae wards either," Eamon pointed out with a shrug. "It's not like it's an easy property to get on to. Only one way to find out."

"Set up a meeting," Arthus ordered. "Each generation of fae is born with less and less magic. It makes sense that those who steal it are looking for another source."

Which would make getting the Assembly on side a lot easier, but our task a whole lot harder.

In the two weeks since we had left the Academy, my magic had improved, but we'd achieved very little of our *impossible* task. Eamon had sent a letter to Brently, but we were still waiting for him to reply, and Arthus had decided that upping my magic training was our priority in the meantime.

They should really create some kind of phone system in Avalon. It took *forever* to contact fae.

I was lying on the couch in the living room, contemplating what I could say to Briallen in my next letter while I waited for Eamon to get back from outside. Today was the day. We were *finally* going to cement our relationship. With everything hanging over us, it had felt a little strange to plan our claiming ceremony, but we'd put it off long enough. As Marlen had pointed out, we should enjoy the calm happy moments while we have them, not feel guilty about them.

Eamon and I hadn't been together long at all, and a month of that time we'd spent apart. But weirdly, it didn't feel like we were moving too fast. The Fi that had arrived in Avalon all those months ago would have run for the hills, but I wasn't the same woman I was when I arrived here.

From the very beginning, Eamon had been totally committed, like we were a foregone conclusion. Even when he'd been worried about how I would react to his ability, he'd never wavered in his affection or his desire to be with me.

He made it easy for me to be all in because he was all in.

The sun shone through the high windows, warming my legs and casting the whole soft white and gray space in a peaceful, romantic light. *I love this house,* I thought with a sigh. I loved the whole Old Adair Estate, or "our place" as Eamon kept referring to it, which I guessed made sense since what was his would belong to our mating circle after the claiming ceremony. It hadn't really come up before since neither Marlen, Arthus or I had anything of real monetary value to contribute, but Eamon was bringing a lot to the table.

I missed the treehouse near the Academy, though. It was tiny and cozy, and I loved that we were all on top of each other all the time while we were there.

Eamon appeared at the foot of the couch, picking up the satchel I'd packed our supplies in. "Ready, cariad?"

"So ready," I assured him with a giddy smile, climbing off the couch and taking his enormous hand in mine.

My big, strong fae looked adorably shy. It gave me butterflies. I said my goodbyes to my two very smug mates at the back door of the house before Eamon and I headed off towards the oak tree where we were to have our claiming ceremony. It was still within the warded section of the grounds, so Marlen and Arthus would hang back at the house—the bells would alert them if anyone was at the gate.

"This is so beautiful," I murmured as Eamon led me through an ancient grove of trees to a trickling stream that looked like something straight out of a fairytale. The water ran slightly downhill around rocks and pebbles, pooling in a small pond at the bottom.

Wildflowers grew around the base of the enormous oak tree and dotted around the trees and rocks were red and white spotted toadstools the size of dinner plates. Bright blue butterflies and shimmering emerald dragonflies flitted around us, and I could just make out tiny fish darting around in the stream between the lily pads.

Even if this place hadn't been Eamon's ancestral home, it would still be the perfect spot for an earth affinity's claiming ceremony. It was teeming with *life*.

"I'm glad you like it," Eamon replied, shooting me a small smile over his shoulder as he guided me right to the edge of the stream where, under the shade of the oak tree, we sat down facing each other on the bare dirt. He absently ran his hand through the soil next to him, a patch of vibrant blue forget-me-nots sprouting in his wake before he picked one and handed it to me with a sheepish smile.

I tucked it behind my ear, glad for the addition of a little something special. I always felt like I was underdressed for these momentous occasions. Though we'd soon be naked, so I suppose it didn't much matter either way.

"Are you sure about this, cariad? You've been through so much recently, I don't want to put more pressure on you."

He was worried about how I'd cope with this? *Cute.* The idea of claiming Eamon had been a beacon of light in a sea of darkness over these past few weeks. I leaned forward and brushed a chaste kiss against his lips, loving the scratchy feeling of his beard on my skin.

"I'm sure," I told him firmly against his mouth and I felt his relief course through me.

I grabbed the satchel that held a blanket and wine for later and rooted around in the pocket for the scrap of leather with the mating vows engraved on it. I handed it to Eamon, who shook his head with a slightly bashful smile.

"I've got them memorized," he admitted.

I let out a surprised laugh. "Shouldn't that be my line? This is my third journey down this lane."

"That doesn't matter," Eamon said with an easy shrug. "Besides, it's nice that you've used this at each of your claiming ceremonies. It's special."

He took my free hand in both of his and recited his claiming vow. "I, Eamon Adair, take you, Ffion Laisren, to be my bonded mate. I pledge you my love, my magic, my loyalty, and my devotion. I vow from this day forward to put the needs of you and our mating circle first, forsaking all others."

Eamon's eyes slid closed as the bond between us solidified in his chest. The potency of the gratitude he was feeling almost had me in tears.

I held the words in one hand and repeated the vow back to him. "I, Ffion Laisren, take you, Eamon Adair, to be my bonded mate. I pledge you my love, my magic, my loyalty, and my devotion. I vow from this day forward to put the needs of you and our mating circle first, forsaking all others."

My bond with Eamon snaked into place right next to the other two like a twisting, coiling vine, and I let out a long sigh of relief at the glorious, fulfilling sensation.

Shoving the claiming vows roughly back into my satchel, I crawled towards Eamon, resting my hands on the top of his thick thighs and craning my neck to capture his mouth in a long, languid kiss, pouring every ounce of feeling I had for him into it.

I want you. *Kiss.*

I need you. *Kiss.*

I'm grateful for you. *Kiss.*

I'd do anything for you. *Kiss.*

I love you. *Kiss.*

"I love you." *Out loud.*

A slow, beautiful smile stretched across Eamon's face. "I love you too, cariad."

"I know." *Kiss.*

I did know. I knew Eamon had loved me from the moment I saw his gift in action and didn't balk way back on New Year's Eve, and I knew it wasn't an ill-conceived or superficial kind of love. The love he had for me was pure and ran as deep as the ocean, and I had treasured it from the moment I felt it, even when I hadn't gotten there yet in my own mind.

I lightly pushed Eamon backwards, encouraging him to shuffle back and lean against the base of the large oak tree, chasing his lips with mine as he moved, desperate to feel him inside me, for our magic to intertwine and bind us together forever.

As soon as Eamon's back hit the tree trunk I was on him, yanking impatiently at the laces of his trousers and freeing his spectacular cock. I bit his lip impatiently, needing to feel him inside me.

Eamon smiled lightly against my lips as his hands slid under my dress. "Patience, cariad. I need to make sure you're ready for me."

As impatient as I was, I knew he was right. Eamon was hung like a godsdamned stallion. If I wasn't fully ready for him, I might end up not walking for a week.

Then again, Marlen could just heal me. Maybe it was worth it…

Eamon hummed quietly under his breath. "Where are your panties, Fi?" he asked as his fingers drifted over my bare pussy, making me squirm.

"They seemed superfluous," I panted as Eamon's wicked fingers brushed against my clit.

"So is the dress, my love. How about we lose it?"

"Lose the shirt," I retorted as I roughly pulled at the buttons on my dress and yanked it over my head. Eamon chuckled as he did the same with his shirt.

"I need to taste you," he purred, and oh my *gods*, I was so here for this sexy, confident version of Eamon. The bond snapping into place had made him feel deeply settled—he was the same fae, yet different. Bolder.

"Okay," I agreed immediately, moving to stand so we could change positions. Eamon's hands gripped my hips tightly, holding me in place. "Allow me, cariad."

Before I could ask what he meant, thick green vines snaked down from the branches above us, making me jump. I gasped as two of the vines bent towards me, wrapping around my torso and lifting me into the air. I squeaked in alarm, but Eamon grabbed my thighs and draped my legs over his shoulders, lining me up perfectly with his mouth.

Okay, I can work with this.

Eamon's grip on my thighs was hard enough to bruise and his tongue felt as magical as the tree branches holding me up as he flattened it against my folds, slowly licking upwards to my clit. My eyes rolled back into my head as I writhed against his face, frantically seeking more friction, chasing my release.

Fuck. Me. The weightlessness added to the cocktail of sensation, and I knew I wasn't going to last long like this. Not when Eamon was sucking in light pulses over my clit in a perfect rhythm like the Fi Whisperer. I exploded against his mouth, fingers digging into the vines as my mind floated happily away from my body. I barely even noticed when they lowered me back onto Eamon's lap, retracting back up into the tree.

After a few minutes—or possibly hours—sensation returned to my limbs, and I leaned up to give Eamon an X-rated kiss as I raised up on my knees and lined my aching pussy over his throbbing cock. He was so hard it looked painful, and *that* I could relate to. I reached down between us, teasingly stroking his shaft a few times until he gave my lower lip a light warning nip.

I eased myself down, my breath catching as I accommodated every massive inch of him. Our magic sparked between us everywhere our naked skin touched and the sensation almost made me come again as every nerve lit up like fireworks on New Year's Eve. It was a blissful achiness that left me wanting more.

Fully seated, I gripped Eamon's shoulders tightly and began lifting myself up as high as I could before dropping back down on his cock. Eamon's muscles were taut, his jaw clenched as he held himself back, letting me set the pace. He'd always let me take the lead, afraid of letting himself go. Afraid of *hurting* me, but that wasn't going to work for me anymore. I was his mate. I needed him to fully let go with me.

"I want all of you," I commanded breathily, my nails digging into his shoulders hard enough to draw blood.

"Cariad," Eamon warned through gritted teeth.

"Let go," I insisted, slamming myself down on him and leaning forward to bite his neck.

Eamon's hands tightened on my hips, keeping me in place as he thrust up into me at a punishing rate. It was more intense, more savage, more passionate than anything we'd ever experienced together, and I reveled in it. I felt like Eamon was satisfying a craving I had that I didn't even know about. I needed this from him.

My arms wrapped around his neck as I held on tight and let him take me where I needed to go. Magic fluttered along my arms, over my breasts where they pressed tightly against his chest, even over my face where it was buried into his neck. By the time my orgasm hit me, I was practically sobbing with need.

Eamon swore loudly as I contracted around him, finding his release after a few more hard, desperate thrusts. Still connected, his arms banded tightly around my back as the last of the magic finished moving between us, overwhelming both of our senses.

My head slipped down to rest against his chest and I barely blinked as the telltale tingling on my wrist alerted me that another line in my mating mark was appearing. Eamon held up his left wrist to inspect the double **XX** mark with awe, peppering light kisses over my hair as he did so.

"Thank you, cariad. I swear I will spend the rest of my life trying to be worthy of this gift," he breathed, his voice full of adoration.

"Shhhhh. Don't have the energy to tell you off for being ridiculous right now," I grumbled. My arm felt like it weighed a ton as I lifted it up to look at my wrist. My mating mark was now one complete X and one half of another X. One more to go until my mating circle was complete.

"You and Arthus could compare notes on hanging me in the air for sexual gratification," I murmured sleepily against his chest, rolling out my shoulders slightly. All this acrobatic sex was very unforgiving on my poor, under-used muscles. Marlen was absolutely going to give me another smug, knowing healing after this.

"I'll be sure to do that," Eamon replied, silently shaking with laughter. "I have something for you," he added, reaching into his pocket.

"Oh?" I sat back on my knees because nothing perked me up more than presents. They were still such a novelty for me after a lifetime of never getting any.

Eamon opened his palm to reveal a ring—a raw piece of amethyst in an almost teardrop shape, set in copper on a thin copper band. It was dainty and perfect, and took my breath away.

"It's imbued with a small amount of my magic," Eamon explained, a thread of vulnerability in his voice. "Enough to temporarily see through glamours when you blood it."

"It's amazing," I assured him, leaning up to kiss him gratefully. I took it from his hand and slid it onto my ring finger, where I'd always imagined I'd wear a wedding band someday.

"Are you sure? I can have one made in a different style—"

"I love it," I cooed, holding my hand up so I could admire the way the amethyst glinted in the light. Saffir had returned the malachite pendant Arthus had given me and it hung proudly around my neck, topped up with another dose of Marlen's healing magic for future use. I was gathering quite the little jewelry collection for myself.

If I could get my hands on some kyanite, I could give the guys some of my empath magic. It irritated me that Glendower had access to some of my magic, but my mates didn't.

Eamon rearranged me so I was sitting on his lap, pulling the blanket over both our naked bodies. I pulled the bottle of wine out of my satchel, uncorked it and took a swig straight from the bottle—I had packed cups, but why make more mess to deal with later?—before handing the bottle to Eamon, who accepted it with a bemused expression.

"I've never drunk wine straight from the bottle before."

"You haven't lived," I slurred, feeling a little love drunk and extremely satisfied. "Do it, go a little crazy."

Eamon gave me an indulgent half-smile before taking a tentative sip from the bottle. Before he had a chance to lower it, my hand shot out to tip the bottle further up. Eamon swatted my hand away playfully, wiping the excess wine from his beard with the back of his hand.

"I think it tastes better from a glass," he mused.

"Oh, it definitely does. But it doesn't have that same rebellious feeling that comes from downing it out the bottle, right?" I grabbed the wine back and took a big gulp to illustrate my point.

Eamon laughed. "You're a bad influence, my mate."

CHAPTER 62

I wanted to bottle this moment, to preserve it and keep it in my pocket forever. This was what perfect happiness felt like. It felt too incredible to last.

My arm tightened slightly around Fi's waist and she giggled, the sound warming me through to my soul. "I'm not going anywhere," she assured me. "Ever. So you best get used to me. You'll be sick of me after two hundred years."

She shuddered slightly, and I knew the fae lifespan was something she still struggled to comprehend, I *felt* her discomfort with it, and while I never wanted her to be unhappy, I was awed at the insight I had into her soul after claiming one another. The mating bond was so much more than I dreamed it would be.

While there was nothing I could say to ease Fi's mind about our life span, I planned to make sure every year was full of so much happiness that she was grateful for each one.

I'll never get sick of you, cariad," I reassured her, pressing a kiss to her temple.

"Even if I drink all your fancy vineyard wine straight out of the bottle?"

"Even then."

Fi snuggled further back against me and I secured the blanket to make sure she was covered and warm. My head tipped back against the tree and my eyes drifted shut as I enjoyed the perfect peace and tranquility of this moment, knowing we'd need to get back to the others soon but enjoying stealing this little moment for myself. After a while, Fi's breathing became soft and even as she dozed in my arms.

I wasn't surprised—the ceremony was intense, and I knew Fi hadn't been sleeping well. Not even all the orgasms we gave her could distract her from the enormity of the task that lay ahead of her. She stirred after an hour of dozing while I relaxed in the shade, and as much as I wanted to keep her there, she wasn't just mine.

"Come on, my love," I said softly, shifting the blanket out of the way and pulling Fi's dress back over her head. "We need to get back to the house. I'm sure Arthus and Marlen are impatient to see you."

"They are," she assured me around a yawn. "I can feel them fretting through the bonds, it woke me up. Let's go put them out of their misery."

We packed up our little picnic into Fi's satchel and I shouldered it on one arm while wrapping the other around her shoulders. As we walked back up to the house together, I marveled at the overwhelming sense of calm and rightness I felt. I always knew the bond would feel good, but I hadn't expected it to fill a space in my soul I didn't know was empty.

I pulled open the back door that led into the kitchen, allowing Fi to enter first.

"Three down, one to go," Marlen announced cheerily, handing Fi a cup of peppermint tea as she slid onto a stool at the kitchen island.

Fi's eyes narrowed at his mischievous expression and I snorted. Marlen was a troublemaker at heart. "I'd ask you to elaborate, but I'm pretty sure I don't want you to."

"I was referring to your mating circle," Marlen elaborated anyway. "Three out of four. So, who gets the coveted final spot, Bryn or Enfys?"

Arthus scoffed loudly at that from his spot at the dining table, and my lips twitched slightly.

"Obviously Bryn," Arthus replied.

"Hopefully Bryn," I muttered.

Fi scowled at the three of us over the top of her teacup and I could admit we probably looked rather smug and infuriating when we ganged up on her like this, though I think she secretly enjoyed it. It was important to Fi that us guys got along well with each other, not just with her. "Maybe I should claim Enfys, he could keep you all in line."

Marlen wrinkled his nose in distaste. "That's hardly a good reason, foxglove. Bryn's a tyrant. I'm sure he'd keep us in line just fine."

"Well, thank you all for your votes, I've noted that there are three in Bryn's favor. Can we talk about something else now?"

"You're not going to drag it out for ages, are you? Bryn would probably love for you to put him out of his misery," Marlen continued, disregarding her attempt to change the subject.

"Plus, it'd give you full access to your empath abilities. Given the task we're undertaking, being able to influence crowds might be an essential tool," Arthus added as if we were talking about something as banal as the weather.

"That's not a good enough reason," she reminded Arthus, shooting him a haughty look as she sipped her tea. "We don't even know what effect claiming Eamon had on my magic yet. And as Bryn is safely tucked up back at the Academy, not here, with me, I will assume he's feeling just fine about me not claiming him. He's not even my suitor," she muttered as an afterthought.

"You know Bryn better than to think he's just sitting around at the Academy, forgetting about you," Arthus chided, and I could have sworn Fi blushed a little. I reached for the bond in my sternum and felt Fi's self-doubt. I didn't think she had anything to worry about—Bryn may not have instantly fallen at her feet the way the three of us did, but he was clearly taken with her. If only the two of them would have an honest and vulnerable conversation with each other, he'd probably be here right now.

It had always baffled me how closely Arthus monitored his bond with Fi—he was forever checking in to see how she was feeling. Now that I had a bond of my own, I completely understood. I always wanted to know how she was, wanted to chase away anything that might upset her and fix anything she felt was broken.

I was 43 years old. The few friends I had from my time at the Academy had all found their mates there. They had been together for over twenty years and were approaching their first fertile cycle. I'd given up hope that I would ever have this connection with anyone.

I didn't think Fi fully realized how much the gift of her love meant to me.

Fi gulped down the rest of her tea, shuddering a little. "Right, now you two have seen me and know I'm okay, Eamon and I are going to go have a little more alone time."

My throat constricted almost painfully with emotion. Fi jumped lightly off the stool and grabbed my hand as she passed, pulling me towards the bedroom.

"You two are on dinner duty tonight, Eamon will be indisposed," she called over her shoulder. By the gods, I think I might have blushed. The sounds of Marlen's laughter followed us down the hallway.

It took three weeks for Brently to respond to my letter, which was fairly standard since he moved around so much for his work. The wait had been driving Fi crazy though, so I was glad he'd set the date for his visit the day after his letter arrived—any longer and Fi would insist we take the griffins from the stables and go track him down ourselves.

Like Bryn, Brently had a tracking gift. He was surprisingly willing to talk to us, given how he usually kept everyone at a distance, treating them all with suspicion, but none of us felt comfortable letting him through the wards past the gates or into the house, so we opted to meet at a hilltop point on the property, overlooking the vineyard. It was isolated but easy to see anyone approaching, so we wouldn't be overheard.

The four of us stood around waiting as we watched his griffin approach. Fi's body language was tense and wary. Once upon a time she would have looked forward to speaking to fae who worked alongside dragons, and we all mourned the loss of her innocent wonder about all things Avalon.

"Mr. Adair," Brently greeted me politely as he approached, inclining his head.

"Mr. Laisren now, actually. But Eamon is fine. My mating circle," I said, gesturing to indicate them. "Ffion, Arthus, and Marlen."

"Brently," he replied, tipping his chin respectfully towards the other three. "I hear we may be able to help each other out." I appreciated his directness.

"I know you were watching the Castell Estate. I also know you were meeting with a group of young dragons," I began, watching his expression closely. His eyes flared slightly, probably surprised I knew as much as I did, but he said nothing. "We believe a dragon is being held on the property."

"I suspected as much, but no one can get onto the property. How do you know that?"

"Because I was being held prisoner there, and I sensed a non-fae presence. Don't ask me how, I'm not going to explain my gift to you," Fi interjected in a dry tone, though it was likely he'd already heard about Ffion the Empath. I checked the bond to gauge her emotional state and found a healthy dose of discomfort at speaking to a strange fae.

Brently sighed and ran a hand over his face. "Why do I feel that your escape was a stroke of luck? I've been watching that property for six months and I'm no closer to figuring out how to get her out."

"Her?" Fi asked curiously.

"I've already said too much, it isn't my place. My clients will want to speak to you directly. I'll arrange a meeting with them on neutral territory."

I would bet my fortune that the clients in question were the female dragon's mates. They could be the key to getting the Assembly on our side, but male dragon shifters were notoriously hotheaded and protective of their mates. They could have been volatile allies.

"How soon?" Arthus asked calmly, his gaze trained on Brently, ever watchful for any sign of danger.

"A week, at least. I will send word through one of my colleagues to confirm."

The dragons had agreed to meet at a quiet grove, only a thirty-minute flight from the Old Adair Estate where we'd been lying low. We'd all tweaked our appearance with glamours, but leaving the property made all of us nervous.

Perhaps I could convince Fi's fathers to visit—Galvyn could load us up with cloaking amulets to cover our tracks next time we left the Estate. Plus, Fi would probably enjoy spending some time talking to them. She hadn't really had a chance yet.

Fi wriggled back against me on the griffin, pressing her back against my chest. Marlen flew solo on a griffin next to us, and Arthus tumbled and glided through the air a few years below, wanting to stretch his wings. He was peacocking for sure, but I couldn't begrudge him the display.

If I had wings, I'd be showing them off for Fi too.

We landed a short walk away from the meeting spot and left the griffins to rest. Arthus and I were both tense and on-guard while Marlen focused on keeping Fi's mind at ease. He pointed out every flower, bird, bug and tiny speck that may be of possible interest to distract her. She definitely knew what he was doing, but she played along, regardless. It was her way of giving us comfort.

By the time we arrived at the clearing, they were already waiting for us.

Five male dragon shifters stood in front of us, each at least seven foot tall, all wearing matching grim expressions. They stood with their arms crossed and feet shoulder-width apart, a stance designed to intimidate rivals. Brently hovered uncomfortably next to them, looking like he wanted to make a dash to us—the less frightening option.

I checked the bond to ensure that Fi was feeling okay but also... not too okay. Male dragons were known throughout the realm for their rugged good looks.

Fi shot me an amused glance, something in my emotions catching her attention. She didn't appear to have any fear of the dragons. Perhaps, underneath all that alpha-male posturing, the emotions Fi was picking up from them were less hostile than they appeared.

The male in the middle of the lineup stepped forward, and it was clear he was the black dragon—the Alpha of the flight. He had deeply tanned skin, like he spent a lot of time outdoors, and dark blonde hair. If the other dragons were seven-foot-tall, this guy was closer to eight. And about as wide. He made me look dainty in comparison.

"My name is Ezra," he announced, looking over each of us clinically as if memorizing our details. "This is my flight—Levi, Hiram, Oren, and Seff." He gestured at the males on either side of him.

Arthus stepped forward without hesitation, and while he was younger than me, I found I didn't mind him taking the lead. He had a naturally commanding presence that made people sit up and pay attention.

"I'm Arthus. This is my mate, Ffion, and her other mates Eamon and Marlen." I inclined my head as Arthus made the introductions. Fi stuck close to Marlen's side but stood tall, chin up and shoulders back.

"Brently here thinks you can help us," Ezra stated.

"We may be able to help each other," Arthus countered. "You are looking for someone, and you suspect they are within the Castell Estate. Am I correct?"

"How did you know we were looking for someone?" Ezra asked, looking at Brently suspiciously.

"You are a young flight of dragons. We assumed you were looking for your mate," Arthus said lightly. We didn't want to give the impression we were getting between the dragons and their mate. If that were the case, they would annihilate us without a second thought.

Ezra grunted. "We came of age and felt called to our mate's location, but we couldn't find her. We can't see the property, and it feels like there's a bubble around it, so we contracted Brently to assist us, assuming a fae would have more luck against fae magic. He determined that the general area is owned by Evalina Castell. How does this concern you?"

Arthus went to speak, but Fi got there first. "I was held as a prisoner on the Castell property. I felt someone nearby, someone non-fae. They were... very unhappy with their conditions."

Ezra's eyes narrowed in on Fi, and I half expected him to ask how she knew that, but he just gave her a curt nod instead. Every creature in Avalon knew that fae couldn't lie.

"How did you escape?" One man behind him asked Fi. Ezra's expression had remained stoic throughout the discussion, but the four men behind him were visibly struggling.

"I didn't escape from there, they took me off the premises. But we have a good idea of how the property is warded, and how we can get in," Fi said, tilting her chin up defiantly, my clever cariad knowing inherently to not show fear in front of a predator.

"Oh?" Ezra asked, giving Fi an assessing glance. "What is it you want in return? You've already escaped."

"We want to make sure everyone being held on the property is freed," Fi began.

"And an introduction," Arthus cut in. "We want a meeting with one of the dragon representatives on the Assembly."

"About this? Because if our mate is being held by fae scum, the Assembly will hear about it with or without your input," Ezra retorted.

"We wouldn't expect any different," Fi said soothingly. "This is bigger than just the Castells, though. We need the Assembly so we can get rid of all the *fae scum* on the Council, as you so eloquently called them."

All five dragons' expressions went blank, and I guessed they were communicating telepathically. Judging by Fi's puzzled face, we must have forgotten to mention to her that dragons could do that.

"Fine," Ezra said suddenly. "Seff's father, Ilia, is on the Assembly. He'll meet with you, but we're not interested in doing anything until our mate is safe."

"Understandable," Arthus conceded. "We have a contact we're working with who will figure out how to get us onto the property. Let's meet again soon to finalize the plan."

"We'll get her out," Fi added quietly, her eyes full of steely resolve. Pain flashed across Ezra's face for a split second before he schooled his features back into a mask of Alpha control.

"With or without you, we will get our mate," he promised.

FFION

CHAPTER 63

After our meeting with the dragons a week ago, we'd sent a letter to Saffir at the Academy asking if she could come out and meet over the weekend. She hadn't replied, and the guys didn't think she'd show, but I was confident she would. Even if she was having second thoughts about our deal, Saffir wasn't a coward.

If she wanted to tell me to shove it, she'd do it right to my face.

I sat on a stool at the kitchen island, picking apart an orange as Eamon prepared the dough for the bread he was making. His cooking had been next level since we'd arrived at the Estate—probably because of the full-sized fancy kitchen. It made the dinky kitchen back at the cabin look like a child's playset.

"How does this whole Councilor gig work? Are there elections?" I mused out loud.

"There were once, I think. They stopped during my grandparents' generation," Eamon replied thoughtfully, slowly adding more water to the bowl of dough he was making.

"What? Why?" I asked, mystified. That seemed like a massive flaw in the system.

"As fewer and fewer powerful fae were born, there was less competition for the positions, and those with gifts ran uncontested. Sometimes, if there were two candidates, they would duel fae-to-fae for the position." He shrugged like it was no big deal.

"Um, that's not going to work for me," I announced. "The Keeper of Balance has decreed that the fae deserve better than tyranny of the mightiest. Who represents the low magic fae like Marlen's family if the Council is made up entirely of gifted strongmen?"

"No one does, cariad," Eamon replied, giving me a sad smile like he didn't really think anything would change either way. Maybe that was why the gods had stuck me with this mission. Fae who had grown up in Avalon were so used to this terrible system that they assumed it would always be this way.

The bell on the outer wall rang indicating there was someone at the gate, and Arthus was striding past me to answer it before I could even get up from my stool.

"As if he would let you answer the door on your own," Marlen snorted as he wandered into the living area, pulling down his shirt. He had just gotten out of the shower and as I watched him, he used his magic to draw the water out of his hair and directed it out the window where it landed in the garden with a splash.

Arthus returned with an apprehensive Saffir in tow, and I gave each of the guys a smug grin. I knew she would show up.

"Hi," I greeted her a little awkwardly, standing up next to the kitchen island.

"Hello," Saffir replied, equally stiffly. She was dressed impeccably in a fitted off-white dress and beige cardigan, her hair neatly braided on each side and secured in a bun at the back. "Nice house," she added, looking around the room. It seemed weird to thank her for the compliment, since it didn't really feel like my house. I smiled politely and waved her towards the dining table instead.

"I'll make some tea," Marlen called from the kitchen, his tone laced with amusement at my discomfort. Arthus stood sentry by the window, giving us the illusion of privacy while watching us like a hawk as we took our seats next to each other at the enormous wooden table.

"How have you been? How are things at the Academy?" I asked, struggling to keep the jealousy out of my tone. I had some great private tutors in Arthus, Marlen and Eamon, but I missed my classes and my friends, and I was more than a little bitter that the opportunity had been taken away from me.

"Fine," Saffir said nonchalantly, shrugging. "Your absence caused quite the stir on campus. It's all anyone can talk about, even now."

"Presumably, your parents know then?" Eamon asked, sitting down across from us.

"I told them myself," Saffir admitted. "Everyone on campus already knew about it, so I didn't see the harm in telling them. It would have been suspicious if I had said nothing."

"Do you think they suspect you of undermining them?" Eamon asked cautiously.

"No. Not yet, anyway. I sent a carefully worded letter to my parents, saying that for all I knew, you were with them again and if so, it wouldn't be my place to question that. I think that reassured them that I was cooperative and knew my place."

Gods, I hate Saffir's parents.

"Smart." I nodded approvingly. I'm glad we hadn't told Saffir that we were leaving. The less she knew, the more she could get away with in her "carefully worded" responses.

"I assume you asked me here because you've got some kind of plan in mind?" Saffir hedged curiously.

"I want to sneak onto your parents' property and disable the wards from the inside," I stated flatly.

"You want to... Okay, sure, I guess. That's... *A* plan."

"Eamon has experience with warding properties, so he can explain how they work," I added. "We just need you to figure out where the warding crystals are located."

"You're all on board with this?" Saffir looked around dubiously between

Eamon, Marlen and Arthus, who all nodded with varying degrees of enthusiasm.

"What about Bryn? How does he feel about this? Where is he?" Saffir asked lightly. My eyes snapped to Saffir's. Her emotions were a mixture of curiosity and apprehension, not a drop of heartsick longing in sight.

Good thing, too. The distance between Bryn and me right now was making me feel weird and irritable. I'd been feeling oddly territorial over him, which was bad because I didn't really have a right to. Or did I have a right to?

"At the Academy, I assume. Why do you ask?" I replied, trying to play it cool. I hadn't heard from Bryn since we'd parted ways at the Academy and he told me he'd be seeing me. Five weeks ago. I should have just kidnapped him when we left the Academy and asked for forgiveness afterwards. The distance between us felt insurmountable.

"Because he left the Academy the same day you did?" Saffir said slowly, looking at me like I was a few crayons short of a box.

The guys' emotions were a weird mixture of surprised and not surprised at all, but they always seemed to read Bryn better than I did. Maybe it was a guy thing? Or maybe it was really just a Fi-and-Bryn thing.

"He's probably staying with Briallen's family in Northgales, foxglove," Marlen called from the kitchen. "That's where he grew up."

"He has a small cabin of his own on their property for when he goes home for visits," Saffir confirmed, and I shoved down a flash of irritation that she knew him better than I did.

"I'd like to discuss the wards now," I announced. I wasn't sure how to feel about Bryn's departure from the Academy.

Actually, yes, I did know how I felt.

Pissed.

Why hadn't he come here? He had to know we'd be here, and he'd been to this house before, it's not like he'd have trouble finding it. Plus, we were in Northgales too. He could only be a thirty-minute flight away at most.

Why was he avoiding me?

"Of course, cariad," Eamon said, shooting me an understanding smile as Marlen set down the tray of tea and scones before setting himself up on the couch.

"To create illusion wards that cloak a property, they arrange large chunks of black tourmaline in a square to cloak the area within. They imbue the crystal with the blood—and therefore magic—of the illusionist, and the blood of whoever can grant entry."

"All four of my parents," Saffir confirmed, pouring herself a cup of tea.

"So once someone has been through the wards once…" I prompted.

"They can enter again indefinitely until the crystals are fully drained or replaced," Eamon concluded.

"Perfect," I said with a grin that probably looked a little sinister, based on Saffir's hesitant smile of a reply.

"I'm guessing this is where I come in," she said with a grimace.

"You're not helping disable them. You'll be at the Academy that day, making sure you're seen by as many fae as possible," I replied, giving her a meaningful look.

"Right. Good idea. It's just… Well, you're sort of free now, aren't you? Why would you want to go back into the Estate?" Saffir asked. I didn't feel any malice from her, just confusion. Though we had a memory altering potion on standby if Saffir went back on the deal we'd made, I really didn't want to use it. That would make me just as bad as her father.

I sighed. "Because I'm pretty sure I wasn't the first or the only resident of the Castell Penitentiary."

"You think there are others still trapped in there? Surely I would have seen or heard *something*. I spent my whole childhood in that house…" Saffir stuttered, looking distraught. I muted my ability temporarily to get a reprieve from her suffocating guilt.

"Look, your parents are older than you and have been at this a lot longer. Don't feel guilty for their decisions, help me try to fix them."

It probably wasn't my finest pep talk, but having experienced the Castell's special form of hospitality firsthand, I needed Saffir to get her head in the game. If there were other prisoners there—and I was confident there was at least one—we had to get them out. It wasn't even about carrying out the gods' quest. It was just the right thing to do.

"Right, you're right." Saffir straightened her spine and tipped her chin up defiantly.

"Are you in?" I asked, just to be sure.

"I'm in."

By the time Ezra, Levi, Hiram, Oren and Seff showed up to discuss the plan two days later, the entire kitchen island was covered in plates of food. Eamon cooked when he was nervous. Originally, Arthus had been adamant that they couldn't enter the property, but I'd pushed back because we couldn't risk being overheard. What we were planning would get us all kinds of locked up if we botched it.

It had been nearly six weeks since Gwyneira had unceremoniously booted us from the Academy, and finally—*finally*—it felt like things were happening, but it also felt like not enough things were happening. As much as I didn't want to become the face of the gods' big plan, in the back of my mind I felt like I needed some sort of big Joan-of-Arc-leading-the-army moment to really kick it all off.

No, that would be awful, I didn't want to be the Leader of the Revolution. I'd happily stick to being the Administrator of the Revolution.

We'd formed an alliance with these dragons, but it was an uneasy one. My fae stood in the dining area facing them, matching their defensive posture and grim expressions. I rolled my eyes impatiently.

"If I didn't know any better, I'd worry that the level of testosterone in this room was a choking hazard," I said drily. I was met with eight puzzled expressions and remembered that they probably didn't know what testosterone was since science wasn't exactly a big part of the magic curriculum.

"What I mean is, there's this whole manly man face-off going on right now and could we just, you know... not? You drink ale, right?" I asked, turning to face the dragons, who nodded slowly. "And you eat food, right?"

"Not fae food," the tanned dragon with light brown hair and honey-colored highlights grumbled.

"Enough, Hiram," Ezra reprimanded, glaring at him. "Yes, we eat food and drink ale."

"Great, then let's go do that and we can chat." I headed over to the kitchen and loaded up my plate with chickpea salad. Hiram sidled up to the counter next to me, sighing as he poked unenthusiastically at a lettuce leaf.

"So, what do dragons eat?" I asked conversationally, trying to get them to relax a little. If we couldn't bond over food, we couldn't bond over anything.

"*Meat*," he replied incredulously, looking at me like I'd sprouted a second head for considering anything different.

"I totally get it. I used to eat meat," I said, nodding sagely. Now that I wasn't restricted to the Academy's raw food diet, I didn't miss meat as much—Eamon was an awesome cook—but sometimes I still craved pepperoni pizza and vodka in a can, though. Humans really had convenient comfort food down to a fine art.

"Really?" Hiram asked dubiously, looking at me like he was seeing me for the first time. "I've never met a fae who eats meat."

"I didn't know I was a fae at the time in my defense. Or that fae even existed. Long story." I shrugged as I moved towards the dining table, trying not to laugh at his baffled face. "Come on, we've got plots to hatch."

I'd made progress with one dragon, at least. Four to go.

I was seated between Arthus on one side and Levi on the other. Levi had rich black skin, buzzed black hair, and a tidy beard—he was quite the looker, as were the other four dragons. I hoped that their mate would feel like she'd won the jackpot when she saw them because I was convinced she had been the person whose emotions I felt echoes of when I was in the cave, and I remembered her loneliness and heartache.

After a couple of drinks and several minor disagreements on the plan, everyone had loosened up a little and I was significantly less worried about a fistfight breaking out. My guys were big and strong, but the dragons were between seven and eight feet of solid muscle each. They looked like they could crush my bones with one of their hands.

"Can I ask how it feels? The draw to your mate?" I asked Levi softly, not wanting to offend him but also being eaten alive by curiosity.

Levi gave me a long, considering look. "It's not like the fae mating pull, or what I know of it anyway. It's more like a subconscious draw to a particular location. Our flight, we all eventually came together for the first time outside the Castell Estate as we'd all felt drawn there."

"You didn't know each other beforehand?" I asked in amazement. It seemed that dragon's fates were a lot more predetermined than the fae's.

"Nope," Levi replied, popping the 'p'.

"Do you have any idea who your mate might be?"

"None at all. We haven't heard of any dragons going missing, either," Levi replied. His eyes glazed over at the same time as Ezra's, whose mouth was set in a firm, tight line. I was kind of glad fae couldn't communicate telepathically. Marlen would always be in my head making me laugh at inopportune moments, followed by Arthus telling us off, then Eamon checking worriedly to make sure Arthus hadn't upset me.

"What if she doesn't like you?" I asked playfully when Levi's eyes lost their glassy look. I framed it as a joke, but I genuinely wanted to know. Were dragons just stuck with whoever the gods gave them?

"Of course she'll like us," Ezra cut in with a frown. "She'll love us as we love her."

I just nodded because what could you say to that? I didn't doubt his conviction, but I didn't share his optimism either. Whoever this girl was, she'd been through hell. I hoped her mates gave her the space to love herself before expecting her to love them in return.

"Why do we need to wait five days from now to go on the property? Surely they will have Council duties away from the Estate before then?" Ezra asked suspiciously. I doubted he'd feel even remotely less hostile towards us until his mate was free, though the other four guys had warmed up to us a little.

Probably because of the ale.

"We have determined that day gives us the greatest window of opportunity," Arthus replied curtly. He hated this plan and everything to do with it.

"Even if we could go sooner, I need a few more days to practice disabling wards," I added in a much calmer tone than Arthus' irate one. "I doubt we'll get a second shot at this, so we've got to get it right the first time."

"Very well," Ezra said with a resigned sigh. "Thank you for your hospitality, but we should go now. We have a lot of training to do ourselves. I'm not leaving anything to chance."

FFION

CHAPTER 64

After the dragons had left, I holed myself up in the study to research the history of the Fae Council. The guys had left me to sleep in this morning after I'd stayed up far too late reading by candlelight, but the more I learned, the more I was convinced that the only way the fae could redeem themselves was if the low-magic fae took back some of the power that they had lost over the centuries. Somehow.

The 'how' was the answer I needed, the one that kept me up at night questioning.

When the words started to blur together on the pages, I shuffled into the bathroom and cranked the shower as forcefully as it could go, grateful for the hot spring that was piped directly into the house. As I stood under the spray, aggressively massaging my temples, I tried to figure out what my role in all of this was supposed to be.

Was it possible to start a revolution while remaining entirely in the background?

Why couldn't the gods give me a little extra direction? Were they even paying attention?

After a long, indulgent shower, I wrapped myself in my pale pink silk robe—another gift from Eamon—and practiced drying my hair with my air magic. Arthus made it look so easy, but whenever I tried it I ended up looking like I'd stuck my finger in a power outlet. I snorted and tied my puffy cloud of hair into a messy high bun instead.

I intended to go back to the bedroom and get dressed, but the smell of cinnamon drew me down the hall into the main living area where I found Eamon pulling cinnamon scones out of the oven, and my mouth watered at the sight of them.

"Intellectually I know you have three mates, but I'd still prefer not to see you wandering around in front of them wearing so little, kid," Attie said drolly, making me shriek in surprise. He and my other father, Galvyn, sat on the sofa, both scowling at my short silk robe.

I must have been completely lost in thought not to have picked up on the presence of two other sets of emotions. Usually I wasn't so easy to sneak up on. I quickly shut down my ability because the force of Marlen's amusement made me want to laugh and I felt like that wouldn't be super well received.

"Um, hello, fathers," I greeted with an awkward little wave. "I'm just going to, er, get dressed."

"Probably a good idea," Arthus agreed, his voice laced with humor. "We'll put some tea on."

A few minutes later, I emerged in my most modest beige linen shirt tucked into a knee-length olive wrap skirt and joined everyone else at the dining table. Eamon pushed a cup of tea and a warm cinnamon scone at me, and I shoved a big pulse of love at him through our bond in response.

"I must say, he is my favorite of your mates so far," Attie remarked, reaching for a scone. "Congratulations, by the way."

"Thanks. One more to go," I replied with a strained laugh. Galvyn grimaced.

"What are you guys doing here?" I asked, hiding behind the rim of my teacup. "How did you know where we were?"

"I sent your fathers a letter, cariad. I thought you might want to spend some time with them now that things are slightly more settled," Eamon interjected. I gave him a grateful smile. I hadn't had a chance to just sit and chat with my fathers after I'd met them, since we always seemed to meet under weird, stressful conditions.

"Though we already knew you weren't at the Academy," Attie added while Galvyn grunted in what I supposed was agreement. "Gwyneira sent a letter the day you left the Academy, saying your priority needed to be your quest from the gods."

"Left the Academy?" Arthus scoffed.

"I suppose we technically *left* the grounds," I conceded bitterly. "After Gwyneira expelled me and Marlen, and fired Arthus."

"She didn't mention that part." Attie frowned.

"I'll just bet she didn't," I muttered.

"What's this task then, daughter?" Galvyn grumbled. Reluctantly, I relayed the full story, fully aware they might go full Gwyneira on me as well.

"Can't catch a break, can you, Ffion?" Galvyn asked, his sympathy rolling over my skin like a soothing balm, and I felt some tension ease from my shoulders. I didn't realize how important their reaction would be to me until I was waiting to hear it.

Maybe it made me selfish or petulant or *something*, but I wanted a bit of sympathy. I didn't ask for any of this shit, and while I was coming around to the idea of making some changes in Avalon, I wasn't feeling particularly gung-ho about it.

"I suppose that's why you wanted some cloaking amulets?" Galvyn asked Eamon, shoving a small, rattling cloth bag towards him as Eamon nodded. "There's enough in there for four each, and I'll make you some more as soon as I can. Glendower Castell has been disturbingly quiet lately."

The guys discussed the conversation we had overheard at the tavern with my fathers as I picked unenthusiastically at my delicious scone.

"I have a question," I began cautiously, looking between my fathers.

Being around them was hard. I always experienced an uncomfortable mixture of loss and hope in their presence—loss at the childhood I didn't have with them, and hope for the relationship we could have now. And that was *with* my ability muted because their sense of loss always fueled mine. After a while, it felt like I was drowning in our combined despair.

"What's your question, daughter?" Galvyn asked in his low, grouchy voice.

Gods, this was going to make me sound like an asshole, but I was salty enough to bring it up anyway.

"Why did you write my name on my arm when you sent me to Albion? The Castells only took me because they were looking for a 'Ffion Laisren'. If I'd gone by a human first name, they might not have ever found me."

Galvyn growled irritably, glaring at me from across the table, but said nothing. I turned to Attie, who gave me a sad smile.

"We were so happy when we realized your mother was pregnant," he began, and my heart sank to my stomach. Marlen grabbed my hand under the table, giving my fingers a supportive squeeze. "We had our bedroom all set up for her labor. A midwife was supposed to come and stay with us for the last few weeks of the pregnancy, to help with your birth."

"Supposed to?" I prodded when he became lost in thought.

"Yes," Attie continued, clearing his throat. "We were all sitting in the front room of the house, the sunniest room, one afternoon when Rhedyn's waters broke. The healer was supposed to arrive the next day, so Galvyn and I were in a panic."

Galvyn grunted his assent, staring determinedly at the table.

"Before we figured out what we should do, you were here."

"How long did you deliberate?" I asked suspiciously, assuming this was standard parental bragging. *Maybe fae babies were just born fast?* I wasn't about to ask the guys about them. My fertile window was another thirty years away, but I still didn't want them getting any crazy ideas.

"Half an hour, perhaps a little less," Galvyn answered quietly.

"Is that a thing? Waters break, half an hour later a baby arrives?" I asked, alarmed. "Is that a fae thing?"

"Certainly not," Marlen chuckled. "My mother claims she labored for days on end with all of her births."

"I wonder now if it was the first sign of the gods' favor," Attie mused thoughtfully. "You were born so quickly, with such little fuss. Rhedyn held you to her breast, sitting in the same chair where she'd just delivered you, and saw the foxgloves growing outside the window. She decided then and there to name you 'Ffion'. Galvyn and I were too stunned to object, even if we wanted to," Attie chuckled.

"Leaving you in Albion was the hardest thing we ever did," Galvyn interjected somberly, finally looking up to meet my eyes. "Your mother was distraught. Even if the Council hadn't captured her, even if she had come home to us... I'm not sure she would have ever recovered."

"A fae's name is sacred, and Rhedyn knew you couldn't keep your last name, but she thought your first name would be safe. Besides, she wanted you to have a piece of your history, your family," Attie continued sadly. "We were convinced she could pass through the portal with you undetected. Had we known what would happen..." he trailed off, his eyes distant, lost in faraway memories.

I'd heard this from my mates, who'd relayed the details of their visit to my fathers with me, but it was so much harder hearing it firsthand. Their pain felt as fresh as though my mother had died yesterday.

"Of course," I replied hoarsely, clearing my throat. "You had no way of knowing. I shouldn't have... I don't blame you or anything."

"You should," Galvyn replied grimly. "We failed at keeping you safe. We failed at keeping your mother safe. You shouldn't forget our failures. The gods know that we never do."

"The fault lies with the Castells and any other corrupt Councilor who had a part in my mother's death," I reprimanded sharply. "Don't accept blame that isn't yours to take. You're depriving the people who deserve it."

"You're very like your mother when you tell us off," Attie said lightly, his eyes flickering with amusement. "We struggle to forgive ourselves because a few months after Rhedyn's death, we found out about a different portal. One that was safe from the Council's eyes. In the end, her death was for nothing."

"There is no other portal," Arthus objected, looking between Galvyn and Attie with his brow furrowed.

"There is no other *sanctioned* portal," Attie allowed, tilting his head. "You really think Ffion is the only fae to be smuggled out of Avalon for their own safety?"

"*Allow those in hiding to find their way home*," I recounted, looking between Eamon, Arthus and Marlen with my eyebrow raised. I assumed the gods had meant those hiding in Avalon. It never even occurred to me that there would be other fae hiding in *Albion*.

I was sure I hadn't encountered any. I knew the second I saw Bryn on that London footpath that there was something not-quite-human about him.

"Where is this unsanctioned portal?" Arthus asked sharply.

Galvyn and Attie exchanged a look. "We're not entirely sure, its location isn't exactly advertised. We assume it's in the Outer Isles," Attie said eventually.

"How do you know about it? Is there someone we could ask who knows the location?" Eamon pushed.

"Seren Parry," Galvyn sighed. "She and her three mates run the portal. They help fae who are in need of protection. We've never met her, but we know her mate, Egan."

"They live on an island in the Outer Isles, which is why we assume the portal is there. They're, er, not the most receptive to visitors," Attie added nervously, looking between the four of us.

Too fucking bad.

Maybe the gods would smite them for me if they didn't cooperate? If not, what was the point of being sanctified? So far, the gods hadn't done a single helpful thing to aid us in this mission they had sent me on.

"We'll try to contact Egan for you," Attie announced, standing up.

"And I'll create more cloaking amulets," Galvyn finished. "You'll contact us if you need anything else in the meantime."

I nodded and gave them both awkward hugs. I needed a crash course in normal parental interaction.

"Until next time, daughter."

The chiming bell that indicated someone was at the main gate had all of us tensing up. My fathers had left a few hours ago and for once, we weren't expecting visitors.

Eamon and Arthus exchanged wary looks. "Stay here with Marlen, sweetheart. We'll go see who it is."

Eamon nodded curtly, and they both headed for the front door. Marlen sidled up behind me, where I was perched on a stool at the kitchen island and languidly wrapped his arms around my shoulders. He nibbled lightly on my neck and I snorted.

"You're obviously not worried," I commented lightly, tipping my head back to give him better access. I wasn't particularly worried either since the wards here were almost impossible to get past. Besides, whoever it was had politely rung the bell, which seemed like a positive sign.

"Nah, the grownups will handle it. We can have some fun here instead."

"You are so irresponsible," I murmured as his hands drifted down to caress my breasts through the thin shirt I was wearing.

Marlen hummed under his breath and gave my hard, achy nipples a firm pinch. "I'd say you like that about me," he replied smugly.

He isn't wrong.

Just when I contemplated stripping off my clothes and climbing up onto the counter to present a Ffion Buffet for him to feast on, Arthus and Eamon returned.

Given the mixture of lust and amusement that preceded their arrival, I guessed our mystery visitor wasn't anyone to worry about.

"Who was it?" I half asked, half moaning as Marlen's hands glided up my thighs and snuck under my skirt.

"A messenger," Arthus replied with a smirk, fanning an envelope in the air.

"Who's it for?" I asked breathily as Marlen deftly unlaced my panties.

"You, cariad," Eamon replied, sounding amused.

"Oh." I swatted Marlen's hands away and reached towards Arthus. "Gimme!"

"Seriously?" Marlen asked incredulously from behind me, snagging my panties and yanking them out abruptly from underneath me. Arthus snorted as he handed over the letter.

"It might be important," I protested, but I grabbed one of his hands and returned it to my upper thigh anyway. Waste not, want not, and all that.

I ripped open the envelope and pulled the letter out as Marlen rubbed torturous circles with his thumbs up and down my legs.

"What is it, sweetheart?" Arthus asked impatiently. I was impressed he'd even handed the letter over.

"An invitation," I squealed as my eyes scanned the paper. "Briallen is having a party at her parents' place to celebrate her completed mating circle in two days' time. She's invited us to stay the night."

I looked up at Arthus and Eamon who were both giving me matching *you cannot be serious* faces. Marlen leaned in close, brushing his lips over the shell of my ear. "Let's soften them up first, foxglove. Then they'll give you anything you want," he whispered conspiratorially.

Marlen was the true strategist among us.

I suppressed a grin and wrapped my arm around the back of his head, pulling him forward to capture his mouth. He smiled against my mouth and I gave his lower lip a possessive bite, hard enough to leave teeth marks.

Marlen's lips moved down against the column of my neck as he gently turned me on the stool so I was facing out towards Arthus and Eamon. His hands made quick work of undoing my skirt, and I happily undid the buttons of my blouse so I could pull it off myself. *We make quite the tantalizing team*, I thought smugly to myself.

Was I sitting on a kitchen stool in just a bra in front of three fully dressed men? *Why, yes.* Yes, I was. Their eyes were all trained entirely on me, darkened with desire, and I don't think I'd ever felt so beautiful.

Marlen wasted no time moving around in front of me and dropping to his knees. He shot me a devilish grin before roughly pushing my thighs apart and *devouring* me. His head was turning from side to side, and the noises he was making were downright *lewd*. My hands quickly moved to grip the edge of the counter behind me as I threw my head back and moaned in ecstasy. Marlen always ate me out like he was on death row and I was his last meal.

My eyes rolled back and by the time I opened them, Eamon's mouth was pressing against my own, his tongue sweeping against my lips, demanding entrance. One of his massive hands coasted lazily up from my hip bone, across my stomach, before cupping my breast, kneading it firmly until I arched into him, silently pleading for more.

As he reached around to unlace my bra, I caught Arthus' movement in my peripheral vision. He'd deposited the small bottle of oil we used as lubricant on the counter next to me and sat himself down on one of the dining chairs he'd turned to face us, and I watched hungrily as he casually pulled his cock free from his pants. He sat there stroking himself lazily while watching me with an infuriatingly smug smirk on his face.

"It's not like you to sit on the sidelines," I teased. He'd never do what I told him to do, but maybe I could taunt him into giving me what I wanted.

"I'll still be calling the shots," he assured me arrogantly.

"You're going to give these two instructions on how to fuck me?" I voiced in disbelief. We generally all deferred to Arthus in and out of the bedroom, but he was usually an active participant. Marlen's laughter vibrated against my sensitive nerves, making me shudder.

"I'll be giving all three of you instructions, sweetheart," Arthus corrected. "Firstly, you're going to come on Marlen's face."

He said it so factually, like he was stating a mundane fact rather than commanding orgasms from my body. Maddening.

As much as I wanted to disobey on principle, Arthus' dominant tone always affected me. His deep, authoritative voice made me *want* to submit. And when Marlen's tongue started flicking hard against my clit faster than I even thought possible, I obeyed spectacularly, announcing my orgasm loud enough for the whole freaking vineyard to hear. Eamon's mouth came down on mine, swallowing my cries and prolonging my ecstasy as his hands worked my nipples.

"Eamon, pick Fi up," Arthus ordered as I laid back against the counter, boneless and happy. "Start fucking her, standing up. Marlen, get the oil."

I practically orgasmed again at the thought of having both of them fucking me in into oblivion while standing in the middle of the kitchen. It was sordid and filthy, and I was all about it.

Eamon lifted me into his strong arms like I weighed nothing at all, and I wrapped my arms around his neck with my legs around his waist as he gripped my ass and lined his enormous cock up with my entrance. It was no accident that Arthus had instructed Eamon to stand in front of me.

He was way too big for my ass. I'd absolutely die. It'd be a happy death, but a death nonetheless.

I moaned obscenely as Eamon sank into me, squirming shamelessly in his arms as he pulled me down onto his cock. It felt *so* good, but it just wasn't enough. As if I'd summoned him with my mind, Marlen's chest pressed up against my back and I could hear the slickness of the oil as he fisted his cock, before his fingers moved to my asshole, teasing me slowly, preparing me for him.

"Hurry up, M," Arthus said impatiently. "Fi's getting greedy."

He was right, I was. Arthus had painted a pretty, erotic picture in my mind, and I wanted it to become a reality.

Marlen held my hip steady with one hand as he used the other to guide his cock into my ass. "Relax, foxglove," he murmured sweetly, leaning forward to place light kisses down my spine. I melted into him, reaching back with one hand to wrap it around his neck.

Holy Fi Sandwich, this is delicious.

I decided I had a *thing* for being held up in the air. The weightlessness heightened all the other sensations my body was feeling.

"Very good," Arthus purred in approval. "Now, make her come."

Marlen and Eamon both laughed quietly as they began to move in tandem, setting every nerve ending in my body on fire. I writhed impatiently between them, chasing my release, mindless with need and entirely reliant on them to move me in this position. My nails raked across the back of Marlen's neck as well as down Eamon's arm and chest. *Mine.*

"That's it, sweetheart. Mark them. Your mates. Show us how much you want us. Come for us."

I realized I'd subconsciously been waiting for his encouragement when Arthus' words sent me spiraling into bliss. Marlen and Eamon's pace didn't lessen as they fucked me into my next orgasm, and another one after that. It was too much. *Too good.* Pleasure that rode the edge of pain.

With a fierce thrust, Eamon groaned his release and stilled as Marlen followed not long after. My head fell forward onto Eamon's chest and I sighed. Messy, sticky, and oh so happy.

I barely even noticed Marlen and Eamon withdrawing and placing me gently into Arthus' arms. He carried me easily through the house into the private bathroom and set me down carefully on my feet in the shower as he stripped and got the water running.

"What are you doing?" I slurred, still a little lust-drunk.

"Taking care of my mate," Arthus replied, as if it should have been obvious.

As he gently ran the bar of shampoo over my hair and lovingly washed every inch of my skin, it was easy to forget that this was the fae who had once shied away from any kind of non-sexual touch. A lifetime of fearing people were only trying to get close to him to cut off his wings had made Arthus very selective about physical intimacy. The fact that he was now comfortable enough to let me touch him whenever I wanted was a gift that meant everything to me.

Satisfied that I was clean, Arthus shut off the water, dried us both off and wrapped me in his bathrobe, which was much larger and comfier than my own. I doubted those were his reasons for dressing me in his clothes, but I wasn't going to complain either way.

He scooped me up and carried me back out to the living room, depositing me on the sofa where Eamon appeared almost immediately with a cup of piping hot peppermint tea.

"Now would be a good time to ask about Briallen's party," Marlen whispered dramatically as he dropped into the spot next to me and threw his arm over the back of the sofa.

I tried to hide my smile behind my teacup, but I was too slow for Arthus. He rolled his eyes, not looking—or feeling—particularly upset. "Fine, we'll go. It isn't far from here anyway, right?"

Eamon shook his head. "Twenty minutes' flight at the most."

"You'll wear a cloaking amulet the whole time, though," Arthus warned. "And you'll need to utilize your gift the entire time we're there, no matter how uncomfortable it gets. If anyone wants to follow in Glendower's footsteps, we'll need as much warning as possible."

"Agreed," I said easily, nodding my head. I wanted to ensure my safety as much as they did.

Arthus' eyes narrowed suspiciously at my acquiescence. "And if we're concerned at any point about your safety, we're leaving."

"Fine," I assented, waving my hand absently. "Do you really think I'm going to put myself at risk for a party? If at any point the situation becomes dangerous, we should leave."

"Good, I'm glad we're in agreement." Seemingly mollified, Arthus disappeared into the kitchen and Marlen chuckled softly in my ear. "Nicely done, foxglove."

"Good teamwork," I added cheerfully, holding out my palm for him to low-five.

Looks like we'd be partying with Briallen and her guys after all. Which meant that, whether I was ready for it or not, Bryn and I were going to have that long overdue chat.

BRYN

CHAPTER 65

A bashing on the door of my cabin woke me up. I'd been staying in my small cabin on my aunt and uncles' property for the past six or so weeks, making plans, biding my time, and just generally wondering what the fuck I was doing with my life.

I pulled a shirt on as I made my way to the door, and Briallen shoved her way inside before I'd even got it open all the way, beaming with excitement.

"I just got word from Fi, they're attending the party tomorrow and they'll be staying the night. They can stay in your cabin, right?" she asked, rocking back and forth on the balls of her feet.

"Where am I supposed to stay?" I grumbled, throwing a larger than necessary ball of fire at the stove so I could put some tea on.

"With them...? Obviously?"

"We haven't discussed anything like that," I snapped, although I *had* stayed with them at Eamon's cabin that one time...

"And whose fault is that?" Briallen asked rhetorically, sounding exasperated as she rifled through the small kitchen area, looking for tea leaves. "Why are you even here? You should have just gone straight to Eamon's place. I bet she's claimed him by now."

"I've been keeping busy here, working on things in the background to assist with Ffion's task," I countered, avoiding her question. Truthfully,

I wasn't sure why I hadn't gone to see her. I'd contemplated it so many times—I knew where she was staying—but every time I considered going, something held me back.

I wanted her to come to me. I wanted to know that she wanted me. I wanted her to take a leap too. Maybe I was a little afraid that she never would. That the damage had already been done.

"Fine, don't tell me." Briallen sighed. "If you two don't have a one-on-one chat this weekend, I'm going to bind you together with vines until you sort your shit out."

"I could just burn them off."

"I'll get Leigh to douse your flames with water every time you try. I'm serious, Bryn. You haven't even told her you left the Academy and insisted I didn't either. For all she knows, you're still there and not upset in the least that she's gone. Imagine how you would feel if she meets another fae she feels a strong mating pull to while she's traveling around Avalon, saving the fae? You'll regret it for the rest of your life."

Tossing me the tin of tea leaves, she waltzed out with one last imperious look. She was right, it would be like losing a limb. I'd feel the echoes of that loss for the rest of my life.

I may not have been the most welcoming to Ffion in the past, but every interaction we'd had since occurred because I went to her, or someone forced us together. It hadn't bothered me in the past—male fae were expected to do all the work for a female they wanted—but something about that system bothered me when it came to Ffion. Probably the knowledge that she wouldn't buy into it. She wasn't from this world, she'd never acted like a female fae who expected males to crawl over broken glass for her attention.

Maybe I just wanted her to want me too.

Gods, I'd get my fucking balls back any day now.

I finished my tea and made some bread and jam for breakfast before heading down the narrow hallway of my cabin to the bathroom for a shower. My aunt and uncles had built it for me when I was 16 and needed a little space from their cozy family dynamic because while I cared about them, I'd never felt like I truly belonged here.

The cabin had a round living area with a small kitchenette, a short hallway with a bedroom off one side, and a bathroom at the end. It'd be a tight fit for Ffion and her three guys in here, but the main house was already full with extended family and Ffion would be more comfortable away from the crowd anyway.

I'd probably sleep under the gazebo on the front lawn. Being around my extended family was an exercise in patience, and I was not in the mood.

At midday, I made my way up the path to the back of the house, then around the side to the front lawn to greet my reluctant visitor. Regardless of where things stood with Ffion and me, I could still help her with her task.

With a face like he'd just sucked a lemon, Enfys stormed across the vast expanse of lawn towards me. I tilted my head towards the gazebo a short distance from the main house, not wanting this conversation to be overheard. Not that my family would be upset, but they were meddlesome by nature, and my uncles would probably enjoy fucking with Enfys for sport.

I strode ahead, dropping onto the bench a few seconds before Enfys got there. He shot me a brief scowl as he sat stiffly on the bench opposite, as far away from me as he could possibly get.

Ffion's emotion scouting ability would be pretty convenient right now. Was Enfys feeling bitterness? Resentment? Vicious loathing? A mixture of all three? Probably.

"Did you discover anything?" I asked sharply, skipping the pleasantries. No point pretending either of us wanted to be around each other.

"I think we have potential allies in three Councilors," Enfys responded just as curtly. "Glendower has the other six firmly under his control, but three appear to oppose him."

"Have you been able to get close to them?"

"Not so far," Enfys replied grimly. "I can't risk Glendower noticing me hanging around. He'll question me about Fi at the very least. At the most, we know he's not above torture."

I nodded, mulling over his words. Enfys was a dick, but torture was probably a bit extreme. Besides, he might end up telling Glendower something about Ffion, and that wasn't an acceptable risk.

Still, this was progress. Allies on the Council might be enough to tip the scales in Ffion's favor.

Enfys watched me closely out of the corner of his eye, his face pinched.

"You're still not good enough for her."

"I know," I replied honestly.

"I still want you to stay away from her," he gritted out.

"I know."

"I would be better for her," Enfys sniped.

"Ah, that's where you're wrong. Your family may be better respected than mine, and your gift may be more useful to Ffion than mine. You may even be better at getting along with her other mates—though given your social skills, I think that's unlikely—but you will never be better for Ffion than I am."

Enfys opened his mouth to object, but I barrelled on. "I understand her on a level you never will—her pride, her stubbornness, her curiosity, and her desire to overcome the obstacles she has faced in her life. I understand what drives her because the same things drive me. From the moment we felt the mating pull in Albion, she was mine, and I was hers. We just had to figure that out."

I wouldn't have been able to speak the words if I didn't believe them to be true, but I hadn't *realized* how much I believed them until I said them to Enfys. I doubted myself a lot, I had strayed from the plan I had for my life, and my future didn't look anything like how I'd planned, especially now that I'd left the Academy.

But underneath all of those concerns, I knew how I felt.

"And you've got it all figured out now?" Enfys taunted, though the tick in his jaw gave him away—my words had gotten to him.

"Does it matter? She's got you all figured out," I replied calmly, avoiding his question because I didn't have it all figured out. I knew how she felt about Enfys, though. That was never going to happen.

"Don't expect me to be happy for you," Enfys sighed, glaring out at the flat stretch of lawn edged with the colorful flowers my aunt adored so much.

It was an oddly peaceful backdrop for this fraught conversation.

"I wouldn't be happy for you if our roles were reversed." I stood up, eager to get rid of Enfys now that I'd said my piece. I was confident he'd continue to work in Ffion's interests regardless of whether or not she was courting him—he had taken Glendower's involvement in her capture as a personal betrayal.

Besides, he probably saw an opportunity for a promotion, the cunning little fucker.

Enfys stood too, and we walked in silence back to the edge of the lawn where his griffin was waiting. It wasn't exactly companionable, but it was the silence of two fae who had reached an agreement.

Enfys turned to me before he mounted the griffin. "Here," he grunted, shoving a piece of paper at me that he'd fished out of his pocket.

"What is this?"

"The location of my cottage in Garrán Naofa. I don't spend a lot of time there, but I thought Fi and her mates may find it useful. It isn't protected like I'm sure the Adair properties are, but it isn't connected to any of them."

"I'll be sure to let them know," I replied, impressed at his generosity. Garrán Naofa was an ancient area in the center of Avalon, home to the oldest temple. The name meant sacred grove, and it was said to be the area where the gods' presence was most strongly felt. If that were true, it would have been the perfect hideout for the Sanctified Empath.

"I'll work on the three rogue Councilors and get back to you. I'm confident we can form a positive working relationship."

I nodded curtly, not entirely knowing if he was talking about working with me, or the three Councilors.

Once I'd gotten that little chore out of the way, I could go back to preparing my cabin for our guests and avoiding my inebriated family in peace.

I slept restlessly knowing that I'd be seeing Ffion the next day, and I paced back and forth through the front garden, impatient for them to arrive. Briallen had invited her to come early, even though she would spend most of the day preparing for the celebration, so I assumed that particular request was for my benefit. Meddlesome cousin.

Six weeks. Six weeks since Ffion had been kicked out of the Academy. Six weeks since I'd told Gwyneira I was giving up my place there. But Ffion didn't know that.

Only the gods knew how she'd react when she realized I'd been here the whole time. A tearful hug would be nice. A slap across the face wouldn't be entirely surprising. I'd settle for anything except her indifference.

The tug of the mating pull in my chest made my stupid heart skip a stupid beat. I didn't realize how much I'd been missing that sensation.

I shielded my eyes from the sun's glare as the two griffins descended, and a twinge of jealousy flared as I noted Eamon's tight grip around her waist, the way Ffion was nestled back between his thighs. Lucky fucker.

I focused on my irritation at having to deal with my entire extended family for Briallen's claiming celebration to smother my jealousy before Ffion could pick up on it.

She swung her leg over the griffin before her mates had a chance to dismount, but I was there to catch her, holding her waist and guiding her to the ground. Possibly holding her a *little* closer than strictly necessary and enjoying the feel of her body sliding down mine.

"Scout," I said quietly, still lightly gripping her hips.

"Bryn," she replied softly, her hands resting on my chest as she peered up at me curiously. "Care to explain what you've been doing here for the past six weeks?"

Straight to the point, that was my Ffion. I took a step back, unwillingly releasing my hold on her so I could guide them around the property to my cabin.

"Why do you think I've been here?" I tossed over my shoulder at her, enjoying her puzzled expression as I strode ahead. I couldn't just walk next to her and not touch her. The temptation was too great, and I didn't know how she felt about me yet. Not really.

"You left the same day we did," Arthus stated quietly, falling into step alongside me.

"Of course," I agreed.

"You've been here the whole time?"

"I have."

"You didn't come to the Old Adair Estate," he said, glancing at me strangely.

"I didn't."

Arthus snorted. "I'd bet ten bronze coins you'll be leaving with us, though."

"Twenty bronze coins says he'll be leaving with us with a claiming mark on his wrist," Marlen added, breezing past us with his satchel flung over one shoulder and Ffion's on the other. She was trailing behind us, arm-in-arm with Eamon, admiring the garden.

"I'm not even courting her yet," I argued, my magic flaring hot under my skin. They were getting more than a few steps ahead of themselves.

"Doesn't matter," Marlen said with a shrug. "That's not how you and Fi work. You two are explosive. It'll be all or nothing."

I shook my head, trying to stop the smile twitching at the corner of my mouth at his absurdity. When Briallen had claimed Leigh and Marlen started hanging around them all the time, I'd initially found him annoyingly chipper. The more I got to know him, the more I got to see him interacting with Ffion, I realized he was growing on me.

Like a fungus.

"Come on. I'll show you to where you'll be staying."

We slowed so Ffion and Eamon could catch up with us and only when I was next to her did I notice the addition of a third line to her claiming mark. I found myself thinking again of how irritating my nosy Great Aunt

Ceara was to smother the sudden surge of jealousy.

"FI!"

Briallen's piercing shriek as she barreled around the corner made all of us wince. I discreetly positioned myself behind Ffion, in case I needed to catch her.

Briallen leaped on Ffion, clinging tightly to her neck. "I missed you, Fi. The Academy has been so boring without you."

Leigh and Hagan rounded the corner, giving their mate indulgent grins. I suppressed an eye roll.

"You totally look at Fi like that," Marlen whispered, leaning in to speak to me.

"The fuck I do," I retorted, scowling at him.

"Deny it all you want, but I've seen it. It's a more ragey version of that expression, but the gist of it is the same," he replied with a chuckle. *Asshole.*

"How are ya', Fi?" Leigh called, moving around her to clap Marlen on the back. "Hasn't been the same at the Academy without you lot."

"I've missed you guys too," Ffion replied with a smile, wrapping her arm around Briallen's shoulders and avoiding Leigh's question. "Are you excited for tonight's celebration?"

"So excited," Briallen sighed, leaning her head against Ffion's shoulder. "I want to stay and catch up properly, but I need to get ready. I have a very specific vision for my dress."

"Naturally," Ffion laughed. "Bryn was just showing us where we'd be staying."

"Oh, with him, in his cabin," Briallen said breezily, absently waving her hand in the air. *Quite the actress, my cousin.* "Anyway, Leigh? Hagan? We should go get ready now."

She threw her arms around Ffion and gave her another quick hug before skipping off back to the house to avoid the fallout of the bomb she'd just dropped.

Ffion turned to look at me with one eyebrow raised and amusement written all over her face.

"Come on," I grunted irritably. "I'll show you to my cabin where you four will be staying."

"That's not what Briallen said," Marlen sang behind me.

"Briallen's too busy with party planning to manage sleeping arrangements," I bit back. Six weeks I'd waited to see Ffion and now that she was here, I had no idea what I was doing.

Gods, the sooner the caterers brought out the ale, the better off I'd be.

FFION

CHAPTER 66

All four guys were monumentally unhelpful when explaining what a mating circle celebration entailed. I'd spent the afternoon grilling them as we lazed around in Bryn's cabin, and they all gave me some variation of "it's a party."

Once we arrived on the stretch of lawn in front of the house, I realized they weren't unhelpful in this instance. It really was just a party—a fancy party—but a party nonetheless. There was nothing ceremonial about it, no aisle, no grand entrance, no first dance. There was a bar however, I noted with amusement.

I wasn't disappointed per se that I'd never have a traditional human wedding, because the wedding had never been the thing I'd fantasized about. I'd spent my whole life hoping I'd be able to build enough of a connection with someone to even *get* to that point, because it seemed like an impossible dream when I was growing up. Now I had *three* someones.

Maybe one day I'd have a mating circle celebration of my own and I'd wear a white dress and make everyone dance and eat cake. I always imagined those were the best bits of a wedding anyway.

Briallen looked ethereal in her enormous lavender dress. The bodice was delicate, with thin spaghetti straps holding it up, but the skirt was at least three feet wide, made up of layers upon layers of fabric. The whole gown was interspersed with live flowers she must have created herself—in the exact same shade of dusky pink as her hair—and brushed with glittering fairy dust. She'd done her hair in some kind of thick, intricate braid with more flowers woven throughout.

She looked majestically beautiful, like a proper fairy princess, and her mates couldn't keep their eyes off her.

Fortunately, my mates only had eyes for me or I'd have to kill them. I'd chosen a slinky emerald dress that fell to mid-calf but had a split up one side that showed off a decent stretch of thigh. It was silky with off-the-shoulder straps, and I'd died a little bit from happiness when Eamon had gifted it to me. My long, curly hair was down, with just the front bits twisted back.

Bryn seemed to materialize next to us out of nowhere as our little group stood on the edge of the grounds, surveying the crowd. These people were Briallen's friends and family. I wasn't overly worried about my safety, but I didn't relish the idea of being in a crowd either. I'd promised Arthus I wouldn't mute my ability, and I intended to keep that promise.

"Come on," Bryn muttered, just loud enough for the group of us to hear him. "They're storing the rest of the alcohol around the side of the house."

We all followed him quite happily, eager to avoid the crowd. Marlen was even whistling like a godsdamned psychopath.

The guys all helped themselves to pitchers of ale while Bryn poured me a glass of fae wine without even asking. *One point for Bryn.*

Instead of leading us back to where we'd been awkwardly hovering, we followed Bryn around the outskirts of the lawn to a gazebo, half-hidden among the masses of tall colorful flowers that ring-fenced the flat expanse of grass. Bryn and Arthus sat on one bench, and I squeezed between Marlen and Eamon on the opposite one, half sitting in both of their laps.

I crossed my legs primly and took a very regal sip of my wine, perched upon my Throne of Hot Fae. Bryn snorted.

"I was sitting here with Enfys recently," Bryn said conversationally, like it was a totally normal occurrence.

"Why?" I asked, totally mystified, taking another swig of my wine because they'd really sprung for the good stuff. Enfys had been a Grade-A asshole to Bryn, so I couldn't imagine what they had to talk about.

"He and I made a deal at the Spring Equinox bonfire. He agreed to report back on the goings-on at the Council."

"In exchange for what?" Arthus asked suspiciously.

"My assurance that I wouldn't advertise the fact he'd been enthusiastically cooperating with Ffion's kidnappers when news of their actions comes to light," Bryn replied lightly.

"That's blackmail," I pointed out, not altogether upset about it. Maybe the torture had broken my moral compass.

"I prefer to think of it as a mutually beneficial agreement." Bryn shrugged.

"I'm sure you do," I murmured, trying to discreetly give Bryn an appreciative once-over, because the wine was going straight to my head and by the gods he looked *good* dressed up.

Leigh appeared abruptly at the entrance to the gazebo, looking like a man dying of thirst who'd just found an oasis in the desert. He leaned his shoulder against the post and scrubbed one hand down his face. His light brown hair was sticking up in every direction like he'd been pulling it.

Or like Briallen had been pulling it. It was hard to say, really.

"By the gods, making all this small talk is exhausting," he groaned, raising his pitcher of ale at us. I raised my wine in cheers and downed half the glass in one. *So delicious. So relaxing.*

"Surely more exhausting for Hagan?" Marlen asked. "You've been around for ages, no one's interested in you anymore. The hazards of being the first mate," Marlen said with a dramatic sigh, elbowing me in the ribs. I felt a little flash of pride from him that warmed my heart.

"They are far more interested in him," Leigh conceded. "Good thing too, he's far more charming than I am, the bastard."

Bryn grumbled something that sounded a lot like "*wouldn't be hard,*" but as he was maybe the least charming fae I'd ever met, he hardly had room to judge.

"So when will your mating circle celebration be, Fi? I assume you'll be taking this grumpy prick with you when you leave." Leigh inclined his head at Bryn, and I choked on a mouthful of wine.

"I think that means we're still discussing the logistics," Marlen replied amiably as Eamon thumped me on the back, peering at me with an alarmed expression. I squeezed his enormous thigh to let him know I was okay.

"Did you want something?" Bryn snarled at Leigh and I wondered for the millionth time where Bryn and I stood. It wasn't enough to read Bryn's emotions—he was too good at manipulating them. I wanted to get inside his head and read his thoughts.

No, I wanted to see inside his soul. I wanted the mating bond.

I shook off that errant thought. I had no idea if that's what Bryn wanted. Well, not no idea. Just not a definite idea. *Gods, this wine is glorious.*

"Your aunt and uncles want to meet this Ffion they've heard so much about. And her mates, of course," he added as an afterthought, making Marlen chuckle.

"Oh," I replied lamely, climbing off Marlen and Eamon to stand and straightening out my dress. "You could have mentioned that before I started on the wine," I muttered. My face felt super hot. Could everyone tell how hot my face was?

"Don't worry about that, scout. If both Briallen and my aunt aren't three glasses in and slurring their words, I'll be your personal servant for the rest of the evening," Bryn grumbled as he strode out of the gazebo and onto the lawn.

I blinked, processing his words. Boy, did I hope he was wrong. I could have a lot of fun with Bryn as my personal servant.

He wasn't wrong. Briallen and her mother were both barely coherent. They were also the happiest drunks I'd ever met, which may be why no one seemed too bothered about all the stumbling and high pitched cackling.

Briallen had mentioned before that her parents were in their seventies, and seeing them fully cemented the long lifespan of fae for me. Tal Edan looked more like Briallen's sister than her mother. She had pink hair too, though it was more of a pale blush shade than Briallen's dusky rose, and Briallen's fathers—Oscar and Quillan—were laughing loudly, palling around with their guests like any young fae at the Academy would. My eyes shot curiously to Bryn, trying to figure out where he fit in this dynamic.

He was smirking while watching his family with an almost indulgent look in his eyes. It was clear that he loved them, but I wondered if he felt like he was truly one of them. They all seemed rather exuberant in comparison to his quiet, brooding nature. Bryn had more layers than an onion.

"This is the girl, is it?" Quillan announced loudly, striding over to greet us. His joy was infectious, it fizzed in my stomach like champagne bubbles. This was definitely who Briallen got her buoyant personality from.

"I don't know about that," I replied, laughing it off because Bryn's face and emotions were entirely unreadable. Had he talked about me?

"I do," Quillan assured me, nodding his head eagerly. "Ffion Laisren, from the Academy of Avalon. Our Bryn's been tied up in knots over you."

"And we're done," Bryn cut in smoothly, resting his hand on my lower back and guiding me towards Briallen's other father, Oscar. "Thanks for that, Uncle Q," Bryn called over his shoulder as his uncle's laughter followed us.

My attention was soon diverted as we reached Oscar, who was setting up a table with shot glasses bunched together in groups of three. He added a drop of different liquids to each one, then pulled out a large bottle of clear alcohol. As he poured it into the shot glasses, the alcohol changed color—one pink, one blue, and one green in each cluster of three.

"One for each member of the mating circle," Eamon explained quietly. "To toast to their good health and a long, happy relationship."

"It's potent though, foxglove," Marlen warned, sounding like he hoped I'd drink it anyway. *I mean, I shouldn't. Right?* Because we might be in danger and all that. But everyone seemed really nice. Plus, I was wearing the cloaking amulet.

And I was already drunk.

"So," Oscar announced, clapping his hands together. "Who will join me in toasting the happy circle?"

"Ooh, you'll join in, won't you, Fi?" Briallen slurred cheerily, appearing next to me and leaning heavily against my side. I was pretty sure she'd be out for the count if she had three shots now, but it was her party, I wasn't judging.

"Sure, B," I announced, stepping up to the table next to Bryn, who gave me an appraising look. Marlen, Arthus and Eamon all hung back watching, blessedly quiet if they were questioning my life choices.

Gods, I need a night off. Just one. A night to be 20 and celebrate my best friend's happily ever after.

Briallen, Bryn, and I all reached for the pink shot first, clinking our glasses together and downing it in one. I was expecting something similar to vodka, or perhaps gin, but I'm pretty sure what I got was paint stripper. I did my best to tamp down my coughing and spluttering as Briallen shuddered lightly and Bryn barely even grimaced.

I threw Marlen a quick glare for laughing at me before grabbing the blue and green shots and downing them one after the other.

This shit is nasty. Best to get it over and done with.

"Fuck, you actually drank all three? We should find you some food," Bryn marveled, sounding both awed and uncharacteristically concerned.

"Bread, preferably," Arthus muttered.

"You're all being dramatic." I waved my hand, aiming for nonchalance and probably failing because gods my head was spinning.

Food sounded good, though. I needed to get the taste of paint stripper out of my mouth.

"What's paint stripper?" Bryn asked, giving me a puzzled look.

"Did I say that out loud? Shit, that was probably really rude."

Like an angel, Eamon appeared in front of me with a plate stacked high with finger food. Pastries! So many pastries. I sunk down onto the grass, leaning back against the shots table and tucked into my snacks.

Bryn and Marlen dropped down on either side of me and I growled under my breath at their quick reflexes as they repeatedly stole food off my plate. Eamon looked amused, but Arthus was giving me his best frowny face. Maybe he'd spank me later.

That would be great.

The sky darkened until eventually Briallen, Leigh and Hagan joined our little friendship circle on the grass, as did Eamon and Arthus, somewhat reluctantly.

Eamon used his earth magic to create a small ring of rocks in the middle of our circle, which Bryn filled with fire. The weather had been warming up and the chirping of crickets mixed in with the clinking of glasses and laughter of the partygoers.

Maybe one day this could be my life all the time. No massive responsibilities, no fate-of-the-fae on my shoulders. Just me, my mates, and my friends getting shitfaced under the stars.

I was definitely too drunk to participate in the conversation, but I smiled like a loon, surrounded by some of my favorite fae in the universe.

Are we even in the universe? How did this whole separate realm thing work in relation to Earth's place in the solar system? Was Avalon a different planet?

"Okay, bedtime for you," Arthus announced. I looked around and found Marlen, Briallen and both her mates howling with laughter while Bryn and Eamon shook their heads.

"Perhaps we'll save the lesson on the complexities of inter-realm travel for when your head's a little clearer, scout," Bryn suggested lightly. *Asshole.* Why wasn't he drunk? He'd had those awful shots too.

Eamon moved behind me and slid his hands under my armpits to pull me to my feet. His arm banded around my waist even though I'd have been totally fine walking on my own. 98% fine.

5% fine?

"Want to ride on my back?" Eamon said softly in my ear, sounding like he was struggling not to laugh.

"Sure." I shrugged, cool as a cucumber. Shaking with silent laughter, Eamon turned so I could jump on his back, wrapping my arms around his neck and my thighs around his waist.

"I'd suggest saying goodbye to Briallen before we go, but she's already asleep." Marlen chortled, watching Leigh and Hagan do their best to lift her without waking her up.

I quite enjoyed our walk back to Bryn's cabin. I rested my cheek on Eamon's broad shoulder and took in the garden by moonlight and the mesmerizing fireflies that hung in the air.

"You're staying, right?" Marlen asked Bryn as we reached the base of the stairs.

Bryn turned to me, raising a questioning eyebrow. Everyone was so quiet, like they were all holding their breath or something. *Weird.* Gods, I needed a glass of water.

"Er, it's your cabin, so you should stay." I gestured absently at said cabin. Bryn's relaxed expression shuttered instantly.

"I'll see you all tomorrow," he said tightly before turning on his heel and leaving.

"You may have screwed that one up, foxglove," Marlen sighed. I didn't reply. I was already almost asleep on Eamon's shoulder.

I'd deal with... whatever the problem was, tomorrow.

FFION

CHAPTER 67

I woke up in a borderline homicidal mood. My eyelids felt gritty, my skull was too small for my brain, and my stomach churned sickeningly.

No more fae wine. Ever.

Definitely no more shots.

This must be what dying feels like.

There was an obscenely loud chuckle from somewhere next to me, and I realized I must have said that out loud.

"Go away," I grumbled, pulling a pillow over my face. "You're too loud."

"You're so mean when you're hungover," Marlen whined, poking me lightly in the ribs like he had a godsdamned death wish.

"Why are you pestering me right now? What did I ever do to you?"

I felt the bed move as Marlen shook with silent laughter. At least he was keeping it down now.

Just as I closed my eyes, trying to fall back asleep and willing the world to stop spinning, I felt Marlen's hand push under my sleep top and rest on my ribcage, fingers brushing light under my breast.

Has he freaking lost it? I have never been less in the mood in my life.

I was about to tell him as much when I felt the delicious warmth of his healing magic spread from under his palm, seeking out all my ills. I let out an indecent groan as my too small skull grew to what felt normal-sized again.

As soon as the magic receded, I was on Marlen, tossing the pillows and blankets off me and straddling his hips.

"Seriously? You could have been healing my hangovers this whole time?" I hissed.

Marlen tossed me back into the center of the bed with a laugh, standing up and straightening his shirt. "Sure, but how would you learn?"

"You're infuriating," I bit back, rolling myself out of bed.

"Probably." Marlen shrugged. "I'd planned on letting you suffer today too, but Leigh dropped by to tell us Bryn slept in the cave he retreats to whenever he's sulking and he hasn't emerged yet. We hoped that maybe you could drag him out. We need to talk to him about Enfys. And everything else."

"Why would I be able to drag him out?" I asked, mystified. Marlen just rolled his eyes in response.

"I'm not going to dignify that with an answer. Besides, you probably need to apologize, I think you might have really hurt his feelings last night, foxglove. You two are as bad as each other when it comes to communicating."

Did I? Shit. Everything after the shots was pretty fuzzy.

"You might want to shower first, though. Healing magic can't cure the wine smell," he said with a cheeky grin, flicking his fingers and catching my cheek with a splash of his water magic. Before I had a chance to blast him with air, he'd disappeared down the hallway, his laughter reverberating through the walls.

I had a super quick shower because the bathroom in Bryn's cabin didn't get hot water, presumably because he could fire magic up some kind of heating system and never had to worry about it. The cold water did an effective job of washing away the remnants of my hangover, at least. I dried my hair with air magic and pulled on a simple plum-colored dress that buttoned from the scooped neckline to where it fell just above my knees.

Unsure about how I was supposed to coax a grumpy Bryn out of his hidey-hole, I pulled out all the spare clothes I'd packed from my satchel and filled it with what was left of the guys' breakfast—bread with jam that I wrapped in cloth, an apple, and a handful of berries. If all else failed, I'd try to entice him out with some food like an animal.

Marlen escorted me through the forest path until the mouth of the cave was in view. The entrance was easily tall enough to walk through, and while the outside and surrounding area was lush and mossy, the inside appeared to be oddly rocky and dry from what I could see. Perhaps Briallen had used her earth magic to make it more comfortable for Bryn—or at least less flammable.

"This is where I leave you, foxglove. It'll only make Bryn grumpier if I hang around. Besides, you'll be safe with him," Marlen said cheerfully, leaning down to plant a firm kiss on my lips before walking away, whistling to himself.

Honestly. They were lucky I found their determination to get me and Bryn together endearing.

Hoping I wasn't entering the wolf's den, I secured my satchel across my body and made my way tentatively into the cave. The entryway was bright, and a fire burned in a small circle of rocks in the center of the 10-foot deep cavern, illuminating the space. It was plain and unfurnished, but it looked like grooves had been carved out to create a seating area in one corner. I wondered how much time Bryn had spent here growing up.

I briefly worried that I was going to panic since the last time I'd been in a cave had been *awful*, but it never eventuated. Maybe it was the brightness of the space and the large open entryway, or maybe it was the mating pull in my chest, keeping me anchored. Bryn had been my knight-in-shining-armor, after all.

The fae in question sat against the cave wall, just inside the entryway, lazily flicking fireballs at the opposing wall. I dropped down next to him, and we sat next to each other on the cave floor in silent reflection.

There was no point trying to get a read on Bryn's emotions when he was doing his level best to hide them.

"Look, I'm sorry if I was a dick to you last night. Honestly, I'm not 100%

sure of the details. The shots were a terrible idea. I'm not making excuses or anything, just... sorry." The words felt like they were being wrenched from my body. I hated apologizing, it made me feel vulnerable. I'd spent my entire life hiding my vulnerabilities.

"Fine," Bryn grunted, as if he hadn't been so upset that he'd slept in a cave all night. I wasn't about to just leave things like this though. It was time for The Big Talk. The moment where I found out if this connection between Bryn and I was going anywhere.

It was a conversation that was long overdue, but we both had to let down our guards for it to happen.

I may have hated being vulnerable, but I couldn't have this conversation without it, and neither could he.

"Alright. Let's do this," I sighed, watching the fireballs fizz out as they hit the rock wall.

"Do what?" Bryn asked drily, not looking at me.

"Talk. About all of it. We are going to clear the air and get on the same page, and neither of us are leaving this cave until that happens."

"Is that so?" Bryn asked, sounding mildly amused.

"It is. I even brought snacks." I patted the satchel slung across my body. "Let's start with why you were so hostile towards me when we first met," I added a little reluctantly. I wasn't entirely sure I wanted to hear the answers he had for me, but it was a question that lingered at the back of my mind, and I needed to know so we could move forward.

Bryn let out a long breath, staring at the cave wall. "What do you know about my parents?"

His shield of anger and irritation dropped, and I chanced a glance at him out of the corner of my eye, finding that his expression perfectly reflected what he was feeling—resigned, tired, subdued.

"Not much. Briallen mentioned some kind of, um, family tragedy? She said it was your story to tell." *Gods, I am awkward.* I'm pretty sure being an empath had somehow made me worse at dealing with sensitive emotions.

Bryn hummed under his breath. "My parents had a strong mating pull.

Like ours, I assume. My mother had claimed both my fathers within two months of each other and they lived happily, as far as I'm aware, for many decades."

He paused, lost in thought, and I gave him space to collect himself.

"They eventually had me, and my few memories of them are mostly good. My fathers went out of their way to spend time with me. One of them ran a sanctuary for griffins who had escaped captivity. It was a place for them to recover and learn to trust the fae again, and I spent a lot of my childhood flying."

That explained why Bryn was such a natural in the air. He'd been flying ever since he could walk.

"And your mother?" I asked hesitantly as Bryn's mood plummeted.

"Distant, mostly. Like she lived in her own world. She stayed in bed a lot," he mused sadly. "One night, I woke up suddenly, I'm not sure why. There were flames in my room, rushing towards the bed. Fae fire. My mother had a fire affinity. She hadn't been well for a long time, and I guess she hit her breaking point that night."

I felt the blood drain from my face. I'd been expecting something awful—everyone had hinted at it without giving me any details—but this was so much worse than I could have even imagined. A "tragedy" would have been losing his parents in some kind of freak accident. There wasn't a word to describe his mother setting fire to his house with him and his fathers inside. It was beyond comprehension.

Tentatively, I placed my hand over Bryn's. He flipped his palm over and linked our fingers together without looking at me, the heat emanating from his skin seeping into mine.

"That night I discovered I had a fire affinity too. I pushed the flames back enough for me to climb out the window. She didn't see me, but I could hear her laughing from the other room."

"Gods, Bryn. I am so sorry, that is horrific."

"The Council Enforcers who came to investigate determined that my mother had tied my fathers to the bed before she set the fire. She laid down with them in the end, and they all died together," he grimaced, although his tone remained factual and detached. "Briallen's parents came to collect me from the Council authorities as soon as they heard. Took me in and raised me as their own."

"You're close with them," I stated, watching his reaction. It was hard to tell with Bryn—he barely spent any time with Briallen, but I knew he adored her. It wasn't too much of a stretch to assume that Bryn had trouble expressing his feelings for others.

"I find them difficult to relate to. As you saw last night, they're very... outgoing. They've always been kind to me though, and I owe them everything." He dropped my hand and stood, pacing back and forth in front of me. I felt the loss of contact keenly. Not wanting to look up at him from the floor, I stood and leaned back against the wall, adjusting the strap of my satchel.

"You said your parents felt a strong mating pull, like we do." I began, not entirely sure if I wanted to know more, but needing to push through my own discomfort. "Is that why you fight this thing between us?"

"Fought, past tense," Bryn retorted, giving me a sharp look. "I never wanted to feel blinded by a strong mating pull like I always thought my fathers were. I blamed them, thinking that if they'd paid closer attention to my mother, seen past the connection they felt with her, they'd have realized she needed help. That she wasn't a suitable mate, or a suitable mother."

I swallowed hard. Even if I disagreed with him, I could hardly argue with him about it. Bryn had his reasons for feeling the way he did, and it wasn't my place to tell him those reasons were wrong.

"And now?" I asked eventually.

"Now, I'm less concerned, though I don't regret not rushing into a courtship with you. I gave the mating pull too much credit for how my fathers acted, but it took a while to realize that. To realize that having a strong mating pull doesn't make you blind, because I see *you*, Ffion. I see your pride, your stubbornness, your unwillingness to ask for help. And I like them. You wouldn't be you without those things."

My heart leaped to my throat. It was the most romantic thing he'd ever said to me, and even if he had just delivered it as factually as if he was reading the newspaper, it was almost too sweet to bear. I didn't know how to respond to a declaration like that.

"If you're waiting for an apology, you'll be waiting a long time," Bryn said drolly like the sweetheart he was, probably taking pity on me as I was still struggling to come up with an answer.

I almost giggled in relief at the out he was giving me. And weirdly, I didn't think I needed an apology. Bryn had to set aside a lot of his hang ups to even get to this point with me, and that meant more to me than just hearing him say the word 'sorry'.

The slate was clear. We could write our own story from here on with nothing left unsaid between us, if we chose to.

"I'm not delusional, and I can leave our past in the past if you can, but I want to know what this thing between us is now. So tell me, Bryn, if you *see* me and you *like* me, why are you here at your aunt and uncles' house?"

"Briallen's mating celebration," Bryn replied gruffly, avoiding eye contact again. He stopped pacing and sat down on a flat rock against the wall, directly opposite me.

"Why have you been here for the past six weeks?" I sighed at his evasiveness. And I thought *I* was bad at talking about my feelings.

Bryn chanced a glance at me but broke eye contact again, almost looking a little sheepish, and something about that made me livid. This isn't what we *did,* it wasn't how we *worked.* I pushed Bryn, and he pushed me back. We tried to out-stubborn each other, out-pride each other, out-awkward each other, but we didn't *back down* from each other.

I pushed off the wall, stormed over and dropped to my knees in front of him where he sat leaning forward with his elbows resting on his knees. Shoving my satchel to the side, I got right up in his personal space like I had every right to be there, daring him to move away.

Bryn's eyes darkened at the challenge in my voice, his stare boring into mine. *Better.* I'd take this version of Bryn over the morose, distant one any day.

"I wasn't going to stay at the Academy after they kicked you out, Ffion," he said in a cutting tone. His anger was running hot, smothering his other emotions.

"Why. Are. You. *Here*?" I pushed, eyes narrowed.

Come on, Bryn. Don't back down.

"Why the fuck do you think, scout?" he retorted in a low voice, mirroring my scowl.

"Don't avoid the question, Bryn. You're stubborn, proud, and a pain in my ass 99% of the time, but you aren't a coward. Well, I didn't think you were until you left the Academy and hid out here, twenty minutes away from me, for the past six weeks."

He stared at me with a burning intensity, his jaw set, giving nothing away. I could feel his anger abating though, feel the undercurrent of fear and embarrassment he was trying to suppress.

I could also feel the pure, burning, unbridled love that he was trying to hide from me. That he'd been hiding with various degrees of success since he held me in his arms on the back of the griffin as we flew away from that ballroom.

Still, he said nothing. We didn't have a great track record of being honest with one another about our feelings. I should have said something way back then, on that griffin. Or in any of the moments I'd seen him since. I should have told him that I felt it too. That I was as scared of those feelings as he was, but that we didn't have to face them alone.

But at that moment, I kind of understood where he was coming from. Bryn had come to my rescue time and time again, and had been a constant presence on the sidelines even when he was denying the connection we felt to one another. He'd held me close, taken care of me, kissed me gently after he'd whisked me away from the Council ball. He'd taken on the guilt for the Castells capturing me, even when it wasn't his to take, and he'd held me in his arms when we'd flown back to the Academy from the Old Adair Estate.

Bryn had once asked me to open myself up to *seeing* what was between us, and I'd been sitting around waiting for him to make some grand gesture. It was my turn to take the next step, my turn to put myself out there and show him how I felt.

I grabbed Bryn around the back of the head and yanked him towards me, slamming my lips against his and breathing him in like he was the oxygen I needed to survive. He didn't miss a beat, his hands immediately gripped my ass, my knees grazing painfully against the cave floor as he pulled me tightly against his body.

This wasn't anything like our first kiss that I'd replayed a million times in my head, so sweet and tender and surprising. This was rough, passionate, feral, and honestly, everything I expected from Bryn.

His hands squeezed my ass possessively and as my mouth parted, he tilted my head further back, wrestling back control, but I'd never concede. Not with him. From the moment I'd met Bryn I had wanted to fuck him and fight him all at once. My hands were gripping his hair so tightly I was surprised I hadn't ripped a chunk out, my nails digging into his scalp as I tried to angle him where I wanted him, teeth scraping his lower lip as surely as his scraped mine.

Eventually, we came up for air, both panting heavily as we held on to each other like we would never let go. *This was it.* We'd finally taken the plunge.

I was never letting him go after this. I would never let him run and hide from me again.

Based on his love rushing through my system like the best kind of drug, he wouldn't let me go either.

"I love you too," I told him softly, letting him see the vulnerability written all over my face, contrasting with the ferocity of how tightly we were holding each other.

The rush of happiness I felt from Bryn was so potent, I semi wondered if I'd spontaneously orgasmed. Even my legs were trembling.

"Too, huh?" His lips twitched as he fought the grin that was trying to take over his face.

"You were thinking it," I said with an unapologetic shrug.

"Spying on my emotions again, hm? Maybe I should punish you for invading my privacy," he teased. *Teased!*

"There's no privacy between mates," I challenged.

"We're not mates yet, scout."

"Yet," I agreed, because when I told myself I'd never let him go, I godsdamned meant it.

I pulled off my satchel and sat it on the ground next to me, digging around in the pocket until my fingers brushed against the small scrap of leather I'd carelessly shoved in there after mine and Eamon's claiming ceremony. I pulled it out and offered it to Bryn, who took it with a cocked eyebrow.

He unfolded it and as his eyes scanned the ancient and magical words embossed on the leather, I felt another rush of pure, undiluted love. Despite already having three mates who loved me dearly, feeling the emotion from Bryn was no less potent, no less addictive.

It was a massive relief because handing him the claiming vows had been a hell of a gamble. He could have panicked. Or worse, laughed.

"Here? Right now?" Bryn asked, looking amused.

"I'm game if you are, Edan." I knew my smile was pretty savage, but I was letting the recklessness take over. Why wait? Five minutes or five years from now, this would always be the result. We were a foregone conclusion. Endgame.

"Oh, I'm game."

"Good. I hope you're not bad in bed," I teased. Bryn barked a laugh, and the sound both startled me and warmed me right down to my bones.

"You'll soon find out," he replied before yanking my head forward to capture my lips in another fierce, competitive kiss. I grinned in satisfaction against his mouth before giving his lower lip a swift, punishing bite.

Because I loved him.

Bryn growled, roughly yanking my satchel off before attacking the buttons that ran all the way down the front of my dress. He slid off the rock onto the floor in front of me and I fumbled with his pants, undoing the laces before climbing onto his lap to straddle him.

"Shit, Fi," Bryn cursed, running his hands over my hips and cupping my ass. It was the first time he'd used my nickname, and it filled me with all the warm and fuzzies.

I grabbed the claiming vows he'd dropped on the ground next to us, but he snatched them out of my hand.

"Me first," he said with a wolfish grin.

I rolled my eyes before moving my attention to his neck. *Oh yes.* I was going to leave some severe love bites there. I was still feeling more than a little possessive when it came to Bryn after everything it had taken to get to this point.

"I, Bryn Edan, take you, Ffion Laisren, to be my bonded mate. I pledge you my love, my magic, my loyalty, and my devotion..."

Bryn groaned as I bit down lightly on his shoulder and tugged his cock free of his unlaced trousers. *I can work with this.*

I had been truly blessed with well-endowed lovers.

"...I vow from this day forward to put the needs of you and our mating circle first, forsaking all others." He finished the vows with a pained sounding sigh that made me grin.

He stilled for a moment, his eyes darting down to his chest where I knew he'd be feeling the mating bond settling into place. I imagined mine felt airy, like the bond I felt with Arthus. It was like a slow-moving hurricane in my sternum.

"My turn," Bryn whispered with a devilish grin as I took the vows from him.

My breath hitched as his fingers stroked teasingly between my legs. Before I could object, Bryn had me flat on my back on the cave floor, unbuttoning my dress all the way until it fell at my sides.

"Well? On with it," Bryn gestured magnanimously at the vows in my hand from his spot, kneeling between my legs before leaning over and blowing a long, torturous breath against my pussy. I didn't even think he was trying to tease me, it felt almost reverent.

"You are such an asshole," I groaned, squirming beneath him.

Determined not to let him see how much he was affecting me, I held the vows in front of my face and recited them.

"I, Ffion Laisren, take you, Bryn Edan, to be my bonded *mate*." My voice broke on the word as Bryn's tongue connected with my clit. I took a long shuddering breath to focus my thoughts and continued.

"I pledge you my love..." *Long, lazy lick.*

"...my magic..." *Light grazing of teeth.*

"...my loyalty..." *Punishingly hard suck.*

"...and my devotion." *Soft, yet somehow devastating bite.*

Gods, this fae was trying to kill me.

"I vow from this day forward to put the needs of you and our mating circle first, forsaking all others."

The bond settled into my chest, and it was everything I thought it would be. Fiery, intense, demanding my attention.

As it took its place next to my three other bonds, a feeling of total completion came over me. No more mating pulls. No more claiming ceremonies. No more what-ifs. I'd made my choices, my mating circle was complete, and now we could move forward with the rest of our lives together.

"You'd better fuck me right this second, Bryn Edan. Don't make me regret claiming you already," I whined, writhing uncomfortably to ease the ache between my thighs as his tongue continued to swirl lazily around my clit as he categorized each reaction, learning my body for the first time.

Oh so slowly, he pulled his mouth away, swiping his tongue over his lips before climbing over me, his hands either side of me supporting his weight.

"Bryn *Laisren*," he corrected smugly before ramming into me so hard my back bowed off the cave floor. Magic exploded between us, sparking off our skin everywhere we touched.

I cursed under my breath that he'd gotten the upper hand whilst simultaneously grinning because Bryn Laisren sounded so good. *Mine, mine, mine.*

"I can feel your possessiveness through the bond," Bryn growled, but I could hear the awe in his voice. He slammed into me again, one hand moving to grip my hip tight enough to leave a bruise. The sparks of magic wrapped around my nerve endings, the sensation riding the edge of pain and pleasure.

I don't know how he had the presence of mind to check the bond while he was doing such magical things with his hips.

"I've waited a long time for you," I panted. "So yeah, I'm feeling a little possessive."

Bryn gave me a slow, sexy smirk before biting his lip and picking up his already punishing pace. He leaned over, his arms caging me in, muscles taut with strain, chest and shoulders rippling with exertion, and it may have been the sexiest fucking thing I'd ever seen.

I met each of his movements, flattening my feet on the ground to get purchase, wanting to feel him as deeply as possible within me. I wanted to bind us as closely together as two fae could ever be bound. *Needed* to.

My hands slid up his arms, and I raked deep lines down his biceps as my orgasm hit me like a freight train. Bryn leaned down and bit hard into my shoulder as he groaned his own release. We stayed locked in that position, trying to catch our breaths.

Holy fucking fae. Bryn and I just claimed each other? We hadn't even been courting when I woke up this morning! Oh gods, the other guys were either going to kill me or laugh until they cried. I wasn't 100% sure which would be worse.

Bryn lifted off my body and rolled onto the ground next to me, and I half expected him to thank me for my services and be on his merry way, even knowing we'd just mated for life. He didn't though. Just tugged me into his side and wrapped his arm around my shoulders.

Honestly, I wasn't expecting Bryn to be a cuddler.

I raised my left wrist to my face and admired the last addition to my mating mark in awe, loving that mine matched the guys' mark now.

Bryn examined his mark with a solemn intensity. There was nary a grumpy scowl or arrogant smirk in sight—he was taking this moment seriously, and it made my eyes a little watery.

"I want to keep you here, but I suspect they didn't send you in here with the intention of you claiming me as your mate," Bryn murmured. Now that he wasn't trying to cover up his emotions, I could feel the full force of his amusement, yet his body language and tone were relatively unaffected. The real Bryn was a lot more lighthearted than he appeared underneath all that stoicism and scowling.

"Yeah, they didn't. I'm pretty sure I was just supposed to apologize and drag you out so we could, you know, plot and stuff."

Bryn snorted. "I'm not mad about this outcome."

"Me neither," I agreed, huffing a quiet laugh at myself for packing snacks like this meeting was ever going to go any other way.

"Alright," Bryn sighed, handing me my dress as he pulled his trousers up. "Let's go discuss your save-the-fae plans. After I have a shower."

"I can't believe I had sex with you after you slept in a cave all night," I half grumbled, half giggled. "Gross."

He wasn't offended, though. We were both feeling so smug I couldn't tell whose emotions were whose.

"Let's try to avoid the word 'gross' in our post-sex descriptors, hm?" Bryn's voice was filled with amusement as he tossed an arm around my shoulders and led me out of the cave.

My mate. All mine. Forever.

TFFION

CHAPTER 68

Bryn and I made our way back to the main house through the lush forest together to share our news with Marlen, Arthus and Eamon. His happiness fed mine, vibrating along my skin.

I reached over to grab his hand and Bryn snorted, batting it away playfully. I rolled my eyes, intending to storm ahead to make my point, but he doubled in front of me, tackling me around the waist and tossing me over his shoulder.

"Bryn!" I shrieked, pounding my fists into his back.

"I'm not the hand-holding type, scout. This works for me though," he added, flipping up my dress and swatting me on the ass.

"You've made your point, manly man. Put me down now," I groused, secretly a little impressed that he was striding along like it was no big deal to have a whole person slung over his shoulder. Bryn was by no means scrawny, but he was the leanest of all four guys. Really, the only one I'd expect to carry me with any ease would be Eamon. He was built like a tank.

Bryn ran his hand over my ass cheek and down my thigh, and I felt his amusement as I shuddered. With no warning, he dropped me back onto my feet with a smirk.

"Asshole," I muttered, elbowing him in the ribs as we continued back to the house. He threw his arm around my neck, pulling me in tight to his side, and chuckled.

I wasn't mad. Playful Bryn was a Bryn I didn't know I needed.

We came around the corner of the path and were met by the smuggest wall of muscle in existence. Marlen, Arthus and Eamon stood shoulder-to-shoulder across the path wearing a mixture of shit-eating grins (Marlen) and arrogant smirks (Eamon and Arthus).

"Wrist," Arthus demanded, eyes twinkling with amusement.

I rolled my eyes but stuck out my left wrist all the same, now complete with the full mating mark that the guys had.

"Pay up," Marlen announced, sticking out his hand and giving both Arthus and Eamon a self-satisfied look. "Twenty bronze coins each, I believe."

"Gods, save me from idiotic fae men," I sighed, trying not to smile at their antics even though they could feel my happiness through the bonds. "Come on, I need some food."

Marlen turned to head back to the house, and I took the opening to jump on his back because cave sex had really taken it out of me.

He caught me easily, and I felt his healing magic travel through me from where his hands gripped my legs, traveling over the bruises that had been forming on my back. I rewarded him with a love bite on the crook of his neck, enjoying the sensation of his sudden spike of lust.

We piled into the cabin where Eamon had been busy in my absence, putting together a snack for us. There wasn't much of a kitchen to speak of, but he'd cut up an array of fruit and had a stack of toast and jam ready for us.

There was a breakfast nook built into the corner of Bryn's cabin that wasn't quite big enough to accommodate me, three full-sized fae men, and Eamon who was probably two full-sized men put together. Arthus stood, leaning against the wall while the others squished in and Bryn pulled me down onto his lap, his plans to shower apparently forgotten in the face of food. I didn't think the PDA would be a regular thing for him, but we were both high on the claiming ceremony buzz right now.

"So," Arthus began. "What did you learn from Enfys? Anything we can use?"

"He's pretty sure there are three Councilors who disagree with Glendower's various... philosophies. But he hasn't been able to get close to them yet. He can't be spotted by any of the Castells and risk an interrogation about Ffion leaving the Academy." Bryn absently drew circles on my thigh as he talked and the surreality of the moment sort of made me want to cry.

Eamon shot me an understanding smile at that moment, and I guessed he was checking the bond. He was almost as bad as Arthus for monitoring me.

"Enfys also gave me the directions to his cabin in Garrán Naofa, should you need a hiding spot."

"*We*," I corrected automatically.

"Should *we* need a hiding spot," Bryn conceded, oozing smugness. "I assume you four haven't been sitting around doing nothing for six weeks?"

"Nope. In a few days' time, we are breaking into the Castell's estate, disabling the wards, and busting out the female dragon imprisoned there, and any other prisoners we can find," I replied casually. It appeared that happy relaxed Bryn had been good while it lasted.

"What did you just say?" he growled in a low, dangerous voice, millimeters away from my ear.

"Don't freak out, it's a good plan," I reassured him, reaching for more fruit. "We've got the insider advantage. Saffir sent us a map of where the four cloaking crystals are on the property. We'll just drain them, then *ta-da!* Big ass dragons bust in and pull off a dramatic rescue."

I was leaving out a significant chunk of the plan, the part I knew he wouldn't like, and based on the judgy eyebrows I was getting from Arthus, Eamon, and even Marlen, I wouldn't get away with it for long.

"You really trust Saffir?" Bryn asked doubtfully.

"We struck a deal before I even left the Academy. She's good to go. Team Fi."

"Yes, but—"

I slid off his lap and pulled on his hand, dragging him to his feet. "Let's go have that shower."

"We'll be right back," I called over my shoulder at the other guys who all looked various levels of amused. It wasn't the most romantic conversation to have an hour after we'd had our claiming ceremony, but it was a necessary one.

Probably one I should have had before the claiming ceremony, if I'd have been sensible and hadn't got all caught up in my feels.

I pulled Bryn down the short hallway into his room, and he sat down on the end of the bed, leaning back on his hands, all broad shoulders and firm chest. *So* godsdamned attractive.

Maybe I should start working out? All four of my fae looked like they melted the body fat right off themselves.

Focus, Fi!

"Let's talk about Saffir."

"I haven't slept with her since I met you," Bryn replied automatically, immediately defensive even though I could feel his shame coursing through my system. It was an ugly, slimy feeling.

"Right, but there was other stuff happening." I held my hand up when he went to argue. "Honestly, it's not even about that. I'm mostly over it. *Mostly*. You used her, she used you, and the whole thing was shitty. But even if you were both using each other, she had different expectations of what that meant than you did."

"I can't take it back, scout," Bryn grunted, glancing at the ground.

"I'm not asking you to. I'm asking you to apologize."

"Sorry." It was so growly, the word was barely discernible.

"Not to me, idiot. To her. And do a better job than that," I added disapprovingly. We had a few centuries to work on his apology game. He'd learn.

Bryn's glare was so heated, I think we were both having trouble figuring out if he wanted to fuck me or fight me.

"Is this important to you?" Bryn gritted out, eventually.

"Yes. It should be important to you, too. Aside from it being the right thing to do, she's an important ally for us. You two need to be able to work together. To trust each other."

"I admire your virtue, but I will never forgive her for telling her parents about you."

"She didn't know I was a wanted fugitive, Bryn. Don't put that on her."

"Regardless, she went to her parents hoping they would bribe me into mating her," he objected. I could see the fight draining out of him.

"And from what Briallen let slip, her connection with the Council was one of the things you liked most about her," I replied impatiently. "Saffir is our ally. We might even be friends one day, once all this business is over. Play nice."

"Fine." Bryn threw his hands up in exasperation. "Now, join me in the shower. That was our first fight as a couple, and it's time for our first make up fuck."

I bit the inside of my cheeks to stop myself from smiling. I'm sure this would be the first of many fights with Bryn —he was my match for stubbornness.

"You say such sweet things to me, my mate," I commented lightly, following him into the bathroom.

Bryn didn't pack much, just a satchel of essentials he could carry on the griffin. We'd agreed after we finished our mission at the Castell Estate, laying low at Enfys' cabin would probably be wise. The Adair-owned properties were the first place they'd come looking for us.

Sorry, Eamon's parents.

We spent the rest of the day hanging out, making plans and sneaking makeout sessions. Bryn and I, that is. Months of denying the connection we had between us had made us a little handsy, though I noticed Bryn wasn't particularly comfortable with affection in front of the others. That was fine by me, maybe he'd get there with time, or maybe he'd always prefer more privacy. I was okay with either option.

I thought he'd want to go up to the main house and tell his family about our bonding straight away, but he was confident Briallen and her mother would be sleeping off their hangovers until early evening. Apparently the Edans knew how to party, and they did it *a lot*. Being at the Academy most of the year probably did wonders for Briallen's liver.

"It's nice to see the bond between you so strong and healthy now," Eamon said softly as we sat curled up on the couch next to each other.

I frowned, remembering how when I'd met Eamon for the first time a few months ago he had told me he could see a bond between Bryn and I, but it had appeared strained and fractured.

"Is that normal? For us to have a bond between us before we were even courting?"

Eamon's split second of hesitation was enough to tell me that *no*, it wasn't normal, and that I probably wouldn't like why.

"No, it isn't normal..."

"What's your theory?" Bryn cut in, reclining on the arm of the chair next to me, getting all up in my personal space like he had every right to be there. Which he kind of did, but it was still an odd change. A lot had happened in 24 hours.

Marlen and Arthus were watching Eamon intently, waiting for his answer. "Perhaps the gods were steering you in a particular direction in regards to your choice of mates, helping your relationships along... Maybe they thought we would be the best equipped to help you with your task."

"It is a little convenient that each of your mates holds a different elemental affinity," Bryn conceded.

"And our gifts have all aided Fi at some point or another," Marlen added thoughtfully.

They were all chatting about it conversationally like it was no big deal. Like they didn't care that we'd been potentially pushed into this relationship by forces beyond our control after everyone had talked such a big game about the freedom to choose. I thought I *had* chosen. The idea of my mates being handpicked by the gods because they served a purpose in this awful mission they had given me sat like a lead weight in my gut.

I'd spent my whole life being ignored, unwanted and overlooked. I thought these four had chosen me for me, just like I thought I'd chosen them for them.

"Stop," Bryn commanded, glaring at me. "Fuck, could you give me one full day before you start questioning our relationship? By the gods."

"Sweetheart, does it matter if the gods thought we'd be good together or not? Does it make you less happy with us?" Arthus asked, looking more than a little offended.

"Aren't you mad that they took the choice away from you?" I challenged, glaring at him. "You more than anyone has railed against the gods getting involved in our lives."

"You would have always been my choice, Fi. I am confident about that."

Even if fae couldn't lie, his sincerity was so intense, I could feel it in my bones. I blinked away the tears that were threatening to fall, mortified I was about to cry about this in front of them.

Eamon lifted me gently off the couch and sat me across his lap, banding his thick arms around my waist and I hid my face in his neck until I could compose myself, since that's probably why he'd sat me there.

"Fuck the gods," Bryn said with a ridiculously casual shrug. "You are ours, and we are yours. How we got here doesn't matter much to me."

"Well said," Marlen said cheerfully, forcefully shoving love at me through the mating bond like he could just love me out of my bad mood. It was sort of working.

"Yes, enough of the self-doubt," Arthus announced. "We need to fly back to the Estate before it gets dark. We'll experiment with your empath abilities tomorrow, now that you have a complete mating circle, Fi."

Dream on. Instinctively, I knew I could influence people's emotions from afar now, and it was the part of my gift I'd always dreaded. I sensed the ability to push emotions on someone skin-to-skin after I claimed Eamon, but I still hadn't tried it out. I'm sure I could figure it out if I was ever in enough trouble to actually need it.

I definitely didn't want to experiment with it on the people I loved most in the world.

"If you want to say your goodbyes to your family, Bryn, now's the time," Arthus added.

Bryn went to grab his satchel of essentials from his room as the guys shuffled around, collecting their things. He reappeared, holding something tightly in his fist, looking oddly shy.

"Did you get me something?" I teased, eyeing his closed fist.

"Yes," he bit out, looking like he deeply regretted it. He sat down on the couch next to me and opened his palm to reveal a thin, dainty bracelet. It was a simple gold chain with a few small blue stones threaded onto it in a row.

Bryn looked at my right wrist expectantly—the one without the mating mark—and I held my arm out curiously. He didn't strike me as much of a gift-giver.

"It's lapis lazuli," he explained quietly as he fastened the catch. "There's a little of my magic in there, you can blood it and it will act as a warning system alerting you to a new presence within ten feet. It's not a very impressive gift for someone with your abilities, but maybe it'll come in handy if you need to mute the emotions."

"I love it," I told him, holding his eyes so he could see the sincerity on my face. "Thank you."

"Whatever, don't make it a big thing. Come on, let's go say goodbye to my family. You can blast Briallen with air magic if she's still passed out."

We found Briallen, Leigh and Hagan lying out on the grass in the sun. She was cuddled up peacefully between the two of them, and the love I felt from them made me weak at the knees. These were three thrilled, incredibly in love, fae.

"You awake cousin?" Bryn asked, shooting a tiny streak of fire an inch above her face.

"Looks like it," Marlen chuckled as Briallen shrieked in surprise.

"Please tell me you're taking him with you, Fi," Briallen begged, sitting up on the grass and squinting up at me as the low sun shone in her eyes.

"He's mine, so yes I'll be taking him with me," I replied, flashing her my mating mark and feeling proud as punch, even while talking about him like he was an errant child. Bryn's ego could barely fit through the door at the best of times, I wasn't about to add to it.

"*FINALLY!*" Briallen shouted, leaping off the ground and flinging her arms around me. "Gods, I shouldn't have moved so fast," she groaned, slumping against me and resting her head on my shoulder. Briallen was so comfortable with casual touch, and after a lifetime without it, I still hadn't got completely used to her easy affection.

Marlen chuckled, resting his glowing hand over her forearm and letting his healing magic flow. Bryn scowled at him.

"Why aren't you hungover?" I asked him, mystified.

"I grew up with these people." He shrugged. Apparently that was the only explanation necessary.

"Are you going to expect us all to do five shots at your celebration? If so, I'm not coming," Leigh interjected, laying back on the grass with his arm flung over his face. All four of my mates looked at me expectantly.

"Are we having one of those? A party?" I asked. Almost everyone I knew was right here, but I guessed they all had families who might want to celebrate with us. I felt kind of selfish that it hadn't occurred to me earlier.

"Someday, right? Now probably isn't the best time," Marlen shrugged as Bryn and Arthus shook their heads at the understatement.

"We can have it at any of the properties you like, cariad. After you've looked at a few more of them," Eamon added.

"Lucky lady," Briallen sighed in my ear, still half leaning on me. "It'll be something to look forward to after you get all the hard stuff over and done with."

"So let's go do it then," Bryn groused impatiently. "Tell your parents Ffion and I claimed each other and I've left with them. Also, if Enfys Owen visits, we're where he advised us to go."

"Enfys Owen?" Briallen blinked slowly. "Uh, sure. We see him around the Academy sometimes. We'll let him know."

"Good. Just make sure no one else hears you," Bryn agreed.

"And whatever you hear about us..." I trailed off, not knowing exactly what to say to my best friend.

"Don't even finish that sentence, Fi," Leigh interjected. "We know you five, we know what the gods tasked you with." Briallen and Hagan nodded supportively.

I pulled Briallen into a hug, not able to articulate in words how much their loyalty and friendship meant to me.

I hoped it wouldn't be long until I saw them again, and without this black cloud of the gods' mission hanging over my head.

FFION

CHAPTER 69

As our motley crew assembled in a secluded forest area near the border of the Castell property, I felt several shades of anxious about this rescue mission.

I can totally do this. I'll be fine. I'm not scared. Actually, I feel great about this.

It sucked that I could only lie in my head because my four mates could do with some false hope right now. I'd muted my empath ability because my mates felt distinctly not good about the whole thing, and their rage was physically uncomfortable for me.

"This is the worst idea you've ever had," Arthus grumbled under his breath. "The worst idea anyone's ever had."

I pushed a pulse of reassurance through our bond and he practically snarled at me, so I let it be. I didn't feel great about what I was about to do either, but it was the best and safest option we had.

"I don't see why Saffir couldn't have done this," Bryn muttered, fire flickering around his fingers at irregular intervals.

"Yes, you do. She's safe at the Academy, surrounded by witnesses. An airtight alibi. We can't risk losing our best informant," I reminded him lightly, keeping my voice barely above a whisper. Besides, Saffir looked like a clone of her mother, and the chance of her being attacked by one of the prisoners we freed was high. At least I could try to influence them to remain calm until we explained the situation to them.

We were waiting in the forest near where we'd left our three griffins and the one which had brought Brently. He hung back, observing us with his arms crossed, leaning against a tree. He didn't need to be an empath to feel the rage and concern coming off my mates. Staying out of the way was an act of self-preservation.

The rustle of leaves and snapping of twigs heralded the arrival of five fierce-looking dragon shifters. Ezra gave us a curt nod, his mouth set in a grim line.

"Good. We're all here," I announced quietly. "Any questions before we begin?"

Is there no other way?" Arthus ground out.

"Any sensible questions?" I clarified. "No? Right. Let's go."

We approached the boundary of the Castell property as a group, with me boxed in by my surly mates. The dragons brought up the rear and I unmuted my gift to check on everyone, gritting my teeth against my guys' fear and anger.

The dragons' determination lapped reassuringly at my skin. Their lack of fear was reassuring because I was fairly close to peeing my pants, plus I was wearing maybe the least badass rescue mission outfit of all time—no shoes, loose khaki linen capris, and a dark brown linen blouse with elbow-length sleeves. I'd tamed my curls into a low bun, secured with a black ribbon. I was going for a fae camo vibe, which bemused all four of my mates. *Good*. I enjoyed keeping them on their toes.

As we neared the boundary line, the impact of the wards became obvious. The guys didn't react at all because they saw nothing to react to. The dread sliding uncomfortably down my spine was all mine as I saw the imposing sandstone mansion in the distance.

I could get through the wards because Glendower and Evalina had brought me through them before. Based on Saffir's explanation and Eamon's understanding of wards, only those that her parents had escorted inside could see through the illusion which Glendower had cast over the property. It's not like the property was invisible with the wards up—the illusion was all in our heads. Bryn couldn't even track any magic behind the wards, and it messed with his radar.

The guys were worried that Glendower would have reset the wards and revoked my access after I left, but I knew he wouldn't, the cocky bastard. He was confident he'd get me back in that cave, eventually.

The barrier felt like a thick bubble that I had to push through, and as soon as we hit it, the guys realized they couldn't go any further. They were all reaching their hands out and running them over the invisible shield, eyes narrowed in irritation.

"This is where I leave you," I announced reluctantly, turning to Eamon, Marlen, Arthus and Bryn. Marlen snatched me up first, lifting me into his arms and encouraging me to wrap my legs around his waist. He kissed me deeply, squeezing me around my middle as if he could fuse our bodies together.

"Come back to me, foxglove," he murmured against my lips.

"Always," I assured him. I pecked his mouth lightly and let Eamon pull me out of Marlen's arms. He held me off the ground, my legs dangling against him with my arms wrapped around his neck.

"I love you, cariad," Eamon whispered softly in my ear. I leaned back to capture his lips in a sweet, soft kiss.

"I love you too."

He placed me gently on the ground and Bryn's arm shot out to wrap around the back of my neck, yanking me into him. He placed a quick, hard kiss on my lips and abruptly let me go with an obnoxious smirk on his face. "Don't fuck this up, scout."

He was so full of it. I could feel his anxiety, and it was through the godsdamned roof.

"I'll take care of the hard stuff, don't you worry your pretty little head about it." I shot him a flirty wink, playing along with his carefree banter. This was practically the sole reason Bryn had tried to avoid a relationship with me—he hated vulnerabilities, and I was his biggest.

I turned to Arthus, who stood with his arms crossed, intense silver stare trained on me. The only thing Arthus valued more than control was me. He was struggling with this even more than the others.

"Arthus," I chided him softly. "Don't make me walk away from you while you're angry with me."

His face softened a fraction, and I took that as an invitation to step into his space, sighing in relief as his arms wrapped around my shoulders. He placed a firm kiss against my forehead before stepping back.

That was practically an obscene public display of affection by Arthus' standards.

"Be back within the hour," he instructed. "Stick to the plan."

"I will," I promised. I didn't want to take unnecessary risks any more than they wanted me to.

I crossed through the barrier of the ward, holding my breath. I'd braced myself for some kind of alarm-bells-blaring worst-case scenario, but all that happened was feeling the faintest brush of magic against my skin which I probably wouldn't have even noticed if I hadn't been so on edge.

I was wearing one of the cloaking amulets my father had given me, so even if there were any trackers on the property, they wouldn't be able to sense my presence.

The front of the estate was all landscaped gardens with tall, flowering bushes and ugly statues, while forest surrounded the rest of the beige mansion on three sides. It was hilly, and I was already feeling the burn from ducking and darting between shrubbery.

I should have probably done some kind of endurance training for this.

Thanks to Saffir, I knew exactly what I was looking for. She'd snuck home repeatedly while her parents were at Council events to scout out the property and find the location of the lumps of black tourmaline that warded the area.

And Bryn called me *'scout'.*

Actually, if he gave Saffir a nickname, I'd probably have to murder him.

She and I were cool now, but I didn't like to reflect on their shared history.

I scurried purposefully around the edge of the grounds, sticking to the shadows and tree cover as much as possible. Glendower and Evalina were both attending a Council session, which meant Kenley and Logan—the other two males in their mating circle—would stick close to them, but the Castells had plenty of staff, and we couldn't afford to gamble on them being disloyal enough to keep our presence quiet.

Just thinking about Glendower had my pulse spiking. Fear trickled down the back of my spine, spreading through my system and turning my veins to ice.

I tried not to think about those weeks I spent in the cave. I'd been working hard on overcoming my fear of daggers—I was carrying Arthus' and I didn't mind it so long as I was the one in control. My aversion to the dark was less potent with my mates to snuggle up to at night, though I knew I'd have to deal with it, eventually.

But being here, so close to the home of all those awful memories... My breathing had sped up, and it had nothing to do with how unfit I was.

Shit. Fi, focus! You cannot do this right now.

However frightened I'd felt in that cave, there was at least one other who was still going through that. Probably more. I owed it to them to get my godsdamned shit together. Plus, I didn't want to freak my mates out by panicking, they were struggling enough as it was.

Saffir had marked the location of each crystal on the map and noted that they all had a white stick over the top of where they were buried. It wasn't very safety-conscious, but I doubted anyone had tried to disable the wards from the inside before. Besides, Glendower needed to locate them easily whenever he topped them up with his blood.

"Shit," I muttered under my breath as I approached the first location. "Couldn't have left them somewhere easily accessible, could you? Asshole."

A white stick caught my attention, sticking out proudly from a clear patch of dirt on a ledge at the bottom of a short yet possibly still deadly slope. The slope itself didn't look too bad, but I couldn't see the drop beyond the

3-foot wide ledge.

I can totally handle getting down a small hill. Gods, if I couldn't handle this, then the rest of the mission would be a total write-off. I hesitated for a moment longer before sitting on my butt and scooting down the slope on my ass, glad Bryn and Marlen weren't here to witness it because I would have never heard the end of it.

I was filthy but unhurt by the time I got to the bottom. I stood up and focused on keeping calm, brushing the debris off my pants. I knew without a doubt that all four of my mates would monitor our bond the entire time I was in here, and I didn't want to give them any reason to worry. The helplessness would be eating them alive.

With a deep, steadying breath, I unsheathed Arthus' dagger from my belt and used it to loosen the dirt around the white stick before shoveling the rest out with my hands. My fingers brushed over the rough edges of the large piece of black tourmaline before I saw it. Feeling invigorated, I frantically shoved more soil aside until I could wriggle my hands down on either side of the crystal. I gritted my teeth as I moved the crystal loose and yanked it out of the ground.

It wasn't as impressive as I'd predicted. It was a little bigger than a loaf of bread, but significantly heavier. The crystal was rough and raw, and from what I could make out under all the dirt, it sort of looked like a chunk of tree branch that had been charred black.

I could feel Glendower's magic on it, though.

The ward would already be faltering, but I wanted to make sure it was down completely. Besides, I had a good use for all that cloaking magic.

I wiped the blade of the dagger on my pants and grimaced as I sliced the pad of my thumb. Hopefully Marlen's healing magic could cure tetanus.

Grimacing slightly, I pressed my bleeding thumb to the crystal. Glendower's potent cloaking magic flooded my system, far more powerful than my father's. By the time I'd bled all the crystals, I'd have enough illusion magic to cloak myself for months and be able to glamour myself into a little green alien, should I so desire.

Fortunately for me, Glendower's magic felt sickly and slimy, and I associated it with terrible things so hopefully that meant there was no chance of me becoming addicted to it. I had to be careful, though. Every fae who had become addicted to other people's magic and gone dark had probably said the same thing, but I was adamant I would not be drinking blood any time... ever.

The ledge seemed to go around the property toward the next crystal, so I stayed at the bottom rather than scrambling back up the hill, especially while I carried the drained crystal in my arms. The least I could do was ditch it somewhere difficult for Glendower to find.

The ledge ended abruptly a few meters on, and the thick patch of undergrowth at the bottom of the drop was perfect. I biffed the crystal into the brush with a quiet grunt before brushing the loose dirt off my hands. Satisfied that it would take them a while to find, I scrambled clumsily up the slope, grabbing at the roots to stop me falling.

Shit, shit, shit! Please don't let anyone notice the amount of noise I'm making.

Puffing with exertion, I doubled over with my hands on my knees, allowing myself a three-second recovery break. After this was over, I would definitely take up jogging. Or at least speed walking. Definitely something.

I quickly pushed a pulse of reassurance down each of the bonds and was slammed with waves of love in return. I suspected they were freaking out, but I couldn't really afford to take time out and check, and dwelling on it would just upset me anyway.

Creeping along the tree-lined edge of the property, I made my way towards the next spot Saffir had marked on Avalon's Most Disappointing Treasure Map. This section of the grounds had thinner tree coverage, and I felt uncomfortably exposed, so I nicked my thumb again on the dagger and ran it over the lapis lazuli bracelet Bryn had given me, just in case. His magic would give me a heads up if anyone was approaching, and I needed all the help I could get.

I moved into a thicker copse of trees and my heart sank when I heard the unmistakable sound of water. I'd really been hoping the oval Saffir had drawn on the map had been literally anything else.

Nope, no such luck.

There was definitely a pond between me and where I needed to be. It didn't look deep, but wading into unknown waters, hoping I wouldn't drown, seemed like the very definition of 'idiotic'.

Arthus would know what to do. He always knew what to do.

What would Arthus do?

Duh, Fi. Fly. I didn't have wings, but...

I eyed the pond warily; it was maybe 10-feet across. This was a terrible idea, but surely no worse than trying to swim it...

I took a few steps back to give myself some room. *Three, two, one, don't scream...*

I ran towards the edge of the pond and jumped as high as I could into the air, shooting a gust of air magic below me to propel me along. Then another, because I was definitely about to land in the pond. Then one more, just in case.

With a thunderous crack, my face collided with an enormous tree trunk and I fell back onto the ground with a howl of agony.

Fuckity fuck fuck, keep quiet, Fi! Oh gods, my face hurts.

Blood ran down from my nose over my mouth, filling it with a revolting coppery taste. I needed to move—I'd just made a huge commotion—but I wanted to curl up in the fetal position and bawl.

My face hurt so bad.

Why the fuck had the gods picked me for this? I was clearly not superhero material.

The familiar warmth of Marlen's healing magic settled around my nose, startling me out of my reverie. *The malachite around my neck.* I was basically an assortment of open wounds all down my front, and the pendant must be resting on one. Convenient.

I was for sure going to do that thing with my tongue Marlen liked if I made it out of here.

The crystal wasn't powerful enough to heal all of my injuries, but my nose wasn't hurting anymore. With a jolt, I realized the marker stick was right next to my hip. *Close call.* I doubt the little malachite healing crystal would have saved me if I'd impaled myself on a stick.

I rolled to my side and pushed up onto my knees, shoving some reassurance down the bonds since no doubt the guys had picked up on my moment of distress. The rush of relief that came back to me almost made me weep. With significantly more difficulty this time, I yanked the marker out of the ground and shoved the dagger into the packed dirt where it had been.

Come on, useless muscles.

I dug deep, both physically and metaphorically, until the blade hit something solid. Sighing in relief, I sheathed the dagger and loosened the lump of crystal with my hands until I pulled it free.

I pulled the dagger up enough from my belt to run my thumb down the edge of the blade and pressed the wound to the crystal, letting the cloaking magic rush through my system.

Gods, if you're listening, I could really use a truck-sized lump of malachite full of healing magic right now.

With a very unladylike grunt, I hefted the drained crystal into the pond. I didn't hear it hit the bottom, so it looks like I'd made the right call not wading in there.

Foster kids in Central London didn't spend a lot of time taking swimming lessons.

I pushed more reassurance down the bonds before inching my way along the edge of the pond, hoping I could make my way to the next crystal whilst keeping my feet firmly on the ground.

Two down, two to go.

CHAPTER 70

"This is absurd," Arthus muttered for the hundredth time as he paced back and forth in front of the invisible barrier. I was keeping my hand on it, feeling it weaken under my fingers as our brave, wonderful, determined mate dismantled the wards from the inside, all by herself.

Arthus had calmed down for a while, bolstered by the pulses of emotion Fi was sending through the bond. We were all watching the bond though, and we knew something had happened that had given her a scare.

I'd never felt so powerless in my life.

Whatever it was that had frightened her, Fi had recovered from it and sent us each another burst of reassurance, but we were more on edge than ever. Arthus was past the edge, floundering somewhere in the deep end.

"What do we do with the other prisoners once we release them?" Marlen asked in a deceptively casual tone, trying to break Arthus out of his panicked state.

"What do you mean *we*? Nothing. Our priority is Fi's safety," Arthus snapped, immediately at attention.

"You know as well as I do she won't be comfortable leaving them if they've got nowhere to go," Marlen pointed out, impressively calm and patient in the face of Arthus' barely restrained anger.

"She won't have a choice," Bryn cut in, his expression grim. Aside from the occasional puff of smoke rising off him, he was coping better than I thought he would. "We'll be on the run once the Castells find out what happened here. They'll assume Fi was the one to cross through the wards."

"I can provide shelter for anyone who needs it," Brently volunteered quietly, taking us all by surprise. "I don't know what you have planned, but I've been watching this property for months, and I know we'll find something awful behind these wards. If your plan means taking down Glendower and Evalina Castell, and any other corrupt Councilors, I want in."

"Do you swear to keep any prisoners who leave with you safe, and not to disclose their whereabouts to anyone?" Bryn asked, taking a step towards Brently and reaching out his hand to strike a deal.

"Of course," Brently replied, looking offended that Bryn had even asked as he clapped his hand into Bryn's and agreed to the terms.

"Glad that's settled," Arthus grunted, mollified that we weren't bringing a bunch of escapees home with us.

The cloaking shield rippled under my hand, followed by another rush of reassurance from Fi.

"That's three down," Marlen said out loud for Brently and the dragons' benefit.

"She was faster that time," Bryn commented quietly.

"Good," Ezra gritted out impatiently. The five of them had been standing in a silent row at the very edge of the barrier, bodies coiled to spring at the first opportunity. They were a standoffish bunch, but I felt for them. Their mate was so close, yet they still couldn't get to her.

At that moment, I could relate to their frustration.

"I think I can see something in the distance," Seff blurted, squinting at the shield. I didn't doubt him—dragons had heightened senses, they could see things we couldn't.

"I see it too. It looks like the outline of a house, but it's kind of fuzzy," Levi added.

"Remember, the house is irrelevant to us," Ezra reminded them. "The prisoners are in a cave on the grounds."

"Bet there's some amazing gold in the house though," Hiram replied wistfully, earning him a withering glare from Ezra.

Dragons were all about their hoards of treasure.

After another twenty minutes of Arthus pacing, the barrier beneath my palm disappeared with a loud pop, like a bubble bursting, and I snatched my hand back instinctively.

"Wow, your girl came through, huh?" '

None of us bothered to respond to whichever dragon had spoken. We were already moving forward and onto the grounds as the dragons partially shifted and took to the air.

If Fi had followed the plan, she'd have disabled the ward closest to the area where we thought the caves were last. It was a hilly, forested area east of the manor which matched Fi's description, and was an area Saffir told us she'd been warned away from as a child.

It was only a short distance away from the manor—not nearly as far away as we'd have liked. There was a very good chance the staff had noticed the wards coming down, and we didn't know what kind of gifts the staff here had. We had to get to Fi, and we had to be silent about it because none of us wanted an all-out battle if we could avoid it.

"I can't track her," Bryn called quietly over his shoulder. Good, at least the cloaking magic she'd absorbed was working.

"Let's split up, the path divides into three up here. Release any prisoners you come across," Arthus whisper-shouted, yanking his shirt off and tucking it into the back of his trousers so he could release his wings. Arthus launched up into the branches, joining the partially shifted dragons in the air. Their enormous wings blocked out the sunlight as they repeatedly circled and dived.

Someone would definitely see them—apparently, they cared about anonymity a lot less than we did.

I took the left-most path and my heart filled with relief so intense it was almost painful when my beautiful, bloodied cariad careened around a corner towards me. That relief turned into horror when I realized she wasn't alone. Before I had a chance to subdue her pursuer, there was a dagger embedded in her back.

A dagger. In her back.

For a moment, it felt like time stood still. Fi's lips parted, her eyes widened with realization, and I forgot how to breathe.

No.

No!

Then everything sped up as my sweet, beautiful mate crumpled on the ground with a scream of agony that ripped my soul in two.

"Fi," I choked out, stumbling towards her and dropping to my knees. In my periphery, I saw her assailant run back the way he came, but I couldn't bring myself to follow him when Fi was bleeding out on the ground in front of me. It scared me to move her in case I made things worse, but when she tried to move onto my lap, I pulled her up gently so her cheek laid against my shoulder with her body draped over mine.

"Cariad, can you try to focus on the bond with Marlen? I know it hurts my love, but if you can get his attention, he'll make it better," I said in my most soothing tone, trying to keep my grip on her lower back light so I didn't hurt her.

"Arthus!" I called at the sky, ignoring Fi's panicked shushing. If any of Glendower's cronies approached us now, I'd create vines strong enough to pull them down under the earth and bury them there.

Come on, Arthus. Please be close by.

"Marlen knows... I need him," Fi gasped out.

"That's good, cariad. That's really good," I whispered, trying to keep the tremor out of my voice. Fi needed me to be calm. She was the one with a godsdamned knife in her back. I wasn't allowed to be more scared than she was.

"Don't be afraid," I whispered, half for her benefit and half for my own.

"I'm not," she rasped, a strange gurgling quality to her voice. "Marlen will come for me."

Her confidence in him was absolute, and it soothed a little of my fear.

"Fi!" Arthus cried hoarsely, dropping from the sky like a stone.

"Find Marlen!" I barked the order.

Arthus gave me a startled look before shooting back into the tree canopy. He hung up in the air above us, but I couldn't focus on him when my hands that rested on Fi's lower back were turning red from the blood that flowed from her wound.

Come on, Marlen!

After a minute that felt like a year, Marlen skidded to a stop behind Fi just as Bryn arrived behind me, his hand softly cupping Fi's cheek. Marlen was cool and focused as he pulled his dagger out and carefully ran it down Fi's top, exposing the skin around the embedded knife.

"Arthus," he clipped, all focus. "Come here, be ready to pull the blade out when I say."

Arthus landed hesitantly next to Marlen, though his gaze became steely as he focused on the protruding knife. Marlen's hands glowed against Fi's back, her natural bronze skin barely visible under the coating of red.

"Bryn," Fi breathed. "Cover my mouth."

"Three..." Marlen began, mouth set in a grim line. "Two..." Arthus moved himself into position next to Marlen. "One."

Bryn's hand clapped over Fi's mouth just in time to smother her harrowing scream. Arthus dropped the bloody knife like it was on fire as Marlen's hands moved directly over the wound, the red blood shining brighter as his magic glowed against it.

It was a serious wound, that much was obvious. I'd never seen Marlen use his gift for more than a few seconds, but he stayed in position for what felt like forever, growing paler by the second.

Fi shuddered in my arms, lifting her head slightly off my shoulder. "No more, Marlen. You're tapped out."

"A little more," he muttered, eyes unfocused.

"No more," Fi insisted. I couldn't see her face, but whatever she'd communicated with Bryn had him moving around her as fast as lightning and hauling Marlen back, breaking the skin-to-skin connection.

Marlen collapsed on the ground next to Fi and me, leaning back on his hands and breathing hard. He was covered in a thin sheen of sweat and his skin had taken on a grayish pallor.

"Sweetheart?" Arthus murmured as he moved closer, his voice laced with vulnerability.

"I'm okay, I'll live," Fi groaned, shifting back in my arms until she was sitting upright on my lap and could look around at all of us. "Thanks to Marlen. Sorry for giving you all a scare."

"A scare? You may have just shaved a century off of our lives," Bryn snapped even as the relief practically poured off him.

"The prisoners!" Fi gasped, raising up on her knees as if she would stand. I yanked her back down onto my lap, tugging her body closer to mine.

"Don't worry, scout. I'm sure the dragons busted open every cave in search of their mate. And Brently's a tracker, he's doing a sweep of the caves to make sure we didn't miss anyone."

Arthus crouched down next to us and helped Fi out of her ruined top, pulling his shirt over her head and rolling up the too-long sleeves, while Bryn immediately torched the ruined one.

"Did they find her?" Fi asked, nails digging slightly into my shoulders.

"They did," a low voice grumbled from down the path behind Fi. Four of the dragons appeared, Ezra in the lead with a petite, sickly looking young woman cradled in his arms. Her clothes were rags, her skin pallid and her thick black hair matted, but there was no disguising the look in her unique, almond-shaped eyes.

Rage. So much rage.

"Put. Me. Down." she ordered, glaring at Ezra. Surprising me, given his prickly nature, he looked at her tenderly and cuddled her closer.

I spotted the fifth dragon as Seff's red fire dragon swooped low in the sky above us, scanning the area. Our cover was well and truly blown, but we still had the advantage for now. If the dragons took off, we'd be outnumbered and in serious trouble.

"Help me up," Fi demanded. Arthus immediately lifted her around the waist, tucking her into his side as naturally as if he took orders from her all the time.

"I'm Fi," she said calmly, focusing on the female dragon. "I was a prisoner here too, until a couple of months ago. I'm an empath. I could feel your emotions sometimes."

The girl looked at her appraisingly. "My name is Shira."

"Shira," all four dragons sighed in unison, earning them another glare from her. Either they hadn't asked her name or—and I had a feeling this was more likely—she'd refused to tell them. She didn't look like someone who was happy to meet her mates for the first time.

"Are you happy to go with them?" Fi asked. "Because you don't have to if you don't want to."

"She's coming with us," Ezra growled.

"Assume nothing—mate or otherwise," Shira snapped. "I don't know you."

Shira was going to give the commanding Ezra a run for his money, that much was obvious.

She gave Fi another appraising look. "I suspect that this whole escapade won't be without repercussions. You've probably got enough going on without worrying about me. As presumptuous as these five are, I'm sure I'll be safe with them. If not, I'll dismember them with my talons."

The four of us joined the dragons in wincing as Fi giggled tiredly. "That's what I like to hear."

Brently appeared at that moment, carrying what appeared to be twins—a boy and a girl—on each hip. Their faces looked solemn and mature, but their tiny bodies were more like a toddler's. A wary, pale adult male fae reluctantly followed him.

"Is that everyone?" Fi asked hesitantly, looking between the newcomers.

"There was a centaur, but he bolted as soon as we broke the shackles," Levi confirmed. My stomach churned. A centaur and a dragon? How did the Castells think they would get away with this?

"Why did you free us?" the male asked. I couldn't tell how old he was, but I couldn't see any mating bonds. Perhaps he'd been here since he was a juvenile.

"I was fortunate enough to have someone come to my rescue," Fi responded cautiously. Whatever she was sensing from him made her wary. "I could hardly rest knowing there were others still here."

"What are you going to do with us?" he asked, his voice disconcertingly flat.

"Nothing." Bryn took over, noticing Fi's discomfort. "You're free to go. If you want to get revenge on the assholes who kept you here, find Enfys Owen at the Council. He's working with us."

The male nodded, walking backwards slowly before vanishing into the shadows like a ghost.

"We should get out of here," Arthus muttered. "We've lingered far too long already."

"We'll be in touch regarding your meeting with a dragon representative," Ezra said shortly. "We took care of the fae who attacked you. He won't be a problem anymore."

Their wings snapped out as the four of them partially shifted and they took to the air without another word, Shira's outraged screech echoing in the trees.

"Come on, let's get off the property at least," Arthus grunted.

"Can you ride on my back, cariad?" Fi's wound may have healed, but she'd lost a lot of blood and she looked unsteady on her feet. Even more so after Ezra's parting words.

"That would be nice," she sighed, allowing Arthus to help her up and wrapping her arms loosely around my neck.

Arthus and Bryn each slung one of Marlen's arms over their shoulders, half carrying him as we practically jogged over the property line and back into the surrounding forest where we'd left the griffins.

We all looked around nervously once we approached the tiny clearing in the forest where the four griffins were grazing, but we could hardly take off without addressing the fact that Brently was holding two children that had just been freed from the-gods-only knew what kind of horror.

"What are your names?" Marlen asked the children kindly, still leaning heavily on Arthus as I hitched Fi higher on my back.

"The man called us Girl and Boy," the little boy said shyly, looking to Brently for comfort. That was good. Perhaps we'd have been able to help some fully grown fae, but we were in no position to look after children.

"You, uh, still okay to look after them?" Bryn asked apprehensively, looking at the children like they might bite.

"My youngest is only a little older than these two, and my mate is wonderful with children. They'll be safe with me," Brently assured us.

"I was more worried about your safety," Bryn muttered, only loud enough for Fi and me to hear. I suppressed a grin. Fatherhood may not be Bryn's calling.

"Are you happy to go with him?" Marlen directed his question at the children. "He'll take good care of you, and we'll be checking in to make sure."

"That's right. You can talk to them whenever you like," Brently assured the children who had wrapped themselves around him like vines. "This is Ffion. They held her here just like you, but she escaped and came back to get you all. We'll track down your family too, we just need to get you somewhere safe for now. And several hot meals," he added, frowning at their tiny figures. Both children nodded, looking more curious than afraid.

"We need to get in the air. We've hung around long enough," Arthus ordered, eyes flitting around the forest anxiously. I'd never seen him so shaken up.

We moved deeper into the forest where the griffins were waiting, and I handed the two kids up to Brently. There wasn't any fear in their eyes, but not a lot of hope either. My gut clenched. These children had seen things that no child should ever have to see. The Castells had to answer for their crimes. It was unconscionable that they didn't.

"Ffion flies with me," Bryn commanded, mounting the griffin and looking at me expectantly. She slid off my back and I lifted her carefully around the waist, passing her easily up to Bryn and earning a startled squeal from Fi for our efforts. I moved to boost Marlen up and climbed on the griffin behind him. He was magically tapped out and while it wasn't anything a good sleep and some time in nature—ideally water—wouldn't cure, he was in no state to fly solo.

Arthus mounted the final griffin solo, and we took to the skies, anxiously glancing behind us the entire way to Garrán Naofa.

It hadn't been without consequences, but we'd done it. We'd freed those being held captive by the Castells, disabled Glendower's wards, and got one over on him. Now we had more witnesses to the atrocities that had been happening there, and not just fae witnesses.

The gods had requested too much of Fi, I had no doubt of that, but we might actually be able to pull it off, nonetheless.

FFION

CHAPTER 71

Well, that had gone... mostly to plan.

We'd freed everyone, that was the most important thing. Glendower would be furious that his wards were down, and in the time it would take him to build new ones, he wouldn't be able to keep anyone else at the property. That was another positive.

Getting stabbed in the back wasn't great.

I'd never experienced pain like that in my *life*, and I hoped to the gods that I never would again. Without Marlen's quick action, I would be deader than dead in Eamon's arms, and my stomach kept churning with nausea at the thought of just how close it had been.

The fear he'd felt in that moment would live in my memory until my dying day.

"You're okay," Bryn murmured softly in my ear, both for his comfort and mine. It wasn't unusual for him to hold me while we were flying on a griffin together, but the way he kept touching and stroking me made me think he was verifying I was still here.

"I'm okay," I agreed, squeezing his forearm. I was shaky, and the adrenaline crash was going to be brutal, but I was okay because I was here and alive, and we'd all made it out of there. That was what mattered.

We had agreed in advance to hide out at Enfys' place, but I still felt a sinking sense of disappointment as the griffins approached the secluded cottage. I loved the Old Adair Estate, it felt like home, just like the treehouse near the Academy had. Only the gods knew when we'd get to see those houses again. If ever.

The cottage was set in a small clearing, so deep in the heart of the forest that I wasn't sure I would have even spotted it from the air if I hadn't been looking for it. As the griffin descended, I could make out the cottage's thatched roof and rough-hewn wooden siding, and it looked *tiny*.

Bryn's arms tightened around my waist as the griffin thudded onto the ground, and I was grateful he'd been holding me more securely than usual the whole trip back because the blood loss had made my head feel kind of woozy.

Eamon was waiting next to the griffin to catch me and I happily slid into his arms, winding myself around him like a koala as he carried me towards the house, pausing outside so Bryn could go in first and ensure that it was safe. Marlen's arm was slung over Arthus' shoulders and it looked like Arthus was holding up most of his weight.

Marlen and I both needed a nap.

Fortunately, it seemed like everyone else had the same idea since they deposited us both into the generously sized bed in the middle of the room. We immediately rolled together, snuggling into each other's embrace.

I had a million things to say to him, a million ways I wanted to express my gratitude, but I was exhausted and words were hard. Instead, I relied on the bond to push all the things I couldn't say towards him, melting into the love he sent back at me.

"Sweetheart, did something else happen while you were taking down the wards? We felt your fear, and we knew you were in pain. Did you run into someone else on the grounds?" Arthus asked gently, a deep furrow between his brows that looked like it had permanently embedded there.

"Yeah, you were pretty banged up even without the knife in your back," Marlen said around a yawn, earning him a scowl from Arthus.

"Are you... embarrassed right now?" Bryn asked, staring at me with a confused frown, trying to interpret whatever he was sensing through our bond.

I was definitely embarrassed.

"I didn't run into anyone else," I replied, hoping that would satisfy their curiosity.

"So what happened?" Marlen prodded, pushing the back of my borrowed shirt up so he could rest his palms against bare skin.

"It felt like you were really hurt, cariad," Eamon added tenderly.

"Gods, fine. I used my air magic to fly over a pond and smashed headfirst into a tree."

If Marlen had any energy left in him, he'd have probably peed his pants laughing. Fortunately for me, he was too tired, and I only had to deal with *feeling* his amusement. It was strong enough to make my own lips twitch.

In hindsight, it *was* sort of funny.

"That is fourth-year air magic, sweetheart," Arthus chastised, though he looked kind of impressed.

"I was trying to think of what you would do in that situation," I replied, trying to bat my lashes at him even though my eyelids felt like they weighed a hundred pounds each because he clearly needed the ego boost right now. I'd never seen Arthus so unsettled.

"Yes, well, he has wings," Bryn cut in drily. "You'd better get some sleep, scout. Once you're recovered, you'll be training from sunrise 'til sunset."

And with that cheery thought, I let my heavy eyelids close and fell into a deep, dreamless sleep.

I awoke to sun streaming through the small windows of the cottage, surprised to find I'd slept all night. I was now very much awake and very much starving.

It must have been early because all four guys were still asleep, two on either side of me. Marlen and I must have clung to each other all night—my face was squished against his chest, with Eamon right at my back.

I wriggled to extricate myself from their grip, but two sets of arms tightened around me. "Let me up, I need to pee," I grumbled.

"I'll carry you into the bathroom, sweetheart," Arthus muttered from Marlen's other side.

"That is entirely unnecessary," I protested.

"You need to rest today, you're only allowed out of bed for bathroom breaks," he ordered.

"You're not staying in the bathroom with me."

I could practically feel Arthus' smirk as Marlen rolled me over his body to the edge of the bed. Fortunately for everyone, he waited outside after I'd ordered him out of the tiny bathroom. He then insisted on carrying me back to bed like an invalid.

By that point, Eamon was up and dressed, rummaging around in the kitchen cupboards.

Now that I wasn't on the verge of passing out, I realized how tiny the cabin really was. The entire thing was one large square, with a small corner taken up by a bathroom and the rest an open room. There was a kitchen of sorts against one wall—some cabinets, a long bench, a sink, and a wood burner stove. There was a two-person table near the kitchen, a large bed in the center of the room and two armchairs against the far wall.

Since I wasn't at risk of dying and was safely cosseted in Enfys' cabin, I could take a second to appreciate how insane yesterday was.

I'd caught a knife in the back.

If Marlen hadn't been there... Well, I wouldn't be here. And as grateful as I was for him and to be alive, it reminded me of Eamon's theory that the gods had chosen my mates for me because their gifts aided my cause.

Marlen's gift had saved my life. Eamon's gift had delivered the gods' message to me. Bryn and Arthus hadn't used their respective gifts to help with this task yet, but I was confident they would have to, eventually.

"You're seriously contemplating your relationships with us now, sweetheart?" Arthus drawled, spying on me through our bond. "Didn't you see us yesterday while Marlen was healing you?"

"I've never been so scared in my life, cariad," Eamon admitted.

My doubt morphed into guilt because I had felt their fear. I'd felt it like it was my own.

"The dragons killed that guy," I croaked, suddenly remembering that horrific detail. I'd seen body bags taken away in London, I'd even arrived at the Tube station when the police were cleaning up the aftermath of a stabbing once, but I'd never been this close to death, though. Never been so aware of my own mortality, and others'.

That guy had been some kind of guard. I'd looked him in the eyes when I'd stumbled across him, too relieved at taking down the wards to realize I'd strayed too close to the main house. His death was on my conscience.

"If that knife had been two inches to the right, you wouldn't be here to feel unnecessarily guilty about his death," Bryn bit out.

"Bryn's right," Marlen sighed. "My healing ability is stronger since our claiming ceremony, but if the injury had been worse or it had taken me a few seconds longer to reach you…"

"Don't feel guilty about his death, cariad. He probably wouldn't have felt guilty about yours," Eamon assured.

"Yes, well, I *was* trespassing," I pointed out drily. The guy had just been doing his job.

"It will only get more dangerous from here on out," Bryn said. "You need to figure out how to use your gift to defend yourself."

It hadn't occurred to me at that moment to influence the guy's emotions. Maybe I could have made him super calm or something and escaped. Then he wouldn't be dead right now.

"No point going through the what ifs," Marlen said around a yawn. His skin was still paler than usual, except for the dark shadows under his eyes that looked like bruises. "Start practicing now and you'll be better prepared for next time."

"I don't want to practice on any of you. I actually like you guys."

"Good to know," Arthus deadpanned, though his cool facade felt forced. He and I needed to have a little chat about yesterday's events.

"That's why you should experiment on us. If you screw it up, we're guaranteed to forgive you," Marlen pointed out like it was the most obvious thing in the world.

"I'm not experimenting on you until you've recovered. Do you need more sleep? Some food?"

"I was thinking I'd take a dip in the pond behind the cottage. A soak in the water will help restore my magic," Marlen said cheerily, seeming a lot less concerned than I was.

"I'll come with you," Bryn said, standing. "Heat the water for your sensitive skin."

"I knew you cared," Marlen shot back with a sly grin.

"We need more firewood too," Eamon mused to himself.

"Perfect. Everyone out," I announced. "Except you. You and I need to have a little chat." I narrowed my eyes at Arthus, who looked oddly shifty.

Bryn, Marlen and Eamon filed out of the room, leaving a dejected-looking Arthus sitting on the end of the bed. His emotions were a potent mixture of guilt and shame, and I would not stand for it.

"You have nothing to feel guilty or ashamed of."

He looked up at me incredulously. "You had a fucking knife sticking out of your back, Fi. Without Marlen, you'd be dead. And I fell apart. When you needed me most, I panicked."

"Arthus, there are lots of times when I need you. Multiple times a day, usually. But in that situation, the person I needed was Marlen, and he totally came through for me like I knew he would. You can't control every situation and, honestly, there will be times where it's better for someone else to take the lead. No one thinks any less of you because of it."

"I've never seen Marlen so focused," Arthus admitted, the chokehold of his guilt easing slightly.

"Right, but this is what he does. His instincts are to heal, that was him entirely in his element. Bryn's been extracting fae from terrible situations for the past couple of years in his work for the Academy. Only the gods know what kinds of twisted things Eamon's seen from his gift. Seeing trauma first hand... you and I are both in new territory here."

Arthus was silent and reflective, but he was feeling lighter.

"I'm glad it was me," I admitted quietly. "I'd much prefer to take the pain myself than ever watch any of you suffer."

Arthus gave me a sharp look before sighing. "I can relate to that sentiment. My whole life I've feared letting anyone near my wings with a blade, but I'd happily take ten knives in my back if it meant keeping at least one off you."

"What about eleven?" I teased. *Come on, Arthus. Give me those dimples.*

"Twelve, if need be," Arthus confirmed. *Ha, I totally saw a dimple.*

"Do I get a cuddle now?" I asked sweetly. I sensed Arthus was feeling more like himself again, and the window of opportunity to give him orders had closed.

"Sure, sweetheart," he replied with an almost playful eye roll, joining me in the bed and pulling me into his chest.

Maybe I didn't care if the gods had chosen them for me. I wouldn't give up a single one of my mates for anything.

I was on forced bedrest for two days, alternating between the actual bed and laying on the grass outside, before I finally put my foot down.

While, *yes*, I almost died, it wasn't like I was out of danger yet. I had to be better prepared next time, and that wasn't going to happen while I was lying in bed all day.

I pulled on my one pair of trousers and a cream linen tank top with thin straps since summer had well and truly arrived in Avalon. Too bad we were on the run, this would have been the perfect time to visit the waterfall where Marlen and I had our claiming ceremony.

"Okay, what are we doing?" I asked, joining the guys outside as I tied my hair up out of my way. All four of my mates were only wearing shorts and the cloaking amulets my father had given us, and there was a truly distracting amount of chiseled chests and defined abdominals on show.

"Our eyes are a little further north," Bryn drawled with the smuggest freaking smirk on his stupidly handsome face.

"Shush, you," I chided, throwing him a scowl for daring to call me out on my obvious perving. "What are we doing?"

"To begin with, you'll practice defending yourself against different elemental attacks. We'll move on to weapons training and using your gift after that," Arthus explained.

"Marlen's up first," Bryn added. "We'll save the fire for when you prove you're not entirely useless at shielding yourself."

"Thanks for the vote of confidence," I responded drily, though I was secretly a little grateful. Fending off water was a lot less intimidating than fending off fire. Plus, I knew Marlen would go easy on me. That practically went against everything Bryn believed in.

Before I could prepare myself, a stream of cold water hit me in the chest.

"Wait!" I shrieked.

"That's not how actual fights work," Marlen pointed out, giving me a shit-eating grin. I shielded myself from his next attack that he'd aimed at my left side, but was too slow to block the second hit to my torso.

Gritting my teeth in irritation, I tried to maintain my shield with one hand while blasting Marlen backwards with the other, but I timed it wrong and caught another blast of water in the chest.

"Is there a reason you're aiming for my tits?"

"Your top is see-through," Marlen replied cheerfully, his eyes trained on my soaked tank top as he formed a massive ball of water between his outstretched hands. *Fucker.*

I forced enough air at Marlen to knock him on his ass, then attempted to use my magic to dry out my top. It was still uncomfortably damp, but I was fairly confident my nips were no longer on display.

"Pin him down, sweetheart," Arthus called. "Three seconds on the ground to win."

That sounded manageable. Before I had the chance, Marlen blasted me square in the chest—again—putting me flat on my back. Streams of water snaked over my wrists and ankles, pulling my limbs towards the ground whenever I tried to raise them.

"And, three. Hard luck, scout," Bryn called from his spot leaning against the cottage. With an exaggerated sigh, Marlen pulled all the water from my clothes and dumped it on the grass. Arthus' air magic wrapped around me, drying me to the bone as he pulled me to his feet.

"Are you okay, Fi? Was that too much?" Eamon's concern wrapped around my insides like a warm, fuzzy blanket.

"I'm okay," I promised him. "Aside from the hurt pride. I thought you'd go easy on me," I said to Marlen, throwing him a filthy look.

"If it were anything else, foxglove, I would. But I was a godsdamned champion in combat class and I don't throw fights." Marlen shrugged, and his unexpectedly confident swagger was a serious turn-on. Marlen joked around a lot, but in the past few days, I was seeing a more serious side of him. I was into it.

The rest of the afternoon and the following day continued with the same pattern. I had been genuinely excited on day one about my increased training schedule. Then I realized it was just all four guys shouting and throwing magic at me all day, and the appeal substantially wore off.

Today was day three, and honestly? Fuck it. I would sit myself in this armchair and enjoy the fresh blueberry scones Eamon had made, and not one of these bossy males was going to tell me otherwise.

If the gods wanted me to "restore the balance", then they could find a way for me to do it that involved zero physical combat because I was *done*.

BRYN

CHAPTER 72

"Come on, scout."

Ffion looked up from the scone she was dismantling with a frown. Her legs were tucked up underneath her on the armchair, her chin resting on her knees. She looked beautiful. And entirely too relaxed.

It was time to do something about that.

"What are we doing?" Ffion asked suspiciously.

"Training."

"I'm taking the morning off," she countered haughtily.

My mate was a sore loser, which I'd always suspected, but had confirmed over the past couple of days. She didn't like being bad at something, and was easily frustrated when she couldn't quickly get *good* at it.

I was exactly the same. It really was no wonder that we were kindred souls.

"You aren't. And I'm taking the decision out of your hands," I replied calmly, smirking at her in the way I knew riled her up the most.

"More elemental sparring?" Arthus asked from the table where he was studying a map of Avalon. I nodded my head. Those training sessions she'd had with Enfys at the Academy hadn't taught her anything—Ffion had a lot of catching up to do and we hadn't even got to weapons training yet, let alone her gift, which she outright refused to try.

"No thanks," Ffion interjected breezily, going back to her scone. *Brat.* I snorted at her rejection, catching Arthus' eye to make sure we were on the same page. He gave me a curt nod as he crept up behind her to snatch the plate out of her hands. Before she could protest, I pulled her up from her seat and tossed her over my shoulder.

I strode out to the patch of grass out the front of the house, enjoying listening to Ffion muttering about all the ways she was going to punish me, before lowering her gently to the ground and ducking out of the way when she took a swing at me.

"Seriously? Your aim is appalling, scout. This is why you need combat training."

Fi huffed, glaring at me but not arguing because she absolutely knew I was right.

"Eamon!" I called to the giant, traipsing across the yard with an armful of firewood. "I believe next up on Ffion's training schedule was deflecting earth magic."

"Asshole," she muttered as Eamon lowered the firewood to the ground and made his way over to us.

I moved back a few feet to give them room to spar as they squared off against each other, neither of them looking thrilled about it. Eamon reluctantly conjured a vine from the ground so obvious that Fi saw it a mile off, blocking it with an air shield with a lazy flick of her hand.

I'd been afraid when I'd escaped my burning house, though it was a childlike version of fear. I'd been afraid when Ffion had disappeared, but I figured they needed her alive and that gave me hope.

Seeing her in Eamon's arms with a knife sticking out of her bloodied back... *that* was fear. If Fi's heart stopped beating, mine would stop right along with it. There was no me without her.

That was why I was throwing motivational fireballs at Eamon. Because I loved my beautiful, messy mate, and I wouldn't let her be off-guard again.

"Stop burning him, Bryn! You are such an asshole!"

She definitely loved me too.

"His vines are two feet away from you, scout. You won't learn if he goes easy on you."

Eamon gave me a pleading face that looked pathetic, given what a mountain of a fae he was. Marlen was healing our cuts and scrapes after each sparring session, anyway—Fi's ego was hurting more than her body.

"Don't punish him because he isn't a sadist like you," Ffion grumbled. I flicked a tiny flame at her that flickered out as it brushed against her bare arm.

She blasted me with a gust of air, then flung up a shield to protect herself from the spray of dirt Eamon was trying to distract her with. I flung a few more small fireballs at her to see if she could keep fending off two attacks at once, but she was far more concerned about fire than earth. Eamon's vines wound around her ankles, pulling her onto her ass before she could even blink.

He was over there in a flash, lifting her carefully into his arms and moving as if he would carry her back into the cottage.

"Don't even think about it," I growled. "By the fucking gods, you know there's a good chance she'll experience worse than falling on her ass if the Council tracks us down. She needs to train."

Ffion buried her face in the crook of Eamon's neck and made a frustrated noise of complaint before patting his chest to put her down. She could complain all she liked, she knew I was right.

"I'll take it from here," I added, raising my brow at Eamon to see if he'd protest. He shot into the cottage, practically oozing relief. *Softie.*

"Okay, scout. That was your warm-up." I gave her my most predatory grin and allowed flames to engulf both of my hands. She smirked back, and I felt the flames stutter as she used her magic to suck the air out of them.

"Better," I commended, shooting thin lines of flames across the grass towards her feet. She yelped as she threw her shield up a second too slowly, concentrating hard to shield and pull the air out of the lines of fire. Her enraged face was maybe my favorite of her facial expressions. She was all venom and righteous fury, like some kind of avenging goddess.

While Ffion focused on the flames, I yanked my shirt over my head, sweating from the heat of my magic. Her eyes traveled greedily over my chest, and I couldn't stop the smug smirk that tugged at my mouth if I tried. It felt so *fucking* good to know I affected her as much as she affected me. Even if she still looked like she wanted to slice my head off.

I directed my magic upwards to rain weak flames down on her, testing her awareness of her surroundings. She caught on quickly, encasing herself in a bubble of air.

"Not bad," I admitted.

Ffion's expression turned calculating as she threw up a blast of air that pushed me back a step. I contemplated checking the bond to see what brought on her change in demeanor, but that would spoil the game.

Besides, I was confident I could handle whatever it was. Let her come at me with everything she had, I'd been doing this a lot longer than Ffion had.

I expected her to attack me with air again, but she dropped the shield and ran at me like there was a fire dragon on her heels. It took me off guard for a split second, and that's all she needed.

Ffion planted her hands firmly on my bare chest, and I caught a flash of her impish grin before the force of her emotion influencing magic hit me. My eyes met hers in surprise as every drop of blood in my body drained into my cock. All of it.

I'd never been so hard in my *life*, and it was agony. I stumbled away from her, doubling over with my need for relief, needing to fuck this ache out of my system.

"Bryn?" Ffion asked hesitantly, standing above me. "Shit, maybe I overdid it. I was just trying to distract you with a bit of lust..."

Gritting my teeth, I wrapped my hand firmly around her elbow and yanked her towards the side of the cottage, behind some bushes for a small amount of privacy.

Was I going to fuck her against the side of Enfys' cottage like a godsdamned animal? *Abso-fucking-lutely.* Her little lust trick had unleashed a monster.

I went to turn her back to the wall and hike her leg around my hip—even that move felt too difficult for the agony I was in—but Ffion pushed me against the wall instead, dropping to her knees with a thud.

"Let me take the edge off," Ffion demanded breathily, her hands already tugging at the laces of my trousers, while I threaded mine through her hair. I'd take anything she was offering.

Ffion pulled my cock free and sucked it deep into her mouth without hesitation. I tightened my grip on her hair, pulling her forward until I hit the back of her throat. This was the first time we'd done this, and I'd planned on savoring the moment, but if I didn't come soon, I'd die. I groaned loudly when she swallowed me down, my perfect little goddess of a mate.

When she wasn't forcing so much lust on me that my balls were at risk of exploding, that is.

It was rough and fast and messy, and the sounds I was making were more animal than fae. Ffion's mouth worked me as one hand wrapped tightly around the base of my cock and her other pulled up her dress and disappeared into her panties. My balls tightened painfully as tingles began at the base of my spine, watching her fingers moving frantically against her clit. Knowing she was getting off on this too was enough to send me over the edge.

"I'm going to come," I gritted out, giving her just enough warning to pull back. Her eyes met mine in challenge and fuck me if it wasn't the sexiest thing I'd ever seen. I came with a pained groan, marveling at the way Ffion swallowed down every drop even though I felt like it was fucking gallons.

I'd never underestimate the potency of her gift again. She could take down an army. Death by horniness.

The first orgasm had taken the edge off, but my cock didn't deflate at all. Without a word, Ffion stood, dropped her panties and bent over, bracing her arms on the side of the cottage and looking back at me with the most glorious pair of bedroom eyes I'd ever seen. I rucked her dress up around her hips and plunged into her, filling her in one smooth movement.

With one hand firmly gripping her hip and the other winding through her hair, I yanked her back against me, encouraging her to use me, to fuck herself on me.

"You better not be muting your gift," I growled. "I want you to feel what you're doing to me."

"I'm not," she gasped. "I know what you need."

Hands splayed against the rough wood, she pushed herself back into me over and over, each thrust easing the ache until it felt more like pleasure than pain. Ffion's breathy pants and quiet moans shot straight to my cock, spurring me on. There was no way I was coming again until she did. I had *some* pride remaining.

My hand on her hip slid around to her front so I could roughly massage and pinch her clit, pushing her over the edge. Ffion's muscles clenched tightly around me, like she could fuse us permanently together, and it felt so fucking good that it set me off again.

I'm pretty sure I wouldn't be able to come again for a year. I was out. Empty. Godsdamned drained.

Panting, I quickly fastened my trousers and pulled Ffion around to face me and tucked her against my chest, banding my arms around her shoulders. I was a little annoyed about her brutal sneak attack, but I'd always hold her close after sex as savage as that. I never wanted her to feel used.

"Sorry," she whispered quietly, mumbling into my chest. "I shouldn't have used my awful gift."

"Of course you should have," I replied, pulling back so I could meet her eyes. "You should have used it earlier. We were sparring. Use every weapon you have at your disposal."

"It was so much stronger than I thought it would be," she said, looking furious at herself. "It *hurt* you. I was just trying to distract you."

"So you practice using it and figure out how to control it. If I was your enemy, *hurting* me would be the entire point."

I shrugged. My annoyance had mostly faded into appreciation for the intensity of the weapon she was wielding.

Once I'd regained some sensation back in my cock, I'd probably be fine about the whole thing. A blow job and sex was the best end to any sparring session I'd ever had.

"I'm not using it again," Ffion said stubbornly, shaking her head.

"You are. But you can experiment on one of the other guys next time. Let's go," I announced, grabbing her hand and pulling her around the cottage towards the front door.

"Wait!" she shrieked, crouching down to grab her panties off the ground where she'd dropped them. I grinned and snatched them out of her hand, stuffing them into my pocket. "We're not practicing now, I need a bath and a minute to recover. That was intense," Ffion added.

"What? I was thinking you could try to influence them to feel happy or sad or something. What did you have in mind, scout? Sordid little thing," I teased as Ffion's face flushed redder than I'd ever seen it.

"Prick," she muttered quietly under her breath, even as she linked her fingers more securely through mine. I'd break my hand-holding rule for her.

As Ffion was in the bath recovering from her fourth day of training—where she'd used her gift to make Marlen feel calm and managed to pin him—I followed Arthus outside, where he'd snuck off when he thought we weren't paying attention. He was sitting on the edge of the clearing at the front of the house on a fallen log, looking contemplative.

"You're struggling," I said bluntly as I dropped down next to him, giving him a flat look. Arthus had probably been struggling from the moment they left the Academy. For a fae who prized control, he hadn't had a lot of it lately.

I thought I'd butt heads with him more, but we worked together surprisingly well. He didn't try to boss me around, and I didn't try to boss him around. I also had no interest in leading the others, so Arthus was free to keep that responsibility.

"We need a plan," Arthus grumbled, not acknowledging what I'd said.

"So we'll make a plan. But what you need right now is to be in charge. So go take charge," I replied, my voice laden with innuendo.

Arthus snorted. "You're suggesting I fuck my problems away?"

"You can't deny it's your favorite form of exercising control." I shrugged.

"No, I can't deny that. Marlen and Eamon quite enjoy taking direction from me, you know." Arthus gave me a smug smirk.

"Ha. You're dreaming if you think I'll listen to you in the bedroom," I scoffed. I barely listened to him out of it, and only when it was convenient to me.

Arthus hummed. "I didn't expect you would. There's something you're not telling us though," he prodded. I scowled at him. Nosy bastard. Though I suppose he had a right to be. Whatever concerned me concerned the rest of my mating circle, and I had followed him out here to nag him about his problems after all.

"I'd never planned on having a magically powerful mate."

"You thought you'd be one of two, not one of four," Arthus deduced. "Does it bother you?"

"Not as much as I thought," I admitted begrudgingly. Maybe I'd hate it more if I had a worse mating circle. These three weren't so awful. Most of the time.

"Except in the bedroom. Well, you'll just have to watch, I suppose," Arthus announced, standing up and clapping me on the shoulder.

"I'll give you pointers." I smirked, standing and following Arthus back to the cottage.

CHAPTER 73

Bryn's little talk had motivated me. There were plenty of things that were out of my control at the moment, but not everything. Sex wasn't the solution to all of my problems, but I'd missed the connection between us over the past few days, and I knew Fi had been missing it too.

I could give her this. *We* could give her this.

Fi was already on the bed—cuddling with Marlen—while Eamon was working at the kitchen table. Things weren't bad between us, but there was a distance that hadn't been there before and I intended to rectify it.

"Strip, sweetheart," I announced casually, hoping to catch her off-guard. Fi's slow blink told me I'd succeeded.

"You heard him," Marlen laughed, elbowing Fi lightly in the ribs.

"Why?" she asked, glancing suspiciously between me and Bryn, who was leaning against the door jamb with a smirk on his face.

"Why do you think?" Bryn snorted.

"We are not having sex on Enfys' bed!" Fi said, looking scandalized at the very suggestion.

"Do it on the floor then," Bryn replied with an arrogant shrug, making his way over to the armchair and sitting himself down in a way that clearly showed he was just going to observe.

"We can keep you comfortable on the floor," Marlen added without missing a beat, sliding onto the ground and pulling Fi down with him onto his lap. With a confident grin, Eamon dropped to one knee in front of them and captured Fi's mouth with his. Within seconds, Fi's hands were wound through Eamon's hair, her back arching, silently pleading for me. So godsdamned responsive. From outraged to needy in two seconds flat, that was my mate.

Marlen kissed up the back of her sensitive neck as his hands made quick work of the front buttons of her dress, relieving her of her dress and bra as Eamon unlaced her panties. Seeing her naked between Marlen and Eamon who were still fully dressed was obscene in the best way.

"You two had better strip," I commented lightly, cocking my head as I took in the scene unfolding in front of me. "You're not much good to Fi wearing all your clothes."

"Yes, boss," Marlen chuckled, shucking his shirt and sliding Fi onto the floor in front of him so he could remove his trousers as Eamon did the same on her other side. The small pause gave Fi enough time to notice Bryn lounging comfortably in the nearby armchair, his gaze trained on her.

Eamon liked to watch, and she always played to his voyeuristic tendencies, performing for him in a way. With Bryn, everything was a challenge to Fi. She tossed him a cocky smirk before sliding her hand between her legs and tipping her head back, the ghost of a smile on her lips. Daring him to move.

He smirked back, unlaced his trousers and lazily pulled his dick out. Fi's eyes narrowed in irritation.

Before she could snap at him, Marlen's hand was pushing hers out of the way and Eamon's mouth was on her nipple, and she forgot all about Bryn as her head fell back onto Marlen's shoulder with her lips parted.

"Make her come," I instructed Marlen, fishing the bottle of oil out of my satchel.

Marlen grinned, his hand moving faster as Eamon pushed Fi's legs until they were bent at the knee, giving him a better view. Fi bit down hard on her lip as an orgasm ripped through her, eyes rolling back into her head. Glorious.

She was glorious.

I handed Marlen the oil, and he wasted no time pouring it into his palm and fisting his cock. Fi's head was thrown back as she panted, her body writhing on the floor, wanting more, the noises coming out of her throat akin to a needy whine. She looked gorgeous—relaxed, euphoric, uninhibited. I wanted to freeze this moment forever.

"You ready for this, sweetheart?" This was a new position for her, and I wanted to make sure she was comfortable with it.

"Oh, yes. I've got a great view from here," she said cheekily, her eyes flicking between Bryn and I on her periphery, Eamon kneeling between her thighs as Marlen nipped her ear from over her shoulder, his fingers disappearing behind her. Fi sucked in a breath as he teased her ass, adjusting her position to give him better access.

I chanced a look at Bryn, half expecting to see smoke wafting off him watching Fi like this. She was uninhibited, comfortable, and irresistible.

"Hop on," Marlen said brazenly, lifting Fi's hips back and guiding his cock to her ass. She relaxed into him, breathing evenly and letting her body adjust as Marlen held himself still until Fi had taken his full length, the backs of her thighs resting over his legs.

"Good?" I asked, checking in again.

"Full," Fi sighed. "It's good. More. I want more."

"Tell me if it gets too much," I warned Fi before turning my attention to Eamon. "Bind her hands behind Marlen's head."

Fi wrapped her arms around the back of Marlen's neck willingly as Eamon's vines snaked around her wrists to secure them. She gyrated slightly in Marlen's lap, seeking more friction as Eamon moved closer, encouraging Marlen to pull her knees up against her chest to make room for Eamon's large frame between her thighs.

He pushed in gradually as Fi arched her back, mumbling words of encouragement as Eamon thrust slowly, rocking her into Marlen.

For a moment, I panicked. Eamon was a broad guy, and I worried the angle would cause Fi pain. I reached for the bond and pulled it to me to check how she was feeling. My balls tightened almost painfully and the base of my spine tingled, her lust feeding mine.

I hurriedly released the bond and swallowed hard, taking a steadying breath to stave off the impending orgasm. I wasn't about to come in my pants like a godsdamned teenager.

"There," Fi panted. "Right there."

Eamon's pelvis ground against her clit and Fi's back arched completely off Marlen's body as she moaned loud enough for the entire forest to hear.

"I'm not going to last, cariad," Eamon groaned.

"Good," I bit out impatiently.

Eamon took the hint, thrusting into Fi with renewed vigor, driving her orgasm into another one. Eamon fell over the edge with her, his mouth buried in her neck, chanting her name against her skin like a prayer.

I cleared my throat impatiently. Eamon looked up at me, his messy brown hair falling over his eyes and skin slicked with sweat. At that moment, no one would guess he was twenty years older than us. He pressed a light kiss against Fi's forehead before pulling out and moving aside, releasing the vines so she could move her hands.

I kneeled in front of her, watching her squirm on Marlen's lap, trying to deepen his shallow thrusts. Bryn tossed me a damp washcloth, and I quickly cleaned Fi up until her shyness about the messiness faded. It helped that I was targeting all of her sensitive spots with pulses of air magic to keep her stimulated. The hard suctioning of air at the apex of her thighs was her favorite—she was writhing on Marlen's cock as she looked up at me pleadingly with those big amber eyes.

"Please, Arthus. Please!" she whimpered as I increased the pulsing of air over her clit. Somewhere in the background, I heard Bryn's groan of satisfaction.

"So fucking pretty when you beg," I whispered approvingly before burying myself in her hot, slick channel. Her muscles contracted around me, and I could see her brief flash of panic.

"One more, sweetheart. Hold back until I say, then give us one more," I commanded.

"I can't," she sobbed. "It's too intense."

"We've got you," Marlen crooned, his soothing tone immediately relaxing her. He picked up his pace to meet mine, and Fi's nails dug into my shoulders hard enough to leave crescent-shaped wounds.

"*Fuck*," Marlen gritted out as Fi's muscles fluttered around us again. Neither of them could last much longer.

"Now," I instructed, pulling the bond to me and embracing the feel of Fi's orgasm. The sensation was so overwhelming I felt like I blacked out for a moment as I emptied myself inside her. I would never get used to how good sex with Fi was now that we were bonded. It had been amazing before, but feeling what she felt heightened everything.

Bryn gave us a couple of moments to recover before demanding we move so he could get Fi in the bath. Despite the gruffness of his words, he scooped Fi up tenderly, his face softening as her head lolled sleepily against his chest.

I cleared up and redressed, feeling more like myself than I had in the past few days. Maybe even weeks. It was time to make a plan. To take the next step.

To talk to the gods.

"I think we should visit the temple," I announced the next morning as we all got ready for the day. "We probably should have gone already."

"But you're avoiding your parents?" Marlen supplied helpfully.

"We don't have to go if it makes you uncomfortable. What would be the benefit, anyway?" Fi asked, her eyebrows drawing down.

"I'm hoping the gods will give us some kind of sign. If nothing else, perhaps they'll take it as a signal that we need some direction." I shrugged. It wasn't the most well-developed theory I had, but it was a starting point.

I wasn't particularly in the mood to listen to my parents fawning over the gods, given what the gods expected Fi to take on, and I doubted they would speak to Fi directly at all—being sanctified was only one step away from the gods themselves. The whole experience would be awkward.

The temple was about an hour's walk through the forest. It'd be faster to take the griffins—they'd been lounging around the woods surrounding the house since we'd arrived here—but all of us felt safer sticking below the tree cover. I barely noticed the journey, too focused on every rustle of a leaf or snapping of a twig. We couldn't be tracked with our cloaking amulets on, but that didn't mean we wouldn't run into someone on the path.

It was a shame we didn't have the luxury of enjoying it because Garrán Naofa was the most beautiful part of Avalon, in my opinion. The trees were gnarled and wizened, as old as the gods, and a thick sheen of glittering O'r Blodau covered almost everything around us, clinging to our feet as we walked. It wasn't harvested and sold from these parts, no one wanted to risk offending the gods.

Fi puffed along next to me as we climbed the small hill that led to the oldest temple in Avalon. We were in the most ancient part of the forest, but the trees stopped growing at the base of the slope, leaving this area exposed to the sun. Six ancient slabs of stone seemed to sprout out of the ground in a circle. They were at least 10-feet tall and had just enough space between the stones to slip through to the center of the circle.

I had played here as a child. My parents' house wasn't too far away from this hill as they were the guardians of the temple. Even my brother didn't live too far away from here with his mating circle, hopeful that one day he would take over when my parents couldn't do it anymore.

My parents' devotion to the gods had always made me excessively uncomfortable, though not as much now as it used to. Now that I had seen the gods in action... Well, I knew I wouldn't be angling for my parents' jobs in my lifetime.

Fi slid between the stones like she was in a trance, the four of us chasing after her in a panic. In the split second it had taken for us to follow her, Fi was already standing in the center of the circle, eyes drifting from stone to stone as if they mesmerized her.

The moment we joined her in the middle of the temple, I felt a wave of magic like nothing I'd ever experienced engulf me, crawling up my body from my toes to the top of my head. It was ancient. Primordial. Divine.

The gods were giving us their favor.

Once every inch of my body had been submerged in the warm, dense magic, time stood still.

Albion.

Albion.

Albion.

The word kept pressing into my brain like it was being forcefully shoved into my head.

My mind slowly cleared, and I noticed Fi looking between the four of us in amazement.

"All four of us were sanctified?" Eamon confirmed, looking at each of us. With his Second Sight, he'd be able to see the gods' magic on us.

"I'm gutted no one got to see my big sanctification moment," Fi said, sounding a little awed. "You were all kind of glowing, it was insane."

Bryn scoffed at her description, but even he looked a little humbled for a change.

Sanctified. Perhaps the gods didn't hold my years of resentment against them after all.

Fi's head whipped around at the same time Bryn's did, and the three of us all tensed to prepare for whoever their gifts had detected.

A tiny fae woman with dark, wrinkled skin and eyes as silver as her hair dropped to her knees a few feet away from us. She wore the dull, pale gray shapeless robes of the temple guardians, and her waist-length hair was pulled back into the same tight bun she'd worn every day of my life.

Had she seen?

"My mother, Meriel Calder," I said, gesturing towards the small but commanding woman that kneeled before us.

"Shouldn't we say hello?" Fi asked tentatively as my mother bent forward to touch her forehead to the earth. It was the ultimate sign of respect to touch your head to the source of magic.

"She won't speak to us," I replied, trying to keep both my expression and emotions in check.

"What? Why?" Fi whispered, her eyes flicking between me and my mother's prone form.

"She won't believe she's worthy." I shrugged as though the thought didn't bother me. "We've got the answers we came for, we shouldn't linger out here."

Fi still looked unsure, but Bryn cupped her elbow and firmly led her back through a gap in the stones to the forest path. I glanced over my shoulder and said a silent goodbye to the woman who gave me life, still prostrated on the ground behind me.

We arrived back at the cabin to find a visitor waiting for us. Fortunately, Bryn's tracking ability picked up Enfys' presence well before we reached the cabin.

The rest of us had warmed to Enfys significantly since he'd started spying on the Council, and we liked him even more when he offered us his cottage to stay in. Bryn's attitude towards Enfys was still icy though, and I imagined the feeling was mutual.

Enfys had seen Bryn as competition, even when Enfys had never been invited to the race.

"Owen," Bryn greeted as we all piled into the cottage behind him.

Enfys was sitting at the small table in the kitchen, nursing a steaming cup of tea. He looked like he'd aged several decades since I last saw him, and I doubted he'd slept much either.

He stood when Fi entered the cabin, surprised to see her. "Fi," he breathed, staring at her with a little too much familiarity. "I didn't feel the pull to you."

"You wouldn't," Bryn replied, his voice void of emotion. "Her mating circle is complete."

Bryn's body language belied his bland tone. He'd pulled Fi tightly against him and was resting a possessive hand on her ass. She rolled her eyes even as she rested her hand reassuringly on Bryn's chest.

I pulled the bond to me and whatever Enfys was feeling had Fi upset, though I couldn't understand why. She'd never once led him to believe there was anything between them.

"I hope you're finding everything here to your liking," Enfys eventually said awkwardly.

"It's wonderful. Thank you so much for letting us stay here," Fi replied sweetly. Bryn's hand flexed on her ass, and Fi shot him a warning look.

"I can't stay long," Enfys said abruptly, standing. "I don't want to risk drawing attention to my absence. But just so you're aware, Glendower Castell has posted a notice in local villages demanding your capture to face trial before the Council on the charges of theft, destruction of property, and murder."

Fi's face paled at the murder accusation, and I felt like I had to physically swallow down my rage.

"Is he fucking *deranged*? He tortured her and stole her magic! He really thinks getting her in front of his peers to testify is the best course of action?" Bryn snapped.

"He has most of the Council at his disposal," Fi reminded him. "Enough for a majority vote."

"He's not going to capture you, sweetheart, so it's irrelevant." Fi's dubious expression reminded me why I let Marlen and Eamon handle the comforting.

"I'm assuming he didn't make any mention of dragons in that notice?" Bryn asked drily.

"Dragons? No. Why?"

"The Castells had captured a female dragon. We worked with her mates to free her, as well as the other prisoners from the Estate," Eamon explained. "One of the dragons has a father on the Assembly. News of this will get out."

"By the gods," Enfys sighed. "I've been steering clear of the Castells, but

I heard they vacated that property and have been lying low. They're very rarely seen at the Council building nowadays."

"They have to know by now that they're in danger," Fi muttered.

"One more thing—someone's been following me. A young male, pale skin, dark hair. He appears out of nowhere and blatantly watches me. No subtlety. I don't know what his aim is, he just hangs back and observes me," Enfys said, looking thoughtful.

"There was a fae we released from the Castell Estate who we directed to speak to you if he wanted to testify about his experience," Bryn said slowly.

"Was he interested in doing so?" Enfys asked, his gaze flicking to Fi, who looked suddenly uncomfortable.

"I couldn't tell you either way. His emotions were like a black hole or a void. There was nothing there. I've never felt anything like it."

"He may have been shielding subconsciously. Fae used to use mental shields that blocked out empath magic," Eamon suggested.

"Yeah, Gwyneira and I worked on that during our mentoring sessions... You think it was some kind of protective instinct? Because of what he's been through?" Fi asked Eamon.

"It's a theory. I imagine that if he's following you, he's seeing for himself if you're trustworthy," Eamon replied, turning to Enfys.

"Or letting you know that he's watching you," Bryn added.

"Do you know his name? Or why he was captured?" Enfys asked, cutting Bryn off with a glare.

"Nothing," Fi admitted.

"Were there any other prisoners?" Enfys asked reluctantly, looking like he'd really rather not know.

"Two children, who our associate is caring for, and a centaur who immediately bolted. We intend to meet with the dragon representative on the Assembly to discuss their involvement in punishing the Castells," I cut in.

"Allow me," Enfys replied thoughtfully. "Aside from the fact that it's risky for you to travel, this could be the motivator I need to spur the three fae Councilors into action. They'll be more inclined to act if they have the support of the Assembly."

"We'd be putting a lot of trust in them..." Fi trailed off, voice filled with doubt. If any of them gave Glendower and his cohorts warning of what we were doing, we'd be in trouble.

"We'd be backing them into a corner," Enfys argued with a calculating gleam in his eye. Perhaps Bryn was right about Enfys having political goals of his own. "Our corner. Regardless of what the fae Councilors do or don't do, the dragons and the centaurs will take action. Either they're on the winning side or they aren't."

"It's not the friendliest way of gaining allies," Fi pointed out wryly.

"It's the fae way," Bryn replied with a feral grin. "Besides, with Owen handling the political arrangements, we can focus on the other part of your task."

"Our task," Fi corrected. "You're all sanctified now, so it's your problem too."

"It was always our problem," Marlen chuckled.

"You're all sanctified? Well, it looks like you picked the right mating circle then," Enfys said a little sadly.

"I did," Fi agreed, sounding resolute. Bryn's grip on her tightened slightly, and I knew it meant something to him that she'd defended her choice.

"Right." Enfys cleared his throat awkwardly. "Well, you're welcome to stay here for as long as you'd like. It is an honor to have the gods' chosen ones in my home." His pompousness was back in full force, but I much preferred this Enfys to the heartbroken version.

"I need to see my dads," Fi declared, looking between us. If Enfys was handling the Council, we could focus on finding the hidden portal to Albion.

"You trust them with your location?" Enfys asked warily.

"I trust them implicitly," Fi confirmed.

"Well, that's good enough for me. I'll get in touch with them within the next couple of days. Visiting your childhood home while you're on the run would be... inadvisable." Bryn snorted as Enfys reached the door, pausing on the threshold to give Fi a lingering look.

"May the gods keep you safe."

FFION

CHAPTER 74

True to his word, Enfys had contacted my fathers with our location. They showed up two days later, relief pouring off them to find us okay after seeing the posters around town labeling us as wanted criminals.

They didn't ask about the murder charge. Hopefully, it was because they knew I wasn't capable of that and not because they were fine with it if it were true.

My fathers had each taken one of the dining chairs and we'd pulled the armchairs up to the table. Eamon sat on one with me on his lap, Bryn was next to us in the other with Marlen perched on the arm of the chair, much to Bryn's dismay. I felt like a rose among thorns with all these prickly men around.

Having my dads observe this seating arrangement with raised eyebrows was the height of awkwardness.

Especially when Arthus sat on the bed. By the dirty looks Galvyn was giving it, he may have been genuinely considering setting it on fire.

"Every time we see you, you've acquired a new mate," Attie mused, giving Bryn an appraising look. Attie was definitely less hot-headed than Galvyn.

"Ah, yes. Well, I'm all done now," I replied with an awkward laugh, waving my wrist a little so they could see the finished mating mark. Galvyn hummed, still glaring at the bed.

While I was glad they'd come here, I was disappointed I couldn't visit them at my childhood home—Marlen, Arthus and Eamon had seen it before I had—but this was still nice. My fathers had brought pastries and ale with them, which we'd set up on the minuscule dining table. When we were all sitting around like this, breaking bread and drinking ale, it was easy to take a mental break from all the other shit I was supposed to focus on.

There were even moments of lightness from my fathers from time to time, cutting through the heavy aura of misery that clung to them. Moments where their grief at losing their mate didn't suffocate them.

"I'm guessing you didn't call us here because you wanted ale?" Attie asked eventually.

"No, but we're grateful for it," I admitted. I wasn't even a massive ale fan, but it was going down a treat. "We need to know more about that portal you mentioned."

"You're going to go through it," Galvyn stated.

"Yes." I met his concerned gaze across the table.

"It could be dangerous," he countered immediately. "It was created in secret by a rebel fae. It isn't maintained like the Council-sanctioned one is."

"Of course it's dangerous." I shrugged.

That's just par for the course at this stage.

"We sent a message to Egan Parry saying our daughter wanted to meet with his mating circle," Attie began. "They know about you, we've talked about you before."

"How did you meet him?"

"The Parrys have an underground network of sorts. That's how we were getting stolen tokens for Galvyn to visit you in London and maintain your glamour," Attie explained.

"Why didn't you go through the unsanctioned portal?" Bryn asked.

"That portal is too far from London." Attie shrugged. "Albion is an enormous place. Bigger than Avalon."

"So did Egan reply?" I interjected, trying to steer the conversation back on topic.

"The Parrys rarely put anything in writing. They sent us a rare pale green shell that is only found on Ardotalia in the Outer Isles, so we assume that's where they are."

Arthus was pulling out his map of Avalon before Attie had even finished speaking.

"It might take longer, but we could stop in Dubris and stay a night at your sister's," he said to Marlen. "It would be a safe place for us to rest and there's a port nearby, we could hire a boat from there to take us to Ardotalia."

Marlen's joy at the idea of seeing Aderyn buzzed pleasantly over my skin.

"We could follow you as far as Dubris, giving you a day or two head start," Attie mused. "That way, we'll be nearby if you need us either before you go through the portal or when you come out on the other side."

"I've always wanted to see the unicorns in the Black Forest," Galvyn grunted. "That's as good a reason as any for us to be in Dubris, if anyone asks."

Amusement tickled at my skin from all four of my mates. Apparently my unicorn fascination was inherited.

Eamon stilled beneath me and his arms that had been resting loosely on my hips fell to his sides. I turned, startled, only to find him staring past me with his cloudy spirit eyes. More gently than I imagined possible, Bryn scooped me out of Eamon's lap and onto his own, his arms banding protectively around me.

"My moon, my sun," Eamon spoke in the strange ethereal voice that the spirits channeled through him. Galvyn and Attie sucked in a breath. Their emotions were too tumultuous to get a clear read on. Hope, grief, surprise, longing, all at once.

"My daughter," Eamon continued. I froze. Bryn's arms tightened around my waist.

"Rhedyn?" Attie whispered hoarsely.

"I am so proud of you, daughter. I am sorry I could not do more to protect you. Stay strong in the face of the challenges yet to come."

Emotion welled up strongly in me, my throat constricted painfully and my eyes burned with unshed tears. I muted my empath ability only to realize the feelings were all my own.

"Hold on, scout. You can fall apart later," Bryn said quietly into my hair. I sucked in a raspy breath, knowing he was right.

"My moon, my sun. Protect our daughter. Come home to me."

Eamon shuddered violently, his eyes snapping shut before opening again, back to a brilliant—but troubled—amethyst. I gave Bryn's arms a quick thank you squeeze before climbing back onto Eamon's lap, wrapping my arms around him and burying my face in the crook of his neck.

He smelled like cinnamon and comfort.

"Cariad? Are you okay?" he asked gently. "I'm so sorry, I didn't know it was your mother until she started speaking. I can never tell who the spirit belongs to."

"It's okay, it's okay," I repeated quietly, nuzzling his neck. It's not like it was his fault. He didn't ask for the spirits to drop into his body.

It had never occurred to me that the spirit of my *dead mother* was going to drop by, and I doubted Eamon had considered that either.

"Come home." Galvyn chanted the two words under his breath like a prayer.

"Perhaps we should go," Attie said hesitantly, glancing at Galvyn. I could tell that it wasn't about getting away from me. Hearing from their mate from the grave after seventeen years rattled them, and they weren't in a socializing mood any longer, which seemed totally reasonable to me.

"Yes, of course," I rasped, climbing off Eamon's lap to walk them out. My voice sounded odd to my own ears.

My mates tactfully spread out, giving us some space. I didn't know what to do with it, but I didn't want to brush the encounter off either. I got the feeling my fathers wanted to talk about her, and I wanted to know everything they had to say.

"So, moon and sun, huh?" I asked with a wistful smile. My parents were kind of cute.

Attie chuckled. "With my black hair and gray eyes, Rhedyn always said

I reminded her of the moon. Galvyn was more like the sun, especially his eyes. Your eyes."

"Was she pretty?"

"Beautiful," Galvyn answered without hesitation. "You look just like her."

My face heated at the unexpected compliment. I liked the idea of looking like the mysterious mother I didn't remember. It made me feel more connected to her in a way.

While the guys walked towards the edge of the grassy patch where my fathers' griffin was grazing, I pulled Galvyn and Attie back towards the cottage a little until we were out of earshot.

"Everything okay, kid?" Attie asked, giving me a perplexed look.

"Need us to rough up those pretty boy mates of yours?" Galvyn added gruffly. "We never got a chance to give them a proper welcome to the family."

"By the sounds of it, that's a good thing," I responded drily, giving him an unimpressed look, though I was glad he'd perked up a little. "I need a favor, actually."

"Anything," Galvyn grunted, ignoring Attie's disapproving look. Galvyn was surly on the outside, but he was definitely a softie at heart. He'd have been the one I had wrapped around my little finger as a kid if I'd grown up with them. A pang of longing shot through my chest at the thought of the childhood I never had.

"I need some kyanite," I said quietly, speaking quickly as Arthus turned back to usher me over. "Enough for each of the guys to have an amulet."

"Done," Attie said readily, with a curt nod.

"Sweetheart?" Arthus asked, giving us a curious once-over.

"Just a second." I'm sure he'd already checked the bond to figure out what was going on. Not wanting him to catch on that I was up to something, I abruptly asked my fathers the first question that came to mind to change the subject.

"Do I have grandparents?"

"Grandparents? Sure," Attie chuckled, looking surprised. "Aunts, uncles, and cousins too."

"Oh," I replied, mulling over how I felt about that. "Do they know about me?"

"Of course, they live all over Avalon, but you'd met most of them in your three years, er, with us," Galvyn said, eyes flitting away uncomfortably.

"We told no one about your gift, just that you had to leave for your own safety," Attie added. "Your grandparents probably suspected something. You used to tell them how their emotions made you feel. Tickles on your skin, bubbles in your tummy, that kind of thing."

"It was cute," Galvyn muttered, his cheeks pinkening a little. *Gods, such a softie.*

"It was," Attie agreed, a smile tugging at his mouth. "We see little of your mother's family now, unfortunately..." he trailed off.

We'd had a moment of levity, but the loneliness and desolation were back in full force. For the first time, I could see how lost they were. I'd always visualized a mating circle as an unbroken chain, but it wasn't, not really. It was more like a solar system. Without their star, my fathers had no orbit.

I didn't feel comfortable telling them I loved them, even though I was confident I did. They were still strangers to me, even if they'd been in the background my entire life, but I could show them though. Surely if there was ever a good use for the gift I'd been cursed with, it was spreading a little love. I'd just be super careful this time. I'd managed it okay with Marlen.

Tentatively, I reached for their hands and isolated that *blanket-made-of-sunshine* feeling that originated in my chest, letting it trickle through my arms and gradually releasing it through my fingertips.

I sensed the moment that the love started flowing into them, temporarily filling the void. They looked at me like they were seeing me for the first time, while my mates stood off to the side, oozing pride that I was using my gift.

It was a heady feeling. I felt powerful, like I could make things happen. Maybe I wasn't as ill-suited for the gods' task as I thought.

I pulled my hands back slowly, following my instincts and letting the trickle of emotion taper off. Once I'd released their hands, I let go of the breath I didn't realize I'd been holding.

"You're incredible, kid," Attie breathed, pulling me into a tight hug.

"Stay safe, daughter," Galvyn added, his voice rough with emotion. "We'll see you soon."

I let Eamon pull me to his side as my fathers mounted their griffin and took to the sky, while Marlen's arm snaked around my waist on my other side.

"That was perfect, cariad. You were amazing," Eamon murmured, his lips brushing against the shell of my ear.

"Nicely done, scout," Bryn announced, patting me on the cheek as he strode past us back towards the cottage. "Now come pack your shit. We've got a long journey ahead of us."

Practically brimming with Glendower's illusion magic, I'd glamoured myself with silky ink blue shoulder-length hair, pale blue eyes, and had even made my facial feature more pixie-like, inspired by Briallen. It was my best glamour yet, but it didn't reassure me in the slightest. Dubris was a full day and night of travel away. We'd be seriously exposed.

All the guys had created their own detailed glamours, and it was weirding me the fuck out. I contemplated activating the amethyst ring Eamon gave me so I could see through them like he could.

"Does this mean you like my hair the best?" blonde Bryn asked as he toyed with my midnight blue tresses. He looked like a surfer.

I shrugged, unable to lie and not wanting to admit that I regularly coveted his unique hair color, but the smug look he gave me told me he already knew.

"Okay, we'll fly to Leodis, then the griffins can travel back to the Old Adair Estate, and we'll go the rest of the way by carriage," a silver-haired Arthus instructed unhappily. No one liked this plan. No one wanted to leave the relative safety of Enfys' little cabin, even with glamours and cloaking amulets to protect us.

Fortunately, it appeared all our worries had been for naught.

We made it to Leodis and parted ways with the griffins with no trouble. It would have looked suspicious for me to travel with four males, so we split up to hire separate carriages to take us to Dubris.

I hated being separated from Arthus and Bryn. I could feel their presence not far behind us, but it didn't prevent the anxiety bubbling in my chest that something would happen to them and we would be too far away to help.

We traveled overnight, each taking turns at napping when we could calm down enough to fall asleep. We farewelled the drivers at a small roadside stop and found new ones, since the horses had needed to rest. For the second stretch, I rode with Bryn and Arthus while fretting about Eamon and Marlen.

Rather than risk the carriage driver seeing where we were staying, we walked the last three miles into the village. Probably attracting all kinds of attention given how late at night it was in the process.

Working for the gods was tiring, sweaty business, and I nearly cried when we reached the base of Aderyn's treetop cabin. I craved a shower and a decent night's sleep. All saving-the-fae tasks were officially on pause until tomorrow, the Keeper of Balance needed a fucking break.

MARLEN

CHAPTER 75

It was after midnight when we finally made it to Aderyn and Lachlan's cabin in Dubris.

I'd never been so happy to see my sister. So much had happened in the weeks since we'd parted at the Academy, it felt more like *years*.

Aderyn wasn't the most expressive or affectionate fae, so when she flung her arms around my neck the second I dropped my glamour on her doorstep, I knew she was happy to see me too. She pulled back, eyes scanning my face, and I wondered if she could *see* how much we'd been through. Fi's brush with death had aged me by decades.

With a small frown, Aderyn ushered us into the cabin, and we all squished in against the walls and the furniture to fit. It was a cozy, comfortable home, but it really wasn't a space designed for seven adults.

Seeing Aderyn with half a claiming mark on her wrist, bustling around the home she shared with Lachlan added to the impression that I hadn't seen her in forever. I barely recognized this confident, capable fae in front of me. She'd truly come into her own.

"I wanted to talk to you all about what you've been doing—there are posters around the village saying the Council are looking for you," Aderyn breathed, biting her lip as Lachlan wrapped a supportive arm around her waist. "You all look so exhausted though."

"We are," I admitted.

"My parents have a bigger cabin just across the clearing," Lachlan interjected. "Addie and I can stay there tonight, you can take our place."

"Are you sure?" Fi asked, looking both guilty and excited at the prospect of sleep.

"Of course," Aderyn assured her with a sad smile. "We'll talk in the morning."

The cabin itself was small—about the size of the student cabins at the Academy—but with a decent-sized kitchen that took up most of the space. The bed was only big enough for three of us, and Eamon and I totally had dibs since we were the spooners of the mating circle.

Within five minutes, Fi had used the bathroom, changed into a nightdress and passed out face down in the middle of the bed. I snuggled in next to her while Eamon and Arthus tried to out-polite each other into taking the bed. Bryn had already kicked his feet up on the couch and closed his eyes. Eventually, Eamon conceded and slid into the bed on Fi's other side.

If we could just get a solid twelve hours of sleep, we'd be able to handle whatever the next step of this journey threw at us, I thought as my heavy eyelids drifted shut.

We were woken up by aggressive pounding on the door well before sunrise. Arthus was up and alert before the rest of us. He jumped off the floor where he must have been sleeping, his wings exploding out of his back defensively. Bryn and Eamon flanked him on either side as he approached the cabin door. Meanwhile, I hauled Fi out of bed and into the corner of the room, positioning myself in front of her.

"Nobody puts baby in the corner," she grumbled, making no sense at all. Maybe she was still half-asleep.

"Who are you?" Arthus called through the door.

"Seren, Cleland, Egan and Merle Parry. I believe you were looking for us," a feminine voice replied, giving us all pause.

"Well?" Fi demanded, striding around me. "Are you going to let her in?"

"You have no sense of self-preservation, scout," Bryn muttered, wrapping his arm around her waist and hauling her back against him.

"How did you find us?" Arthus demanded, his irritation coming through loud and clear in his voice. I was impressed he hadn't had some kind of stroke by now with all the surprises and changes of plans we'd had.

"The spirits did," a low masculine voice replied. "Through me."

I couldn't see Eamon's face from where I was standing, but his spine stiffened slightly. He'd told us before that he'd never met anyone else with Second Sight—it was a fairly rare gift, and those who possessed it were usually shunned.

"I want to talk to them," Fi said determinedly. "This is the whole reason we traveled here."

Arthus sighed in resignation. He may play at being the boss, but he ultimately answered to Fi just as willingly as the rest of us did.

"Give us five minutes," Arthus called through the door. I could tell he didn't feel any better about letting them in here than I did, but we couldn't risk being overheard. Besides, none of us had glamours on right now. It was best to stay out of sight.

Fi moved to Arthus' side, softly murmuring something in his ear as she stroked the edge of his wing. He shuddered slightly before letting out a deep breath, his wings retracting with more ease than I'd ever seen.

"Did you just *empath* him?" I gaped.

"If you mean did I use my emotion influencing ability to relax him enough to retract his wings, yes I did. I told him beforehand," Fi shot back defensively.

"Shut up," Arthus groaned before I could reply. "That felt good, don't ruin it for me."

I sniggered and tossed him a shirt, letting him lounge in his happy buzz a little longer. It'd disappear as soon as we had to talk to the newcomers, anyway.

We finished dressing quickly and silently, and I wrapped one of Aderyn's shawls around Fi's shoulders as Bryn moved to open the door. After weeks of small steps and what-ifs, the past two days had been a blur of activity and it didn't look like we'd be slowing down any time soon.

Fi slid between Eamon and I, while Bryn and Arthus stood in front of us like bodyguards, all scowls and crossed arms.

"My name is Seren Parry," a tiny woman with silvery lavender hair and inky black eyes said, looking critically between us. "This is Cleland, Egan, and Merle."

Merle's eyes were a similar shade of amethyst to Eamon's but the cloudiness of the spirits lurked around the edges of his irises, like the spirits were hovering right on the periphery. It was... unsettling, to say the least.

"What do you know about us?" Arthus asked in a louder, far more relaxed tone than usual. Maybe Fi had overdone it on the happy magic. She glanced at him nervously like she might have been thinking the same thing.

"We can't speak here," Seren hissed, eyes darting between the cabin windows.

"We're not going anywhere with you until we know your intentions," Bryn countered, as amiable as ever.

"Likewise," Egan gritted out. He was totally the Bryn of their mating circle. "Swear that you mean no harm to us or the fae in hiding. We swear that we will not harm you—unless it's in self-defense." He reached out his hand towards Bryn.

"Fine, we swear it," Bryn took his hand, striking the deal without a second's hesitation.

"Right, then let's go to Ardotalia. We can talk openly there. Put your glamours on," Seren announced, pulling the front door open.

We hadn't had a chance to get much out of our satchels, so all we had to do was add our outer layers, quickly put our glamours back in place and head out the door. There was no way I'd be leaving without saying goodbye to my sister, though.

I looked around the treetop cabins that circled the clearing, trying to figure out which one Aderyn could be in. Damn it, I should have asked her for more details yesterday.

"Her magical signature is coming from that room," Bryn grunted, pointing at a window across the clearing. I smiled at him, clapping his shoulder as I jogged past because I always knew we were friends under all his grumpiness. I stopped at the base of the cabin, gently tossing balls of water at the window until Lachlan stuck his head out, narrowly missing one.

"We've got to go, can you guys come down?" I whisper-shouted up at him. He gave me a quick nod, appearing at the base of the cabin a few minutes later with my disheveled-looking twin in tow.

"You're leaving?" she asked around a yawn as Fi sidled up next to me. "Already?"

"Sorry, sis." I grimaced. I knew we had a lot going on, but I'd been feeling like a neglectful brother lately. Aderyn had started a whole new life, and I knew nothing about it.

"I wish we could stay," I told her seriously. "I want to hear everything about your life here in Dubris and what you've been doing."

"You have to go *right* now," Aderyn stated rather than asked, looking dubiously between us and the Parrys, who were waiting impatiently a few feet away.

"I'm so sorry, Aderyn," Fi mumbled. Arthus made a grumbling sound behind us, staring at Fi's back. Whatever he was picking up through the bond had made him unhappy. "We'll come back for a visit as soon as we can. You're doing okay though, right? Are you happy?"

"Me?" my sister asked, surprised. "Of course. I'm incredibly happy. You're the ones wanted by the Council, off gallivanting with... whoever those people are. I just... You know what you're doing, right?"

"Some of the time," I told her reassuringly, pulling her into a hug. "As soon as we can, we'll be back," I promised again.

"Please be careful," Aderyn implored, pulling Fi in for a quick hug.

Fi gave her a watery smile, but said nothing. That was hardly a promise she could make. I mean, she'd wandered onto the Castell Estate and ripped apart the wards all on her own. And gotten herself stabbed in the process. Careful had gone out the window awhile ago.

As we headed towards the main road from the cluster of cabins Aderyn's place was located in, Arthus scowled at me before shooting a pointed look at Fi's back. I pulled the bond towards me and my stomach churned when I realized what Arthus was so worked up about.

Guilt. She felt guilty.

I'd met Fi on her first morning at the Academy, and I'd been there almost every step of the way as she transformed from a quiet, curious student to *the Sanctified Empath*, the reluctant *Keeper of Balance*, and whatever other titles the gods planned to heap on her. I knew better than anyone that Fi had never asked for any of this.

She had nothing to feel guilty about.

I jogged a few steps to close the distance between us and wrapped my arm around Fi's shoulders, tucking her into my side and planting a firm kiss against her temple.

"If we weren't here, we'd still be at the Academy—it's term time—and we wouldn't be seeing Aderyn anyway. So you're not allowed to feel guilty," I teased, though I was pretty serious about it.

"I'm not allowed?" Fi asked, looking up at me with a cocked brow.

"Nope. I would prefer you never feel guilty, especially on my behalf. You're breaking my heart here, foxglove."

"I've dragged you all away from your lives," she lamented quietly.

"Never doubt that, no matter what crazy adventures the gods send you—and therefore us—on, our lives are better because you're in them," I assured her, leaning down to brush my lips over hers.

"I don't deserve any of you," she murmured.

Eamon made a quiet strangled sound, his desire to comfort Fi getting the best of him. I chuckled and tipped my head to encourage him closer. Within seconds, he appeared on her other side, tucking her arm into the crook of his elbow.

I pulled my arm back and let them walk in front of me. Seeing Aderyn again, seeing how normal her life was, had thrown me for a loop. While I felt secure in Fi's affections, I also didn't know how not to be 'the fun one' of the mating circle. No one wanted Morose Marlen.

The port was a 45-minute walk from Dubris, the Parrys took their privacy seriously and weren't willing to risk a carriage ride. The sun was only just beginning to rise and the cool air was pleasant after spending the past two days cooped up. We were all running low on sleep, though. Fi, in particular, was shuffling more than walking. Her arm was linked through Eamon's and her head rested against his bicep, eyes half closed, letting him guide her.

A few months ago, she hadn't been comfortable enough to tell anyone she was getting threatening notes. Now, her trust in us was absolute. I don't think she realized how amazing that was. She'd come so far.

We didn't speak the whole journey. I tried to start a few conversations, but one of the Parrys always shushed me. I hoped our lives didn't turn out like this—forever balancing on the knife edge of paranoia. I didn't want that for any of us, but particularly for Fi, who'd spent her entire childhood trying to disguise the fact that she was different.

She deserved centuries of being unapologetically herself.

Fi lifted her head sleepily and gave me a dozy smile, shoving love at me through our bond. Exhausted as she was, she was still checking on us.

Before we reached the port, the Parrys led us off the main road into a patch of forest where griffin heads seemed to peer around from every tree, catching us all off-guard. As they moved out towards us, I realized there were five griffins—enough for us to ride two astride with one spare.

"Ardotalia is one of the closer islands, only an hour flight," one of the guys told us. "Faster than going by boat."

That was fine by me. I'd never been on a boat. I didn't want to freak out in front of my girl.

Bryn tugged Fi out of Eamon's grip and helped her onto the griffin before climbing on behind her. Arthus climbed up behind Eamon and I flew solo.

The griffins kicked off smoothly, following the Parrys up into the air. They were the most placid group of griffins I'd ever met—almost like they were used to transporting skittish fae. It seemed like the Parrys had quite the operation going here.

The hour-long flight passed in a blur and was over too quickly. Even though the view below was mostly crystal blue water with other islands barely visible in the distance, I didn't get sick of it. The ocean was awesome.

The griffins landed on an almost invisible-from-the-air patch of grass between thick, green foliage and bright, exotic flowers. This was my first trip to the Outer Isles, and it was like a different world. More than anything, I wanted to head back to the beach and stick my toes in the sand, but the fun stuff would have to wait.

We dismounted the griffins and followed the Parrys through some overgrown brush, the barest evidence of a pathway under our feet. The sun was fully up now, and I felt the sweat trickle down the back of my neck. It was definitely hotter here than it was on the mainland.

Eventually a cabin came into view, mostly obscured by trees. It wasn't like any home I'd ever seen on the mainland—the walls were more glass than wood, and a low porch wrapped around the whole house. I pulled the bond towards me and felt Fi's awe as she took everything in.

"Come in," Seren's mate—*Cleland, was it?*—called over his shoulder as he pulled a glass door to the side and stood back to let us pass. There was a lot of plant life inside too, enormous pots with exotic flowers covered every surface and took up half the floor space. Four white couches were arranged in a square surrounding a round wicker coffee table, and I slid onto the couch next to Fi with Bryn on her other side. Everyone else dropped onto the remaining three couches. Fi sunk back slightly in the pillows and I knew she was resisting the urge to lay her head back and have a little nap.

"So, what do you know about Ffion?" Bryn started, skipping the pleasantries.

"The spirits told us about you. That the gods sanctified you, chose you to restore the balance between light and dark," Seren said, assessing Fi intently.

She didn't seem hostile, but she wasn't friendly either.

"You have your doubts," Fi replied bluntly, giving Seren a flat look. Fi had plenty of doubts of her own, but apparently she was the only one allowed to voice those.

"My parents gave their lives to protect the portal. It's the only way out of Avalon for those who need it," Seren replied evenly, her eyes still narrowed on Fi.

"It's important to you," my foxglove surmised, letting out a long exhale. She was as beautiful as ever, but she hadn't glamoured the black circles under her eyes and she couldn't disguise the exhausted slump of her shoulders.

"My aunt, Úna, looks after the, er, community there. She's an elder of sorts. That's who you must speak to."

"The gods want me to bring them home," Fi said cautiously, testing the waters.

"Make it safe for them here and they will come," Seren replied simply as Fi's shoulders slumped even further. That was the plan, but we hadn't managed it yet.

"Look," Seren added sympathetically. "No fae wants to hide out in Albion, away from the source of their magic, surrounded by all those suffocating human toxins." She shuddered at the thought.

"There's your angle, scout," Bryn muttered, too quietly for the Parrys to hear.

"Well, it would be futile to go against the gods' wishes, even if I question their logic," Seren sighed, making Fi bristle. "I'll take you to the portal. Be warned, it's an unpleasant journey, I'll show you where you can rest and wash up first."

EAMON

CHAPTER 76

Seren led us down a short corridor with huge window panes that covered most of the walls. The high, thick vegetation outside the windows hid us from view, though from the air, it hadn't looked like there were any other properties nearby anyway.

"You can stay in this room," Seren announced, pushing the door open. "Or even if you don't, you can leave your things here. Our portal is much smaller than the Council one. You won't be able to bring it all with you."

Bryn, who'd had the most experience with portal travel, gave her an alarmed look. I'd never been through the portal myself, but I knew it was a large pond that many fae could pass through at once, but this one didn't sound like that at all.

I hoped we knew what we were getting ourselves into here.

The room was simply furnished with a large circular bed, a plain wooden bench against the wall, and a single chest of drawers. Windows dominated one wall, and the remaining walls were whitewashed. The floors and furniture were a glossy dark wood, and the bedding was a crisp white, as were the gauzy curtains that framed the windows.

Fi sighed longingly at the bed as we each offloaded our satchels onto the wooden bench.

"There's a bathroom down the hall," Seren added.

"I think we should freshen up and head to the portal straight away," Fi sighed.

"You're exhausted, cariad."

Worry for her wellbeing gnawed at me. She needed sleep and a hot meal after all the travel we'd been doing.

"I'm not going to sleep," Fi replied, looking at me like I'd lost my mind. I had to admit, as tired as I was, I doubted I'd be able to rest with our upcoming journey playing on my mind. "Besides, as wanted criminals, won't we be safer in Albion?"

"Depends on the fae in Albion," Bryn grumbled, earning him a scowl from Seren.

"They're far more polite than you," she snarked, crossing her arms over her chest.

"I don't doubt that," Bryn agreed solemnly as Fi stifled a giggle.

"Do you know all the fae hiding in Albion?" Fi asked Seren curiously.

"Almost all of them. There are some who have been there longer than I've been alive. In recent years, my mates have assisted the younger ones out of their, er, situations. I'd take care of them here until they were ready to travel to Albion."

It was difficult to tell, but Seren didn't look much older than Fi. There was a hardness in her black eyes that Fi didn't have, though. Not yet, anyway. Hopefully never.

"We'll bring in some food for you. Let us know what you decide to do. If you want to go through the portal today, dress warm," Seren added, earning her another puzzled glance from Bryn.

Seren left us alone and Arthus looked intently at Fi for a long moment, searching for something in the bond, or perhaps just her expression.

"You want to get this over with?"

"I want to control my own life," she shot back, eyes blazing with determination. "Up to now, I've been sitting back and just letting things happen. I'm done with waiting around, hoping it all works out. I'm going to *make* it work out."

The relief in the room was palpable. If Fi noticed it, she said nothing as she collected an armful of clean clothes and disappeared down the hallway.

Whether or not she realized it, she'd just embraced her role for the first time. No hedging words. No jokes about the gods choosing wrong. She'd taken the next step forward of her own volition.

Arthus blinked slowly at the door before shaking his head and rolling his shoulders back. "You heard her. Carry the amulets in your belts, we'll leave the satchels here," he instructed.

The Parrys brought us a tray of vegetable wraps and freshly sliced fruit, and we all took turns showering as each of us grazed. By the time we set out into the Parrys back garden for the portal, the sun was high overhead and sweat beaded on my forehead.

As per Seren's instructions, we'd worn the warmest clothes we had with us, which wasn't much, considering the time of year. Each of us males had a long pair of linen trousers and a long-sleeved shirt, but if we were going somewhere freezing, we'd be uncomfortable. Fi was wearing what she'd dubbed her "ass-kicking pants"—the only pants she owned—and I vowed to buy her ten more pairs when we got back to Avalon.

We followed Seren into their back garden, across a small patch of grass, before delving right into the heart of the overgrown vegetation that surrounded their property. The Council-sanctioned portal was set in a meadow of wildflowers. It was open, spacious, and exposed. The complete opposite of where we were heading now, though this was no less beautiful.

After pushing some enormous leaves aside, we ended up on a narrow sloping walkway that was almost hidden by the lush foliage. The Outer Isles were warmer than central Avalon, and the exotic plant life had always fascinated me.

Fi looked like she was in paradise. Someday soon, I'd take her to the Adair house on Maglona, one of the bigger islands. It wasn't as tranquil as this, but she deserved a chance to relax on the beach. Eventually.

We heard the splash of running water before we saw it. The portal was a narrow—though probably deep—pool at the base of a small, rocky waterfall. A circle of knee-high boulders surrounded it and it was shrouded by leaves as big as my torso in the deepest of emerald greens. Every inch of the rock beneath was visible through the crystalline water.

All of us were eying the portal apprehensively. Seren's description had been accurate—there was no way we'd all fit through at the same time.

"Ffion and I should go through together, first," Bryn sighed, cutting Arthus a quick glance out of the corner of his eye.

"Absolutely not," Arthus countered.

"It makes the most sense," Fi said quickly, resting her hand on Arthus' arm. "Bryn can sense approaching magic signatures, I can pick up surrounding emotions. We're harder to sneak up on."

Bryn nodded in agreement, though he didn't look any happier with the idea than we did.

"Can you both fit?" Marlen asked dubiously, leaning over the rocky barrier that surrounded the narrow pool.

"We'll cuddle," Fi replied cheerfully, trying to ease some tension. Bryn rolled his eyes, though the corner of his mouth twitched.

"This is where I leave you," Seren said from the path behind us.

"Thank you for your help," I told her. They had sought us out, and brought us all the way here. It was more than we expected.

"Who are we to challenge the gods?" Seren replied easily, giving Fi a curt nod before she left.

"Let's do this," Bryn grumbled, perching on the large rock at the edge of the portal and reaching his hand back to Fi expectantly. He helped her up on the rock, then pulled her leg over his lap so she was straddling him.

"Hold on tight, scout," Bryn instructed. Fi's legs wrapped around his back with her arms around his neck, and she gave us each a reassuring smile over Bryn's shoulder.

"See you on the other side," she said softly as Bryn pushed off the rocks and disappeared into the rushing water. Arthus was climbing onto the rocks before Bryn's head had fully submerged. He pushed off the rocks with his feet too, followed by Marlen who dived off the rocks head first.

I lowered myself cautiously, feeling the swirl of the magic pulling at my legs the moment they hit the water. With a quick silent prayer to the gods, I let the water take me under, releasing my body to the sensation.

This portal had been created in secret by rebel fae, and the experience of passing through it reflected that. It was rough, churning and erratic, and by the time I emerged in some kind of lake on the Albion end, Fi and Bryn were doubled over on the shore, trying not to throw up, while Arthus and Marlen were making their way to them.

My stomach heaved uncomfortably and my head spun with dizziness. I could see why Seren and her mates hadn't insisted on accompanying us on this trip. I wouldn't go through that portal again by choice either.

The portal must have been centered on this particular spot in an enormous lake. My clothes were dry, but I could see the others were soaking wet from swimming to the shore. With a sigh of irritation, I left the dry bubble and headed straight into the icy water. There was a brush of magic as I swam away—a glamour probably, repelling humans from this spot. It was a more sophisticated setup than I'd envisioned.

I hauled myself up to standing next to the others on the rocky shore. We were all dripping water and shivering so loud our teeth chattered.

It was very undignified.

"Don't heal us," Fi gasped out, giving Marlen a sharp look as he stumbled towards her with his hand outstretched. "You need to reserve your magic while we're here. Just in case."

He gave her a pained look, but nodded in agreement. It went against every one of his instincts to watch someone suffer. Especially the woman he loved.

"We need to dry off, at least," Arthus gritted out, aggressively rubbing his temple. Marlen immediately began pulling the water out of our clothes, chased by Arthus' air magic whipping around us. I almost groaned in relief at feeling dry fabric against my skin again.

After a few minutes, we straightened ourselves out and took in our surroundings. Fi frowned, looking at the mountain range ahead of us.

"Don't use too much magic," Bryn cautioned. "We're running on reserves in Albion, and we don't want to draw any attention to ourselves."

We all nodded reluctantly. I could feel the remnants of magic swirling in my veins, but nothing like the potency I felt in Avalon. It was awful. Like a missing limb.

The fae who lived here must be truly desperate to give it up.

"Does any of this look familiar at all, cariad?" I asked cautiously.

"They don't have mountains like this anywhere near London," Bryn said quietly.

"Yeah, we're definitely not in the United Kingdom," Fi agreed, blowing out a long breath. "I'm not sure where we are. Switzerland maybe? It's kind of stunning, though. And cold," she added, shivering slightly as she looked around.

"The seasons have always been the same between realms when I traveled to Albion," Bryn replied, his brow furrowed. "I was expecting summer."

We were standing on the rocky shore of a lake as bright blue as any I'd ever seen in Avalon. Behind us was a thick cluster of trees, and beyond that were tall, snow-capped mountains. They were reflected in almost perfect clarity in the lake water below. This place looked pristine, untouched by humans.

It was nothing like what I expected. I assumed Albion's landscapes to be as dead as the magic that was once rampant here.

"We've got company," Bryn said quietly, his eyes darting towards the thick copse of trees behind us.

The four of us circled Fi instinctively, and I tried to suppress my smile at her indignant huff. I could no more deny my need to protect her than I could deny my need to breathe.

Fortunately, whoever was approaching wasn't trying to sneak up on us. Twigs crunched under their feet and leaves rustled loudly as they pushed through the undergrowth. A young fae male emerged from the treeline, watching us as warily as we watched him. He had a mop of bright orange hair, pale skin flushed with exertion, and a slight build.

Young. Awfully young to be in hiding.

"What's your business here?" he asked cautiously, eyes jumping between us four guys. He looked like he was sizing us up, trying to determine who was the biggest threat. It didn't bode well for the fae hiding here if this was one of their guards—the kid couldn't be older than fifteen.

"We're here to speak to Úna," Arthus replied coolly.

"Why?" I had to give the kid credit for not backing down.

"We're going to take down the Fae Council and lock up all those fuckers who steal gifted magic. Gods' orders," Fi deadpanned, getting right to the point. Arthus and Bryn grumbled under their breath.

"Oh." The kid blinked at her a few times. "Well, um, I guess you'd better come talk to Úna then?"

"Marvelous idea," Fi replied cheerfully, scowling at Arthus when she tried to stride past him and he moved deftly in front of her.

"Follow me" the kid mumbled, shaking his head.

FFION

CHAPTER 77

"What's your name?" I asked the orange-haired teenager in front of us as he led us into the copse of trees, weaving easily through the undergrowth until he found a narrow dirt path.

"Osian," he replied, eventually. He was a brave kid. I could feel how nervous he was, but he kept his voice even and held his head high when he spoke to us. I hadn't expected to come across someone so young here, and it unsettled me, despite my own childhood spent in Albion. My stomach churned uneasily, remembering the little twins from the Castell Estate that Brently was caring for. Had Osian endured a childhood like that?

"We're nearly there," he added.

"I don't see anything," Arthus said. I knew he was struggling with being in a foreign setting around strange fae, but I also thought he just needed a decent nap. The past two days were a blur, and we were fucking exhausted.

"There's a weak glamour over the village, enough to repel humans," Osian replied as he led us up the loose dirt path. The trees on either side of us didn't look like any I'd seen in London. I trailed my fingers along an overhanging fern whose leaves were pale green on top and a silvery white underneath.

"Where are we?" I called ahead to our guide. Both Bryn and Arthus were walking single-file in front of me, and I could just make out the occasional flash of orange from Osian's hair. "On Earth, I mean. This doesn't look like the UK."

"We're at the base of the Southern Alps," he replied over his shoulder. *Southern Alps?* "New Zealand," he added.

Holy fucking fae! Everything I knew about New Zealand came from the Lord of the Rings movies. Given that we were following a mysterious fae to a hidden part of a forest to meet with some kind of elder figure, maybe the whole Middle Earth thing wasn't as fantastical as I had thought.

The path ended at a large, hilly clearing with what appeared to be a campsite on it. There was a large wooden building in the center of it that looked sort of like a house, with doors off each side leading out to the grounds. Small cabins were scattered around the periphery of the site, some closer to the communal building while others were more private, partially obscured by the encroaching treeline.

Each cabin was made of the same dark wood, with coppery red paint around the window and door frames, and simple sheet metal roofs that were probably deafening in a rainstorm.

It wasn't luxurious, but there was evidence of old campfires, children's toys on the ground, and well cared for vegetable plots dotted around the clearing. It felt homey, and the fae who lived here had gone to a great deal of effort to make it so.

Unease slithered over me at the idea of asking them to leave this community they'd built for themselves. Why would the gods even ask them to? They'd be taking an enormous risk returning to Avalon.

The grounds appeared deserted, but I could sense a sizable group of fae in the central building. They didn't feel afraid so much as apprehensive, mixed with a healthy dose of curiosity.

As we approached the building, the double front doors swung open and a small contingency of ten fae came forward to greet us. The elderly woman leading them could only be Úna.

She was the ultimate hippie. Her waist-length hair was probably once a rich plum color all over, but now it was interspersed with thick streaks of silver. Her eyes were the same striking shade of plum, and while her body still appeared fit and strong, her skin was papery and wrinkled.

She wore a floor-length halter neck dress, tie-dyed in distinct shades of aqua blue. It was way too cold here for a cotton halter neck dress that was better suited for the beach, but homegirl needed it. There was no way she was fitting those pink and purple fae wings under any clothes.

I wondered for a moment why she didn't just retract them until she turned slightly and I spotted the mangled joint where the wing connected to her back. It looked like someone came at her wings with a hacksaw, but she'd come out on top. *Just barely.*

Úna flitted rather than walked, much like the butterflies her wings resembled. I was dying to ask her how old she was because she looked as old as Noah, but she moved like a Zumba instructor.

Bryn gave me a judgy side-eye like he could read my mind, though he'd probably just checked the bond and got a sense of my burning curiosity.

"Living in Albion, away from magic, affects a fae. She's probably not as old as you think," he murmured, leaning in close so only I could hear him.

"Really?" My head whipped towards him in alarm. "Is that going to happen to me? I spent seventeen years here."

Bryn shrugged. "You look fine. She's probably been here longer than seventeen years."

I couldn't decide if his casual attitude reassured or irritated me. If I was going to suddenly start aging like milk because of the time I'd spent in this realm, I wanted to know.

Úna was flanked protectively by two fae who appeared to be around my age. I was a fully mated lady nowadays, but I could still appreciate a handsome man when I saw one. And holy fucking fae, right now I was seeing double.

Twin guys stood on either side of Úna, both tall, broad shoulders, and impressively built. They had identical messy jet black hair and olive skin that looked like it saw a lot of sun. Their only distinguishing feature was their eyes, which were striking and creepy in their intensity.

One twin had eyes of the palest gray, the other had irises as black as pitch. It didn't detract from their masculine beauty, but added to their commanding presence.

"Welcome," Úna said eventually, looking curiously between the five of us. "My name is Úna. This is Finnian," she indicated the pale-eyed twin, "and Conn," she said, gesturing to the dark-eyed twin.

"My name is Ffion Laisren," I replied, figuring it was best to go for formality. "These are my mates—Arthus, Marlen, Eamon, and Bryn Laisren." I gestured to each of them.

"You here seeking sanctuary, Ffion Laisren?" the pale-eyed twin asked, cocking his head to the side and scrutinizing me. Arthus and Bryn bristled defensively, and I quickly shot a pulse of reassurance through our bonds to calm them down.

"Ah, no." *Crap*, I should have rehearsed a proper speech or something. Something rousing that stirred a patriotic desire to return to Avalon.

Why wasn't there a handbook on this shit? *How to Revolution: 101.*

"No?" Úna repeated with a slight smile. I didn't sense any animosity from her, and if she'd been here a while, she'd probably seen all sorts of fae come out of that portal. I doubted much would have fazed her at this point.

Bryn cleared his throat and gave me a pointed look that clearly said *get your shit together.*

"The gods tasked me with bringing the fae in hiding back to Avalon," I began, watching the eyes of the spectators widen in alarm. "Not because you're in trouble," I added quickly. "They want all the fae to feel safe living in Avalon again."

"Not fucking happening," Conn interjected, his black eyes flashing dangerously.

"I'm afraid it is impossible for us to feel safe living in Avalon again," Úna replied softly, giving me a pitying look.

"There's a little more to our mission than that," Arthus grumbled. My heart skipped a beat that he'd called it our mission. "Ffion here has been named the *Keeper of Balance* by the gods, she's restoring the balance between dark and light magic in Avalon."

"Why? What's so special about her?" A male near the back of the crowd called out.

"What isn't special about her?" Marlen replied amiably, ever the peacekeeper. "She is an Empath—I'm sure you know they've been extinct for centuries—and the gods have sanctified her. Plus, she grew up in Albion too, so not only does she understand your situation, she has all kinds of human ideas about how we should run things in Avalon to make things fair for all fae. It's revolutionary," Marlen finished with a wink in my direction. My face was probably as red as a beetroot.

"Oh my," Úna said after a long and awkward silence. *Thanks, Marlen.*

"We're not expecting you to decide right now, or leave with us today," I said placatingly, holding up my hands in the universal *we come in peace* gesture. "I was hoping we could just talk a little, explain more about what we have planned..."

There was a lengthy pause as they all looked among themselves, deciding whether we could be trusted.

"Do you really think Seren would have sent us here if we had ill intentions?" Eamon asked quietly.

"No," Úna admitted with a sigh. "My niece is protective of our community. Let's move to the firepit, you're hardly dressed for this weather."

She was right. It clearly wasn't summer in New Zealand, because I was freezing. We followed Úna, Conn and Finnian to a round firepit next to the large communal building. There were logs arranged all around it so I sat down between Eamon and Marlen, with Úna and the twins on the log opposite. Bryn and Arthus stood sentry behind us, forever watching our back. Osian stacked up a pile of wood in the center of the pit and as he stepped back, Bryn lit it with his fire magic.

Something akin to longing emanated from Conn. I'd bet money that he had a fire affinity that he wasn't able to use after being here for so long.

"So, you mentioned you want to take down the Council?" Osian asked conversationally. The twins' eyes whipped to him, but Úna's stayed intently on me.

"They're corrupt," I shrugged. "The gods were vague on the whole restoring-the-balance thing, but I figure that taking out the rot at the top is a good way to kick things off. To get fae to rise up on their own and fight for a better society."

"You really are a revolutionary," Finnian replied drily.

"Very reluctantly," I admitted. Though perhaps I wasn't as reluctant as I had been.

"You probably should have led with fucking up the Council," Conn said, cracking his neck. "Finnian and I aren't the only ones that have personal grudges with them. In fact, almost everyone here has either been targeted by a Councilor or someone under a Councilor's protection."

I felt the sharp uptick in optimism from my four mates, and I was right there with them. I'd sensed Conn's longing when he saw Bryn's magic, and I doubted he was the only one missing it. Knowing we had a common enemy... Maybe this is why I was here. Maybe this is what the gods meant by bringing them home.

Perhaps I wasn't supposed to create a haven for these fae, but give them a chance for revenge. I was okay with that.

"It's personal for me too," I told them, looking up so they could see the sincerity on my face. "Two of the Councilors, Glendower and Evalina Castell, kidnapped me from the Academy grounds and kept me captive on their property. If it weren't for Bryn, I'd probably still be there." I looked up to shoot him a small grateful smile, but he shifted uncomfortably. He could take every insult I threw at him, but gods forbid I ever give him a compliment.

There had been a steady, curious presence hiding in the shadows of a nearby tree since we'd sat down. That curiosity had only gotten stronger since we'd mentioned the Council. My eyes adjusted to the light until I could just make out a young girl watching us warily from the shadows, eyes so fixated on us it looked like she wasn't blinking.

She shifted closer and the more I looked, the more I realized she wasn't as young as I'd assumed. More like a teenager, in fact. The sunlight briefly flashed across her, and her striking appearance took me off guard.

Her skin was a rich deep brown and her black hair fell around her shoulders in a sleek wave, but her eyes... her eyes were like two orbs of captured lightning. As she moved her head, they seemed to flash icy blue, to brilliant silver, then almost gold.

All fae had some pretty crazy eyes, but they usually resembled crystals. I was positive there was no crystal in existence the color of this fae's eyes.

"By the gods. Storm fae," Eamon whispered next to me. His tone was awed, almost reverent. Whatever this girl's gift was, it must be impressive.

"That's Riona," Osian said defensively, and the intense rush of love he felt for her warmed my heart.

"She really hates the Council," Finnian muttered.

"You've given us a lot to think about, Sanctified Empath," Úna said slowly. I wanted to tell her to just call me Ffion, but I didn't want to offend anyone. The whole Sanctified Empath thing was a little much. Úna blew out a long, exhausted breath. "We better find you somewhere to stay. You all look tired, and we need time to think."

I definitely was not objecting to that idea. I was exhausted.

Úna led us to one of the larger cabins, a little further back from the main building, nestled among some trees.

"There's clean linen on the shelf," she told us, pausing at the threshold. "Dinner isn't for a couple of hours, but there are snacks in the main kitchen. Help yourself."

Úna gave us a long measured look before leaving us to settle in, while Bryn and Arthus insisted on going in first to do their usual, over-the-top security sweep before giving us the all clear to follow.

I was disappointed to see twin double beds, but I could hardly expect everywhere to accommodate five adults sleeping together—even by Avalon standards, we were a rarity. It just made me want to get home faster, either to the cabin by the Academy or the Old Adair Estate, I wasn't fussy. They were both just big enough to accommodate the five of us and housed all of my favorite memories.

There wasn't much else in the cabin. A bedside table, some shelves on either side of the front door, and another door off one side that presumably led to the bathroom.

Marlen and I pulled folded sheets off the shelves and started making up the two beds. With the two of us moving around, there was barely enough room for the other three guys to stand without getting in the way.

"Why don't you three go get us some snacks from the main kitchen?" I suggested politely instead of telling them to get out because their enormous muscles were taking up all the room.

Bryn snorted. "We'll leave you to it, I want to look around, anyway."

"So do I," Arthus replied.

"I'll find us some food," Eamon volunteered.

With only two of us in the room, we finished making the bed quickly, and I kicked off my shoes, flopping back sideways across the bed. Meeting unfamiliar people hadn't got any less stressful for me, and combined with the portal travel, I was done. I didn't know how I was supposed to convince these people to come back to Avalon with me, but I wasn't in the mood for shaking hands and kissing babies or whatever.

Marlen's hands dropped on either side of my head, caging me in as he leaned down to run his nose softly along my jaw.

"You're exhausted, foxglove. How can I help you get to sleep, hm?" Marlen asked, his lips brushing temptingly over my collarbone. "Massage? Orgasm? Or should I just fuck you to sleep?"

"One of each, please," I breathed, tipping my head back to give him better access. His hands deftly removed my blouse and bra before pushing at the waistband of my pants. I lifted my butt off the bed so he could work them the rest of the way down my legs. Maybe this was why fae females always wore dresses.

Marlen trailed a teasing line of soft kisses up my neck before guiding me onto my stomach. He straddled my legs, careful not to put too much weight on me, and I groaned indecently when his magic thumbs pressed into my tight shoulders.

"Good?" Marlen chuckled.

"So good," I moaned. Hopefully, if anyone showed up to say hello, they'd knock first. I had a thin pair of panties on and nothing else, and Marlen's magical hands were both relaxing me and firing me up in the best kind of way.

His hands dug into my aching muscles, moving slowly down my back before drifting outwards to my hips where the laces of my panties were. Teasingly slowly, he unthreaded them and pulled the scrap of fabric away, leaving me facedown on the bed completely bare.

"I'm done with the massage, I think you need your orgasm now," Marlen practically growled as he shifted off my legs and spread them apart, his fingers lightly stroking my inner thighs.

Usually, some part of me objected to Marlen taking charge in the bedroom, but I was so tired and it felt so good that I spread my legs a little further apart and let myself enjoy what he was doing.

His fingers drifted up further to exactly where I wanted them, and he cursed lightly as he found me wet and wanting. "One orgasm on my fingers, then I'll fuck you to sleep," he chuckled. I pushed back against his hand in response, too tired to be witty but letting him know how incredibly okay I was with that plan.

Marlen's other hand stroked tenderly over my back and I smiled into the mattress. Arthus would have used his to pin me to the bed, immobilizing me. Bryn would have fisted my hair, fighting me for control. Eamon would sit me up so he had a better view. But Marlen's gentle ministrations were exactly what I needed right now.

He teased me softly, tenderly, until I was achy and whining before plunging two fingers into my pussy and finding that magical spot inside me that made my vision blur. There was a part of me that wanted to draw this out because when it came to my mates, I could never get enough. At the same time, I was exhausted and highly aware that we could be discovered at any moment.

"Relax," Marlen instructed, his fingers crooking at that perfect angle until

I was muffling my moans in the comforter, rocking my hips wildly against his hand. "That's it, let go. I've got you."

His gentle words were at odds with his fierce movements, but the combination of sweet and intense was exactly what I needed. My pussy clenched around his fingers as I fisted the blanket below me for purchase, my body shaking with release.

"I need you, foxglove," Marlen croaked, his voice hoarse with lust as he quickly undressed. Still boneless, I didn't object when he pulled me up onto my knees—angling me so I faced the door—and climbed on the bed behind me. I pushed up onto my elbows and gave him my best seductive smile over my shoulder.

Marlen grinned in response, eyes filled with heat as he lined up behind me, bumping his cock teasingly against my clit before guiding himself smoothly into me. He rocked back and forth infuriatingly slowly, and I could feel how much he was enjoying riling me up.

"I thought you meant fuck me to sleep as in I'd be exhausted, not bored," I drawled in challenge.

Marlen barked a laugh. "I can take a hint. Hold on, beautiful," he chuckled.

Marlen's grip on my hips tightened as he started thrusting into me at a punishing rate. My head fell to the mattress, and I bit into the comforter again to keep myself quiet. I felt Bryn's approach, but I didn't raise my head as he entered the cabin.

"Company," Marlen announced cheerfully. "Maybe he can help you keep quiet," he teased, his hand drifting around to my front to stimulate my clit as if to illustrate his point.

We'd never explicitly talked about it, but I sensed Bryn's hesitance when it came to sharing me intimately. I'd have bet money that he'd happily drop onto the twin bed and watch, but he took me entirely by surprise when he strode over to the edge of the bed, unlacing his pants as he went.

Barely able to form a coherent thought as my body hovered on the precipice of orgasm, I had just enough presence of mind to check Bryn's emotions for signs of concern. I found none, and he didn't seem shy at all when he tangled his hands in my hair and lifted my head until I was mouth-level with his painful-looking erection.

"Don't bite," he said with an infuriating smirk, even as his eyes blazed with lust. Determined to wipe that cocky expression off his face, I took him into my mouth as far as I could go and swallowed.

Marlen stilled, giving me a moment to adjust. I wriggled back against him, needing him to move—I was so close I was *aching*. My eyes met Bryn's as I sucked him down deep, refusing to break our gaze, and I could feel how much it turned him on to feel like I was submitting to him, even though we both knew I wasn't. I may have been the one on my hands and knees, but he was the one without any power. He wasn't submitting to me, yet I was taking control of his pleasure.

They both moved in tandem as I focused on keeping myself upright. Pleasure was building low in my belly, coiled tight like a spring. I was so tired, and this felt so good. Was it possible to die by orgasm?

Bryn's hands tangled in my hair, controlling my movements. I hummed around him and enjoyed the way he shuddered in response.

"Sorry, foxglove. You're going to sleep now because I'm not going to last," Marlen muttered. His hand slipped around my hip to my clit again, working rough circles with his finger until I was a panting, moaning, frenzy of need. His cock hit the perfect spot and I shattered, back arching, muscles contracting. With a curse, Bryn's release filled my throat, and he quickly pulled back before I gagged. Marlen whispered my name like a prayer as he stilled behind me, pulling my hips back tightly against him.

My eyes were drooping before he even pulled out. I was vaguely aware of a warm cloth cleaning me up and my body being gently moved underneath the heavy comforter before the world went black.

FFION

CHAPTER 78

I woke up sandwiched between two snoring males, squished in so tightly I could barely move. Aside from the fact that I was starving and 3.7 seconds away from peeing my metaphorical pants, I felt weirdly good. The sleep had definitely helped, but it was more than that.

I felt resolved. Determined. Invigorated, even. Ready to kick ass and take names to redeem the fucking fae.

"Gods, what are you thinking about?" Bryn groaned from the opposite bed. "You're so fucking peppy, the bond practically woke me up."

I snorted dismissively at the exaggeration. He'd checked the bond first thing when he woke up purely because he wanted to. Because he was a big ol' marshmallow under that grumpy exterior, but only for me.

Ignoring his question, I shoved some love at him through the bond and extricated myself from the tangle that was Marlen and Eamon's limbs. As lovely as their cuddles were, I now had roughly 1.4 seconds before I peed myself.

I freshened up while I was in the bathroom, then let myself back into the room, diving on the bed between the two mates I hadn't spent the night snuggled up to. Despite being the pushiest in every other respect, Bryn and Arthus didn't demand regular physical affection the way Marlen and Eamon did, so I wanted to make sure I didn't inadvertently neglect them.

Bryn pulled me into him and I flung my leg over his hip, resting my head on his chest. Arthus rested a hand lazily on my ass before shoving his head under the pillow. He really was not a morning person. *Morning fae?* Whatever.

"Are you going to tell me what you were thinking about?" Bryn asked, staring up at the ceiling with one hand behind his head, the other playing with my hair.

"Everything and nothing, I guess."

"You were happy," Bryn pointed out.

"I woke up and it all just felt... easier, somehow."

"Because you're not fighting it anymore. You know it has to be you. That even if you disagree with the gods' choice, you're still the one they chose." I hummed under my breath, not ready to admit out loud that his theory was probably right. Whether or not I wanted to be here, here I was.

Arthus' hand flexed slightly on my ass in what may have been a gesture of support, or potentially just a good-morning grope.

"You must be hungry, cariad," Eamon said, his voice hoarse with sleep. The sheet pooled around his waist as he sat up. He looked so deliciously rumpled in the morning. "You didn't eat last night."

"I'm starving," I admitted.

"Then let's get out there," Bryn decided, shoving me off him so he could climb out of bed. "The sooner we get this over with, the sooner we can go back to Avalon. The lack of magic here is awful. I don't understand how the fuck you lived here, scout," he continued as he strode into the bathroom.

"I hope you enjoyed that brief romantic moment while it lasted," Marlen laughed.

By the time we emerged from the cabin, dressed and ready to argue our case, the entire community was already gathered in the dining hall. There were at least thirty fae here, of varying ages. Some looked ancient, one was a toddler, snuggled up on a woman's lap. I hoped it was her mother and that they had stayed together. We seemed to have interrupted a heated debate, judging by the awkward silence that greeted our presence.

Úna stood to welcome us, gesturing for us to sit at the central table with her, though her smile was strained. I tried to get a read on her emotions, but everyone in the room was filled with such strong opinions about whatever they'd been discussing that it was impossible to separate one person's emotions from another's. I gritted my teeth against the onslaught and focused on Arthus' calm, steady control to center myself. As much as I wanted to mute my ability, I didn't want to risk missing something important.

"What is it that we've interrupted here, Úna?" Arthus asked, cutting directly to the point as always.

"We're trying to decide if we will follow you back to Avalon, risking the lives of the innocent fae here who have already suffered enough, to complete your probably impossible task," Conn answered.

"So... did you decide?" I asked hopefully. Maybe I wouldn't have to sell my soul to convince them to come with me.

"Conn and Finnian will return to Avalon with you," Úna cut in. "They have struggled the most being away from the source of their magic, and they are old enough to make their own decisions. The rest of us will return only when you can assure our safety."

There was a rumble of dissatisfaction from around the room, mostly from the younger fae. They were clearly itching for a fight, and I completely understood why.

Úna's request seemed like an impossible task. Could I ever really assure their safety? There would always be fae ruled by greed, even if they weren't sitting on the Council.

An enormous platter of cut-up fruit, bread and jam was set in front of us, ending the conversation. I exchanged a nervous look with Eamon as we ate. Bringing two fae back from Albion was better than no fae, but it didn't really fulfill the gods' mission either. *Baby steps.*

Conn and Finnian had a better chance of reassuring the fae that lived here than we did, we were strangers to them. If we could *show* the twins that it was safe, they could come back and pass that message on.

My conflicting thoughts must have been written all over my face as Finnian observed me with amusement. "You could do a lot worse than us as your travel companions, Sanctified Empath. We've got some useful tricks up our sleeves."

"Such as?" Bryn shot back, resting his hand heavily on the nape of my neck. It was a possessive gesture, and it almost made me giggle since Finnian wasn't flirting with me in the slightest.

"See for yourself," Finnian replied with a smirk. He didn't drop eye contact as he faded into nothingness.

"What the hell?" I gaped, staring at the spot opposite me where Finnian had just been sitting.

"Light bender," Arthus supplied, sounding impressed. "Let me guess," he continued, turning to Conn. "Shadow bender?"

"Correct," Finnian answered on his behalf, reappearing in the same spot, grinning like the Cheshire cat.

"Show off," Bryn groused.

"How does it work?" I asked, intrigued. Why couldn't I get a cool gift like that? Invisibility had always been my number one most wanted superpower.

"I can wrap the light around myself so it reflects off me," Finnian said with a shrug. "Conn does the opposite with the shadows."

Arthus hummed thoughtfully. "You might be useful after all."

Riona shot the twins a filthy glare while Osian tried fruitlessly to distract her with conversation, but she wasn't so much angry as she was envious. Despite her slight stature, Riona might have been the most bloodthirsty fae there.

We finished our breakfast and stood awkwardly to the side while the twins said their goodbyes to everyone. They were clearly an important part of the community here, and guilt twinged uncomfortably in my gut at taking them away from the home they'd found here.

Riona appeared behind us as silently as a cat, startling all five of us, which was no mean feat. She toed the ground uncomfortably, and I gave her a moment to build up her courage again after approaching us. I quickly shot a pulse of calming emotions down each of the bonds so the guys would stand down a little. They looked like menacing fuckers when they were being all scowling and broody.

Riona finally cleared her throat and looked up at me. "Dark fae kept me as a prisoner. They'd drink from my veins every day to harness my gift. You cannot reason with them, you cannot save them. The bloodlust destroys their mind. You should be prepared for that."

I knew the *that* she was referring to was a violent, savage kind of justice that I wanted no part of. I'd see them pay for their crimes, but I didn't want anyone's blood on my hands. Before I could formulate a response, Riona was gone. I was grateful. I didn't really know how to reply to that, anyway.

Thanks for the tip, I'll be sure to murder them all?

The seven of us made our way back down the dirt path to the lake we'd emerged from yesterday, with Marlen and Finnian making just enough small talk to break the awkwardness.

I groaned in dread as we approached the edge of the lake. I wasn't in any rush to jump back into the whirlpool of death again.

"You're coming with me this time," Arthus announced, making me smile. I could handle the portal part on my own, but I was less confident about swimming through the lake to get to it. If my mates wanted to help me, I wasn't about to object.

My pride wasn't worth drowning over.

Bryn insisted on going first, followed by Arthus and I. He used small, barely noticeable bursts of air magic to propel us through the water, and I felt the resistance of the portal's glamour before we broke through, then the rapid, unpleasant suck of the magic yanking us below the surface. I emerged on the other side, gulping for air as Bryn's muscular arms yanked me out of the little pool before I'd even opened my eyes.

I scrambled over the rocky ledge with his help and collapsed on all fours on the ground, trying to keep my breakfast down. I heard Arthus helping Marlen up behind me and they both dropped to the ground next to me. After a few uncomfortable minutes, Marlen's hand covered my own and his healing magic spread throughout my body.

Once all seven of us were through and Marlen had spread his healing goodness around, we started on the path up to Seren's house. I hoped she wouldn't mind us bringing the twins back. I also wondered if she remembered them, they were definitely younger than her.

Merle, Seren's Second-Sighted mate, was waiting for us halfway up the path, not looking surprised in the least to see us. He seemed to have a very chatty relationship with the spirits.

"Conn, Finnian," he said, giving them each a nod. They didn't look surprised that he knew their names as they greeted him in return.

"Come, you've got visitors," Merle instructed, turning towards the house. Arthus bristled, but Bryn shook his head slightly.

"It's just Enfys and Saffir," he said quietly, striding past us towards the house. I stumbled behind him, taken by surprise. How did they know we were here? Why were they here?

As we entered the house, Seren and her three mates sat away from the main group on a window bench, observing us.

"Fi," Enfys greeted me grimly, sparing my mates a curt nod. He was sitting on a couch on his own in the middle of the room, like he belonged there.

"Enfys?" I replied questioningly. I sat on the closest couch between Eamon and Marlen, with Arthus and Bryn standing behind us. Conn and Finnian leaned against a wall near the doorway, arms crossed, looking brooding and intimidating.

Saffir appeared from the hallway, looking around the room nervously.

"Hi Saffir," I said with a small, awkward wave.

She barely acknowledged me. Her wide eyes were too busy flicking between Finnian and Conn, lust practically oozing from her pores. Lust that was very much reciprocated by the two handsome, intimidating as hell twins staring right back at her. A very petty part of me was happy about this development. If Saffir was involved with the twins, hopefully she'd forget all about Bryn.

With a lingering, uncertain look at the twins, Saffir sat herself hesitantly in an armchair at the opposite end of the room from them.

"Enfys? What are you doing here?" Surprise didn't even begin to cover it. How had he known where to find us? "Something's happened," I realized, fear trickling down my spine.

"Your fathers were picked up by Council Enforcers in Dubris for questioning regarding your whereabouts."

My heart felt like it was falling through my stomach. I realized dimly that I was being shifted onto someone's lap and strong arms had wrapped around me, physically pulling me back together.

My fathers had only been in Dubris because they wanted to help me. I should have told them to stay home.

"Have they been questioned yet?" Arthus' sharp tone broke me out of my reverie.

"They'll be brought before all ten Councilors tomorrow in a closed session."

"So we make our move tomorrow," Conn said nonchalantly from somewhere behind me. I'd forgotten they were even there.

"Er, yes," Enfys agreed, his eyes flicking curiously to the intimidating twins behind me. "I've got five Assembly representatives ready to show up at the Council session. The dragon representatives were already willing to act regardless, and the centaurs also received a complaint from one of their own. All you need to do is testify."

Like that wasn't a massive deal.

"There was a centaur being held at the Castell Estate," Arthus confirmed, and Saffir winced.

"We can hardly stroll up to the Council building, we'll be arrested before we get to the door," Bryn scoffed.

"Right," Enfys conceded. "You'll need to make your way into the main chamber without being seen... It's a closed session so you can hide on the observation deck until it's time."

"We can get through the main door unseen," Finnian pointed out. Enfys looked like he was about to question that, but must have thought better of it.

"Your fathers are due in the chambers at eleven am, make sure you're on the observation deck by then," Enfys instructed as he stood.

"You're leaving?" I couldn't keep the disbelief out of my voice. Who drops a bombshell like that and wanders off? The ghost of a smile flickered over Enfys' face.

"I need to stop by and see your dragon friends. They'll be furious if they're not there tomorrow to avenge their mate's honor."

"Saffir, can I give you a ride back to the Academy?" Both Conn and Finnian stiffened at Enfys' question.

"Stay here," I urged her. "You can come with us to the Council building in the morning."

"I may as well," she sighed. "Doesn't much matter what I do now. My parents will soon find out I betrayed them. It's all going to be over by tomorrow."

Hopefully.

We all stood as Enfys left. I muted my ability, unable to make sense of the swirling mess of emotions around me and feeling more than a little overwhelmed by them.

"How did he even find us?" Bryn muttered.

"Ah, that was me," Merle admitted. "The spirits urged me to go to Dubris and find him. He was there looking for you." Bryn nodded in satisfaction.

"I'll put on some tea," Seren announced, moving towards the kitchen. A petulant part of me wanted to rage at her for even making such a banal suggestion right now. *My fathers are being held by the Council! They're going to be questioned tomorrow!* Only the gods knew what kind of fate would befall them if we didn't pull off our... coup. Or whatever it was we were even doing. Who the fuck cared about tea right now?

Unable to sit still, I climbed off Eamon's lap and paced behind the couch. I wanted to go now. Why were we just sitting around chatting?

"Ffion, you should also know about the rumors I've been hearing about my father," Saffir said tentatively, even as she pushed her shoulders back and did her best to present her usual confident front.

"What rumors? From who?" Arthus pressed as I tried to force my scrambled brain to form actual words.

"From the staff mostly, and neighbors. My parents have been staying at other properties since, you know, the break in. My father's behavior has attracted a lot of attention recently. He's been... erratic. Twitchy."

Her declaration didn't really set off any alarm bells for me because the one thing I remembered most clearly about Glendower Castell is that he was erratic. He mostly existed in a state of deranged glee, but occasionally the darkness would take over and his emotions would morph into pure malice.

Everyone else in the room looked a lot more concerned by this news than I did, though. "We're worried he's gone dark, scout," Bryn muttered quietly in my ear. "If he's been draining fae directly from the vein instead of using crystals... Well, twitchy is a good descriptor for how dark fae behave between feedings."

"What would that mean for his magic?" I asked, alarmed as I stopped pacing and turned to face him. Riona's warning echoed in my mind. *You cannot reason with them, you cannot save them.*

"If he's fed recently, he'll have abilities we don't know about," Bryn replied through gritted teeth. I didn't need to unmute my ability to sense his worry. It was in every tense word, the tight clenching of his fists, and the prominent tick in his jaw. My hand drifted up to his face, I could see my fingers gliding over his jaw but they didn't feel like mine. My head was a mess, but my body was instinctively seeking comfort.

Bryn wrapped an arm around my waist and tugged me against his body, giving me a tight, one-armed hug and resting his chin on my ducked head.

Out of the corner of my eye, I noticed Saffir had drifted towards Conn and Finnian, who had wasted no time in protectively boxing her in. Good, she needed someone in her corner. Two someones were even better. Saffir may well be going to sleep tomorrow with at least one less parent than she woke up with.

"Hey," Bryn called out to Conn and Finnian. I had an embarrassing moment of panic that he was jealous of the attention they were giving Saffir. "That storm kid followed us through the portal. She's skulking around in the garden."

"Riona?" Conn snapped, pushing off the wall.

"I'll go," Finnian said quickly, resting a hand on his brother's chest. "You'll piss her off, and she's not used to Avalon's magic. She could rain lightning down on this entire island."

Finnian set out through the front door as Seren re-emerged with a tray of steaming hot cups of tea. She paused in front of us and lowered her voice so only the five of us could hear.

"Egan recovered Riona personally," she whispered. "She was being drained by three dark fae. Egan killed them, and Councilor Grigor was livid at the mysterious deaths of his close friends."

"Unsurprising," I sighed.

Before she could say anything further, Finnian appeared, dragging a sulking Riona through the front door. She was nervous, but felt more settled when she noticed Egan in the corner giving her a kind smile.

"Care to tell us what the fuck you're doing here, Rio?" Conn drawled, his eyes narrowing dangerously at her. He had about as much tact as Bryn.

"Don't call me that," Riona snapped, glaring at him and crossing her arms over her chest. She looked every inch the petulant teenager. "I'm here to help."

"It would have been helpful if you'd stayed in Albion, out of the fucking way," Conn grumbled. Riona practically snarled as flashes of lightning slid around her fingertips.

"Come, Riona. I'll show you to one of the guest rooms," Seren said quickly, gently guiding her to the hallway.

"She's not leaving the property unless it's to go back to Albion," Conn grunted. Saffir whispered something to him and he visibly relaxed.

"We'd better start preparing dinner, since there's so many extra mouths to feed tonight," Seren's mates were saying in the background. Eamon moved to help them as one of her other mates showed Conn and Finnian to the room they'd be staying in.

"Sweetheart," Arthus asked gently as he moved in front of me, gripping my chin lightly and keeping my eyes in on his. "Are you ready for this?"

"Yes," I replied, surprising myself with my conviction. Arthus searched my face for a long moment before giving me a satisfied nod.

"Good," he said quietly, looking grim.

It was good, because I didn't have any choice. It was time, whether I wanted it to be or not.

# CHAPTER 79

Dinner was fucking awkward.

Ffion was so lost in her own thoughts, she felt impossible to reach. I was checking the bond constantly, watching her waver between guilt and self-doubt. Part of me wanted to force her out of her shell, but another part of me resisted. She could have one night to wallow, so long as she got her shit together when it mattered.

Only our mating circle seemed to be worried about Ffion right now. Seren, her mates, and the twins were all concerned about the little storm-fae girl possibly burning the house to a crisp. It was easier to use gifted magic in Albion than our elemental affinities—both Ffion and I could use our gifts there just fine—but the abundance of magic in the air in Avalon had overwhelmed the kid. Lightning was practically bursting out of her skin.

"I could be useful tomorrow. If someone attacks you, I could fight back," she attempted to argue with the twins.

"You'd be as likely to kill us as to kill them," Conn muttered.

"You don't have great control of your gift right now," Finnian said at the same time.

Saffir choked slightly on her chickpea salad and I almost jumped. I forgot she was even there—she'd been doing her best to disappear since the conversation with Enfys. As the twins renewed their argument with Riona,

Saffir slipped away from the table. I hesitated for a moment, watching Marlen dutifully try to get Ffion to eat, before I stood and followed Saffir into the hallway.

Because Ffion apparently owned my testicles, I was going to apologize. Because Ffion had told me to apologize. And I probably owed Saffir.

"Hey," I called quietly after her, not wanting to draw everyone's attention from the main room. Saffir paused, waiting for me to catch up to her. It was the least put-together I'd ever seen her. She looked like she hadn't slept in days.

"What is it you want, Bryn?" she asked tiredly.

"I want to clear the air. We're on the same side."

"I presume this was Ffion's idea?" Saffir quirked her eyebrow at me, and I almost smiled seeing her usual haughty demeanor coming through. I didn't have any romantic feelings for her, but she was going through a fucking rough time and I felt bad for her.

"I shouldn't have pursued a courtship with you while my feelings for Ffion were so conflicted. It was disrespectful to both of you," I replied, ignoring her question.

"I didn't actually hear an apology in there, but fine. I get what you're trying to say. I shouldn't have asked my parents to give you a Council internship to get you to stay with me. I thought if I could get you to choose me over her, it would soothe my pride, but I only ended up humiliating myself more. Plus, everything else that happened..."

That wasn't an apology either, but I didn't particularly care. Saffir had already apologized to Ffion. It was Ffion that had borne the brunt of Saffir and my bad decisions.

"So, allies?" Saffir asked, holding out her hand.

"Allies," I agreed, giving her hand a quick shake.

With a sad smile, she disappeared down the hallway. I made my way back into the main room, secretly grateful that Ffion had suggested I do this. Saffir was an important ally in this struggle, sure, but it also felt like we'd closed a chapter.

"I'm going to run Fi a bath," Arthus muttered while he strode past me as I rejoined the rest of my mating circle at the dining table. Ffion's eyes met mine for a moment and saw the briefest glimmer of approval, before she went back to aimlessly pushing food around her plate.

Hang in there, scout. We'll be at your side every step of the way.

If there was one thing Ffion and I were good at, it was tension. There had been tension between us from the moment we met until the moment we claimed each other.

Those months of tension had nothing on this morning. Ffion was a fucking wreck. None of us knew what to say or do to make it better, even though we were all obsessively watching the bond. The gulf between us felt about a thousand miles wide as we all contemplated what today would bring.

Seren had pulled Ffion aside to find her some suitable clothes to wear since we only had the few things we'd packed in our satchels to take to Albion. The guys and I wore our usual clothes, but for the most antisocial fae I'd ever met, Seren understood optics.

When Ffion emerged half an hour later, she looked like a fae chosen by the gods. The gods were always depicted in white robes, and Ffion looked like a miniature version in a knee-length white dress with floaty sleeves that tied around the middle. The front of her hair was pulled back and tied with a matching white ribbon, the rest of her long curls left loose. The look in her eyes was all fiery resolve, though. She was the perfect mixture of grit and innocence.

I sighed in exasperation. It would be a fucking nightmare trying to keep her hidden in a white dress.

Ffion refused to eat, eager to head out as soon as possible—it was an hour flight over the water and the griffins would take us one hour further to Vertis. The traditional Council building was ancient and closer to Inver, and we'd have never made it there in time from Ardotalia. Fortunately, these Councilors were arrogant and had erected their own monstrosity for meetings in a warmer part of Avalon.

We all formed our glamours and hovered around Ffion as she said her strained goodbyes to the Parrys. They had no interest in being part of what was about to happen with the Council, but swore to keep the fae in Albion updated. If today went well... hopefully it would be enough to draw them home. Hopefully the gods would be satisfied that Ffion had done enough.

She needed a fucking break. We all did.

We made our way through the lush gardens of the Parry's property to a clearing where their griffins were waiting for us. We needed four as Saffir, Conn, and Finnian were flying with us. Without hesitation, Ffion followed me, waiting patiently for me to help her mount the griffin—I had the most experience flying, and I'd always preferred Ffion to fly with me, but it did something to my insides that she assumed she would.

Ffion paused before I could help her up, looking around the four griffins in confusion. "You're not coming with us?" she asked Seren in surprise, having been lost in her thoughts all morning.

"Dubris is the furthest I've traveled in my entire life. I stay on Ardotalia and protect the portal, it's what I do. Like my mother and grandmother before me." Seren gave Ffion a wistful smile.

"What kind of gift do you have?" I asked curiously. She had three mates, it had to be a powerful one.

"Guardian magic." *Like Gwyneira.* "As did my mother and grandmother before me. The gods knew what they were doing. They know what they're doing with you too," she said, looking at Ffion.

"Let's hope so," she murmured, giving Seren a tight smile. "Thank you for all your help."

"I imagine we'll be seeing you again soon," Arthus added, climbing up on the griffin behind Eamon. "Hopefully, with good news."

We all dropped our glamours into place, though Ffion still stood out in her white dress. The twins didn't seem to know how to create a glamour. It probably seemed like an unnecessary skill when they could disappear entirely.

I wrapped my hands around Ffion's small waist and lifted her up onto the griffin before climbing up behind her. She'd gone back into her weird, tense headspace and didn't react at all as the griffin took to the air, surrounded by three others.

A cheerful Marlen was flying with Finnian, while Conn and a subdued Saffir had a griffin to themselves. Marlen never met a stranger—he was chatting and laughing with Finnian like they'd known each other their whole lives.

As the water below us turned into rocky coastline and green trees, the silence wore thin on my patience.

Fuck it, I wasn't going to let this weird tension stop me from talking to my godsdamned mate. I didn't want to think things would go badly today, but just in case... Tense silence wasn't how I wanted to spend this calm before the storm.

"One of the Outer Isles, Isannavantia, is a dormant volcano," I said casually, letting Ffion join the conversation in her own time.

"What about it?" Ffion asked eventually with a begrudging sigh. I hid my grin in her hair, even though she'd be able to sense my satisfaction at drawing her into the conversation. She was too curious not to ask.

"There are geysers and hot springs all around the base."

"Are you suggesting a vacation right now?" Ffion snapped irritably.

"Not right at this moment," I drawled, enjoying her fire. She sighed in exasperation. "It's where I'd planned for us to have our claiming ceremony one day. Except you ambushed me at home and all my plans went to shit."

"You seemed to enjoy our claiming ceremony just fine," she retorted, a hint of teasing back in her voice.

"I did," I conceded, though I still regretted that it wasn't more special for her. Ffion deserved better than a cave at the back of my aunt and uncles' property.

"You'd thought about our claiming ceremony?" Ffion asked softly after a beat of silence.

"Sure," I shrugged. "We may have taken the long road, but it was always going to be you and me."

Ffion wriggled back against me, finally relaxing in my arms. "I thought so too," she said, sniffling.

Well, fuck. She wasn't supposed to cry. If I didn't cheer her up before we got off this griffin, Arthus would have my balls on a platter.

Or he'd try, anyway. I could take him.

"They're happy tears, mostly. Relax," Ffion sighed.

I could have checked the bond, read into her feelings, but this seemed like something she needed to say out loud.

"Are you scared?"

Ffion shifted slightly in my arms, but didn't answer for a long moment. I wrapped one of my arms around her waist and used my other hand to grip her long hair to stop it whipping into my face.

"I'm not scared for me. I'm scared that the gods chose wrong. I'm scared I'll let everyone down. I'm scared for my fathers. I'm scared I've dragged you, Arthus, Marlen and Eamon into this mess with me."

I almost snorted. As if we would have ever let her go into this alone.

"If the gods gave us the choice to leave, each one of us would choose to be right here," I told her with absolute confidence. This girl was a godsdamned magnet for trouble, and there's no place any of us would rather be than by her side. "As for the other stuff—you've already done more for the fae than anyone else has in centuries, just by virtue of trying to make a difference. So, fuck it. If you fail today, you fail. At least you didn't give up."

"You probably shouldn't be a motivational speaker," Ffion replied drily, but I could hear the smile in her voice. Perfect timing, too. I could see the Council building looming in the distance.

We were landing behind a grove of orange trees where five agitated-looking dragons and a nervous Brently were waiting for us. Enfys was with them, his magical signature obvious to me, but his glamour had probably thrown the others.

"It's Enfys," I told Ffion. "Blood your amethyst ring. Now would be an excellent time to be able to see through glamours." Ffion nodded as she accepted the dagger I unsheathed and handed to her. She slid the pad of her thumb across the blade and pressed it to the ring Eamon had given her, then across the lapis lazuli bracelet that I'd topped up with my magic.

"I love you, Bryn," Ffion breathed as our griffin began its descent. It was only the second time she'd ever said it to me.

"As I love you," I replied sharply, unwilling to let her get any ideas about this being goodbye. We were just getting started.

The griffin landed clumsily, legs buckling slightly underneath it. I thanked it as we dismounted—two hours spent carrying two fully grown adults was a big ask. None of the griffins moved to find food once they landed, choosing to lie down in the grass for a rest instead.

The grove hid us, but we could just make out the imposing Council building through the gaps in the trees. The Fae Council building was a grand mansion, made of a creamy stone, with elaborate turrets rising from the roof and glittering windows covering every wall. The acres surrounding the building were all flat grass with small pockets of landscaped flowering bushes around. None of it offered much protection for a stealthy approach.

"That is the least fae-looking building I've ever seen," Ffion observed disdainfully, peering past the trees.

"It's new," Eamon replied ruefully as the others dismounted and we gathered together. The traditional Council building was an ancient wooden structure in the forest that looked like it was part of the trees.

"Not easy to sneak up on either," Ezra noted, his mouth set in a grim line. "We'll have to approach from the air."

"Easy for you to say," I grumbled.

"Don't worry, we'll give you a lift," Hiram shot back with an arrogant grin. It'd be just my luck that Ffion would want to hang out with their dragon mate after all this was said and done, and I'd be stuck spending time with these smug assholes for the rest of my long life.

"We'll make our own way inside," Conn and Finnian said in unison. Their twin bond was fucking creepy. "We have our own ways of not being seen,"

Conn added when the dragons gave them disbelieving looks.

"I'll fly with Fi," Arthus said immediately, making me feel marginally better. At least some random guy's arms wouldn't be around her. "The rest of you can transport Marlen, Bryn, Eamon and Saffir."

Finnian made a low growling noise in his chest that caught everyone's attention. Even more surprisingly, it only eased when Saffir started soothingly stroking his arm. *Huh, when did that happen?*

I threw Ffion a smirk when I felt her eyes burning into the side of my head. If she was looking for signs of jealousy from me, she wouldn't find any. I had everything I wanted.

"There's a small balcony on the top floor of the east side. It leads into an office that isn't occupied at the moment. If I could get up there and unlock it for you..." Enfys trailed off.

"We can handle that," Conn replied confidently.

"If you're sure," Enfys replied dubiously, fishing a set of keys out of his pocket and twisting them between his fingers. "The entrance to the observational deck of the chamber is a few doors down from that office. You can wait up there until it's time. I'll bar the doors to the Councilor's floor once they're inside and stay close to grant the Assembly members entry."

"Give them the keys, they can handle the door," Saffir said impatiently, flushing slightly when everyone's attention turned to her. "Enfys, you need to get inside. Don't sneak around. If the Councilors suspect you of anything, you'll be locked up in the dungeons and the whole plan falls apart."

"She's right," Ffion said, nodding.

Enfys reluctantly handed over the keys, giving us each a long parting look as he turned to leave.

"Remember, stay hidden on the observation deck until the Assembly members arrive," Enfys called over his shoulder, dropping his glamour as he strode through the grove.

"We'll take point," Finnian said quietly, watching Enfys' retreating form. "Guard duty is something we're familiar with, and we can stay out of sight."

Saffir looked distressed at the suggestion. Conn was leaning in close, murmuring in her ear like he was reassuring her.

"Brently will join us, too," Ezra offered. "He's not under suspicion, so he'll enter through the main doors and make his own way to the observation deck."

I pulled the bond towards me and sensed the small waves of Ffion's relief. The more support we had, the more likely it would be to tip the balance between light and dark magic. Success today would forever change the course of fae history.

No pressure, scout.

With lingering looks at Saffir, the twins followed Enfys through the grove and took off in different directions once they reached the manicured grounds—Conn towards the shadows cast by the topiary bushes and Finnian disappearing into the bright sunlit path that led directly to the grand entrance.

"Come on," Ezra said quietly. "We need to find somewhere less conspicuous to take off from," he explained, leading us away from the Council building.

"Where's Shira?" Ffion called after Ezra suspiciously. Ezra bristled as the other four dragons shifted uncomfortably.

"This is no place for her," he answered curtly. "It's too dangerous."

Ffion snorted dismissively. "I'm assuming she disagreed, judging by the guilt rolling off you."

"She's safer staying with my parents," Ezra replied, clearing his throat.

"I hope you haven't imprisoned her with your parents, given her history of being locked up against her will," Ffion said lightly, though there was a dangerous edge to her voice.

The silence that met her words was deafening.

We headed further back into a forested area that put us about 50-feet away from the building. Honestly, I didn't feel great about Arthus flying that far with Ffion. I mean, he was strong, but she was an adult sized fae...

"We're going to partially shift," Ezra announced once the trees fully hid us. "Just wings. Minimize the chances of someone seeing us."

I didn't like our odds. And I didn't like being carried through the air like an infant by a partially shifted dragon.

The dragons and Arthus all removed their shirts and tied them around their waists with practiced ease. As the whooshing and rustling of unfurling wings filled the air, I did my best to stifle my laugh at Arthus' delicate butterfly-like fae wings next to the heavy, leathery dragon ones. The glare he was giving me made me think he already knew what I was thinking.

"Alright, fire fae. You're with me," Seff, the fire dragon, announced, striding over to me. "I can handle the heat, so if you freak out and blast me, I won't die."

"I won't freak out," I muttered, offended.

"How are you going to carry them?" Ffion asked, looking worriedly at all of us. She didn't need to worry. As big as we were, the dragons were bigger and stronger, the bastards.

"Like this," Seff replied cheerfully, slinging my arm over his neck and grabbing me under the knees and shooting up to the treetops before I could object.

"Bridal style?" Ffion asked, stifling a laugh. I didn't know what that meant, but at least she was animated.

"I dislike you," I grumbled to Seff, who laughed like I'd just told the funniest joke he'd ever heard. Arthus scooped Ffion up with ease, Oren took Marlen, and Levi gently lifted Saffir, both looking equally uncomfortable about it. With an irritated huff, Ezra—by far the biggest of the dragons as their flight alpha—picked up Eamon.

"We'll go first. We'll be less conspicuous as a group," Ezra grumbled, shooting into the air far higher than I thought he would and soaring over the grounds.

"We're next," Seff announced, still cradling me like a fucking baby in midair.

"They're really high," Ffion called from the ground, snuggling into Arthus.

"Less likely to be seen," Oren replied in a low, raspy voice and I realized it was the first time I'd heard him speak. Judging by the surprise on Ffion's face, she'd never heard him talk either.

Once Ezra and Eamon had cleared the grounds, Seff took off after them. Fae definitely weren't meant to fly at these high altitudes. My vision swam as the air thinned, and although I tried to focus on where the building was, I ended up closing my eyes. Just for a moment. Just until everything stopped spinning.

"You can stop cuddling me now, fire fae. You're not really my type," Seff chuckled, landing with a thud. To my horror, I realized my head had drifted to his shoulder. I practically launched myself out of his grip, stumbling a bit as I found my feet.

Seff laughed quietly as he grabbed me by the elbow and hauled me through the open doors into a dusty, unused office. Ezra was looking impatiently past us, scanning the sky, but Eamon, Finnian, and Conn were all smirking infuriatingly at me.

"Shut up," I muttered as I stormed past them to stand guard at the door to the hallway.

A few moments later, Levi landed on the balcony with Saffir. Conn snatched her out of Levi's arms instantly, gently placing her on the ground and moving in front of her like a guard dog. Arthus landed next with Ffion in his arms, looking slightly ill even with the glamour on. Arthus was rolling his shoulders and cracking his neck discreetly—or what he thought was discreet because Ffion kept shooting him apologetic looks. She wasn't easy to hide things from.

A cheerful Marlen and a stoic Oren followed them. Finnian ushered them in and locked the door behind him, securing us in the dark, dusty office.

The building was all dark wood paneling, and the corridor had no windows, so Conn vanished into the shadows with ease. While he checked the hallway for Council workers, Marlen used his healing magic to counter the effects of the high altitude. We couldn't afford any distractions. Conn reappeared a few minutes later and nodded silently, guiding us out into the hallway towards the observation deck of the Chamber.

We made our way down the hallway in total silence. Ffion would never mute her ability in such a dangerous situation, even though the anxiety she would pick up on from the rest of us was probably making her feel ill.

Fortunately, it seemed like the top-floor rooms were mostly empty as we made our way down the hallway, encountering no one.

We slipped silently into the observation deck, hugging the wall so we didn't catch the candlelight from the room below us. The candelabras on the deck hadn't been lit, since observers weren't allowed to witness today's session. In the darkness, we waiting fae dropped our glamours.

My heart felt like it stopped for a full beat when the door to the observation deck opened again, and I let out a lengthy breath when I recognized it was Brently slipping in and shutting the door silently behind him. He must have been wearing a cloaking amulet too, since I hadn't picked up his presence. He greeted us with a curt nod, backing up against the wall next to the dragons.

The chamber was a suffocating room, located right in the middle of the building, so there were no windows, and the dark wood paneling that covered the walls emphasized the lack of natural light. The room itself was rectangular, with a large round table in the center and ten seats for the Councilors. The observation deck wrapped around the walls on the second story, allowing an audience to stand and look down on the discussions below.

We watched patiently as the Councilors chatted among themselves, getting comfortable in their elaborate, high-backed chairs while making small talk. So far, they were oblivious to our presence, which meant our cloaking amulets were holding up. There were six Enforcers guarding the doors, but either they hadn't realized we were here or Enfys had gotten them on our side.

"Shall we begin?" Glendower called lazily, drawing the meeting to order. There were a few murmurs of assent from his shady Councilor buddies— one of them even reached for a bottle of wine in the center of the table which only aggravated me further. They were going to have a glass of *wine* while they sentenced Fi's fathers for some made up crime?

Disgusting. That the "good" Councilors we'd allied with didn't blink an eye demonstrated this wasn't an irregular occurrence. *Burn it all down.* This whole institution was fucking broken.

Before Glendower could speak again, Enfys moved. Glendower watched him with a frown as Enfys quickly unlocked the large double doors he had been guarding, throwing them open before stepping back.

Five members of the Assembly strode confidently into the now silent chamber—two dragons, two centaurs, and a goblin carrying a sheaf of paper.

"What is the meaning of this?" Glendower asked, rising to his feet. The muscles in his face twitched sporadically and his hands flexed continuously, like he couldn't control them. He didn't look like the same fae who'd languidly moved through the Council ball with a half-dead Ffion on his arm a few months ago.

He had definitely gone dark.

"Ilia?" One of the other fae Councilors addressed the big-ass dragon shifter at the front of the delegation. He must be Seff's father—he looked just like him, but with deep lines in his face and thinning hair.

The Councilor who spoke was a ruddy, portly man with a greasy face and greasy hair to match. Conn's shadows slipped for a moment when the man spoke, and his expression was fucking murderous. I'd bet coin that this was the "personal grudge" they'd mentioned. "This is a closed session concerning the whereabouts of a wanted fae. It's not an Assembly matter," he added.

"If it is regarding the whereabouts of one Ffion Laisren, it very much concerns us," Ilia rumbled.

"Why? Did our little troublemaker kill one of your guards? Or did she steal from you too?" Greasy chuckled. A few of the other Councilors tittered in the background, but not Glendower or Evalina Castell. They were silent, stony-faced, and practically dripping with nerves.

"She returned something, actually. Something very precious to my son and his flight." The tittering died down instantly. The three Councilors Enfys had been working with sat comfortably in their seats, taking in the unfolding scene. None of the other seven looked quite so relaxed.

"How interesting," Glendower interjected drolly. "Let's get her fathers in and find out where she's hiding. Then perhaps you'll get the chance to thank her personally."

"*Perhaps*, hm?" Ilia said, cocking his head. This was a man familiar with the vague terms fae used to get around lying.

A door below the deck creaked, and the sound of footsteps and rattling chains filled the tense silence. There must have been a separate entrance from the dungeons to the Chamber. Ffion's fathers were brought to stand against the wall, illuminated by candlelight.

I pushed some reassurance at Ffion through the bond and saw her spine straighten out of the corner of my eye.

That's it, scout. This is your show now.

FFION

CHAPTER 80

All the nerves, all the self-doubt disappeared the moment my fathers were escorted through the double doors by two Enforcers. They'd bound their wrists in the same magic-suppressing chains that had shackled me to the cave wall at the Castell Estate, and anger coursed through me at seeing them dragged in like criminals when all they'd done was protect their child. What made it worse is that I didn't sense any fear from my fathers. They were despondent. *Resigned.* Either they weren't hopeful that I'd come for them, or they weren't confident I'd succeed if I did.

It was difficult to get a good read on them with all the other emotions in the room. Some of the Councilors were so intensely gleeful that it made my skin crawl.

"Galvyn Laisren, Attie Laisren," Glendower began cheerfully. He'd been rattled by the unexpected guests showing up, but he was finding his footing now. "We have brought you in front of the Fae Council for questioning regarding the whereabouts of the Empath, Ffion Laisren. You were picked up in Dubris, miles away from your home village, with a small supply of kyanite amulets on you. A gift for your daughter, perhaps? I'm sure I need not tell you that kyanite is the best crystal for absorbing empath magic."

He would know, I thought bitterly as my heart sank to my stomach. Was the kyanite the justification the Council used for arresting them? They'd only got it because I'd asked them to.

Where were the gods now? Why, when innocent fae were suffering, were *they* silent? Why was it on *me* to do something about this?

Galvyn bristled, and the Enforcer's grip on his chain tightened enough to pull my father's shoulders back. Reflexively, I took a step forward, disgusted with this whole charade, but Bryn and Arthus had one hand around each of my arms, hauling me back before I had the chance to move.

"Soon," Arthus breathed in my ear.

"Can you confirm the location of your daughter, Ffion Laisren?" Glendower continued.

"No," Galvyn grunted, scowling at Glendower.

"Tell us where her last known location was," Glendower drawled, looking a little bored with the proceedings. The fucking *audacity* of this guy!

"No," Attie replied, eyebrows in his hairline and voice dripping with disbelief. "Do you expect us to believe that if we tell you her location, it would make a difference? You'll imprison her and kill us, regardless. Just like you killed her mother." There were a handful of muffled gasps and enough shock in the room to feel like someone had doused my skin in ice water.

"The death of your mate isn't relevant to the topic at hand," Glendower replied callously, making some observing Enforcers around the room wince.

"Isn't it though? She was the first casualty in your quest to get your hands on Ffion's magic, and you didn't even know what it was. But even when you had access to her gift, you couldn't keep it," Attie goaded. "The gods chose her. She is sanctified. Your time is coming."

"The gods abandoned the fae," Evalina hissed, speaking for the first time. The fear filling the room was so potent, I could almost smell it.

For the first time, I really understood what it meant to be *sanctified*. It wasn't that it had given me any special abilities, but it was a seal of approval that everyone in Avalon recognized, legitimizing me in their eyes. Evalina hadn't felt fear until she'd heard those words.

That knowledge bolstered me, giving me the strength I needed to speak up when I would have much rather stayed silent.

"The fae abandoned the gods."

I barely raised my voice, but I didn't need to. You could have heard a pin drop, the room was so quiet. "Fae like you treated magic like a right instead of the gift from the gods it is."

I'm not ashamed to admit that I paused for dramatic effect before stepping out of the shadows, resting my hands on the balcony railing and surveying the room. Seeing the surprise on most of the fae Councilors' faces made it entirely worth it. They were so used to their absolute control, who knows how long it had been since they'd been taken off guard, protected as they were in their gilded palace.

"Please share your experience with us, Ms. Laisren," Ilia commanded. The five Assembly members were standing in front of the door, arms crossed with displeasure written all over their features, but Ilia's voice was kind and sympathetic when it was directed at me.

"Glendower and Evalina Castell kidnapped me from the Academy of Avalon and kept me prisoner in a cave on their property. I was there for over a month while they repeatedly cut me with daggers to steal my blood and my magic," I stated calmly, proud that I kept the shakiness out of my voice.

The silence was deafening. Evalina and Glendower had their eyes locked on each other, communicating with their eyes. Evalina looked panicked, but Glendower was *enraged*. His hands shook and there was a tic in his cheek I'd never noticed before. He didn't look good. I understood why his neighbors and staff had pointed it out to Saffir.

"I can verify Ffion's story," Saffir's quiet voice practically echoed around the room. "I can attest to her injuries. I saw her there at the end of her... imprisonment. At my family's estate."

The disgust of the Assembly members licked uncomfortably at my skin, but I knew it wasn't directed at me. The only emotion I felt more strongly was Saffir's parents' anger at what they saw as betrayal. I really hoped I'd read the dynamic between her, Conn, and Finnian right because she would not be safe from here on out.

"You are no longer a daughter of mine!" Glendower hissed, eyes flashing dangerously as he stared up at Saffir on the balcony. She held her head high even as her limbs trembled and tears welled in her eyes. Glendower went to raise his hand, but Bryn and Marlen immediately stepped up next to her protectively, and Glendower's arm twitched as he lowered it, sneaking glances at the Assembly members behind him.

"Who else wishes to share their testimony?" Ilia spoke into the uncomfortably silent room.

Conn released the shadows cloaking him, materializing out of nowhere in the corner of the room, on the ground level with the Councilors. An Enforcer lunged at him reflexively, but Conn had vanished. He appeared again, leaning against the opposite wall with a smug grin on his face.

"Ellis Rowlands demanded my brother and I be released to his care when we started presenting signs of our gift at age three."

"That's right," Finnian added, appearing suddenly sitting on the balcony railing, releasing the light he'd bent around him. "He killed our parents afterwards, too. Couldn't leave anything to chance right, Ellis?"

The man's face had turned red as soon as Conn had appeared. It was becoming an impressive shade of purple.

Brently stepped up next to me. "I am testifying on behalf of two young children who were imprisoned by the Castells. Their proper names and ages are still unknown, and they have no recollection of their family."

Outraged mutterings broke out amongst those in the room, the horror and disgust growing more potent. My heart broke at that update on the little twins, and I struggled to keep my composed facade in place. No one should have to experience horror like what Glendower Castell inflicted with his dagger, especially not such tiny children.

One of the Councilors on our side looked ready to square off with the Castells over that, but before she could, the mysterious fae we had freed from the Castell Estate appeared behind Enfys, making him jump. The mystery fae let the shadows surrounding his body unravel slowly, making no attempt to hide the black tourmaline cloaking amulet around his neck. His emotions were still a complete blank slate to me, just a void where a normal person's feelings would be. It was... terrifying.

The fae stepped forward, eyes darting around suspiciously. Gods, he moved around like a ghost. No wonder he'd been so good at shadowing Enfys—he could literally bend the shadows to his will.

"The Castells also imprisoned me," he said quietly, his moon-pale face glowing in the shadows. "Ffion, her mates, Brently, and the dragons set us free." As quickly as he appeared, the mysterious shadow bender vanished into the darkness, undoubtedly still there though. Waiting and watching.

"Those dragons were freeing their mate who had been kept on the Castell Estate since she was sixteen," Ezra grunted, stepping forward with all four other dragons and crossing his arms over his enormous barrel chest. A flicker of nervousness went around the Councilors' faces. I, for one, would not want to fuck with this guy.

"A centaur who had been missing for three years came to the Centaur Council to report the Castells had imprisoned him and experimented with his magic," a dark-skinned centaur representative with pale green eyes said. His hooves shuffled impatiently on the varnished wooden floors as he stared intently at the Fae Councilors.

"Since we know the fae can't lie, this seems like a rather straightforward trial," the centaur added coldly. "I vote that the seven fae Councilors who didn't bring this issue to the attention of the Assembly are executed and made an example of. Whether or not they are guilty of stealing magic, they let this depravity go unchecked."

Gods, centaurs are ruthless.

There was a silent pause, and it was the moment I had been waiting for. I would step forward. Command the room. Throw down the gauntlet. I'd planned out this whole spiel about how things would be different from now on. But I didn't have a chance to use it because the room erupted into chaos a split second later.

The Councilors screamed at the Assembly representatives, at the wavering

Enforcers guarding the room, at us, but mostly at each other. A burst of fire aimed at the centaur Assembly member spurred the Enforcers into action, enough to separate the two sides at least. Enfys was blocking the door, his combat gift coming in handy as two of the Councilors sought to get around him.

While Enfys was distracted, another Councilor attempted to slip past him, but Ilia picked the portly man up by the front of his shirt and *threw* him clean into the table the Councilors had been sitting at like he weighed nothing. One of the dragons whooped supportively—probably Hiram.

Whatever vague sense of control we'd had over the room, we were losing. The Councilors who were on our side, the ones who were meant to be helping us, were too caught up in their anger. The Assembly members were livid, rightly so, and they didn't particularly care about the fate of the fae.

They were going to kill them right here and be done with it, and I knew in my heart that wasn't going to be enough. It would be swift justice, but it wouldn't change the *balance*.

"Come on, scout. You're the Keeper of Balance," Bryn urged quietly as he sidled up to me, reading my mind. "The Sanctified Empath. Embrace your destiny. *Empath them*," he added, glancing at me from the corner of his eye. Almost as an afterthought, he sent a pulse of encouragement through the bond.

I blew out a long breath as I surveyed the carnage spreading across the floor below me.

"I never thought I'd hear you of all people say that," I murmured, heart pounding in my chest. I'd never used these supposed crowd influencing abilities I had. I wasn't even sure how to use them. Swaying people's emotions en masse sat incredibly badly with me.

But the idea of any of these assholes taking advantage of the chaos to escape was far worse. We needed a reprieve, a pause button, and I could do that.

"Fuck it," I sighed. "I guess I'm doing this."

My four mates must have been monitoring the bond between us closely because the moment I made my decision, they all crowded in closer, lending me their support.

I closed my eyes and focused on a feeling of total calm and tranquility, forcing my mind to go blank. I rolled back my shoulders and flexed my fingers, trying to ease some of the tension in my body.

Calm.

Waves crashing against the shore. The rustle of leaves in the breeze. Laying on the grass, watching the clouds pass me by. Waking up each morning surrounded by the four men I love.

I took a deep steadying breath as blissful, perfect calm radiated out from my chest along every inch of my body. This was the feeling I wanted to share.

Almost unconsciously, I felt my arms rising at my sides. My arms brushed against whoever was standing either side of me, and I heard them suck in a breath as my magic washed over them.

Good. Now I just needed more.

Isolating that sense of calm within me, I shoved it out into the world with as much force as I could muster. The impact had me doubled over, gripping the balcony to keep me on my feet.

I took a deep gasping breath, my head feeling uncomfortably light and my muscles uncomfortably heavy, and forced myself to look at the room below me. There was no fighting, no movement. The fae in the room were luxuriating in the high of emotions I'd just thrown at them, while the non-fae weren't quite as blissed out, but they weren't entirely unaffected either.

Enfys slumped against the wall, a dopey smile on his face, while the other Enforcers stretched out on the ground and Councilors sank back into their seats. A chill ran through me at the fact that I had done this, that I was controlling their behaviors, but I forced my own discomfort away because as powerful as I felt, it hadn't worked entirely.

Glendower Castell looked up at me triumphantly, the corners of his mouth curling into a sinister grin that made chills race down my spine. This was Glendower Castell without the mad hatter mask and showy veneer. A depraved, rotten husk of a fae.

"I've been busy these past few weeks since we unfortunately parted," Glendower called up to me, his eyes gleaming with malice. "Looks like you have too," he added snidely, looking between my four mates.

Of course he'd have practiced mental shields to block out my power. I should have known he would. Exhausted, I focused my magic towards him and I could feel the wall he'd put up. It felt... spongy. Like if I pushed hard enough, I could probably break through it and force my influence. Even though he'd gone dark and I could practically see his bloodlust, the idea made my stomach turn.

"Stop this!" I demanded, wondering if it was possible to both keep everyone else in the room calm and push through Glendower's barrier to make him more compliant. "Enough. You're outnumbered, witnesses have testified to the Assembly members what you've done. You're only making things worse for yourself."

You cannot reason with them, you cannot save them.

Maybe I couldn't reason with him right now, but if I could just get him to calm down enough...

"There is no making things *better* now, little empath."

I was too fucking slow. Too slow and stupid. Because I felt Glendower's malice, and I didn't have the wits to react and do something about it.

One second he was standing there, baring his teeth at me like a rabid animal, and the next... It was like lightning exploded out of him. It was crackling all around his body, wrapping around his arms and legs like vines. It looked *painful*. Why was he hurting himself? This must be storm fae magic, but this isn't how I imagined it was supposed to work.

Time stopped as he lifted his hands directly at my cuffed and vulnerable fathers standing in front of him. Their faces froze in shock before the convulsions started. Someone was screaming, and I realized with a start it was me. Screaming, screaming, screaming so loud that it reverberated in my ears and my throat ached.

My influence released the others in the room with a snap, and everyone on the observation deck was rushing down the stairs at once. I was vaguely aware of someone gripping my arm, stopping me from falling headfirst down the stairs, but it was just another obstacle preventing me from getting to my fathers.

If I could just get close enough...

Before I could jump in front of my fathers and do something, anything, a glittering golden shield appeared out of nowhere, criss-crossing like a wire fence. It knitted itself together into a dome shape, and I threw myself against it with everything I had, but it wouldn't give.

No matter how viciously I fought, I couldn't get through. This strange magic was keeping my fathers inside and Glendower with them.

"It's keeping us out," Eamon croaked. "This is divine magic. The gods are protecting us."

"I hate the gods!" I screamed, beating the shield with my fists. "Stop this! Let me through!" I wailed, tipping my head to the sky.

My fathers were dying, I could feel it. Sense it. Their love for me, their relief at knowing I was okay, and something... more. An emotion I'd never felt or experienced before and I wasn't entirely sure how to identify. Something very final.

Glendower's stolen magic was burning him alive. He collapsed to the ground in a barely recognizable heap. As the remnants of the lightning disappeared, the shield vanished along with it. I tried to run to my fathers, their bodies still twitching with the aftereffects of the lightning, but Bryn grabbed me around the waist, pulling me tightly back against his chest.

"Heal them," I begged Marlen, struggling to choke out the words. "Heal them!"

Why was he just standing there? Bryn's arms tightened around me as I struggled against his hold.

"Heal them!" My scream pierced the shocked silence around us. Marlen's face was etched with agony, but he still didn't move.

"I can't," he whispered hoarsely. "I can't move." With a start, I realized the gold net-like magic had twined around his legs, holding him in place.

Icy dread trickled over every inch of my skin. No, no, no, this couldn't be happening. This wasn't the end. I'd just found them, I couldn't lose them now.

"Sweetheart," Arthus said softly from somewhere next to me, his voice filled with pain. "The gods are bringing them home, like your mother said. She told them to come home to her. This was always how it was going to be."

Guilt knifed through my chest. Of course. They wanted to be with her. They'd dedicated the past seventeen years of their lives to keeping me hidden and safe. I didn't need them to protect me anymore. They were free to move forward.

To move on.

The fight left my body, and Bryn's arms went from restraining me to holding me up.

"They can hear you, scout," he murmured in my ear. "Don't let them go without saying goodbye."

"I love you. Both of you," I called out, speaking the words for the first time as loud as my broken voice could go. "Thank you for keeping me safe. I'm so grateful you're my parents and that you get to spend eternity with your mate even though I'm not ready to let you go..."

I knew before I finished speaking that they were gone. This was my first experience of losing someone I loved, and it wasn't the profound, earth-tilting moment that movies and books had led me to believe.

It was raw, hollow, anticlimactic. Their lives were just... over.

Glendower Castell lay in a charred heap on the ground. Evalina Castell was howling, already restrained by an Enforcer. My anger had nowhere to go, the grief had transformed from raw agony to a numb emptiness.

We had won the battle; the war had only begun, and I felt like I'd never be happy again.

The shocks wore off and my fathers finally lay still. The five of us moved towards the two prone bodies on the floor as a unit, Bryn mostly carrying me as I willed my feet to move.

As we got closer, I fought Bryn's hold, turning in his arms to bury my face in the crook of his neck.

"I don't want to see. This isn't how I want to remember them."

Bryn's arms tightened. "Okay, scout."

Vaguely, I was aware of a commotion outside. The enormous double doors to the Chamber had opened at some point. With my face tucked into Bryn's neck, I heard the Enforcers restraining the rest of the guilty Councilors at the Assembly members' request. Judging by the chaos outside, the Assembly members had brought backup of their own.

Subconsciously, I muted my ability as a crush of fae appeared at the doors, burning with curiosity. It was all too much. I was feeling too much, yet somehow feeling nothing at all.

"Ffion Laisren." I closed my eyes in dread when I heard the haunting voice of the spirit who had commandeered Eamon's body. I wasn't in the mood to chat to the gods.

"Head up, Fi," Bryn whispered. "Just a little longer. Put on a show."

Reluctantly, I lifted my head and turned in Bryn's arms, facing out to face the crowd. He pulled me tightly back against his chest as Marlen and Arthus materialized on either side of me and we all looked at Eamon with rapt attention.

Just a few more minutes.

"Sanctified Empath."

I scrunched my eyes shut for a moment, shoring up my defenses as a wave of fear, surprise and curiosity directed right at me hit from all the fae watching.

"Your sacrifices have not been for nothing. You were given a choice. You fought for the fae, to show them the path to redemption. Let them put the lessons you have taught them into practice."

I gave the spirit inhibiting my mate's body a curt nod, my throat tight and aching with the effort of holding back tears. If the gods wanted my gratitude, they'd be waiting for a long time. As far as I was concerned, they'd chosen a random fae baby out of a hat, dumped an extinct gift on me, and validated ruining my life by "sanctifying" me. Maybe something good would come of this, maybe the low magic fae would rise up, show strength in numbers, and fae like Glendower wouldn't get away with stealing power any longer.

Maybe the fae would show the gods that they could be responsible enough with magic to get it back.

Or maybe not.

I'd find the energy to care about the future later—right now, I just wanted to grieve. Grieve for all the things I had lost, for the things I'd never asked for but been forced to endure, for the time I'd never get with the fathers I'd only recently gotten to know.

"It is their time now, Keeper of Balance."

ARTHUS

CHAPTER 81

Fi had spoken before about starting a revolution. I'd envisioned her leading an army, flanked by her mates on each side, her amber eyes shining with determination as she led the charge on a mysterious enemy.

But as outraged fae spread word throughout the Council building of what they'd witnessed, and Fi's head lay against Bryn's shoulder, her face the picture of heartbreak, I understood.

This wouldn't be glorious.

It wouldn't be poetic, even if people one day made up poems about it. It would be bloody, and long, and miserable. It was the cruel and gruesome revolution the fae deserved after their centuries-long cruel and gruesome treatment of magic.

Galvyn and Attie Laisren wouldn't be the only innocent casualties.

The riots had begun before we had even left the building. There were more low-magic fae than gifted fae everywhere in Avalon—including in the Council building—and the gods' message was spreading. Learn from Fi's battle. Take up the mantle. *Fight.*

And they were, but none of that mattered to me right now because my love had just watched her fathers die right in front of her eyes. Bryn had picked her up and pulled her legs around his waist, striding purposefully from the building with Marlen and Eamon flanking him on either side and me covering his back as he carried our precious cargo. It wasn't the most dignified exit for Ffion Laisren—Sanctified Empath and Keeper of Balance—but I didn't need to check the bond to know that she was seconds away from falling apart.

It took me a moment to realize that the reason no one was approaching us was because we had five intimidating dragon shifters at our backs.

Instead, the fae who worked in the building lined the walls, giving us plenty of room. I don't think I imagined a few of them bowing their heads as we passed.

"We'll fly you wherever you need to go," Ezra said in his most commanding voice as soon as we got out of the building, blinking against the harsh sunlight. It was an unexpected offer—dragons did not like to be seen as transportation.

"Sweetheart? Where do you want to go?" I asked softly, hoping she'd request the Old Adair Estate.

"Northgales." The one muffled word she spoke into Bryn's neck was barely audible, but it was all the instruction we needed. The dragons had visited the Old Adair Estate before, they already knew how to find it.

A small, possessive part of me was grateful that Fi's head was buried against Bryn so she couldn't see the five disrobing males in front of her right now. One-by-one they shifted fully. In their dragon forms, they were at least twenty-foot long and fucking terrifying.

Some of the fae who'd left the building scurried back inside, and I hoped Fi was muting her gift against their fear.

Hiram's silver air-dragon looked between Bryn and I with his enormous eyes and tilted his head back as if to say *"get on."* Out of the corner of my eye, I noticed Oren's blue water-dragon doing the same to Eamon and Marlen. Levi's green earth-dragon was looking expectantly at Finnian and Conn, who had never seen a dragon before judging by the awed looks on their faces.

Conn was carrying an unconscious Saffir in his arms, and pity twinged in the recesses of my mind. Fi's fathers hadn't been the only ones to die here today.

"Come with us," I called out to Conn and Finnian as I mounted the silver dragon and pulled Fi up from Bryn's arms. Conn nodded, a flicker of gratitude passing over his face. I wasn't sure they had anywhere else to go.

Fi's forehead rested between my shoulderblades as Bryn's arms banded around her from behind, securing her in place. The fact that we were sitting astride a silver dragon and Fi hadn't reacted in the least spoke volumes about how she was feeling.

Hiram kicked off into the air as the sound of Fi's silence roared in my ears.

We landed in the vineyard of the Estate and to no one's surprise, Eamon took over carrying a catatonic Fi into the house. Bryn had done well keeping it together at the Council building, but he was starting to let off smoke and Eamon was practically vibrating with the need to take care of her.

"Thank you," I told Ezra tightly. He gave a slow nod before the five of them launched themselves into the sky, undoubtedly eager to get back to the mate they'd left behind.

I led the way, gesturing for Conn, Finnian, and a now-conscious Saffir to follow. They could stay in the guest room upstairs for as long as they liked, but that was about as much consideration as I could spare them at the moment. Through the bond, I could feel Fi's pain calling to us, and it demanded all of my attention.

"Shower," Eamon muttered, more to himself than anyone as he carried Fi through the house to the downstairs bathroom and Bryn directed Saffir and the twins upstairs. Eamon didn't even bother removing their clothes, just waited until the water was hot and steam was filling the small space before walking under the spray with Fi in his arms.

She nestled further against him, not reacting otherwise as the hot water washed away the ugliness of the day, turning the white dress she was wearing transparent. I knew from the bond that despite her lack of reaction, the shower was helping her feel better, and she stood on her own feet when

Eamon put her down to strip them both out of their wet clothes.

Bryn stood out in the hallway, tipping his head slightly to encourage me and Marlen to follow him out. Marlen pulled the door closed behind him as we joined Bryn, but none of us were able to bring ourselves to move further than the hallway, even knowing Fi was safe and comfortable with Eamon.

I scrubbed a hand over my face, noticing that Bryn was doing the same. Marlen had been silent since the Council building, and I knew he was struggling with the fact that he hadn't been able to save Fi's fathers even though there was nothing he could have done.

"There are going to be expectations," Bryn sighed eventually. "People are going to want things from Fi now."

"From all of us, probably," I muttered. "But Fi comes first, and she's in no position to be making statements or answering questions now, let alone *leading*, or whatever it is they'll expect from her."

At the very least, Gwyneira was going to want to speak to Fi, probably thrilled with herself at the way this had all turned out.

"Marlen?" Bryn prompted, crossing his arms over his chest.

Marlen startled, but Bryn was right to ask for his opinion. Marlen was more observant than we gave him credit for, hiding behind his jokes and mischievous smiles.

"Enfys," Marlen rasped, clearing his throat. "Enfys will hold them off."

Bryn and I exchanged a look. Why hadn't we thought of that?

"I'll write him a letter," Bryn said decisively. The shower cut off, and we heard Eamon's quiet murmuring as he and Fi got out, all three of us pausing to listen. "We can't rush her," Bryn added quietly, a deep crease between his brows.

"Agreed," I replied, my chest aching at just the hint of what I was getting through the bond. Fi had been cautiously optimistic about the direction her relationship with her fathers was heading in. There had been a future there. Now she'd never get to know them, never spend holidays with them, or introduce them to our children...

"Sacrifice," Marlen said quietly, staring down at the mating mark on his wrist. "The gods demanded sacrifice."

And they'd taken it.

It took three weeks for us to even consider leaving the Old Adair Estate. Fi had barely left the *bed* during that time. It wasn't just the loss of her fathers she was coming to terms with—it was everything. Fi had experienced more in the past few months than many fae experienced in five centuries.

By silent agreement, Marlen, Eamon, Bryn and I were getting Fi out of bed and back to real life today. If I had my way, we'd be on our way back to the Academy by nightfall. Saffir's latest letter informed us that Gwyneira had been taking far more credit than she was due for the fae uprisings that had broken out across Avalon.

Saffir had gone back to the Academy with Conn and Finnian the day after everything had happened at the Council. None of us blamed her for Galvyn's and Attie's deaths, but it was obvious that she felt out of place with us. Perhaps getting Conn and Finnian a place at the Academy—where, as gifted fae, they should have been all along—was her way of coping.

Plus, there was something between them. Whether that was a good thing while Saffir was grieving and her life had been turned upside down was yet to be seen.

Enfys had slipped seamlessly into the power vacuum left by the abrupt exit of seven Councilors. Between him and Brently, who we'd contracted to be our eyes and ears on the ground, we were pretty well informed for five fae who never left the house.

"Today's the day, scout," Bryn announced, striding into the room and ripping the blankets off the bed. Our sweet, beautiful, broken little mate didn't even flinch. She stayed curled up in a ball on her side, her gaze drifting absently over each of us.

"Are you calling time on my emotional recovery?" she asked after a long pause.

There was a dangerous edge to her calm voice that made my cock twitch. I wanted to see her full of fire again, then voluntarily taming that fire and giving me her beautiful submission.

"You've got your entire life ahead of you to recover from this and whatever other terrible shit lies ahead of us. You don't need to cram all your recovery in now," Bryn groused impatiently. In the resounding silence that followed, Eamon and Marlen gaped at him like he'd lost his mind.

Faster than she'd moved in weeks, Fi sat up and blasted Bryn onto his ass with her air magic. There was a stunned pause before Bryn chuckled and set the rest of us off. As Fi's peals of laughter turned into pained sobs that wrecked her body, we took turns lying in the bed next to her, offering her whatever comfort she needed from us.

I never understood more why the mating mark the gods had given us symbolized sacrifice than when I saw my mate so broken. All the parts that made Fi who she was—her curiosity, her quick wit, her fierce independent streak—had been scattered into the wind to pursue the gods' agenda. But she would find them again because she had four mates who'd protect her from anything, including her own self-destruction.

Eventually, she fell asleep lying atop Marlen's chest, cheeks red and stained with tears, but calmer than she'd been in weeks. Eamon disappeared into the kitchen to make the butternut pasta she liked so much, and when she stirred, I ran her a steaming hot bath she got into gratefully.

And just like that, we had hope.

Thank the gods for Briallen. Reverent silence mostly met our arrival back on Academy grounds. I was watching the bond obsessively, seeing how Fi reacted to everyone's emotions to make sure nothing alarming came up. She was mostly feeling varying levels of discomfort until Briallen showed up and leaped on her, then she was all relief.

"Where have you been? It's been weeks!" Briallen said with an exaggerated sigh. "I wondered if you were ever coming back."

"I just needed some time..." Fi trailed off awkwardly, and Briallen's face blanched.

"Oh gods. That was stupid of me. I'm so sorry about your dads, Fi. I know you didn't get to spend much time with them..." Briallen looked anxiously back at her mates, seemingly at a loss for words.

"Hey, don't feel weird about it," Fi said softly, resting her hand on Briallen's forearm. "I didn't grow up with them, but I am grieving them. I'm grieving the time I spent with them and all the memories I assumed we'd make one day."

Fi let out a long exhale, gathering her thoughts before giving Briallen a watery smile. "This is what they wanted, though. To be with my mother. So I'm happy that they got what they wanted, even if I'm not happy. You know?"

"I get it," Briallen replied gently, giving Fi a sympathetic smile. "My fathers would be lost without my mother, too."

"What brings you all back to the Academy?" Hagan asked, deftly changing the subject. I liked him already.

"The guys are outraged on my behalf about Gwyneira taking some credit for the gods' attention to the fae and the uprisings." Fi shrugged. "Apparently we're here to, um, discuss it with her."

That was a far too polite description for what I had in mind.

"You don't seem all that upset about it," Leigh observed, tilting his head curiously.

"There are bigger things going on," Fi replied nonchalantly, thinking of the fae uprisings that were sprouting all across Avalon. Many of the estates belonging to Councilors had been torched, and powerful fae across the realm had gone into hiding. "That being said, I'd quite like the magical education she denied me, so I'll be letting Gwyneira know all about that."

"I'd expect nothing less," Leigh chuckled.

"Come find us after? In the commons?" Briallen asked eagerly, and I knew there was no way Fi would turn her down. Or that she'd want to. Fi hadn't ever complained, but we had starved her for female company these past few months and I knew she was craving some time with her friends.

"If we aren't being escorted off the premises, then yes, definitely."

"You're the Sanctified Empath, Keeper of Balance, and probably some other important shit," Leigh called after us. "Don't let anyone push you around, Ffion Laisren!"

Fi buried her face against Marlen's arm as he shook with laughter. The brief walk to Gwyneira's cabin felt like it took forever with so many eyes trailing us. Maybe returning to the Academy wasn't the best idea, given how famous Fi was now.

"Ffion."

Gwyneira was waiting for us at the top of the stairs that led to her treetop cabin as we rounded the corner. Standing above us, looking magnanimously down with her arms spread wide in welcome, she looked every inch a benevolent leader. Irritation rippled down my spine as my wings threatened to break free. Where was Gwyneira the past few months? She'd unceremoniously kicked us out, told us to prioritize the gods' task, and had offered no kind of help. Yet here she was, taking credit like she deserved any of it.

Fi was calmer than I was as she led us up the stairs, shoulders back and chin up. She wasn't the same unsure, overwhelmed fae that had left the Academy, and the hint of surprise in Gwyneira's gaze told me she recognized that too.

"Please, come in."

We filed into the sitting room where Gwyneira's mates were all standing obediently against the wall, waiting. We moved to sit, but before we even got that far, a choked sound from Eamon caught everyone's attention.

Fi moved to his side as his eyes shifted from purple to swirling smoke. There was no way a spirit dropping in right as we entered Gwyneira's cabin was a coincidence.

"Gwyneira. The gods convey their gratitude for your many years of dedication to this Academy," the spirit speaking through Eamon began. My hopes rose with that one line as Bryn threw Gwyneira a grin that bordered on savage. "Over the past two centuries, you have contributed to the education of gifted fae throughout Avalon. However, fae without gifts went ignored. They gave you the opportunity to do more—the Keeper of Balance was under your care—yet you continued on your path rather than help her."

I'd never seen Gwyneira look anything less than calm and collected before, but she was definitely looking *rattled* now. Her eyes darted between Eamon and her mates, who had gathered around closer the longer the spirit spoke.

"It was for her own good," Gwyneira protested weakly. "She needed to focus entirely on her quest..."

"That was not your decision to make!" the spirit thundered, making all of us jump. Fi collected herself and quickly sidled back up to Eamon, looking guilty for moving away from him in the first place. "Your gratitude for the gods, your appreciation of your gift and the position you hold is hollow."

"What would you have me do?" Gwyneira whispered.

"Step aside. It is time for another to guide and nurture the young fae at the Academy of Avalon."

With that, Eamon's eyes shuttered, and he shook his head slightly before taking in the uncomfortably silent room with his amethyst eyes.

"Gwyneira..." Mawrth, one of her mates, said softly. She was staring vacantly out of the window, saying nothing.

"I will not argue with the gods," Gwyneira sighed. "For what it is worth, I still believe I did the right thing in sending you away," she added, turning to face Fi.

"I know you believe that," Fi replied, with far more grace and dignity than I possessed. "I believe all sorts of things, but that doesn't mean I'm right."

Perhaps not *that* much more grace and dignity.

Fi turned with a flourish, heading towards the door. "Be sure to mention to the new dean that Marlen, Bryn and I will be resuming our studies, and I expect to see Arthus' position reinstated. If you have any questions, I'll be in the commons with my friends, eating a revolting salad. Thanks for everything."

FFION

EPILOGUE 1

Twelve years later...

The fae technically don't do bridesmaids, but as I got myself ready in the upstairs guest bedroom of the Old Adair Estate, surrounded by my favorite ladies, I found myself not particularly caring about that rule.

It had taken us *twelve years* to finally get around to having our mating circle celebration. We could do whatever we wanted at this point.

Besides, if the Keeper of Balance had bridesmaids for her mating circle celebration, every female fae in Avalon would probably follow suit. I had a bit of a following, and it never ceased to make me uncomfortable.

"So, why exactly are we here, *Sanctified Empath*?" Saffir teased from her spot lounging on the bed, sipping her glass of sparkling fae wine, produced right here at the vineyard. She got a massive kick out of using my titles to irritate me.

"We're here to *drink wine and be merry*. Those were her exact words," Riona drawled. She was almost as famous as me—the storm fae who had been held by dark fae. Against Conn and Finnian's wishes, she'd led a huge uprising in her hometown, which had been a den of iniquity unlike anything Avalon had ever seen. It was the most devastating battle of the past twelve years, not just because of the number of casualties, but because of the atrocities we'd uncovered.

Riona, the teenage storm fae who led the charge, was the stuff of legends. As soon as she and Osian came of age, they felt the mating pull, surprising no one when they turned out to be kindred souls. She'd since picked up two more mates from her fellow rebels.

Conn and Finnian had eventually calmed down because Saffir kept her mates on a tight leash and Riona was practically a little sister to her. Saffir, Conn and Finnian didn't have compatible magic as Saffir had no gift, but they were kindred souls and it was true love. Bucking fae convention, Saffir had taken their surname—the Castell family name was beyond ruined.

"I thought we were here to help you get ready," Briallen said from behind me as she wrangled my curls into an elaborate side-do that cascaded over one shoulder, interspersed with delicate white flowers.

"Well, you are," I admitted. "You're the best at doing my hair." Briallen gave my strands a playful tug as she laughed.

"Lucky that I like you." We didn't get to spend as much time together now. After being a major part of the revolution—traveling between uprisings and keeping everyone informed—she, Leigh and Hagan had settled at her parents' home in Northgales.

My mates and I were still mostly based out of the Academy, where Arthus was an Air Master, and Marlen was a Combat Instructor and Healer. Now that they were training female fae for guard duty as well, he was busier than ever with students. It wasn't Marlen's dream job but, much like Eamon, he was hanging out for fatherhood in a few years. By the gods, those two were broody.

Bryn and I were still working with the reformed Council to uncover any dark fae still in hiding—Bryn using his tracking magic to locate them while I used my empath gift to distract them from the bloodlust and offer them some comfort. It was the only time I got any joy out of influencing emotions.

It was uncomfortable for my other three mates when Bryn and I had to travel, though, and I didn't want to keep doing it forever. I hadn't even expected to be doing it this long, but it turns out, change really doesn't happen overnight.

Or even after a few nights. Or a few months.

It took ten *years* of violence, voting, arrests, and executions for the revolution to end. Towards the end, fae children were increasingly showing signs of rare gifts, which helped our cause. Now, twelve years after the big showdown with the Council and the death of my fathers, a large number of fae babies were being born with wings again.

Despite the notoriety my mates and I had found over the course of the revolution, the five of us still lived in our one-bedroom cabin close to the Academy grounds like nothing had changed. At the end of each day, we would sit around the dining table, sipping on our respective wines and ales, and go through the astounding amount of correspondence we received each day.

We had *fans*. It was weird. Especially because, while we may have kicked things off, the fae fought for their own redemption. I'd just been there to supervise.

"Here you go," Aderyn announced, emerging with my dress draped over her arm. Aderyn, Lachlan, and her second mate, Carrick, still lived in Dubris so we didn't get to spend as much time with them. But, on our last visit I finally saw a real live unicorn in the forest, so I was selfishly glad they'd never moved.

Saffir choked slightly on her wine. "That's the sexiest dress I've ever seen for a mating circle celebration."

I threw her a wink as I stood to take the dress from Aderyn and pour myself into it. Not only would my mates love it, Eamon's ancient, snobby parents would absolutely *hate* it. A petty part of me lived to antagonize my judgy mother-in-law.

I ditched my robe and worked the dress up my legs and torso, slipping my arms into the almost nonexistent straps. I definitely couldn't wear a bra with this one. The dress was entirely made of silk, pooling on the ground to give me a small train, but with a slit that came almost up to my hip bone on one side. The back dropped to just above my ass, and the top was a drapey, wraparound V-neck that showed a generous amount of cleavage.

All in virginal white, of course.

"Why did you even invite guests?" Riona complained, huffing exasperatedly. "One look at you in that dress and your mates will drag you straight to bed."

"I made a bet with them that they wouldn't last two hours at this party." I shrugged. "I wanted to give them a challenge."

"Evil," Briallen laughed, lightly brushing fairy dust strategically over my dress to catch the light.

"Ready to go?" Saffir asked, moving towards the door.

"Let's do it," I replied confidently.

My mates, and my friends' mates, were gathered in the garden where the party was being held. My various in-laws were down there too, except for Arthus' parents who were still pretty funny about us. His brother was here though, which meant a lot to Arthus. Marlen's parents, who lived on an island property we'd purchased for them in the Outer Isles, were talking animatedly to Bryn's aunt and uncles, who'd already gotten the party started, setting up the shots while Eamon's parents looked on, lips pursed in disapproval.

Brently was around here somewhere with his mating circle, child, and the twins he'd raised as his own. It had taken years to figure out where they'd come from and, to no one's surprise, their parents had long since "mysteriously vanished." Brently's mating circle had been more than happy to keep them and protect their rare telekinetic gift.

In the distance, I could see Úna and a few of the other fae from Albion talking to some of my cousins I'd connected with over the years. Being back in Avalon, reconnecting with her magic, had done wonders for Úna. She looked far younger than she had when we'd first met her in Albion.

"What the fuck are you wearing?" Bryn growled, stalking over to me. He pulled me tight against his front, his hand resting possessively over the curve of my ass, his go-to move for marking his territory.

"Don't you like it?" I purred in his ear, pressing my breasts against his chest. I was determined to win this bet. I didn't care much for parties, anyway.

"Foxglove," Marlen said with a low whistle. "Playing dirty, I see."

"Just keeping the spark alive," I replied, looking back at him over my shoulder and blowing him a kiss.

"I wasn't aware that had ever been a problem for us," Arthus drawled. I smiled, tilting my chin slightly for him, exposing my throat. It was as good as pushing lust on him with my gift.

"Let her have her fun," Marlen chuckled, throwing his arm around Arthus' shoulder. "It's only two hours, we've got this."

My heart warmed seeing the affection between them. It had taken years for Arthus to be truly comfortable with physical touch and even then, only within our mating circle. Which was fine by me.

"Only two hours," Eamon groaned, emerging from the kitchen and handing me a glass of wine. I didn't know what they were complaining about—I had temptation times four. All of my mates looked fucking edible in their dark dress clothes and the kyanite pendants that were a constant fixture against their chests. We'd recovered them from my fathers' belongings and my mates hadn't taken them off since.

In the center of the food table were six candles. Bryn guided me towards them, lighting each with small flames to get started. I focused on growing my three while he expanded his with ease. One in honor of each of our parents who couldn't be here to celebrate with us.

"Marlen," Leigh called across the yard. "I forgot to tell you, our neighbor just had a baby boy and named him after you."

"Really? That never happens. I reckon every second girl baby is called 'Ffion' and every second boy is called 'Bryn'," Marlen groused good-naturedly. "I don't know why he's the favorite."

"Because I'm the best looking," Bryn replied like it should have been obvious.

"Fi is the best looking," Arthus corrected. "And she will look even better out of that dress so fuck the bet, let's get out of here."

I laughed as Bryn threw me over his shoulder, ruining all the hard work Briallen had done on my hair.

"We'll save you some shots, see you in a few hours!" Uncle Oscar yelled after us, our guests' amusement tickling pleasantly at my skin.

"I won," I reminded my mates as we headed down the hallway.

"We all did," Bryn murmured.

FFION

EPILOGUE 2

1 8 years later…

"That's it, Fi," Eamon said softly, his voice cracking slightly on my name as I squeezed his hand tight enough to break his fingers. Even with Marlen's healing magic pulsing steadily into me from where he sat behind me, his palms resting on my shoulders, this fucking *hurt*.

"I can't do this!" I sobbed, shaking my head. "I can't."

Bryn made a distressed noise from where he and Arthus were pacing against the far wall, criss-crossing in front of each other, both too wound up to get any closer.

Arthus had already blown out a window when a particularly bad contraction hit and he lost control of his air magic, and his wings had been out since the second my waters broke.

"You can," Marlen assured me, his voice soft next to my ear. I didn't have a choice, this baby was coming out whether I thought I could do it or not. "Deep breaths. Just focus on that, one breath after another."

"And pushing," the midwife added, no-nonsense but not unkind. She'd seemed like a steady pair of hands which was why I'd chosen her. Now I was wishing I'd chosen someone willing to coddle me a bit more. "You're ready. Next contraction, you need to push. All of Avalon is waiting for this baby."

"No pressure or anything," I muttered, wrinkling my nose. "Is something burning?"

"Gods, Bryn," Arthus snapped. "You're burning footprints into the floor, get it together."

"*Me* get it together?" Bryn exclaimed, gesturing at the paneless window. "*You* godsdamned get it together."

"Both of you get it together," Eamon commanded, shooting them a warning glare over his shoulder as my hand tightened around his again. He was going to be such a good dad. He had the best dad voice.

"Come on, foxglove," Marlen murmured, ignoring everyone else in the room. His magic was like an old friend, wrapping around me like a hug and easing the aches as they appeared. "One more big push. Let's meet our little girl."

I was concentrating too hard to remind him for the millionth time that it could be a boy, but his mind was already made up.

"Good," the midwife clipped, standing between my legs and getting a really good look at parts of me that I usually reserved for my mates. My modesty had vanished somewhere around the tenth contraction. "Push, Fi. Push, push, push! I can see the head."

I grimaced at that somewhat horrifying visual, bearing down with every ounce of strength in my body. *Out, out, out. This tenancy is done, Baby Laisren. I am evicting you.*

"That's it!" the midwife exclaimed. "Eamon, get over here and catch."

He scrambled up like there was a fire under his ass, sidling up next to the midwife. We'd talked about one of them possibly doing this, if it was all progressing well, and I got some comfort that the midwife obviously thought it was to pull Eamon in.

I bit down hard enough on my lip to bleed, Marlen's magic quickly healing it up as I gave one final exhausted push, collapsing back against Marlen as Baby Laisren made their noisy entry into the world.

"Girl," Eamon choked out, holding the tiny bright red squalling creature in his enormous hands. "It's a girl."

"A girl," I repeated dreamily, eyes welling with tears. "A baby girl."

"I knew it," Marlen said smugly, his healing magic still flowing through me. "Eira Laisren. Unless you've changed your mind, mama?"

"No," I whispered, as Eamon carefully brought her up to my chest under the midwife's careful supervision, laying her on my breast. "Eira Laisren."

I'd never seen a newborn in person before, and I hadn't expected her to be quite so... tomato-colored, but the midwife didn't seem worried so I guessed it was fine? I smoothed my thumb over the shock of dark hair matted against her scalp, and sighed at her delightfully pudgy cheeks. And her fingers! They were so teeny!

Bryn and Arthus moved closer, and I was relieved to see that Arthus had managed to retract his wings and Bryn was no longer leaving scorch marks on our bedroom floor.

"You two good?" I teased tiredly, glancing up at them before returning my gaze to little Eira.

"Sorry, sweetheart," Arthus said gruffly, staring at our daughter. "It's hard seeing you in pain.

"Fucking awful," Bryn agreed, his voice softer than usual.

"Am I supposed to be doing something?" I asked the midwife nervously. "Is she hungry? Oh my gods, I don't know how to do this."

The stern, matronly midwife cracked the first smile I'd seen in all the months she'd been monitoring me. "Just cuddle her for now, and we'll try feeding soon. Let out that breath you've been holding, Ffion. You did it."

I did release a breath before inhaling fresh cool air, courtesy of Arthus who was circulating it around the room, blowing away the stench of stress and sweat.

Eira made a small snuffling noise, immediately attracting the eyes of all of her parents, before settling against my chest. For being brand new to the world, she was adjusting remarkably well. Soon she'd be settled in her own bed, then she'd be crawling, then walking, talking, running through the fields with her friends, leaving home...

I burst into tears—great, big proper ones.

Bryn started smoking out of his ears.

"There there, Fi," Marlen soothed, rubbing my shoulders. "It's alright, just let it all out."

And so I did. I cried, and I laughed, and I held the most precious gift I'd ever been entrusted with in my arms, surrounded by the love and contentment of my mates.

BRYN

EPILOGUE 3

4 years later...

"Eira!" I yelled, leaping forward to snatch our hellion of a child before she launched herself out of the godsdamned window. She growled like a furious kitten, attempting to squirm out of my grip.

No matter that she was four years old now and fae wings appeared at birth, Eira was adamant they'd sprout from her back if she just *fell* from high enough.

"Dad!" she complained, giving up on her attempt to get free, but I'd fallen for that trick before so I hauled her up on my chest, flipping her around so she faced me. I knew the lower lip was coming before she unleashed it. As powerful as Eira's pout was, there was nothing in this realm or any other that could tempt me to let her launch herself out of the window.

"You do not have wings, daughter," I told her patiently. "That's not a bad thing, you'll have a different gift. A better one, like tracking magic."

She wrinkled her nose, decidedly unimpressed. Out of all five of her parents, the only gift Eira had ever coveted was Arthus' pretty silver wings.

"I don't want tracking magic," she said bluntly, wriggling for me to put her down. I held her closer and made for the stairs that led down to the ground outside, not quite trusting her with heights when she was in this mood. Marlen was down there, he'd blast her with water magic until she was a giggling mess and forgot whatever she had been mad about. "When will I get my gift?"

"Your next birthday, probably," I assured her, spotting Marlen's grin as he leaned against the shovel he'd been using, helping Eamon out with the vegetable garden while our earth fae was busy with administrative work for the various estates.

Fi and I had finished our positions at the Council when she'd fallen pregnant with Eira, and while we'd considered moving full time to the ancient estate at Northgales which was easily big enough to house a family, none of us had wanted to ask Arthus to give up his position at the Academy. He was the Head of Air Mastery now, and he'd worked too hard for the position to give it up.

Besides, Fi liked the treehouse-style of home, and building a family-friendly extension had been a much needed distraction for her during the long months of pregnancy.

"Have you come to see me, trouble?" Marlen asked as I deposited Eira on the ground. She stomped across the grass, though some of her grumpiness was fading already in the face of her most playful father.

"Dad wouldn't let me fly."

My lips twitched as I crossed my arms over my chest.

"Ah, that's because you *can't* fly, Eira. Perhaps you'll be a healer," Marlen suggested, already flicking water at her to make her smile. Fi and Eamon emerged from the cabin where she'd been helping him with paperwork, watching with amusement from the top step.

"I don't want to be a healer. Do you think I'll have a water 'finity?" Eira asked, trying to snatch the droplets of liquid out of the air.

Marlen and I exchanged a knowing look, him grinning from ear to ear. With Eira's temper, I'd be *shocked* if she had anything other than a fire affinity. I didn't think Eira was my daughter by blood—she looked mostly like Fi with her mass of golden brown curls and amber eyes, and her bone structure and height were all Eamon—but affinities were assigned by the gods, not parentage.

"Maybe," Marlen replied eventually, shooting streams of water at her feet that she dodged with loud shrieks. Eira laughed as she attempted to kick the liquid back at him, and it was the best sound I ever heard. Despite her fiery temper and determination to try flattening herself on the ground every time we weren't looking, Eira was a happy child. She enjoyed a wonderful life here, and had close friends in Saffir and Briallen's kids, and enjoyed trips to Dubris to visit her Aunt Aderyn and cousin, Alys.

Through the bond, I knew that Fi was struck by the same feeling of gratitude that I was whenever Eira laughed. The same gratefulness that she was enjoying a happy childhood so different from our own miserable ones.

And then all progress was lost because Arthus had finished work for the day, and landed among us in the clearing, wings outstretched. Eira crossed her arms, mimicking my posture, and glared at them like Arthus had been flying just to upset her.

"Hello, little one," Arthus said warmly, giving Eira his closest thing to a smile, obviously thrilled to see her after a long day teaching. She promptly burst into tears, and he gave us all a bewildered look.

"Wings," I said, not bothering to elaborate. He retracted them instantly, heading straight for Eira and scooping her up, his air magic swirling around to dry off her damp clothes.

Fi sighed happily, leaning on the railing with Eamon at her back watching as Arthus placated the true head of this household, rocking her side to side until she smiled again.

Thank the gods for that.

The deities had thrown us plenty of challenges over the years, but they'd also given us this life, and I knew none of us would exchange it for anything.

Looking at the faces of my mate and our mating circle, I knew we were all thinking the exact same thing.

AUTHOR'S NOTE

And they lived happily ever after. The end.

For real, this time! It's been such a joy to revisit Avalon to put the complete trilogy together. It's been two years since the series came out, and I missed these characters a lot. These were my very first books, so they'll always hold a particularly special place in my heart!

Thank you to absolutely everyone who read this series—both when they were first released and now. I'm constantly amazed and grateful that you took a chance on my books, and it's because of you that I get to spend my days telling the weird stories that float around my head.

There are a few other thank you's I need to mention—to my husband, for everything. My alpha reader, bestie, all-around-wonderful human, Lucy, for always believing in me. To Trish and Kari, the amazing betas and friends who tackled this manuscript when it was first published and have been such incredible supports for me ever since. And to the amazing bookish friends I've since made who got me through the boxset editing and bonus content writing process: TS, Rachel, Rory, and Ashley in particular! One of the unexpectedly wonderful things about falling into this career are the all people within the writing community that I've met.

I hope you enjoyed the Empath Found series, and if you'd like more from Avalon, the Deadly Dragons duet is complete—Fi and the guys make an appearance in Shira's story as well. You can find my full list of books on my website coletterhodes.com, or head over to the Colette Rhodes Reader Group on Facebook for the latest news.

Colette R. xx

ALSO BY COLETTE RHODES

AGATHOS UNIVERSE

Run Riot (State of Grace #1)

Silver Bullet (State of Grace #1)

Wild Game (State of Grace #1)

Dead of Spring (Hades and Persephone retelling)

CHEEKY FAIRY TALES

Gilded Mess (Three Bears #1)

Golden Chaos (Three Bears #2)

Scarlet Disaster (Little Red #1)

Seeing Red (Little Red #2)

KNOTTY BY NATURE OMEGAVERSE

Allure Part 1

Allure Part 2

AVALON UNIVERSE

Empath Found: The Complete Trilogy

The ~~Not~~ Cursed Dragon (Deadly Dragons #1)

The ~~Not~~ Satisfied Dragon (Deadly Dragons #2)

STANDALONES

Luxuria

Blood Nor Money

Fire & Gasoline